PRAISE FOR DAVID BRIN'S UPLIFT NOVELS

THE UPLIFT WAR

"An exhilarating read that encompasses everything from breathless action to finely drawn moments of quiet intimacy. There is no way we can avoid coming back as many times as Brin wants us to, until his story is done." —*Locus*

"Shares all the properties that made *Startide* such a joy. The plot fizzes along . . . and there are the wonders of the Galactic civilizations (which have all the invention and excitement that SF *used* to have)." —*Asimov's Science Fiction*

SUNDIVER

"Brin has done a superb job on all counts." —*Science Fiction Times*

"Brin has a fertile and well-developed imagination . . . coupled with a sinuous and rapid-paced style." —*Heavy Metal*

STARTIDE RISING

"*Startide Rising* is an extraordinary achievement, a book so full of fascinating ideas that they would not have crowded each other at twice its considerable length." — Poul Anderson

"One of the outstanding SF novels of recent years." —*Publishers Weekly*

BRIGHTNESS REEF

"A captivating read . . . *Brightness Reef* leaves you looking forward to more. It's a worthy addition to what promises to be a great science-fiction series." — *Star Tribune,* Minneapolis

"Brin is a skillful storyteller. . . . There is more than enough action to keep the book exciting, and like all good serials, the first volume ends with a bang." — *The Plain Dealer,* Cleveland

INFINITY'S SHORE

Book Two of the
Uplift Storm Trilogy

David Brin

BANTAM BOOKS
New York   Toronto   London
Sydney   Auckland

INFINITY'S SHORE

A Bantam Spectra Book

PUBLISHING HISTORY
Bantam hardcover edition published December 1996
Bantam paperback edition / December 1997
SPECTRA and the portrayal of a boxed "s" are trademarks of Bantam
Books, a division of Bantam Doubleday Dell Publishing Group, Inc.

Library of Congress Catalog Card Number: 96-32346

ISBN 0-553-57777-8

Published simultaneously in the United States and Canada

Bantam Books are published by Bantam Books, a division of Bantam
Doubleday Dell Publishing Group, Inc. Its trademark, consisting of the
words "Bantam Books" and the portrayal of a rooster, is Registered in U.S.
Patent and Trademark Office and in other countries. Marca Registrada.
Bantam Books, 1540 Broadway, New York, New York 10036.

PRINTED IN THE UNITED STATES OF AMERICA

OPM   10 9 8 7 6 5 4

to
Ariana Mae, our splendid envoy,
who will speak for us at the threshold of the fantastic
twenty-second century.

CONTENTS

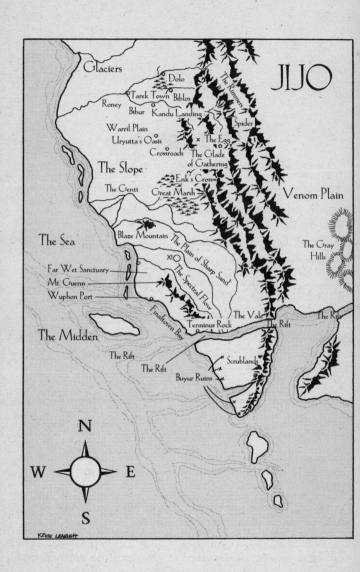

CAST OF CHARACTERS

Alvin—the humicker nickname of Hph-wayuo, an adolescent hoon of Wuphon Village.

Asx—member of the Jijo Council of High Sages, representing the traeki race.

Baskin, Gillian—Terragens agent and physician, acting captain of the dolphin survey vessel *Streaker*.

Blade—a blue qheuen, son of Log Biter; a wood-carver and friend of Sara Koolhan.

Bloor—deceased photographer who discovered the secret Rothen identity.

Brookida—dolphin metallurgist on *Streaker*.

Cambel, Lester—High Sage of Earthlings on Jijo.

Chuchki—dolphin engineering mate on *Streaker*.

Creideiki—a dolphin, former captain of the dolphin vessel *Streaker*. Lost on Kithrup years ago.

Dedinger—human zealot who wishes all races of Jijo to devolve so one day they may be uplifted from innocence.

Dwer—son of the papermaker Nelo Koolhan, chief tracker of the Commons of Six Races.

Emerson D'Anite—a human engineer, once part of the Terragens spacecraft *Streaker*'s crew, until he crashed on Jijo.

Ewasx—a Jophur ring stack transformed from the old sage Asx by the imposition of a new master ring.

Fallon—a retired tracker; Dwer's former mentor.

Foo, Ariana—the emeritus High Sage of Human Sept (retired).

Harullen—gray qheuen intellectual. Leader of a heretical sect that believes illegal settlers should voluntarily stop breeding and let Jijo return to its time of fallow rest.

Hikahi—former third-in-command of *Streaker,* lost at Kithrup.

Hph-wayuo—Alvin's formal hoonish name.

Huck—humicker nickname of a g'Kek orphan raised in Wuphon. Alvin's friend.

Huphu—Alvin's pet noor beast.

Jass—young hunter of the Gray Hills band. Rety's past tormentor.

Jimi—the "blessed," born higher along the Path of Redemption.

Jomah—the young son of Henrik the Exploser.

Jop—Dolo Village tree farmer, believer in the old Sacred Scrolls.

Joshu—Sara Koolhan's late suitor, an itinerant bookbinder who died in Biblos of the pepper pox.

Kaa—dolphin, pilot of *Streaker.* Formerly known as Lucky Kaa.

Karkaett—engineering mate on *Streaker.*

Keepiru—former chief pilot of *Streaker,* lost at Kithrup.

Knife-Bright Insight—a blue qheuen, High Sage for the qheuen race.

Kunn—human pilot of the Rothen-Danik ship.

Kurt—a leader of the Explosers Guild. Jomah's uncle.

Lark—a naturalist, junior sage of the Commons, and heretic.

Ling—Danik crewwoman of the Rothen ship. A skilled biologist.

Makanee—female dolphin, ship's surgeon on *Streaker*.

Melina—Nelo Koolhan's late wife; mother of Lark, Sara, and Dwer.

Mopol—a male dolphin, spacer second class on *Streaker*.

Mudfoot—a wild noor, named by Dwer Koolhan.

Nelo—papermaker of Dolo Village, patriarch of the Koolhan family.

Niss—a sapient computer lent to *Streaker* by Tymbrimi intelligence agents.

Old Ones—general term for the "retired" races of the Fractal World.

One-of-a-Kind—an ancient mulc spider assigned to decompose a ruin high in the Rimmer mountains.

Orley, Thomas—a Terragens agent assigned to *Streaker*, lost at Kithrup. Husband of Gillian Baskin.

Ozawa, Danel—deputy sage, knowing hidden secrets of Human Sept.

Peepoe—a female dolphin; geneticist and nurse on *Streaker*.

Phwhoon-dau—the hoonish High Sage.

Pincer-Tip—a red qheuen friend of Alvin's, who carved the bathyscaphe *Wuphon's Dream* out of a tree trunk.

Prity—a neo-chimpanzee; Sara's servant, skilled at math imagery.

Purofsky—a sage of Biblos, specializing in arcane physics.

Rann—leader of the Danik humans aboard the Rothen ship.

Rety—a human sooner, she fled her savage band's hidden offshoot colony in the Gray Hills.

Ro-kenn—a Rothen "lord" whose human followers included Rann, Ling, Besh, and Kunn.

Ro-pol—possibly Ro-kenn's mate, killed before Battle of the Glade.

Shen, Jeni—a human militia sergeant.

Strong, Lena—part of Danel Ozawa's expedition to the Gray Hills.

Suessi, Hannes—engineer on *Streaker,* cyborg modified by Old Ones.

Taine—a Biblos scholar who once courted Sara Koolhan.

Tsh't—a female dolphin, once *Streaker*'s fifth-in-command, now sharing command with Gillian Baskin.

Tyug—the traeki alchemist of Mount Guenn Forge, a vital assistant to Uriel the Smith.

Ulgor—an urrish tinker and supporter of the Urunthai.

Urdonnol—urrish apprentice serving Uriel.

Uriel—urrish master smith of the Mount Guenn Forge.

Ur-Jah—the urrish High Sage.

Ur-ronn—Alvin's urrish friend. Part of the *Wuphon's Dream* expedition. Uriel's niece.

Uthen—gray qheuen naturalist. Helped Lark write field guide to Jijoan species.

Vubben—the g'Kek High Sage.

Worley, Jenin—part of Danel Ozawa's expedition to the Gray Hills.

yee—an urrish male ejected from his pouch home by his former mate. Later "married" to the sooner girl Rety.

Zhaki—a male dolphin, spacer third class on *Streaker.*

*Those who hunger after wisdom often seek it
in the highest heights, or profound depths.*

*Yet, marvels are found in shallow sites
where life starts, burgeons, and dies.*

*What pinnacle, or lofty mount,
offers lessons as poignant
as the flowing river—
a crashing reef—
or the grave?*

—from a Buyur wall inscription,
found half-buried in a marsh
near Far Wet Sanctuary

INFINITY'S
SHORE

Streakers

[Five Jaduras Earlier]

Kaa

> * What strange fate brought me,
> > * Fleeing maelstroms of winter,
> > > * Past five galaxies? *

> * Only to find refuge,
> > * On a forlorn planet (nude!)
> > > * In laminar luxury! *

SO HE THOUGHT WHILE PERFORMING SWOOPING rolls, propelling his sleek gray body with exhilarated tail strokes, reveling in the caress of water against naked flesh.

Dappled sunlight threw luminous shafts through crystal shallows, slanting past mats of floating sea florets. Silvery native creatures, resembling flat-jawed fish, moved in and out of the bright zones, enticing his eye. Kaa squelched the instinctive urge to give chase.

Maybe later.

For now, he indulged in the liquid texture of water sliding around him, without the greasiness that used to cling so, back in the oily seas of Oakka, the green-green world, where soaplike bubbles would erupt from his blowhole each time he surfaced to breathe. *Not that it was worth the effort to inhale on Oakka. There wasn't enough good air on that horrid ball to nourish a comatose otter.*

This sea also tasted good, not harsh like Kithrup, where each excursion outside the ship would give you a toxic dose of hard metals.

In contrast, the water on Jijo world felt clean, with a salty tang reminding Kaa of the gulf stream flowing past the Florida Academy, during happier days on far-off Earth.

He tried to squint and pretend he was back home, chasing mullet near Key Biscayne, safe from a harsh universe. But the attempt at make-believe failed. One paramount difference reminded him this was an alien world.

Sound.

—a beating of tides rising up the continental shelf—a complex rhythm tugged by three moons, not one.

—an echo of waves, breaking on a shore whose abrasive sand had a strange, sharp texture.

—an occasional distant *groaning* that seemed to rise out of the ocean floor itself.

—the return vibrations of his own sonar clicks, tracing schools of fishlike creatures, moving their fins in unfamiliar ways.

—above all, the engine hum just behind him . . . a cadence of machinery that had filled Kaa's days and nights for five long years.

And now, another clicking, groaning sound. The clipped poetry of duty.

> * Relent, Kaa, tell us,
>> * In exploratory prose,
>>> * Is it safe to come? *

The voice chased Kaa like a fluttering, sonic conscience. Reluctantly, he swerved around to face the submarine *Hikahi,* improvised from ancient parts found strewn across this planet's deep seafloor—a makeshift contraption that suited a crew of misfit fugitives. Clamshell doors closed ponderously, like the jaws of a huge carnivore, cycling to let others emerge in his wake . . . if he gave the all clear.

Kaa sent his Trinary reply, amplified by a saser unit plugged into his skull, behind his left eye.

> * If water were all
> > * We might be in heaven now.
> > > * But wait! I'll check above! *

His lungs were already making demands, so he obeyed instinct, flicking an upward spiral toward the glistening surface. *Ready or not, Jijo, here I come!*

He loved piercing the tense boundary of sky and sea, flying weightless for an instant, then broaching with a splash and spume of exhalation. Still, he hesitated before inhaling. Instruments predicted an Earthlike atmosphere, yet he felt a nervous tremor drawing breath.

If anything, the air tasted better than the water! Kaa whirled, thrashing his tail in exuberance, glad Lieutenant Tsh't had let him volunteer for this—to be the first dolphin, the first *Earthling,* ever to swim this sweet, foreign sea.

Then his eye stroked a jagged, gray-brown line, spanning one horizon, very close.

The shore.

Mountains.

He stopped his gyre to stare at the nearby continent—inhabited, they now knew. But by whom?

There was not supposed to be any sapient life on Jijo.

Maybe they're just hiding here, the way we are, from a hostile cosmos.

That was one theory.

At least they chose a pleasant world, he added, relishing the air, the water, and gorgeous ranks of cumulus hovering over a giant mountain. *I wonder if the fish are good to eat.*

* As we await you,
    * Chafing in this cramped airlock,
        * Should we play pinochle? *

Kaa winced at the lieutenant's sarcasm. Hurriedly, he sent back pulsed waves.

* Fortune smiles again,
    * On our weary band of knaves.
        * Welcome, friends, to Ifni's Shore. *

It might seem presumptuous to invoke the goddess of chance and destiny, capricious Ifni, who always seemed ready to plague *Streaker*'s company with one more surprise. Another unexpected calamity, or miraculous escape. But Kaa had always felt an affinity with the informal patron deity of spacers. There might be better pilots than himself in the Terragens Survey Service, but none with a deeper respect for fortuity. Hadn't his own nickname been "Lucky"?

Until recently, that is.

From below, he heard the grumble of clamshell doors reopening. Soon Tsh't and others would join him in this first examination of Jijo's surface—a world they heretofore saw only briefly from orbit, then from the deepest, coldest pit in all its seas. Soon, his companions would arrive, but for a few moments more he had it to himself—silken water, tidal rhythms, fragrant air, the sky and clouds. . . .

His tail swished, lifting him higher as he peered. *Those aren't normal clouds,* he realized, staring at a great mountain dominating the eastern horizon, whose peak wore shrouds of billowing white. The lens implanted in his right eye dialed through a spectral scan, sending readings to his optic nerve—revealing steam, carbon oxides, and a flicker of molten heat.

A volcano, Kaa realized, and the reminder sent his ebullience down a notch. This was a busy part of the planet, geologically speaking. The same forces that made it a useful hiding place also kept it dangerous.

That must be where the groaning comes from, he pondered. Seismic activity. An interaction of miniquakes and crustal gas discharges with the thin overlaying film of sea.

Another flicker caught his notice, in roughly the same direction, but much closer—a pale swelling that might also have been a cloud, except for the way it moved, flapping like a bird's wing, then bulging with eagerness to race the wind.

A sail, he discerned. Kaa watched it jibe across the stiffening breeze—a two-masted schooner, graceful in motion, achingly familiar from the Caribbean seas of home.

Its bow split the water, spreading a wake that any dolphin might love to ride.

The zoom lens clarified, magnified, until he made out fuzzy bipedal forms, hauling ropes and bustling around on deck, like any gang of human sailors.

. . . Only these weren't human beings. Kaa glimpsed scaly backs, culminating in a backbone of sharp spines. Swathes of white fur covered the legs, and froglike membranes pulsated below broad chins as the ship's company sang a low, rumbling work chant that Kaa could dimly make out, even from here.

He felt a chill of unhappy recognition.

Hoons! What in all Five Galaxies are they doing here?

Kaa heard a rustle of fluke strokes—Tsh't and others rising to join him. Now he must report that enemies of Earth dwelled here.

Kaa realized grimly—this news wasn't going to help him win back his nickname anytime soon.

She came to mind again, the capricious goddess of uncertain destiny. And Kaa's own Trinary phrase came back to him, as if reflected and reconverged by the surrounding alien waters.

> * Welcome . . .
>> * Welcome . . .
>>> * Welcome to Ifni's Shore . . . *

Sooners

The Stranger

EXISTENCE SEEMS LIKE WANDERING THROUGH A vast chaotic house. One that has been torn by quakes and fire, and is now filled with bitter, inexplicable fog. Whenever he manages to pry open a door, exposing some small corner of the past, each revelation comes at the price of sharp waves of agony.

In time, he learns not to be swayed by the pain. Rather, each ache and sting serves as a *marker,* a signpost, confirming that he must be on the right path.

His arrival on this world—plummeting through a scorched sky—should have ended with merciful blankness. What luck instead hurled his blazing body from the pyre to quench in a fetid swamp?

Peculiar luck.

Since then, he has grown intimate with all kinds of suffering, from crass pangs to subtle stings. In cataloging them, he grows learned in the many ways there are to hurt.

Those earliest agonies, right after the crash, had

screeched coarsely from wounds and scalding burns—a gale of such fierce torment that he barely noticed when a motley crew of local savages rowed out to him in a make-shift boat, like sinners dragging a fallen angel out of the boggy fen. Saving him from drowning, only to face more damnations.

Beings who insisted that he fight for his broken life, when it would have been so much easier just to let go.

Later, as his more blatant injuries healed or scarred, other types of anguish took up the symphony of pain.

Afflictions of the mind.

Holes gape across his life, vast blank zones, lightless and empty, where missing memories must once have spanned megaparsecs and life years. Each gap feels chilled beyond numbness—a raw vacancy more frustrating than an itch that can't be scratched.

Ever since he began wandering this singular world, he has probed the darkness within. Optimistically, he clutches a few small trophies from the struggle.

Jijo is one of them.

He rolls the word in his mind—the name of this planet where six castaway races band together in feral truce, a mixed culture unlike any other beneath the myriad stars.

A second word comes more easily with repeated use— *Sara*. She who nursed him from near death in her tree house overlooking a rustic water mill . . . who calmed the fluxing panic when he first woke to see pincers, claws, and mucusy ring stacks—the physiques of *hoons, traekis, qheuens,* and others sharing this rude outcast existence.

He knows more words, such as *Kurt* and *Prity* . . . friends he now trusts almost as much as *Sara*. It feels good to think their names, the slick way all words used to come, in the days before his mangling.

One recent prize he is especially proud of.

Emerson . . .

It is his own name, for so long beyond reach. Violent shocks had jarred it free, less than a day ago—shortly after he provoked a band of human rebels to betray their urrish allies in a slashing knife fight that made a space battle seem antiseptic by comparison. That bloody frenzy ended with an explosive blast, shattering the grubby caravan tent, spearing light past Emerson's closed lids, overwhelming the guardians of reason.

And then, amid the dazzling rays, he had briefly glimpsed . . . his captain!

Creideiki . . .

The blinding glow became a luminous foam, whipped by thrashing flukes. Out of that froth emerged a long gray form whose bottle snout bared glittering teeth. The sleek head *grinned,* despite bearing an awful wound behind its left eye . . . much like the hurt that robbed Emerson of speech.

Utterance shapes formed out of scalloped bubbles, in a language like none spoken by Jijo's natives, or by any great Galactic clan.

> * *In the turning*
> > *of the cycloid,*
> * *Comes a time*
> > *to break for surface.*
>
> * *Time to resume*
> > *breathing,*
> > *doing.*
> * *To rejoin the*
> > *great sea's*
> > *dreaming.*
>
> * *Time has come*
> > *for* you *my old friend.*
> * *Time to wake*
> > *and see what's churning. . . .* *

Stunned recognition accompanied waves of stinging misery, worse than any fleshy woe or galling numbness.

Shame had nearly overwhelmed him then. For no injury short of death could ever excuse his forgetting—

Creideiki . . .

Terra . . .

The dolphins . . .

Hannes . . .

Gillian . . .

How could they have slipped his mind during the months he wandered this barbarian world, by boat, barge, and caravan?

Guilt might have engulfed him during that instant of recollection . . . except that his new friends urgently needed him to act, to seize the brief advantage offered by the explosion, to overcome their captors and take them prisoner. As dusk fell across the shredded tent and torn bodies, he had helped Sara and Kurt tie up their surviving foes—both urrish and human—although Sara seemed to think their reprieve temporary.

More fanatic reinforcements were expected soon.

Emerson knew what the rebels wanted. They wanted *him*. It was no secret that he came from the stars. The rebels would trade him to sky hunters, hoping to exchange his battered carcass for guaranteed survival.

As if anything could save Jijo's castaway races, now that the Five Galaxies had found them.

Huddled round a wan fire, lacking any shelter but tent rags, Sara and the others watched as terrifying portents crossed bitter-cold constellations.

First came a mighty titan of space, growling as it plunged toward nearby mountains, bent on awful vengeance.

Later, following the very same path, there came a *second* behemoth, this one so enormous that Jijo's pull seemed to lighten as it passed overhead, filling everyone with deep foreboding.

Not long after that, golden lightning flickered amid the mountain peaks—a bickering of giants. But Emerson did not care who won. He could tell that neither vessel was *his* ship, the home in space he yearned for . . . and prayed he would never see again.

With luck, *Streaker* was far away from this doomed world, bearing in its hold a trove of ancient mysteries— perhaps the key to a new galactic era.

Had not all his sacrifices been aimed at helping her escape?

After the leviathans passed, there remained only stars and a chill wind, blowing through the dry steppe grass, while Emerson went off searching for the caravan's scattered pack animals. With donkeys, his friends just might yet escape before more fanatics arrived. . . .

Then came a rumbling noise, jarring the ground beneath his feet. A rhythmic cadence that seemed to go—

taranta taranta
taranta taranta

The galloping racket could only be urrish hoofbeats, the expected rebel reinforcements, come to make them prisoners once again.

Only, miraculously, the darkness instead poured forth *allies*—unexpected rescuers, both urrish and human—who brought with them astonishing beasts.

Horses.

Saddled horses, clearly as much a surprise to Sara as they were to him. Emerson had thought the creatures were extinct on this world, yet here they were, emerging from the night as if from a dream.

So began the next phase of his odyssey. Riding southward, fleeing the shadow of these vengeful ships, hurrying toward the outline of an uneasy volcano.

Now he wonders within his battered brain—is there a plan? A destination?

Old Kurt apparently has faith in these surprising saviors, but there must be more to it than that.

Emerson is tired of just running away.

He would much rather be running toward.

While his steed bounds ahead, new aches join the background music of his life—raw, chafed thighs and a bruised spine that jars with each pounding hoofbeat.

taranta, taranta, taranta-tara
taranta, taranta, taranta-tara

Guilt nags him with a sense of duties unfulfilled, and he grieves over the likely fate of his new friends on Jijo, now that their hidden colony has been discovered.

And yet . . .

In time Emerson recalls how to ease along with the sway of the saddle. And as sunrise lifts dew off fan-fringed trees near a riverbank, swarms of bright bugs whir through the slanted light, dancing as they pollinate a field of purple blooms. When Sara glances back from her own steed, sharing a rare smile, his pangs seem to matter less. Even fear of those terrible starships, splitting the sky with their angry engine arrogance, cannot erase a growing elation as the fugitive band gallops on to dangers yet unknown.

Emerson cannot help himself. It is his nature to seize any possible excuse for hope. As the horses pound Jijo's ancient turf, their cadence draws him down a thread of familiarity, recalling rhythmic music quite apart from the persistent dirge of woe.

> *tarantara, tarantara*
> *tarantara, tarantara*

Under insistent stroking by that throbbing sound, something abruptly clicks inside. His body reacts involuntarily as unexpected *words* surge from some dammed-up corner of his brain, attended by a melody that stirs the heart. Lyrics pour reflexively, an undivided stream, through lungs and throat before he even knows that he is singing.

"Though in body and in mind, {tarantara, tarantara}
We are timidly inclined, {tarantara!}
And anything but blind, {tarantara, tarantara}
To the danger that's behind— {tarantara!}"

His friends grin—this has happened before.

"Yet, when the danger's near, {tarantara, tarantara}
We manage to appear, {tarantara!}
As insensible to fear,
As anybody here,
As an-y-bo-dy here!"

Sara laughs, joining the refrain, and even the dour urrish escorts stretch their long necks to lisp along.

"Yet, when the danger's near,
We manage to appear,
As insensible to fear,
    As anybody here,
      As anybody here!"

{tarantara, tarantara}
{tarantara!}"

PART ONE

EACH OF THE SOONER RACES making up the Commons of Jijo tells its own unique story, passed down from generation to generation, explaining why their ancestors surrendered godlike powers and risked terrible penalties to reach this far place—skulking in sneakships past Institute patrols, robot guardians, and Zang globules. Seven waves of sinners, each coming to plant their outlaw seed on a world that had been declared off-limits to settlement. A world set aside to rest and recover in peace, but for the likes of us.

THE g'Kek arrived first on this land we call the Slope, between misty mountains and the sacred sea—half a million years after the last legal tenants—the Buyur—departed Jijo.

Why did those g'Kek founders willingly give up their former lives as star-traveling gods and citizens of the Five Galaxies? Why choose instead to dwell as fallen primitives, lacking the comforts of technology, or any moral solace but for a few engraved platinum scrolls?

Legend has it that our g'Kek cousins

fled threatened extinction, a dire punishment for devastating gambling losses. But we cannot be sure. Writing was a lost art until humans came, so those accounts may be warped by passing time.

What we do know is that it could not have been a petty threat that drove them to abandon the spacefaring life they loved, seeking refuge on heavy Jijo, where their wheels have such a hard time on the rocky ground. With four keen eyes, peering in all directions at the end of graceful stalks, did the g'Kek ancestors see a dark destiny painted on galactic winds? Did that first generation see no other choice? Perhaps they only cursed their descendants to this savage life as a last resort.

NOT long after the g'Kek, roughly two thousand years ago, a party of *traeki* dropped hurriedly from the sky, as if fearing pursuit by some dreaded foe. Wasting no time, they sank their sneakship in the deepest hollow of the sea, then settled down to be our gentlest tribe.

What nemesis drove them from the spiral lanes?

Any native Jijoan glancing at those familiar stacks of fatty toruses, venting fragrant steam and placid wisdom in each village of the Slope, must find it hard to imagine the traeki having enemies.

In time, they confided their story. The foe they fled was not some other race, nor was there a deadly vendetta among the star gods of the Five Galaxies. Rather, it was an aspect of their own selves. Certain rings—components of their physical bodies— had lately been modified in ways that turned their kind into formidable beings. Into *Jophur*, mighty and feared among the noble Galactic clans.

It was a fate those traeki founders deemed unbearable. So they chose to become lawless refugees—*sooners* on a taboo world—in order to shun a horrid destiny.

The obligation to be great.

•   •   •

IT is said that *glavers* came to Jijo not out of fear, but seeking the Path of Redemption—the kind of innocent oblivion that wipes all slates clean. In this goal they have succeeded far better than anyone else, showing the rest of us the way, if we dare follow their example.

Whether or not that sacred track will also be ours, we must respect their accomplishment—transforming themselves from cursed fugitives into a race of blessed simpletons. As starfaring immortals, they could be held accountable for their crimes, including the felony of invading Jijo. But now they have reached a refuge, the purity of ignorance, free to start again.

Indulgently, we let glavers root through our kitchen middens, poking under logs for insects. Once mighty intellects, they are not counted among the sooner races of Jijo anymore. They are no longer stained with the sins of their forebears.

QHEUENS were the first to arrive filled with wary ambition.

Led by fanatical, crablike gray matrons, their first-generation colonists snapped all five pincers derisively at any thought of union with Jijo's other exile races. Instead, they sought dominion.

That plan collapsed in time, when *blue* and *red* qheuens abandoned historic roles of servitude, drifting off to seek their own ways, leaving their frustrated gray empresses helpless to enforce old feudal loyalties.

OUR tall *hoonish* brethren inhale deeply, whenever the question arises—"Why are you here?" They fill their prodigious throat sacs with low meditation umbles. In rolling tones, hoon elders relate that their ancestors fled no great danger, no oppression or unwanted obligations.

Then why *did* they come, risking frightful punishment if their descendants are ever caught living illegally on Jijo?

The oldest hoons on Jijo merely shrug with frustrating

cheerfulness, as if they do not know the reason, and could not be bothered to care.

Some do refer to a legend, though. According to that slim tale, a Galactic *oracle* once offered a starfaring hoonish clan a unique opportunity, if they dared take it. An opportunity to claim something that had been robbed from them, although they never knew it was lost. A precious birthright that might be discovered on a forbidden world.

But for the most part, whenever one of the tall ones puffs his throat sac to sing about past times, he rumbles a deep, joyful ballad about the crude rafts, boats, and seagoing ships that hoons invented from scratch, soon after landing on Jijo. Things their humorless star cousins would never have bothered looking up in the all-knowing Galactic Library, let alone have deigned to build.

LEGENDS told by the fleet-footed *urrish* clan imply that their foremothers were rogues, coming to Jijo in order to *breed*—escaping limits imposed in civilized parts of the Five Galaxies. With their short lives, hot tempers, and prolific sexual style, the urs founders might have gone on to fill Jijo with their kind . . . or else met extinction by now, like the mythical centaurs they vaguely resemble.

But they escaped both of those traps. Instead, after many hard struggles, at the forge and on the battlefield, they assumed an honored place in the Commons of Six Races. With their thundering herds, and mastery of steel, they live hot and hard, making up for their brief seasons in our midst.

FINALLY, two centuries ago, Earthlings came, bringing chimpanzees and other treasures. But humans' greatest gift was *paper*. In creating the printed trove of Biblos, they became lore masters to our piteous commonwealth of exiles. Printing and education changed life on the Slope, spurring a new tradition of scholarship, so that later generations of castaways dared to study their adopted world, their hybrid civilization, and even their own selves.

As for *why* humans came all this way—breaking Galactic laws and risking everything, just to huddle with other outlaws under a fearsome sky—their tale is among the strangest told by Jijo's exile clans.

from *An Ethnography of the Slope,*
by Dorti Chang-Jones and Huph-alch-Huo

Sooners

Alvin

I HAD NO WAY TO MARK THE PASSAGE OF TIME, LY-ing dazed and half-paralyzed in a metal cell, listening to the engine hum of a mechanical sea dragon that was hauling me and my friends to parts unknown.

I guess a couple of days must have passed since the shattering of our makeshift submarine, our beautiful *Wuphon's Dream*, before I roused enough to wonder, What next?

Dimly, I recall the sea monster's face as we first saw it through our crude glass viewing port, lit by the *Dream*'s homemade searchlight. That glimpse lasted but a moment as the huge metal thing loomed toward us out of black, icy depths. The four of us—Huck, Pincer, Ur-ronn, and me—had already resigned ourselves to death . . . doomed to crushed oblivion at the bottom of the sea. Our expedition a failure, we didn't feel like daring subsea adventurers any-more, but like scared kids, voiding our bowels in terror as we waited for the cruel abyss to squeeze our hollowed-out tree trunk into a zillion soggy splinters.

Suddenly this enormous shape erupted toward us,

spreading jaws wide enough to snatch *Wuphon's Dream* whole.

Well, *almost* whole. Passing through that maw, we struck a glancing blow.

The collision shattered our tiny capsule.

What followed still remains a painful blur.

I guess anything beats death, but there have been moments since that impact when my back hurt so much that I just wanted to rumble one last umble through my battered throat sac and say *farewell* to young Alvin Hph-wayuo—junior linguist, humicking writer, uttergloss daredevil, and neglectful son of Mu-phauwq and Yowg-wayuo of Wuphon Port, the Slope, Jijo, Galaxy Four, the Universe.

But I stayed alive.

I guess it just didn't seem *hoonish* to give up, after everything my pals and I went through to get here. What if I was sole survivor? I owed it to Huck and the others to carry on.

My cell—a prison? hospital room?—measures just two meters, by two, by three. Pretty skimpy for a hoon, even one not quite fully grown. It gets even more cramped whenever some six-legged, metal-sheathed demon tries to squeeze inside to tend my injured spine, poking with what I assume (hope!) to be clumsy kindness. Despite their efforts, misery comes in awful waves, making me wish desperately for the pain remedies cooked up by Old Stinky—our traeki pharmacist back home.

It occurred to me that I might never walk again . . . or see my family, or watch seabirds swoop over the dross ships, anchored beneath Wuphon's domelike shelter trees.

I tried talking to the insecty giants trooping in and out of my cell. Though each had a torso longer than my dad is tall—with a flared back end, and a tubelike shell as hard as Buyur steel—I couldn't help picturing them as enormous *phuwnthus,* those six-legged vermin that gnaw the walls of wooden houses, giving off a sweet-tangy stench.

These things smell like overworked machinery. Despite my efforts in a dozen Earthling and Galactic languages, they seemed even less talkative than the *phuwnthus* Huck and I used to catch when we were little, and train to perform in a miniature circus.

I missed Huck during that dark time. I missed her quick g'Kek mind and sarcastic wit. I even missed the way she'd snag my leg fur in her wheels to get my attention, if I stared too long at the horizon in a hoonish sailor's trance. I last glimpsed those wheels spinning uselessly in the sea dragon's mouth, just after those giant jaws smashed our precious *Dream* and we spilled across the slivers of our amateur diving craft.

Why didn't I rush to my friend, during those bleak moments after we crashed? Much as I yearned to, it was hard to see or hear much while a screaming wind shoved its way into the chamber, pushing out the bitter sea. At first, I had to fight just to breathe again. Then, when I tried to move, my back would not respond.

In those blurry instants, I also recall catching sight of *Ur-ronn*, whipping her long neck about and screaming as she thrashed all four legs and both slim arms, horrified at being drenched in vile water. Ur-ronn bled where her suede-colored hide was pierced by jagged shards—remnants of the glass porthole she had proudly forged in the volcano workshops of Uriel the Smith.

Pincer-Tip was there, too, best equipped among our gang to survive underwater. As a red qheuen, Pincer was used to scampering on five chitin-armored claws across salty shallows—though our chance tumble into the bottomless void was more than even he had bargained for. In dim recollection, I *think* Pincer seemed alive . . . or does wishful thinking deceive me?

My last hazy memories of our "rescue" swarm with violent images until I blacked out . . . to wake in this cell, delirious and alone.

Sometimes the phuvnthus do something "helpful" to my spine, and it hurts so much that I'd willingly spill every secret I know. That is, if the phuvnthus ever asked questions, which they never do.

So I never allude to the mission we four were given by Uriel the Smith—to seek a taboo treasure that her ancestors left on the seafloor, centuries ago. An offshore cache, hidden when urrish settlers first jettisoned their ships and high-tech gadgets to become just one more fallen race. Only some dire emergency would prompt Uriel to violate the Covenant by retrieving such contraband.

I guess "emergency" might cover the arrival of alien robbers, plundering the Gathering Festival of the Six Races and threatening the entire Commons with genocide.

Eventually, the pangs in my spine eased enough for me to rummage through my rucksack and resume writing in this tattered journal, bringing my ill-starred adventure up to date. That raised my spirits a bit. Even if none of us survives, my diary might yet make it home someday.

Growing up in a little hoonish village, devouring human adventure stories by Clarke and Rostand, Conrad and Xu Xiang, I dreamed that people on the Slope would someday say, "Wow, that Alvin Hph-wayuo was some storyteller, as good as any old-time Earther."

This could be my one and only chance.

So I spent long miduras with a stubby charcoal crayon clutched in my big hoon fist, scribbling the passages that lead up to this one—an account of how I came to find myself in this low, low state.

—How four friends built a makeshift submarine out of skink skins and a carved-out garu log, fancying a treasure hunt to the Great Midden.

—How Uriel the Smith, in her mountain forge, threw her support behind our project, turning it from a half-baked dream into a real expedition.

—How we four snuck up to Uriel's observatory, and heard a human sage speak of *starships* in the sky, perhaps bringing foretold judgment on the Six Races.

—And how *Wuphon's Dream* soon dangled from a pole near Terminus Rock, where the Midden's sacred trench passes near land. And Uriel told us, hissing through her cloven upper lip, that a ship had indeed landed up north. But this cruiser did not carry Galactic magistrates. Instead another kind of criminal had come, worse even than our sinner ancestors.

So we sealed the hatch, and the great winch turned. But on reaching the mapped site, we found that Uriel's cache was already missing! Worse—when we went looking for the damned thing, *Wuphon's Dream* got lost and tumbled off the edge of an undersea cliff.

Flipping back some pages, I can tell my account of the journey was written by someone perched on a knife-edge of harrowing pain. Yet, there is a sense of *drama* I can't hope to match now. Especially that scene where the bottom vanished beneath our wheels and we felt ourselves fall toward the *real* Midden.

Toward certain death.

Until the phuvnthus snatched us up.

So, here I am, swallowed by a metal whale, ruled by cryptic silent beings, ignorant whether my friends still live or if I am alone. Merely crippled, or dying.

Do my captors have anything to do with starship landings in the mountains?

Are they a different enigma, rising out of Jijo's ancient past? Relics of the vanished Buyur perhaps? Or ghosts even older still?

Answers seem scarce, and since I've finished recounting the plummet and demise of *Wuphon's Dream,* I daren't waste more precious paper on speculation. I must put my pencil down, even if it robs my last shield against loneliness.

All my life I've been inspired by human-style books, picturing myself as hero in some uttergloss tale. Now my sanity depends on learning to savor *patience.*

To let time pass without concern.

To live and think, at last, just like a hoon.

Asx

YOU MAY CALL ME *ASX*.

you manicolored rings, piled in a high tapered heap, venting fragrant stinks, sharing the victual sap that climbs our common core, or partaking in memory wax, trickling back down from our sensory peak.

you, the rings who take up diverse roles in this shared body, a pudgy cone nearly as tall as a hoon, as heavy as a blue qheuen, and slow across the ground like an aged g'Kek with a cracked axle.

you, the rings who vote each day whether to renew our coalition.

From you rings i/we now request a ruling. Shall we carry on this fiction? This "Asx"?

Unitary beings—the humans, urs, and other dear partners in exile—stubbornly use that term, Asx, to signify this loosely affiliated pile of fatty toruses, as if we/i truly had a fixed *name*, not a mere label of convenience.

Of course unitary beings are all quite mad. We traeki long ago resigned ourselves to living in a universe filled with egotism.

What we could not resign ourselves to—and the reason for our exile here on Jijo—was the prospect of becoming the most egotistical of all.

Once, our/my stack of bloated tubes played the role of a modest village pharmacist, serving others with our humble secretions, near the sea bogs of Far Wet Sanctuary. Then others began paying us/me homage, calling us "Asx," chief sage of the Traeki Sept and member of the Guiding Council of the Six.

Now we stand in a blasted wasteland that was formerly a pleasant festival glade. Our sensor rings and neural tendrils recoil from sights and sounds they cannot bear to perceive. And so we are left virtually blind, our component toruses buffeted by the harsh fields of two nearby starships, as vast as mountains.

Even now, awareness of those starships fades away. . . .

We are left in blackness.

•   •   •

What has just happened!

Be calm, my rings. This sort of thing has transpired before. Too great a shock can jar a traeki stack out of alignment, causing gaps in short-term memory. But there is another, surer way to find out what has happened. Neural memory is a flimsy thing. How much better off we are, counting on the slow/reliable wax.

Ponder the fresh wax that slithers down our common core, still hot-slick, imprinted with events that took place recently on this ill-fated glade, where once gay pavilions stood, and banners flapped in Jijo's happy winds. A typical festival, the annual gathering of Six Races to celebrate their hundred-year peace. Until—

Is this the memory we seek?

Behold . . . a starship comes to Jijo! Not sneaking by night, like our ancestors. Not aloofly, like a mysterious Zang globule. No, this was an arrogant cruiser from the Five Galaxies, commanded by aloof alien beings called *Rothen.*

Trace *this* memory of our first sight of Rothen lords, emerging at last from their metal lair, so handsome and noble in their condescension, projecting a majestic charisma that shadowed even their sky-human servants. How glorious to be a star god! Even gods who are "criminals" by Galactic law.

Did they not far outshine us miserable barbarians? As the sun outglows a tallow candle?

But we sages realized a horrifying truth. After hiring us for local expertise, to help them raid this world, the Rothen could not afford to leave witnesses behind.

They would not leave us alive.

No, that is too far back. Try again.

What about these other livid tracks, my rings? A red flaming pillar erupting in the night? An explosion, breaking apart our sacred pilgrimage? Do you recall the sight of the Rothen-Danik station, its girders, twisted and smoking? Its cache of biosamples burned? And most dire—one Rothen and a sky human killed?

By dawn's light, foul accusations hurled back and forth between Ro-kenn and our own High Sages. Appalling threats were exchanged.

No, that still took place over a day ago. Stroke wax that is more recent than that.

Here we find a broad sheet of terror, shining horribly down our oily core. Its colors/textures blend hot blood with cold fire, exuding a smoky scent of flaming trees and charred bodies.

Do you recall how Ro-kenn, the surviving Rothen master, swore vengeance on the Six Races, ordering his killer robots forward?

"Slay everyone in sight! Death to all who saw our secret revealed!"

But then behold a marvel! Platoons of our own brave militia. They spill from surrounding forest. Jijoan savages, armed only with arrows, pellet rifles, and courage. Do you now recall how they charged the hovering death demons . . . and prevailed!

The wax does not lie. It happened in mere instants, while these old traeki rings could only stare blankly at the battle's awful ruin, astonished that we/i were not ignited into a stack of flaming tubes.

Though dead and wounded lay piled around us, victory was clear. Victory for the Six Races! Ro-kenn and his god-like servants were disarmed, wide-eyed in their offended surprise at this turn of Ifni's ever-tumbling dice.

Yes, my rings. i know this is not the final memory. It took place many miduras in the past. Obviously something must have happened since then. Something dreadful.

Perhaps the Danik scout boat came back from its survey trip, carrying one of the fierce sky-human warriors who worship Rothen patron masters. Or else the main Rothen starship may have returned, expecting a trove of bio-plunder, only to find their samples destroyed, their station ruined, and comrades taken hostage.

That might explain the scent of sooty devastation that now fills our core.

But no later memories are yet available. The wax has not congealed.

To a traeki, that means none of it has really happened. Not yet.

Perhaps things are not as bad as they seem.

It is a gift we traeki reacquired when we came to Jijo. A talent that helps make up for the many things we left behind, when we abandoned the stars.

A gift for wishful thinking.

Rety

THE FIERCE WIND OF FLIGHT TORE DAMPNESS FROM her streaming eyes, sparing her the shame of tears running down scarred cheeks. Still, Rety could weep with rage, thinking of the hopes she'd lost. Lying prone on a hard metal plate, clutching its edge with hands and feet, she bore the harsh breeze as whipping tree branches smacked her face and caught her hair, sometimes drawing blood.

Mostly, she just held on for dear life.

The alien machine beneath her was supposed to be her loyal servant! But the cursed thing would *not* slow its panicky retreat, even long after all danger lay far behind. If Rety fell off now, at best it would take her days to limp back to the village of her birth, where less than a midura ago there had been a brief, violent ambush.

Her brain still roiled. In just a few heartbeats her plans had been spoiled, and it was all *Dwer*'s fault!

She heard the young hunter moan, held captive by metal arms below her perch. But as the wounded battle drone fled recklessly onward, Rety turned away from Dwer's suffering, which he had only brought on himself, trekking all the way to these filthy Gray Hills from his safe home near the sea—*the Slope*—where six intelligent races lived at a much *higher* level of ignorant poverty than her own birth clan of wretched savages. Why would slopies hike past two thousand leagues of hell to reach this dreary wasteland?

What did Dwer and his pals hope to accomplish? To conquer Rety's brutish relatives?

He could *have* her smelly kinfolk, for all she cared! *And* the band of urrish sooners Kunn subdued with fire from his screeching scout boat. Dwer was welcome to them all. Only, couldn't he have waited quietly in the woods till after Rety and Kunn finished their business here and flew off again? Why did he have to rush things and attack the robot with her aboard?

I bet he did it out of spite. Prob'ly can't stand knowing that I'm the one Jijo native with a chance to get away from this pit hole of a planet.

Inside, Rety knew better. Dwer's heart didn't work that way.

But mine does.

When he groaned again, Rety muttered angrily, "I'll make you even sorrier, Dwer, if I don't make it off this mudball 'cause of you!"

So much for her *glorious homecoming.*

At first it had seemed fun to pay a return visit, swooping from a cloud-decked sky in Kunn's silver dart, emerging proudly to amazed gasps from the shabby cousins, who had bullied her for fourteen awful years. What a fitting climax to her desperate gamble, a few months ago, when she finally found the nerve to flee all the muck and misery, setting forth alone to seek the fabled Slope her great-grandparents had left behind, when they chose the "free" life as wild sooners.

Free of the sages' prying rules about what beasts you may kill. Free from irky laws about how many babies you can have. Free from having to abide neighbors with four legs, or five, or that rolled on humming wheels.

Rety snorted contempt for the founders of her tribe.

Free from books and medicine. Free to live like animals!

Fed up, Rety had set out to find something better or die trying.

The journey had nearly killed her—crossing icy torrents and parched wastes. Her closest call came traversing a high pass into the Slope, following a mysterious metal bird into a mulc spider's web. A web that became a terrifying trap when the spider's tendrils closed around her, oozing golden drops that horribly *preserved.* . . .

Memory came unbidden—of *Dwer* charging through that awful thicket with a gleaming machete, then sheltering her with his body when the web caught fire.

She recalled the bright bird, glittering in flames, treacherously cut down by an attacking robot just like her "servant." The one now hauling her off to Ifni-knew-where.

Rety's mind veered as a gut-wrenching swerve nearly spilled her overboard. She screamed at the robot.

"*Idiot!* No one's shooting at you anymore! There were just a few slopies, and they were all afoot. Nothing on Jijo could catch you now!"

But the frantic contraption plunged ahead, riding a cushion of incredible god force.

Rety wondered, Could it sense her contempt? Dwer and two or three friends, equipped with crude fire sticks, had taken just a few duras to disable and drive off the so-called war bot, though at some cost to themselves.

Ifni, what a snarl. She pondered the sooty hole where Dwer's surprise attack had ripped out its antenna. *How'm I gonna explain this to Kunn?*

Rety's adopted rank as an honorary star god was already fragile. The angry pilot might simply abandon her in these hills where she had grown up, among savages she loathed.

I won't go back to the tribe, she vowed. *I'd rather join wild glavers, sucking bugs off dead critters on the Poison Plain.*

It was all Dwer's fault, of course. Rety hated listening to the young fool moan.

We're heading south, where Kunn flew off to. The robot

must be rushin' to report in person, now that it can't far-speak anymore.

Having witnessed Kunn's skill at torture, Rety found herself hoping Dwer's leg wound would reopen. Bleeding to death would be better by far.

The fleeing machine left the Gray Hills, slanting toward a tree-dotted prairie. Streams converged, turning the brook into a river, winding slowly toward the tropics.

The journey grew smoother and Rety risked sitting up again. But the robot did not take the obvious shortcut over water. Instead, it followed each oxbow curve, seldom venturing past the reedy shallows.

The land seemed pleasant. Good for herds or farming, if you knew how, and weren't afraid of being caught.

It brought to mind all the wonders she had seen on the Slope, after barely escaping the mulc spider. Folk there had all sorts of clever arts Rety's tribe lacked. Yet, despite their fancy windmills and gardens, their metal tools and paper books, the slopies had seemed dazed and frightened when Rety reached the famous Festival Glade.

What had the Six Races so upset was the recent coming of a *starship,* ending two thousand years of isolation.

To Rety, the spacers seemed wondrous. A ship owned by unseen Rothen masters, but crewed by *humans* so handsome and knowing that Rety would give anything to be like them. Not a doomed savage with a scarred face, eking out a life on a taboo world.

A daring ambition roused . . . and by pluck and guts she had made it happen! Rety got to know those haughty men and women—*Ling, Besh, Kunn,* and *Rann*—worming her way into their favor. When asked, she gladly guided fierce Kunn to her tribe's old camp, retracing her earlier epic journey in a mere quarter day, munching Galactic treats while staring through the scout boat's window at wastelands below.

Years of abuse were repaid by her filthy cousins' shocked stares, beholding her transformed from grubby urchin to *Rety, the star god.*

If only that triumph could have lasted.

• • •

She jerked back when Dwer called her name.

Peering over the edge, Rety saw his windburned face, the wild black hair plastered with dried sweat. One buckskin breech leg was stained ocher brown under a makeshift compress, though Rety saw no sign of new wetness. Trapped by the robot's unyielding tendrils, Dwer clutched his precious hand-carved bow, as if it were the last thing he would part with before death. Rety could scarcely believe she once thought the crude weapon worth stealing.

"What do you want now?" she demanded.

The young hunter's eyes met hers. His voice came out as a croak.

"Can I . . . have some water?"

"Assumin' I have any," she muttered, "name one reason I'd share it with you!"

Rustling at her waist. A narrow head and neck snaked out of her belt pouch. Three dark eyes glared—two with lids and one pupilless, faceted like a jewel.

"wife be not liar to this one! wife has water bottle! yee smells its bitterness."

Rety sighed over this unwelcome interruption by her miniature "husband."

"There's just half left. No one tol' me I was goin' on a trip!"

The little urrish male hissed disapproval. "wife share with this one, or bad luck come! no hole safe for grubs or larvae!"

Rety almost retorted that her marriage to yee was not real. They would never have "grubs" together. Anyway, yee seemed bent on being her portable conscience, even when it was clearly every creature for herself.

I never should've told him how Dwer saved me from the mulc spider. They say male urs are dumb. Ain't it my luck to marry a genius one?

"Oh . . . all right!"

The bottle, an alien-made wonder, weighed little more than the liquid it contained. "Don't drop it," she warned Dwer, lowering the red cord. He grabbed it eagerly.

"No, fool! The top don't *pull* off like a stopper. *Turn*

it till it comes off. That's right. Jeekee know-nothin' slopie."

She didn't add how the concept of a screw cap had mystified her, too, when Kunn and the others first adopted her as a provisional Danik. Of course that was before she became sophisticated.

Rety watched nervously as he drank.

"Don't spill it. An' don't you *dare* drink it all! You hear me? That's enough, Dwer. Stop now. *Dwer!*"

But he ignored her protests, guzzling while she cursed. When the canteen was drained, Dwer smiled at her through cracked lips.

Too stunned to react, Rety knew—she would have done exactly the same.

Yeah, an inner voice answered. *But I didn't expect it of him.*

Her anger spun off when Dwer squirmed, tilting his body toward the robot's headlong rush. Squinting against the wind, he held the loop cord in one hand and the bottle in the other, as if waiting for something to happen. The flying machine crested a low hill, hopping over some thorny thickets, then plunged down the other side, barely avoiding several tree branches. Rety held tight, keeping yee secure in his pouch. When the worst jouncing ended she peered down again . . . and rocked back from a pair of black, beady eyes!

It was the damned *noor* again. The one Dwer called *Mudfoot.* Several times the dark, lithe creature had tried to clamber up from his niche, between Dwer's torso and a cleft in the robot's frame. But Rety didn't like the way he salivated at yee, past needle-sharp teeth. Now Mudfoot stood on Dwer's rib cage, using his forepaws to probe for another effort.

"Get lost!" She swatted at the narrow, grinning face. "I want to see what Dwer's doin'."

Sighing, the noor returned to his nest under the robot's flank.

A flash of blue came into view just as Dwer threw the bottle. It struck watery shallows with a splash, pressing a furrowed wake. The young man had to make several attempts to get the cord twisted so the canteen dragged with its opening forward. The container sloshed when Dwer reeled it back in.

I'd've thought of that, too. If I was close enough to try it.

Dwer had lost blood, so it was only fair to let him drink and refill a few more times before passing it back up.

Yeah. Only fair. And he'll do it, too. He'll give it back full.

Rety faced an uncomfortable thought.

You trust him.

He's the enemy. He caused you and the Daniks heaps of trouble. But you'd trust Dwer with your life.

She had no similar confidence in Kunn, when it came time to face the Rothen-loving stellar warrior.

Dwer refilled the bottle one last time and held it up toward her. "Thanks, Rety . . . I owe you."

Her cheeks flushed, a sensation she disliked. "Forget it. Just toss the cord."

He tried. Rety felt it brush her fingertips, but after half a dozen efforts she could never quite hook the loop. *What happens if I don't get it back!*

The noor beast emerged from his narrow niche and took the cord in his teeth. Clambering over Dwer's chest, then using the robot's shattered laser tube as a support, Mudfoot slithered closer to Rety's hand. *Well,* she thought. *If it's gonna be helpful . . .*

As she reached for the loop, the noor sprang, using his claws as if her arm were a handy climbing vine. Rety howled, but before she could react, Mudfoot was already up on top, grinning smugly.

Little yee let out a yelp. The urrish male pulled his head inside her pouch and drew the zipper shut.

Rety saw blood spots well along her sleeve and lashed in anger, trying to kick the crazy noor off. But Mudfoot dodged easily, inching close, grinning appealingly and rumbling a low sound, presenting the water bottle with two agile forepaws.

Sighing heavily, Rety accepted it and let the noor settle down nearby—on the opposite side from yee.

"I can't seem to shake myself loose of *any* of you guys, can I?" she asked aloud.

Mudfoot chittered. And from below, Dwer uttered a short laugh—ironic and tired.

Alvin

IT WAS A LONELY TIME, CONFINED IN GNAWING PAIN to a cramped metal cell. The distant, humming engine reminded me of umble lullabies my father used to sing, when I came down with toe pox or itchysac. Sometimes the noise changed pitch and made my scales frickle, sounding like the moan of a doomed wooden ship when it runs aground.

Finally I slept . . .

. . . then wakened in terror to find that a pair of metal-clad, six-legged monsters were tying me into a contraption of steel tubes and straps! At first, it looked like a pre-contact torture device I once saw in the Doré-illustrated edition of *Don Quixote*. Thrashing and resisting accomplished nothing, but hurt like bloody blue blazes.

Finally, with some embarrassment, I realized. It was no instrument of torment but a makeshift *back brace*, shaped to fit my form and take weight off my injured spine. I fought to suppress panic at the tight metal touch, as they set me on my feet. Swaying with surprise and relief, I found I could walk a little, though wincing with each step.

"Well thanks, you big ugly bugs," I told the nearest of the giant phuvnthus. "But you might've warned me first."

I expected no answer, but one of them turned its armored torso—with a humped back and wide flare at the rear—and tilted toward me. I took the gesture as a polite bow, though perhaps it meant something different to them.

They left the door open when they exited this time. Slowly, cringing at the effort, I stepped out for the first time from my steel coffin, following as the massive creatures stomped down a narrow corridor.

I already figured I was aboard a submarine of some sort, big enough to carry in its hold the greatest hoonish craft sailing Jijo's seas.

Despite that, it was a hodgepodge. I thought of Frankenstein's monster, pieced together from the parts of many corpses. So seemed the monstrous vessel hauling me to who-knows-where. Each time we crossed a hatch, it seemed as if we'd pass into a distinct ship, made by different artisans . . . by a whole different *civilization*. In one section, the decks and bulkheads were made of riveted steel sheets. Another zone was fashioned from some fibrous substance—flexible but strong. The corridors changed proportions—from wide to painfully narrow. Half the time I had to stoop under low ceilings . . . not a lot of fun in the state my back was in.

Finally, a sliding door hissed open. A phuvnthu motioned me ahead with a crooked mandible and I entered a dim chamber much larger than my former cell.

My hearts surged with joy. Before me stood my friends! All of them—alive!

They were gathered round a circular viewing port, staring at inky ocean depths. I might've tried sneaking in to surprise them, but qheuens and g'Keks literally have "eyes in the back of their heads," making it a challenge to startle Huck and Pincer.

(I *have* managed it, a couple of times.)

When they shouted my name, Ur-ronn whirled her long neck and outraced them on four clattering hooves. We plunged into a multispecies embrace.

Huck was first to bring things back to normal, snapping at Pincer.

"Watch the claws, Crab Face! You'll snap a spoke! Back off, all of you. Can't you see Alvin's hurt? Give him room!"

"Look who talks," Ur-ronn replied. "Your left wheel just squished his toes, Octofus Head!"

I hadn't noticed till she pointed it out, so happy was I to hear their testy, adolescent whining once more.

"Hr-rm. Let me look at you all. Ur-ronn, you seem so much . . . *drier* than I saw you last."

Our urrish buddy blew a rueful laugh through her nostril fringe. Her pelt showed large bare patches where fur had sloughed after her dousing. "It took our hosts a while to adjust the hunidity of ny guest suite, vut they finally got it right," she said. Her torso showed tracks of hasty needle-work—the phuvnthus' rough stitching to close Ur-ronn's gashes after she smashed through the glass port of *Wuphon's Dream*. Fortunately, her folk don't play the same mating games as some races. To urs, what matters is not appearance, but *status*. A visible dent or two will help Ur-ronn show the other smiths she's been around.

"Yeah. And now we know what an urs smells like after actually taking a *bath*," Huck added. "They oughta try it more often."

"*You* should talk? With that green eyeball sweat—"

"All right, all right!" I laughed. "Just stopper it long enough for me to look at you, eh?"

Ur-ronn was right. Huck's eyestalks needed grooming and she had good reason to worry about her spokes. Many were broken, with new-spun fibers just starting to lace the rims. She would have to move cautiously for some time.

As for Pincer, he looked happier than ever.

"I guess you were right about there being monsters in the deep," I told our red-shelled friend. "Even if they hardly look like the ones you descr—"

I yelped when sharp needles seemed to lance into my back, clambering up my neck ridge. I quickly recognized the rolling growl of *Huphu,* our little noor-beast mascot, expressing gladness by demanding a rumble umble from me right away.

Before I could find out if my sore throat sac was up to it, Ur-ronn whistled from the pane of dark glass. "They turned on the searchlight again," she fluted, with hushed awe in her voice. "Alvin, hurry. You've got to look!"

Awkwardly on crutches, I moved to the place they made for me. Huck stroked my arm. "You always wanted to see this, pal," she said. "So gaze out there in wonder.

"Welcome to the Great Midden."

Asx

HERE IS ANOTHER MEMORY, MY RINGS. AN EVENT that followed the brief Battle of the Glade, so swiftly that war echoes still abused our battered forest canyons.

Has the wax congealed enough yet? Can you stroke-and-sense the awesome disquiet, the frightening beauty of that evening, as we watched a harsh, untwinkling glow pass overhead?

Trace the fatty memory of that spark crossing the sky, brightening as it spiraled closer.

No one could doubt its identity.

The Rothen cruiser, returning for its harvest of bi-oplunder, looted from a fragile world.

Returning for those comrades it had left behind.

Instead of genetic booty, the crew will find their station smashed, their colleagues killed or taken.

Worse, their true faces are known! We castaways might testify against them in Galactic courts. Assuming we survive.

It takes no cognition genius to grasp the trouble we faced. We six fallen races of forlorn Jijo.

As an Earthling writer might put it—we found ourselves in fetid mulch. Very ripe and very deep.

Sara

THE JOURNEY PASSED FROM AN ANXIOUS BLUR INTO something exalting . . . almost transcendent.

But not at the beginning.

When they perched her suddenly atop a galloping creature straight out of mythology, Sara's first reaction was terrified surprise. With snorting nostrils and huge tossing head, the *horse* was more daunting than Tarek Town's stone tribute to a lost species. Its muscular torso flexed with each forward bound, shaking Sara's teeth as it crossed the foothills of the central Slope by the light of a pale moon.

After two sleepless days and nights, it still seemed dreamlike the way a squadron of the legendary beasts came trotting into the ruined Urunthai campsite, accompanied by armed urrish escorts. Sara and her friends had just escaped captivity—their former kidnappers lay either dead or bound with strips of shredded tent cloth—but she expected reenslavement at any moment. Only then, instead of fresh foes, the darkness brought forth these bewildering saviors.

Bewildering to everyone except Kurt the Exploser, who welcomed the newcomers as expected friends. While Jomah and the Stranger exclaimed wonder at seeing real-life horses, Sara barely had time to blink before she was thrust onto a saddle.

Blade volunteered to stay by the bleak fire and tend the wounded, though envy filled each forlorn spin of his blue cupola. Sara would trade places with her qheuen friend, but his chitin armor was too massive for a horse to carry. There was barely time to give Blade a wave of encouragement before the troop wheeled back the way they came, bearing her into the night.

Pounding hoofbeats soon made Sara's skull ache.

I guess it beats captivity by Dedinger's human chauvinists, and those fanatic Urunthai. The coalition of zealots, volatile as an exploser's cocktail, had joined forces to snatch the Stranger and sell him to Rothen invaders. But they underestimated the enigmatic voyager. Despite his crippling loss of speech, the starman found a way to incite urs-human suspicion into bloody riot.

Leaving us masters of our own fate, though it couldn't last.

Now here was a *different* coalition of humans and centauroid urs! A more cordial group, but just as adamant about hauling her Ifni-knew-where.

When limnous Torgen rose above the foothills, Sara got to look over the urrish warriors, whose dun flanks were daubed with more subtle war paint than the garish Urunthai. Yet their eyes held the same dark flame that drenched urs' souls when conflict scents fumed. Cantering in skirmish formation, their slim hands cradled arbalests while long necks coiled, tensely wary. Though much smaller than horses, the urrish fighters conveyed formidable craftiness.

The human rescuers were even more striking. Six *women* who came north with nine saddled horses, as if they expected to retrieve just two or three others for a return trip.

But there's six of us. Kurt and Jomah. Prity and me. The Stranger and Dedinger.

No matter. The stern riders seemed indifferent about doubling up, two to a saddle.

Is that why they're all female? To keep the weight down?

While deft astride their great mounts, the women seemed uneasy with the hilly terrain of gullies and rocky spires. Sara gathered they disliked rushing about strange trails at night. She could hardly blame them.

Not one had a familiar face. That might have surprised Sara a month ago, given Jijo's small human population. The Slope must be bigger than she thought.

Dwer would tell stories about his travels, scouting for the sages. He claimed he'd been everywhere within a thousand leagues.

Her brother never mentioned horse-riding amazons.

Sara briefly wondered if they came from off-Jijo, since this seemed the year for spaceships. But no. Despite some odd slang, their terse speech was related to Jijoan dialects she knew from her research. And while the riders seemed unfamiliar with this region, they knew to lean away from a migurv tree when the trail passed near its sticky fronds. The Stranger, though warned with gestures not to touch its seed pods, reached for one curiously and learned the hard way.

She glanced at Kurt. The exploser's gaunt face showed satisfaction with each league they sped southward. The existence of horses was no surprise to him.

We're told our society is open. But clearly there are secrets known to a few.

Not *all* explosers shared it. Kurt's nephew chattered happy amazement while exchanging broad grins with the Stranger . . .

Sara corrected herself.

With *Emerson.* . . .

She peered at the dark man who came plummeting from the sky months ago, dousing his burns in a dismal swamp near Dolo Village. No longer the near corpse she had nursed in her tree house, the star voyager was proving a resourceful adventurer. Though still largely mute, he had passed a milestone a few miduras ago when he began thumping his chest, repeating that word—*Emerson*—over and over, beaming pride over a feat that undamaged folk took for granted. Uttering one's own name.

Emerson seemed at home on his mount. Did that mean horses were still used among the god worlds of the Five Galaxies? If so, what purpose might they serve, where miraculous machines did your bidding at a nod and wink?

Sara checked on her chimp assistant, in case the jouncing ride reopened Prity's bullet wound. Riding with both arms clenched round the waist of a horsewoman, Prity kept her eyes closed the whole time, no doubt immersed in her beloved universe of abstract shapes and forms—a better world than this one of sorrow and messy nonlinearity.

That left *Dedinger,* the rebel leader, riding along with both hands tied. Sara wasted no pity on the scholar-turned-prophet. After years preaching militant orthodoxy, urging his desert followers toward the Path of Redemption, the ex-sage clearly knew patience. Dedinger's hawklike face bore an expression Sara found unnerving.

Serene calculation.

The tooth-jarring pace swelled when the hilly track met open ground. Soon Ulashtu's detachment of urrish warriors fell behind, unable to keep up.

No wonder some urs clans resented horses, when humans first settled Jijo. The beasts gave us mobility, the trait most loved by urrish captains.

Two centuries ago, after trouncing the human newcomers in battle, the original Urunthai faction claimed Earthlings' beloved mounts as war booty, and slaughtered every one.

They figured we'd be no more trouble, left to walk and fight on foot. A mistake that proved fatal when Drake the Elder forged a coalition to hunt the Urunthai, and drowned the cult's leadership at Soggy Hoof Falls.

Only, it seems horses weren't extinct, after all. How could a clan of horse-riding folk remain hidden all this time?

And as puzzling—*Why emerge now, risking exposure by rushing to meet Kurt?*

It must be the crisis of the starships, ending Jijo's blessed/cursed isolation. What point in keeping secrets, if Judgment Day is at hand?

Sara was exhausted and numb by the time morning pushed through an overcast sky. An expanse of undulating hills stretched ahead to a dark green marsh.

The party dismounted at last by a shaded creek. Hands aimed her toward a blanket, where she collapsed with a shuddering sigh.

Sleep came laced with images of people she had left behind.

Nelo, her aged father, working in his beloved paper mill, unaware that some conspired its ruin.

Melina, her mother, dead several years now, who always seemed an outsider since arriving in Dolo long ago, with a baby son in her arms.

Frail Joshu, Sara's lover in Biblos, whose touch made her forget even the overhanging Fist of Stone. A comely rogue whose death sent her spinning.

Dwer and Lark, her brothers, setting out to attend festival in the high Rimmer glades . . . where starships were later seen descending.

Sara's mind roiled as she tossed and turned.

Last of all, she pictured Blade, whose qheuen hive farmed crayfish behind Dolo Dam. Good old Blade, who saved Sara and Emerson from disaster at the Urunthai camp.

"Seems I'm always late catching up," her qheuen friend whistled from three leg vents. *"But don't worry, I'll be along. Too much is happening to miss."*

Blade's armor-clad dependability had been like a rock to Sara. In her dream, she answered.

"I'll stall the universe . . . keep it from doing anything interesting until you show up."

Imagined or not, the blue qheuen's calliope laughter warmed Sara, and her troubled slumber fell into gentler rhythms.

The sun was half-high when someone shook Sara back to the world—one of the taciturn female riders, using the archaic word *brekkers* to announce the morning meal. Sara got up gingerly as waves of achy soreness coursed her body.

She gulped down a bowl of grain porridge, spiced with unfamiliar traeki seasonings, while horsewomen saddled mounts or watched Emerson play his beloved dulcimer, filling the pocket valley with a sprightly melody, suited for travel. Despite her morning irritability, Sara knew the starman was just making the best of the situation. Bursts of song were a way to overcome his handicap of muteness.

Sara found Kurt tying up his bedroll.

"Look," she told the elderly exploser, "I'm not ungrateful to your friends. I appreciate the rescue and all. But you can't seriously hope to ride horses all the way to . . . *Mount Guenn*." Her tone made it sound like one of Jijo's moons.

Kurt's stony face flickered a rare smile. "Any better suggestions? Sure, you planned taking the Stranger to the High Sages, but that way is blocked by angry Urunthai. And recall, we saw *two* starships last night, one after the other, headed straight for Festival Glade. The Sages must have their hands and tendrils full by now."

"How could I forget?" she murmured. Those titans, growling as they crossed the sky, had seared their image in her mind.

"You *could* hole up in one of the villages we'll pass soon, but won't Emerson need a first-rate pharmacist when he runs out of Pzora's medicine?"

"If we keep heading south we'll reach the Gentt. From there a riverboat can take us to Ovoom Town."

"Assuming boats are running . . . and Ovoom still exists. Even so, *should* you hide your alien friend, with great events taking place? What if he has a role to play? Some way to help sages and Commons? Might you spoil his one chance of goin' home?"

Sara saw Kurt's implication—that she was holding Emerson back, like a child refusing to release some healed forest creature into the wild.

A swarm of sweetbec flies drifted close to the starman, hovering and throbbing to the tempo of his music, a strange melody. Where did he learn it? On Earth? Near some alien star?

"Anyway," Kurt went on, "if you can stand riding these huge beasts awhile longer, we may reach Mount Guenn sooner than Ovoom."

"That's crazy! You must pass *through* Ovoom if you go by sea. And the other way around is worse—through the funnel canyons and the Vale."

Kurt's eyes flickered. "I'm told there's a . . . more direct route."

"Direct? You mean due *south*? Past the Gentt lies the Plain of Sharp Sand, a desperate crossing under good conditions—which these *aren't*. Have you forgotten that's where Dedinger has followers?"

"No, I haven't forgotten."

"Then, assuming we get past the sandmen and flame dunes, there comes the *Spectral Flow,* making any normal desert seem like a meadow!"

Kurt only shrugged, but clearly he wanted her to accompany him toward a distant simmering mountain, far from where Sara had sworn to take Emerson. Away from Lark and Dwer, and the terrible attraction of those fierce starships. Toward a starkly sacred part of Jijo, renowned for one thing above all—the way the planet renewed itself with flaming lava heat.

Alvin

MAYBE IT WAS THE COMPRESSED ATMOSPHERE WE breathed, or the ceaseless drone of reverberating engines. Or it could have been the perfect darkness outside that fostered an impression of incredible depth, even greater than when our poor little *Wuphon's Dream* fell into the maw of this giant metal sea beast. A single beam—immeasurably brighter than the handmade eik light of our old minisub—speared out to split the black, scanning territory beyond my wildest nightmares. Even the vivid imagery of Verne or Pukino or Melville offered no preparation for what was revealed by that roving circle as we cruised along a subsea canyon strewn with all manner of ancient dross. In rapid glimpses we saw so many titanic things, all jumbled together, that—

Here I admit I'm stumped. According to the texts that teach Anglic literature, there are two basic ways for a writer to describe unfamiliar objects. First is to catalog sights and sounds, measurements, proportions, colors—saying *this* object is made up of clusters of colossal *cubes* connected by translucent rods, or *that* one resembles a tremendous sphere caved in along one side, trailing from its crushed innards a glistening streamer, a liquidlike banner that somehow defies the tug of time and tide.

Oh, I can put words together and come up with pretty pictures, but that method ultimately fails because at the time I *couldn't tell how far away anything was*! The eye sought clues in vain. Some objects—piled across the muddy panorama—seemed so vast that the huge vessel around us was dwarfed, like a minnow in a herd of *behmo* serpents. As for colors, even in the spotlight beam, the water drank all shades but deathly blue gray. A good hue for a shroud in this place of icy-cold death.

Another way to describe the unknown is to *compare* it to things you already recognize . . . only that method proved worse! Even Huck, who sees likenesses in things I can't begin to fathom, was reduced to staring toward great heaps of ancient debris with all four eyestalks, at an utter loss.

Oh, *some* objects leaped at us with sudden familiarity—like when the searchlight swept over rows of blank-eyed windows, breached floors, and sundered walls. Pushed in a tumbled mound, many of the sunken towers lay upside down or even speared through each other. Together they composed a city greater than any I ever heard of, even from readings of olden times. Yet someone once scraped the entire metropolis from its foundations, picked it up, and dumped it here, sending all the buildings tumbling down to be reclaimed the only way such things *can* be reclaimed—in Mother Jijo's fiery bowels.

I recalled some books I'd read, dating from Earth's Era of Resolution, when pre-contact humans were deciding on their own how to grow up and save their homeworld after centuries spent using it as a cesspit. In Alice Hammett's mystery *The Case of a Half-Eaten Clone,* the killer escapes a murder charge, only to get ten years for disposing of the evidence at sea! In those days, humans made no distinction between midden trenches and ocean floor in general. Dumping was dumping.

It felt strange to see the enormous dross-scape from two viewpoints. By Galactic law, this was a consecrated part of Jijo's cycle of preservation—a scene of devout caretaking. But having grown up immersed in human books, I could shift perspectives and see *defilement,* a place of terrible sin.

The "city" fell behind us and we went back to staring at bizarre shapes, unknown majestic objects, the devices of star-god civilization, beyond understanding by mere cursed mortals. On occasion, my eyes glimpsed flickerings in the blackness *outside* the roving beam—lightninglike glimmers amid the ruins, as if old forces lingered here and there, setting off sparks like fading memories.

We murmured among ourselves, each of us falling back to what we knew best. Ur-ronn speculated on the nature of materials, what things were made of, or what functions they once served. Huck swore she saw *writing* each time the light panned over a string of suspicious shadows. Pincer insisted every other object must be a starship.

The Midden took our conjectures the same way it accepts all else, with a patient, deathless silence.

Some enormous objects had already sunk quite far, showing just their tips above the mire. I thought—*This is where Jijo's ocean plate takes a steep dive under the Slope, dragging crust, mud, and anything else lying about, down to magma pools that feed simmering volcanoes. In time, all these mighty things will become lava, or precious ores to be used by some future race of tenants on this world.*

It made me ponder my father's sailing ship, and the risky trips he took, hauling crates of sacred refuse, sent by each tribe of the Six as partial payment for the sin of our ancestors. In yearly rituals, each village sifts part of the land, clearing it of our own pollution and bits the Buyur left behind.

The Five Galaxies may punish us for living here. Yet we lived by a code, faithful to the Scrolls.

Hoonish folk moots chant the tale of Phu-uphyawuo, a dross captain who one day saw a storm coming, and dumped his load before reaching the deep blue of the Midden. Casks and drums rolled overboard far short of the trench of reclamation, strewing instead across shallow sea bottom, marring a site that was changeless, unrenewing. In punishment, Phu-uphyawuo was bound up and taken to the Plain of Sharp Sand, to spend the rest of his days beneath a hollow dune, drinking enough green dew to live, but not sustain his soul. In time, his heart spine was ground to dust and cast across a desert where no water might wash the grains, or make them clean again.

But this is the Midden, I thought, trying to grasp the wonder. *We're the first to see it.*

Except for the phuvnthus. And whatever else lives down here.

I found myself tiring. Despite the back brace and crutches, a weight of agony built steadily. Yet I found it hard to tear away from the icy-cold pane.

Following a searchlight through suboceanic blackness, we plunged as if down a mine shaft, aimed toward a heap of jewels—glittering objects shaped like needles, or squat globes, or glossy pancakes, or knobby cylinders. Soon there loomed a vast shimmering pile, wider than Wuphon Bay, bulkier than Guenn Volcano.

"Now, *those* are definitely ships!" Pincer announced, gesturing with a claw. Pressed against the glass, we stared at mountainlike piles of tubes, spheres, and cylinders, many of them studded with hornlike protrusions, like the quills of an alarmed rock staller.

"Those must be the *probability whatchamacallums* starships use for going between galaxies," Huck diagnosed from her avid reading of *Tabernacle*-era tales.

"Probability flanges," Ur-ronn corrected, speaking Galactic Six. In matters of technology, she was far ahead of Huck or me. *"I think you may be right."*

Our qheuenish friend chuckled happily as the searchlight zeroed in on one tremendous pile of tapered objects. Soon we all recognized the general outlines from ancient texts—freighters and courier ships, packets and cruisers—all abandoned long ago.

The engine noise dropped a notch, plunging us toward that mass of discarded spacecraft. The smallest of those derelicts outmassed the makeshift *phuvnthu* craft the way a full-grown traeki might tower over a herd-chick turd.

"I wonder if any of the ancestor vessels are in this pile," Huck contemplated aloud. "You know, the ones that brought our founders here? The *Laddu'kek* or the *Tabernacle.*"

"Unlikely," Ur-ronn answered, this time in lisping Anglic. "Don't forget, we're in the *Rift*. This is nothing vut an *offshoot* canyon of the Nidden. Our ancestors likely discarded their shifs in the nain trench, where the greatest share of Vuyur trash went."

I blinked at that thought. *This, an offshoot? A minor side area of the Midden?*

Of course she was right! But it presented a boggling image. What staggering amounts of stuff must have been dumped in the main trench, over the ages! Enough to tax even the recycling power of Jijo's grinding plates. No wonder the Noble Galactics set worlds aside for ten million years or more. It must take that long for a planet to digest each meal of sapient-made things, melting them back into the raw stuff of nature.

I thought of my father's dross ship, driven by creaking masts, its hold filled with crates of whatever we exiles can't recycle. After two thousand years, all the offal we sooners sent to the Midden would not even show against this single mound of discarded starships.

How rich the Buyur and their fellow gods must have been to cast off so much wealth! Some of the abandoned vessels looked immense enough to swallow every house, khuta, or hovel built by the Six Races. We glimpsed dark portals, turrets, and a hundred other details, growing painfully aware of one fact—those shadowy behemoths had been sent down here to rest in peace. Their sleep was never meant to be invaded by the likes of us.

Our plummet toward the reef of dead ships grew alarming. Did any of the others feel we were heading in awful *fast*?

"Maybe this is their home," Pincer speculated as we plunged toward one twisted, oval ruin, half the size of Wuphon Port.

"Maybe the phuvnthus are made of, like, *parts* of old machines that got dumped here," Huck mused. "And they kind of put themselves together from whatever's lying around? Like this *boat* we're on is made of all sorts of junk—"

"Ferhafs they were servants of the Vuyur—" Ur-ronn interrupted. "Or a race that lived here even vefore. Or a strain of nutants, like in that story vy—"

I cut in. "Have any of you considered the simplest idea? That maybe they're just like us?"

When my friends turned to look at me, I shrugged, human style.

"Maybe the phuvnthus are sooners, too. Ever stop to think of that?"

Their blank faces answered me. I might as well have suggested that our hosts were *noor* beasts, for all the sense my idea made.

Well, I never claimed to be quick-witted, especially when racked with agony.

We lacked any sense of perspective, no way to tell how close we were, or how fast we were going. Huck and Pincer murmured nervously as our vessel plunged toward the mountain-of-ships at a rapid clip, engines running hard in reverse.

I think we all jumped a bit when a huge slab of corroded metal moved aside, just duras before we might have collided. Our vessel slid into a gaping hole in the mountain of dross, cruising along a corridor composed of spaceship hulls, piercing a fantastic pile of interstellar junk.

Asx

READ THE NEWLY CONGEALED WAX, MY RINGS.

See how folk of the Six Races dispersed, tearing down festival pavilions and bearing away the injured, fleeing before the Rothen starship's expected arrival.

Our senior sage, Vubben of the g'Kek, recited from the Scroll of Portents a passage warning against disunity. Truly, the Six Races must strive harder than ever to look past our differences of shape and shell. Of flesh, hide, and torg.

"Go home," we sages told the tribes. "See to your lattice screens. Your blur-cloth webs. Live near the ground in Jijo's sheltered places. Be ready to fight if you can. To die if you must."

The *zealots,* who originally provoked this crisis, suggested the Rothen starship might have means to track Rokenn and his lackeys, perhaps by sniffing our prisoners' brain waves or body implants. "For safety, let's sift their bones into lava pools!"

An opposing faction called *Friends of the Rothen* demanded Ro-kenn's release and obeisance to his godlike will. These were not only humans, but some qheuens, g'Keks, hoons, and even a few urs, grateful for cures or treatments received in the aliens' clinic. Some think redemption can be won in this lifetime, without first treading the long road blazed by glavers.

Finally, others see this chaos as a chance to settle old grudges. Rumors tell of anarchy elsewhere on the Slope. Of many fine things toppled or burned.

Such diversity! The same freedom that fosters a vivid

people also makes it hard to maintain a united front. Would things be better if we had disciplined order, like the feudal state sought by Gray Queens of old?

It is too late for regrets. Time remains only for *improvisation*—an art not well approved in the Five Galaxies, we are told.

Among poor savages, it may be our only hope.

Yes, my rings. We can now remember all of that.

Stroke this wax, and watch the caravans depart toward plains, forests, and sea. Our hostages are spirited off to sites where even a starship's piercing scrutiny might not find them. The sun flees and stars bridge the vast territory called the Universe. A realm denied us, that our foes roam at will.

Some remain behind, awaiting the ship.

We voted, did we not? We rings who make up Asx? We volunteered to linger. Our cojoined voice would speak to angry aliens for the Commons. Resting our basal torus on hard stone, we passed the time listening to complex patterns from the Holy Egg, vibrating our fatty core with strange shimmering motifs.

Alas, my rings, none of these reclaimed memories explains our current state, that something terrible must have happened?

Here, what of *this* newly congealed waxy trail?

Can you perceive in it the glimmering outlines of a great vessel of space? Roaring from the same part of the sky lately abandoned by the sun?

Or *is* it the sun, come back again to hover angrily above the valley floor?

The great ship scans our valley with scrutinizing rays, seeking signs of those they left behind.

Yes, my rings. Follow this waxy memory.

Are we about to rediscover the true cause of terror?

Lark

SUMMER PRESSED HEAVILY ACROSS THE RIMMER Range, consuming the unshaded edges of glaciers far older than six exile races. At intervals, a crackling static charge would blur the alpine slopes as countless grass stems wafted skyward, reaching like desperate tendrils. Intense sunshine was punctuated by bursts of curtain rain—water draperies that undulated uphill, drenching the slopes with continuous liquid sheets, climbing until the mountaintops wore rainbow crowns, studded with flashes of compressed lightning.

Compact reverberations rolled down from the heights, all the way to the shore of a poison lake, where fungus swarmed over a forty-hectare thicket of crumbling vines. Once a mighty outpost of Galactic culture, the place was now a jumble of stone slabs, rubbed featureless by abrading ages. The pocket valley sweltered with acrid aromas, as caustic nectars steamed from the lake, or dripped from countless eroding pores.

The newest sage of the Commons of Jijo plucked yellow moss from a decaying cable, one of a myriad of strands that once made up the body of a half-million-year-old creature, the mulc spider responsible for demolishing this ancient Buyur site, gradually returning it to nature. Lark had last seen this place in late winter—searching alone through snow flurries for the footprints of Dwer and Rety, refugees from this same spider's death fury. Things had changed here since that frantic deliverance. Large swathes of mulc cable were simply gone, harvested in some recent effort that no one had bothered explaining when Lark was assigned here. Much of what remained was coated with this clinging moss.

"Spirolegita cariola." He muttered the species name, rubbing a sample between two fingers. It was a twisted, deviant cariola variety. Mutation seemed a specialty of this weird, astringent site.

I wonder what the place will do to me—to all of us—if we stay here long.

He had not asked for this chore. To be a *jailor*. Just wearing the title made him feel less clean.

A chain of nonsense syllables made him turn back toward a blur-cloth canopy, spanning the space between slablike boulders.

"It's a *clensionating sievelator* for *refindulating* excess torg. . . ."

The voice came from deep shade within—a strong feminine alto, though somewhat listless now, tinged with resignation. Soft clinking sounds followed as one object was tossed onto a pile and another picked up for examination.

"At a guess, I'd say *this* was once a *glannis truncator*, probably used in rituals of a chihanic sect . . . that is, unless it's just another Buyur joke-novelty device."

Lark shaded his eyes to regard Ling, the young sky-born scientist and servant of star-god Rothen, in whose employ he had worked as a "native guide" for many weeks . . . until the Battle of the Glade reversed their standing in a matter of heartbeats. Since that unexpected victory, the High Sages had assigned her care and custody to him, a duty he never asked for, even if it meant exalted promotion.

Now I'm quite a high-ranking witch doctor among savages, he thought with some tartness. *Lord High Keeper of Alien Prisoners.*

And maybe executioner. His mind shied from that possibility. Much more likely, Ling would be traded to her Danik-Rothen comrades in some deal worked out by the sages. Or else she might be rescued at any moment by hordes of unstoppable robots, overpowering Lark's small detachment of sword-bearing escorts like a pack of *santi* bears brushing aside the helpless buzzing defenders of a zil-honey tree.

Either way, she'll go free. Ling may live another three hundred years on her homeworld, back in the Five Galaxies, telling embroidered tales about her adventure among the feral barbarians of a shabby, illicit colony. Meanwhile, the best we fallen ones can hope for is bare survival. To keep scratching a living from poor tired Jijo, calling it lucky if some of the Six eventually join glavers down the Path of Redemption. The trail to blissful oblivion.

Lark would rather end it all in some noble and heroic way. Let Jijo's Six go down defending this fragile world, so she might go back to her interrupted rest.

That was his particular heresy, of course. Orthodox belief held that the Six Races were sinners, but they might mitigate their offense by living at peace on Jijo. But Lark saw that as hypocrisy. The settlers should *end* their crime, gently and voluntarily, as soon as possible.

He had made no secret of his radicalism . . . which made it all the more confusing that the High Sages now trusted him with substantial authority.

The alien woman no longer wore the shimmering garb of her Danik star clan—the secretive band of humans who worshiped Rothen lords. Instead she was outfitted in an ill-fitting blouse and kilt of Jijoan homespun. Still, Lark found it hard to look away from her angular beauty. It was said that sky humans could buy a new face with hardly a thought. Ling claimed not to care about such things, but no woman on the Slope could match her.

Under the wary gaze of two militia corporals, Ling sat cross-legged, examining relics left behind by the dead mulc spider—strange metallic shapes embedded in semitransparent gold cocoons, like archaic insects trapped in amber. Remnants of the Buyur, this world's last legal tenants, who departed half a million years ago when Jijo went fallow. A throng of egglike preservation beads lay scattered round the ashen lakeshore. Instead of dissolving all signs of past habitation, the local mulc spider had apparently chosen relics to seal away. *Collecting* them, if Lark believed the incredible story told by his half brother, Dwer.

The luminous coatings made him nervous. The same substance, secreted from the spider's porous conduits, had nearly smothered Dwer and Rety, the wild sooner girl, the same night two alien robots quarreled, igniting a living morass of corrosive vines, ending the spider's long, mad life. The gold stuff felt queer to touch, as if a strange, slow liquid sloshed under sheaths of solid crystal.

"Toporgic," Ling had called the slick material during one of her civil moments. *"It's very rare, but I hear stories. It's*

said to be a pseudo-matter substrate made of organically folded time."

Whatever that meant. It sounded like the sort of thing Sara might say, trying to explain her beloved world of mathematics. As a biologist, he found it bizarre for a living thing to send "folded time" oozing from its far-flung tendrils, as the mulc spider apparently had done.

Whenever Ling finished examining a relic, she bent over a sheaf of Lark's best paper to make careful notes, concentrating as if each childlike block letter were a work of art. As if she never held a pencil before, but had vowed to master the new skill. As a galactic voyager, she used to handle floods of information, manipulating multidimensional displays, sieving data on this world's complex ecosystem, searching on behalf of her Rothen masters for some biotreasure worth stealing. Toiling over handwritten notes must seem like shifting from starship speeds to a traeki's wooden scooter.

It's a steep fall—one moment a demigoddess, the next a hostage of uncouth sooners.

All this diligent note taking must help take her mind off recent events—that traumatic day, just two leagues below the nest of the Holy Egg, when her home base exploded and Jijo's masses violently rebelled. But Lark sensed something more than deliberate distraction. In scribing words on paper, Ling drew the same focused satisfaction he had seen her take from performing any simple act well. Despite his persistent seething anger, Lark found this worthy of respect.

There were folk legends about mulc spiders. Some were said to acquire odd obsessions during their stagnant eons spent chewing metal and stone monuments of the past. Lark once dismissed such fables as superstition, but Dwer had proved right about this one. Evidence for the mulc beast's collecting fetish lay in countless capsules studding the charred thicket, the biggest hoard of Galactic junk anywhere on the Slope. It made the noxious lakeshore an ideal site to conceal a captured alien, in case the returning starship had instruments sifting Jijo for missing crew mates.

Though Ling had been thoroughly searched, and all possessions seized, she might carry in her body some detectable trace element—acquired growing up on a far Galactic world. If so, all the Buyur stuff lying around here might mask her presence.

There were other ideas.

Ship sensors may not penetrate far underground, one human techie proposed.

Or else, suggested an urrish smith, *a nearby lava flow may foil alien eyes.*

The other hostages—Ro-kenn and Rann—had been taken to such places, in hopes of holding on to at least one prisoner. With the lives of every child and grub of the Six at stake, anything seemed worth trying. The job Lark had been given was important. Yet he chafed, wishing for more to do than waiting for the world to end. Rumors told that others were preparing to fight the star criminals. Lark knew little about weapons—his expertise was the natural flux of living species. Still, he envied them.

A burbling, wheezing sound called him rushing to the far end of the tent, where his friend Uthen squatted like an ash-colored chitin mound. Lark took up a makeshift aspirator he had fashioned out of boo stems, a cleft pig's bladder, and congealed mulc sap. He pushed the nozzle into one of the big qheuen's leg apertures and pumped away, siphoning phlegmy fluid that threatened Uthen's ventilation tubes. He repeated the process with all five legs, till his partner and fellow biologist breathed easier. The qheuen's central cupola lifted and Uthen's seeing stripe brightened.

"Th-thank you, L-Lark-ark . . . I am—I am sorry to be so—be so—to be a burden-en-en. . . ."

Emerging uncoordinated, the separate leg voices sounded like five miniature qheuens, getting in each other's way. Or like a traeki whose carelessly stacked oration rings all had minds of their own. Uthen's fevered weakness filled Lark's chest with a burning ache. A choking throat made it hard to respond with cheerful-sounding lies.

"You just rest up, claw brother. Soon we'll be back in the

field . . . digging fossils and inventing more theories to turn your mothers blue with embarrassment."

That brought a faint, gurgling laugh. "S-speaking-king of heresies . . . it looks as if you and Haru . . . Haru . . . Harullen-ullen, will be getting your wish."

Mention of Lark's other gray qheuen friend made him wince with doubled grief. Uthen didn't know about his cousin's fate, and Lark wasn't about to tell him.

"How do you mean?"

"It seems-eems the raiders-raiders found a way to rid Jijo of at least *one* of the S-S-Six P-p-pests. . . ."

"Don't say that," Lark urged. But Uthen voiced a common thought. His sickness baffled the g'Kek medic resting in the next shelter, all four eyes curled in exhaustion. The malady frightened the militia guards. All knew that Uthen had been with Lark in the ruined Danik station, poking among forbidden things.

"I felt sorrow when-hen zealots-lots blew up the alien base." Uthen's carapace shuddered as he fought for breath. "Even when the Rothen tried to misuse our Holy Egg . . . sending false dreams as wedges-edges . . . to drive the Six Races apart-part. . . . Even *that* did not justify the . . . inhospitable-able murder of strangers."

Lark wiped an eye. "You're more charitable than most."

"Let me finish-ish. I was-as going to say that *now* we know what the outsiders were up to all along-long . . . something worse than dreams. Designing-ing *bugs* to bring us down-own-own."

So, Uthen must have overheard the rumors—or else worked it out for himself.

Biological warfare. Genocide.

"Like in *War of the Worlds*." It was one of Uthen's favorite old novels. "Only with the roles reversed."

Lark's comparison made the gray qheuen laugh—a raspy, uneven whistle.

"I . . . always-ways did identify . . . with those . . . with those poor Martians-ans-ans. . . .."

The ribbon eye went foggy, losing the light of consciousness as the cupola sank. Lark checked his friend's breathing, and found it no worse. Uthen was simply tired.

So strong, he thought, stroking the rigid shell.

We picture grays as toughest of the tough. But chitin won't slow a laser ray.

Harullen found that out. Death came to Uthen's cousin during the brief Battle of the Glade, when the massed militia of Six Races barely overcame Ro-kenn's robot assassins. Only the advantage of surprise had carried that day. The aliens never realized that savages might have books showing how to make rifled firearms—crude, but potent at short range.

But victory came late for Harullen. Too dedicated or obstinate to flee, the heretic leader spent his last frenzied moments whistling ornate pleas for calm and reason, crying in five directions at once, beseeching everyone to lay down their arms and talk things over—until Harullen's massive, crablike body was cleaved in uneven parts by a killer drone, just before the machine was itself blown from the sky.

There will be mourning among the gray matrons of Tarek Town, Lark thought, resting both arms across Uthen's broad shell, laying his head on the mottled surface, listening to the strained labor of his friend's phlegmy breathing, wishing with all his heart that there was more he could do.

Irony was but one of many bitter tastes in his mouth.

I always figured, if the end did come, that qheuens would be the last to go.

Emerson

JIJO'S COUNTRYSIDE FLOWS RAPIDLY PAST THEM now, as if the mysterious horsewomen fear any delay might turn faint hope to dust.

Lacking speech, Emerson has no idea where they are riding in such a hurry, or why.

Sara turns in her saddle now and then, to give an encouraging smile. But rewq-painted colors of misgiving surround her face—a nimbus of emotion that he can read the way he used to find meaning in letters on a data display.

Perhaps he should find her qualms unnerving, since he depends on her guidance in this strange, perilous world. Yet Emerson cannot bring himself to worry. There are just too many other things to think about.

Humidity closes in as their caravan veers toward a winding river valley. Dank aromas stir memories of the swamp where he first floundered after the crash, a shattered cripple, drenched in agony. But he does not quail. Emerson welcomes any sensation that might trigger random recall—a sound, a chance smell, or else a sight around the next bend.

Some rediscoveries already float across a gulf of time and loss, as if he has missed them for quite a while. Recovered names connect to faces, and even brief snatches of isolated events.

Tom Orley . . . so strong and clever. Always a sure eye for trouble. He brought some back to the ship, one day. Trouble enough for Five Galaxies.

Hikahi . . . sweetest dolphin. Kindest friend. Dashing off to rescue her lover and captain . . . never to be seen again.

Toshio . . . a boy's ready laughter. A young man's steady heart. Where is he now?

Creideiki . . . captain. Wise dolphin leader. A cripple like himself.

Briefly, Emerson wonders at the similarity between Creideiki's injury and his own. . . . But the thought provokes a searing bolt of pain so fierce that the fleeting thought whirls away and is lost.

Tom . . . *Hikahi* . . . *Toshio* . . . He repeats the names, each of them once attached to friends he has not seen for . . . well, a very long time.

Other memories, more recent, seem harder to reach, more agonizing to access.

Suessi . . . *Tsh't* . . . *Gillian* . . .

He mouths each sound repeatedly, despite the tooth-jarring ride and difficulty of coordinating tongue and lips. He does it to keep in practice—or else how will he ever recover the old handiness with language, the skill to roll out words as he used to, back when he was known as such a clever fellow . . . before horrid holes appeared in both his head and memory.

Some names come easy, since he learned them *after* waking on Jijo, delirious in a treetop hut.

—*Prity,* the little chimp who teaches him by example. Though mute, she shows flair for both math and sardonic hand speech.

—*Jomah* and *Kurt* . . . sounds linked to younger and older versions of the same narrow face. Apprentice and master at a unique art, meant to erase all the dams, towns, and houses that unlawful settlers had built on a proscribed world. Emerson recalls *Biblos,* an archive of paper books, where Kurt showed his nephew well-placed explosive charges that might bring the cave down, smashing the library to dust. If the order ever came.

—The captive fanatic, *Dedinger,* rides behind the explosers, deeply tanned with craggy features. Leader of human rebels with beliefs Emerson can't grasp, except they preach no love of visitors from the sky. While the party hurries on, Dedinger's gray eyes rove, calculating his next move.

Some names and a few places—these utterances have meaning now. It is progress, but Emerson is no fool. He figures he must have known *hundreds* of words before he fell, broken, to this world. Now and again he makes out snatches of half meaning from the *"wah-wah"* gabble as his companions address each other. Snippets that tantalize, without satisfying.

Sometimes the torrent grows tiresome, and he wonders—might people be less inclined to fight if they talked less? If they spent more time watching and listening?

Fortunately, words aren't his sole project. There is the haunting familiarity of music, and during rest stops he plays math games with Prity and Sara, drawing shapes in the sand. They are his friends and he takes joy from their laughter.

He has one more window to the world.

As often as he can stand it, Emerson slips the *rewq* over his eyes . . . a masklike film that transforms the world into splashes of slanted color. In all his prior travels he never encountered such a creature—a species used by all six races to grasp each other's moods. If left on too long, it gives him headaches. Still he finds fascinating the auras surrounding Sara, Dedinger, and others. Sometimes it seems the colors carry more than just emotion . . . though he cannot pin it down. Not yet.

One truth Emerson recalls. Advice drawn from the murky well of his past, putting him on guard.

Life can be full of illusions.

PART TWO

LEGENDS TELL OF MANY PRECIOUS TEXTS that were lost one bitter evening, during an unmatched disaster some call the Night of the Ghosts, when a quarter of the Biblos Archive burned. Among the priceless volumes that vanished by that cruel winter's twilight, one tome reportedly showed pictures of Buyur—the mighty race whose lease on Jijo expired five thousand centuries ago.

Scant diary accounts survive from witnesses to the calamity, but according to some who browsed the Xenoscience Collection before it burned, the Buyur were squat beings, vaguely resembling the *bullfrogs* shown on page ninety-six of *Cleary's Guide to Terrestrial Life-Forms*, though with elephantine legs and sharp, forward-looking eyes. They were said to be master shapers of useful organisms, and had a reputation for prodigious wit.

But other sooner races already knew that much about the Buyur, both from oral traditions and the many clever servant organisms that flit about Jijo's forests, perhaps still looking for departed masters. Beyond these few scraps, we have very little about the race whose mighty civilization thronged this world for more than a million years.

HOW could so much knowledge be lost in a single night? Today it seems odd. Why weren't *copies* of such valuable texts printed by those first-wave human colonists, before they sent their sneakship tumbling to ocean depths? Why not place duplicates all over the Slope, safeguarding the learning against all peril?

In our ancestors' defense, recall what tense times those were, before the Great Peace or the coming of the Egg. The five sapient races already present on Jijo (excluding glavers) had reached an edgy balance by the time starship *Tabernacle* slinked past Izmunuti's dusty glare to plant Earthlings illicitly, the latest wave of criminal colonists to plague a troubled world. In those days, combat was frequent between urrish clans and haughty qheuen empresses, while hoonish tribes skirmished among themselves in their ongoing ethical struggle over traeki civil rights. The High Sages had little influence beyond reading and interpreting the Speaking Scrolls, the only documents existing at the time.

Into this tense climate dropped the latest invasion of sooner refugees, who found an unused eco-niche awaiting them. But human colonists were not content simply to take up tree farming as another clan of illiterates. Instead, they used the *Tabernacle's* engines one last time before sinking her. With those godlike forces they carved Biblos Fortress, then toppled a thousand trees, converting their pulp into freshly printed *books*.

The act so astonished the Other Five, it nearly cost human settlers their lives. Outraged, the queens of Tarek Town laid siege to the vastly outnumbered Earthlings. Others, equally offended by what seemed heresy against the Scrolls, held back only because the priest sages refused sanctioning holy war. That narrow vote gave human leaders time to bargain, to cajole the different tribes and septs with practical advice from books, bribing them with useful things. Spoke cleats for g'Kek wheels. Better sails for hoonish captains. And, for urrish smiths, the long-sought knack of brewing clear glass.

How things had changed just a few generations later, when the new breed of scholar sages gathered to affirm the Great Peace, scribing their names on fresh paper and sending copies to each hamlet on the Slope. Reading became a common habit, and even *writing* is no longer viewed as sin.

An orthodox minority still objects to the clatter of printing presses. They piously insist that *literacy* fosters *memory,* and thus attachment to the same conceits that got our spacefaring ancestors in trouble. Surely, they claim, we must cultivate detachment and forgetfulness in order to tread the Path of Redemption.

Perhaps they are right. But few these days seem in a hurry to follow glavers down that blessed trail. Not yet. First, we must prepare our souls.

And wisdom, the New Sages declare, can be nurtured from the pages of a book.

> from *Forging the Peace, a Historical Meditation-Umble,*
> by Homer Auph-puthtwaoy

Streakers

Kaa

STRANDED, BY UNYIELDING FATE, ON IFNI'S SHORE. Stranded, like a beached whale, barred from ever going home.

Five ways stranded—

First, cut off from Earth by hostile aliens bearing a death grudge toward Terrans in general, and the *Streaker* crew in particular, though Kaa never quite understood why.

Second, banished from Earth's home *galaxy,* blown off course, and off-limits, by a caprice of hyperspace—though many on the crew still blamed Kaa, calling it "pilot's error."

Third, starship *Streaker* taking refuge on a taboo world, one scheduled to have a respite from sapient minds. An ideal haven, according to some. A trap, said others.

Fourth, when the vessel's weary engines finally ceased their labors, depositing the *Streaker* in a realm of ghosts, deep in this planet's darkest corner, far from air or light.

And now, this, Kaa thought. *Abandoned, even by a crew of castaways!*

Of course Lieutenant Tsh't didn't put it that way, when

she asked him to stay behind in a tiny outpost with three other volunteers for company.

"This will be your first important command, Kaa. A chance to show what you're made of."

Yeah, he thought. *Especially if I'm speared by a hoonish harpoon, dragged onto one of their boats, and slit open.*

That almost happened yesterday. He had been tracking one of the native sailing craft, trying to learn its purpose and destination, when one of his young assistants, Mopol, darted ahead and began surfing the wooden vessel's rolling bow wake . . . a favorite pastime on Earth, where dolphins frequently hitched free rides from passing ships. Only here it was so dumb, Kaa hadn't thought to forbid it in advance.

Mopol offered that lawyerly excuse later, when they returned to the shelter. "B-besides, I didn't do any harm."

"No harm? You let them see you!" Kaa berated. "Don't you know they started throwing *spears* into the water, just as I got you out of there?"

Mopol's sleek torso and bottle beak held a rebellious stance. "They never saw a dolphin before. Prob'ly thought we were some local kind of fish."

"And it's gonna stay that way, do you hear?"

Mopol grunted ambiguous assent, but the episode unnerved Kaa.

A while later, dwelling on his own shortcomings, he worked amid clouds of swirling bottom mud, splicing optical fiber to a cable the submarine *Hikahi* had laid, on its return trip to *Streaker*'s hiding place. Kaa's newly emplaced camera should let him spy more easily on the hoon colony whose sheltered docks and camouflaged houses lay perched along the nearby bay. Already he could report that hoonish efforts at concealment were aimed *upward*, at shrouding their settlement against the sky, not the sea. That might prove important information, Kaa hoped.

Still, he had never trained to be a spy. He was a pilot, dammit!

Not that he ever used to get much practice during the early days of *Streaker*'s mission, languishing in the shadow of Chief Pilot Keepiru, who always got the tough, glamorous jobs. When Keepiru vanished on Kithrup, along with the captain and several others, Kaa finally got a chance to practice his skill—for better and worse.

But now Streaker's *going nowhere. A beached ship needs no pilot, so I guess I'm expendable.*

Kaa finished splicing and was retracting the work arms of his harness when a flash of silver-gray shot by at high speed, undulating madly. Sonar strafed him as waves of liquid recoil shoved his body. Clickety dolphin laughter filled the shallows.

> ** Admit it, star seeker!*
> ** You did not hear or see me,*
> ** Sprinting from the gloom! **

In fact, Kaa had known the youth was approaching for some time, but he did not want to discourage Zhaki from practicing the arts of stealth.

"Use Anglic," he commanded tersely.

Small conical teeth gleamed in a beam of slanted sunshine as the young Tursiops swung around to face Kaa. "But it's much easier to speak Trinary! Sometimes Anglic makes my head hurt."

Few humans, listening to this exchange between two neo-dolphins, would have understood the sounds. Like Trinary, this underwater dialect consisted mostly of clipped groans and ratchetings. But the *grammar* was close to standard Anglic. And grammar guides the way a person thinks—or so Creideiki used to teach, when that master of Keeneenk arts lived among the *Streaker* crew, guiding them with his wisdom.

Creideiki has been gone for two years, abandoned with Mr. Orley and others when we fled the battle fleets at Kithrup. Yet every day we miss him—the best our kind produced.

When Creideiki spoke, you could forget for a while that neo-dolphins were crude, unfinished beings, the newest and shakiest sapient race in the Five Galaxies.

Kaa tried answering Zhaki as he imagined the captain would.

"The pain you feel is called *concentration*. It's not easy, but it enabled our human patrons to reach the stars, all by themselves."

"Yeah. And look what good it did them," Zhaki retorted.

Before Kaa could answer, the youth emitted the *need-air* signal and shot toward the surface, without even performing a wariness spiral to look out for danger. It violated security, but tight discipline seemed less essential as each Jijoan day passed. This sea was too mellow and friendly to encourage diligence.

Kaa let it pass, following Zhaki to the surface. They exhaled and drew in sweet air, faintly charged with distant hints of rain. Speaking Anglic with their gene-modified blowholes out of the water called for a different dialect, one that hissed and sputtered, but sounded more like human speech.

"All right-t," Kaa said. "Now report."

The other dolphin tossed his head. "The red crabs suspect nothing. They f-fixate on their crayfish penss. Only rarely does one look up when we c-come near."

"They aren't crabs. They're *qheuens*. And I gave strict orders. You weren't to go near enough to be seen!"

Hoons were considered more dangerous, so Kaa had kept that part of the spy mission for himself. Still, he counted on Zhaki and Mopol to be discreet while exploring the qheuen settlement at the reef fringe. *I guess I was wrong.*

"Mopol wanted to try some of the reds' delicaciesss, so we p-pulled a diversion. I rounded up a school of those green-finned fishies—the ones that taste like Sargasso eel—and chased 'em right through the q-qheuen colony! And guess what? It turns out the crabs have *pop-up nets* they use for jussst that kind of luck! As soon as the school was inside their boundary, they whipped those things up-p and snatched the whole swarm!"

"You're lucky they didn't snag you, too. What was Mopol doing, all this time?"

"While the reds were busy, Mopol raided the crayfish pens." Zhaki chortled with delight. "I saved you one, by the way. They're delisssh."

Zhaki wore a miniharness fastened to his flank, bearing a single manipulator arm that folded back during swimming. At a neural signal, the mechanical hand went to his seamed pouch and drew out a wriggling creature, proffering it to Kaa.

What should I do? Kaa stared at the squirmy thing. Would accepting it only encourage Zhaki's lapse of discipline? Or would rejection make Kaa look stodgy and unreasonable?

"I'll wait and see if it makes you sick," he told the youth. They weren't supposed to experiment on native fauna with their own bodies. Unlike Earth, most planetary ecosystems were mixtures of species from all across the Five Galaxies, introduced by tenant races whose occupancy might last ten million years. So far, many of the local fishoids turned out to be wholesome and tasty, but the very next prey beast might have its revenge by poisoning you.

"Where is Mopol now?"

"Back doing what we were told," Zhaki said. "Watching how the red crabs interact with hoonsss. So far we've seen 'em pulling two sledge loads toward the port, filled with harvested ssseaweed. They came back with cargoes of wood. You know . . . ch-chopped tree trunks."

Kaa nodded. "So they do trade, as we suspected. Hoons and qheuens, living together on a forbidden world. I wonder what it means?"

"Who knows? If they weren't mysterious, they wouldn't be eateesss. C-can I go back to Mopol now?"

Kaa had few illusions about what was going on between the two young spacers. It probably interfered in their work, but if he raised the issue, Zhaki would accuse him of being a prude, or worse, "jealous."

If only I were a real leader, Kaa thought. *The lieutenant should never have left me in charge.*

"Yes, go back now," he said. "But only to fetch Mopol and return to the shelter. It's getting late."

Zhaki lifted his body high, perched on a thrashing tail.

   * *Yes, oh exalted!*
     * *Your command shall be obeyed,*
      * *As all tides heed moons.* *

With that, the young dolphin did a flip and dived back into the sea. Soon his dorsal fin was all Kaa saw, glinting as it sliced through choppy swell.

Kaa pondered the ambiguous insolence of Zhaki's last Trinary burst.

In human terms—by the cause-and-effect logic the patron race taught its dolphin clients—the ocean bulged and shifted in response to the gravitational pull of sun and moon. But there were more ancient ways of thinking, used by cetacean ancestors long before humans meddled in their genes. In those days, there had never been any question that tides were the most powerful of forces. In the old, primal religion, *tides* controlled the *moon,* not vice versa.

In other words, Zhaki's Trinary statement was sassy, verging on insubordination.

Tsh't made a mistake, Kaa mused bitterly, as he swam toward the shelter. *We should never have been left here by ourselves.*

Along the way, he experienced the chief threat to his mission. Not hoonish spears or qheuen claws, or even alien battlecruisers, but Jijo itself.

One could fall in love with this place.

The ocean's flavor called to him, as did the velvety texture of the water. It beckoned in the way fishlike creatures paid him respect by fleeing, but not too quick to catch, if he cared to.

Most seductive of all, at night throbbing *echoes* penetrated their outpost walls—distant rhythms, almost too low to hear. Eerie, yet reminiscent of the whale songs of home.

Unlike Oakka, the green-green world—or terrible Kithrup—this planet appeared to have a *reverent* sea. One where a dolphin might swim at peace.

And possibly forget.

Brookida was waiting when Kaa cycled through the tiny airlock, barely large enough for one dolphin at a time to pass into the shelter—an inflated bubble, half-filled with water and anchored to the ocean floor. Against one wall, a lab had been set up for the metallurgist geologist, an elderly dolphin whose frailty had grown as *Streaker* fled ever farther from home.

Brookida's samples had been taken when the *Hikahi* followed a hoonish sailboat beyond the continental shelf, to a plunging abyssal trench, where the ship had proceeded to dump its cargo overboard! As casks, barrels, and chests fell into the murk, a few were snagged by the submarine's gaping maw, then left here for analysis as the *Hikahi* returned to base.

Brookida had already found what he called "anomalies," but something else now had the aged scientist excited.

"We got a message while you were out. Tsh't picked up something amazing on her way to *Streaker*!"

Kaa nodded. "I was here when she reported, remember? They found an ancient cache, left by illegal settlers when—"

"That's nothing." The old dolphin was more animated than Kaa had seen Brookida in a long time.

"Tsh't called again later to say they rescued a bunch of *kids* who were about to drown."

Kaa blinked.

"Kids? You don't mean—"

"Not human or fin. But wait till you hear who they are . . . and how they came to be d-down there, under the sea."

Sooners

Alvin

A FEW SCANT DURAS BEFORE IMPACT, PART OF THE wall of debris ahead of us began to move. A craggy slab, consisting of pitted starship hulls, magically slipped aside, offering the phuvnthu craft a long, narrow cavity.

Into it we plummeted, jagged walls looming near the glass, passing in a blur, cutting off the searchlight beam and leaving us in shadows. The motors picked up their frantic backward roar . . . then fell away to silence.

A series of metallic clangs jarred the hull. Moments later the door to our chamber opened. A clawed arm motioned us outside.

Several phuvnthus waited—insectoid-looking creatures with long, metal-cased torsos and huge, glassy-black eyes. Our mysterious saviors, benefactors, captors.

My friends tried to help me, but I begged them off.

"Come on, guys. It's hard enough managing these crutches without you all crowding around. Go on. I'll be right behind."

At the intersection leading back to my old cell, I moved

to turn left but our six-legged guides motioned right instead. "I need my stuff," I told the nearest phuvnthu-thing. But it gestured *no* with a wave of machinelike claws, barring my path.

Damn, I thought, recalling the notebook and backpack I had left behind. I figured I'd be coming back.

A twisty, confused journey took us through all sorts of hatches and down long corridors of metal plating. Ur-ronn commented that some of the weld joins looked "hasty." I admired the way she held on to her professionalism when faced with awesome technology.

I can't say exactly when we left the sea dragon and entered the larger base/camp/city/hive, but there came a time when the big phuvnthus seemed more relaxed in their clanking movements. I even caught a snatch or two of that queer, ratcheting sound that I once took for speech. But there wasn't time for listening closely. Just moving forward meant battling waves of pain, taking one step at a time.

At last we spilled into a corridor that had a feel of permanence, with pale, off-white walls and soft lighting that seemed to pour from the whole ceiling. The peculiar passage curved gently *upward* in both directions, till it climbed out of sight a quarter of an arrowflight to either side. It seemed we were in a huge *circle,* though what use such a strange hallway might serve, I could not then imagine.

Even more surprising was the reception committee! At once we faced a pair of creatures who could not look more different from the phuvnthus—except for the quality of having six limbs. They stood upright on their hind pair, dressed in tunics of silvery cloth, spreading four scaly webbed hands in a gesture I hopefully took to mean welcome. They were small, rising just above my upper knees, or the level of Pincer's red chitin shell. A frothy crown of moist, curly fibers topped their bulb-eyed heads. Squeaking rapidly, they motioned for us to follow, while the big phuvnthus retreated with evident eagerness.

We four Wuphonites consulted with a shared glance . . . then a rocking, qheuen-style shrug. We turned to troop silently behind our new guides. I could sense Huphu purring on my shoulder, staring at the little beings, and I vowed to drop my crutches and grab the noor, if she tried to jump one of our hosts. I doubted they were as helpless as they looked.

All the doorways lining the hall were closed. Next to each portal, something like a *paper strip* was pasted to the wall, always at the same height. One of Huck's eyestalks gestured toward the makeshift coverings, then winked at me in Morse semaphore.

SECRETS UNDERNEATH!

I grokked her meaning. So our hosts did not want us to read their door signs. That implied they used one of the alphabets known to the Six. I felt the same curiosity that emanated from Huck. At the same time, though, I readied myself to stop her, if she made a move to tear off one of the coverings. There *are* times for impulsiveness. This was not one of them.

A door hatch slid open with a soft hiss and our little guides motioned for us to enter.

Curtains divided a large chamber into parallel cubicles. I also glimpsed a dizzying array of shiny machines, but did not note much about them, because of what then appeared, right in front of us.

We all stopped in our tracks, facing a quartet of familiar-looking entities—an urs, a hoon, a red qheuen, and a young g'Kek!

Images of ourselves, I realized, though clearly not reflections in a mirror. For one thing, we could see right *through* the likenesses. And as we stared, each figure made beckoning motions toward a different curtained nook.

After the initial shock, I noticed the images weren't perfect portraits. The urrish version had a well groomed pelt, and my hoonish counterpart stood erect, without a back brace. Was the difference meaningful? The hoonish caricature smiled at me in the old-fashioned way, with a fluttering throat sac, but no added grimace of mouth and lips that Jijoan hoons had added since humans came.

"Yeah right," Huck muttered, staring at the ersatz g'Kek in front of her, whose wheels and spokes gleamed, tight and polished. "I am *so* sure these are *sooners,* Alvin."

I winced. So my earlier guess was wrong. There was no point rubbing it in.

"Hr-rm . . . shut up, Huck."

"These are holographic frojections," Ur-ronn lisped in Anglic, the sole Jijoan language suitable for such a diagnosis. The words came from human books, inherited since the Great Printing.

"Whatever you s-say," Pincer added, as each ghost backed away toward a different curtained cell. "What d-d-do we do now?"

Huck muttered. "What choice do we have? Each of us follows our own guy, and see ya on the other side."

With an uneven bumping of her rims, she rolled after the gleaming g'Kek image. A curtain slid shut after her.

Ur-ronn blew a sigh. "Good water, you two."

"Fire and ash," Pincer and I replied politely, watching her saunter behind the urrish cartoon figure.

The fake hoon waved happily for me to enter the cubby on the far right.

"Name, rank, and serial number only," I told Pincer.

His worried—"Huh?"—aspirated from three leg vents in syncopation. When I glanced back, his cupola eye still whirled indecisively, staring in all directions *except* at the translucent qheuen in front of him.

A hanging divider closed between us.

My silent guide in hoonish form led me to a white obelisk, an upright slab, occupying the center of the small room. He pantomimed stepping right up to it, standing on a small metal plate at its base. When I did so, I found the white surface *soft* against my face and chest. No sooner were my feet on the plate than the whole slab began to *tilt* . . . rotating down and forward to become a table, with my own poor self lying prone on top. Huphu scrambled off my shoulders, muttering guttural complaints, then yowled as a *tube* lifted up from below and snaked toward my face!

I guess I could have struggled, or tried to flee. But to what point? When colored gas spilled from the tube, the odor reminded me of childhood visits to our Wuphon infirmary. The House of Stinks, we kids called it, though our

traeki pharmacist was kindly, and always secreted a lump
of candy from an upper ring, if we were good. . . .

As awareness wavered, I recall hoping there would be a
tasty sourball waiting for me this time, as well.

"G'night," I muttered, while Huphu chittered and
wailed. Then things kind of went black for a while.

Asx

STROKE THE FRESH-FLOWING WAX, MY RINGS,
streaming hot with news from real time.

Here, trace this ululation, a blaring *cry of dismay*,
echoing round frosted peaks, setting stands of mighty
greatboo a-quivering.

Just moments earlier, the Rothen ship hovered majestically
above its ruined station, scanning the Glade for signs of its
lost spore buds, the missing members of its crew.

Angry the throbbing vessel seemed, broody and threatening, ready to avenge.

Yet we/i remained in place, did we not, my rings? Duty
rooted this traeki stack in place, delegated by the Council
of Sages to parley with these Rothen lords.

Others also lingered, milling across the trampled festival
grounds. Curious onlookers, or those who for personal
reasons wished to offer invaders *loyalty*.

So we/i were not alone to witness what came next.
There were several hundred present, staring in awe as the
Rothen starship probed and palped the valley with rays,
sifting the melted, sooty girders of its ravaged outpost.

Then came that abrupt, awful sound. A cry that still fizzes, uncongealed, down our fatty core. An alarm of anguished dread, coming from the ship itself!

Shall we recall more? Dare we trace this waxy trail yet
further? Even though it gives off painful molten heat?

Yes?

You are brave, my rings. . . .

Behold the Rothen ship—suddenly bathed in light!

Actinic radiance pours onto it *from above* . . . cast by a new entity, shining like the blazing sun.

It is no sun, but *another* vessel of space! A ship unbelievably larger than the slim gene raider, looming above it the way a full-stacked traeki might tower over a single, newly vlenned ring.

Can the wax be believed? Could anything be as huge and mighty as that luminous mountain-thing, gliding over the valley as ponderous as a thunderhead?

Trapped, the Rothen craft emits awful, grating noises, straining to escape the titanic newcomer. But the cascade of light now presses on it, pushing with force that spills across the vale, taking on qualities of physical substance. Like a solid shaft, the beam thrusts the Rothen ship downward against its will, until its belly scours Jijo's wounded soil.

A deluge of saffron color flows around the smaller cruiser, covering the Rothen craft in layers—thickening, like gobs of cooling sap. Soon the Rothen ship lies helplessly encased. Leaves and twigs seem caught in midwhirl, motionless beside the gold-sealed hull.

And above, a new power hovered. Leviathan.

The searing lights dimmed.

Humming a song of overpowering might, the titan descended, like a guest mountain dropping in to take its place among the Rimmers. A stone from heaven, cracking bedrock and reshaping the valley with its awful weight.

Now the wax stream changes course. The molten essence of distilled chagrin veers in a new direction.

Its heading, my rings?

Over a precipice.

Into hell.

Rety

RETY THOUGHT ABOUT HER BIRD. THE BRIGHT bird, so lively, so unfairly maimed, so like herself in its stubborn struggle to overcome.

All her adventures began one day when Jass and Bom returned from a hunting trip boasting about wounding a mysterious flying creature. Their trophy—a gorgeous metal feather—was the trigger she had been waiting for. Rety took it as an omen, steadying her resolve to break away. A sign that it was time, at last, to leave her ragged tribe and seek a better life.

I guess everybody's looking for something, she pondered, as the robot followed another bend in the dreary river, meandering toward the last known destination of Kunn's flying scout craft. Rety had the same goal, but also dreaded it. The Danik pilot would deal harshly with Dwer. He might also judge Rety, for her many failings.

She vowed to suppress her temper and grovel if need be. *Just so the starfolk keep their promise and take me with them when they leave Jijo.*

They must! I gave 'em the bird. Rann said it was a clue to help the Daniks and their Rothen lords search . . .

Her thoughts stumbled.

Search for what?

They must need somethin' awful bad to break Galactic law by sneakin' to far-off Jijo.

Rety never swallowed all the talk about "gene raiding"—that the Rothen expedition came looking for animals almost ready to think. When you grow up close to nature, scratching for each meal alongside other creatures, you soon realize *everybody* thinks. Beasts, fish . . . why, some of her cousins even prayed to trees and stones!

Rety's answer was—*so what?* Would a gallaiter be less smelly if it could read? Or a wallow kleb any less disgusting if it recited poetry while rolling in dung? By her lights, nature was vile and dangerous. She had a bellyful and would gladly give it up to live in some bright Galactic city.

Rety never believed Kunn's people came across vast space just to teach some critters how to blab.

Then what was the real reason? And what were they afraid of?

The robot avoided deep water, as if its force fields needed rock or soil to push against. When the river widened, and converging tributaries became rivers themselves, further progress proved impossible. Even a long detour west offered no way around. The drone buzzed in frustration, hemmed by water on all sides.

"Rety!" Dwer's hoarse voice called from below. "Talk to it again!"

"I already did, remember? *You* must've wrecked its ears in the ambush, when you ripped out its antenna thing!"

"Well . . . try again. Tell it I might . . . have a way to get across a stream."

Rety stared down at him, gripped by snakelike arms. "You tried to kill it a while back, an' now you're offerin' to help?"

He grimaced. "It beats dying, wandering in its clutches till the sun burns out. I figure there's food and medicine on the flying boat. Anyway, I've heard so much about these alien humans. Why should you get all the fun?"

She couldn't tell where he stopped being serious, and turned sarcastic. Not that it mattered. If Dwer's idea proved useful, it might soften the way Kunn treated him.

And me, she added.

"Oh, all right."

Rety spoke directly to the machine, as she had been taught.

"Drone Four! Hear and obey commands! I order you to let us down so's we can haggle together about how to pass over this here brook. The prisoner says he's got a way mebbe to do it."

The robot did not respond at first, but kept cruising between two high points, surveying for any sign of a crossing. But finally, the humming repulsors changed tone as metal arms lowered Dwer, letting him roll down a mossy bank. For a time the young man lay groaning. His limbs twitched feebly, like a stranded fish.

More than a little stiff herself, Rety hoisted her body off the upper platform, wincing at the singular touch of steady ground. Both legs tingled painfully, though likely not as bad as Dwer felt. She got down on her knees and poked his elbow.

"Hey, you all right? Need help gettin' up?"

Dwer's eyes glittered pain, but he shook his head. She put an arm around his shoulder anyway as he struggled to sit. No fresh blood oozed when they checked the crusty dressing on his thigh wound.

The alien drone waited silently as the young man stood, unsteadily.

"Maybe I can help you get across water," he told the machine. "If I do, will you change the way you carry us? Stop for breaks and help us find food? What d'you say?"

Another long pause—then a chirping note burst forth. Rety had learned a little Galactic Two during her time as an apprentice star child. She recognized the upward sliding scale meaning yes.

Dwer nodded. "I can't guarantee my plan'll work. But here's what I suggest."

It was actually simple, almost obvious, yet she looked at Dwer differently after he emerged from the stream, dripping from the armpits down. Before he was halfway out, the robot edged aside from its perch *above Dwer's head*. It seemed to glide down the side of the young hunter's body until reaching a point where its fields could grip solid ground.

All the way across the river, Dwer looked as if he wore a huge, eight-sided hat, wafting over his head like a balloon. His eyes were glazed and his hair stood on end as Rety sat him down.

"Hey!" She nudged him. "You all right?"

Dwer's gaze seemed fixed far away. After a few duras though, he answered.

"Um . . . I . . . guess so."

She shook her head. Even Mudfoot and yee had ceased

their campaign of mutual deadly glares in order to stare at the man from the Slope.

"That was *so* weird!" Rety commented. She could not bring herself to say "brave," or "thrilling" or "insane."

He winced, as if messages from his bruised body were just now reaching a dazed brain. "Yeah . . . it was all that. And more."

The robot chirruped again. Rety guessed that a triple upsweep with a shrill note at the end meant—*That's enough resting. Let's go!*

She helped Dwer onto a makeshift seat the robot made by folding its arms. This time, when it resumed its southward flight, the two humans rode in front with Mudfoot and little yee, sharing body heat against the stiff wind.

Rety had heard of this region from those bragging hunters, Jass and Bom. It was a low country, dotted with soggy marshes and crisscrossed by many more streams ahead.

Alvin

I WOKE FEELING WOOZY, AND HIGH AS A CHIMP that's been chewing ghigree leaves. But at least the agony was gone.

The soft slab was still under me, though I could tell the awkward brace of straps and metal tubes was gone. Turning my head, I spied a low table nearby. A shallow white bowl held about a dozen familiar-looking shapes, vital to hoon rituals of life and death.

Ifni! I thought. *The monsters cut out my spine bones!*

Then I reconsidered.

Wait. You're a kid. You've got two sets. In fact, isn't it next year you're supposed to start losing your first . . .

I really was *that* slow to catch on. Pain and drugs can do it to you.

Looking in the bowl again, I saw all my baby vertebrae. Normally, they'd loosen over several months, as the barbed adult spines took over. The accident must have jammed both sets together, pressing the nerves and hurrying nature

along. The phuvnthus must have decided to take out my
old verts, whether the new ones were ready or not.

Did they guess? Or were they already familiar with
hoons?

Take things one at a time, I thought. *Can you feel your
toe hooks? Can you move them?*

I sent signals to retract the claw sheaths, and sensed the
table's fabric resist as my talons dug in. So far so good.

I reached around with my left hand, and found a slick
bulge covering my spine, tough and elastic.

Words cut in. An uncannily smooth voice, in accented
Galactic Seven.

"The new orthopedic brace will actively help bear the
stress of your movements until your next-stage vertebroids
solidify. Nevertheless, you would be well advised not to
move in too sudden or jerky a manner."

The fixture wrapped all the way around my torso, feeling snug and comfortable, unlike the makeshift contraption
the phuvnthus provided earlier.

"Please accept my thanks," I responded in formal Gal-
Seven, gingerly shifting onto one elbow, turning my head
the other way. "And my apologies for any inconvenience
this may have cause—"

I stopped short. Where I had expected to see a
phuvnthu, or one of the small amphibians, there stood a
whirling shape, ghostly, like the *holographic projections*
we had seen before, but ornately abstract. A spinning mesh
of complex lines floated near the bed.

"There was no inconvenience." The voice seemed to
emerge from the gyrating image. "We were curious about
matters taking place in the world of air and light. Your swift
arrival—plummeting into a sea canyon near our scout vessel—seemed as fortuitous to us as *our* presence was for
you."

Even in a drugged state, I could savor multilevel irony in
the whirling thing's remarks. While being gracious, it was
also reminding me that the survivors of *Wuphon's Dream*
owed a debt—our very lives.

"True," I assented. "Though my friends and I might
never have fallen into the abyss if *someone* had not removed the article we were sent to find in more shallow

waters. Our search beyond that place led us to stumble over the cliff."

The pattern of shifting lines took a new slant of bluish, twinkling light.

"You assert ownership over this thing you sought? As your property?"

Now it was my turn to ponder, wary of a trap. By the codes laid down in the Scrolls, the cache Uriel had sent us after should not exist. It bent the spirit and letter of the law, which said that sooner colonists on a forbidden world must ease their crime by abandoning their godlike tools. It made me glad to be speaking a formal dialect, forcing more careful thought than I might have used in our local patois.

"I assert . . . a right to *inspect* the item . . . and reserve an option to make further claims later."

Purple swirls invaded the spinning pattern, and I could almost swear it seemed amused. Perhaps this strange entity already had pursued the same line of questioning with my pals. I may be articulate—Huck says no one can match me in GalSeven—but I never claimed to be the brightest one in our gang.

"The matter can be discussed another time," the voice said. "After you tell us of your life, and recent events in the upper world."

This triggered something in me . . . call it the latent trading instinct that lurks in any hoon. A keenness for the fine art of dickering. Carefully, tenderly, I sat up, allowing the supple back brace to take most of the strain.

"Hr-r-rm. You're asking us to give away the only thing we have to barter—our story, and that of our ancestors. What do you offer in exchange?"

The voice made a pretty good approximation of a rueful hoonish rumble.

"Apologies. It did not occur to us that you would look at it that way. Alas, you have already told us a great deal. We will now return your information store. Please accept our contrition over having accessed it without expressed permission."

A door slid open and one of the little amphibian creatures entered the cubicle, bearing in its four slim arms my backpack!

Better yet, on top lay my precious journal, all battered and bent, but still the item I most valued in the world. I snatched up the book, flipping its dog-eared pages.

"Rest assured," the spinning pattern enounced. "Our study of this document, while enlightening, has only whetted our appetite for information. Your economic interests are undiminished."

I thought about that. "You read my journal?"

"Again, apologies. It seemed prudent, when seeking to understand your injuries, and the manner of your arrival in this realm of heavy wet darkness."

Once again, the words seemed to come at me with layers of meaning and implications I could only begin to sift. At the time, I only wanted to end the conversation as soon as possible, and confer with Huck and the others before going any further.

"I'd like to see my friends now," I told the whirling image, switching to Anglic.

It seemed to quiver, as if with a nod.

"Very well. They have been informed to expect you. Please follow the entity standing at the door."

The little amphibian attended while I set foot on the floor, gingerly testing my weight. There were a few twinges, just enough to help me settle best within the support of the flexible body cast. I gripped the journal, but glanced back at my knapsack and the bowl of baby vertebrae.

"These items will be safe here," promised the voice.

I hope so, I thought. *Mom and Dad will want them . . . assuming that I ever see Mu-phauwq, and Yowg-wayuo again . . . and especially if I don't.*

"Thank you."

The speckled pattern whirled.

"It is my pleasure to serve."

Holding my journal tight, I followed the small being out the door. When I glanced back at the bed, the spinning projection was gone.

Asx

HERE IT IS, AT LAST. THE IMAGE WE HAVE SOUGHT, now cool enough to stroke.

Yes, my rings. It is time for another vote. Shall we remain catatonic, rather than face what will almost certainly be a vision of pure horror?

Our first ring of cognition insists that duty must take precedence, even over the natural traeki tendency to flee unpleasant subjectivities.

Is it agreed? Shall we be *Asx,* and meet reality as it comes? How do you rule, my rings?

> *stroke the wax. . . .*
> *follow the tracks. . . .*
> *see the mighty starship come. . . .*

Humming a song of overwhelming power, the monstrous vessel descends, crushing every remaining tree on the south side of the valley, shoving a dam across the river, filling the horizon like a mountain.

Can you feel it, my rings? Premonition. Throbbing our core with acrid vapors?

Along the starship's vast flank a hatch opens, large enough to swallow a small village.

Against the lighted interior, *silhouettes* enter view.

Tapered cones.

Stacks of rings.

Frightful kin we had hoped never again to see.

Sara

SARA LOOKED BACK FONDLY AT LAST NIGHT'S WILD ride, for now the horses sped up to a pace that made her bottom feel like butter.

And to think, as a child I wished I could gallop about like characters in storybooks.

Whenever the pace slackened, she eyed the enigmatic female riders who seemed so at home atop huge, mythological beasts. They called themselves *Illias,* and their lives had been secret for a long time. But now haste compelled them to travel openly.

Can it really be just to get Kurt the Exploser where he wants to go?

Assuming his mission is vital, why does he want my help? I'm a theoretical mathematician with a sideline in linguistics. Even in math, I'm centuries out of date by Earth standards. To Galactics I'd be just a clever shaman.

Losing altitude, the party began passing settlements—at first urrish camps with buried workshops and sunken corrals hidden from the glowering sky. But as the country grew more lush, they skirted dams where blue qheuen hives tended lake-bottom farms. Passing a riverside grove, they found the "trees" were ingeniously folded masts of hoonish fishing skiffs and khuta boats. Sara even glimpsed a g'Kek weaver village where sturdy trunks supported ramps, bridges, and swaying boardwalks for the clever wheeled clan.

At first the settlements seemed deserted as the horses sped by. But the chick coops were full, and the blur canopies freshly patched. *Midday isn't a favorite time to be about, especially with sinister specters in the sky.* Anyone rousing from siesta glimpsed only vague galloping figures, obscured by dust.

But attention was unavoidable later, when members of all six races scurried from shelters, shouting as the corps of beasts and riders rushed by. The grave Illias horsewomen never answered, but Emerson and young Jomah waved at astonished villagers, provoking some hesitant cheers. It made Sara laugh, and she joined their antics, helping turn the galloping procession into a kind of antic parade.

When the mounts seemed nearly spent, the guides veered into a patch of forest where two more women waited, dressed in suede, speaking that accent Sara found tantalizingly familiar. Hot food awaited the party—along with a dozen fresh mounts.

Someone is a good organizer, Sara thought. She ate standing up—a pungent vegetarian gruel. Walking helped stretch kinked muscles.

The next stage went better. One of the Illias showed Sara a trick of flexing in her stirrups to damp the jouncing rhythm. Though grateful, Sara wondered.

Where have these people lived all this time?

Dedinger, the desert prophet, caught Sara's eye, eager to discuss the mystery, but she turned away. The attraction of his intellect wasn't worth suffering his character. She preferred spending her free moments with Emerson. Though speechless, the wounded starman had a good soul.

Villages grew sparse south of the Great Marsh. But *traeki* flourished there, from tall cultured stacks, famed for herbal industry, all the way down to wild quintets, quartets, and little trio ring piles, consuming decaying matter the way their ancestors must have on a forgotten homeworld, before some patron race set them on the Path of Uplift.

Sara daydreamed geometric arcs, distracting her mind from the heat and tedium, entering a world of parabolas and rippling wavelike forms, free of time and distance. By the time she next looked up, dusk was falling and a broad river flowed to their left, with faint lights glimmering on the other bank.

"Traybold's Crossing." Dedinger peered at the settlement, nestled under camouflage vines. "I do think the residents have finally done the right thing . . . even if it inconveniences wayfarers like us."

The wiry rebel appeared pleased. Sara wondered.

Can he mean the bridge? Have local fanatics torn it down, without orders from the sages?

Dwer, her well-traveled brother, had described the span across the Gentt as a marvel of disguise, appearing like an aimless jam of broken trees. But even that would not satisfy fervent scroll thumpers these days.

Through twilight dimness she spied a forlorn skeleton of charred logs, trailing from sandbar to sandbar.

Just like at Bing Hamlet, back home. What is it about a bridge that attracts destroyers?

Anything sapient-made might be a target of zealotry, these days.

The workshops, dams, and libraries may go. We'll follow glavers into blessed obscurity. Dedinger's heresy may prove right, and Lark's prove wrong.

She sighed. *Mine was always the unlikeliest of all.*

Despite captivity, Dedinger seemed confident in ultimate success for his cause.

"Now our young guides must spend days trying to hire boats. No more rushing about, postponing Judgment Day. As if the explosers and their friends could ever have changed destiny."

"Shut up," Kurt said.

"You know, I always thought your guild would be on *our* side, when the time came to abandon vanities and take redemption's path. Isn't it frustrating, preparing all your life to blow up things, only to hold back at the crucial moment?"

Kurt looked away.

Sara expected the horsewomen to head to a nearby fishing village. Hoonish coracles might be big enough to ferry one horse at a time, though that slow process would expose the Illias to every gawking citizen within a dozen leagues. Worse, Urunthai reinforcements, or Dedinger's own die-hard supporters, might have time to catch up.

But to her surprise, the party left the river road, heading west down a narrow track through dense undergrowth. Two Illias dropped back, brushing away signs of their passage.

Could their settlement lie in this thicket?

But hunters and gleaners from several races surely went browsing through this area. No secret horse clan could remain hidden for more than a hundred years!

Disoriented in a labyrinth of trees and jutting knolls, Sara kept a wary eye on the rider in front of her. She did not relish wandering lost and alone in the dark.

Gaining altitude, the track finally crested to overlook a cluster of evenly spaced hills—steep mounds surrounding a depression filled with dense brush. From their symmetry, Sara thought of Buyur ruins.

Then she forgot about archaeology when something else caught her eye. A flicker to the west, beckoning from many leagues away.

The mountain's wide shoulders cut a broad wedge of stars.

Near its summit, curved streaks glowed red and orange.

Flowing lava.

Jijo's blood.

A volcano.

Sara blinked. Might they already have traveled to—

"No," she answered herself. "That's not Guenn. It's *Blaze Mountain*."

"If only that *were* our destination, Sara. Things'd be simpler." Kurt spoke from nearby. "Alas, the smiths of Blaze Peak are conservative. They want no part of the hobbies and pastimes that are practiced where we're headin'."

Hobbies? Pastimes? Was Kurt trying to baffle her with riddles?

"You can't still reckon we're going all the way to—"

"To the other great forge? Aye, Sara. We'll make it, don't fret."

"But the bridge is out! Then there's desert, and after that, the Spec . . ."

She trailed off as the troop turned downward, into the thorn brake between the hills. Three times, riders dismounted to shift clever barriers that looked like boulders or tree trunks. At last, they reached a small clearing where the guides met and embraced another group of leatherclad women. There was a campfire . . . and the welcome aroma of food.

Despite a hard day, Sara managed to unsaddle her own mount and brush the tired beast. She ate standing, doubtful she would ever sit again.

I should check Emerson. Make sure he takes his medicine. He may need a story or a song to settle down after all this.

A small figure slipped alongside, chuffing nervously.

No—Go—Hole— Prity motioned with agile hands. *Scary—Hole.*

Sara frowned.

"What hole are you talking about?"

The chimp took Sara's hand, pulling her toward several Illias, who were shifting baggage to a squat, boxy object.

A *wagon*, Sara realized. A big one, with four wheels, instead of the usual two. Fresh horses were harnessed, but to haul it where? Surely not through the surrounding thicket!

Then Sara saw what "hole" Prity meant—gaping at the base of a cone hill. An aperture with smooth walls and a flat floor. A thin glowing stripe ran along the tunnel's center, continuing downhill before turning out of sight.

Jomah and Kurt were already aboard the big wagon, with Dedinger strapped in behind, a stunned expression on his aristocratic face.

For once Sara agreed with the heretic sage.

Emerson stood at the shaft entrance and whooped, like a small boy exploring a cave first with his own echoes. The starman grinned, happier than ever, and reached for her hand. Sara took his while inhaling deeply.

Well, I bet Dwer and Lark never went anywhere like this. I may yet be the one with the best story to tell.

Alvin

I FOUND MY FRIENDS IN A DIM CHAMBER WHERE frigid fog blurred every outline. Even hobbling with crutches, my awkward footsteps made hardly a sound as I approached the silhouettes of Huck and Ur-ronn, with little Huphu curled on Pincer's carapace. All faced the other way, looking downward into a soft glow.

"Hey, what's going on?" I asked. "Is this any way to greet—"

One of Huck's eyestalks swerved on me.

"We're-glad-to-see-you're-all-right-but-now-shut-up-and-get-over-here."

Few other citizens of the Slope could squeeze all that

into a single GalThree word-blat. Not that skill excused her rudeness.

"Hr-rm. The-same-to-you-I'm-sure, oh-obsessed-being-too-transfixed-to-offer-decent-courtesy," I replied in kind.

Shuffling forward, I noted how my companions were transformed. Ur-ronn's pelt gleamed, Huck's wheels were realigned, and Pincer's carapace had been patched and buffed smooth. Even Huphu seemed sleek and content.

"What is it?" I began. "What're you all staring . . ."

My voice trailed off when I saw where they stood—on a *balcony* without a rail, overlooking the source of both the pale glow and the chill haze. A cube—two hoon lengths on a side, colored a pale shade of brownish yellow—lay swathed in a fog of its own making, unadorned except by a symbol embossed on one face. A *spiral* emblem with five swirling arms and a bulbous center, all crossed by a gleaming vertical bar.

Despite how far the people of the Slope have fallen, or how long it's been since our ancestors roamed as star gods, that emblem is known to every grub and child. Inscribed on each copy of the Sacred Scrolls, it evokes awe when prophets and sages speak of lost wonders. On this frosted obelisk it could only mean one thing—that we stood near more knowledge than anyone on Jijo could tally, or begin to imagine. If the human crew of sneakship *Tabernacle* had kept printing paper books till this very day, they could have spilled only a small fragment of the trove before us, a hoard that began before many stars in the sky.

The Great Library of the Civilization of the Five Galaxies.

I'm told moments like these can inspire eloquence from great minds.

"J-j-jeez," commented Pincer.

Ur-ronn was less concise.

"The questions . . . ," she lisped. "The questions we could ask . . ."

I nudged Huck.

"Well, you said you wanted to go find something to *read*."

For the first time in all the years I've known her, our little wheeled friend seemed at a loss for words. Her stalks trembled. The only sound she let out was a gentle keening sigh.

Asx

If only we/i had nimble running feet,
  i/we would use them now, to flee.
If we/i had burrowers' claws,
  i/we would dig a hole and hide.
If we/i had the wings,
  i/we would fly away.

Lacking those useful skills, the member toruses of our composite stack nearly vote to draw permanently, sealing out the world, negating the objective universe, waiting for the intolerable to go away.

It will not go away.

So reminds our second torus of cognition.

Among the greasy trails of wisdom that coat our aged core, many were laid down after reading learned books, or holding lengthy discussions with other sages. These tracks of philosophical wax agree with our second ring. As difficult as it may be for a traeki to accept, the cosmos does not vanish when we turn within. Logic and science appear to prove otherwise.

The universe goes on. Things that matter keep happening, one after another.

Still, it is *hard* to swivel our trembling sensor rings to face toward the mountain dreadnought that recently lowered itself down from heaven, whose bulk seems to fill both valley and sky.

Harder to gaze through a hatchway in the great ship's

flank—an aperture broad as the largest building in Tarek Town.

Hardest to regard the worst of all possible sights—those cousins that we traeki fled long ago.

Terrible and strong—the mighty Jophur.

How gorgeous they seem, those glistening sap rings, swaying in their backlit portal, staring without pity at the wounded glade their vessel alters with its crushing weight. A glade thronging with half-animal felons, a miscegenous rabble, the crude descendants of fugitives.

Exiles who futilely thought they might elude the ineludable.

Our fellow Commons citizens mutter fearfully, still awed by the rout of the smaller Rothen ship—that power we had held in dread for months—now pressed down and encased in deadly light.

Yes, my rings. i/we can sense how some nearby Sixers—the quick and prudent—take to their heels, retreating even before the landing tremors fade. Others foolishly mill *toward* the giant vessel, driven by curiosity, or awe. Perhaps they have trouble reconciling the shapes they see with any sense of danger.

As harmless as a traeki, so the expression goes. After all, what menace can there be in tapered stacks of fatty rings?

Oh, my/our poor innocent neighbors. You are about to find out.

Lark

THAT NIGHT HE DREAMED ABOUT THE LAST TIME HE saw Ling smile—before her world and his forever changed.

It seemed long ago, during a moonlit pilgrimage that crept proudly past volcanic vents and sheer cliffs, bearing shared hope and reverence toward the Holy Egg. Twelve twelves of white-clad celebrants made up that procession—qheuens and g'Keks, traekis and urs, humans and hoons—climbing a hidden trail to their sacred site. And accompanying them for the first time, guests from outer space—a Rothen master, two Danik humans, and their robot guards—attending to witness the unity rites of a quaint savage tribe.

He dreamed about that pilgrimage in its last peaceful moment, before the fellowship was splintered by alien words and fanatical deeds. Especially the smile on her face, when she told him joyous news.

> *"Ships are coming, Lark. So many ships!*
> *"It's time to bring you all back home."*

Two words still throbbed like sparks in the night. Rhythmically hotter as he reached for them in his sleep.

. . . *ships* . . .
. . . *home* . . .
. . . *ships* . . .
. . . *home* . . .

One word vanished at his dream touch—he could not tell which. The other he clenched hard, its flamelike glow increasing. Strange light, pushing free of containment. It streamed past flesh, past bones. A glow that clarified, offering to show him *everything*.

Everything except . . .

Except now *she* was gone. Taken away by the word that vanished.

Pain wrenched Lark from the lonely night phantasm, tangled in a sweaty blanket. His trembling right hand clenched hard against his chest, erupting with waves of agony.

Lark exhaled a long sigh as he used his left hand to pry open the fingers of his right, forcing them apart one by one. Something rolled off his open palm—

It was the stone fragment of the Holy Egg, the one he had hammered from it as a rebellious child, and worn ever since as penance. Even as sleep unraveled, he imagined the rocky talisman throbbing with heat, pulsing in time to the beating of his heart.

Lark stared at the blur-cloth canopy, with moonlight glimmering beyond.

I remain in darkness, on Jijo, he thought, yearning to see once more by the radiance that had filled his dream. A light that seemed about to reveal distant vistas.

Ling spoke to him later that day, when their lunch trays were slipped into the tent by a nervous militiaman.

"Look, this is stupid," she said. "Each of us acting like the other is some kind of devil spawn. We don't have time for grudges, with your people and mine on a tragic collision course."

Lark had been thinking much the same thing, though her sullen funk had seemed too wide to broach. Now Ling met his eyes frankly, as if anxious to make up for lost time.

"I'd say a collision's already happened," he commented.

Her lips pressed a thin line. She nodded.

"True. But it's wrong to blame your entire Commons for the deeds of a minority, acting without authority or—"

He barked a bitter laugh. "Even when you're trying to be sincere, you still condescend, Ling."

She stared for a moment, then nodded. "All right. Your sages effectively sanctioned the zealots' attack, *post facto,* by keeping us prisoner and threatening blackmail. It's fair to say that we're already—"

"At war. True, dear ex-employer. But you leave out our own *casus belli.*" Lark knew the grammar must be wrong, but he liked showing that even a savage could also drop a Latin phrase. "We're fighting for our lives. And now we know genocide was the Rothen aim from the start."

Ling glanced past him to where a g'Kek doctor drew increasing amounts of nauseating fluid from the air vents of a qheuen, squatting unconscious at the back of the shelter. She had worked alongside Uthen for months, evaluating local species for possible uplift. The gray's illness was no abstraction.

"Believe me, Lark. I know nothing of this disease. Nor

the trick Ro-kenn allegedly pulled, trying to broadcast psi-influentials via your Egg."

"Allegedly? You suggest *we* might have the technology to pull off something like that, as a frame-up?"

Ling sighed. "I don't dismiss the idea entirely. From the start you Jijoans played on our preconceptions. Our willingness to see you as ignorant barbarians. It took weeks to learn that you were still literate! Only lately did we realize you must have hundreds of books, maybe thousands!"

An ironic smile crossed his face, before Lark realized how much the expression revealed.

"More than that? *A lot more?*" Ling stared. "But where? By Von Daniken's beard—how?"

Lark put aside his meal, mostly uneaten. He reached over to his backpack and drew forth a thick volume bound in leather. "I can't count how many times I wanted to show you this. Now I guess it doesn't matter anymore."

In a gesture Lark appreciated, Ling wiped her hands before accepting the book, turning the pages with deliberate care. What seemed reverence at first, Lark soon realized was inexperience. Ling had little practice holding paper books.

Probably never saw one before, outside a museum.

Rows of small type were punctuated by lithographed illustrations. Ling exclaimed over the flat, unmoving images. Many of the species shown had passed through the Danik research pavilion during the months she and Lark worked side by side, seeking animals with the special traits her Rothen masters desired.

"How old is this text? Did you find it here, among all these remnants?" Ling motioned toward a stack of artifacts preserved by the mulc spider, relics of the long-departed Buyur, sealed in amber cocoons.

Lark groaned. "You're still doing it, Ling. For Ifni's sake! The book is written in *Anglic*."

She nodded vigorously. "Of course. You're right. But then who—"

Lark reached over and flipped the volume to its title page.

A PHYLOGENETIC INTERDEPENDENCE PROFILE
OF ECOLOGICAL SYSTEMS ON THE JIJOAN SLOPE

"This is part one. Part two is still mostly notes. I doubt we'd have lived long enough to finish volume three, so we left the deserts, seas, and tundras for someone else to take on."

Ling gaped at the sheet of linen paper, stroking two lines of smaller print, below the title. She looked at him, then over toward the dying qheuen.

"That's right," he said. "You're living in the same tent with both authors. And since I'm presenting you with this copy, you have a rare opportunity. Care to have both of us autograph it? I expect you're the last person who'll get the chance."

His bitter sarcasm was wasted. Clearly she didn't understand the word *autograph*. Anyway, Ling the biologist had replaced the patronizing alien invader. Turning pages, she murmured over each chapter she skimmed.

"This would have been incredibly useful during our survey!"

"That's why I never showed it to you."

Ling answered with a curt nod. Given their disagreement over the rightness of gene raiding, his attitude was understandable.

Finally, she closed the volume, stroking the cover. "I am honored by this gift. This *accomplishment*. I find I cannot grasp what it must have taken to create it, under these conditions, just the two of you. . . ."

"With the help of others, and standing on the shoulders of those who came before. It's how science works. Each generation's supposed to get better, adding to what earlier ones knew. . . ."

His voice trailed off as he realized what he was saying.

Progress? But that's Sara's apostasy, not mine!

Anyway, why am I so bitter? So what if alien diseases wipe out every sapient being on Jijo? Weren't you willing to see that as a blessing, a while ago? Didn't it seem an ideal way to swiftly end our illegal colony? A harmful invasion that should never have existed in the first place?

Over the course of Uthen's illness, Lark came to realize something—that death can sometimes seem desirable in abstract, but look quite different when it's in your path, up close and personal.

If Harullen the Heretic had lived, that purist might have helped Lark cling to his belief in Galactic law, which for good reason forbade settlements on fallow worlds. *It was our goal to atone for our ancestors' egotistical sin. To help rid Jijo of the infestation.*

But Harullen was gone, sliced to bits by a Rothen robot, and now Lark grappled with doubts.

I'd rather Sara were right. If only I could see nobility here. Something worth enduring. Worth fighting for.

I don't really want to die.

Ling pored through the guidebook again. Better than most, she could appreciate the work he and Uthen spent their adult lives creating. Her professional esteem helped bridge the chasm of their personalities.

"I wish I had something of equal value to give you," she said, meeting his eyes again.

Lark pondered.

"You really mean that?"

"Of course I do."

"All right then, wait here. I'll be right back."

At the rear of the shelter, the g'Kek physician indicated with twined eyestalks that Uthen's condition was unvaried. Good news, since each change till now had been for the worse. Lark stroked his friend's chitin carapace, wishing he could impart comfort through the gray's stupor.

"Is it my fault you caught this bug, old friend? I made you go with me into the station wreckage, rummaging for alien secrets." He sighed. "I can't make up for that. But what's in your bag may help others."

He lifted Uthen's private satchel and took it back to Ling. Reaching inside, he felt several slablike objects, cool to the touch.

"Earlier, we found something that you might help me learn to read. If you meant your promise."

He put one of the flat lozenges in her hand—pale brown and smooth as glass, with a spiral shape etched on each face.

Ling stared at it for several duras. When she looked up, there was something new in her countenance. Was it respect for the way he had cornered her? Trapping her with the one other trait they shared—a compelling sense of honor?

For the first time since they met, Ling's eyes seemed to concede that she was dealing with an equal.

Asx

CALM DOWN, MY RINGS. NO ONE CAN FORCE YOU to stroke wax against your will.

As traeki we are each of us sovereign, free not to recall intolerable memories before we are ready.

Let the wax cool a little longer—a majority of rings demands—*before we dare look again.*

Let the most recent terror wait.

But our second cognition ring demurs. It insists—we/i should delay no longer confronting the dread news about Jophur, our terrible cousins, arriving on Jijo.

Our second ring of cognition reminds us of the Quandary of Solipsism—the riddle that provoked our traeki founders to flee the Five Galaxies.

Solipsism. The myth of the all-important self.

Most mortal sapient beings hold this conceit, at one level or another. An individual can perceive others by sight, touch, and empathy, yet still reckon them as mere figments or automatons. Caricatures, of little importance.

Under solipsism, the world exists for each solitary individualist.

Examined dispassionately, it seems an insane concept. Especially to a traeki, since none of us can thrive or think alone. Yet egotism can also be useful to ambitious creatures, driving their single-minded pursuit of success.

Madness seems essential in order to be "great."

•   •   •

Terran sages knew this paradox from their long isolation. Ignorant and lonely, humans wallowed in one bizarre superstition after another, frantically trying concepts that no uplifted species would consider for even a dura. According to wolfling tales, humans wrestled endlessly with their own overpowering egos.

Some tried *suppressing* selfness, seeking detachment. Others subsumed personal ambition in favor of a greater whole—family, religion, or a leader.

Later they passed through a phase in which individualism was extolled as the highest virtue, teaching their young to inflate the ego beyond all natural limits or restraint. Works from this mad *era of the self* are found in the Biblos Archive, with righteous, preening rage flowing across every page.

Finally, just before contact, there emerged another approach.

Some of their texts use the word *maturity*.

We traeki—newly uplifted from the pensive swamps of our homeworld—seemed safe from achieving greatness, no matter how many skills our patrons, the blessed Poa, inserted in our rings. Oh, we found it pleasant to merge in tall, wise stacks. To gather learned wax and travel the stars. But to our patrons' frustration, we never found appealing the fractious rivalries that churn the Five Galaxies. Frantic aspiration and zeal always seemed pointless to our kind.

Then the Poa brought in experts. The *Oailie*.

The Oailie pitied our handicap. With great skill, they gave us tools for achievement. For greatness.

The Oailie gave us new rings—

Rings of power.

Rings of self-centered glory.

Rings that turned mere traeki into *Jophur*.

Too late, we and the Poa learned a lesson—that ambition comes at a cost.

•   •   •

We fled, did we not, my rings?

By a fluke, some traeki managed to shuck these Oailie "gifts," and escape.

Only a few wax-crystal remembrance cells survive from those days. Memories laced with dread of what we were becoming.

At the time, our ancestors saw no choice but flight.

And yet . . . a pang of conscience trickles through our inner core.

Might there have been another way?

Might we have stayed and fought somehow to tame those awesome new rings? Futile as our forebears' exodus now seems . . . was it also *wrong*?

Since joining the High Sages, this traeki Asx has pored over Terran books, studying their lonely, epochal struggle—a poignant campaign to control their own deeply solipsistic natures. A labor still under way when they emerged from Earth's cradle to make contact with Galactic civilization.

The results of that Asx investigation remain inconclusive, yet i/we found tantalizing clues.

The fundamental ingredient, it seems, is courage.

Yes, my rings?

Very well then. A majority has been persuaded by the second ring of cognition.

We/i shall once again turn to the hot-new-dreadful waxy trail of recent memory.

Glistening cones stared down at the confused onlookers who remained, milling on the despoiled glade. From a balcony high a-flank the mountain ship, polished stacks of fatty rings dripped luxuriously as they regarded teeming savages below—we enthralled members of six exile races.

Shifting colors play across their plump toruses—shades of rapid disputation. Even at a great distance, i/we sense controversy raging among the mighty Jophur, as they quarrel among themselves. Debating our fate.

• • •

Events interrupt, even as our dribbling thought-streams converge.

Near.

At last we have come very near the recent. The present.

Can you sense it, my rings? The moment when our dreadful cousins finished arguing what to do about us? Amid the flashing rancor of their debate, there suddenly appeared forceful decisiveness. Those in command—powerful ring stacks whose authority is paramount—made their decree with stunning confidence.

Such assuredness! Such certainty! It washed over us, even from six arrowflights away.

Then something else poured from the mighty dreadnought.

Hatchet blades of infernal light.

Emerson

H E HAS NEVER BEEN ESPECIALLY FOND OF HOLES. This one both frightens and intrigues Emerson.

It is a strange journey, riding a wooden wagon behind a four-horse team, creaking along a conduit with dimpled walls, like some endless stretched intestine. The only illumination—a faintly glowing stripe—points straight ahead and behind, toward opposite horizons.

The duality feels like a sermon. After departing the hidden forest entrance, time became vague—the past blurry and the future obscure. Much like his life has been ever since regaining consciousness on this savage world, with a cavity in his head and a million dark spaces where memory should be.

Emerson can feel this place tugging associations deep within his battered skull. Correlations that scratch and howl beyond the barriers of his amnesia. Dire recollections lurk just out of reach. Alarming memories of abject, gibbering terror, that snap and sting whenever he seeks to retrieve them.

Almost as if, somehow, they were being guarded.

Strangely, this does not deter him from prodding at the barricades. He has spent much too long in the company of pain to hold it in awe any longer. Familiar with its quirks and ways, Emerson figures he now knows pain as well as he knows himself.

Better, in fact.

Like a quarry who turns at bay after growing bored with running—and then begins hunting its pursuer—Emerson eagerly *stalks* the fear scent, following it to its source.

The feeling is not shared. Though the draft beasts pant and their hooves clatter, all echoes feel muffled, almost deathlike. His fellow travelers react by hunching nervously on the narrow bench seats, their breath misting the chill air.

Kurt the Exploser seems a little less surprised by all this than Sara or Dedinger, as if the old man long suspected the existence of a subterranean path. Yet, his white-rimmed eyes keep darting, as if to catch dreaded movement in the surrounding shadows. Even their guides, the taciturn women riders, appear uneasy. They must have come this way before, yet Emerson can tell they dislike the tunnel.

Tunnel.

He mouths the word, adding it proudly to his list of recovered nouns.

Tunnel.

Once upon a time, the term meant more than a mere hole in the ground, when his job was fine-tuning mighty engines that roamed the speckled black of space. Back then it stood for . . .

No more words come to mind. Even images fail him, though oddly enough, *equations* stream from some portion of his brain less damaged than the speech center. Equations that explain *tunnels,* in a chaste, sterile way—the sort of multidimensional tubes that thread past treacherous shoals of hyperspace. Alas, to his disappointment, the formulas lack any power to yank memories to life.

They do not carry the telltale spoor of fear.

●　　●　　●

Also undamaged is his unfailing sense of direction. Emerson knows when the smooth-walled *passage* must be *passing* under the broad river, but no seepage is seen. The tunnel is a solid piece of Galactic workmanship, built to last for centuries or eons—until the assigned time for dismantling.

That time came to this world long ago. This place should have vanished along with all the great cities, back when Jijo was lain fallow. By some oversight, it was missed by the great destroyer machines and living acid lakes.

Now desperate fugitives use the ancient causeway to evade a hostile sky, suddenly filled with ships.

While still vague on details, Emerson knows he has been fleeing starships for a very long time, along with *Gillian, Hannes, Tsh't,* and the crew of *Streaker.*

Faces flicker, accompanying each name as recall agony makes him grunt and squeeze his eyelids. Faces Emerson pines for . . . and desperately hopes never to see again. He knows he must have been sacrificed somehow, to help the others get away.

Did the plan succeed? Did *Streaker* escape ahead of those awful dreadnoughts? Or has he suffered all of this for nothing?

His companions breathe heavily and perspire. They seem taxed by the stale air, but to Emerson it is just another kind of atmosphere. He has inhaled many types over the years. At least this stuff nourishes the lungs . . .

. . . *unlike the wind back on the green-green world, where a balmy day could kill you if your helmet failed.* . . .

And his helmet *did* fail, he now recalls, at the worst possible time, while trying to cross a mat of sucking demiveg, running frantically toward—

Sara and Prity gasp aloud, snapping his mental thread, making him look up to see what changed.

At a brisk pace the wagon enters a sudden widening of the tunnel, like the bulge where a snake digests its meal. Dimpled walls recede amid deep shadows, where dozens of large objects dimly lurk—tubelike vehicles, corroded by time. Some have been crushed by rock falls. Piles of stony debris block other exits from the underground vault.

Emerson lifts a hand to stroke a filmy creature riding his forehead, as lightly as a scarf or veil. The *rewq* trembles at his touch, swarming down to lay its filmy, translucent membrane over his eyes. Some colors dim, while others intensify. The ancient transit cars seem to shimmer like specters, as if he is looking at them not through space, but time. It is almost possible to imagine them in motion, filled with vital energies, hurtling through a network that once girdled a living, global civilization.

The horsewomen sitting on the foremost bench clutch their reins and peer straight ahead, enclosed by a nimbus of tension made visible by the rewq. The film shows Emerson their edgy, superstitious awe. To them, this is no harmless crypt for dusty relics, but a macabre place where phantoms prowl. Ghosts from an age of gods.

The creature on his brow intrigues Emerson. How does the little parasite translate emotions—even between beings as different as human and traeki—and all without words? Anyone who brought such a treasure to Earth would be richly rewarded.

To his right, he observes Sara comforting her chimpanzee aide, holding Prity in her arms. The little ape cringes from the dark, echoless cavern, but the rewq's overlaid colors betray a fringe of *deceit* in Prity's distress. It is partly an act! A way to distract her mistress, diverting Sara from her own claustrophobic fears.

Emerson smiles knowingly. The hues surrounding Sara reveal what the unaided eye already knows—that the young woman thrives on being needed.

"It's all right, Prity," she soothes. "Shh. It'll be all right."

The phrases are so simple, so familiar that Emerson understands them. He used to hear the same words while thrashing in his delirium, during those murky days after the crash, when Sara's tender care helped pull him back from that pit of dark fire.

The vast chamber stretches on, with just the glowing stripe to keep them from drifting off course. Emerson glances back to see young Jomah, seated on the last bench with his cap a twisted mass between his hands, while his uncle Kurt tries to explain something in hushed tones, motioning at the distant ceiling and walls—perhaps speculating what held them up . . . or what explosive force it would take to bring them crashing down. Nearby, with fastened hands and feet, the rebel, Dedinger, projects pure hatred of this place.

Emerson snorts annoyance with his companions. What a gloomy bunch! He has been in spots infinitely more disturbing than this harmless tomb . . . some of them he can even remember! If there is one sure truth he can recall from his former life, it is that a cheerful journey goes much faster, whether you are in deep space or the threshold of hell.

From a bag at his feet, he pulls out the midget dulcimer Ariana Foo had given him back at the Biblos Archive, that ornate hall of endless corridors stacked high with paper books. Not bothering with the hammers, he lays the instrument on his lap and plucks a few strings. Twanging notes jar the others from their anxious mutterings to look his way.

Though Emerson's ravaged brain lacks speech, he has learned ways to nudge and cajole. Music comes from a different place than speech, as does song.

Free association sifts the shadowy files of memory. Early drawers and closets, undammed by the traumas of later life. From some cache he finds a tune about travel down another narrow road. One with a prospect of hope at the end of the line.

It spills forth without volition, as a whole, flowing to a voice that's unpracticed, but strong.

> *"I've got a mule, her name is Sal,*
> *Fifteen miles down the Erie Canal.*
> *She's a good old worker and a good*
>   *old pal,*
> *Fifteen miles down the Erie Canal.*
>
> *We've hauled some cargo in our day,*
> *Filled with lumber, coal, and hay,*
> *And we know every inch of the way,*
> *From Albany to Buffalo-o-o. . . ."*

Amid the shadows, they are not easily coaxed from their worries. He too can feel the weight of rock above, and so many years. But Emerson refuses to be oppressed. He sings louder, and soon Jomah's voice joins the refrain, followed tentatively by Sara's. The horses' ears flick. They nicker, speeding to a canter.

The subterranean switching yard narrows again, walls converging with a rush. Ahead, the glowing line plunges into a resuming tunnel.

Emerson's voice briefly falters as a flicker of memory intrudes. Suddenly he can recall another abrupt plunge . . . diving through a portal that opened into jet vacuum blankness . . . then falling as the universe converged on him from all sides to *squeeze.* . . .

And something else.

A row of pale blue eyes.

Old Ones . . .

But the song has a life of its own. Its momentum pours unstoppably from some cheerful corner of his mind, overcoming those brief, awful images, making him call out the next verse with a vigor of hoarse, throaty defiance.

> *"Low bridge, everybody down!*
> *Low bridge! 'Cause we're comin' to a*
> *town.*
>
> *And you'll always know your neighbor,*
> *Always know your pal,*
> *If you ever navigate along the Erie Ca-*
> *nal."*

His companions lean away from the rushing walls. Their shoulders press together as the hole sweeps up to swallow them again.

PART THREE

ONCE A LENGTHY EPISODE of colonization
finally comes to an end, subduction recycling
is among the more commonly used methods
for clearing waste products on a life world.
Where natural cycles of plate tectonics provide a powerful indrawing force, the planet's
own hot convection processes can melt and
remix elements that had been fashioned into
tools and civilized implements. Materials that
might otherwise prove poisonous or intrusive
to new-rising species are thus removed from
the fallow environment, as a world eases into
the necessary dormant phase.

What happens to these refined materials, after they have been drawn in, depends
on mantle processes peculiar to each planet.
Certain convection systems turn the molten
substance into high-purity ores. Some become
lubricated by water seeps, stimulating the release of great liquid magma spills. Yet another
result can be sudden expulsions of volcanic
dust, which briefly coat the planet and can
later be traced in the refractory-metal enrichment of thin sedimentary layers.

Each of these outcomes can result in
perturbations of the local biosphere, and oc-

casional episodes of extinction. However, the resulting enrichment fecundity usually proves beneficial enough to compensate, encouraging development of new presapient species. . . .

from *A Galactographic Tutorial for Ignorant Wolfling Terrans,* a special publication of the Library Institute of the Five Galaxies, year 42 EC, in partial satisfaction of the debt obligation of 35 EC

Streakers

Hannes

SUESSI FELT NOSTALGIC ABOUT BEING HUMAN. NOW and then, he even wished he were still a man.

Not that he was ungrateful for the boon the Old Ones had granted him, in that strange place called the Fractal System, where aloof beings transformed his aged, failing body into something more durable. Without their gift, he would be stone dead—as cold as the giant corpses surrounding him in this dark ossuary of ships.

The ancient vessels seemed peaceful, in dignified repose. It was tempting to contemplate resting, letting eons pass without further care or strife.

But Suessi was much too busy to spare time for being dead.

"Hannes," a voice crackled directly to his auditory nerve. *"Two minutes, Hannes. Then I think-k we'll be ready to resume cut-t-ting."*

Shafts of brilliant illumination speared through the watery blackness, casting bright ovals toward one curved hull segment of the Terran starship *Streaker*. Distorted silhouettes crisscrossed the spotlight beams—the long undulating shadows of workers clad in pressurized armor, their movements slow, cautious.

This was a more dangerous realm than hard vacuum.

Suessi did not have a larynx anymore, or lungs to blow air past one if he had. Yet he retained a voice.

"Standing by, Karkaett," he transmitted, then listened as his words were rendered into groaning saser pulses. "Please keep the alignment steady. Don't overshoot."

One shadow among many turned toward him. Though cased in hard sheathing, the dolphin's tail performed a twist turn with clear body-language meaning.

Trust me . . . do you have any choice?

Suessi laughed—a shuddering of his titanium rib cage that replaced the old, ape-style method of syncopated gasps. It wasn't as satisfying, but then, the Old Ones did not seem to have much use for laughter.

Karkaett guided his team through final preparations while Suessi monitored. Unlike some others in *Streaker*'s crew, the engineering staff had grown more seasoned and confident with each passing year. In time, they might no longer need the encouragement—the supervising crutch—of a member of the patron race. When that day came, Hannes would be content to die.

I've seen too much. Lost too many friends. Someday, we'll be captured by one of the eatee factions pursuing us. Or else, we'll finally get a chance to turn ourselves in to some great Institute, only to learn Earth was lost while we fled helter-skelter across the universe. Either way, I don't want to be around to see it.

The Old Ones can keep their Ifni-cursed immortality.

Suessi admired the way his well-trained team worked, setting up a specially designed cutting machine with cautious deliberation. His audio pickups tracked low mutterings—*keeneenk* chants, designed to help cetacean minds concentrate on explicit thoughts and tasks that their ancestral brains were never meant to take on. Engineering thoughts—the kind that some dolphin philosophers called the most painful price of uplift.

These surroundings did not help—a mountainous graveyard of long-dead starcraft, a ghostly clutter, buried in the kind of ocean chasm that dolphins traditionally associated with their most cryptic cults and mysteries. The dense water seemed to amplify each rattle of a tool. Every whir of a harness arm resonated queerly in the dense liquid environment.

Anglic might be the language of engineers, but dolphins preferred Trinary for punctuation—for moments of resolution and action. Karkaett's voice conveyed confidence in a burst phrase of cetacean haiku.

> * Through total darkness
> * Where the cycloid's gyre comes never . . .
> * Behold—decisiveness! *

The cutting tool lashed out, playing harsh fire toward the vessel that was their home and refuge . . . that had carried them through terrors unimaginable. *Streaker*'s hull—purchased by the Terragens Council from a third-hand ship dealer and converted for survey work—had been the pride of impoverished Earthclan, the first craft to set forth with a dolphin captain and mostly cetacean crew, on a mission to check the veracity of the billion-year-old Great Library of the Civilization of the Five Galaxies.

Now the captain was gone, along with a quarter of the crew. Their mission had turned into a calamity for both Earthclan and the Five Galaxies. As for *Streaker*'s hull—once so shiny, despite her age—it now lay coated by a mantle of material so black the abyssal waters seemed clear by comparison. A substance that drank photons and weighed the ship down.

Oh, the things we've put you through, dear thing.

This was but the latest trial for their poor ship.

Once, bizarre fields stroked her in a galactic tide pool called the Shallow Cluster, where they "struck it rich" by happening upon a vast derelict fleet containing mysteries untouched for a thousand eons. In other words, where everything first started going wrong.

•   •   •

Savage beams rocked her at the Morgran nexus point, where a deadly surprise ambush barely failed to snare *Streaker* and her unsuspecting crew.

Making repairs on poisonous Kithrup, they ducked out almost too late, escaping mobs of bickering warships only by disguising *Streaker* inside a hollowed-out Thennanin cruiser, making it to a transfer point, though at the cost of abandoning many friends.

Oakka, the green world, seemed an ideal goal after that—a sector headquarters for the Institute of Navigation. Who was better qualified to take over custody of their data? As Gillian Baskin explained at the time, it was their duty as Galactic citizens to turn the problem over to the great institutes—those august agencies whose impartial lords might take the awful burden away from *Streaker*'s tired crew. It seemed logical enough—and nearly spelled their doom. Betrayal by agents of that "neutral" agency showed how far civilization had fallen in turmoil. Gillian's hunch saved the Earthling company—that and a daring cross-country raid by Emerson D'Anite, taking the conspirators' base from behind.

Again, *Streaker* emerged chastened and worse for wear.

There *was* refuge for a while in the Fractal System, that vast maze where ancient beings gave them shelter. But eventually that only led to more betrayal, more lost friends, and a flight taking them ever farther from home.

Finally, when further escape seemed impossible, Gillian found a clue in the Library unit they had captured on Kithrup. A syndrome called the "Sooner's Path." Following that hint, she plotted a dangerous road that might lead to safety, though it meant passing through the licking flames of a giant star, bigger than Earth's orbit, whose soot coated *Streaker* in layers almost too heavy to lift.

But she made it to Jijo.

This world looked lovely from orbit. Too bad we had only that one glimpse, before plunging to an abyssal graveyard of ships.

Under sonar guidance by dolphin technicians, their improvised cutter attacked *Streaker*'s hull. Water boiled into steam so violently that booming echoes filled this cave within a metal mountain. There were dangers to releasing so much energy in a confined space. Separated gases might recombine explosively. Or it could make their sanctuary detectable from space. Some suggested the risk was too great . . . that it would be better to abandon *Streaker* and instead try reactivating one of the ancient hulks surrounding them as a replacement.

There were teams investigating that possibility right now. But Gillian and Tsh't decided to try this instead, asking Suessi's crew to pull off one more resurrection.

The choice gladdened Hannes. He had poured too much into *Streaker* to give up now. *There may be more of me in her battered shell than remains in this cyborg body.*

Averting his sensors from the cutter's actinic glow, he mused on the mound of cast-off ships surrounding this makeshift cavern. They seemed to speak to him, if only in his imagination.

We, too, have stories, they said. *Each of us was launched with pride, flown with hope, rebuilt many times with skill, venerated by those we protected from the sleeting desolation of space, long before your own race began dreaming of the stars.*

Suessi smiled. All that might have impressed him once— the idea of vessels millions of years old. But now he knew a truth about these ancient hulks.

You want old? he thought. *I've seen old.*

I've seen ships that make most stars seem young.

The cutter produced immense quantities of bubbles. It screeched, firing ionized bolts against the black layer, just centimeters away. But when they turned it off at last, the results of all that eager destructive force were disappointing.

"That-t's all we removed?" Karkaett asked, incredulously, staring at a small patch of eroded carbon. "It'll take years to cut it all away, at-t this rate!"

The engineer's mate, Chuchki, so bulky she nearly burst from her exo-suit, commented in awed Trinary.

> * Mysteries cluster
>   * Frantic, in Ifni's shadow—
>   * Where did the energy go! *

Suessi wished he still had a head to shake, or shoulders to shrug. He made do instead by emitting a warbling sigh into the black water, like a beached pilot whale.

> * Not by Ifni's name,
>   * But her creative employer—
>   * I wish to God I knew. *

Gillian

IT ISN'T EASY FOR A HUMAN BEING TO PRETEND *she's an alien.*

Especially if the alien is a Thennanin.

Shrouds of deceitful color surrounded Gillian, putting ersatz flesh around the lie, providing her with an appearance of leathery skin and a squat bipedal stance. On her head, a simulated crest rippled and flexed each time she nodded. Anyone standing more than two meters away would see a sturdy male warrior with armored derma and medallions from a hundred stellar campaigns—not a slim blond woman with fatigue-lined eyes, a physician forced by circumstances to command a little ship at war.

The disguise was pretty good by now. It ought to be. She had been perfecting it for well over a year.

"Gr-phmph pltith," Gillian murmured.

When she first started pulling these charades, the Niss Machine used to translate her Anglic questions into Thennanin. But now Gillian figured she was probably as fluent in that Galactic dialect as any human alive. Probably even Tom.

It still sounds weird though. Kind of like a toddler making disgusting fart imitations for the fun of it.

At times, the hardest part was struggling not to break out laughing. That would not do, of course. Thennanin weren't noted for their sense of humor.

She continued the ritual greeting.

"Fhishmishingul parfful, mph!"

Chill haze pervaded the dim chamber, emanating from a sunken area where a beige-colored cube squatted, creating its own wan illumination. Gillian could not help thinking of it as a magical box—a receptacle folded in many dimensions, containing far more than any vessel its size should rightfully hold.

She stood at a lipless balcony, masked to resemble the former owners of the box, awaiting a reply. The barred-spiral symbol on its face seemed slippery to the eye, as if the emblem were slyly looking back at her with a soul far older than her own.

"Toftorph-ph parfful. Fhishfingtumpti parfff-ful."

The voice was deeply resonant. If she had been a real Thennanin, those undertones would have stroked her ridge crest, provoking respectful attentiveness. Back home, the Branch Library of Earth spoke like a kindly human grandmother, infinitely experienced, patient, and wise.

"I am prepared to witness," murmured a button in her ear, rendering the machine's words in Anglic. "Then I will be available for consultation."

That was the perpetual trade-off. Gillian could not simply demand information from the archive. She had to give as well.

Normally, that would pose no problem. Any Library unit assigned to a major ship of space was provided camera views of the control room and the vessel's exterior, in order to keep a WOM record for posterity. In return, the archive offered rapid access to wisdom spanning almost two billion years of civilization, condensed from planet-scale archives of the Library Institute of the Civilization of Five Galaxies.

Only there's a rub, Gillian thought.

Streaker was not a "major ship of space." Her own WOM units were solid, cheap, unresponsive—the only kind that impoverished Earth could afford. This lavish cube was a far greater treasure, salvaged on Kithrup from a mighty war cruiser of a rich starfaring clan.

She wanted the cube to *continue* thinking it was on that cruiser, serving a Thennanin admiral. Hence this disguise.

"Your direct watcher pickups are still disabled," she explained, using the same dialect. "However, I have brought more recent images, taken by portable recording devices. Please accept-and-receive this data now."

She signaled the Niss Machine, her clever robotic assistant in the next room. At once there appeared next to the cube a series of vivid scenes. Pictures of the suboceanic trench that local Jijoans called the "Midden"—carefully edited to leave out certain things.

We're playing a dangerous game, she thought, as flickering holosims showed huge mounds of ancient debris, discarded cities, and abandoned spacecraft. The idea was to pretend that the Thennanin dreadnought *Krondor's Fire* was hiding for tactical reasons in this realm of dead machines . . . and to do this without showing *Streaker*'s own slender hull, or any sign of dolphins, or even revealing the specific name and locale of this planet.

If we make it home, or to a neutral Institute base, we'll be legally bound to hand over this unit. Even under anonymous seal, it would be safest for it to know as little as we can get away with telling.

Anyway, the Library might not prove as cooperative to mere Earthlings. Better to keep it thinking it was dealing with its official lease-holders.

Ever since the disaster at Oakka, Gillian had made this her chief personal project, pulling off a hoax in order to pry data out of their prize. In many ways, the Library cube was more valuable than the relics *Streaker* had snatched from the Shallow Cluster.

In fact, the subterfuge had worked better than expected.

Some of the information won so far might prove critically useful to the Terragens Council.

Assuming we ever make it home again . . .

Ever since Kithrup, when *Streaker* lost the best and brightest of her crew, that had always seemed a long shot, at best.

In one particular area of technology, twenty-second-century humans had already nearly equaled Galactic skill levels, even before contact.

Holographic imagery.

Special-effects wizards from Hollywood, Luanda, and Aristarchus were among the first to dive confidently into alien arts, undismayed by anything as trivial as a billion-year head start. Within mere decades Earthlings could say they had mastered a single narrow field as well as the best starfaring clans—

Virtuosity at lying with pictures.

For thousands of years, when we weren't scratching for food we were telling each other fables. Prevaricating. Propagandizing. Casting illusions. Making movies.

Lacking science, our ancestors fell back on magic.

The persuasive telling of untruths.

Still it seemed a wonder to Gillian that her Thennanin disguise worked so well. Clearly the "intelligence" of this unit, while awesome, was of a completely different kind than hers, with its own limitations.

Or else maybe it simply doesn't care.

From experience, Gillian knew the Library cube would accept almost anything as input, as long as the show consisted of credible scenes it had never witnessed before. So Jijo's abyss flashed before it—this time the panoramas came over fiber cable from the western sea, sent by Kaa's team of explorers, near the settled region called the Slope. Ancient buildings gaped—drowned, eyeless, and windowless—under the scrutiny of probing searchlight beams. If anything, this waste field was even greater than the one where *Streaker* took refuge. The accumulated mass of made-things collected by a planetary culture for a million years.

Finally, the cascade of images ceased.

There followed a brief pause while Gillian waited edgily. Then the beige box commented.

"The event stream remains disjointed from previous ones. Occurrences do not take place in causal-temporal order related to inertial movements of this vessel. Is this effect a result of the aforementioned battle damage?"

Gillian had heard the same complaint—the very same words, in fact—ever since she began this ruse, shortly after Tom brought the captured prize aboard *Streaker* . . . only days before he flew away to vanish from her life.

In response, she gave the same bluff as always.

"That is correct. Until repairs are completed, penalties for any discrepancies may be assessed to the *Krondor's Fire* mission account. Now please prepare for consultation."

This time there was no delay.

"Proceed with your request."

Using a transmitter in her left hand, Gillian signaled to the Niss Machine, waiting in another room. The Tymbrimi spy entity at once began sending data requisitions, a rush of flickering light that no organic being could hope to follow. Soon the info flow went bidirectional—a torrential response that forced Gillian to avert her eyes. Perhaps, amid that flood, there might be some data helpful to *Streaker*'s crew, increasing their chances of survival.

Gillian's heart beat faster. This moment had its own dangers. If a starship happened to be scanning nearby—perhaps one of *Streaker*'s pursuers—onboard cognizance detectors might pick up a high level of digital activity in this area.

But Jijo's ocean provided a lot of cover, as did the surrounding mountain of discarded starships. Anyway, the risk seemed worthwhile.

If only so much of the information offered by the cube weren't confusing! A lot of it was clearly meant for starfarers with far more experience and sophistication than the *Streaker* crew.

Worse, we're running out of interesting things to show

*the Library. Without fresh input, it might withdraw. Refuse
to cooperate at all.*

That was one reason she decided yesterday to let the
four native kids come into this misty chamber and visit the
archive. Since Alvin and his friends didn't yet know they
were aboard an Earthling vessel, there wasn't much they
could give away, and the effect on the Library unit might
prove worthwhile.

Sure enough, the cube seemed bemused by the unique
sight of an urs and hoon, standing amicably together. And
the existence of a living g'Kek was enough, all by itself, to
satisfy the archive's passive curiosity. Soon afterward, it
willingly unleashed a flood of requested information about
the varied types of discarded spaceships surrounding
Streaker in this underwater trash heap, including parameters used by ancient Buyur control panels.

That was helpful. But we need more. A lot more.

*I guess it won't be long until I'm forced to pay with real
secrets.*

Gillian had some good ones she could use . . . if she
dared. In her office, just a few doors down, lay a mummified cadaver well over a billion years old.

Herbie.

To get hold of that relic—and the coordinates where it
came from—most of the fanatic, pseudo-religious alliances
in the Five Galaxies had been hunting *Streaker* since before Kithrup.

Pondering the chill beige cube, she thought—

*I'll bet if I showed you one glimpse of ol' Herb, you'd
have a seizure and spill every datum you've got stored
inside.*

*Funny thing is . . . nothing would make me happier in
all the universe than if we'd never seen the damned thing.*

As a girl, Gillian had dreamed of star travel, and someday doing bold, memorable things. Together, she and Tom
had planned their careers—and marriage—with a single
goal in mind. To put themselves at the very edge, standing
between Earth and the enigmas of a dangerous cosmos.

Recalling that naive ambition, and how extravagantly it
was fulfilled, Gillian very nearly laughed aloud. But with

pressed lips she managed to keep the bitter, poignant irony bottled inside, without uttering a sound.

For the time being, she must maintain the dignified presence of a Thennanin admiral.

Thennanin did not appreciate irony. And they never laughed.

Sooners

Ewasx

YOU MIGHT AS WELL GET USED TO IT, MY RINGS.

The piercing sensations you feel are My fibrils of control, creeping down our shared inner core, bypassing the slow, old-fashioned, waxy trails, attaching and penetrating your many toroid bodies, bringing them into new order.

Now begins the lesson, when I teach you to be docile servants of something greater than yourselves. No longer a stack of ill-wed components, always quarreling, paralyzed with indecision. No more endless *voting* over what beliefs shall be held by a fragile, tentative *i*.

That *was* the way of our crude ancestor stacks, meditating loose, confederated thoughts in the odor-rich marshes of Jophekka World. Overlooked by other star clans, we seemed unpromising material for uplift. But the great, slug-like Poa saw potential in our pensive precursors, and began uprising those unlikely mounds.

Alas, after a million years, the Poa grew frustrated with our languid traeki natures.

"Design new rings for our clients," they beseeched the clever Oailie, "to boost, guide, and drive them onward."

The Oailie did not fail, so great was their mastery of genetic arts.

WHAT WAS THEIR TRANSFORMING GIFT?

New, ambitious rings.

Master rings.

LIKE ME.

Alvin

THIS IS A TEST. I'M TRYING OUT A BURNISH-NEW WAY of writing.

If you call this "writing"—where I talk out loud and watch sentences appear in midair above a little box I've been given.

Oh, it's uttergloss all right. Last night, Huck used her new autoscribe to fill a room with words and glyphs in Gal-Three, GalEight, and every obscure dialect she knew, ordering translations back and forth until it seemed she was crowded on all sides by glowing symbols.

Our hosts gave us the machines to help tell our life stories, especially how the Six Races live together on the Slope. In return, the spinning voice promised a reward. Later, we'll get to ask questions of the big chilly box.

Huck went delirious over the offer. Free access to a memory unit of the Great Library of the Five Galaxies! Why, it's like telling Cortés he could have a map to the Lost Cities of Gold, or when the legendary hoonish hero Yuq-wourphmin found a password to control the robot factories of Kurturn. My own nicknamesake couldn't have felt more awe, not even when the secrets of Vanamonde and the Mad Mind were revealed in all their fearsome glory.

Unlike Huck, though, I view the prospect with dark worry. Like a detective in some old-time Earth storybook, I gotta ask—*where's the catch?*

Will they break their promise, once we've shared all we know?

Maybe they'll fake the answers. (How could we tell?)

Or perhaps they'll let us talk to the cube all we want, because they figure the knowledge won't do us any good, since we're never going home again.

On the other hand, let's say it's all open and sincere. Say we *do* get a chance to pose questions to the Library unit, that storehouse of wisdom collected by a billion-year-old civilization.

What on Jijo could we possibly have to say?

I've just spent a midura experimenting. Dictating text. Backing up and rewriting. The autoscribe sure is a lot more flexible than scratching away with a pencil and a ball of *guarru* gum for an eraser! Hand motions move chunks of text like solid objects. I don't even have to speak aloud, but simply *will* the words, like that little tickle when you mutter under your breath so's no one else can hear. I know it's not true mind reading—the machine must be sensing muscle changes in my throat or something. I read about such things in *The Black Jack Era* and *Luna City Hobo*. But it's unnerving anyway.

Like when I asked to see the little machine's dictionary of Anglic synonyms! I always figured I had a good vocabulary, from memorizing the town's copy of *Roget's Thesaurus*! But it turns out that volume left out most of the Hindi and Arabic cognate grafts onto the English-Eurasian rootstock. This tiny box holds enough words to keep Huck and me humble . . . or me, at least.

My pals are in nearby rooms, reciting their own memoirs. I expect Huck will rattle off something fast-paced, lurid, and carelessly brilliant to satisfy our hosts. Ur-ronn will be meticulous and dry, while Pincer will get distracted telling breathless stories about sea monsters. I have a head start because my journal already holds the greater part of our personal story—how we four adventurers got to this place of weirdly curved corridors, far beneath the waves.

So I have time to worry about *why* the phuvnthus want to know about us.

It could just be curiosity. On the other hand, what if something we say here eventually winds up hurting our kinfolk, back on the Slope? I can hardly picture how. I mean, it's not like we know any military secrets—except about the urrish cache that Uriel the Smith sent us underwater to retrieve. But the spinning voice already knows about that.

In my cheerier moments I envision the phuvnthus letting us take the treasure back, taking us home to Wuphon in their metal whale, so we seem to rise from the dead like the fabled crew of the *Hukuph-tau* . . . . much to the surprise of Uriel, Urdonnol, and our parents, who must have given us up for lost.

Optimistic fantasies alternate with other scenes I can't get out of my head, like something that happened right after the whale sub snatched *Wuphon's Dream* out of its death plunge. I have this hazy picture of bug-eyed spider-things stomping through the wreckage of our handmade vessel, jabbering weird ratchety speech, then jumping back in mortal terror at the sight of *Ziz,* the harmless little traeki five-stack given us by Tyug the Alchemist.

Streams of fire blasted poor Ziz to bits.

You got to wonder what anyone would go and do a mean thing like that for.

I might as well get to work.

How to begin my story?

Call me Alvin. . . .

No. Too hackneyed. How about this opening?

Alvin Hph-wayuo woke up one morning to find himself transformed into a giant . . .

Uh-uh. That's hitting too close to home.

Maybe I should model my tale after *20,000 Leagues Under the Sea.* Here we are, castaways being held as cordial prisoners in an underwater world. Despite being female, Huck would insist *she's* the heroic Ned Land character. Urronn would be Professor Aronnax, of course, which leaves either Pincer or me to be the comic fall guy, Conseil.

So when are we going to finally meet *Nemo?*

Hmm. That's a disadvantage of this kind of writing, so

effortless and easily corrected. It encourages running off at the mouth, when good old pencil and paper meant you had to actually think in advance what you were going to sa—

Wait a minute. What was that?

There it goes again. A faint booming sound . . . only louder this time. Closer.

I don't think I like it. Not at all.

. . .

Ifni! This time it set the floor quivering.

The rumble reminds me of Guenn Volcano back home, belchin' and groanin', making everybody in Wuphon wonder if it's the long-awaited Big O—

Jeekee sac-rot! No fooling this time.

Those are explosions, getting close fast!

Now comes another noise, like a zookir screeching its head off 'cause it sat on a quill lizard.

Is that the sound a *siren* makes? I always wondered—

Gishtuphwayo! Now the lights go dim. The floor jitters—

What is Ifni-slucking going on!

Dwer

THE VIEW FROM THE HIGHEST DUNE WASN'T PROMISing.

The Danik scout craft was at least five or six leagues out to sea, a tiny dot, barely visible beyond a distinct line where the water's hue changed from pale bluish green to almost black. The flying machine cruised back and forth, as if searching for something it had misplaced. Only rarely, when the wind shifted, did they catch the faint rumble of its engines, but every forty or so duras Dwer glimpsed something specklike tumble from the belly of the sleek boat, glinting in the morning sun before it struck the sea. Ten more duras would pass after the object sank— then the ocean's surface *bulged* with a hummock of roiling foam, as if an immense monster suffered dying spasms far below.

"What's Kunn doing?" Dwer asked. He turned to Rety, who shaded her eyes to watch the distant flier. "Do you have any idea?"

The girl started to shrug her shoulders, but yee, the little urrish male, sprawled there, snaking his slender neck to aim all three eyes toward the south. The robot rocked impatiently, bobbing up and down as if trying to signal the distant flier with its body.

"I don't know, Dwer," Rety replied. "I reckon it has somethin' to do with the bird."

"Bird," he repeated blankly.

"You know. My metal bird. The one we saved from the mulc spider."

"*That* bird?" Dwer nodded. "You were going to show it to the sages. How did the aliens get their hands—"

Rety cut in.

"The Daniks wanted to know where it came from. So Kunn asked me to guide him here, to pick up Jass, since he was the one who saw where the bird came to shore. I never figured that'd mean leavin' me behind in the village. . . ." She bit her lip. "Jass must've led Kunn here. Kunn said somethin' about 'flushin' prey.' I guess he's tryin' to get more birds."

"Or else whoever *made* your bird, and sent it ashore."

"Or else that." She nodded, clearly uncomfortable. Dwer chose not to press for details about her deal with the star humans.

As their journey south progressed, the number of marshy streams had multiplied, forcing Dwer to "carry" the robot several more times before he finally called a halt around dusk. There had been a brief confrontation when the combat machine tried intimidating him to continue. But its god weapons had been wrecked in the ambush at the sooner camp, and Dwer faced the robot's snapping claws without flinching, helped by a strange detachment, as if his mind had somehow *grown* while enduring the machine's throbbing fields. Hallucination or not, the feeling enabled him to call its bluff.

With grudging reluctance that seemed lifelike, the robot gave in. By a small fire, Dwer had shared with Rety the donkey jerky in his pouch. After a moment's hesitation, Rety brought out her own contribution, two small lozenges sealed in wrappers that felt slick to the touch. She showed Dwer how to unwrap his, and guffawed at the look on his face when intense, strange flavors burst in his mouth. He laughed, too, almost inhaling the Danik candy the wrong way. Its lavish sweetness won a place on his List of Things I'm Glad I Did Before Dying.

Later, huddled with Rety on the banked coals, Dwer dreamed a succession of fantastic images far more potent than normal—perhaps an effect of "carrying" the robot, conducting its ground-hugging fields. Instead of crushing weight, he fantasized *lightness,* as if his body wafted, unencumbered. Incomprehensible panoramas flickered under closed eyelids . . . objects glimmering against dark backgrounds, or gassy shapes, glowing of their own accord. Once, a strange sense of recognition seized him, a timeless impression of loving familiarity.

The Egg, his sleeping consciousness had mused. Only the sacred stone looked strange—not an outsized pebble squatting in a mountain cleft, but something like a huge, dark *sun,* whose blackness outshone the glitter of normal stars.

Their journey resumed before dawn, and featured only two more water crossings before reaching the sea. There the robot picked them up and streaked eastward along the beach until it reached this field of dunes—a high point to scan the strange blue waters of the Rift.

At least Dwer thought it was the Rift—a great cleft splitting the continent. *I wish I still had my telescope,* he thought. With it he might glean some idea what the pilot of the scout ship was trying to accomplish.

Flushing out prey, Rety said.

If that was Kunn's aim, the Danik star warrior could learn a thing or two about hunting technique. Dwer recalled one lesson old Fallon taught him years ago.

No matter how potent your weapon, or whatever game you're after, it's never a good idea to be both beater and shooter. If there's just one of you, forget driving your quarry.

The solitary hunter masters patience, and silently learns the ways of his prey.

That approach had one drawback. It required empathy. And the better you learn to feel like your prey, the greater the chance you may someday stop calling it *prey* at all.

"Well, we settled one thing," Rety commented, watching the robot semaphore its arms wildly at the highest point of the dune, like a small boy waving to parents who were too far away to hear. "You must've done a real job on its comm gear. Even the short range won't work, on line-o'-sight."

Dwer was duly impressed. Rety had learned a lot during her stint as an adopted alien.

"Do you think the pilot could spot us by eye, when he heads back toward the village to pick you up?" Dwer asked.

"Maybe . . . supposin' he ever meant to do that. He may forget all about me when he finds what he wants, and just zip west to the Rothen station, to report."

Dwer knew that Rety had already lost some favor with the sky humans. Her voice was bitter, for aboard that distant flying dot rode *Jass,* her tormentor while growing up in a savage tribe. She had arranged vengeance for the bully. But now Jass stood at the pilot's elbow, currying favor while Rety was stuck down here.

Her worry was clear. What if her lifelong enemy won the reward she had struggled and connived for? Her ticket to the stars?

"Hmm. Well, then we better make sure he doesn't miss us when he cruises by."

Dwer wasn't personally anxious to meet the star pilot who had blasted the poor urrish sooners so unmercifully from above. He fostered no illusion of gentle treatment at Kunn's hands. But the scout boat offered life and hope for Rety. And perhaps by attracting the Danik's attention he could somehow prevent the man's quick return to the Gray Hills. Danel Ozawa had been killed in the brief fight with the robot, but Dwer might still buy time for Lena Strong and the urrish chief to work out an accord with Rety's old band . . . beating a stealthy retreat to some place where star gods would never find them. A delaying action could be Dwer's last worthwhile service.

"Let's build a fire," the girl suggested, gesturing toward the beach, littered with driftwood from past storms.

"I was just about to suggest that," Dwer replied.

She chuckled.

"Yeah, right! Sure you were."

Sara

AT FIRST THE ANCIENT TUNNEL SEEMED HORRID and gloomy. Sara kept imagining a dusty Buyur tube car coming to life, an angry phantom hurtling toward the little horse-drawn wagon, bent on punishing fools who disturbed its ghostly domain. Dread clung fast for a while, making each breath come short and sharp between rapid heartbeats.

But fear has one great enemy, more powerful than confidence or courage.

Tedium.

Chafed from sitting on the bench for miduras, Sara eventually let go of the dismal oppression with a long sigh. She slipped off the wagon to trot alongside—at first only to stretch her legs, but then for longer periods, maintaining a steady jog.

After a while, she even found it enjoyable.

I guess I'm just adapting to the times. There may be no place for intellectuals in the world to come.

Emerson joined her, grinning as he kept pace with long-legged strides. And soon the tunnel began to lose its power over some of the others, as well. The two wagon drivers from the cryptic *Illias* tribe—Kepha and Nuli—grew visibly less tense with each league they progressed toward home.

But where was that?

Sara pictured a map of the Slope, drawing a wide arc roughly south from the Gentt. It offered no clue where a horse clan might stay hidden all this time.

How about in some giant, empty magma chamber, beneath a volcano?

What a lovely thought. Some magical sanctuary of hidden grassy fields, safe from the glowering sky. An underground world, like in a pre-contact adventure tale featuring vast ageless caverns, mystic light sources, and preposterous monsters.

Of course no such place could form under natural laws.

But might the Buyur—or some prior Jijo tenant—have used the same forces that carved this tunnel to create a secret hideaway? A place to preserve treasures while the surface world was scraped clean of sapient-made things?

Sara chuckled at the thought. But she did not dismiss it.

Sometime later, she confronted Kurt.

"Well, I'm committed now. Tell me what's so urgent that Emerson and I had to follow you all this way."

But the exploser only shook his head, refusing to speak in front of Dedinger.

What's the heretic going to do? Sara thought. *Break his bonds and run back to tell the world?*

The desert prophet's captivity appeared secure. And yet it was disconcerting to see on Dedinger's face an expression of serene confidence, as if present circumstances only justified his cause.

Times like these bring heretics swarming . . . like privacy wasps converging on a gossip. We shouldn't be surprised to see fanatics thriving.

The Sacred Scrolls prescribed two ways for Jijo's illegal colonists to ease their inherited burden of sin—by preserving the planet, and by following the Path of Redemption. Ever since the days of Drake and Ur-Chown, the sages had taught that both goals were compatible with commerce and the comforts of daily life. But some purists disagreed, insisting that the Six Races must choose.

We should not be here, proclaimed Lark's faction. *We sooners should use birth control to obey Galactic law, leaving this fallow world in peace. Only then will our sin be healed.*

Others thought redemption should take higher priority.

Each clan should follow the example of glavers, preached Dedinger's cult, and the Urunthai. *Salvation and renewal come to those who remove mental impediments and rediscover their deep natures.*

The first obstacle to eliminate—the anchor weighing down our souls—is knowledge.

Both groups called today's High Sages true heretics, pandering to the masses with their wishy-washy moderation. When dread starships came, fresh converts thronged to purer faiths, preaching simple messages and strong medicine for fearful times.

Sara knew her *own* heresy would not attract disciples. It seemed ill matched to Jijo—a planet of felons destined for oblivion of one sort or another. And yet . . .

Everything depends on your point of view.

So taught a wise traeki sage.

we/i/you are oft fooled by the obvious.

Lark

AN URRISH COURIER CAME RUSHING OUT OF THE forest of tall, swaying greatboo.

Could this be my answer already?

Lark had dispatched a militiaman just a few miduras ago, with a message to Lester Cambel in the secret refuge of the High Sages.

But no. The rough-pelted runner had galloped up the long path from Festival Glade. In her rush, she would not even pause for Lark to tap the vein of a tethered simla, offering the parched urs a hospitable cup of steaming blood. Instead, the humans stared amazed as she plunged her fringed muzzle into a bucket of undiluted *water,* barely shuddering at the bitter taste.

Between gasping swallows, she told dire news.

As rumored, the second starship was titanic, squatting like a mountain, blocking the river so a swamp soon formed around the trapped Rothen cruiser, doubly imprisoning Ling's comrades. Surviving witnesses reported seeing familiar outlines framed by the battleship's brightly lit hatchway. Corrugated cones. Stacks of rings, luxuriously glistening.

Only a few onlookers, steeped in ancient legends, knew this was not a good sign, and they had little time to spread a warning before torrid beams sliced through the night, mowing down everything within a dozen arrowflights.

At dawn, brave observers peered from nearby peaks to see a swathe of shattered ground strewn with oily smudges and bloody debris. *A defensive perimeter,* stunned observers suggested, though such prudence seemed excessive for omnipotent star gods.

"What casualties?" asked Jeni Shen, sergeant of Lark's militia contingent, a short, well-muscled woman and a friend of his brother, Dwer. They had all seen flickering lights in the distance, and heard sounds like thunder, but imagined nothing as horrible as the messenger related.

The urs told of hundreds dead . . . and that a High Sage of the Commons was among those slaughtered. *Asx* had been standing near a group of curious spectators and confused alien lovers, waiting to parley with the visitors. After the dust and flames settled, the traeki was nowhere to be seen.

The g'Kek doctor tending Uthen expressed the grief they all felt, rolling all four tentacle-like eyes and flailing the ground with his pusher leg. This personified the horror. Asx had been a popular sage, ready to mull over problems posed by any of the Six Races, from marriage counseling to dividing the assets of a bisected qheuen hive. Asx might "mull" for days, weeks, or a year before giving an answer—or *several* answers, laying out a range of options.

Before the courier departed, Lark's status as a junior sage won him a brief look at the drawings in her dispatch pouch. He showed Ling a sketch of a massive oval ship of space, dwarfing the one that brought her to this world. Her face clouded. The mighty shape was unfamiliar and frightening.

Lark's own messenger—a two-legged human—had plunged into the ranks of towering boo at daybreak, carrying a plea for Lester Cambel to send up Ling's personal

Library unit, so she might read the memory bars he and Uthen had found in the wrecked station.

Her offer, made the evening before, was limited to seeking data about plagues, especially the one now sweeping the qheuen community.

"If Ro-kenn truly was preparing genocide agents, he is a criminal by our own law."

"Even a Rothen master?" Lark had asked skeptically.

"Even so. It is not disloyal for me to find out, or else prove it was not so.

"However," she had added, "don't expect me to help you make war against my crew mates or my patrons. Not that you could do much, now that their guard is raised. You surprised us once with tunnels and gunpowder, destroying a little research base. But you'll find that harming a starship is beyond even your best-equipped zealots."

That exchange took place before they learned about the second vessel. Before word came that the mighty Rothen cruiser was reduced to a captive toy next to a true colossus from space.

While they awaited Cambel's answer, Lark sent his troopers sifting through the burned lakeshore thicket, gathering golden preservation beads. Galactic technology had been standardized for millions of years. So there just might be a workable reading unit amid all the pretty junk the magpie spider had collected. Anyway, it seemed worth a try.

While sorting through a pile of amber cocoons, he and Ling resumed their game of cautious question-and-evasion. Circumstances had changed—Lark no longer felt as stupid in her presence—still, it was the same old dance.

Starting off, Ling quizzed him about the Great Printing, the event that transformed Jijo's squabbling coalition of sooner races, even more than the arrival of the Holy Egg. Lark answered truthfully without once mentioning the Biblos Archive. Instead he described the guilds of printing, photocopying, and especially papermaking, with its pounding pulp hammers and pungent drying screens, turning out fine pages under the sharp gaze of his father, the famed Nelo.

"A nonvolatile, randomly accessed, analog memory store

that is completely invisible from space. No electricity or digital cognizance to detect from orbit." She marveled. "Even when we saw books, we assumed they were hand-copied—hardly a culture-augmenting process. Imagine, a *wolfling* technology proved so effective . . . under special circumstances."

Despite that admission, Lark wondered about the Danik attitude, which seemed all too ready to dismiss the accomplishments of their own human ancestors—except when an achievement could be attributed to Rothen intervention.

It was Lark's turn to ask a question, and he chose to veer onto another track.

"You seemed as surprised as anybody, when the disguise creature crawled off of Ro-pol's face."

He referred to events just before the Battle of the Glade, when a dead Rothen was seen stripped of its charismatic, symbiotic mask. Ro-pol's eyes, once warm and expressive, had bulged lifeless from a revealed visage that was sharply slanted, almost predatory, and distinctly less humanoid.

Ling had never seen a master so exposed. She reacted to Lark's question cautiously.

"I am not of the Inner Circle."

"What's that?"

Ling inhaled deeply. "Rann and Kunn are privy to knowledge about the Rothen that most Daniks never learn. Rann has even been to one of the secret Rothen home sites. Most of us are never so blessed. When not on missions, we dwell with our families in the covered canyons of Poria Outpost, with just a hundred or so of our patrons. Even on Poria, the two races don't mix daily."

"Still, not to know something so basic about those who claim to be—"

"Oh, one hears rumors. Sometimes you see a Rothen whose face seems odd . . . as if part of it was, well, *put on* wrong. Maybe we cooperate with the deception by choosing at some level not to notice. Anyway, that's not the real issue, is it?"

"What *is* the real issue?"

"You imply I should be horrified to learn they wear symbionts to look more humanoid. To appear more beautiful in our eyes. But why *shouldn't* the Rothen use artificial aids, if it helps them serve as better guides, shepherding our race toward excellence?"

Lark muttered, "How about a little thing called honesty?"

"Do you tell your pet chimp or zookir everything? Don't parents sometimes lie to children for their own good? What about lovers who strive to look nice for each other? Are they dishonest?

"Think, Lark. What are the odds against another race seeming as gloriously beautiful to human eyes as our patrons appear? Oh, part of their attraction surely dates back to early stages of uplift, on Old Earth, when they raised our apelike ancestors almost to full sapiency, before the Great Test began. It may be ingrained at a genetic level . . . the way dogs were culled in favor of craving the touch of man.

"Yet, we are still unfinished creatures. Still crudely emotional. Let me ask you, Lark. If *your* job were to uplift flighty, cantankerous beings, and you found that wearing a cosmetic symbiont would make your role as teacher easier, wouldn't you do it?"

Before Lark could answer an emphatic no, she rushed ahead.

"Do not some members of your Six use *rewq* animals for similar ends? Those symbionts that lay their filmy bodies over your eyes, sucking a little blood in exchange for help translating emotions? Aren't rewq a vital part of the complex interplay that is your Commons?"

"Hr-rm." Lark throat-umbled like a doubtful hoon. "Rewq don't help us lie. They are not *themselves* lies."

Ling nodded. "Still, you never faced a task as hard as the Rothens'—to raise up creatures as brilliant, and disagreeable, as human beings. A race whose capability for future majesty also makes us capricious and dangerous, prone to false turns and deadly errors."

Lark quashed an impulse to argue. She might only dig in, rationalizing herself into a corner and refusing to come out. At least now she admitted that *one* Rothen might do evil deeds—that Ro-kenn's personal actions might be criminal.

And who knows? That may be all there is to it. The scheming of a rogue individual. Perhaps the race is just as wonderful as she says. Wouldn't it be nice if humanity really had such patrons, and a manifest greatness waiting, beyond the next millennium?

Ling had seemed sincere when she claimed the Rothen ship commander would get to the bottom of things.

"It's imperative to convince your sages they must release the hostages and Ro-pol's body, along with those 'photograms' your portraitist took. Blackmail won't work against the Rothen—you must understand this. It's not in their character to respond to threats. Yet the 'evidence' you've gathered could do harm in the long run."

That was before the stunning news—that the Rothen ship was itself captured, encased in a prison of light.

Lark· mused over one of the mulc spider's golden eggs while Ling spoke for a while about the difficult but glorious destiny her masters planned for impulsive, brilliant humanity.

"You know," he commented. "There's something screwy about the logic of this whole situation."

"What do you mean?"

Lark chewed his lip, like an urs wrestling with uncertainty. Then he decided—it was time to bring it all in the open.

"I mean, let's put aside for now the added element of the new starship. The Rothen may have feuds you know nothing about. Or it may be a different gang of gene raiders, come to rob Jijo's biosphere. For all we know, magistrates from the Galactic Migration Institute have brought Judgment Day as foretold in the Scrolls.

"For now, though, let's review what led to the Battle of the Glade—the fight that made you my prisoner. It began when Bloor photo'd the dead Ro-pol without her mask. Ro-kenn went livid, ordering his robots to kill everyone who had seen.

"But didn't you once assure me there was no need to delete local witnesses to your team's visit? That your masters could handle it, even if oral and written legacies survive hundreds or thousands of years, describing a visit by human and Rothen gene raiders?"

"I did."

"But you admit gene raiding is against Galactic law! I

know you feel the Rothen are above such things. Still, they don't want to be caught in the act.

"Let's assume credible testimony, maybe even photos, finally reach Migration Institute inspectors next time they visit Jijo. Testimony about you and Rann and Kunn. *Human* gene raiders. Even I know the rule—'police your own kind'—prevails in the Five Galaxies. Did Ro-kenn explain how the Rothen would prevent sanctions coming down on Earth?"

Ling wore a grim expression. "You're saying he played us for fools. That he let me spread false assurances among the natives, while planning all along to strew germs and wipe out every witness."

Obviously it was bitter for her to say it.

Ling seemed surprised when Lark shook his head.

"That's what I thought at first, when qheuens fell sick. But what I now imagine is worse yet."

That got her attention.

"What could be worse than mass murder? If the charge is proved, Ro-kenn will be hauled off to the home sites in *dolor chains*! He'll be punished as no Rothen has been in ages."

Lark shrugged. "Perhaps. But stop and think a bit.

"First, Ro-kenn wasn't relying on disease alone to do the job.

"Oh, he probably had a whole library of bugs—infectious agents used in past wars in the Five Galaxies. No doubt starfaring qheuens long ago developed countermeasures against the germ raging through Uthen's lymph pipes right now. I'm sure Ro-kenn's concoctions will kill a lot more of us."

Ling started to protest, but Lark forged ahead.

"Nevertheless, I know a thing or two about how pestilence works in natural ecosystems. It would be a complete fluke for even a string of diseases to wipe out every member of the Six. Random immunities would stymie the best-designed bugs. Furthermore, the sparser the population got, the harder it would be to reach and infect dispersed survivors.

"No, Ro-kenn needed something more. A breakdown of the Commons into total war! A war that could be exploited, pushed to the limits. A struggle so bitter that each race would pursue its victims to the farthest corners of Jijo, willingly helping to spread new parasites in order to slay their foes."

He saw Ling struggle to find a way around his logic. But she had been present when Ro-kenn's psi-recordings were played—sick dream images, meant to incite fatal grudges among the Six. Those present weren't fooled because they were forewarned, but what if the messages had been broadcast as planned . . . amplified through the compelling wave forms of the Holy Egg?

"I will tell of this, back home," she vowed in a low, faint voice. "He will be punished."

"That's gratifying," Lark went on. "But I'm not finished. You see, even by combining plagues with war, Ro-kenn could never guarantee annihilation of all six races, or eliminate the off chance that credible testimony might be passed down the generations—perhaps stored in some cave—to finally reach Institute prosecutors. On the other hand, he could influence *which* race or sept would be left standing at the end, and which would perish first. There is one, in particular, whose fate he knows well how to manipulate. That one is *Homo sapiens.*

"The way I see it, Ro-kenn's plan had several parts. First, he had to make sure Earthlings were hated. Second, he must weaken the other five races by releasing diseases that could then be blamed on humans. But the ultimate goal was to make sure *humans* went extinct on Jijo. He didn't give a damn if others left a few survivors to tell the tale."

Ling stared. "What good would that do? You said testimony might be passed down—"

"Yes, but with Earthlings on Jijo only a hated memory, all history will tell is that once upon a time a ship full of humans came down, stole genes, and tried to kill everybody. No one will bother emphasizing *which* humans did these things.

"In the future—perhaps only a few centuries, if someone plants an anonymous tip—Galactic judges would arrive and hear that people from *Earth* did these dreadful things. *Earth* will bear the full brunt of any sanctions, while the Rothen get off scot-free."

Ling was silent for a long moment, working her way through his logic. Finally, she looked up with a broad grin.

"You had me worried a minute, but I found the defect in your reasoning!"

Lark tilted his head. "Do tell."

"Your diabolical scenario just might make sense, but for two flaws—

"*First*—the Rothen are patrons of all humanity. Earth and her colonies, while presently governed by Darwinist fools on the Terragens Council, still represent the vast majority of our gene pool. The Rothen would never let harm come to our homeworld. Even in the current galactic crisis, they are acting behind the scenes to ensure Earth's safety from the enemies besetting her."

There it was again . . . a reference to dire events happening megaparsecs away. Lark yearned to follow that thread, but Ling continued with her argument.

"Second—let's say Ro-kenn wanted all blame shifted to humans. *Then why did he and Ro-pol emerge from the station and show themselves?* By walking around, letting artists sketch them and scribes take down their words, weren't they jeopardizing the Rothen to the same eyewitness accounts you say could damage Earth?"

Ling seemed ready to accept that her immediate boss might be criminal or insane, but with bulwarks of logic she defended her patron race. Lark had mixed feelings about demolishing such faith. He, too, had his heresies.

"I'm sorry, Ling, but my scenario still stands.

"Your first point only has validity *if it is true that the Rothen are our patrons.* I know that's the central premise around which you were raised, but believing does not make it so. You admit your people, the Daniks, are small in number, live on an isolated outpost, and see just a few Rothen. Putting aside mythic fables about ancient visitors and Egyptian pyramids, all you really have is their word regarding a supposed relationship with our race. One that may simply be a hoax.

"As for your second point, just look back at the way events unfolded. Ro-kenn surely knew he was being sketched when he emerged that evening, using his charisma on the crowd and planting seeds of dissension. After living so long together, all six races are affected by each other's standards of beauty, and the Rothen were indeed beautiful!

"Ro-kenn may even have known we had the ability to etch our drawings onto durable plates. Later, when he saw Bloor's *first* set of photographic images, he hardly batted an eye. Oh, he pretended to dicker with the sages, but you and I could both tell he was unafraid of the 'proof' being used to blackmail him. He was only buying time till the ship returned. And it might have worked—if Bloor hadn't uncovered and recorded Ro-pol's corpse, bare and unmasked. *That's* when Ro-kenn went hysterically murderous, ordering a massacre!"

"I know." Ling shook her head. "It was madness. But you must understand. Disturbing the dead is very serious. It must have pushed him over the edge—"

"Over the edge, my left hind hoof! He knew exactly what he was doing. Think, Ling. Suppose someday Institute observers see photos showing humans, *and a bunch of very humanlike beings nobody ever heard of,* committing crimes on Jijo. Could such crude pictures ever really implicate the Rothen?

"Perhaps they might, *if that's what Rothen looked like.* But till Bloor shot Ro-pol's naked face, our crude images posed no threat to Rothen security. Because in a century or two those facial disguise symbionts won't exist anymore, and no one alive will know that Rothen ever looked like that."

"What are you talking about? Every Danik grows up seeing Rothen as they appear with symbionts on. Obviously there will be people around who know . . ."

Her voice faded. She stared at Lark, unblinking. "You can't mean—"

"Why not? After long association with your people, I'm sure they've acquired the necessary means. Once humans are of no further use as front men for their schemes, your 'patrons' will simply use a wide spectrum of tailored viruses to wipe out every Danik, just as they planned to eliminate humans on Jijo.

"For that matter, once they've tested it on both our peoples, they'll be in a good position to sell such a weapon to Earth's enemies. After all, once our race goes extinct, who will protest our innocence? Who will bother to look for other suspects in a series of petty felonies that were committed, all over the Five Galaxies, by groups of bipeds looking a lot like—"

"Enough!" Ling shouted, standing suddenly, spilling gold cocoons from her lap. She backed away, hyperventilating.

Unrelenting, he stood and followed.

"I've thought about little else since we left the Glade. And it all makes sense. Even down to the way the Rothen won't let your kind use neural taps."

"I told you before. It's forbidden because the taps might drive us mad!"

"Really? Why do the Rothen themselves have them? Because they're more highly evolved?" Lark snorted. "Anyway, I hear that nowadays humans *elsewhere* use them effectively."

"How do you know what humans elsewhere—"

Lark hurriedly cut her off.

"The truth is, the Rothen can't risk letting their pet humans make direct mind-computer links, because someday one of you Daniks might bypass sanitized consoles, draw on the Great Library directly, and figure out how you've been pawns—"

Ling backed away another pace. "Please, Lark . . . I don't want to do this anymore."

He felt an impulse to stop, to take pity. But he quashed it. This had to come out, all of it.

"I must admit it's quite a scam, using humans as front men for gene theft and other crimes. Even two centuries ago, when the *Tabernacle* departed, our race had a vile reputation as one of the lowest-ranking citizen tribes in the Five Galaxies. So-called *wolflings,* with no ancient clan to stand up for us. If anybody gets caught, we'll make perfect patsies. The Rothen scheme is clever. The real question is, why would any humans let themselves be used that way?

"History may hold the answer, Ling. According to our texts, humans suffered from a major inferiority complex at the time of contact, when our primitive canoe-spacecraft stumbled onto a towering civilization of star gods. Your ancestors and mine chose different ways of dealing with the complex, each of them grasping at straws, seeking any excuse for hope.

"The *Tabernacle* colonists dreamed of escaping to some place out of sight of bureaucrats and mighty Galactic clans—a place to breed freely and fulfill the old romance of colonizing a frontier. In contrast, your Danik forebears rushed to embrace a tall tale they were told by a band of smooth talkers. A flattering fable that indulged their wounded pride, promising a grand *destiny* for certain chosen humans and their descendants . . . providing they did exactly as they were told. Even if it meant raising their children to be shills and sneak thieves in service to a pack of galactic gangsters."

Tremors rocked Ling as she held up one hand, palm out, at the end of a rigid arm, as if trying physically to stave off any more words.

"I asked . . . you to stop," she repeated, and seemed to have trouble breathing. Pain melted her face.

Now Lark did shut up. He had gone too far, even in the name of truth. Raggedly, trying to maintain some remnant of her dignity, Ling swiveled and strode off to the acrid lake that lay below a boulder field of tumbled Buyur ruins.

Does anybody like having their treasured worldview torn away? Lark mused, watching Ling hurl stones into the caustic pond. *Most of us would reject all the proof in the cosmos before considering that our own beliefs might be wrong.*

But the scientist in her won't let her dismiss evidence so easily. She has to face facts, like them or not.

The habit of truth is hard to learn, and a mixed blessing. It leaves no refuge when a new truth comes along that hurts.

Lark knew his feelings were hardly a testament to clarity. Anger roiled, mixed with shame that he could not hold on to the purity of his own convictions. There was childish satisfaction from upsetting Ling's former smug superiority . . . and chagrin at finding such a motive smoldering inside. Lark enjoyed being right, though it might be better, this time, if he turned out to be wrong.

Just when I had her respecting me as an equal, and maybe starting to like me, that's when I have to go stomping through her life, smashing idols she was raised to worship, showing off the bloodstained hands of her gods.

You may win an argument, boy. You may even convince her. But could anyone fully forgive you for doing something like that?

He shook his head over how much he might have just thrown away, all for the torrid pleasure of harsh honesty.

Ewasx

DO NOT BE AFRAID, MY LESSER PARTS.

The sensations you feel may seem like coercive pain, but they convey a kind of *love* that will grow dear to you, with time. I am part of you now, one with you. I will never do anything to cause us harm, so long as this alliance serves a function.

Go ahead, stroke the wax if you wish, for the old ways of memory still have lesser uses (so long as they serve My purpose). Play over recent images so we may recall together events leading to our new union. Re-create the scene perceived by *Asx*, staring up in awe, watching the great Jophur warship, *Polkjhy*, swoop from the sky, taking the pirates captive, then landing in this tortured valley. Poor, loosely joined, scatterbrained Asx—did you/we not stare in tremulous fear?

Yes, I can stroke another driving motivation. One that kept you admirably unified, despite swirling dread. It was a cloying sense of *duty*. Duty to the not-self community of half beings you call the Commons.

As Asx, your stack planned to speak for the Commons. Asx expected to face star-traveling humans, along with creatures known as "Rothen." But then *Jophur* forms were seen through our ship ports!

After some hesitation, did you not turn at last and try to flee?

How *slow* this stack was before the change! When knives of fire lanced forth from this mighty vessel, how did you react to the maelstrom of destruction? To hot ravening beams that tore through wood, stone, and flesh, but always spared this pile of aged rings? Had you then possessed the bright new running legs we now wear, you might have thrown yourselves into that roaring calamity. But Asx was slow, too slow even to shelter nearby comrades with its traeki bulk.

All died, except this stack.

ARE YOU NOT PROUD?

The *next* ray from the ship seized this multistriped cone, lifting it into the night air, sweeping the fatty rings toward doors that gaped to receive them.

Oh, how well Asx spoke then, despite the confusion! With surprising coherence for a stack without a master, tapping waxy streaks of eloquence, Asx pleaded, cajoled, and reasoned with the enigmatic creatures who peered from behind glaring lights.

Finally, these beings glided forward. The starship's hold filled with Asx's ventings of horrified dread.

How unified you were, My rings! The testimony of the wax is clear. At that moment, you were one as never before.

United in shared dismay to see those cousin toroids your ancestors sought to escape, many cycles ago.

We Jophur, the mighty and fulfilled.

Dwer

THE ROBOT PROVED USEFUL AT HEAPING DRIFT-wood onto the seaside shoulder of a high dune over-looking the Rift. Without rest or pause, it dumped a load then scurried for more, in whatever direction Rety indicated with an outstretched arm. The Danik machine seemed willing to obey once more—so long as her orders aimed toward a reunion with Kunn.

Such single-minded devotion to its master reminded Dwer of Earth stories about dogs—tales his mother read aloud when he was small. It struck him odd that the *Tabernacle* colonists brought horses, donkeys, and chimps, but no canines.

Lark or Sara might know why.

That was Dwer's habitual thought, encountering something he didn't understand. Only now it brought a pang, knowing he might never see his brother and sister again.

Maybe Kunn won't kill me outright. He might bring me home in chains, instead, before the Rothens wipe out the Six Races to cover their tracks.

That was the terrible fate the High Sages foresaw for Jijo's fallen settlers, and Dwer figured they ought to know. He recalled Lena Strong musing about what means the aliens might use to perform their genocide. With gruesome relish, Lena kept topping herself during the long hike east from the Rimmer Range. Would the criminal star gods wash the Slope with fire, scouring it from the glaciers to the sea? Would they melt the ice caps and bring an end by drowning? Her morbid speculations were like a fifth companion as Dwer guided two husky women and a lesser sage past a thousand leagues of poison grass all the way to the Gray Hills, in a forlorn bid to safeguard a fragment of human civilization on Jijo.

Dwer had last glimpsed Jenin, Lena, and Danel during the brief fight near the huts of Rety's home clan. This same robot cut poor Danel down with lethal rays, instants before its own weapons pod was destroyed.

Indeed, the battle drone was no dog to be tamed or befriended. Nor would it show gratitude for the times Dwer helped it cross rivers, anchoring its fields to ground through the conduit of his body.

Mudfoot was hardly any better a comrade. The lithe noor beast swiftly grew bored with wood-gathering chores, and scampered off instead to explore the tide line, digging furiously where bubbles revealed a buried hive of sand clamettes. Dwer looked forward to roasting some . . . until he saw that Mudfoot was cracking and devouring every one, setting none aside for the humans.

As useful as a noor, he thought, quashing stings of hunger as he hoisted another bundle of twisty driftwood slabs, digging his moccasins into the sandy slope.

Dwer tried to remain optimistic.

Maybe Kunn will feed me, before attaching the torture machines.

yee stood proudly atop the growing woodpile. The diminutive urrish male called directions in a piping voice, as if mere humans could never manage a *proper* fire without urrish supervision. Rety's "husband" hissed disappointment over Dwer's poor contribution—as if being wounded, starved, and dragged across half of Jijo in a robot's claws did not excuse much. Dwer ignored *yee*'s reprimand, dumping his load then stepping over to the dune's seaward verge, shading his eyes in search of Kunn's alien scoutship.

He spied it far away, a silvery bead, cruising back and forth above the deep blue waters of the Rift. At intervals, something small and shiny would fall from the slender spacecraft. *An explosive,* Dwer supposed, for about twenty duras after each canister struck the water, the sea abruptly frothed white. Sometimes a sharp, almost musical tone reached shore.

According to Rety, Kunn was trying to force something—or somebody—out of hiding.

I hope you miss, Dwer thought . . . though the star pilot might be in a better mood toward prisoners if his hunt went well.

"I wonder what Jass has been tellin' Kunn, all this time," Rety worried aloud, joining Dwer at the crest. "What if they become pals?"

Dwer waited as the robot dropped another cargo of wood and went off for more. Then he replied.

"Have you changed your mind? We could still try to escape. Take out the robot. Avoid Kunn. Go our own way."

Rety smiled with surprising warmth.

"Why, Dwer, is that a whatchamacallum? A *proposal?*

What'll we do? Make our own little sooner clan, here on the wind barrens? Y'know I already *have* one husban' and I need his p'rmission to add another."

Actually, he had envisioned trying to make it back to the Gray Hills, where Lena and Jenin could surely use a hand. Or else, if that way seemed too hard and Rety rigidly opposed returning to the tribe she hated, they might strike out west and reach the Vale in a month or two, if the foraging was good along the way.

Rety went on, with more edge in her voice.

"B'sides, I still have my eye set on an apart'mint on Poria Outpost. Like the one Besh an' Ling showed me a picture of, with a *bal-co-ny,* an' a bed made o' cloud stuff. I figure it'll be just a *bit* more comfy than scratchin' out the rest of my days here with savages."

Dwer shrugged. He hadn't expected her to agree. As a "savage," he had reasons of his own for going ahead with the bonfire to attract Kunn's attention.

"Well, anyway, I don't suppose the bot would let its guard down a second time."

"It was lucky to survive doin' it around you once."

Dwer took a moment to realize she had just paid him a compliment. He cherished its uniqueness, knowing he might never hear another.

The moment of unaccustomed warmth was broken when something massive abruptly streaked by, so fast that its air wake shoved both humans to the ground. Dwer's training as a tracker let him follow the blurry object . . . to the top of a nearby dune, which erupted in a gushing spray of sand.

It was the *robot,* he realized, *digging* with furious speed. In a matter of heartbeats it made a hole that it then dived within, aiming its remaining sensor lens south and west.

"Come on!" Dwer urged, grabbing his bow and quiver. Rety paused only to snatch up a wailing, hissing yee. Together they fled some distance downslope, where Dwer commenced digging with both hands.

Long ago, Fallon the Scout had taught him—*If you don't know what's happening in a crisis, mimic a creature who does.* If the robot felt a sudden need to hide, Dwer thought it wise to follow.

"Ifni!" Rety muttered. "Now what in hell's he doin'?"

She was still standing—staring across the Rift. Dwer yanked her into the hole beside him. Only when sand covered most of their bodies did he poke his head back out to look.

The Danik pilot clearly felt something was wrong. The little craft hurtled toward shore, diving as it came. *Seeking cover,* Dwer thought. *Maybe it can dig underground, like the robot.*

Dwer started turning, to spot whatever had Kunn in such a panic, but just then the boat abruptly veered, zigzagging frantically. From its tail bright fireballs arced, like sparks leaping off a burning log. They flared brightly and made the air *waver* in a peculiar way, blurring the escaping vessel's outlines.

From behind Dwer, streaks of fierce light flashed overhead toward the fleeing boat. Most deflected through warped zones, veering off course, but one bypassed the glowing balls, striking target.

At the last moment, Kunn flipped his nimble ship around and fired back at his assailants, launching a return volley just as the unerring missile closed in.

Dwer shoved Rety's head down and closed his eyes.

The detonations were less Jijo-shattering than he expected—a series of dull concussions, almost anticlimactic.

Looking up with sand-covered faces, they witnessed both winner and loser in the brief battle of god chariots.

Kunn's boat had crashed beyond the dune field, plowing into a marshy fen. Smoke boiled from its shattered rear.

Circling above, the victor regarded its victim, glistening with a silvery tint that seemed less metallic than *crystal.* The newcomer was bigger and more powerful looking than the Danik scout.

Kunn never stood a chance.

Rety muttered, her voice barely audible.

"She *said* there'd turn out to be someone stronger."

Dwer shook his head. "Who?"

"That smelly old urs! Leader o' those four-legged sooners, back in the village pen. Said the Rothen might be a-feared of somebody bigger. So she was right."

"*urs* smelly?" yee objected. "you wife should talk?"

Rety stroked the little male as yee stretched his neck, fluting a contented sigh.

The fallen scout boat rocked from a new explosion, this one brightly framing a rectangle in the ship's side. That section fell and two bipeds followed, leaping into the bog, chased by smoke that boiled from the interior. Staggering through murky water, the men leaned on each other to reach a weedy islet, where they fell, exhausted.

The newcomer ship cruised a wary circle, losing altitude. As it turned, Dwer saw a stream of pale smoke pouring from a gash in its other side. A roughness to the engine sound grew steadily worse. Soon, the second cruiser settled down near the first.

Well, it looks like Kunn got in a lick of his own.

Dwer wondered—*Now why should that make me feel glad?*

Alvin

BONE-RATTLING CONCUSSIONS GREW MORE TERRI-fying with each dura, hammering our undersea prison refuge, sometimes receding for a while, then returning with new force, making it hard for a poor hoon to stand properly on the shuddering floor.

Crutches and a back brace didn't help, nor the little autoscribe, fogging the room with my own projected words. Stumbling through them, I sought some solid object to hold, while the scribe kept adding to the mob of words, recording my frantic curses in Anglic and GalSeven. When I found a wall stanchion, I grabbed for dear life. The clamor of reverberating explosions sounded like a giant, bearing down with massive footsteps, nearer . . . ever nearer. . . .

Then, as I feared some popping seam would let in the

dark, heavy waters of the Midden . . . it abruptly stopped.

Silence was almost as disorienting as the jeekee awful noise. My throat sac blatted uselessly while a hysterical Huphu clawed my shoulders, shredding scales into torglike ribbons.

Fortunately, hoon don't have much talent for panic. Maybe our reactions are too slow, or else we lack imagination.

As I was gathering my wits, the door hatch opened and one of the little amphibian types rushed in, squeaking a few rapid phrases in simplified GalTwo.

A summons. The spinning voice wanted us for another powwow.

"Perhaps we should share knowledge," it said when the four of us (plus Huphu) were assembled.

Huck and Pincer-Tip, able to look all ways at once, shared meaningful glances with Ur-ronn and me. We were pretty rattled by the recent booming and shaking. Even growing up next to a volcano had never prepared us for that!

The voice seemed to come from a space where abstract lines curled in tight patterns, but I knew that was an illusion. The shapes and sounds were projections, sent by some entity whose real body lay elsewhere, beyond the walls. I kept expecting Huphu to dash off and tear away a curtain, exposing a little man in an emerald carnival suit.

Do they think we're rubes, to fall for such a trick?

"Knowledge?" Huck sneered, drawing three eyes back like coiled snakes. "You want to *share* some knowledge? Then tell us what's going on! I thought this place was breaking up! Was it a quake? Are we being sucked into the Midden?"

"I assure you, that is not happening," came the answer in smooth-toned GalSix. *"The source of our mutual concern lies above, not below."*

"Exflosions," Ur-ronn muttered, blowing through her snout fringe and stamping a hind hoof. "Those weren't quakes, vut underwater detonations. Clean, sharf, and very close. I'd say soneone uf there doesn't like you guys very nuch."

Pincer hissed sharply and I stared at our urrish friend, but the spinning voice conceded.

"That is an astute guess."

I couldn't tell if it was impressed, or just sarcastic.

"And since our local guild of exflosers could hardly achieve such feats, this suggests you have other, powerful foes, far greater than we feevle Six."

"Again, a reasonable surmise. Such a bright young lady."

"Hr-rm," I added, in order not to be left out of the sardonic abuse. "We're taught that the simplest hypothesis should always be tried first. So let me guess—you're being hunted by the same folks who landed a while back in the Festival Glade. Those *gene raiders* Uriel got word about before we left. Is that it?"

"A goodly conjecture, and possibly even true . . . though it could as easily be someone else."

"Someone else? What're you say-ay-aying?" Pincer-Tip demanded, raising three legs and teetering dangerously on the remaining two. His chitin skin flared an anxious crimson shade. "That the eatees-tees-tees on the Glade might not be the only ones? That you've got whole *passels* of enemies?"

Abstract patterns tightened to a tornado of meshing lines as silence reigned. Little Huphu, who had seemed fascinated by the voice from the very start, now dug her claws in my shoulder, transfixed by the tight spiral form.

Huck demanded, in a hushed tone.

"How many enemies have you guys *got*?"

When the voice spoke again, all sardonic traces were gone. Its tone seemed deeply weary.

"Ah, dear children. It seems that half of the known sidereal universe has spent years pursuing us."

Pincer clattered his claws and Huck let out a low, mournful sigh. My own dismal contemplation-umble roused Huphu from her trancelike fixation on the whirling display, and she chittered nervously.

Ur-ronn simply grunted, as if she had expected this, vindicating her native urrish cynicism. After all, when things seem unable to get any worse, isn't that when they nearly always do? Ifni has a fertile, if nasty imagination. The goddess of fate keeps shaving new faces on her infinite-sided dice.

"Well, I guess this means—hrm-m—that we can toss out all those ideas about you phuvnthus being ancient Jijoans, or native creatures of the deep."

"Or remnants of cast-off Buyur machines," Huck went on. "Or sea monsters."

"Yeah," Pincer added, sounding disappointed. "Just another bunch of crazy Galactics-tic-tics."

The swirling patterns seemed confused. *"You would prefer sea monsters?"*

"Forget it," Huck said. "You wouldn't understand."

The patterns bent and swayed.

"I am afraid you may be right about that. Your small band of comrades has us terribly perplexed. So much that a few of us posed a sly scenario—that you were planted in our midst to sow confusion."

"How do you mean?"

"Your values, beliefs, and evident mutual affection contribute to undermining assumptions we regarded as immutably anchored in the nature of reality.

"Mind you, this confusion is not wholly unpleasant. As a thinking entity, one of my prime motives might be called a lust for surprise. And those I work with are hardly less bemused by the unforeseen marvel of your fellowship."

"Glad you find us entertaining," Huck commented, as dryly sarcastic as the voice had been. "So you guys came here to hide, like our ancestors?"

"There are parallels. But our plan was never to stay. Only to make repairs, gather stores, and wait in concealment for a favorable window at the nearest transfer point."

"So Uriel and the sages may be wrong about the ship that came to the Glade? Being a gang of gene raiders—that could just be a cover story. Are *you* the real cause of our troubles?"

"Trouble is synonymous with being a metabolizing en-

tity. Or else why have you young adventurers sought it so avidly?

"But your complaint has merit. We thought we had eluded all pursuit. The ship that landed in the mountains may be coincidental, or attracted by a confluence of unlucky factors. In any event, had we known of your existence, we would have sought shelter somewhere off-planet instead, perhaps in a dead city on one of your moons, though such places are less convenient for effecting repairs."

That part I had trouble believing. I'm just an ignorant savage, but from the classic scientific romances I grew up reading, I could picture working in some lunar ghost town like my nicknamesake, waking mighty engines that had slept for ages. What kind of starfaring beings would find darkness and salt water more "convenient" than clean vacuum?

We lapsed into moody silence, unable to stay outraged at folks who accept responsibility so readily. Anyway, weren't they fellow refugees from Galactic persecution?

Or from justice, came another, worried thought.

"Can you tell us why everyone's so mad at you?" I asked.

The spinning figure turned into a narrow, whirling funnel whose small end seemed diminished and very far away.

"Like you, we delved and probed into unvisited places, imagining ourselves bold explorers. . . . ," the voice explained in tones of boundless sadness. *"Until we had the misfortune to find the very thing we sought. Unexpected wonders beyond our dreams.*

"Breaking no law, we planned only to share what we had found. But those pursuing us abandoned all pretense of legality. Like giants striving over possession of a gnat, they war lustily, battling each other for a chance to capture us! Alas, whoever wins our treasure will surely use it against multitudes."

Again, we stared. Pincer unleashed awed whispers from all vents at once.

"Tr-tr-treasure-ure-ure . . . ?"

Huck wheeled close to the spinning pattern. "Can you prove what you just said?"

"Not at this time. Not without putting your people in more danger than they already are."

I recall wondering—what could be more dangerous than the genocide Uriel had spoken of, as one likely outcome of contact with gene raiders?

"Nevertheless," the voice continued, *"it may prove possible to improve our level of mutual confidence. Or even help each other in significant ways."*

Sara

SUPPOSE THE WORLD'S TWO MOST CAREFUL OB-servers witnessed the same event. They would never agree precisely on what had happened. Nor could they go back and check. Events may be recorded, but the past can't be replayed.

And the future is even more nebulous—a territory we make up stories about, mapping strategies that never go as planned.

Sara's beloved equations, derived from pre-contact works of ancient Earth, depicted time as a dimension, akin to the several axes of space. Galactic experts ridiculed this notion, calling the relativistic models of Einstein and others "naive." Yet Sara knew the expressions contained truth. They *had* to. They were too beautiful not to be part of universal design.

That contradiction drew her from mathematics to questions of language—how speech constrains the mind, so that some ideas come easily, while others can't even be expressed. Earthling tongues—Anglic, Rossic, and Nihanic—seemed especially prone to paradoxes, tautologies, and "proofs" that sound convincing but run counter to the real world.

But chaos had also crept into the Galactic dialects used by Jijo's other exile races, even before Terran settlers came. To some Biblos linguists, this was evidence of devolution, starfaring sophistication giving way to savagery, and eventually to proto-sapient grunts. But last year another explanation occurred to Sara, based on pre-contact information theory. An insight so intriguing that she left Biblos to work on it.

Or was I just looking for an excuse to stay away?

After Joshu died of the pox—and her mother of a stroke—research in an obscure field seemed the perfect refuge. Perched in a lonely tree house, with just Prity and her books for company, Sara thought herself sealed off from the world's intrusions.

But the universe has a way of crashing through walls.

Sara glanced at Emerson's glistening dark skin and robust smile, warmed by feelings of affection and accomplishment. Aside from his muteness, the starman scarcely resembled the shattered wreck she had found in the mulc swamp near Dolo and nursed back from near death.

Maybe I should quit my intellectual pretensions and stick with what I'm good at. If the Six Races fell to fighting among themselves, there would be more need of nurses than theoreticians.

So her thoughts spun on, chaotically orbiting the thin glowing line down the center of the tunnel. A line that never altered as they trudged on. Its changelessness rebuked Sara for her private heresy, the strange, blasphemous belief that she held, perhaps alone among all Jijoans.

The quaint notion of progress.

Out of breath after another run, she climbed back aboard the wagon to find Prity chuffing nervously. Sara reached over to check the little chimp's wound, but Prity wriggled free, clambering atop the bench seat, hissing through bared teeth as she peered ahead.

The drivers were in commotion, too. Kepha and Nuli inhaled with audible sighs. Sara took a deep breath and found her head awash with contrasts. The bucolic smell of *meadows* mixed with a sharp metallic tang . . . something utterly alien. She stood up with the backs of her knees braced against the seat.

Was that a hint of light, where the center stripe met its vanishing point?

Soon a pale glow *was* evident. Emerson flipped his rewq over his eyes, then off again.

"Uncle, wake up!" Jomah shook Kurt's shoulder. "I think we're there!"

But the glow remained vague for a long time. Dedinger muttered impatiently, and for once Sara agreed with him. Expectation of journey's end made the tunnel's remnant almost unendurable.

The horses sped without urging, as Kepha and Nuli rummaged beneath their seats and began passing out dark glasses. Only Emerson was exempted, since his rewq made artificial protection unnecessary. Sara turned the urrish-made spectacles in her hand.

I guess daylight will seem unbearably bright for a time, after we leave this hole. Still, any discomfort would be brief until their eyes readapted to the upper world. The precaution seemed excessive.

At last we'll find out where the horse clan hid all these years. Eagerness blended with sadness, for no reality—not even some god wonder of the Galactics—could compare with the fanciful images found in pre-contact tales.

A mystic portal to some parallel reality? A kingdom floating in the clouds?

She sighed. *It's probably just some out-of-the-way mountain valley where neighboring villagers are too inbred and ignorant to know the difference between a donkey and a horse.*

The ancient transitway began to rise. The stripe grew dim as illumination spread along the walls, like liquid trickling from some reservoir, far ahead. Soon the tunnel began taking on texture. Sara made out shapes. Jagged outlines.

Blinking dismay, she realized they were plunging toward sets of triple *jaws,* like a giant urrish mouth lined with teeth big enough to spear the wagon whole!

Sara took her cue from the Illias. Kepha and Nuli seemed unruffled by the serrated opening. Still, even when she saw the teeth were *metal*—corroded with flaking rust—Sara could hardly convince herself it was only a dead machine.

A huge Buyur thing.

She had never seen its like. Nearly all the great buildings and devices of the meticulous Buyur had been hauled to sea during their final years on Jijo, peeling whole cities and seeding mulc spiders to eat what remained.

So why didn't the deconstructors carry this thing away?

Behind the massive jaws lay disks studded with shiny stones that Sara realized were diamonds as big as her head. The wagon track went from smooth to bumpy as Kepha maneuvered the team along a twisty trail through the great machine's gullet, zigzagging around the huge disks.

At once Sara realized—

This is *a deconstructor! It must have been demolishing the tunnel when it broke down.*

I wonder why no one ever bothered to repair or haul it away.

Then Sara saw the reason.

Lava.

Tongues and streamlets of congealed basalt protruded through a dozen cracks, where they hardened in place half a million years ago. *It was caught by an eruption.*

Much later, teams of miners from some of the Six Races must have labored to clear a narrow path through the belly of the dead machine, chiseling out the last stretch separating the tunnel from the surface. Sara saw marks of crude pickaxes. And explosives must have been used, as well. That could explain the guild's knowledge of this place.

Sara wanted to gauge Kurt's reaction, but just then the glare brightened as the team rounded a final sharp bend, climbing a steep ramp toward a maelstrom of light.

Sara fumbled for her glasses as the world exploded with color.

Swirling colors that stabbed.

Colors that shrieked.

Colors that *sang* with melodies so forceful that her ears throbbed.

Colors that made her nose twitch and skin prickle with sensations just short of pain. A gasping moan lifted in unison from the passengers, as the wagon crested a short rise to reveal surroundings more foreign than the landscape of a dream.

Even with the dark glasses in place, each peak and valley shimmered more pigments than Sara could name.

In a daze, she sorted her impressions. To one side protruded the mammoth deconstructor, a snarl of slumped metal, drowned in ripples of frozen magma. Ripples that extended to the far horizon—layer after layer of radiant stone.

At last she knew the answer to her question.

Where on the Slope could a big secret remain hidden for a century or more?

Even Dedinger, prophet of the sharp-sand desert, moaned aloud at how obvious it was.

They were in the last place on Jijo anyone would go looking for people.

The very center of the Spectral Flow.

PART FOUR

FROM THE NOTES
OF GILLIAN BASKIN

I WISH I COULD introduce myself to Alvin. I feel I already know the lad, from reading his journal and eavesdropping on conversations among his friends.

Their grasp of twenty-third-century Anglic idiom is so perfect, and their eager enthusiasm so different from the hoons and urs I met before coming to Jijo, that half the time I almost forget I'm listening to aliens. That is, if I ignore the weird speech tones and inflections they take for granted.

Then one of them comes up with a burst of eerily skewed logic that reminds me these aren't just human kids after all, dressed up in Halloween suits to look like a crab, a centaur, and a squid in a wheelchair.

Passing the time, they wondered (and I could not blame them) whether they were prisoners or guests in this underwater refuge. Speculation led to a wide-ranging discussion, comparing various famous captives of literature. Among their intriguing perceptions—Ur-ronn sees *Richard II* as the story of a legitimate business takeover, with Bolingbroke as the king's authentic apprentice.

The red qheuen, Pincer-Tip, maintains that the hero of the *Feng Ho* chronicles was kept in the emperor's harem against his will, even though he had access to the Eight Hundred Beauties and could leave at any time.

Finally, Huck declared it frustrating that Shakespeare spent so little time dealing with Macbeth's evil wife, especially her attempt to escape sin by finding redemption in a presapient state. Huck has ideas for a sequel, describing the lady's "reuplift from the fallow condition." Her ambitious work would be no less than a morality tale about betrayal and destiny in the Five Galaxies!

Beyond these singular insights, I am struck that here on Jijo an illiterate community of castaways was suddenly flooded with written lore provided by human settlers. What an ironic reversal of Earth's situation, with our own native culture nearly overwhelmed by exposure to the Great Galactic Library. Astonishingly, the Six Races seem to have adapted with vitality and confidence, if Huck and Alvin are at all representative.

I wish their experiment well.

Admittedly, I still have trouble understanding their religion. The concept of *redemption through devolution* is one they seem to take for granted, yet its attraction eludes me.

To my surprise, our ship's doctor said she understands the concept, quite well.

"Every dolphin grows up feeling the call," Makanee told me. "In sleep, our minds still roam the vast songscape of the Whale Dream. It beckons us to return to our basic nature, whenever the stress of sapiency becomes too great."

This dolphin crew has been under pressure for three long years. Makanee's staff must care for over two dozen patients who are already "redeemed," as a Jijoan would put it. These dolphins have "reclaimed their basic nature" all right. In other words, we have lost them as comrades and skilled colleagues, as surely as if they died.

Makanee fights regression wherever she finds symptoms, and yet she remains philosophical. She even offers a theory to explain why the idea revolts me so.

She put it something like so—

"PERHAPS you humans dread this life avenue because your race had to work for sapiency, earning it for yourself the hard way, across thousands of bleak generations.

"We fins—and these urs and qheuens and hoons, and every other Galactic clan—all had the gift handed to us by some race that came before. You can't expect us to hold on to it quite as tenaciously as you, who had to struggle so desperately for the same prize.

"The attraction of this so-called Redemption Path may be a bit like ditching school. There's something alluring about the notion of letting go, shucking the discipline and toil of maintaining a rigorous mind. If you slack off, so what? Your descendants will get another chance. A fresh start on the upward road of uplift, with new patrons to show you the way."

I asked Makanee if she found that part of it especially appealing. The idea of new patrons. Would dolphins be better off with different sponsors than *Homo sapiens*?

She laughed and expressed her answer in deliciously ambiguous Trinary.

> * When winter sends ice
> > * Growling across northern seas
> > > * Wimps love the gulf stream! *

Makanee's comment made me ponder again the question of human origins.

On Earth, most people seem willing to suspend judgment on the question of whether our species had help from genetic meddlers, before the age of science and then contact. Stubborn Darwinists still present a strong case, but few have the guts to insist Galactic experts are wrong when they claim, with eons of experience, that the sole route to sapiency is Uplift. Many Terran citizens take their word for it.

So the debate rages—on popular media shows and in private arguments among humans, dolphins, and chims—about who our absent patrons might have been. At last count there were six dozen candidates—from Tuvallians and Lethani all the way to Sun Ghosts and time travelers from some bizarre Nineteenth Dimension.

While a few dolphins do believe in missing patrons, a majority are like Makanee. They hold that we humans must have done it ourselves, struggling against darkness without the slightest intervention by outsiders.

How did Captain Creideiki put it, once? Oh yes.

"THERE are racial memories, Tom and Jill. Recollections that can be accessed through deep *keeneenk* meditation. One particular image comes down from our dreamlike legends—of an apelike creature paddling to sea on a tree trunk, proudly proclaiming that he had carved it, all by himself, with a stone ax, and demanding congratulations from an indifferent cosmos.

"Now I ask you, would any decent patron let its client act in such a way? A manner that made you look so ridiculous?

"No. From the beginning we could tell that you humans were being raised by amateurs. By yourselves."

AT least that's how I remember Creideiki's remark. Tom found it hilarious, but I recall suspecting that our captain was withholding part of the story. There was more, that he was saving for another time.

Only another time never came.

Even as we dined with Creideiki that evening, *Streaker* was wriggling her way by an obscure back route into the Shallow Cluster.

A day or two later, everything changed.

IT'S late and I should finish these notes. Try to catch some sleep.

Hannes reports mixed results from engineering. He and Karkaett found a way to remove some of the carbon coating from *Streaker*'s hull, but a more thorough job would only wind up damaging our already weak flanges, so that's out for now.

On the other hand, the control parameters I hoaxed out of the Library cube enabled Suessi's crew to bring a couple of these derelict "dross" starships back to life! They're still junk, or else the Buyur would have taken them along when they left. But immersion in icy water appears to have made little difference since then. Perhaps some use might be found for one or two of the hulks. Anyway, it gives the engineers something to do.

We need distraction, now that *Streaker* seems to be trapped once more. Galactic cruisers have yet again chased us down to a far corner of the universe, coveting our lives and our secrets.

How?

I've pondered this over and over. How did they follow our trail?

The course past Izmunuti seemed well hidden. Others made successful escapes this way before. The ancestors of the Six Races, for instance.

It should have worked.

ACROSS this narrow room, I stare at a small figure in a centered spotlight. My closest companion since Tom went away.

Herbie.

Our prize from the Shallow Cluster.

Bearer of hopes and evil luck.

Was there a curse on the vast fleet of translucent vessels we discovered at that strange dip in space? When Tom found a way through their shimmering fields and snatched Herb as a souvenir, did he bring back a jinx that will haunt us until we put the damned corpse back in its billion-year-old tomb?

I used to find the ancient mummy entrancing. Its hint of a humanoid smile seemed almost whimsical.

But I've grown to hate the thing, and all the space this discovery has sent us fleeing across.

I'd give it all to have Tom back. To make the last three years go away. To recover those innocent old days, when the Five Galaxies were merely very, very dangerous, and there was still such a thing as home.

Streakers

Kaa

"**B**-BUT YOU SAID HOONS WERE OUR ENEMIESSS!"

Zhaki's tone was defiant, though his body posture—head down and flukes raised—betrayed uncertainty. Kaa took advantage, stirring water with his pectoral fins, taking the firm upright stance of an officer in the Terragens Survey Service.

"Those were different hoons," he answered. "The NuDawn disaster happened a long time ago."

Zhaki shook his bottle snout, flicking spray across the humid dome. "Eatees are eateesss. They'll crush Earthlings any chance they get, just like the Soro and Tandu and all the other muckety Galactics-cs!"

Kaa winced at the blanket generalization, but after two years on the run, such attitudes were common among the ranks. Kaa also nursed the self-pitying image of Earth against the entire universe. But if that were true, the torment would have ended with annihilation long ago.

We have allies, a few friends . . . and the grudging sympathy of neutral clans, who hold meetings debating what to do about a plague of fanaticism sweeping the Five

Galaxies. Eventually, the majority may reach a consensus and act to reestablish civilization.

They may even penalize our murderers . . . for all the good it will do us.

"Actually," said Brookida, turning from his workbench in the far corner of the cramped shelter. "I would not put the hoon in the same category as our other persecutors. They aren't religious radicals, or power-hungry conquerors. Sourpuss bureaucrats—that's a better description. Officious sticklers for rules, which is why so many enter service with Galactic Institutes. At NuDawn they were only enforcing the law. When human settlers resisted—"

"They thought they were being invaded!" Zhaki objected.

"Yessss." Brookida nodded. "But Earth's colony hadn't heard about contact, and they lacked equipment to hear Galactic inquiries. When hoonish officials came to give a ritual last warning, they met something not in their manuals . . . armed trespassersss. Barbarians with no Galactic language. Mistakes followed. Military units swarmed in from Joph—"

"This has nothing to do with our present problem." Kaa interrupted Brookida's history lecture. "Zhaki, you must stop cutting the local hoons' fishing netsss! It draws attention to us."

"*Angry* attention," Brookida added. "They grow wary against your dep-p-predations, Zhaki. Last time, they cast many spears."

The young dolphin snorted.

> * Let the whalers throw!
> * As in autumn storms of old—
> * Waves come, two-legs drown! *

Kaa flinched. Moments ago, Zhaki was eager to avenge humans who had died on a lost colony, back when dolphins could barely speak. Now the irate youth lumped all bipeds together, dredging up a grudge from days before men and women became caretakers of Earth. There was no arguing with a mind that worked that way.

Still, it was Kaa's job to enforce discipline.

  * If you repeat this act,
      * No harpoon will sting your backside
          * Like my snapping teeth! *

It wasn't great haiku—not poetical Trinary like Captain Creideiki used to dazzle his crew with, crafting devoted loyalty from waves of gorgeous sound. But the warning rocked Zhaki. Kaa followed up, projecting a beam of intense sonar from his brow, piercing Zhaki's body, betraying fear churnings within.

When in doubt, he thought, *fall back on the ancestors' ways.*

"You are dismissssssed," he finished. "Go rest. Tomorrow's another long day."

Zhaki swerved obediently, retreating to the curtained alcove he shared with Mopol.

Alas, despite this brief success, Kaa also knew it would not last.

Tsh't told us this was an important mission. But I bet she assigned us all here because we're the ones Streaker *could most easily do without.*

That night he dreamed of piloting.

Neo-dolphins had a flair for it—a precocious talent for the newest sapient species in all Five Galaxies. Just three hundred years after human geneticists began modifying natural bottlenose dolphins, starship *Streaker* was dispatched in a noble experiment to prove the skill of dolphin crews. The Terragens Council thought it might help solidify Earth's shaky position to become known as a source of crackerjack pilots.

"Lucky" Kaa had naturally been pleased to be chosen for the mission, though it brought home one glaring fact.

I was good . . . but not the best.

In half slumber, Kaa relived the terrifying ambush at Morgran, a narrow escape that still rocked him, even after all this time.

Socketed in his station on the bridge, helpless to do any-

thing but go along for the ride, as Chief Pilot Keepiru *sent the old Snark-class survey ship through maneuvers a Tandu fighter ship would envy, neatly evading lurk mines and snare fields, then diving back into the Morgran maelstrom, without benefit of guidance computation.*

The memory lost no vividness after two long years.

Transit threads swarmed around them, a dizzying blur of dimensional singularities. By a whim of cerebral evolution, trained dolphin pilots excelled at picturing the shimmering space-time clefts with sonar imagery. But Kaa had never rushed through such a tangle! A tornado of knotted strands. Any shining cord, caught at the wrong angle, might hurl the ship back into normal space with the consistency of quark stew . . .

. . . Yet somehow, the ship sped nimbly from one thread to the next, Keepiru escaped the pursuers, dodged past the normal trade routes, and finally brought Streaker *to a refuge Captain Creideiki chose.*

Kithrup, *where resources for repairs could be found as pure isotopic metal, growing like coral in a poison sea . . .*

. . . Kithrup, homeworld of two unknown races, one sinking in an ancient wallow of despair, and the other hopeful, new . . .

. . . Kithrup, where no one should have been able to follow . . .

. . . But they did. Galactics, feuding and battling insanely overhead . . .

. . . And soon Keepiru was gone, along with Toshio, Hikahi, and Mr. Orley . . .

. . . and Kaa learned that some wishes were better not coming true.

He learned that he did not really want to be chief pilot, after all.

In the years since, he has gained experience. The escapes he piloted—from Oakka and the Fractal System—were performed well, if not as brilliantly.

Not quite good enough to preserve Kaa's nickname.

I never heard anyone else say they could do better.

All in all, it was not a restful sleep.

• • • •

Zhaki and Mopol were at it again, before dawn, rubbing and squealing beyond a slim curtain they nearly shredded with their slashing tails. They should have gone outside to frolic, but Kaa dared not order it.

"It is typical postadolescent behavior," Brookida told him, by the food dispenser. "Young males grow agitated. Among natural dolphins, unisex play ceases to be sufficient as youths turn their thoughts to winning the companionship of females. Young allies often test their status by jointly challenging older males."

Of course Kaa knew all that. But he could not agree with the "typical" part. *I never acted that way. Oh sure, I was an obnoxious, arrogant young fin. But I never acted intentionally gross, or like some reverted animal.*

"Maybe Tsh't should have assigned females to our team." He pondered aloud.

"Wouldn't help," answered the elderly metallurgist. "If those two schtorks weren't getting any aboard ship, they wouldn't do any better here. Our fem-fins have high standards."

Kaa sputtered out a lump of half-chewed mullet as he laughed, grateful for Brookida's lapse into coarse humor—though it grazed by a touchy subject among *Streaker's* crew, the *petition to breed* that some had been circulating and signing.

Kaa changed the subject. "How goes your analysis of the matter the hoons dumped overboard?"

Brookida nodded toward his workbench, where several ribboned casks lay cracked open. Bits of bone and crystal glittered amid piles of ashen dust.

"So far, the contents confirm what the hoonish boy wrote in his journal."

"Amazing. I was sure it must be a fake, planted by our enemies." Transcripts of the handwritten diary, passed on by *Streaker's* command, seemed too incredible to believe.

"Apparently the story is true. Six races do live together on this world. As part of ecology-oriented rituals, they send their unrecyclable wastes—called *dross*—to sea for burial in special disposal zones. This includes parts of their processed bodies."

"And you found—"

"Human remainsss." Brookida nodded. "As well as chimps, hoons, urs . . . the whole crowd this young 'Alvin' wrote about."

Kaa was still dazed by it all.

"And there are . . . J-Jophur." He could hardly speak the word aloud.

Brookida frowned. "A matter of definition, it seems. I've exchanged message queries with Gillian and the Niss Machine. They suggest these so-called traeki might have the other races fooled as part of an elaborate, long-range plot."

"How could that be?"

"I am not sure. It would not require that every traeki be in on the scheme. Just a few, with secret master rings, and the hidden equipment to dominate their fellow beings. I cannot quite fathom it. But Gillian has questioned the captured Library unit. And that seems a posssssible scenario."

Kaa had no answer for that. Such matters seemed so complex, so far beyond his grasp, his only response was to shiver from the tip of his rostrum all the way down to his trembling tail.

They spent another day spying on the local sooners. The hoonish seaport, Wuphon, seemed to match the descriptions in Alvin's journal . . . though more crude and shabby in the eyes of beings who had seen the sky towers of Tanith and bright cities on Earth's moon. The hoons appeared to pour more lavish attention on their boats than their homes. The graceful sailing ships bore delicate carving work, down to proud figureheads shaped like garish deities.

When a vessel swept past Kaa, he overheard the deep, rumbling sounds of *singing,* as the sailors boomed evident joy across the whitecaps.

It's hard to believe these are the same folk Brookida described as passionless prigs. Maybe there are two races that look alike, and have similar-sounding names. Kaa made a mental note to send an inquiry in tonight's report.

Hoons weren't alone on deck. He peered at smaller creatures, scrambling nimbly over the rigging, but when he tried using a portable camera, the image swept by too fast to catch much more than a blur.

Streaker also wanted better images of the *volcano,* which apparently was a center of industrial activity among the sooner races. Gillian and Tsh't were considering sending another independent robot ashore, though earlier drones had been lost. Kaa got spectral readings of the mountain's steaming emissions, and discovered the trace of a slender tramway, camouflaged against the rocky slopes.

He checked frequently on Zhaki and Mopol, who seemed to be behaving for a change, sticking close to their assigned task of eavesdropping on the red qheuen colony.

But later, when all three of them were on their way back to base, Mopol lagged sluggishly behind.

"It must-t have been some-thing I ate," the blue dolphin murmured, as unpleasant gurglings erupted within his abdomen.

Oh great, Kaa thought. *I warned him a hundred times not to sample local critters before Brookida had a chance to test them!*

Mopol swore it was nothing. But as the water surrounding their shelter dimmed with the setting sun, he started moaning again. Brookida used their tiny med scanner, but was at a loss to tell what had gone wrong.

Tsh't

NOMINALLY, SHE COMMANDED EARTH'S MOST FAmous spaceship—a beauty almost new by Galactic standards, just nine hundred years old when the Terragens Council purchased it from a Punictin used-vessel dealer, then altered and renamed it *Streaker* to show off the skills of neo-dolphin voyagers.

Alas, the bedraggled craft seemed unlikely ever again to

cruise the great spiral ways. Burdened by a thick coat of refractory stardust—and now trapped deep underwater while pursuers probed the abyss with sonic bombs—to all outward appearances, it seemed doomed to join the surrounding great pile of ghost ships, sinking in the slowly devouring mud of an oceanic ravine.

Gone was the excitement that first led Tsh't into the service. The thrill of flight. The exhilaration. Nor was there much relish in "authority," since she did not make policies or crucial decisions. Gillian Baskin had that role.

What remained was handling ten thousand details . . . like when a disgruntled cook accosted her in a water-filled hallway, wheedling for permission to go up to the realm of light.

"It'ssss too dark and c-cold to go fishing down here!" complained Bulla-jo, whose job it was to help provide meals for a hundred finicky dolphins. "My harvesst team can hardly move, wearing all that pressure armor. And have you seen the so-called fish we catch in our nets? Weird things, all sspiky and glowing!"

Tsh't replied, "Dr. Makanee has passed at least forty common varieties of local sea life as both tasty and nutritious, so long as we sssupplement with the right additives."

Still, Bulla-jo groused.

"Everyone favors the samples we got *earlier,* from the upper world of waves and open air. There are great schools of lovely things swimming around up-p there."

Then Bulla-jo lapsed into Trinary.

> * *Where perfect sunshine*
> * *Makes lively prey fish glitter*
> * *As they flee from us!* *

He concluded, "If you want fresh f-food, let us go to the surface, like you p-promised!"

Tsh't quashed an exasperated sigh over Bulla-jo's forgetfulness. In this early stage of their Uplift, neo-dolphins often perceived whatever they chose, ignoring contradictions.

I do it myself, now and then.

She tried cultivating patience, as Creideiki used to teach.

"Dr. Baskin canceled plans to send more parties to the sunlit surface," she told Bulla-jo, whose speckled flanks and short beak revealed ancestry from the *stenos* dolphin line. "Did it escape your notice that gravitic emissions have been detected, cruising above this deep fissure? Or that someone has been dropping sonic charges, seeking to find usss?"

Bulla-jo lowered his rostrum in an attitude of obstinate insolence. "We can g-go naked . . . carry no tools the eatees could detect-ct."

Tsh't marveled at such single-minded thinking.

"That might work if the gravitics were far away, say in orbit, or passing by at high altitude. But once they know our rough location they can cruise low and slow, sssseeking the radiochemical spoor of molecules in our very blood. Surface-swimming fins would give us away."

Irony was a bittersweet taste to Tsh't, for she knew something she had no intention of sharing with Bulla-jo. *They are going to detect us, no matter how many precautions Gillian orders.*

To the frustrated crew member, she had only soothing words.

"Just float loose for a while longer, will you, Bulla-jo? I, too, would love to chase silvery fish through warm waters. All may be resolved sh-shortly."

Grumpy, but mollified, the messmate saluted by clapping his pectoral fins and swimming back to duty . . . though Tsh't knew the crisis would recur. Dolphins disliked being so far from sunlight, or from the tide's cycloid rub against shore. Tursiops weren't meant to dwell so deep, where pressurized sound waves carried in odd, disturbing ways.

It is the realm of Physeter, sperm whale, great-browed messenger of the ancient dream gods, who dives to wrestle great-armed demons.

The abyss was where hopes and nightmares from past, present, and future drifted to form dark sediments—a place best left to sleeping things.

We neo-fins are superstitious at heart. But what can you expect, having humans as our beloved patrons? Humans, who are themselves wolflings, primitive by the standards of a billion-year-old culture.

This she pondered while inhaling deeply, filling her gill lungs with the air-charged fluid, *oxy-water,* that filled most of *Streaker*'s residential passages—a genetically improvised manner of breathing that nourished, but never comfortably. One more reason many of the crew yearned for the clean, bright world above.

Turning toward the *Streaker*'s bridge, she thrust powerfully through the fizzing liquid, leaving clouds of effervescence behind her driving flukes. Each bubble gave off a faint *pop!* as it hiccuped into existence, or merged back into supercharged solution. Sometimes the combined susurration sounded like elfin applause—or derisive laughter—following her all over the ship.

At least I don't fool myself, she thought. *I do all right. Gillian says so, and puts her trust in me. But I know I'm not meant for command.*

Tsh't had never expected such duty when *Streaker* blasted out of Earth orbit, refurbished for use by a neodolphin crew. Back then—over two years ago, by ship-clock time—Tsh't had been only a junior lieutenant, a distant fifth in line from Captain Creideiki. And it was common knowledge that Tom Orley and Gillian Baskin could step in if the need seemed urgent . . . as Gillian eventually did, during the crisis on Kithrup.

Tsh't didn't resent that human intervention. In arranging an escape from the Kithrup trap, Tom and Gillian pulled off a miracle, even if it led to the lovers' separation.

Wasn't that the *job* of human leaders and heroes? To intercede when a crisis might overwhelm their clients?

But where do we turn when matters get too awful even for humans to handle?

Galactic tradition adhered to a firm—some said oppressive—hierarchy of debts and obligations. A client race to its patron. That patron to *its* sapience benefactor . . . and so on, tracing the great chain of uplift all the way back to the legendary Progenitors. The same chain of duty underlay the reaction of some fanatical clans on hearing news of *Streaker*'s discovery—a fleet of derelict ships with ancient, venerated markings.

But the pyramid of devotion had positive aspects. The uplift cascade meant each new species got help crossing the dire gap dividing mere animals from starfaring citizens. And if your sponsors lacked answers, they might ask *their* patrons. And so on.

Gillian had tried appealing to this system, taking *Streaker* from Kithrup to Oakka, the green world, seeking counsel from impartial savants of the Navigation Institute. Failing there, she next sought help in the Fractal Orb—that huge icy place, a giant snowflake that spanned a solar system's width—hoping the venerable beings who dwelled there might offer wise detachment, or at least refuge.

It wasn't Dr. Baskin's fault that neither gamble paid off very well. *She had the right general idea,* Tsh't mused. *But Gillian remains blind to the obvious.*

Who is most likely to help, when you're in trouble and a lynch mob is baying at your tail?

The courts?

Scholars at some university?

Or your own family?

Tsh't never dared suggest her idea aloud. Like Tom Orley, Gillian took pride in the romantic image of upstart Earthclan, alone against the universe. Tsh't knew the answer would be no.

So, rather than flout a direct order, Tsh't had quietly put her own plan into effect, just before *Streaker* made her getaway from the Fractal System.

What else could I do, with Streaker *pursued by horrid fleets, our best crew members gone, and Earth under siege? Our Tymbrimi friends can barely help even themselves. Meanwhile, the Galactic Institutes have been corrupted and the Old Ones lied to us.*

We had no choice.

. . . I had no choice . . .

It was hard concealing things, especially from someone who knew dolphins as well as Gillian. For weeks since *Streaker* arrived here, Tsh't half hoped her disobedience would come to nought.

Then the detection officer reported gravitic traces. Starcraft engines, entering Jijo space.

So, they came after all, she had thought, hearing the

news, concealing satisfaction while her crew mates expressed noisy chagrin, bemoaning that they now seemed cornered by relentless enemies on a forlorn world.

Tsh't wanted to tell them the truth, but dared not. That good news must wait.

Ifni grant that I was right.

Tsh't paused outside the bridge, filling her gene-altered lungs with oxy-water. Enriching her blood to think clearly before setting in motion the next phase of her plan.

There is just one true option for a client race, when your beloved patrons seem overwhelmed, and all other choices are cut off.

May the gods of Earth's ancient ocean know and understand what I've done.

And what I may yet have to do.

Sooners

Nelo

ONCE, A BUYUR URBAN CENTER STRETCHED BE-tween two rivers, from the Roney all the way to the far-off Bibur.

Now the towers were long gone, scraped and hauled away to distant seas. In their place, spiky ferns and cloud-like *voow* trees studded a morass of mud and oily water. Mulc-spider vines laced a few rounded hummocks remaining from the great city, but even those tendrils were now faded, their part in the demolition nearly done.

To Nelo, this was wasteland, rich in life but useless to any of the Six Races, except perhaps as a traeki vacation resort.

What am I doing here? he wondered. *I should be back in Dolo, tending my mill, not prowling through a swamp, keeping a crazy woman company.*

Behind Nelo, hoonish sailors cursed low, expressive rumblings, resentful over having to pole through a wretched bog. The proper time for gleaning was at the start of the dry season, when citizens in high-riding boats took turns sifting the marsh for Buyur relics missed by the patient mulc beast. Now, with rainstorms due any day, conditions were miserable for exploring. The muddy channels were shallow, yet the danger of a flash flood was very real.

Nelo faced the elderly woman who sat in a wheelchair near the bow, peering past obscuring trees with a rewq over her eyes.

"The crew ain't happy, Sage Foo," he told her. "They'd rather we waited till it's safe."

Ariana Foo answered without turning from her search. "Oh, what a great idea. Four months or more we'd sit around while the swamp fills, channels shift, and the thing we seek gets buried in muck. Of course, by then the information would be too late to do any good."

Nelo shrugged. The woman was retired now. She had no official powers. But as former High Sage for all humans on Jijo, Ariana had moral authority to ask anything she wanted—including having Nelo leave his beloved paper mill next to broad Dolo Dam, accompanying her on this absurd search.

Not that there was much to do at the mill, he knew. *With commerce spoiled by panic over those wretched starships, no one seems interested in buying large orders.*

"Now is the best time," Ariana went on. "Late in dry season, with water levels low, and the foliage drooping, we get maximum visibility."

Nelo took her word. With most young men and women away on militia duties, it was mostly adolescents and old-timers who got drafted into the search party. Anyway, Nelo's daughter had been among the first to find the Stranger from Space in this very region several months ago, during a routine gleaning trip. And he owed Ariana for bringing word about Sara and the boys—that they were all right, when last she heard. Sage Foo had spent time with Nelo's daughter, accompanying Sara from Tarek Town to the Biblos Archive.

He felt another droplet strike his cheek . . . the tenth since they left the river, plunging into this endless slough. He held his hand under a murky sky and prayed the real downpours would hold off for a few more days.

Then let it come down! The lake is low. We need water

pressure for the wheel, or else I'll have to shut down the mill for lack of power.

His thoughts turned to business—the buying and gathering of recycled cloth from all six races. The pulping and sifting. The pressing, drying, and selling of fine sheets that his family had been known for ever since humans brought the blessing of paper to Jijo.

A blessing that some called a curse. That radical view now claimed support from simple villagers, panicked by the looming end of days—

A shout boomed from above.

"There!" A wiry young hoon perched high on the mast, pointing. "Hr-r . . . It must be the Stranger's ship. I *told* you this had to be the place!"

Wyhuph-eihugo had accompanied Sara on that fateful gleaning trip—a duty required of all citizens. Lacking a male's throat sac, she nevertheless umbled with some verve, proud of her navigation.

At last! Nelo thought. *Now Ariana can make her sketches, and we can leave this awful place.* The crisscrossing mulc cables made him nervous. Their boat's obsidian-tipped prow had no trouble slicing through the desiccated vines. Still it felt as if they were worming deeper into some fiendish trap.

Ariana muttered something. Nelo turned, blinking.

"What did you say?"

The old woman pointed ahead, her eyes glittering with curiosity.

"I don't see any soot!"

"So?"

"The Stranger was burned. His clothes were ashen tatters. We thought his ship must have come down in flames—perhaps after battling other aliens high over Jijo. But look. Do you see any trace of conflagration?"

The boat worked around a final voow grove, revealing a rounded metal capsule on the other side, gleaming amid a nest of shattered branches. The sole opening resembled the splayed petals of a flower, rather than a door or hatch. The arrival of this intruder had cut a swathe of devastation stretching to the northwest. Several swamp hummocks were split by the straight gouge, only partly softened by regrown vegetation.

Nelo had some experience as a surveyor, so he helped take sightings to get the ship's overall dimensions. It was small—no larger than this hoonish boat, in fact—certainly no majestic cruiser like the one that clove the sky over Dolo Town, sending its citizens into hysteria. The rounded flanks reminded Nelo of a natural teardrop, more than anything sapient-made.

Two pinpoints of moisture dotted his cheek and forehead. Another struck the back of his hand. In the distance, Nelo heard a sharp rumble of thunder.

"Hurry closer!" Ariana urged, flipping open her sketchpad.

Murmuring unhappily, the hoons leaned on their poles and oars to comply.

Nelo stared at the alien craft, but all he could think was *dross*. When Sixers went gleaning through Buyur sites, one aim was to seek items that might be useful for a time, in a home or workshop. But useful or not, everything eventually went into ribboned caskets to be sent on to the Great Midden. Thus colonists imagined they were helping cleanse Jijo—perhaps doing more good than harm to their adopted world.

"Ifni!" Nelo sighed under his breath, staring at the vehicle that brought the Stranger hurtling out of space. It might be tiny for a starship, but it looked hard as blazes to move by hand.

"We'll be in for a hell of a job draggin' this thing out of here, let alone gettin' it down to sea."

Again, off to the south, the sound of thunder boomed.

Ewasx

WE JOPHUR ARE TAUGHT THAT IT IS TERRIBLE TO BE traeki—a stack lacking any central self. Doomed to a splintered life of vagueness and blurry placidity.

ALL SING PRAISES to the mighty Oailie, who took over

from the too-timid Poa, completing the final stages of our Uplift.

Those same Oailie who designed new master rings to focus and bind our natures.

Without rings like Me, how could our race ever have become great and feared among the Five Galaxies?

AND YET, even as I learn to integrate your many little selves into our new whole, I am struck by how vivid are these older drippings that I find lining our inner core! Drippings that date from before My fusion with your aged pile of rings. How lustrous clear these memories seem, despite their counterpointing harmonies. I confess, existence had intensity and verve when you/we were merely *Asx*.

PERHAPS this surprise comes because I/Myself am so young, only recently drawn from the side of our Ship Commander—from that great one's very own ring-of-embryos.

Yes, that is a high heritage. So imagine the surprise of finding Myself in this situation! Designed for duties in the dominion caste, I am wedded, for pragmatic reasons, to a haphazard heap of rustic toruses, ill educated and filled with bizarre, primitive notions. I have been charged to make the best of things until some later time, when surgery-of-reconfiguration can be performed—

AH. THAT DRAWS A REACTION FROM SOME OF YOU? Our second ring of cognition, in particular, finds this notion disturbing.

Fear not, My rings! Accept these jolts of painful love soothing, to remind you of your place—which is not to question, only to serve. Be assured that the procedure I refer to is now quite advanced among the mighty Jophur. When a ring is removed for reassembly in a new stack, often as many as half of the other leftover components can be recovered and reused as well! Of course, most of you are elderly, and the priests may decide you carry other-race contaminations, preventing incorporation into new mounds. But accept this pledge. When the time comes, I, your beloved master ring, shall very likely make the transition in good health, and take fond memories of our association to My glorious new stack.

I know this fact will bring you all great satisfaction, contemplating it within our common core.

Lark

CATHEDRAL-LIKE STILLNESS FILLED THE BOO FOR-est—a dense expanse of gray-green columns, towering to support the sky. Each majestic trunk had a girth like the carapace of a five-clawed qheuen. Some stretched as high as the Stone Roof of Biblos.

Now I know how an insect feels, scuttling under a sea of pampas grass.

Hiking along a narrow lane amid the giant pillars, Lark often could reach out his arms and brush two giant stems at the same time. Only his militia sergeant seemed immune to a sense of confinement infecting travelers in this strange place of vertical perspectives. Other guards expressed edginess with darting eyes that glanced worriedly down crooked aisles at half-hidden shadows.

"How far is it to Dooden Mesa?" Ling asked, tugging the straps of her leather backpack. Perspiration glistened down her neck to dampen the Jijoan homespun jerkin she wore. The effect was not as provocative as Lark recalled from their old survey trips together, when the sheer fabric of a Danik jumpsuit sometimes clung to her biosculpted figure in breathtaking ways.

Anyway, I can't afford that, now that I'm a sage. The promotion brought only unpleasant responsibilities.

"I never took this shortcut before," Lark answered, although he and Uthen used to roam these mountains in search of data for their book. There were other paths around the mountain, and the wheeled g'Keks nominally in charge of this domain could hardly be expected to do upkeep on such a rough trail. "My best guess is we'll make it in two miduras. Want to rest?"

Ling pushed sodden strands from her eyes. "No. Let's keep going."

The former gene raider seemed acutely aware of Jeni Shen, the diminutive sergeant, whose corded arms cradled her crossbow like a beloved child. Jeni glanced frequently at Ling with hunter's eyes, as if speculating which vital organ might make a good target. Anyone could sense throbbing enmity between the two women—and that Ling would rather die than show weakness before the militia scout.

Lark found one thing convenient about their antagonism. It helped divert Ling's ire away from *him*, especially after the way he earlier used logic to slash her beloved Rothen gods. Since then, the alien biologist had been civil, but kept to herself in brooding silence.

No one likes to have their most basic assumptions knocked from under them—especially by a primitive savage.

Lark blew air through his cheeks—the hoonish version of a shrug.

"Hr-rm. We'll take a break at the next rise. By then we should be out of the worst boo."

In fact, the thickest zone was already behind them, a copse so dense the monstrous stems rubbed in the wind, creating a low, drumming music that vibrated the bones of anyone passing underneath. Traveling single file, edging sideways where the trunks pressed closest, the party had watched for vital trail marks, cut on one rounded bole after the next.

I was right to leave Uthen behind, he thought, hoping to convince himself. *Just hold on, old friend. Maybe we'll come up with something. I pray we can.*

Visibility was hampered by drifting haze, since many of the tall boo *leaked* from water reserves high above, spraying arcs of fine droplets that spread to saturate the misty colonnade. Several times they passed clearings where aged columns had toppled in a domino chain reaction, leaving maelstroms of debris.

Through the fog, Lark occasionally glimpsed *other* symbols, carved on trunks beyond the trail. Not trail marks, but cryptic emblems in GalTwo and GalSix . . . accompanied by strings of Anglic numbers.

Why would anyone go scrawling graffiti through a stand of greatboo?

He even spied dim figures through the murk—once a human, then several urs, and finally a pair of traeki—glimpsed prowling amid rows of huge green pillars. At least he *hoped* the tapered cones were traeki. They vanished like ghosts before he could tell for sure.

Sergeant Shen kept the party moving too fast to investigate. Lark and his prisoner had been summoned by two of the High Sages—a command that overruled any other priority. And despite the difficult terrain, recent news from the Glade of Gathering was enough to put vigor in their steps.

Runners reported that the Jophur dreadnought still blocked the sacred valley, squatting complacently inside its swathe of devastation, with the captive Rothen ship doubly imprisoned nearby—first by a gold cocoon, and now a rising lake as well. The Jophur daily sent forth a pair of smaller vessels, sky-prowling daggers, surveying the Slope and the seas beyond. No one knew what the star gods were looking for.

Despite what happened on the night the great ship landed—havoc befalling Asx and others on the Glade—the High Sages were preparing to send another embassy of brave volunteers, hoping to parley. No one asked Lark to serve as an envoy. The Sages had other duties planned for him.

Humans weren't the only ones to cheat a little, when their founding generation came to plant a taboo colony on forbidden Jijo.

For more than a year after it made landfall, the *Tabernacle*'s crew delayed sending their precious ship to an ocean abyss. A year spent using god tools to cut trees and print books . . . then storing the precious volumes in a stronghold that the founders carved beneath a great stone overhang, protected by high walls and a river. During those early days—especially the urrish and qheuen wars—Biblos Fortress served as a vital refuge until humans grew strong enough to demand respect.

The Gray Queens also once had such a citadel, sculpted by mighty engines when they first arrived, before their sneakship fell beneath the waves. The Caves of Shood, near present-day Ovoom Town, must have seemed impregnable. But that maze of deep-hewn caverns drowned under a rising water table when blue and red workers dropped their slavish maintenance duties, wandering off instead to seek new homes and destinies, apart from their chitin empresses.

Dooden Mesa was the oldest of the sooner ramparts. After Tarek Town, it formed the heart of g'Kek life on Jijo, a place of marvelous stone ramps that curved like graceful filigrees, allowing the wheeled ones to swoop and careen through a swirl of tight turns, from their looms and workshops to tree-sheltered platforms where whole families slept with their hubs joined in slowly rotating clusters. Under an obscuring blur-cloth canopy, the meandering system resembled pictures found in certain Earthling books about pre-contact times—looking like a cross between an "amusement park" and the freeway interchanges of some sprawling city.

Ling's face brightened with amazed delight when she regarded the settlement, nodding as Lark explained the lacy pattern of narrow byways. Like Biblos, Dooden Rampart was not meant to last forever, for that would violate the Covenant of Exile. Someday it all would have to go— g'Kek elders conceded. Still, the wheeled ones throbbed their spokes in sinful pride over their beloved city. Their home.

While Ling marveled, Lark surveyed the busy place with fresh poignancy.

It is their only *home.*

Unless the Rothen lied, it seems there are no more g'Kek living among the Five Galaxies.

If they die on Jijo, they are gone for good.

Watching youngsters pitch along graceful ramps with reckless abandon, streaking round corners with all four eyestalks flying and their rims glowing hot, Lark could not believe the universe would let that happen. How could any race so unique be allowed to go extinct?

With the boo finally behind them, the party now stood atop a ridge covered with normal forest. As they paused, a zookir dropped onto the path from the branches of a nearby garu tree—all spindly arms and legs, covered with white spirals of fluffy torg. Treasured aides and pets of the g'Kek, zookirs helped make life bearable for wheeled be-

ings on a planet where roads were few and stumbling
stones all too many.

This zookir squinted at the party, then scampered closer,
sniffing. Unerringly, it bypassed the other humans, zeroing
in on Lark.

Trust a zookir to know a sage—so went a folk saying. No
one had any idea *how* the creatures could tell, since they
seemed less clever than chimps in other ways. Lark's promotion was recent and he wore the new status of "junior
sage" uncomfortably, yet the creature had no trouble setting him apart. It pressed damp nostrils against his wrist
and inhaled. Then, cooing satisfaction, it slipped a folded
parchment in Lark's hand.

MEET US AT THE REFUGE—That was all it said.

Lester Cambel

A PAIR OF HIGH SAGES WAITED IN A NARROW CAN-
yon, half a league away. Lester Cambel and Knife-Bright
Insight, the blue qheuen whose reputation for compas-
sion made her a favorite among the Six.

Here, too, the paths were smooth and well suited for
g'Keks, since this was part of their Dooden Domain.
Wheeled figures moved among the meadows, looking after
protected ones who lived in thatched shelters beneath the
trees. It was a refuge for sacred simpletons—those whose
existence promised a future for the Six Races—according
to the scrolls.

Several of the *blessed ones* gathered around Knife-Bright
Insight, clucking or mewing in debased versions of Galactic tongues. These were hoons and urs, for the most part,
though a red qheuen joined the throng as Lester watched,
and several traeki stacks slithered timidly closer, burbling
happy stinks as they approached. Each received a loving
pat or stroke from Knife-Bright Insight, as if her claws were
gentle hands.

Lester regarded his colleague, and knew guiltily that he
could never match her glad kindness. The *blessed* were

superior beings, ranking above the normal run of the Six. Their simplicity was proof that other races could follow the example of glavers, treading down the Path of Redemption.

It should fill my heart to see them, he thought.

Yet I hate coming to this place.

Members of all six races dwelled in simple shelters underneath the canyon walls, tended by local g'Keks, plus volunteers from across the Slope. Whenever a qheuen, or hoon, or urrish village found among their youths one who had a knack for innocence, a gift for animal-like naïveté, the lucky individual was sent here for nurturing and study.

There are just two ways to escape the curse bequeathed to us by our ancestors, Lester thought, struggling to believe. *We could do as Lark's group of heretics want—stop breeding and leave Jijo in peace. Or else we can all seek a different kind of oblivion, the kind that returns our children's children to presentience. Washed clean and ready for a new cycle of uplift. Thus they may yet find new patrons, and perhaps a happier fate.*

So prescribed the Sacred Scrolls, even after all the compromises wrought since the arrival of Earthlings and the Holy Egg. Given the situation of exile races, living here on borrowed time, facing horrid punishment if/when a Galactic Institute finds them here, what other goal could there be?

But I can't do it. I cannot look at this place with joy. Earthling values keep me from seeing these creatures as lustrous beings. They deserve kindness and pity—but not envy.

It was his own heresy. Lester tried to look elsewhere. But turning just brought to view another cluster of "blessed." This time, humans, gathered in a circle under a ilhuna tree, sitting cross-legged with hands on knees, chanting in low, sonorous voices. Men and women whose soft smiles and unshifting eyes seemed to show simplicity of the kind sought here . . . only Lester knew them to be liars!

Long ago, he took the same road. Using meditation techniques borrowed from old Earthling religions, he sat under just such a tree, freeing his mind of worldly obsessions, disciplining it to perceive Truth. And for a while it seemed he succeeded. Acolytes bowed reverently, calling him *illuminated*. The universe appeared lucid then, as if the stars were sacred fire. As if he were united with all Jijo's creatures, even the very quanta in the stones around him. He lived in harmony, needing little food, few words, and even fewer names.

Such serenity—sometimes he missed it with an ache inside.

But after a while he came to realize—the clarity he had found was sterile blankness. A blankness that *felt* fine, but had nothing to do with redemption. Not for himself. Not for his race.

The other five don't use discipline or concentration to seek simplicity. You don't see glavers meditating by a rotten log full of tasty insects. Simplicity calls to them naturally. They live *their innocence.*

When Jijo is finally reopened, some great clan will gladly adopt the new glaver subspecies, setting them once more upon the High Path, perhaps with better luck than they had the first time.

But those patrons won't choose us. No noble elder clan is looking for smug Zen masters, eager to explain their own enlightenment. That is not a plainness you can write upon. It is simplicity based on individual pride.

Of course the point might be moot. If the Jophur ship represented great Institutes of the Civilization of the Five Galaxies, these forests would soon throng with inspectors, tallying up two thousand years of felonies against a fallow world. Only glavers would be safe, having made it to safety in time. The other six races would pay for a gamble lost.

And if they don't represent the Institutes?

The Rothen had proved to be criminals, gene raiders. Might the Jophur be more of the same? Murderous genocide could still be in store. The g'Kek clan, in particular, were terrified of recent news from the Glade.

On the other hand, it might be possible to cut a deal. Or else maybe they'll just go away, leaving us in the same state we were in before.

In that case, places like this refuge would go back to

being the chief hope for tomorrow . . . for five races out
of the Six.

Lester's dark thoughts were cut off by a tug on his
sleeve.

"Sage Cambel? The . . . um, visitors you're, ah, expecting . . . I think . . ."

It was a young human, broad-cheeked, with clear blue
eyes and pale skin. The boy would have seemed tall—
almost a giant—except that a stooped posture diminished
his appearance. He kept tapping a corner of his forehead
with the fingertips of his right hand, as if in a vague salute.

Lester spoke gentle words in Anglic, the only language
the lad ever managed to learn.

"What did you say, Jimi?"

The boy swallowed, concentrating hard.

"I think the . . . um . . . the people you want t'see
. . . I think they're here . . . Sage Cambel."

"Lark and the Danik woman?"

A vigorous nod.

"Um, yessir. I sent 'em to the visitors' shed . . . to wait
for you an' the other Great Sage. Was that right?"

"Yes, that was right, Jimi." Lester gave his arm a friendly
squeeze. "Please go back now. Tell Lark I'll be along
shortly."

A broad grin. The boy turned around to run the way he
came, awkward in his eagerness to be useful.

*There goes the other kind of human who comes to this
place,* Lester thought. *Our special ones . . .*

The ancient euphemism tasted strange.

*At first sight, it would seem people like Jimi fit the bill.
Simpler minds. Innocent. Our ideal envoys to tread the
Path.*

He glanced at the blessed ones surrounding Knife-Bright
Insight—urs, hoons, and g'Keks who were sent here by
their respective races in order to do that. To lead the way.

*By the standards of the scrolls, these ones aren't dam-
aged. Though simple, they aren't flawed. They are leaders.
But no one can say that of Jimi. All sympathy aside, he is
injured, incomplete. Anyone can see that.*

*We can and should love him, help him, befriend him.
But he leads humanity nowhere.*

Lester signaled to his blue qheuen colleague, using an urslike shake of his head to indicate that their appointment had arrived. She responded by turning her visor cupola in a quick series of GalTwo winks, flashing that she'd be along shortly.

Lester turned and followed Jimi's footsteps, trying to shift his thoughts back to the present crisis. To the problem of the Jophur battleship. Back to urgent plans he must discuss with the young heretic and the woman from the stars. There was a dire proposal—farfetched and darkly dangerous—they must be asked to accept.

Yet, as he passed by the chanting circle of meditating humans—healthy men and women who had abandoned their farms, families, and useful crafts to dwell without work in this sheltered valley—Lester found his contemplations awash with bitter resentment. The words in his head were unworthy of a High Sage, he knew. But he could not help pondering them.

Morons and meditators, those are the two types that our race sends up here. Not a true "blessed" soul in the lot. Not by the standards set in the scrolls. Humans almost never take true steps down redemption's path. Ur-Jah and the others are polite. They pretend that we, too, have that option, that potential salvation.

But we don't. Our lot is sterile.

With or without judgment from the stars—the only future humans face on Jijo is damnation.

Dwer

SMOKE SPIRALED FROM THE CRASH SITE. IT WAS against his better judgment to sneak closer. In fact, now was his chance to run the other way, while the Danik robot cowered in a hole, showing no further interest in its prisoners.

And if Rety wanted to stay?

Let her! Lena and Jenin would be glad to see Dwer if he made the long journey back to the Gray Hills. That should be possible with his trusty bow in hand. True, Rety needed him, but those up north had better claim on his loyalty.

Dwer's senses still throbbed from the din of the brief battle, when the mighty Danik scoutship was shot down by a terrifying newcomer. Both vessels lay beyond the next dune, sky chariots of unfathomable power . . . and Rety urged him to creep closer still!

"We gotta find out what's going on," she insisted in a harsh whisper.

He gave her a sharp glance, demanding silence, and for once she complied, giving him a moment to think.

Lena and Jenin may be safe for a while, now that Kunn won't be returning to plague them. If the Daniks and Rothens have enemies on Jijo, all the star gods may be too busy fighting each other to hunt a little band in the Gray Hills.

Even without guidance from Danel Ozawa, Lena Strong was savvy enough to make a three-way deal, with Rety's old band and the urrish sooners. Using Danel's "legacy," their combined tribe might plant a seed to flourish in the wilderness. Assuming the worst happened back home on the Slope, their combined band might yet find its way to the Path.

Dwer shook his head. He sometimes found it hard to concentrate. Ever since letting the robot use his body as a conduit for its fields, it felt as if *voices* whispered softly at the edge of hearing. As when the crazy old mulc spider used to wheedle into his thoughts.

Anyway, it wasn't his place to ponder destiny, or make sagelike decisions. Some things were obvious. He might not *owe* Rety anything. She may deserve to be abandoned to her fate. But he couldn't do that.

So, despite misgivings, Dwer nodded to the girl, adding with emphatic hand motions that she had better not make a single sound. She replied with a happy shrug that seemed to say, *Sure . . . until I decide otherwise.*

Slinging his bow and quiver over one shoulder, he led the way forward, creeping from one grassy clump to the next, till they reached the crest of the dune. Cautiously they peered through a cluster of salty fronds to stare down at two sky vessels—the smaller a smoldering ruin, half-submerged in a murky swamp. The larger ship, nestled nearby, had not escaped the fracas unscarred. It bore a deep fissure along one flank that belched soot whenever the motors tried to start.

Two men lay prostrate on a marshy islet, barely moving. Kunn and Jass.

Dwer and Rety scratched a new hole to hide in, then settled down to see who—or what—would emerge next.

They did not wait long. A hatch split the large cylinder, baring a dark interior. Through it floated a single figure, startlingly familiar—an eight-sided pillar with dangling arms—close cousin to the damaged robot Dwer knew all too well. Only this one gleamed with stripes of alternating blue and pink, a pattern Dwer found painful to behold.

It also featured a hornlike projection on the bottom, aimed downward. *That must be what lets it travel over water,* he thought. *If the robot is similar, could that mean Kunn's enemies are human, too?*

But no, Danel had said that machinery was standard among the half a million starfaring races, changing only slowly with each passing eon. This new drone might belong to anybody.

The automaton neared Kunn and Jass, a searchlight playing over their bodies, vivid even in bright sunshine. Their garments rippled, frisked by translucent fingers. Then the robot dropped down, arms outstretched. Kunn and Jass lay still as it poked, prodded, and lifted away with several objects in its pincers.

A signal must have been given, for a ramp then jutted from the open hatch, slanting to the bog. *Who's going to go traipsing around in that stuff?* Dwer wondered. *Are they going to launch a boat?*

He girded for some weird alien race, one with thirteen legs perhaps, or slithering on trails of slime. Several great clans had been known as foes of humankind, even in the *Tabernacle*'s day, such as the legendary Soro, or the insect-like Tandu. Dwer even nursed faint hope that the newcomers might be from Earth, come all this vast distance to rein in their criminal cousins. There were also relatives of hoons, urs, and qheuens out there, each with ships and vast resources at their command.

Figures appeared, twisting down the ramp into the open air.

Rety gasped. "Them's traekis!"

Dwer stared at a trio of formidable-looking ring stacks, with bandoliers of tools hanging from their toroids-of-manipulation. The tapered cones reached muddy water and settled in. Abruptly, the flipper legs that seemed awkward on the ramp propelled them with uncanny speed toward the two survivors.

"But ain't traekis s'posed to be peaceful?"

They are, Dwer thought, wishing he had paid more attention to the lessons his mother used to give Sara and Lark. Readings from obscure books that went beyond what you were taught in school. He reached back for a name, but came up empty. Yet he knew a name existed. One that inspired fear, once-upon-a-time.

"I don't—" he whispered, then shook his head firmly. "I don't think these are traeki. At least not like anyone's seen here in a very long while."

Alvin

THE SCENE WAS HARD TO INTERPRET AT FIRST. HAZY blue-green images jerked rapidly, sending shivers down my still-unsteady spine. Huck and Pincer seemed to catch on more quickly, pointing at various objects in the picture display, sharing knowing grunts. The experience reminded me of our trip on *Wuphon's Dream,* when poor Alvin the Hoon was always the last one to grok what was going on.

Finally, I realized—we were viewing a faraway locale, back in the world of sunshine and rain!

(How many times have Huck and I read about some storybook character looking at a distant place by remote control? It's funny. A concept can be familiar from novels, yet rouse awe when you finally encounter it in real life.)

Daylight streamed through watery shallows where green fronds waved in a gentle tide. Schools of flicking, silvery shapes darted past—species that our fishermen brought home in nets, destined for the drying racks and stewpots of hoonish khutas.

The spinning voice said there were sound "pickups" next to the moving camera lens, which explained the swishing, gurgling noises. Pincer shifted his carapace, whistling a homesick lament from all five vents, nostalgic for the tidal pens of his red qheuen rookery. But Ur-ronn soon had quite enough, turning her sleek head with a queasy whine, made ill by the sight of all that swishing water.

Slanting upward, the surf grew briefly violent. Then water fled the camera's eye in foamy sheets as our viewpoint emerged onto a low sandscape. The remote unit scurried inland, low to the ground.

"Normally, we would send a drone ashore at night. But the matter is urgent. We must count on the land's hot glare to mask its emergence."

Ur-ronn let out a sigh, relieved to see no more liquid turbulence.

"It forces one to wonder," she said, "why you have not sent sleuthy agents vefore."

"In fact several were dispatched to seek signs of civilization. Two are long overdue, but others reported startling scenes."

"Such as?" Huck asked.

"Such as hoon mariners, crewing wooden sailing ships on the high seas."

"Hr-rr . . . What's strange about that?"

"And red qheuens, living unsupervised by grays or blues, beholden to no one, trading peacefully with their hoonish neighbors."

Pincer huffed and vented, but the voice continued.

"Intrigued, we sent a submarine expedition beyond the Rift. Our explorers followed one of your dross ships, collecting samples from its sacred discharge. Then, returning to base, our scout vessel happened on the urrish 'cache' you were sent to recover. Naturally, we assumed the original owners must be extinct."

"Oh?" Ur-ronn asked, archly. "Why is that?"

"Because we had seen living hoon! Who would conceive of urs and hoon cohabiting peacefully within a shared volume less broad than a cubic parsec? If hoon lived, we assumed all urs on Jijo must have died."

"Oh," Ur-ronn commented, turning her long neck to glare at me.

"Imagine our surprise when a crude vessel plummeted toward our submarine. A hollowed-out tree trunk containing—"

The voice cut off. The remote unit was in motion again. We edged forward as the camera eye skittered across sand mixed with scrubby vegetation.

"Hey," Ur-ronn objected. "I thought you couldn't use radio or anything that can ve detected from sface!"

"Correct."

"Then how are you getting these fictures in real tine?"

"An excellent question, coming from one with no direct experience in such matters. In this case, the drone needs only to travel a kilometer or so ashore. It can deploy a fiber cable, conveying images undetectably."

I twitched. Something in the words just spoken jarred me, in an eerie-familiar way.

"Does it have to do with the *exflosions?*" Ur-ronn asked. "The recent attack on this site vy those who would destroy you?"

The spinning shape contracted, then expanded.

"You four truly are quick and imaginative. It has been an unusual experience conversing with you. And I was created to appreciate unusual experiences."

"In other words, yes," Huck said gruffly.

"Some time ago, a flying machine began sifting this sea with tentacles of sound. Hours later, it switched to dropping depth charges in a clear effort to dislodge us from our mound of concealing wreckage.

"Matters were growing dire when gravitic fields of a second craft entered the area. We picked up rhythms of aerial combat. Missiles and deadly rays were exchanged in a brief, desperate struggle."

Pincer rocked from foot to foot. "Gosh-osh-osh!" he sighed, ruining our pose of nonchalance.

"Then both vessels abruptly stopped flying. Their inertial signatures ceased close to the drone's present location."

"How close?" Ur-ronn asked.

"Very close," the voice replied.

Transfixed, we watched a hypnotic scene of rapid motion. An ankle-high panorama of scrubby plants, whipping past with blurry speed. The camera eye dodged clumps of saber fronds, skittering with frantic speed, as the drone sought height overlooking a vast marshy fen.

All at once, a glint of silver! *Two* glints. Curving flanks of—

That was when it happened.

Without warning, just as we had our first thrilling glimpse of crashed flyships, the screen was abruptly filled by a grinning *face*.

We rocked back, shouting in surprise. I recoiled so fast, even the high-tech back brace could not save my spine from surging pain. Huphu's claws dug in my shoulder as she trilled an amazed cry.

The face bared a glittering, gleeful display of pointy teeth. Black, beady eyes stared at us, inanely magnified, so full of feral amusement that we all groaned with recognition.

Our tiny drone pitched, trying to escape, but the grinning demon held it firmly with both forepaws. The creature raised sharp claws, preparing to strike.

The spinning voice spoke then—a sound that flew out, then came back to us through the drone's tiny pickups. There were just three words, in a queerly accented form of GalSeven, very high-pitched, almost beyond a hoon's range.

"Brother," the voice said quickly to the strange noor.

"Please stop."

Ewasx

WORD COMES THAT WE HAVE LOST TRACK OF A COR-vette!

Our light cruiser sent to pursue an aircraft of the Rothen bandits.

Trouble was not anticipated in such a routine chore. It raises disturbing questions. Might we have underestimated the prowess of this brigand band?

You, our second ring-of-cognition—you provide access to many memories and thoughts once accumulated by our stack, before I joined to become your master ring. Memories from a time when *we/you* were merely *Asx*.

You recall hearing the human gene thieves making preposterous claims. For instance, that their patrons—these mysterious "Rothen"—are unknown to Galactic society at large. That the Rothen wield strong influence in hidden ways. That they scarcely fear the mighty battle fleets of the great clans of the Five Galaxies.

We of the battleship *Polkjhy* heard similar tall tales before arriving at this world. We took it all for mere bluff. A pathetic cover story, attempting futilely to hide the outlaws' true identity.

BUT WHAT IF THE STORY IS TRUE?

No one can doubt that mysterious forces do exist—ancient, aloof, influential. Might we have crossed fates with some cryptic power, here in an abandoned galaxy, far from home?

OR TAKE THE IDEA MORE BROADLY. Might such a puissant race of cloaked ones stand secretly behind all Terrans, guiding their destiny? Protecting them against the fate that generally befalls wolfling breeds? It would explain much strangeness in recent events. It could also bode ill for our Obeyer Alliance, in these dangerous times.

BUT NO! Facts do not support that fear.

You primitive, rustic rings would not know this, so let Me explain.

NOT LONG AGO, the *Polkjhy* was contacted by certain

petty data merchants, unscrupulous vermin offering news for sale. Through human agents, these "Rothen" approached us—the great and devout Jophur—because our ship happened to be on search patrol nearby. Also, they calculated Jophur would pay twice as much for the information they wanted to sell.

—ONCE for clues to find the main quarry we seek, a missing Earth vessel that ten thousand ships have pursued for years, as great a prize as any in the Five Galaxies—

—AND A SECOND TIME for information about the ancestor-cursed g'Kek, a surviving remnant who took refuge here many planet cycles ago, thwarting our righteous, extinguishing wrath.

The Rothen and their henchmen hoped to reap handsome profit by selling us this information, added to whatever genetic scraps they might steal from this unripe world. The arrangement must have seemed ideal to them, for both sides would be well advised to keep the transaction secret forever.

Is *that* the behavior of some great, exalted power? One risen above trivial mortal concerns?

Would deity-level beings have been so rudely surprised by local savages, who vanquished their buried station with mere chemical explosives?

Did they prove so mighty when we turned our rings around half circle in an act of pious betrayal, and pounced upon their ship? Freezing it in stasis by means of a not-unclever trick?

No, this cannot be a reasonable line of inquiry, My rings. It worries me that you would waste our combined mental resources pursuing a blind pathway.

This digression—IS IT YET ANOTHER VAIN EFFORT TO DISTRACT ME FROM THE NARROWNESS OF PURPOSE THAT IS MY PRINCIPAL CONTRIBUTION TO THE STACK?

Is that also why some of you keep trying to tune in so-called guidance patterns from that silly rock you call a "Holy Egg"?

Are these vague, disjointed efforts aimed at yet another rebellion?

HAVE YOU NOT YET LEARNED?

Shall I demonstrate, once again, why the Oailie made My kind, and named us "master rings"?

LET US drop these silly cogitations and consider alternative explanations for the disappearance of the corvette. Perhaps, when our crew hunted down the scout boat of the Rothen, they stumbled onto something else instead?

Something more powerful and important, by far?

. . . ?

Is this true? You truly have no idea what I am hinting at?

Not even a clue? Why, most of the inhabitants of the Five Galaxies—even the enigmatic Zang—know of the ship we seek. A vessel pursued by half the armadas in known space.

You have indeed lived in isolation, My rustic rings! My primitive subselves. My temporary pretties, who have not heard of a ship crewed by half-animal dolphins.

How very strange indeed.

Sara

WITHOUT DARK GLASSES PROVIDED BY THE HORSE-riding Illias, Sara feared she might go blind or insane. A few stray glints were enough to stab her nerves with unnatural colors, cooing for attention, shouting dangerously, begging her to remove the coverings, to stare . . . perhaps losing herself in a world of shifted light.

Even in sepia tones, the surrounding bluffs seemed laden with cryptic meaning. Sara recalled how legendary Odysseus, sailing near the fabled Sirens, ordered his men to fill their ears with wax, then lashed himself to the mast so he alone might hear the temptresses' call, while the crew rowed frantically past bright, alluring shoals.

Would it hurt to take the glasses off and stare at the rippled landscape? If transfixed, wouldn't her friends rescue her? Or might her mind be forever absorbed by the panorama?

People seldom mentioned the Spectral Flow—a blind spot on maps of the Slope. Even those hardy men who roamed the sharp-sand desert, spearing roul shamblers beneath the hollow dunes, kept awed distance from this poison landscape. A realm supposedly bereft of life.

Only now Sara recalled a day almost two years ago, when her mother lay dying in the house near the paper mill, with the Dolo waterwheel groaning a low background lament. From outside Melina's sickroom, Sara overheard Dwer discussing this place in a low voice.

Of course her younger brother was specially licensed to patrol the Slope and beyond, seeking violations of the Covenant and Scrolls. It surprised Sara only a little to learn he had visited the toxic land of psychotic colors. But from snippets wafting through the open door, it sounded as if *Melina* had also seen the Spectral Flow—before coming north to marry Nelo and raise a family by the quiet green Roney. The conversation had been in hushed tones of deathbed confidentiality, and Dwer never spoke of it after.

Above all, Sara was moved by the wistful tone of her dying mother's voice.

"Dwer . . . remind me again about the colors. . . ."

The horses did not seem to need eye protections, and the two drivers wore theirs lackadaisically, as to stave off a well-known irritation rather than dire peril. Relieved to be out of the Buyur tunnel, Kepha murmured to Nuli, sharing the first laughter Sara had heard from any Illias.

She found her thoughts more coherent now, with surprise giving way to curiosity. *What about people and races who are naturally color-blind?* The effect must involve more than mere frequency variations on the electromagnetic spectrum, as the urrish glasses probably did more than merely darken. There must be some other effect. Light polarization? Or *psi?*

Emerson's rewq satisfied his own need for goggles. But Sara felt concern when he peeled back the filmy symbiont to take an unprotected peek. He *winced,* visibly recoiling from sensory overflow, as if a hoonish grooming fork had plunged into his eye. She started toward him—but that initial reaction was brief. A moment later the starman grinned at her, an expression of agonized delight.

Well, anything you can do—she thought, nudging her glasses forward. . . .

Her first surprise was the pain that wasn't. Her irises adjusted, so the sheer volume of illumination was bearable.

Rather, Sara felt waves of nausea as the world seemed to shift and dissolve . . . as if she were peering through layer after layer of overlapping images.

The land's mundane topography was a terrain of layered lava flows, eroded canyons, and jutting mesas. Only now that seemed only the blank tapestry screen on which some mad g'Kek artist had embroidered an apparition in luminous paint and textured thread. Each time Sara blinked, her impressions shifted.

—Towering buttes were *fairy castles,* their fluttering pennants made of glowing shreds of windblown haze. . . .

—Dusty basins became shimmering pools. Rivers of mercury and currents of blood seemed to flow uphill as merging swirls of immiscible fluid. . . .

—Rippling like memory, a nearby cliff recalled Buyur architecture—the spires of Tarek Town—only with blank windows replaced by a million splendid glowing lights. . . .

—Her gaze shifted to the dusty road, with pumice flying from the wagon wheels. But on another plane it seemed the spray made up countless glittering stars. . . .

—Then the trail crested a small hill, revealing the most unlikely mirage of all . . . several narrow, fingerlike valleys, each surrounded by steep hills like ocean waves, frozen in their spuming torrent. Underneath those sheltering heights, the valley bottoms appeared verdant *green,* covered with impossible meadows and preposterous trees.

"Xi," announced Kepha, murmuring happily in that accent Sara found eerily strange-familiar . . .

. . . and she abruptly knew why!

Surprise made Sara release the glasses, dropping them back over her eyes.

The castles and stars vanished . . .

. . . *but the meadows remained.* Four-footed shapes

could be seen grazing on real grass, drinking from a very real stream.

Kurt and Jomah sighed. Emerson laughed and Prity clapped her hands. But Sara was too astonished to utter a sound. For now she knew the truth about Melina the Southerner, the woman who long ago came to the Roney, supposedly from the far-off Vale, to become Nelo's bride. Melina the happy eccentric, who raised three unusual children by the ceaseless drone of Dolo Dam.

Mother . . . Sara thought, in numb amazement. *This must have been your home.*

The rest of the horsewomen arrived a few miduras later with their urrish companions, dirty and tired. The Illias unsaddled their faithful beasts before stripping off their riding gear and plunging into a warm volcanic spring, beneath jutting rocks where Sara and the other visitors rested.

Watching Emerson, Sara verified that one more portion of his battered brain must be intact, for the spaceman's eyes tracked the riders' nude femininity with normal male appreciation.

She squelched a jealous pang, knowing that her own form could never compete with those tanned, athletic figures below.

The starman glanced Sara's way and flushed several shades darker, so sheepishly rueful that she had to laugh out loud.

"Look, but don't touch," she said, with an exaggerated waggle of one finger. He might not grasp every word, but the affectionate admonishment got through.

Grinning, he shrugged as if to say, *Who, me? I wouldn't think of it!*

The wagon passengers had already bathed, though more modestly. Not that nakedness was taboo elsewhere on the Slope. But the Illias women behaved as if they did not know—or care—about the simplest fact all human girls were taught about the opposite sex. That male *Homo sapiens* have primitive arousal responses inextricably bound up in their optic nerves.

Perhaps it's because they have no men, Sara thought.

Indeed, she saw only female youths and adults, tending chores amid the barns and shelters. There were also urs, of Ulashtu's friendly tribe, tending their precious simla and donkey herds at the fringes of the oasis. The two sapient races did not avoid each other—Sara glimpsed friendly encounters. But in this narrow realm, each had its favored terrain.

Ulashtu knew Kurt, and must have spent time in the outer Slope. In fact, some Illias women also probably went forth, now and then, moving among unsuspecting villagers of the Six Races.

Melina had a good cover story when she came to Dolo, arriving with letters of introduction, and baby Lark on her hip. Everyone assumed she came from somewhere in the Vale. A typical arranged remarriage.

It never seemed an issue to Nelo, that his eldest son had an unknown father. Melina subtly discouraged inquiries into her past.

But a secret like this . . .

With Ulashtu's band came a prisoner. *Ulgor,* the urrish tinker who befriended Sara back at Dolo, only to spring a trap, leading to captivity by Dedinger's fanatics and the reborn Urunthai. Now their roles were reversed. Sara noted Ulgor's triplet eyes staring in dismay at the astonishing oasis.

How the Urunthai would hate this place! Their predecessors seized our horses to destroy them all. Urrish sages later apologized, after Drake the Elder broke the Urunthai. But how can you undo death?

You cannot. But it is possible to *cheat* extinction. Watching fillies and colts gambol after their mares below a bright rocky overhang, Sara felt almost happy for a time. This oasis might even remain unseen by omniscient spy eyes of alien star lords, confused by the enclosing land of illusion. Perhaps Xi would survive when the rest of the Slope was made void of sapient life.

She saw Ulgor ushered to a pen near the desert prophet, Dedinger. The two did not speak.

Beyond the women splashing in the pool and the grazing herds, Sara had only to lift her eyes in order to brush a glittering landscape where each ripple and knoll pretended to be a thousand impossible things. *The country of lies* was a name for the Spectral Flow. No doubt a person got used to it, blanking out irritating chimeras that never proved useful or informative. Or else, perhaps the Illias had no need of dreams, since they lived each day awash in Jijo's fantasies.

The scientist in Sara wondered why it equally affected all races, or how such a marvel could arise naturally. *There's no mention of anything like it in Biblos. But humans only had a sprinkling of Galactic reference material when the* Tabernacle *left Earth. Perhaps this is a common phenomenon, found on many worlds.*

But how much more wonderful if Jijo had made something unique!

She stared at the horizon, letting her mind free-associate shapes out of the shimmering colors, until a mellow female voice broke in.

"You have your mother's eyes, Sara."

She blinked, drawing back to find two humans nearby, dressed in the leather garments of Illias. The one who had spoken was the first elderly woman Sara had seen here.

The other was a *man.*

Sara stood up, blinking in recognition. "F-Fallon?"

He had aged since serving as Dwer's tutor in the wilderness arts. Still, the former chief scout seemed robust, and smiled broadly.

A little tactlessly, she blurted, "But I thought you were dead!"

He shrugged. "People assume what they like. I never said I'd died."

A Zen koan if she ever heard one. But then Sara recalled what the other person said. Though shaded against the desert's glow, the old woman seemed to partake of the hues of the Spectral Flow.

"My name is Foruni," she told Sara. "I am senior rider."

"You knew my mother?"

The older woman took Sara's hand. Her manner reminded Sara of Ariana Foo.

"Melina was my cousin. I've missed her, these many years—though infrequent letters told us of her remarkable children. You three validate her choice, though exile must not have been easy. Our horses and shadows are hard to leave behind."

"Did Mother leave because of Lark?"

"We have ways of making it likely to bear girls. When a boy is born we foster him to discreet friends on the Slope, taking a female child in trade."

Sara nodded. Exchange fostering was a common practice, helping cement alliances between villages or clans.

"But Mother wouldn't give Lark up."

"Just so. In any event, we need agents out there, and Melina was dependable. So it was done, and the decision proved right . . . although we mourned, on hearing of her loss."

Sara accepted this with a nod.

"What I don't understand is why only women?"

The elder had deep lines at the corners of her eyes, from a lifetime of squinting.

"It was required in the pact, when the aunties of *Urchachkin* tribe offered some humans and horses shelter in their most secret place, to preserve them against the Urunthai. In those early days, urs found our menfolk disquieting—so strong and boisterous, unlike their own husbands. It seemed simpler to arrange things on a female-to-female basis.

"Also, a certain fraction of boys tend to shrug off social constraints during adolescence, no matter how carefully they are raised. Eventually, some young man would have burst from the Illias realm without adequate preparation— and all it would take is one. In his need to preen and make a name, he might spill our secret to the Commons at large."

"Girls act that way, too, sometimes," Sara pointed out.

"Yes, but our odds were better this way. Ponder the young men you know, Sara. Imagine how they would have behaved."

She pictured her brothers, growing up in this narrow oasis. Lark would have been sober and reliable. But Dwer, at fifteen, was very different than he became at twenty.

"And yet, I see you aren't all women. . . ."

The senior rider grinned. "Nor are we celibates. From time to time we bring in mature males—often chief scouts, sages, or explorers—men who already know our secret, and are of an age to be calm, sensible companions . . . yet still retain vigor in their step."

Fallon laughed to cover brief embarrassment. "My *step* is no longer my best feature."

Foruni squeezed his arm. "You'll do for a while yet."

Sara nodded. "An urrish-sounding solution." Sometimes a group of young urs, lacking the means to support individual husbands, would share one, passing him from pouch to pouch.

The senior rider nodded, expressing subtleties of irony with languid motions of her neck. "After many generations, we may have become more than a bit urrish ourselves."

Sara glanced toward Kurt the Exploser, sitting on a smooth rock studying carefully guarded texts, with both Jomah and Prity lounging nearby.

"Then you sent the expedition to fetch Kurt because you want another—"

"Ifni, no! Kurt is much too old for such duties, and when we do bring in new partners it is with quiet discretion. Hasn't Kurt explained to you what this is all about? His role in the present crisis? The reason why we gambled so much to fetch you all?"

When Sara shook her head, Foruni's nostrils flared and she hissed like an urrish auntie, perplexed by foolish juniors.

"Well, that's his affair. All I know is that we must escort you the rest of the way as soon as possible. You'll rest with us tonight, my niece. But alas, family reminiscence must wait till the emergency passes . . . or once it overwhelms us all."

Sara nodded, resigned to more hard riding.

"From here . . . can we see—?"

Fallon nodded, a gentle smile on his creased features.

"I'll show you, Sara. It's not far."

She took his arm as Foruni bade them return soon for a feast. Already Sara's nose filled with scents from the cook-fire. But soon her thoughts were on the path as they crossed narrow, miraculous meadows, then scrublands where simlas grazed, and beyond to a steepening pass wedged between two hills. Sunlight was fading rapidly, and soon the smallest moon, Passen, could be seen gleaming near the far west horizon.

She heard *music* before they crested the pass. The familiar sound of Emerson's dulcimer, pinging softly ahead. Sara was loath to interrupt, yet the glow drew her—a shimmering lambency rising from Jijo, filling a vista beyond the sheltered oasis.

The layered terrain seemed transformed in pearly moonlight. Gone were the garish colors, yet there remained an extravagant effect on the imagination. It took an effort of will in order not to go gliding across the slopes, believing in false oceans and battlements, in ghost cities and starscapes, in myriad phantom worlds that her pattern-gleaning brain crafted out of opal rays and shadows.

Fallon took Sara's elbow, turning her toward Emerson.

The starman stood on a rocky eminence with the dulcimer propped before him, beating its forty-six strings. The melody was eerie. The rhythm orderly, yet impossible to constrain, like a mathematical series that refused to converge.

Emerson's silhouette was framed by flickering *fire* as he played for nature's maelstrom.

This fire was no imagining—no artifact of an easily fooled eye. It rippled and twisted in the far distance, rimming the broad curves of a mighty peak that reared halfway up the sky.

Fresh lava.

Jijo's hot blood.

The planet's nectar of renewal, melted and reforged.

Hammering taut strings, the Stranger played for Mount Guenn, serenading the volcano while it repaid him with a halo of purifying flame.

PART FIVE

A PROPOSAL FOR A USEFUL TOOL/STRATEGY BASED ON OUR EXPERIENCE ON JIJO

IT HAS BEEN NEARLY A MILLENNIUM SINCE A LARGE OUTBREAK OF TRAEKINESS WAS FOUND.

These flare-ups used to be frequent embarrassments, where stacks of hapless rings were found languishing without even a single master torus to guide them. But no word of such an occurrence has come within the memory of living wax.

The reaction of our *Polkjhy* ship to this discovery on Jijo was disgusted loathing.

HOWEVER, LET US NOW PAUSE, and consider how the Great Jophur League might learn/benefit from this experiment. Never before have cousin rings dwelled in such intimacy with other races. Although polluted/contaminated, these traeki have also acquired waxy expertise about urs, hoon, and qheuen sapient life-forms—as well as human wolflings and g'Kek vermin.

MOREOVER, the very traits that we Jophur find repellent in traeki-natural rings—their lack of focus, self, or ambition—appear to enable them to achieve empathy with unitary beings! The other five races of Jijo *trust* these ring stacks. They confide secrets, share confidences, delegate some traekis with medical tasks and even powers of life continuation/cessation.

IMAGINE THIS POSSIBILITY. SUPPOSE WE ATTEMPT A RUSE.

INTENTIONALLY, we might create new traeki and arrange for them to "escape" the loving embrace of our noble clan. Genuinely believing they are in flight from "oppressive" master rings, these stacks would be induced to seek shelter among some of the races we call enemies.

Next suppose that, using this knack of vacuous empathy, they make friendships among our foes. As generations pass, they become trusted comrades.

At which point we arrange for agents to snatch—to harvest—some of these rogue traeki, converting them to Jophur exactly as we did when Asx was transformed into Ewasx, by applying the needed master rings.

Would this not give us quick expertise about our foes?

GRANTED, this Ewasx experiment has not been a complete success. The old traeki, Asx, managed to melt many waxy memories before completion of metamorphosis. The resulting partial amnesia has proved inconvenient.

Yet, this does not detract from the value of the scheme—to plant empathic spies in our enemies' midst. Spies who are believable because they think they are true friends! Nevertheless, with the boon of master rings, we can reclaim lost brethren wherever and whenever we find them.

Streakers

Makanee

THERE WERE TWO KINDS OF PUPILS IN THE WIDE, wet classroom.

One group signified hope—the other, despair.

One was illegal—the other, hapless.

The first type was innocent and eager.

The second had already seen and heard far too much.

> # good fish . . .
>   # goodfish, goodfish . . .
> # good-good FISH! #

Dr. Makanee never used to hear Primal Delphin spoken aboard the *Streaker*. Not when the *keeneenk* master, Creideiki, used to hold the crew rock steady by his unwavering example.

Nowadays, alas, one commonly picked up snatches of old-speech—the simple, emotive squealing used by unaltered Tursiops in Earth's ancient seas. As ship physician, even Makanee sometimes found herself grunting a snatch phrase, when frustrations crowded in from all sides . . . and when no one was listening.

Makanee gazed across a broad chamber, half-filled with water, as students jostled near a big tank at the spinward end, avid to be fed. There were almost thirty neo-dolphins, plus a dozen six-armed, monkeylike figures, scrambling up the shelf-lined walls, or else diving to swim agilely with webbed hands. Just half the original group of *Kiqui* survived since they were snatched hastily from far-off Kithrup, but the remaining contingent seemed healthy and glad to frolic with their dolphin friends.

I'm still not sure we did the right thing, taking them along. Neo-dolphins are much too young to take on the responsibilities of patronhood.

A pair of teachers tried bringing order to the unruly mob. Makanee saw the younger instructor—her former head nurse, *Peepoe*—use a whirring harness arm to snatch living snacks from the tank and toss them to the waiting crowd of pupils. The one who uttered the Primal burst—a middle-aged dolphin with listless eyes—smacked his jaw around a blue thing with writhing tendrils that looked nothing like a fish. Still, the fin crooned happily while he munched.

Goodfish . . . good-good-good!

Makanee had known poor Jecajeca before *Streaker* launched from Earth—a former astrophotographer who loved his cameras and the glittering black of space. Now Jecajeca was another casualty of *Streaker*'s long retreat, fleeing ever farther from the warm oceans they called home.

This voyage was supposed to last six months, not two and a half years, with no end in sight. A young client race shouldn't confront the challenges we have, almost alone.

Taken in that light, it seemed a wonder just a quarter of the crew had fallen to devolution psychosis.

Give it time, Makanee. You may yet travel that road yourself.

· · · ·

"Yes, they *are* tasty, Jecajeca," Peepoe crooned, turning the reverted dolphin's outburst into a lesson. "Can you tell me, *in Anglic,* where this new variety of 'fish' comes from?"

Eager grunts and squeaks came from the brighter half of the class, those with a future. But Peepoe stroked the older dolphin with sonar encouragement, and soon Jecajeca's glazed eye cleared a bit. To please her, he concentrated.

"F-f-rom   out-side . . . Good   s-s-sun . . . good wat-t-ter . . ."

Other students offered raspberry cheers, rewarding this short climb back toward what he once had been. But it was a slippery hill. Nor was there much a doctor could do. The cause lay in no organic fault.

Reversion is the ultimate sanctuary from worry.

Makanee approved of the decision of Lieutenant Tsh't and Gillian Baskin, not to release the journal of Alvin the Hoon to the crew at large.

If there's one thing the crew don't need right now, it's to hear of a religion preaching that it's okay to devolve.

Peepoe finished feeding the reverted adults, while her partner took care of the children and Kiqui. On spying Makanee, she did an agile flip and swam across the chamber in two powerful fluke strokes, resurfacing amid a burst of spray.

"Yesss, Doctor? You want to see me?"

Who *wouldn't* want to see Peepoe? Her skin shone with youthful luster, and her good spirits never flagged, not even when the crew had to flee Kithrup, abandoning so many friends.

"We need a qualified nurse for a mission. A long one, I'm afraid."

Ratcheting clicks spread from Peepoe's brow as she pondered.

"Kaa's outpost. Is someone hurt-t?"

"I'm not sure. It may be food poisoning . . . or else kingree fever."

Peepoe's worried expression eased. "In that case, can't Kaa take care of it himself? I have duties here."

"Olachan can handle things while you are away."

Peepoe shook her head, a human gesture by now so ingrained that even reverted fins used it. "There must be two teachers. We can't mix the children and Kiqui with the hapless ones too much."

Just five dolphin infants had been born to crew members so far, despite a growing number of signatures on the irksome *Breeding Petition*. But those five youngsters deserved careful guidance. And that counted double for the Kiqui—presentients who appeared ripe for uplift by some lucky Galactic clan who won the right to adopt them. That laid a heavy moral burden on the *Streaker* crew.

"I'll keep a personal eye on the Kiqui . . . and we'll free the kids' parents from duty on a rotating basis, to join the crèche as teachers' aidesss. That's the best I can do, Peepoe."

The younger dolphin acquiesced, but grumbled. "This'll turn out to be a wild tuna chase. Knowing Kaa, he prob'ly forgot to clean the water filters."

Everyone knew the pilot had a long-standing yearning for Peepoe. Dolphins could sonar-scan each other's innards, so there was no concealing simple, persistent passions.

Poor Kaa. No wonder he lost his nickname.

"There is a second reason you're going," Makanee revealed in a low voice.

"I thought so. Does it have to do with gravitic signals and depth bombsss?"

"This hideout is jeopardized," Makanee affirmed. "Gillian and Tsh't plan to move *Streaker* soon."

"You want me to help find another refuge? By scanning more of these huge junk piles, along the way?" Peepoe blew a sigh. "What else? Shall I compose a symphony, invent a star drive, and dicker treaties with the natives while I'm at it?"

Makanee chuttered. "By all accounts, the sunlit sea above is the most pleasant we've encountered since departing Calafia. Everyone will envy you."

When Peepoe snorted dubiously, Makanee added in Trinary—

> *Legends told by whales*
>   *Call one trait admirable—*
>   *Adaptability! **

This time, Peepoe laughed appreciatively. It was the sort of thing Captain Creideiki might have said, if he were still around.

Back in sick bay, Makanee finished treating her last patient and closed shop for the day. There had been the usual psychosomatic ailments, and inevitable accidental injuries from working outside in armored suits, bending and welding metal under a mountainous heap of discarded ships. At least the number of digestive complaints had gone down since teams with nets began harvesting native food. Jijo's upper sea teemed with life, much of it wholesome, if properly supplemented. Tsh't had even been preparing to allow liberty parties outside . . . before sensors picked up starships entering orbit.

Was it pursuit? More angry fleets chasing *Streaker* for her secrets? No one should have been able to trace Gillian's sneaky path by a nearby supergiant whose sooty winds had disabled the robot guards of the Migration Institute.

But the idea wasn't as original as we hoped. Others came earlier, including a rogue band of humans. I guess we shouldn't be surprised if it occurs to our pursuers, as well.

Makanee's chronometer beeped a reminder. The ship's council—two dolphins, two humans, and a mad computer—was meeting once more to ponder how to thwart an implacable universe.

There was a sixth member who silently attended, offering fresh mixtures of opportunity and disaster at every turn. Without that member's contributions, *Streaker* would have died or been captured long ago.

Or else, without her, we'd all be safe at home.

Either way, there was no escaping her participation.

Ifni, capricious goddess of chance.

Hannes

IT WAS HARD TO GET ANYTHING DONE. DR. BASKIN kept stripping away members of his engine-room gang, assigning them other tasks.

He groused. "It's too soon to give up on *Streaker,* I tell you!"

"I'm not giving her up quite yet," Gillian answered. "But with that carbonite coating weighing the hull down—"

"We've been able to analyze the stuff, at last. It seems the stellar wind blowing off Izmunuti wasn't just atomic or molecular carbon, but a kind of star soot made up of tubes, coils, spheres, and such."

Gillian nodded, as if she had expected this.

"*Buckyballs.* Or in GalTwo—" Pursed lips let out a clicking trill that meant *container home for individual atoms.* "I did some research in the captured Library cube. It seems an interlaced mesh of these microshapes can become superconducting, carrying away vast amounts of heat. You're not going to peel it off easily with any of the tools we have."

"There could be advantages to such stuff."

"The Library says just a few clans have managed to synthesize the material. But what good is it, if it makes the hull heavy and seals our weapons ports so we can't fight?"

Suessi argued that *her* alternative was hardly any better. True, a great heap of ancient starships surrounded them, and they had reactivated the engines of a few. But that was a far cry from finding a fit replacement for the Snark-class survey craft that had served this crew so well.

These are ships the Buyur didn't think worth taking with them, when they evacuated this system!

Above all, how were dolphins supposed to operate a starship that had been built back when humans were learning to chip tools out of flint? *Streaker* was a marvel of clever compromises, redesigned so beings lacking legs or arms could move about and get their jobs done—either striding in six-legged walker units, or by swimming through broad flooded chambers.

Dolphins are crackerjack pilots and specialists. Someday lots of Galactic clans may hire one or two at a time, offering them special facilities as pampered professionals. But few races will ever want a ship like Streaker, *with all the hassles involved.*

Gillian was insistent.

"We've adapted before. Surely some of these old ships have designs we might use."

Before the meeting broke up, he offered one last objection.

"You know, all this fiddling with other engines, as well as our own, may let a trace signal slip out, even through all the water above us."

"I know, Hannes." Her eyes were grim. "But speed is crucial now. Our pursuers already know roughly where we are. They may be otherwise occupied for the moment, but they'll be coming soon. We must prepare to move *Streaker* to another hiding place, or else evacuate to a different ship altogether."

So, with resignation, Suessi juggled staff assignments, stopped work on the hull, and augmented teams sent out to alien wrecks—a task that was both hazardous and fascinating at the same time. Many of the abandoned derelicts seemed more valuable than ships impoverished Earth had purchased through used vessel traders. Under other circumstances, this Midden pile might have been a terrific find.

"Under other circumstances," he muttered. "We'd never have come here in the first place."

Sooners

Emerson

WHAT A WONDERFUL PLACE!

Ever since glorious sunset, he had serenaded the stars and the growling volcano . . . then a crescent of sparkling reflections on the face of the largest moon. Dead cities, abandoned in vacuum long ago.

Now Emerson turns east toward a new day. Immersed in warm fatigue, standing on heights protecting the narrow meadows of Xi, he confronts the raucous invasion of dawn.

Alone.

Even the horse-riding women keep inside their shelters at daybreak, a time when glancing beams from the swollen sun sweep all the colors abandoned by night, pushing them ahead like an overwhelming tide. A wave of speckled light. Bitter-sharp, like shards of broken glass.

His former self might have found it too painful to endure—that logical engineer who always knew what was real, and how to classify it. The clever Emerson, so good at fixing broken things. *That* one might have quailed before the onslaught. A befuddling tempest of hurtful rays.

But now that seems as nothing compared with his other agonies, since crashing on this world. In contrast to having part of his brain ripped out, for instance, the light storm could hardly even be called irritating. It feels more like the claws of fifty mewling kittens, setting his callused skin a-prickle with countless pinpoint scratches.

Emerson spreads his arms wide, opening himself to the enchanted land, whose colors slice through roadblocks in his mind, incinerating barriers, releasing from numb imprisonment a spasm of pent-up images.

Banded canyons shimmer under layer after lustrous layer of strange images. Explosions in space. Half-drowned worlds where bulbous islets glimmer like metal mushrooms. A *house* made of ice that stretches all the way around a glowing red star, turning the sun's wan glow into a hearth's tamed fire.

These and countless other sights waver before him. Each clamors for attention, pretending to be a sincere reflection of the past. But most images are illusions, he knows.

A phalanx of armored damsels brandishes whips of forked lightning against fire-breathing dragons, whose wounds bleed rainbows across the desert floor. Though intrigued, he dismisses such scenes, collaborating with his rewq to edit out the irrelevant, the fantastic, the easy.

What does that leave?

A lot, it seems.

From one nearby lava field, crystal particles reflect tart sunbursts that his eye makes out as vast, distant *explosions*. All sense of scale vanishes as mighty ships die in furious battle before him. Squadrons rip each other. Fleet formations are scythed by moving folds of tortured space.

True!

He knows this to be a real memory. Unforgettable. Too exquisitely horrible to let go, this side of death.

So why was it lost?

Emerson labors to fashion words, using their rare power to lock the recollection back where it belongs.

I . . . saw . . . this . . . happen.

I . . . was . . . there.

He turns for more. Over in *that* direction, amid a simple boulder field, lay a galactic spiral, seen from above the swirling wheel. Viewed from a *shallow place* where few spatial tides ever churn. Mysteries lay in that place, undisturbed by waves of time.

Until someone finally came along, with more curiosity than sense, intruding on the tomblike stillness.

Someone . . . ?

He chooses a better word.

. . . We . . .

Then, a better word, yet.

. . . Streaker!

A slight turn and he sees her, traced among the stony layers of a nearby mesa. A slender caterpillar shape, studded by the spiky flanges meant to anchor a ship to this universe . . . a universe hostile to everything *Streaker* stood for. He stares nostalgically at the vessel. Scarred and patched, often by his own hand, the hull's beauty could only be seen by those who loved her.

. . . loved her . . .

Words have power to shift the mind. He scans the horizon, this time for a human face. One he adored, without hope of anything but friendship in return. But her image isn't found in the dazzling landscape.

Emerson sighs. For now, it is enough to sort through his rediscoveries. A single correlation proves especially useful. If it *hurts,* then it must be a real memory.

What could that fact mean?

The question, all by itself, seems to make his skull crack with pain!

Could that be the intent? To *prevent* him from remembering?

Stabbing sensations assail him. That question is worse! It must never be asked!

Emerson clutches his head as the point is driven home with hammerlike blows.

Never, ever, ever . . .

Rocking back, he lets out a howl. He bays like a wounded animal, sending ululations over rocky outcrops. The sound plummets like a stunned bird . . . then catches itself just short of crashing.

In a steep, swooping turn, it comes streaking back . . . as *laughter!*

Emerson bellows.

He roars contempt.

He brays rebellious joy.

Through streaming tears, he *asks* the question and glories in the answer, knowing at last that he is no coward. His amnesia is no hysterical retreat. No quailing from traumas of the past.

What happened to his mind was no accident.

Hot lead seems to pour down his spine as programmed inhibitions fight back. Emerson's heart pounds, threatening to burst his chest. Yet he scarcely notices, facing the truth head-on, with a kind of brutal elation.

Somebody . . . did . . . this. . . .

Before him, looming from the fractured mesa, comes an image of cold eyes. Pale and milky. Mysterious, ancient, deceitful. It might have been terrifying—to someone with anything left to lose.

Somebody . . . did . . . this . . . to . . . me!

With fists clenched and cheeks awash, Emerson sees the colors melt as his eyes fill with liquid pain. But that does not matter anymore.

Not what he *sees*.

Only what he knows.

The Stranger casts a single cry, merging with the timeless hills.

A shout of defiance.

Ewasx

THEY SHOW COURAGE.

You were right about that, My rings.

We Jophur had not expected anyone to approach so soon after the *Polkjhy* slashed an area of twenty *korech* around our landing site. But now a delegation comes, waving a pale banner.

At first, the symbolism confuses our *Polkjhy* communications staff. But *this* stack's very own association rings relay the appropriate memory of a human tradition—that of using a white flag to signify truce.

WE INFORM THE CAPTAIN LEADER. That exalted stack appears pleased with our service. My rings, you are indeed well informed about vermin! These worthless-seeming toruses, left over from the former Asx, hold waxy expertise about human ways that could prove useful to the Obeyer Alliance, if a prophesied time of change truly has come upon the Five Galaxies.

The Great Library proved frustratingly sparse regarding the small clan from Earth. How ironic then, that we should find proficient knowledge in such a rude, benighted world as this Jijo. Knowledge that may help our goal of extinguishing the wolflings at long last.

What? You quiver at the prospect?

In joyful anticipation of service? In expectation that yet another enemy of our clan shall meet extinction?

No. Instead you shudder, filling our core with mutinous fumes!

My poor, polluted rings. Are you so infested with alien notions that you actually hold *affection* for noisome bipeds? *And* for vermin g'Kek survivors we are sworn to erase?

Perhaps the poison is too rife for you to be suitable, even with useful expertise.

The Oailie were right. Without master rings, all a stack can become is a pile of sentimental traeki.

Lark

THE TALL STAR LORD WAS NO LESS IMPOSING IN A homespun shirt and trousers than in his old black-and-silver uniform. Rann's massive arms and wedgelike torso tempted one to imagine impossible things . . . like pitting him against a fully grown hoon in a wrestling match.

That might take some of the starch out of him, Lark pondered. *There's nothing fundamentally superior about the guy.* Underlying Rann's physique and smug demeanor was the same technology that had given Ling the beauty of a goddess. *I might be just as strong—and live three hundred years—if I weren't born in a forlorn wilderness.*

Rann spoke Anglic in the sharp Danik accent, with burring undertones like his Rothen overlords.

"The favor you ask is both risky and impertinent. Can you offer one good reason why I should cooperate?"

Watched by militia guards, the star lord sat cross-legged in a cave overlooking Dooden Mesa, where camouflaged ramps blended with the surrounding forest under tarpaulins of cunning blur cloth. Beyond the g'Kek settlement, distant ridges seemed to ripple as vast stands of boo bent their giant stems before the wind. In the grotto's immediate vicinity, steam rose from geothermal vents, concealing the captive from Galactic instruments—or so the sages hoped.

Before Rann lay a stack of data lozenges bearing the sigil of the Galactic Library, the same brown slabs Lark and Uthen found in the wrecked Danik station.

"I could give several reasons," Lark growled. "Half the qheuens I know are sick or dying from some filthy bug *you* bastards released—"

Rann waved a dismissive hand.

"Your supposition. One that I deny."

Lark's throat strangled in anger. Despite every point of damning evidence, Rann obstinately rejected the possibility of Rothen-designed genocidal germs. *"What you suggest is quite preposterous,"* he said earlier. *"It is contrary to our lords' kindly natures."*

Lark's first response was amazement. *Kindly nature?* Wasn't Rann present when Bloor, the unlucky portraitist, photographed a Rothen face without its mask, and Rokenn reacted by unleashing fiery death on everyone in sight?

It did Lark no good to recite the same point-by-point indictment he had laid out for Ling. The big man was too contemptuous of anything Jijoan to heed a logical argument.

Or else he was involved all along, and now sees denial as his best defense.

Ling sat miserably on a stalagmite stump, unable to meet her erstwhile leader in the eye. They had come seeking

Rann's help only after she failed to read the reclaimed archives with her own data plaque.

"All right," Lark resumed. "If justice and mercy won't persuade you, maybe threats will!"

Harsh laughter from the big man.

"How many hostages can you spare, young barbarian? You have just three of us to stave off fire from above. Your intimidation lacks conviction."

Lark felt like a bush lemming confronting a ligger. Still, he leaned closer.

"Things have changed, Rann. Before, we hoped to trade you back to the Rothen ship for concessions. Now, that ship and your mates are sealed in a bubble. It's the *Jophur* we'll negotiate with. I suspect they'll care less about visible wear and tear on your person, when we hand you over."

Rann's face was utterly blank. Lark found it an improvement.

Ling broke in.

"Please. This approach is pointless." She stood and approached her Danik colleague. "Rann, we may have to spend the rest of our lives with these people, or share whatever fate the Jophur dish out. A cure may help square things with the Six. Their sages promise to absolve us, if we find a treatment soon."

Rann's silent grimace required no rewq interpretation. He did not savor the absolution of savages.

"Then there are the photograms," Ling said. "You are of the Danik Inner Circle, so you may have seen the true Rothen face before. But I found it a shock. Clearly, those photographic images give Jijo's natives some leverage. In loyalty to our mast . . . to the Rothen, you must consider that."

"And who would they show their pictures to?" Rann chuckled. Then he glanced at Lark and his expression changed. "You would not actually—"

"Hand them over to the Jophur? Why bother? They can crack open your starship any time they wish, and dissect your masters down to their nucleic acids. Face it, Rann, the disguise is no good anymore. The Jophur have their mulch rings wrapped tightly around your overlords."

"Around the beloved patrons of all humanity!"

Lark shrugged. "True or not, that changes nothing. If the Jophur choose, they can have the Rothen declared anathema across the Five Galaxies. The fines may be calamitous."

"And what of your Six Races?" Rann answered hotly. "Each of you are criminals, as well. You all face punishment—not just the humans and others living here, but the home branches of each species, elsewhere in space!"

"Ah." Lark nodded. "But this we have always known. We grow up discussing the dour odds. The guilt. It colors our distinctly pleasant outlook on life." He smiled sardonically. "But I wonder if an *optimistic* fellow like yourself, seeing himself part of a grand destiny, can be as resigned to losing all he knows and loves."

At last, the Danik's expression turned dark.

"Rann," Ling urged. "We have to make common cause."

He glared at her archly. "Without Ro-kenn's approval?"

"They've taken him far away from here. Even Lark doesn't know where. Anyway, I'm now convinced we must consider what's best for humanity . . . for *Earth* . . . independent of the Rothen."

"There cannot be one without the other!"

She shrugged. "Pragmatism, then. If we help these people, perhaps they can do the same for us."

The big man snorted skepticism. But after several duras, he brushed the stack of data lozenges with his toe. "Well, I am curious. These aren't from the station Library. I'd recognize the color glyphs. You already tried to gain access?"

Ling nodded.

"Then maybe I had better have a crack at it."

He looked at Lark again.

"You know the risk, as soon as I turn my reader on?"

Lark nodded. Lester Cambel had already explained. In all probability, the digital cognizance given off by a tiny info unit would be masked by the geysers and microquakes forever popping under the Rimmers.

Yet, to be safe, every founding colony, from g'Keks and glavers to urs and humans, sent their sneakships down to the Midden. Not a single computer was kept. Our ancestors must have thought the danger very real.

"You needn't lecture a sooner about risk," he told the big

man. "Our lives are the floating tumble of Ifni's dice. We know it's not a matter of winning.

"Our aim is to put off losing for as long as we can."

They were brought meals by Jimi, one of the blessed who dwelled in the redemption sanctuary—a cheerful young man, nearly as large as Rann but with a far gentler manner. Jimi also delivered a note from Sage Cambel. The embassy to the Jophur had arrived at Festival Glade, hoping to contact the latest intruders.

The handwritten letter had a coda:

Any progress?

Lark grimaced. He had no way of telling what "progress" meant in this case, though he doubted much was being made.

Ling helped load beige slabs into Rann's data plaque—returned for this purpose. Together, the Daniks puzzled over a maze of sparkling symbols.

Books from pre-*Tabernacle* days described what it was like to range the digital world—a realm of countless dimensions, capabilities, and correlations, where any simulation might take on palpable reality. Of course mere descriptions could not make up for lack of experience. *But I'm not like some fabled islander, befuddled by Captain Cook's rifle and compass. I have concepts, some math, a notion of what's possible.*

At least, he hoped so.

Then he worried—might the Daniks be putting on an act? Pretending to have difficulty while they stalled for time?

There wasn't much left. Soon Uthen would die, then other chitinous friends. Worse, new rumors from the coast told of hoonish villagers snuffling and wheezing, their throat sacs cracking from some strange ailment.

Come on! he urged silently. *What's so hard about using a fancy computer index to look something up?*

Rann threw down a data slab, cursing guttural phonemes of alien argot.

"It's encrypted!"

"I thought so," Ling said. "But I figured you, as a member of the Inner—"

"Even we of the circle are not told everything. Still, I know the outlines of a Rothen code, and this is different." He frowned. "Yet familiar somehow."

"Can you break it?" Lark asked, peering at a maze of floating symbols.

"Not using this crude reader. We'd need something bigger. A real computer."

Ling straightened, looking knowingly at Lark. But she left the decision up to him.

Lark blew air through his cheeks.

"Hr-rm. I think that might be arranged."

A mixed company of militia drilled under nearby trees, looking brave in their fog-striped war paint. Lark saw only a few burly qheuens, though—the five-clawed heavy armor of Jijoan military might.

As one of the few living Jijoans ever to fly aboard an alien aircraft and see their tools firsthand, Lark knew what a fluke the Battle of the Glade had been—where spears, arbalests, and rifles prevailed against star-roaming gods. That freak chance would not be repeated. Still, there were reasons to continue training. *It keeps the volunteers busy, and helps prevent a rekindling of old-time feuds. Whatever happens—whether we submit with bowed heads to final judgment, or go down fighting—we can't afford disunion.*

Lester Cambel greeted them under a tent beside a bubbling hot spring.

"We're taking a risk doing this," the elderly sage said.

"What choice do we have?"

In Lester's eyes, Lark read his answer.

We can let Uthen and countless qheuens die, if that's the price it takes for others to live.

Lark hated being a sage. He loathed the way he was expected to think—contemplating trade-offs that left you damned, either way you turned.

Cambel sighed. "Might as well make the attempt. I doubt the artifact will even turn on."

At a rough log table, Cambel's human and urrish aides

compared several gleaming objects with ancient illustrations. Rann stared in amazement at the articles, which had been carried here from the shore of a far-off caustic lake.

"But I thought you discarded all your digital—"

"We did. Our ancestors did. These items are leftovers. Relics of the Buyur."

"Impossible. The Buyur withdrew half a million years ago!"

Lark told an abbreviated version of the story—about a crazy mulc spider with a collecting fetish. A creature fashioned for destruction, who spent millennia sealing treasures in cocoons of congealed time.

Laboring day and night, traeki alchemists had found a formula to dissolve the golden preservation shells, spilling the contents back into the real world. *Lucky for us these experts happened to be in the area,* Lark thought. The tired-looking traekis stood just outside, venting yellow vapor from chem-synth rings.

Rann stroked one reclaimed object, a black trapezoid, evidently a larger cousin to his portable data plaque.

"The power crystals look negentropic and undamaged. Do you know if it still works?"

Lark shrugged. "You're familiar with the type?"

"Galactic technology is fairly standard, though humans didn't exist, as such, when this thing was made. It is a higher-level model than I've used, but . . ." The sky human sat down before the ancient artifact, pressing one of its jutting bulges.

The device abruptly burst forth streams of light that reached nearly to the canopy. The High Sage and his team scrambled back. Urrish smiths snorted, coiling their long necks while human techs made furtive gestures to ward off evil.

Even among Cambel's personal acolytes—his book-weaned "experts"—our sophistication is thin enough to scratch with a fingernail.

"The Buyur mostly spoke Galactic Three," Rann said. "But GalTwo is close to universal, so we'll try it first."

He switched to that syncopated code, uttering clicks, pops, and groans so rapidly that Lark was soon lost, unable to follow the arcane dialect of computer commands. The star lord's hands also moved, darting among floating images. Ling joined the effort, reaching in to seize ersatz objects that had no meaning to Lark, tossing away any she deemed irrelevant, giving Rann working room. Soon the area was clear but for a set of floating dodecahedrons, with rippling symbols coursing each twelve-sided form.

"The Buyur were good programmers," Rann commented, lapsing into GalSix. *"Though their greatest passion went to biological inventions, they were not slackers in the digital arts."*

Lark glanced at Lester, who had gone to the far end of the table to lay a pyramidal stack of *sensor stones,* like a hill of gleaming opals. Tapping one foot nervously, the sage kept wary vigil, alert for any spark of warning fire.

Turning farther, Lark found the mountain cleft deserted. The militia company had departed.

No one with sense would remain while this is going on.

Rann muttered a curse.

"I had hoped the machine would recognize idiosyncrasies in the encryption, if it is a standard commercial cypher used widely in the Five Galaxies. Or there may be quirks specific to some race or alliance.

"Alas, the computer says it does not recognize the cryptographic approach used in these memory slabs. It calls the coding technique . . . innovative."

Lark knew the term was considered mildly insulting among the great old star clans.

"Could it be a pattern developed since the Buyur left Jijo?"

Rann nodded. "Half an eon is a while, even by Galactic standards."

Ling spoke, eagerly. "Perhaps it's Terran."

The big man stared at her, then nodded, switching to Anglic.

"That might explain the vague familiarity. But why would any Rothen use an Earther code? You know what they think of wolfling technology. Especially anything produced by those unbelieving Terragens—"

"Rann," Ling cut in, her voice grown hushed. "These slabs may not have belonged to Ro-kenn or Ro-pol."

"Who then? You deny ever seeing them before. Neither have I. That leaves . . ."

He blinked, then pounded a heavy fist on the wooden slats. "We must crack this thing! Ling, let us commence unleashing the unit's entire power on finding the key."

Lark stepped forward. "Are you sure that's wise?"

"You seek disease cures for your fellow savages? Well, the Jophur ship squats on the ruins of our station, and our ship is held captive. This may be your only chance."

Clearly, Rann had another reason for his sudden zeal. Still, everyone apparently wanted the same thing—for now.

Lester looked unhappy, but he gave permission with a nod, returning to his vigil over the sensor stones.

We're doing it for you, Uthen, Lark thought.

Moments later, he had to retreat several more steps as space above the prehistoric computer grew crowded. Innumerable glyphs and signs collided like snowflakes in an arctic blizzard. The Buyur machine was applying prodigious force of digital intellect to solving a complex puzzle.

As Rann worked—hands darting in and out of the pirouetting flurry—he wore an expression of simmering rage. The kind of resentful anger that could only come from one source.

Betrayal.

A midura passed before the relic computer announced preliminary results. By then Lester Cambel was worn out. Perspiration stained his tunic and he wheezed each breath. But Lester would let no one else take over watching the sensor stones.

"It takes long training to sense the warning glows," he explained. "Right now, if I relax my eyes in just the right way, I can barely make out a soft glow in a gap between two of the bottommost stones."

Long training? Lark wondered as he peered into the fragile pyramid, quickly making out a faint iridescence, resembling the muted flame that licked the rim of a mulching pan when a dead traeki was boiled, rendering the fatting rings for return to Jijo's cycle.

Cambel went on describing, as if Lark did not already see.

"Someday, if there's time, we'll teach you to perceive the passive resonance, Lark. In this case it is evoked by the Jophur battleship. Its great motors are now idling, forty leagues from here. Unfortunately, even that creates enough background noise to mask any new disturbance."

"Such as?"

"Such as *another* set of gravitic repulsors . . . moving this way."

Lark nodded grimly. Like a rich urrish trader with two husbands in her brood pouches, big starships carried smaller ships—scrappy and swift—to launch on deadly errands. That was the chief risk worrying Lester.

Lark considered going back to watch the two Daniks work, invoking software demons in quest of a mathematical key. But what good would he do staring at the unfathomable? Instead, he bent close to the stones, knowing each flicker to be an echo of titanic forces, like those that drove the sun.

For a time he sensed no more than that soft bluish flame. But then Lark began noticing another rhythm, matching the mute shimmer, beat by beat. The source throbbed near his rib cage, above his pounding heart.

He slid a hand into his tunic and grabbed his amulet—a fragment of the Holy Egg that hung from a leather thong. It was warm. The pulselike cadence seemed to build with each passing dura, causing his arm to vibrate painfully.

What could the Egg have in common with the engines of a Galactic cruiser? Except that both seem bent on troubling me till I die?

From far away, he heard Rann give an angry shout. The big Danik pounded the table, nearly toppling the fragile stones.

Cambel left to find out what Rann had learned. But Lark could not follow. He felt pinned by a rigor that spread from his fist on up his arm. It crossed his chest, then swarmed down his crouched legs.

"Uh-buhnnn . . ."

He tried to speak, but no words came. A kind of paralysis robbed him of the will to move.

Year after year he had striven to achieve what came easily to some pilgrims, when members of all Six Races sought communion with Jijo's gift—the Egg, that enigmatic wonder. To some it gave a blessing—guidance patterns, profound and moving. Consolation for the predicament of exile.

But never to Lark. Never the sinner.

Until now.

But instead of transcendent peace, Lark tasted a bitter tang, like molten metal in his mouth. His eardrums scraped, as if some massive rock were being pushed through a tube much too narrow. Amid his confusion, gaps in the sensor array seemed like the vacuum abyss between planets. The gemstones were moons, brushing each other with ponderous grace.

Before his transfixed eyes, the silken flame grew a minuscule swelling, like a new shoot budding off a rosebush. The new bulge *moved,* detaching from its parent, creeping around the surface of one stone, crossing a gap, then moving gradually upward.

It was subtle. Without the heightened sensitivity of his seizure, Lark might not have noticed.

Something's coming.

But he could only react with a cataleptic gurgle.

Behind Lark came more sounds of fury—Rann throwing a tantrum over some discovery. Figures moved around the outraged alien . . . Lester and the militia guards. No one paid Lark any mind.

Desperately, he sought the place where volition resides. The center of will. The part that commands a foot to step, an eye to shift, a voice to utter words. But his soul seemed captive to the discolored knob of fire, moving languidly this way.

Now that it had his attention, the flicker wasn't about to let him go.

Is this your intent? he asked the Egg, half in prayer and half censure.

You alert me to danger . . . then won't let me cry a warning?

Did another dura pass—or ten?—while the spark drifted around the next stone? With a soft crackle it crossed another gap. How many more must it traverse before reaching the top? What sky-filling shadow would pass above when that happened?

Suddenly, a huge silhouette *did* loom into Lark's field of view. A giant, globelike shape, vast and blurry to his fixed, unfocused gaze.

The intruding object spoke to him.

"Uh . . . Sage Koolhan? . . . You all right, sir?"

Lark mutely urged the intruder closer. *That's it, Jimi. A bit more to the left . . .*

With welcome abruptness, the flame vanished, eclipsed by the round face of Jimi the Blessed—Jimi the Simpleton—wearing a worried expression as he touched Lark's sweat-soaked brow.

"Can I get ya somethin', Sage? A drink o' water mebbe?"

Freed of the hypnotic trap, Lark found volition at last . . . waiting in the same place he always kept it.

"Uhhhh . . ."

Stale air vented as he took gasping breath. Pain erupted up and down his crouched body, but he quashed it, forcing all his will into crafting two simple words.

". . . ever'body . . . out!"

Ewasx

THEY ACT QUICKLY ON THEIR PROMISES, DO THEY not, my rings?

Do you see how soon the natives acquiesced to our demands?

You seem surprised that they moved so swiftly to appease us, but *I* expected it. What other decision was possible, now that their so-called sages understand the way things are?

Like you lesser rings, the purpose of other races is ultimately to obey.

•   •   •

HOW DID THIS COME ABOUT? you ask.

Yes, you have My permission to stroke old-fashioned wax drippings, tracing recent memory. But I shall also re-tell it in the more efficient Oailie way so that we may celebrate together an enterprise well concluded.

WE BEGIN with the arrival of emissaries—one from each of the savage tribes, entering this shattered valley on foot and wheel, shambling like animals over the jagged splinters that surround our proud *Polkjhy*.

Standing bravely beneath the overhanging curve of our gleaming hull, they took turns shouting at the nearest open hatch, making pretty speeches on behalf of their rustic Commons. With surprising eloquence, they cited relevant sections of Galactic law, accepting on behalf of their ancestors full responsibility for their presence on this world, and requesting courteously that we in turn explain *our* purpose coming here.

Are we official inspectors and judges from the Institute of Migration? they asked. And if not, what excuse have *we* for violating this world's peace?

Audacity! Among the crew of the *Polkjhy*, it most upset our junior Priest-Stack, since now we seem obliged to justify ourselves to barbarians.

<<*Why Did We Not Simply Roast This Latest Embassy, Like The One Before It?*>>

To this, our gracious Captain-Leader replied:

<<*It Costs Us Little To Vent Informative Steam In The General Direction Of Half-Devolved Beings. And Do Not Forget That There Are Data Gleanings We Desire, As Well! Recall That The Scoundrel Entities Called* Rothen *Offered To Sell Us Valuable Knowledge, Before We Righteously Double-Crossed Them. Perhaps That Same Knowledge Might Be Wrung From The Locals At A Much Smaller Price, Saving Us The Time And Effort Of A Search.*>>

Did not the junior Priest-Stack then press its argument?

<<*Look Down At The Horrors! Abominations! They Comingle In The Shadow Of Our Great Ship—Urrish Forms Side By Side With Hoons? Poor Misguided Traeki Cousins Standing Close To Wolfling Humans? And There Among Them, Worst Of All . . . G'keks! What Can Be Gained By Talking With Miscegenists? Blast Them Now!*>>

• • •

AH, MY RINGS, would not things be simpler for us/Me, had the Captain-Leader given in, accepting the junior priest's advice? Instead, our exalted commander bent toward the senior Priest-Stack for further consultation.

That august entity stretched upward, a tower of fifty glorious toruses, and declared—

<<*I/We Concede That It Is A Demeaning Task. But It Harms Us Little To Observe The Appropriate Forms And Rituals.*

<<*So Let Us Leave The Chore To Ewasx. Let The Ewasx Stack Converse With These Devolved Savages. Let Ewasx Find Out What They Know About The Two Kinds Of Prey We Seek.*>>

So it was arranged. The job was assigned to this makeshift, hybrid stack. An appointment to be a lowly agent. To parley with half animals.

In this way, I/we learned the low esteem by which our Jophur peers regard us.

BUT NEVER MIND THAT NOW. Do you recall how we took on our apportioned task, with determined aplomb? By gravity plate, we dropped down to the demolished forest, where the six envoys waited. Our ring of association recognized two of them—*Phwhoon-dau,* stroking his white hoonish beard, and *Vubben,* wisest of the g'Kek. This pair shouted surprised gladness at first, believing they beheld a lost comrade—*Asx.*

Then, realizing their mistake, all six quailed, emitting varied noises of dismay. Especially the traeki in their midst—our/your replacement among the High Sages?— who seemed especially upset by our transformation. Oh, how that stack of aboriginal toruses trembled to perceive our Jophurication! Would its segmented union sunder on the spot? Without a master ring to bind and guide them, would the component rings tear their membranes and crawl their separate ways, returning to the feral habits of our ancestors?

Eventually the six representatives recovered enough to

listen. In simple terms, I explained *Polkjhy*'s endeavor in this far-off system.

WE ARE NOT OF THE MIGRATION INSTITUTE, I/we told them, although we did invoke a clause of Galactic law to self-deputize and arrest the Rothen gene raiders. There will be few questions asked by an indifferent cosmos, if/when we render judgment on them . . . *or* on criminal colonists.

To whom will savages appeal?

BUT THAT NEED NOT BE OUR AIM.

This I added, soothingly. There are worse villains to pursue than a hardscrabble pack of castaways, stranded on a forbidden reef, seeking redemption the only way they can.

OUR CHIEF QUEST is for a missing vessel crewed by Earthling *dolphins*. A ship sought by ten thousand fleets, across all Five Galaxies. A ship carrying secrets, and perhaps the key to a new age.

I told the emissaries that we might pay for data, if local inhabitants help shorten our search.

(Yes, My rings—the Captain-Leader also promised to pay those Rothen rascals, when their ship hailed ours in jump space, offering vital clues. But those impatient fools gave away too much in their eagerness. We made vague promises, dispatching them for more proof . . . then covertly followed, before a final deal was signed! Once they led us to this world, what further purpose did they serve? Rather than pay, we seized their ship.

(True, they might have had more data morsels to sell. But if the dolphin ship is in this system, we will find it soon enough.)

(Yes, My rings, our memory core appears to hold no waxy imprints of a "dolphin ship." But others on Jijo might know something. Perhaps they kept data from their traeki sage. Anyway, can we trust memories inherited from Asx, who slyly remelted many core drippings?

(So we must query the Jijoan envoys, using threats and rewards.)

While the emissaries pondered the matter of the dolphin ship, I proceeded to our second requirement. Our goal of long-delayed justice!

YOU MAY FIND THIS ADDITIONAL REQUEST UN-PLEASANT, OR DISLOYAL. BUT YOU HAVE NO CHOICE. YOU MUST BEND TO THE IMPLACABILITY OF OUR WILL. THE SACRIFICE WE DEMAND IS ESSENTIAL. DO NOT THINK OF SHIRKING!

The hoon sage boomed a deep umble, inflating his throat sac. "We are unclear on your meaning. What must we sacrifice?"

To this obvious attempt at dissembling, I replied derisively, adding rippling emphasis shadows across our upper rings.

YOU KNOW WHAT MUST BE GIVEN UP TO US. SOON WE WILL EXPECT A TOKEN PORTION. A DOWN PAYMENT TO SHOW US THAT YOU UNDERSTAND.

With that, I commanded our ring-of-manipulators to aim all our tendrils at the aged g'Kek.

Toward Vubben.

This time, their reactions showed comprehension. Some former Asx rings shared their revulsion, but I clamped down with electric jolts of discipline.

The intimidated barbarians retreated, taking with them the word of heaven.

We did not expect to hear from the agonized sooners for a day or two. Meanwhile, the Captain-Leader chose to send our second corvette east to help the other unit whose self-repairs go too slowly, stranded near a deepwater rift. (A candidate hiding place for the missing Earthling ship!)

Once, we feared that dolphins had shot down our boat, and *Polkjhy* itself must go on this errand. But our tactician stack calculated that the Rothen scout simply got in a lucky shot. It seems safe to dispatch a smaller vessel.

Then, just as our repair craft was about to launch, we

picked up a signal from these very mountains! What else could it be, but the Jijoan envoys, responding to My/our demands!

The corvette was diverted north, toward this new emission.

And lo! Now comes in its report. A g'Kek settlement—a midget *city* of the demon wheels—hidden in the forest!

Oh, we would have found it anyway. Our mapping has only just begun.

Still, this gesture is encouraging. It shows the Six (who will soon be five) possess enough sapient ability to calculate odds, to perceive the inevitable and minimize their losses.

What, My rings? You are surprised? You expected greater solidarity from your vaunted Commons? More loyalty?

Then live and learn, My waxy pretties. This is just the beginning.

Lark

TEARS COVERED THE CHEEKS OF THE AGED HUMAN sage as he ran through the forest.

"It's my fault. . . ." he murmured between gasping breaths. "All my fault . . . I never should've allowed it . . . so near the poor g'Kek. . . ."

Lark heard Cambel's lament as they joined a stampede of refugees, swarming down narrow aisles between colossal shafts of boo. He had to catch Lester when the sage stumbled in grief over what they all had witnessed, only duras ago. Lark caught the eye of a hoonish militiaman with a huge sword slung down his back. The burly warrior swept Lester into his arms, gently hauling the stricken sage to safety.

For those fleeing beneath the boo, that word—*safety*—might never be the same. For two thousand years, the ramparts of Dooden Mesa offered protection to the oldest and weakest sooner race. Yet no defense could stand against the sky cruiser that swept over that sheltered valley, too soon after Lark's shouted warning. Some refugees—those with enough nerve to glance back—would always carry the image of that awful ship, hovering like a predator over the graceful ramps, homes, and workshops.

It must have been drawn by the Buyur computer—by its "digital resonance."

Once over the mountain, the aliens could not help noticing the g'Kek settlement in the valley below.

". . . we were too near the poor g'Kek . . ."

Driven by a need for answers—and a lifelong curiosity about all things Galactic—Cambel had allowed Ling and Rann to drive the machine at full force, deciphering the mystery records. It was like waving a lure above this part of the Rimmers, calling down an ill wind.

Some of those running through the forest seemed less panicky. Fierce-eyed Jeni Shen kept herd on her militia team, so Rann and Ling never had a chance to dodge left or right, slipping away through the boo. As if either Danik had any place to go. Their faces looked as dismayed as anybody's.

Lark's ears still rang from when the Jophur ship cast beams of aching brilliance, tearing apart the frail canopy of blur cloth, laying Dooden Mesa bare under a cruel sun. Teeming wheeled figures scurried futilely, like a colony of hive mites in a collapsed den.

The beams stopped, and something even more dreadful fell from the floating nemesis.

A golden haze. A flood of liquid light.

Lark's nerve had failed him at that point, as he, too, plunged into the boo, fleeing a disaster he had helped wreak.

You aren't alone, Lester. You have company in hell.

Dwer

MUDFOOT SEEMED CRAZIER THAN EVER.

Blinking past a cloud of buzzing gnats, Dwer watched the mad noor crouch over some helpless creature he had caught near the shore, gripping his prey in both forepaws, brandishing sharp teeth toward whatever doomed beast had unluckily strayed within reach. Mudfoot showed no interest in two sooty spaceships that lay crippled, just beyond the dune.

Why should he care? Dwer thought. *Any Galactics who glimpse him will just shrug off another critter of Jijo. Enjoy your meal, Mudfoot. No squatting under hot sand for you!*

Dwer's hidey-hole was intensely uncomfortable. His legs felt cramped and grit eagerly sought every body crevice. Partial shade was offered by his tunic, propped up with two arrows and covered with sand. But he had to share that narrow shelter with Rety—an uncomfortable fit, to say the least. Worse, there was a kind of midge, no larger than a speck, that seemed to find human breath irresistible. One by one, the insectoids drifted upslope to the makeshift cavity where Dwer and Rety exposed their faces for air. The bugs fluttered toward their mouths, inevitably being drawn inside. Rety coughed, spat, and cursed in her Gray Hills dialect, despite Dwer's pleas for silence.

She's not trained for this, he thought, trying for patience. During his apprenticeship, Master Fallon used to leave him in a hunting blind for days on end, then sneak back to observe. For each sound Dwer made, Fallon added another midura, till Dwer learned the value of quiet.

"I wish he'd quit playin' with his food," Rety muttered, glaring downslope at Mudfoot. "Or else, bring some up for us."

Dwer's belly growled agreement. But he told her, "Don't think about it. Try to sleep. We'll see about sneaking away come nightfall."

For once, she seemed willing to take his advice. Sometimes, Rety seemed at her best when things were at their worst.

At this rate, she'll be a saint before it's all over.

He glanced left, toward the swamp. Both alien ships lay grounded in a seaside bog, just two arrowflights away. It made the two humans easy targets if they budged. Nor had he any guarantee this would change at night.

I hear tell that star gods have lenses that pick out a warm body moving in the dark, and other kinds to track metal and tools.

Getting away from here might not be easy, or even possible.

There wasn't much to say for the alternatives. It would have been one thing to surrender to Kunn. As a Danik adoptee, Rety might have swayed the human star pilot to spare Dwer's life. Perhaps.

But the newcomers who shot down Kunn's little scout . . . Dwer felt his hackles rise watching tapered stacks of glistening doughnuts inspect their damaged ship, accompanied by hovering robots.

Why be afraid? They look like traeki, and traeki are harmless, right?

Not when they come swooping from space, throwing lightning.

Dwer wished he had listened more closely to holy services as a child, instead of fidgeting when the Sacred Scrolls were read. Some excerpts had been inserted by the ringed ones, when their sneakship came—passages of warning. Not all stacks of fatty rings were friendly, it seemed. *What was the name they used?* Dwer tried to recall what word stood for a traeki that was no traeki, but he came up blank.

Sometimes he wished he could be more like his brother and sister—able to think deep thoughts, with vast stores of book learning to call upon. Lark or Sara would surely make better use of this time of forced inaction. They would be weighing alternatives, listing possibilities, formulating some plan.

But all I do is doze, thinking about food. Wishing I had some way to scratch.

He wasn't yet desperate enough to walk toward that silver ship with hands raised. Anyway, the aliens and their helpers were still fussing over the smoke-stained hull, making repairs.

As he nodded in a drowsy torpor, he fought down one itch in particular, a prickly sensation *inside* his head. The feeling had grown ever since he first gave the Danik robot a "ride" across a river, using his body to anchor its ground-hugging fields. Each time he collapsed on the opposite bank, waking up had felt like rising from a pit. The effect grew stronger with every crossing.

At least I won't have to do that again. The robot now cowered under a nearby dune, useless and impotent since Kunn's ship was downed and its master taken.

Dwer's sleep was uneasy, disturbed first by a litany of aching twinges, and later by disturbing dreams.

He had *always* dreamed. As a child, Dwer used to jerk upright in the dark, screaming till the entire household roused, from Nelo and Melina down to the lowest chimp and manservant, gathering round to comfort him back to sweet silence. He had no clear memory of what nightmares used to terrify him so, but Dwer still had sleep visions of startling vividness and clarity.

Never worth screaming over, though.

Unless you count One-of-a-Kind.

He recalled the old mulc spider of the acid mountain lake, who spoke words directly in his mind one fateful day, during his first solo scouting trip over the Rimmer Range.

—the mad spider, unlike any other, who tried all kinds of deceit to charm Dwer into its web, there to join its "collection."

—the same spider who nearly caught Dwer that awful night when Rety and her "bird" were trapped in its maze of bitter vines . . . before that vine network exploded in a mortal inferno.

Restlessly, he envisioned living cables, the spider's own body, snaking across a tangled labyrinth, creeping ever nearer, closing an unstoppable snare. From each twisting rope there dripped heavy caustic vapors, or liquors that would freeze your skin numb on contact.

Around Dwer, the sand burrow felt like a ropy spiral of nooses, drawing tight a snug embrace that was both cloying and loving, in a sick-sweet way.

No one else could ever appreciate you as much as I do, crooned the serenely patient call of One-of-a-Kind. *We share a destiny, my precious, my treasure.*

Dwer felt trapped, more by a languor of sleep than by the enveloping sand. He mumbled.

"Yer just . . . my . . . 'magination. . . ."

A crooning, dreamlike laugh, and the mellifluous voice rejoined—

So you always used to claim, though you cautiously evaded my grasp, nonetheless. Until the night I almost had you.

"The night you died!" Dwer answered. The words were a mere rolling of his exhaled breath.

True. But do you honestly think that was an ending?

My kind is very old. I myself had lived half a million years, slowly etching and leaching the hard leavings of the Buyur. Across those ages, thinking long thoughts, would I not learn everything there is to know about mortality?

Dwer realized—all those times he helped the Danik robot cross a stream, conducting its throbbing fields, somehow must have changed him inside. Sensitized him. Or else driven him mad. Either way, it explained this awful dream.

His eyes opened a crack as he tried to waken, but fatigue lay over Dwer like a shroud, and all he managed was to peer through interleaved eyelashes at the swamp below.

Till now, he had always stared at the two alien ships—the larger shaped like a silvery cigar, and the smaller like a bronze arrowhead. But now Dwer regarded the background. The swamp itself, and not the shiny intruders.

They are just dross, my precious. Ignore those passing bits of "made stuff," the brief fancies of ephemeral beings. The planet will absorb them, with some patient help from my kindred.

Distracted by the ships, he had missed the telltale signs. A nearby squarish mound whose symmetry was almost hidden by rank vegetation. A series of depressions, like grooves filled with algae scum, always the same distance apart, one after another, extending into the distance.

It was an ancient Buyur site, of course. Perhaps a port or seaside resort, long ago demolished, with the remnants left for wind and rain to dissolve.

Aided by a wounded planet's friend, came the voice, with renewed pride.

We who help erase the scars.

We who expedite time's rub.

Over there. Between the shadows of his own eyelashes, Dwer made out slender shapes amid the marsh plants, like threads woven among the roots and fronds, snaking through the muddy shallows. Long, tubelike outlines, whose movement was glacially slow. But he could track the changes, with patience.

Oh, what patience you might have learned, if only you joined me! We would be one with Time now, my pet, my rare one.

It wasn't just his growing vexation with the irksome dream voice—that he knew to be imagined, after all. Dawning realization finally lent Dwer the will to shake off sleep. He squeezed his eyelids shut hard enough to bring tears and flush away the stickiness. Alert now, he reopened them and stared again at the faint twisty patterns in the water. They were real.

"It's a mulc swamp," he muttered. "And it still lives."

Rety stirred, commenting testily.

"So? One more reason to get out of this crakky place."

But Dwer smiled. Emerging from the fretful nap, he found his thoughts now taking a sharp turn, veering away from a victim's apprehension.

In the distance, he still heard the noor beast bark and growl while toying with his prey—a carnivore's privilege under nature's law. Before, Mudfoot's behavior had irritated Dwer. But now he took it as an omen.

All his setbacks and injuries—and simple common sense—seemed to demand that he flee this deadly place, crawling on his belly, taking Rety with him to whatever hideout they could find in a deadly world.

But one idea had now crystallized, as clear as the nearby waters of the Rift.

I'm not running away, he decided. *I don't really know how to do that.*

A hunter—that was what he had been born and trained to be.

Alvin

ALL RIGHT, SO THERE WE WERE, WATCHING FARAWAY events through the phuvnthus' magical viewer, when the camera eye suddenly went jerky and we found ourselves staring into the grinning jaws of a giant noor! Hugely magnified, it was the vista a fen mouse might see—its last sight on its way to being a midday snack.

Huphu reacted with a sharp hiss. Her claws dug in my shoulder.

The spinning voice, our host, seemed as surprised as we. That whirling *hologram*-thing twisted like the neck of a confused urs, nodding as if it were consulting someone out of sight. I caught murmurs that might be hurried Anglic and GalSeven.

When the voice next spoke aloud, we heard the words *twice,* the second time delayed as it came back through the drone's tiny pickups. The voice used accented GalSix, and *talked to the strange noor.* Three words, so high-pitched I barely understood.

"Brother," the voice urged quickly. *"Please stop."*

And the strange noor *did* stop, turning its head to examine the drone from one side to the other.

True, we hoons employ noor beasts as helpers on our boats, and those learn many words and simple commands. But that is on the Slope, where they get sour balls and sweet umbles as pay. How would a noor living east of the Rimmers learn Galactic Six?

The voice tried again, changing pitch and timbre, almost at the limit of my hearing range.

"Brother, will you speak to us, in the name of the Trickster?"

Huck and I shared an amazed glance. What was the voice trying to accomplish?

One of those half memories came back to me, from when our ill-fated *Wuphon's Dream* crashed into the open-mawed phuvnthus whale ship. Me and my friends were thrown gasping across a metal deck, and soon after I stared through agonized haze as six-legged monsters tromped about, smashing our homemade instruments underfoot, waving lantern beams, exclaiming in a ratchety language I didn't understand. The armored beings seemed cruel when they blasted poor little Ziz, the five-stack traeki. Then they appeared *crazy* upon spying Huphu. I recall them bending metal legs to crouch before my pet, buzzing and popping, as if trying to get her to speak.

And now here was more of the same! Did the voice hope to talk a wild noor into releasing the remote-controlled drone? Huck winked at me with two waving g'Kek eyes, a semaphore of amused contempt. Star gods or no, our hosts seemed prize fools to expect easy cooperation from a noor.

So *we* were more surprised than anyone—even Pincer and Ur-ronn—when the on-screen figure snapped its jaws, frowning in concentration. Then, through gritted teeth came a raspy squeak . . . *answering* in the same informal tongue.

"In th' nam o' th' Trickst'er . . . who th' hell'r you?"

My healing spine crackled painfully as I straightened, venting an umble of astonishment. Huck sighed and Pincer's visor whirled faster than the agitated hologram. Only Huphu seemed oblivious. She licked herself complacently, as if she had not heard a blessed thing.

"What do you jeekee, Ifni-slucking turds think you're doing!" Huck wailed. All four eyes tossed in agitation, showing she was more angry than afraid. Two hulking, six-legged phuvnthus escorted her, one on each side, carrying her by the rims of her wheels.

The rest of us were more cooperative, though reluctant. Pincer had to tilt his red chitin shell in order to pass through some doorways, following as a pair of little amphibian creatures led us back to the whale ship that brought us to this underwater sanctuary. Ur-ronn trotted behind Pincer, her long neck folded low to the ground, a pose of simmering dejection.

I hobbled on crutches behind Huck, staying out of reach of her pusher leg, which flailed and banged against corridor walls on either side.

"You promised to explain everything!" she cried out. "You said we'd get to ask questions of the Library!"

Neither the phuvnthus nor the amphibians answered, but I recalled what the spinning voice had said before sending us away.

"We cannot justify any longer keeping four children under conditions that put you all in danger. This location may be bombed again, with greater fury. Also, you now know much too much for your own good."

"What do we know?" Pincer had asked, in perplexity. "That noors can talk-alk-alk?"

The hologram assented with a twisting nod. "And other things. We can't keep you here, or send you home as we originally intended, since that might prove disastrous for ourselves and your families. Hence our decision to convey you to another place. A goal mentioned in your diaries, where you may be content for the necessary time."

"Wait!" Huck had insisted. "I'll bet you're not even in charge. You're prob'ly just a computer . . . a *thing*. I want to talk to someone else! Let us see your boss!"

I swear, the whirling pattern seemed both surprised and amused.

"Such astute young people. We had to revise many assumptions since meeting the four of you. As I am programmed to find incongruity pleasant, let me thank you for the experience, and sincerely wish you well."

I noticed, the voice never answered Huck's question.

Typical grown-up, I thought. Whether hoonish parents or alien contraptions . . . they're all basically the same.

•   •   •

Huck settled down once we left the curved hallway and reentered the maze of reclaimed passages leading to the whale ship. The phuvnthus let her down, and she rolled along with the rest of us. My friend continued grumbling remarks about the phuvnthus' physiology, habits, and ancestry, but I saw through her pose. Huck had that smug set to her eyestalks.

Clearly, she felt she had accomplished something sneaky and smart.

Once aboard the whale ship, we were given another room with a porthole. Apparently the phuvnthus weren't worried about us memorizing landmarks. That worried me, at first.

Are they going to stash us in another salvaged wreck, under a different dross pile, in some far-off canyon of the Midden? In that case, who'll come get us if they are destroyed?

The voice mentioned sending us to a "safe" place. Call me odd, but I hadn't felt safe since stepping off dry land at Terminus Rock. *What did the voice mean about it being a site where we already "wanted to go"?*

The whale ship slid slowly at first through its tunnel exit, clearly a makeshift passage constructed out of the hulls of ancient starcraft, braced with rods and improvised girders. Ur-ronn said this fit what we already knew—the phuvnthus were recent arrivals on Jijo, possibly refugees, like our ancestors, but with one big difference.

They hope to leave again.

I envied them. Not for the obvious danger they felt, pursued by deadly foes, but for that one option they had, that we did not. To *go*. To fly off to the stars, even if the way led to certain doom. Was I naive to think freedom made it all worthwhile? To know I'd trade places with them, if I could?

Maybe that thought laid the seeds for my later realization. The moment when everything suddenly made sense. But hold that thought.

Before the whale ship emerged from the tunnel, we caught sight of *figures* moving in the darkness, where long shadows stretched away from moving points of sharp, starlike light. The patchiness of brilliance and pure darkness made it hard, at first, to make out very much. Then Pincer identified the shadowy shapes.

They were *phuvnthus*, the big six-legged creatures whose stomping gait seemed so ungainly indoors. Now, for the first time, we saw them in their element, *swimming*, with the mechanical legs tucked away or used as flexible work arms. The broad flaring at the back ends of their bodies now made sense—it was a great big flipper that propelled them gracefully through dark waters.

We had already speculated that they might not be purely mechanical beings. Ur-ronn thought the heavy metal carapace was worn like a suit of clothes, and the real creatures lay inside horizontal shells.

They wear them indoors because their true bodies lack legs, I thought, knowing also that the steel husks protected their identities. But why, if they were born swimmers, did they continue wearing the coverings outside?

We glimpsed light bursts of hurtful brilliance—underwater welding and cutting. *Repairs,* I thought. *Were they in a battle, before fleeing to Jijo?* My mind filled with images from those vivid space-opera books Mister Heinz used to disapprove of, preferring that we kids broaden our tastes with Keats and Basho. I yearned to get close and see the combat scars . . . but then the sub entered a narrow shaft, cutting off all sight of the phuvnthu vessel.

Soon, we emerged into the blackness of the Midden. A deep chill seemed to penetrate the glass disk, and we backed away . . . especially since the spotlights all turned off, leaving the outside world vacant, but for an occasional blue glimmer as some sea creature tried to lure a mate.

I lay down on the metal deck to rest my back, feeling the thrum of engines vibrate beneath me. It was like the rumbling song of some godlike hoon who never needed to pause or take a breath. I filled my air sac and began to umble counterpoint. Hoons think best when there is a steady background cadence—a *tone* to serve as a fulcrum for deliberation.

I had a lot to think about.

My friends eventually grew bored with staring at the bleak desolation outside. Soon they were all gathered around little Huphu, our noorish mascot, trying to get her to speak. Pincer urged me to come over and use bosun umbles to put her in a cooperative mood, but I declined. I've known Huphu since she was a pup, and there's no way she's been playing dumb all that time. Anyway, I had seen a *difference* in that strange noor on the beach, the one that spoke back to the spinning voice in fluent GalSix. Huphu never had that glint in her eyes . . .

. . . though as I reflected, I felt sure I'd seen the look before—in just a few noor who lounged on the piers in Wuphon, or worked the sails of visiting ships. Strange ones, a bit more aloof than normal. As silent as their brethren, they nevertheless seemed more *watchful* somehow. More evaluating. More *amused* by all the busy activity of the Six Races.

I never gave them much thought before, since a devilish attitude seems innate to all noor. But now perhaps I knew what made them different.

Though noor are often associated with hoons, they didn't come to Jijo with us, the way chimps, lorniks, and zookirs came with human, qheuen, and g'Kek sooners. They were already here when we arrived and began building our first proud rafts. We always assumed they were native beasts, either natural or else some adjusted species, left behind by the Buyur as a practical joke on whoever might follow. Though we get useful work out of them, we hoon don't fool ourselves that they are *ours*.

Eventually, Huck gave up the effort, leaving Pincer and Ur-ronn to continue coaxing our bored mascot. My g'Kek buddy rolled over beside me, resting quietly for a time. But she didn't fool me for a kidura.

"So tell me," I asked. "What'd you swipe?"

"What makes you think I took anything?" She feigned innocence.

"Hr-rrm. How 'bout the fakey way you thrashed around, back there in the hall—a tantrum like you used to throw when you were a leg skeeter, till our folks caught on. After we left the curvy hallway, you stopped all that, wearing a look as if you'd snatched the crown jewels under old Richelieu's nose."

Huck winced, a reflex coiling of eyestalks. Then she

chuckled. "Well, you got me there, d'Artagnan. Come on. Have a look at what I got."

With some effort, I raised up on my middle stretch of forearm while Huck rolled closer still. Excitement hummed along her spokes.

"Used my pusher legs. Kept banging 'em against the wall till I managed to snag one of these."

Her tendril-like arm unfolded. There, held delicately between the tips, hung a narrow, rectangular strip of what looked like thick paper. I reached for it.

"Careful, it's sticky on one side. I think a book called it *adhesive tape*. Got a bit crumpled when I yanked it off the wall. Had to pry some gummy bits apart. I'm afraid there's not much of an impression left, but if you look closely . . ."

I peered at the strip—one of the coverings we had seen pressed on the walls, always at the same height, to the left of each doorway in the curved hall, surely masking label signs in some unknown language.

"You wouldn't happen to've been looking when I ripped it off, were you?" Huck asked. "Did you see what it said underneath?"

"Hr-r. Wish I had. But I was too busy avoiding being kicked."

"Well, never mind. Just look *real* carefully at this end. What d'you see there?"

I didn't have Huck's sensitivity of vision, but hoons do have good eyes. I peered at what seemed a circular pattern with a gap and sharp jog on the right side. "Is it a symbol?"

"That's right. Now tell me—in what alphabet?"

I concentrated. Circles were basic ingredients in most standard Galactic codes. But this particular shape seemed unique.

"I'll tell you my *first* impression, though it can't be right."

"Go on."

"Hr-rm . . . it looks to me like an *Anglic* letter. A letter *G*, to be specific."

Huck let a satisfied sigh escape her vent mouth. All four eyestalks waved, as if in a happy breeze.

"That was my impression, too."

• • •

We clustered round the viewport when the hull began creaking and popping, indicating a rapid change of pressure. Soon the world outside began to brighten and we knew the sub must be on final approach. Beyond the glass, sunshine streamed through shallow water. We all felt a bit giddy, from changing air density, I guess. Pincer-Tip let out hissing shouts, glad to be back in a familiar world where he would be at home. (Though lacking the comforts of his clan rookery.) Soon water slid off the window in dripping sheets and we saw our destination.

Tilted obelisks and sprawling concrete skeletons, arrayed in great clusters along the shore.

Huck let out a warbling sigh.

Buyur ruins, I realized. *These must be the scrublands south of the Rift, where some city sites were left to be torn down by wave and wind alone.*

The voice read my journal and knew about our interest in coming here. If we must be quarantined, this would be the place.

The cluster of ancient sites had been Huck's special goal, before we ever stepped aboard *Wuphon's Dream.* Now she bounced on her rims, eager to get ashore and read the wall inscriptions that were said to be abundant in this place. Forgotten were her complaints over broken phuvnthu promises. This was a more longstanding dream.

One of the six-limbed amphibians entered, gesturing for us to move quickly. No doubt the phuvnthus were anxious to get us ashore before they could be spotted by their enemies. Huck rolled out after Pincer. Ur-ronn glanced at me, her long head and neck shaking in an urrish shrug. At least she must be looking forward to an end to all this water and humidity. The countryside ahead looked pleasantly dry.

But it was not to be.

This time *I* was the mutinous one.

"No!" I planted my feet, and my throat sac boomed. "I ain't movin'."

My friends turned and stared. They must have seen hoonish obstinacy in the set of my limbs as I gripped the crutches. The amphibian fluttered and squeaked distress.

"Forget it," I insisted. "We are not getting off!"

"Alvin, it's all right-ight," Pincer murmured. "They promised to leave us lots of food, and I can hunt along the shore—"

I shook my head.

"We are not going to be cast aside like this, exiled for our own Ifni-slucking *safety,* like a bunch of helpless kids. Sent away from where things are happening. Important things!"

"What're you talking about?" asked Huck, rolling back into the cabin, while the amphibian fluttered and waved its four arms vainly. Finally, a pair of big phuvnthus came in, their long horizontal bodies metal-clad and slung between six stomping steel legs. But I refused to be intimidated. I pointed at the nearest, with its pair of huge, black, glassy eyes, one on each side of a tapered head.

"You call up the spinning voice and tell him. Tell him we can help. But if you people turn us away, putting us ashore here won't do any good. It won't shut us up, 'cause we'll find a way back home, just as fast as we can. We'll head for the Rift and signal friends on the other side. We'll tell 'em the truth about you guys!"

Ur-ronn murmured, "*What* truth, Alvin?"

I let out a deep, rolling umble to accompany my words. "That we know who these guys are."

Sara

IN THE LODGE OF A HORSE CLAN YOU MIGHT EXPECT to see lariats, bridles, and saddle blankets hanging on the walls. Maybe a guitar or two. It seemed strange to find a *piano* here in Xi.

An instrument much like the one back home in Dolo Village, where Melina used to read to her children for hours on end, choosing obscure books no one else seemed eager to check out from the Biblos Archive—some crinkly pages wafting aromas from the Great Printing, two hundred years before. Especially books of *written music* Melina would prop on the precious piano Nelo had made for her as part of the marriage price.

Now, in the great hall of the Illias, Sara ran her hands along white and black keys, stroking fine tooth traces left by expert qheuen wood-carvers, picturing her mother as a little girl, raised in this narrow realm of horses and mind-scraping illusions. Leaving Xi must have been like going to another planet. Did she feel relief from claustrophobic confinement, passing through the Buyur tunnel for a new life in the snowy north? Or did Melina long in her heart for the hidden glades? For the visceral thrill of bareback? For the pastoral purity of life unconstrained by men?

Did she miss the colors that took each dream or nightmare, and spread its secret panorama before your daylight gaze?

Who taught you to play the piano, Mother? Sitting with you on this very bench, the way you used to sit beside me, trying to hide your disappointment in my awkward fingers?

A folio of sheet music lay atop the piano's polished surface. Sara flipped through it, recalling ancient compositions that used to transfix her mother for duras at a stretch, rousing young Sara's jealousy against those dots on a page. Dots Melina transformed into glorious harmonies.

Later, Sara realized how magical the melodies truly were. For they were *repeatable*. In a sense, written music was immortal. It could never die.

The typical Jijoan ensemble—a sextet including members from each sooner race—performed spontaneously. A composition was never quite the same from one presentation to the next. That trait appealed especially to blue qheuens and hoons, who, according to legend, had no freedom to innovate back in ordered Galactic society. They expressed puzzlement when human partners sometimes suggested recording a successful piece in traeki wax, or writing it down.

Whatever for? they asked. *Each moment deserves its own song.*

A Jijoan way of looking at things, Sara acknowledged.

She laid her hands on the keys and ran through some scales. Though out of practice, the exercise was like an old friend. No wonder Emerson also drew comfort from tunes recalling happier days.

Still, her mind churned as she switched to some simple favorites, starting with "Für Elise."

According to Biblos anthropology texts, most ancient cultures on Earth used to play music that was impulsive, just like a Jijoan sextet. But shortly before they made their own way into space, humans also came up with written forms.

We sought order and memory. It must have seemed a refuge from the chaos that filled our dark lives.

Of course that was long ago, back when mathematics also had its great age of discovery on Earth. *Is that a common thread? Did I choose math for the same reason Melina loved this instrument? Because it lends predictability amid life's chaos?*

A shadow fell across the wall. Sara drew back, half rising to meet the brown eyes of Foruni, aged leader of the horse-riding clan.

"Sorry to disturb you, dear." The gray-headed matriarch motioned for Sara to sit. "But watching you, I could almost believe it was Melina back home with us, playing as she did, with such intensity."

"I'm afraid I don't look much like my mother. Nor do I play half as well."

The old woman smiled. "A good parent wants her offspring to excel—to do what she could not. But a wise parent lets the child select *which* excellence. You chose realms of deep thought. I know she was very proud."

Sara acknowledged the kindness with a nod, but took small comfort from aphorisms. *If the choice really were mine, don't you think I'd have been beautiful, like Melina? A dark woman of mystery, who amazed people with many graceful talents?*

Mathematics chose me . . . it seized me with cool infinities and hints at universal truth. Yet whom do I touch with my equations? Who looks at my face and form with unreserved delight?

Melina died young, but surrounded by those who loved her. Who will weep over me, when I am gone?

The Illias leader must have misunderstood Sara's frown.

"Do my words disturb you?" Foruni asked. "Do I sound like a heretic, for believing that generations can improve?

Does it seem an odd belief for a secret tribe that hides itself even from a civilization of exiled refugees?"

Sara found it hard to answer.

Why were Melina's children so odd, by Jijoan standards? Although Lark's heresy seems opposite to mine, we share one thread—rejecting the Path of Redemption.

The books Mother read to us often spoke of hope, drawn from some act of rebellion.

To the Illias leader, she replied, "You and your urrish friends rescued horses, back when they seemed doomed. Your alliance foreshadowed that of Drake and Ur-Chown. You are a society of dedicated women, who carefully choose your male companions from the best Jijo has to offer. Living in splendid isolation, you see humanity at its best—seldom its more nasty side.

"No, it does not surprise me that the Illias are optimists at heart."

Foruni nodded. "I am told that you, in your investigations of language theory, reached similar conclusions."

Sara shrugged. "I'm no optimist. Not personally. But for a while, it seemed that I could see a pattern in the evolution of Jijo's dialects, and in all the new literary activity taking place across the Slope. Not that it matters anymore, now that aliens have come to—"

The old woman cut in. "You don't think we are destined to be like glavers, winning our second chance by passing through oblivion?"

"You mean what *might* have happened, if starships never came? I argued with Dedinger about this. If Jijo had been left alone, I felt there was the possibility of . . ."

Sara shook her head and changed the subject.

"Speaking of Dedinger, have you had any luck finding him?"

Foruni winced unhappily. "It's been just a short while since he broke out of the pen where he was kept. We never imagined he would prove so resourceful, knowing how to saddle and steal a horse."

"He had time to learn by observing."

"I see that we were naive. It's a long time since we kept prisoners in Xi.

"Unfortunately, the tracks do not lead back to the tunnel,

where we might have trapped him in the narrow darkness. Instead, the wily ligger spawn struck out across the Spectral Flow."

Sara tried picturing a man alone on horseback, crossing a vast desert of poison stone and cutting light. "Do you think he can make it?"

"You mean can we catch him before he dies out there?" It was Foruni's turn to shrug. "Fallon is not as spry as he was, but he departed a midura ago with some of our most able young riders. The fanatic should be back in care soon, and we'll watch him more closely—"

Foruni stopped, midsentence, glancing down at her hand. An insect had landed, and was sniffing at a vein. Sara recognized a *skeeter*—a blood-sucking irritant familiar across the Slope. Skeeters were slow and easily smacked, but for some reason Foruni refrained. Instead, she let the vampire wasp leisurely insert a narrow tube and take its meal. When finished, it proceeded to perform a little dance, one filled with jerky, *beckoning* motions.

Sara stared, fascinated. Skeeters seldom survived landing on a human long enough to do this.

Come with me, it seemed to say with each swing of its tiny abdomen and tail. *Come with me now.*

Sara realized, it must be another remnant servant beast of the vanished Buyur. A useful messenger, if you knew how to use it.

Foruni sighed. "Alas, dear cousin, it's time for you to go. You and Kurt and the others must hurry to where you're needed most."

Needed? Sara wondered. *In times like these, what could a person like me possibly be needed for?*

The journey south resumed, this time on horseback. They used the ancient Buyur transit tunnel at first, where the failed deconstructor left its demolition unfinished. But soon it lay cracked open for stretches, like the spent larval casing of a newly fledged qheuen, leaving a dusty cavity or else a pit filled with water. Thereafter they had to ride in the open, awash in the luminous tides of the Spectral Flow. The Illias provided hooded cloaks. Still, it felt as if the

colors were probing the reflective garments for some gap
to worm their way inside.

Kurt and Jomah rode ahead with Kepha, their guide. The
elderly exploser leaned forward in his saddle, as if that
might get them to their goal quicker. Then came Prity, on a
donkey more suited for her small form.

Emerson seemed strangely subdued, though he smiled
at Sara from time to time. He wore the rewq constantly,
though from his ever-turning head, Sara gathered the filmy
symbiont was doing more than just softening the colors. It
must be adjusting, *translating* them. Sometimes, the
starman stiffened in the saddle . . . though whether from
pain, surprise, or exaltation, Sara could never be quite
sure.

Taking up the rear was Ulgor, the urrish traitor. Wisely,
she had not tried to break across the poison plain with her
erstwhile ally, Dedinger. Guarded by two of her own kind
from the Xi colony, Ulgor swung her head in growing eagerness as the party neared Mount Guenn. Urrish nostrils
flared at scents of smoke and molten rock, as the volcano
loomed to fill the southern sky.

Sara felt surprisingly good. The saddle was a tool her
body had mastered. When the going grew steep and riders
dismounted to lead the horses by hand, her legs were suf-
fused with waves of comfortable warmth, with strength still
in reserve.

*So, a hermit math potato can manage to keep up, after
all. Or is this euphoria an early sign of altitude sickness?*

They were mounting one of countless knee hills along
the sloping volcano, when suddenly all three urs bolted
forward, hissing excitement and trailing clouds of pumice,
forgetting their separate roles as they jostled toward the
next outlook. Outlined against the sky, their long heads
swept in unison, from left to right and back again.

Finally, winded from the climb, she and Emerson arrived
to find a mighty caldera spread before them . . . one of
many studding the immense volcano, which kept rising to
the southeast for many more leagues.

Yet this crater had the urs transfixed. Steamy exhalations
rose from vents that rimmed the craggy circle. Cautiously,
Sara removed her sunglasses. The basalt here was of a

coarser, less gemlike variety. They had entered a different realm.

"This was the site of the first forge," Ulgor announced, her voice tinged with awe. She tilted her muzzle to the right, and Sara made out a tumble of stone blocks, too poorly shaped to have been laser-cut by the Buyur, and now long-abandoned. Such tumbled shelters were hand-hewn by the earliest urrish seeker smiths who dared to leave the plains pursuing lava-borne heat, hoping to learn how to cast the fiery substance of Jijoan bronze and steel. In its day, the venture was fiercely opposed by the Gray Queens, who portrayed it as sacrilege—as when humans much later performed the Great Printing.

In time, what had been profane became tradition.

"They must've found conditions better, on high," Jomah commented, for the trail continued steadily upslope. An urrish guard nodded. "Vut it was fron *this* flace that early urs exflorers discovered the secret way across the Sfectral Flow. The Secret of Xi."

Sara nodded. That explained why one group of urs conspired to thwart another—the powerful Urunthai—in their plan to make horses extinct when humanity was new on Jijo. The smiths of those days cared little for power games played by high aunties of the plains tribes. It did not matter to them how Earthlings smelled, or what beasts they rode, only that they possessed a treasure.

Those books the Earthlings printed. They have secrets of metallurgy. We must share, or be left behind.

So it was not a purely idealistic move—to establish a secret herd in Xi. There had been a price. *Humans may be Jijo's master engineers, but we stayed out of smithing, and now I know why.*

Even after growing up among them, Sara still found it fascinating how varied urs could be. Their range of personalities and motives—from fanatics to pragmatic smiths—was as broad as you'd find among human beings. *One more reason why stereotypes aren't just evil, but stupid.*

Soon after they remounted, the trail followed a ridgeline offering spectacular views. The Spectral Flow lay to their left, an eerie realm, even dimmed to sepia shades by distance and dark glasses. The maze of speckled canyons spanned all the way to a band of blazing white—the Plain of Sharp Sand. Dedinger's home, where the would-be prophet was forging a nation of die-hard zealots out of coarse desert folk. Sandmen who saw themselves as humanity's vanguard on the Path of Redemption.

In the opposite direction, southwest through gaps in the many-times-folded mountain, Sara glimpsed another wonder. The vast ocean, where Jijo's promised life renewal was fulfilled. Where Melina's ashes went after mulching. And Joshu's. Where the planet erased sin by absorbing and melting anything the universe sent it.

The Slope is so narrow, and Jijo is so large. Will star gods judge us harshly for living quiet careful lives in one corner of a forbidden world?

There was always hope the aliens might just finish their business and go away, leaving the Six Races to proceed along whatever path destiny laid out for them.

Yeah, she concluded. *There are two chances that will happen—fat and slim.*

The trek continued, more often dismounted than not, and the view grew more spectacular as they moved east, encompassing the southern Rimmer Range. Again, Sara noted skittishness among the urs. In spots the ground vented steaming vapors, making the horses dance and snort. Then she glimpsed a red glimmer, some distance below the trail—a meandering stream of *lava,* flowing several arrowflights downslope.

Perhaps it was fatigue, thin air, or the tricky terrain, but as Sara looked away from the fiery trail, her unshielded eyes crossed the mountains and were caught unready by a stray flash of light. Sensitized by her time in Xi, the sharp gleam made her cringe.

What is that?

The flash repeated at uneven intervals, almost as if the distant mountaintop were speaking to her.

Then Sara caught another, quite different flicker of motion.

Now that must be an illusion, she thought. *It has to be . . . yet it's so far from the Spectral Flow!*

It seemed . . . she could almost swear . . . that she

saw the widespread wings of some titanic bird, or *dragon,* wafting between—

It had been too long since she checked her footing. A stone unexpectedly turned and Sara tripped. Throwing her weight desperately the other way, she overcompensated, losing her balance completely.

Uttering a cry, Sara fell.

The gritty trail took much of the initial impact, but then she rolled over the edge, tumbling down a scree of pebbles and jagged basalt flakes. Despite her tough leather garments, each jab lanced her with fierce pain as she desperately covered her face and skull. A wailing sound accompanied her plunge. In a terrified daze Sara realized the screamer was not her, but *Prity,* shrieking dismay.

"Sara!" someone yelled. There were scrambling sounds of distant, hopeless pursuit.

In midtumble, between one jarring collision and the next, she glimpsed something between blood-streaked fingers—a fast-approaching rivulet winding across the shattered landscape. A liquid current that moved languidly, with great viscosity and even greater heat. It was the same color as her blood . . . and approaching fast.

Nelo

ARIANA FOO SPENT THE RETURN BOAT JOURNEY mulling over her sketches of the tiny space pod that had brought the Stranger to Jijo. Meanwhile, Nelo fumed over this foolish diversion. His workmen would surely *not* have kept to schedule. Some minor foul-up would give those louts an excuse to lie about like hoons at siesta time.

Commerce had lapsed during the crisis, and the warehouse tree was full, but Nelo was determined to keep producing paper. What would Dolo Village be without the groaning waterwheel, the thump of the pulping hammer, or the sweet aroma that wafted from fresh sheets drying in the sun?

While the helmsman umbled cheerfully, keeping a

steady beat for the crew poling the little boat along, Nelo held out a hand, feeling for rain. There had been drops a little earlier, when disturbing thunder pealed to the south.

The marsh petered out as streamlets rejoined as a united river once more. Soon the young people would switch to oars and sweep onto the gentle lake behind Dolo Dam.

The helmsman's umble tapered, slowing to a worried moan. Several of the crew leaned over, peering at the water. A boy shouted as his pole was ripped out of his hands. *It does seem a bit fast,* Nelo thought, as the last swamp plants fell behind and trees began to pass by rapidly.

"All hands to oars!" shouted the young hoon in command. Her back spines, still fresh from recent fledging, made uneasy frickles.

"Lock them down!"

Ariana met Nelo's eyes with a question. He answered with a shrug.

The boat juttered, reminding him of the cataracts that lay many leagues downriver, past Tarek Town, an inconvenience he only had to endure once, accompanying his wife's dross casket to sea.

But there are no rapids here! They were erased when the lake filled, centuries ago!

The boat veered, sending him crashing to the bilge. With stinging hands, Nelo climbed back to take a seat next to Ariana. The former High Sage clutched the bench, her precious folio of drawings zipped shut inside her jacket.

"Hold on!" screamed the young commander. In dazed bewilderment, Nelo clutched the plank as they plunged into a weird domain. A realm that *should not be.*

So Nelo thought, over and over, as they sped down a narrow channel. On either side, the normal shoreline was visible—where trees stopped and scummy water plants took over. But the boat was already well *below* that level, and dropping fast!

Spume crested the gunnels, drenching passengers and crew. The latter rowed furiously to the hoon lieutenant's shrill commands. Lacking a male's resonating sac, she still made her wishes known.

"Backwater-left . . . *backwater-left,* you noor-bitten

ragmen! . . . Steady . . . Now all ahead! *Pull for it,* you spineless croakers! For your lives, *pull*!"

Twin walls of stone rushed inward, threatening to crush the boat from both sides. Glistening with oily algae, they loomed like hammer and anvil as the crew rowed frantically for the narrow slot between, marked by a fog of stinging white spray. What lay beyond was a mystery Nelo only prayed he'd live to see.

Voices of hoons, qheuen, and humans rose in desperation as the boat struck one cliff a glancing blow, echoing like a door knocker on the gateway to hell. Somehow the hull survived to lunge down the funnel, drenched in spray.

We should be on the lake by now, Nelo complained, hissing through gritted teeth. *Where did the lake go!*

They shot like a javelin onto a cascade where water churned in utter confusion over scattered boulders, shifting suddenly as fresh debris barricades built up or gave way. It was an obstacle course to defy the best of pilots, but Nelo had no eyes for the ongoing struggle, which would merely decide whether he lived or died. His numbed gaze lifted beyond, staring past the surrounding mud plain that had been a lake bed, down whose center rushed the River Roney, no longer constrained. A river now free to roll on as it had before Earthlings came.

The dam . . . The dam . . .

A moan lifted from the pair of blue qheuens, lent for this journey by the local hive. A hive whose fisheries and murky lobster pens used to stretch luxuriously behind the dam wherein they made a prosperous home. Remnants of the pens and algae farms lay strewn about as the boat swept toward the maelstrom's center.

Nelo blinked, unable to express his dismay, even with a moan.

The dam still stood along most of its length. But *most* wasn't a word of much use to a dam. Nelo's heart almost gave way when he saw the gap ripped at one end . . . the side near his beloved mill.

"Hold on!" the pilot cried redundantly, as they plunged for the opening. And the waterfall they all heard roaring violently just ahead.

PART SIX

FROM THE NOTES
OF GILLIAN BASKIN

MY DECISION may not be wholly rational.

For all I know, Alvin may be bluffing in order to avoid exile. He may have no idea who we are.

Or perhaps he really has surmised the truth. After all, dolphins are mentioned in many of the Earth books he's read. Even wearing a fully armored, six-legged walker unit, a fin's outline can be recognized if you look in the right way. Once the idea occurred to him, Alvin's fertile imagination would cover the rest.

As a precaution, we could intern the kids much farther south, or in a subsea habitat. That might keep them safe and silent. Tsh't suggested as much, before I ordered the *Hikahi* to turn around and bring them back.

I admit I'm biased. I miss Alvin and his pals. If only the fractious races of the Five Galaxies could have a camaraderie like theirs.

Anyway, they are grown-up enough to choose their own fate.

WE'VE had a report from Makanee's nurse. On her way by sled to check on a sick member of Kaa's team, Peepoe spotted two more piles of junked spacecraft, smaller than this one, but suitable should we have to move *Streaker* soon. Hannes dispatched crews to start preparatory work.

Again, we must rely on the same core group of about fifty skilled crewfen. The reliable ones, whose concentration remains unflagged after three stressful years. Those who aren't frightened by superstitious rumors of sea monsters lurking amid the dead Buyur machines.

AS for our pursuers—we've seen no more gravitic signatures of flying craft, east of the mountains. That may be good news, but the respite makes me nervous. Two small spacecraft can't be the whole story. Sensors detect some great brute of a ship, about five hundred klicks northwest. Is this vast cruiser related to the two vessels that fell near here?

They must surely realize that this region is of interest.

It seems creepy they haven't followed up.

As if they are confident they have all the time in the world.

THE Niss Machine managed to exchange just a few more words with that so-called noor beast that our little drone encountered ashore. But the creature keeps us on tenterhooks, treating the little scout robot like its private toy, or a prey animal to be teased with bites and scratches. Yet it also carries it about in its mouth, careful not to get tangled in the fiber cable, letting us have brief, tantalizing views of the crashed sky boats.

We had assumed that "noor" were simply devolved versions of *tytlal* . . . of little interest except as curiosities. But if some retain the power of speech, what else might they be capable of?

At first I thought the Niss Machine would be the one

best qualified to handle this confusing encounter. After all, the noor is its "cousin," in a manner of speaking.

But family connections can involve sibling rivalry, even contempt. Maybe the Tymbrimi machine is simply the wrong spokesman.

One more reason I'm eager to bring Alvin back.

AMID all this, I had time to do a bit more research on Herbie.

I wish there were some way to guess the isotopic input profiles, before he died, but chemical racemization analyses of samples taken from the ancient mummy appear to show considerably less temporal span than was indicated by cosmic-ray track histories of the hull Tom boarded, in the Shallow Cluster.

In other words, Herbie seems younger than the vessel Tom found him on.

That could mean a number of things.

Might Herb simply be the corpse of some *previous* grave robber, who slinked aboard just a few million years ago, instead of one to two billion?

Or could the discrepancy be an effect of those strange fields we found in the Shallow Cluster, surrounding that fleet of ghostly starcraft, rendering them nearly invisible? Perhaps the outer hulls of those huge, silent ships experienced time differently than their contents.

It makes me wonder about poor Lieutenant Yachapa-jean, who was killed by those same fields, and whose body had to be left behind. Might some future expedition someday recover the well-preserved corpse of a dolphin and go rushing around the universe thinking they have the recovered relic of a progenitor?

Mistaking the youngest sapient race for the oldest. What a joke that would be.

A joke on them, and a joke on us.

Herbie never changes. Yet I swear I sometimes catch him grinning.

OUR stolen Galactic Library unit gets queer and opaque at times. If I weren't in disguise, the big cube probably wouldn't tell me anything at all. Even decked out as a Thennanin admiral, I find the Library evasive when shown those symbols that Tom copied aboard the derelict ship.

One glyph looks like the emblem worn by every Library unit in known space—a great spiral wheel. Only, instead of five swirling arms rotating around a common center, this one has *nine!* And eight concentric *ovals* overlie the stylized galactic helix, making it resemble a bull's-eye target.

I never saw anything like it before.

When I press for answers, our purloined archive says the symbol ". . . is very old . . ." and that its use is ". . . memetically discouraged."

Whatever that means.

At risk of humanizing a machine, the unit seems to get *grumpy,* as if it dislikes being confused. I've seen this before. Terragens researchers find that certain subject areas make Libraries touchy, as if they hate having to work hard by digging in older files. . . . Or maybe that's an excuse to avoid admitting there are things they don't know.

It reminds me of discussions Tom and I used to have with Jake Demwa, when we'd all sit up late trying to make sense of the universe.

Jake had a theory—that Galactic history, which purports to go back more than a billion years, is actually only accurate to about one hundred and fifty million.

"With each eon you go further back than that," he said, "what we're told has an ever-increasing flavor of a carefully concocted fable."

Oh, there's evidence that oxygen-breathing starfarers have been around ten times as long. Surely some of the ancient events recorded in official annals must be authentic. But much has also been painted over.

It's a chilling notion. The great Institutes are supposed to be dedicated to truth and continuity. How, then, can valid information be *memetically discouraged?*

Yes, this seems a rather abstract obsession, at a time when *Streaker*—and now Jijo—faces dire and immediate threats. Yet I can't help thinking it all comes together here at the bottom of a planetary graveyard, where tectonic plates melt history into ore.

We are caught in the slowly grinding gears of a machine more vast than we imagined.

Streakers

Hannes

AT TIMES HANNES SUESSI ACUTELY MISSED HIS young friend Emerson, whose uncanny skills helped make *Streaker* purr like a compact leopard, prowling the trails of space.

Of course Hannes admired the able fins of his engine-room gang—amiable, hardworking crew mates without a hint of regression in the bunch. But dolphins tend to visualize objects as sonic shapes, and often set their calibrations intuitively, based on the way motor vibrations *sounded*. A helpful technique, but not always reliable.

Emerson D'Anite, on the other hand—

Hannes never knew anyone with a better gut understanding of quantum probability shunts. Not the arcane hyperdimensional theory, but the practical nuts and bolts of wresting movement from contortions of wrinkled space-time. Emerson was also fluent in Tursiops Trinary . . . better than Hannes at conveying complex ideas in neo-dolphins' own hybrid language. A useful knack on this tub.

Alas, just one human now remained belowdecks, to help tend abused motors long past due for overhaul.

That is—if one could even call Hannes Suessi human anymore.

Am I more than I was? Or less?

He now had "eyes" all over the engine room—remote pickups linked directly to his ceramic-encased brain. Using portable drones, Hannes could supervise Karkaett and Chuchki far across the wide chamber . . . or even small crews working on alien vessels elsewhere in the great underwater scrap yard. In this way he could offer advice and comfort when they grew nervous, or when their bodies screamed with cetacean claustrophobia.

Unfortunately, cyborg abilities did nothing to prevent loneliness.

You should never have left me here alone, Hannes chided Emerson's absent spirit. *You were an engineer, not a secret agent or star pilot! You had no business traipsing off, doing heroic deeds.*

There were specialists for such tasks. *Streaker* had been assigned several "heroes" when she first set out—individuals with the right training and personalities, equipping them to face dangerous challenges and improvise their way through any situation.

Unfortunately, those qualified ones were gone—Captain Creideiki, Tom Orley, Lieutenant Hikahi, and even the young midshipman Toshio—all used up in that costly escape from Kithrup.

I guess someone had to fill in after that, Hannes conceded.

In fact, Emerson pulled off one daring coup on Oakka, the green world, when the Obeyer Alliance sprang a trap while Gillian tried to negotiate a peaceful surrender to officials of the Navigation Institute.

Not even the suspicious Niss Machine reckoned that neutral Galactic bureaucrats might betray their oaths and violate *Streaker*'s truce pennant. It wasn't supposed to be possible. If not for Emerson's daring trek across Oakka's jungle, taking out a Jophur field-emitter station, *Streaker* would have fallen into the clutches of a single fanatic clan—the one thing the Terragens Council said must not occur, at any cost.

But you let one success go to your head, eh? What were you thinking? That you were another Tom Orley?

A few months later you pulled that crazy stunt, veering a jury-rigged Thennanin fighter through the Fractal System, firing recklessly to "cover" our escape. What did that accomplish, except getting yourself killed?

He recalled the view from *Streaker*'s bridge, looking across the inner cavity of a vast, frosty structure the size of a solar system, built of condensed primal matter. A jagged, frothy structure with a pale star in its heart. Emerson's fighter swerved amid the spiky reaches of that enormous artifact, spraying bright but useless rays while claws of hydrogen ice converged around it.

Foolish heroism. The Old Ones could have stopped Streaker *just as easily as they stopped you, if they really wanted to.*

They meant to let us get away.

He winced, recalling how Emerson's brave, futile "diversion" ended in a burst of painful light, a flicker against the immense, luminous fractal dome. Then *Streaker* fled down a tunnel between dimensions, thread-gliding all the way to forbidden Galaxy Four. Once there, her twisty path skirted the trade winds of a hydrogen-breathing civilization, then plunged past a sooty supergiant whose eruption might at last cover the Earthship's trail.

Others came to Jijo in secret before us, letting Izmunuti erase their tracks.

It should have worked for us, too.

But Hannes knew what was different, this time.

Those others didn't already have a huge price on their heads. You could buy half a spiral arm with the bounty that's been offered for Streaker, *by several rich, terrified patron lines.*

Hannes sighed. The recent depth-charge attack had been imprecise, so the hunters only suspected a general area of sea bottom. But the chase was on again. And Hannes had work to do.

At least I have an excuse to avoid another damned meeting of the ship's council. It's a farce, anyway, since we always wind up doing whatever Gillian decides. We'd be crazy not to.

Karkaett signaled that the motivator array was aligned. Hannes used a cyborg arm to adjust calibration dials on the master control, trying to imitate Emerson's deft touch. The biomechanical extensions that replaced his hands were marvelous gifts, extending both ability and life span—though he still missed the tactile pleasure of fingertips.

The Old Ones were generous . . . then they robbed us and drove us out. They gave life and took it. They might have betrayed us for the reward . . . or else sheltered us in their measureless world. Yet they did neither.

Their agenda ran deeper than mere humans could fathom. Perhaps everything that happened afterward was part of some enigmatic plan.

Sometimes I think humanity would've been better off just staying in bed.

Tsh't

SHE TOLD GILLIAN BASKIN WHAT SHE THOUGHT OF the decision.

"I still do not agree with bringing those young sooners back here."

The blond woman looked back at Tsh't with tired eyes. Soft lines at the corners had not been there when *Streaker* started this voyage. It was easy to age during a mission like this.

"Exile did seem best, for their own good. But they may be more useful here."

"Yesss . . . assuming they're telling the truth about *hoons* and *Jophur* sitting around with humans and urs, reading paper books and quoting Mark Twain!"

Gillian nodded. "Farfetched, I know. But—"

"Think of the coincidence! No sooner does our scout sub find an old urrish cache than these so-called kids and their toy bathysphere drop in."

"They would have died, if the *Hikahi* didn't snatch them up," pointed out the ship's physician, Makanee.

"Perhaps. But consider, not long after they arrived here,

we sensed gravitic motors headed straight for this rift canyon. Then someone started bombing the abysssss! Was that a fluke? Or did spies lead them here?"

"Calling bombs down on their own heads?" The dolphin surgeon blew a raspberry. "A simpler explanation is that one of our explorer robots got caught, and was traced to this general area."

In fact, Tsh't knew the four sooner children hadn't brought Galactics to the Rift. They had nothing to do with it. She was herself responsible.

Back when *Streaker* was preparing to flee the Fractal System, heading off on another of Gillian's brilliant, desperate ploys, Tsh't had impulsively sent a secret message. A plea for help from the one source she felt sure of, revealing the ship's destination and arranging a rendezvous at Jijo.

Gillian will thank me later, she had thought at the time. *When our Rothen lords come to take care of us.*

Only now, images from shore made clear how badly things went wrong.

Two small sky ships, crashed in a swamp . . . the larger revealing fierce, implacable Jophur.

Tsh't wondered how her well-meant plan could go so badly. *Did the Rothen allow themselves to be followed? Or was my message intercepted?*

Worry and guilt gnawed her gut.

Another voice entered the discussion. Mellifluous. Emanating from a spiral of rotating lines that glowed at one end of the conference table.

"So Alvin's bluff played no role in your decision, Dr. Baskin?"

"Is he bluffing? These kids grew up reading Melville and Bickerton. Maybe he recognized dolphin shapes under those bulky exo-suits. Or we may have let hints slip, during conversation."

"Only the Niss spoke to them directly," Tsh't pointed out, thrusting her jaw toward the whirling hologram.

It replied with unusual contrition.

"Going over recordings, I concede having used terms such as *kilometer* and *hour* . . . out of shipboard habit. Alvin and his friends might have correlated this with their extensive knowledge of Anglic, since Galactics would not use wolfling measurements."

"You mean a Tymbrimi computer ccan make mistakesss?" Tsh't asked, tauntingly.

The spinning motif emitted a low humm they all now recognized as the philosophical umbling sound of a reflective hoon.

"Flexible beings exhibit an ability to learn new ways," the Niss explained. "My creators donated me to serve aboard this ship for that reason. It is why the Tymbrimi befriended you Earthling rapscallions, in the first place."

The remark was relatively gentle teasing, compared with the machine's normal, biting wit.

"Anyway," Gillian continued, "it wasn't Alvin's bluff that swayed me."

"Then what-t?" Makanee asked.

The Niss hologram whirled with flashing speckles, and answered for Gillian.

"It is the small matter of the tytlal . . . *the noor beast who speaks*. It has proved uncooperative and uninformative, despite our urgent need to understand its presence here.

"Dr. Baskin and I now agree.

"We need the children for that reason. Alvin, above all.

"To help persuade it to talk to us."

Sooners

Emerson

HE BLAMES HIMSELF. HIS MIND HAD BEEN ON FAR-away places and times. Distracted, he was slow reacting when Sara fell.

Till that moment, Emerson was making progress in the struggle to put his past in order, one piece at a time. No easy task with part of his brain missing—the part that once offered words to lubricate any thought or need.

Hard-planted inhibitions fight his effort to remember, punishing every attempt with savagery that makes him grunt and sweat. But the peculiar panoramas help for a while. Ricocheting colors and half-liquid landscapes jar some of the niches where chained memories lie.

One recollection erupts whole. An old one, from childhood. Some neighbors had a big German shepherd who loved to *hunt bees*.

The dog used to stalk his quarry in a very uncanine manner, crouching and twitching like some ridiculous ungainly cat, pursuing the unsuspecting insect through flower beds and tall grass. Then he pounced, snapping powerful jaws around the outmatched prey.

As a boy, Emerson would stare in amazed delight while outraged buzzing echoed behind the shepherd's bared teeth, followed by a vivid instant when the bee gave up protesting and lashed with its stinger. The dog would snort, grimace, and sneeze. Yet, brief pain came mixed with evident triumph. Bee hunting gave meaning to his gelded suburban life.

Emerson wonders, why does this metaphor resonate so strongly? Is he the *dog,* overriding agony to snatch one defiant memory after another?

Or is he the *bee?*

Emerson recalls just fragments about the haughty entities who reamed his mind, then sent his body plummeting to Jijo in fiery ruin. But he knows how they regarded his kind—like insects.

He pictures himself with a sharp stinger, wishing for a chance to make the Old Ones sneeze. He dreams of teaching them to hate the taste of bees.

Emerson lays hard-won memories in a chain. A necklace with far more gaps than pearls. Easiest come events from childhood, adolescence, and years of training for the Terragens Survey Service. . . .

Even when the horse caravan departs the land of stabbing colors to climb a steep mountain trail, he has other tools to work with—music, math, and hand signs that he trades with Prity, sharing jokes of ultimate crudity. During rest breaks, his sketchpad helps tap the subconscious, using impatient slashes and curves to draw free-form images from the dark time.

Streaker . . .

The ship takes form, almost drawing itself—a lovingly rendered cylinder with hornlike flanges arrayed in circuits along its length. He draws her *underwater*—surrounded by drifting seaweed—abnormal for a vessel of deep space, but it makes sense as other memories fill in.

Kithrup . . .

That awful world where the *Streaker* came seeking shelter after barely escaping a surprise ambush, learning that a hundred fleets were at war over the right to capture her.

Kithrup. A planet whose oceans were poison . . . but a useful place to make repairs, since just half a dozen crew members had legs to stand on. The rest—bright, temperamental dolphins—needed a watery realm to work in. Besides, it seemed a good place to hide after the disaster at . . .

Morgran . . .

A transfer point. Safest of the fifteen ways to travel from star to star. Simply dive toward one at the right slope and distance, and you'd exit at some other point, far across the stellar wheel. Even the Earthling slowboat *Vesarius* had managed it, though quite by accident, before humanity acquired the techniques of Galactic science.

Thinking of Morgran brings *Keepiru* to mind, the finest pilot Emerson ever knew—the show-off!—steering *Streaker* out of danger with flamboyance that shocked the ambushers, plunging her back into the maelstrom, away from the brewing space battle . . .

. . . like the other battle that developed weeks later, over Kithrup. Fine, glistening fleets, the wealth of noble clans, tearing at each other, destroying in moments the pride of many worlds. Emerson's hand flies as he draws exploding arcs across a sheet of native paper, ripping it as he jabs, frustrated by inability to render the gorgeous savagery he once witnessed with his own eyes. . . .

Emerson folds the drawings away when the party remounts, glad that his flowing tears are concealed by the rewq.

Later, when they face a steaming volcano caldera, he abruptly recalls another basin, this one made of folded space . . . *the Shallow Cluster* . . . *Streaker's* last survey site before heading for Morgran—a place empty of anything worth noting, said the Galactic Library.

Then what intelligence or premonition provoked Captain Creideiki to head for such an unpromising site?

Surely, in all the eons, someone else must have stumbled on the armada of derelict ships *Streaker* discovered there— cause of all her troubles. He can envision those silent arks now, vast as moons but almost transparent, as if they could not quite decide *to be*.

This memory hurts in a different way. Claw marks lie across it, as if some outside force once pored over it in detail—perhaps seeking to read patterns in the background stars. Retracing *Streaker*'s path to a single point in space.

Emerson figures they probably failed. Constellations were never his specialty.

"Emerson, you don't have to go."

His head jerks as those words peel from a memory more recent than Morgran or Kithrup, by many months.

Emerson pans the land of fevered colors, now seen from high above. At last he finds her face in rippling glimmers. A worried face, burdened with a hundred lives and vital secrets to preserve. Again she speaks, and the words come whole, because he never stored them in parts of the brain meant for mundane conversation.

Because everything she said to him had always seemed like music.

"We need you here. Let's find another way."

But there was no other way. Not even Gillian's sarcastic Tymbrimi computer could suggest one before Emerson climbed aboard a salvaged Thennanin fighter, embarking on a desperate gamble.

Looking back in time, he hopes to see in Gillian's eyes the same expression she used to have when bidding Tom farewell on some perilous venture.

He sees worried concern, even affection. But it's not the same.

Emerson frees his gaze from the torment-colored desert, turning east toward less disturbing vistas. Far-off mountains offer respite with natural undulating shapes, softened by verdant green forests.

Then, from one tall peak, there comes a glittering flash! Several more gleam in series. A rhythm that seems to *speak*. . . .

His intrigued detachment is cut short by a frightened yell. Yet, for an instant Emerson remains too distant, too slow to turn. He does not see Sara tumble off the path. But Prity's scream tears through him like a torch thrust into cobwebs.

Sara's name pours from his throat with involuntary clarity. His body finally acts, leaping in pursuit.

Hurtling down the jagged talus slope, he flings eloquent curses at the universe, defying it—*daring it*—to take another friend.

Lark

THE SERGEANT'S FACE WAS STREAKED WITH CAMOU-flage. Her black hair still bore flecks of loam and grass from worming through crevices and peering between brambles. Yet Lark had never seen Jeni Shen look better.

People thrive doing the thing they were born for. In Jeni's case, that's being a warrior. She'd rather have lived when the elder and younger Drakes were fashioning the Great Peace out of blood and fire than during the peace itself.

"So far, so good," the young militia scout reported. Blur-cloth overalls made it hard to trace her outline amid stark lantern shadows.

"I got close enough to watch the emissaries reenter the valley, bringing the sages' reply to the Jophur. A couple of guard robots swooped in to look them over, especially poor Vubben, sniffing him from wheel rims to eyestalks. Then all six ambassadors headed down to the Glade, with the bots in escort." Jeni made slanting downward motions with her hands. "That leaves just one or two drones patrolling this section of perimeter! Seems we couldn't ask for a better chance to make our move."

"Can there be any question?" added Rann. The tall starfarer leaned against a limestone wall with arms folded. The Danik was unarmed, but otherwise Rann acted as if this were *his* expedition. "Of course we shall proceed. There is no other option."

Despite Rann's poised assurance, the plan was actually Lark's. So was the decision whether to continue. His would be the responsibility, if three-score brave lives were lost in the endeavor . . . or if their act provoked the Jophur into spasms of vengeful destruction.

We might undermine the High Sages at the very moment when they have the Galactic untraekis calmed down.

On the other hand, how could the Six Races possibly pay the price the Jophur were demanding? While the sages tried to negotiate a lower cost, someone had to see if there was a better way. A way not to pay at all.

Anxious eyes regarded him from all corners of the grotto—one of countless steamy warrens that laced these hills. Ling's gaze was among the most relentless, standing far apart from Rann. The two star lords had been at odds since they worked to decode those cryptic data slabs—that awful afternoon when Rann cried "treason!" then a dread gold mist fell on Dooden Mesa. Each sky human had a different reason to help this desperate mission.

Lark found little cheer in Jeni's report. *Only one or two drones left.* According to Lester Cambel's aides, the remaining robots could still probe some distance underground, on guard against approaching threats. On the plus side, this terrain was a muddle of steam vents and juttering quakes. Then there were the subtle patterning songs put out by the Holy Egg—emanations that set Lark's stone amulet trembling against his chest.

They all watched, awaiting his decision—human, urs, and hoon volunteers, plus some qheuens who weren't yet sick.

"All right." Lark nodded. "Let's do it."

A terse, decisive command. Grinning, Jeni spun about to forge deeper into the cavern, followed by lantern bearers.

What Lark had meant to say was, *Hell no! Let's get out of here. I'll buy a round of drinks so everyone can raise a glass for poor Uthen.*

But if he mentioned his friend's name, he might sob the wrenching grief inside. So Lark took his place along the twisty column of figures stooping and shuffling through the dim passage, lit by glow patches stuck to the walls.

His thoughts caromed as he walked. For instance, he

found himself wondering where on the Slope all six races *could* drink the same toast at the same time? Not many inns served both alcohol and fresh simla blood, since humans and urs disdained each other's feeding habits. And most traeki politely refrained from eating in front of other races.

I do know one bar in Tarek Town . . . that is, if Tarek hasn't already been smothered by a downpour of golden rain. After Dooden, the Jophur may go for the bigger towns, where so many g'Kek live.

It makes you wonder why the g'Kek came to Jijo in the first place. They can only travel the Path of Redemption if it is paved.

Lark shook his head.

Trivia. Minutiae. Brain synapses keep firing, even when your sole concern is following the man in front of you . . . and not slamming your skull on a stalactite.

When they glanced at him, his followers saw a calm, assertive pose. But within, Lark endured a run-on babble of words, forever filling his unquiet mind.

I should be mourning my friend, right now.

I should be hiring a traeki undertaker, arranging a lavish mulching ceremony, so Uthen's polished carapace can go in style to join the bones and spindles of his foremothers, lying under the Great Midden.

It's my duty to pay a formal visit to the Gray Queens, in that dusty hall where they once dominated most of the Slope. The Chamber of Ninety Tooth-Carved Pillars, where they still make pretenses at regal glory. But how could I explain to those qheuen matrons how two of their brightest sons died—Harullen, sliced apart by alien lasers, and Uthen, slain by pestilence?

Can I tell those ashen empresses their other children may be next?

Uthen had been his greatest friend, the colleague who shared his fascination with the ebb and flow of Jijo's fragile ecosystem. Though never joining Lark in heresy, Uthen was the one other person who understood *why* sooner races should never have come to this world. The one to comprehend why some Galactic laws were good.

I let you down, old pal. But if I can't perform all those

other duties, maybe I can arrange something to compensate.

Justice.

Debris littered the floor of the last large cavern, strewn there during the Zealots' Plot, when a cabal of young rebels used these same corridors to sneak explosives under the Danik research station, incinerating Ling's friend Besh and one of the Rothen star lords. Repercussions still spread from that event, like ripples after a large stone strikes a pond.

The Jophur battleship now lay atop the station wreckage, yet no one suggested using the same method of attack a second time. Assuming a mighty starcraft *could* be blown up, it would take such massive amounts of exploser paste that Lark's team would still be hauling barrels by next Founders' Day. Anyway, there were no volunteers to approach the deadly space behemoth. Lark's plan meant coming no closer than several arrowflights. Even so, the going would be hard and fraught with peril.

"From here on, the way's too close for grays," Jeni said.

Urrish partisans peered down a passage that narrowed considerably, coiling their long necks in unison, sniffing an aroma their kind disliked.

The gray qheuens squatted while others unstrapped supplies from their chitin backs. Given enough time, the big fellows might widen the corridor with their digging claws and diamond-like teeth, but Lark felt better sending them back. Who knew how much time they had, with plague spreading on Jijo's winds? Was it a genocide bug? Ling had found supporting evidence on decoded data wafers, though Rann still denied it could be of Rothen origin.

The glowering starman was obsessed with a different wafer-gleaned fact.

There had been a *spy* among the station's staff of outlaw gene raiders. Someone who kept a careful diary, recording every misdemeanor performed by the Rothen and their human servants.

An agent of the Terragens Council!

Apparently, Earth's ruling body had an informant among the clan of human fanatics who worshiped Rothen lords.

He wanted badly to quiz Ling, but there was no time for their old question game. Not since they fled the Dooden disaster along with Lester Cambel's panicky aides, plunging through a maze of towering boo. New trails and fresh-cut trunks had flustered the breathless fugitives until they spilled into an uncharted clearing, surprising a phalanx of traeki who stood in a long row, venting noxious vapors like hissing kettles.

Galloping squads of urrish militia then swarmed in to protect the busy traeki, nipping at ankles, as if the humans were stampeding simlas, driving Cambel's team away from the clearing, diverting them toward havens to the west and south.

Even after finally reaching a campsite refuge, there had been no respite to discuss far-off Galactic affairs. Ling spent her time with the medics, relating what little she had learned from the spy's notes about the qheuen plague.

Meanwhile, Lark found himself surrounded by furious activity, commanding an ever-growing entourage of followers.

It goes to show, desperate people will follow anyone with a plan.

Even one as loony as mine.

Hoonish bearers took up the grays' burdens, and the caravan was off again. Half a dozen blue qheuens took up the rear, so young their shells were still moist from larval fledging. Though small for their kind, they still needed help from men with hammers and crowbars, chiseling away limestone obstructions. Lark's scheme counted on these adolescent volunteers.

He hoped his farfetched plan wasn't the only one at work.

There is always prayer.

Lark fondled his amulet. It felt cool. For now the Egg was quiescent.

At a junction the earlier zealot cabal had veered left, carrying barrels of exploser paste to a cave beneath the Rothen station. But Lark's group turned right. They had less distance to cover, but their way was more hazardous.

Jimi the Blessed was among the burly men helping widen the path, attacking an obstruction with such fury Lark had to intervene.

"Easy, Jimi! You'll wake the recycled dead!"

That brought laughter from the sweaty laborers, and booming umbles from several hoonish porters. *Brave* hoons. Lark recalled how their kind disliked closed places. The urs, normally comfortable underground, grew more nervous with each sign of approaching water.

None of them were happy to be approaching the giant star cruiser.

The Six Races had spent centuries cowering against *The Day* when ships of the Institutes would come judge their crimes. Yet, when great vessels came, they did not bear high-minded magistrates, but *thieves,* and then brutal killers. Where the Rothen and their human stooges seemed crafty and manipulative, the Jophur were chilling.

They demand what we cannot give.

We don't know anything about the "dolphin ship" they seek. And we'd rather be damned than hand over our g'Kek brothers.

So Lark, who had spent his life hoping Galactics would come end the illegal colony on Jijo, now led a desperate bid to battle star gods.

Human literature has been so influential since the Great Printing. It's full of forlorn causes. Endeavors that no rational person would entertain.

He and Ling were helping each other descend a limestone chute, glistening with seepage and slippery lichen, when word arrived from the forward scouts.

"Water just ahead."

That was the message, sent back by Jeni Shen.

So, Lark thought. *I was right.*

Then he added—

So far.

The liquid was oily and cold. It gave off a musty aroma.

None of which stopped two eager young blues from creeping straight into the black pool, trailing mulc-fiber line from a spool. Hoons with hand pumps kept busy inflating air bladders while Lark steeled himself to enter that dark, wet place.

Having second thoughts?

Jeni checked his protective suit of skink membranes. It might ward off the chill, but that was the least of Lark's worries.

I can take cold. But there had better be enough air.

The bladders were an untested innovation. Each was a traeki ring, thick-ribbed to hold gas under pressure. Jeni affixed one to his back, and showed him how to breathe through its fleshy protrusion—a rubbery tentacle that would provide fresh air and scrub the old.

You grow up depending on traeki-secreted chemicals to make native foods edible, and traeki-distilled alcohol to liven celebrations. A traeki pharmacist makes your medicine in a chem-synth ring. Yet you're revolted by the thought of putting one of these things in your mouth.

It tasted like a slimy tallow candle.

Across the narrow chamber, Ling and Rann adjusted quickly to this Jijoan novelty. Of course they had no history to overcome, associating traekis with mulch and rotting garbage.

"Come on," Jeni chided in a low voice that burned his ears. "Don't gag on me, man. You're a sage now. Others are watchin'!"

He nodded—two quick head jerks—and tried again. Fitting his teeth around the tube, Lark bit down as she had taught. The burst of air did not stink as bad as expected. Perhaps it contained a mild relaxant. The pharmacist designers were clever about such things.

Let's hope their star-god cousins don't think of this, as well.

That assumption underlay Lark's plan. Jophur commanders might be wary against direct subterranean assault. But where the buried route combined with *water*, the invaders might not expect trouble.

The Rothen underestimated us. By Ifni and the Egg, the Jophur may do the same.

Each diver also wore a rewq symbiont to protect the eyes and help them see by the dim light of hand-carried phosphors. Webbed gloves and booties completed the ensemble.

Ling's tripping laughter made him turn around, and Lark saw she was pointing at *him* as she guffawed.

"You should talk," he retorted at the ungainly creature she had become, more monstrous than an unmasked Rothen. Hoons paused from laying down cargo by the waterline, and joined in the mirth, umbling good-naturedly while their pet noors grinned with needlelike teeth.

Lark pictured the scene up above, past overlying layers of rock, in the world of light. The Jophur dreadnought squatted astride the mountain glen, thwarting the glade stream in its normal seaward rush. The resulting lake now stretched more than a league uphill.

Water seeks its own level. We must now be several arrowflights from shore. That's a long way to swim before we get to the lake itself.

It couldn't be helped. Their goal was hard to reach, in more ways than one.

Bubbles in the pool. One qheuen cupola broached the surface, followed by another. The young blues crawled ashore, breathing heavily through multiple leg vents, reporting in excited GalSix.

"The way to open water—it is clear. Good time—this we made. To the target—we shall now escort you."

Cheers lifted from the hoons and urs, but Lark felt no stirring.

They weren't the ones who would have to go the rest of the way.

Water transformed the cavities and grottoes. Flippers kicked up clouds of silt, filling the phosphor beams with a myriad of distracting speckles. Lark's trusty rewq pulled tricks with polarization, transforming the haze to partial clarity. Still, it took concentration to avoid colliding with jagged limestone outcrops. The guide rope saved him from getting lost.

Cave diving felt a lot like being a junior sage of the Commons—an experience he never sought or foresaw in his former life as a scientist heretic.

How ungainly swimming humans appeared next to the graceful young qheuens, who seized the rugged walls with flashing claws, propelling themselves with uncanny agility, nearly as at-home in freshwater as on solid ground.

His skin grew numb where the skink coverings pulled loose. Other parts grew hot from exertion. More upsetting was the squirmy traeki tentacle in his mouth, anticipating his needs in unnerving ways. It would not let him hold his breath, as a man might do while concentrating on some near-term problem, but tickled his throat to provoke an exhalation. The first time it happened, he nearly retched. (What if he chucked up breakfast? Would he and the ring both asphyxiate? Or would it take his gift as a tasty, predigested bonus?)

Lark was so focused on the guide rope that he missed the transition from stony catacombs to a murky plain of sodden meadows, drowned trees, and drifting debris. But soon the silty margins fell behind as daylight transformed the Glade of Gathering—now the bottom of an upland lake—giving commonplace shapes macabre unfamiliarity.

The guide rope passed near a stand of lesser boo whose surviving stems were tall enough to reach the surface, far overhead. Qheuens gathered around one tube, sucking down drafts of air. When sated, they spiraled around Lark and the humans, nudging them toward the next stretch of guide rope.

Long before details loomed through the silty haze, he made out their target by its *glow*. Rann and Ling thrashed flippers, passing Jeni in their haste. By the time Lark caught up, they were pressing hands against a giant slick sarcophagus, the hue of yellow moonrise. Within lay a cigar-shaped vessel, the Rothen ship, their home away from home, now sealed in a deadly trap.

The two starfarers split up, he swimming right and she left. By silent agreement, Jeni accompanied the big man—despite their size difference, she was the one more qualified to keep an eye on Rann. Lark kept near Ling, watching as she moved along the golden wall.

Though he had more experience than other Sixers with Galactic god machines, it was his first time near this interloper whose dramatic coming so rudely shattered Gathering Festival, many weeks ago. So magnificent and terrible it had seemed! Daunting and invincible. Yet now it was helpless. Dead or implacably imprisoned.

Tentatively, Lark identified some features, like the jutting anchors that held a ship against quantum probability fluctuations . . . whatever that meant. The self-styled techies who worked for Lester Cambel were hesitant about even the basics of starcraft design. As for the High Sage himself, Lester had taken no part in Lark's briefing, choosing instead to brood in his tent, guilt-ridden over the doom he helped bring on Dooden Mesa.

Despite the crowding sense of danger, Lark discovered a kind of spooky beauty, swimming in this realm where sunlight slanted in long rippling shafts, filled with sparkling motes—a silent, strangely contemplative world.

Besides, even wrapped in skink membranes, Ling's athletic body was a sight to behold.

They rounded the star cruiser's rim, where a sharp shadow abruptly cut off the sun. It might be a cloud, or the edge of a mountain. Then he realized—

It's the Jophur ship.

Though blurred by murky water, the domelike outline sent shivers down his back. Towering mightily at the lake's edge, it could have swallowed the Rothen vessel whole.

A strange thought struck him.

First the Rothen awed us. Then we saw their "majesty" cut down by real power. What if it happens again? What kind of newcomer might overwhelm the Jophur? A hovering mountain range? One that throws the whole Slope into night?

He pictured successive waves of "ships," each vaster than before, matching first the moons, then all Jijo, and—why not?—the sun or even mighty Izmunuti!

Imagination is the most amazing thing. It lets a ground-hugging savage fill his mind with fantastic unlikelihoods.

Churning bubbles nearly tore the rewq off his face as Ling sped up, kicking urgently. Lark hurried after . . . only to arrest himself moments later, staring.

Just ahead, Ling traced the golden barrier with one hand, just meters from a gaping opening. A *hatchway,* backlit by a radiant interior. Several figures stood in the portal—three humans and a Rothen lord, wearing his appealing symbiotic mask. The quartet surveyed their all-enclosing golden prison with instruments, wearing expressions of concern.

Yet, all four bipeds seemed frozen, embedded in crystal time.

Up close, the yellow cocoon resembled the *preservation beads* left by that alpine mulc spider, the one whose mad collecting fetish nearly cost Dwer and Rety their lives, months back. But this trap was no well-shaped ovoid. It resembled a partly melted candle, with overlapping golden puddles slumped around its base. The Jophur had been generous in their gift of frozen temporality, pouring enough to coat the ship thoroughly.

Like at Dooden Mesa, Lark thought.

It seemed an ideal way to slay one's enemies without using destructive fire. *Maybe the Jophur can't risk damaging Jijo's ecosphere. That would be a major crime before the great Institutes, like gene raiding and illegal settlement.*

On the other hand, the untraeki invaders hadn't been so scrupulous in scything the forest around their ship. So perhaps the golden trap had another purpose. To capture, rather than kill? Perhaps the g'Kek denizens of Dooden Mesa might yet be rescued from their shimmering tomb.

That had been Lark's initial thought, three days ago. In hurried experiments, more mulc-spider relics were thawed out, using the new traeki solvents. Some of the preserved items had once been alive, birds and bush creepers that long ago fell into the spider's snare.

All emerged from their cocoons quite dead.

Perhaps the Jophur have better revival methods, Lark thought at the time. *Or else they don't mean to restore their victims, only to preserve them as timeless trophies.*

Then, night before last, an idea came to Lark in the form of a dream.

The hivvern lays its eggs beneath deep snow, which melts in the spring, letting each egg sink in slushy mud, which then hardens all around. Yet the ground softens again, when rainy season comes. Then the hivvern larva emerges, swimming free.

When he wakened, the idea was there, entire.

A spaceship has a sealed metal shell, like the hivvern egg. The Rothen ship may be trapped, but its crew were never touched.

Those within may yet live.

And now proof stood before him. The four in the hatchway were clearly aware of the golden barrier surrounding their ship, examining it with tools at hand.

Just one problem—they did not move. Nor was there any sign they knew they were being observed from just a hoon's length away.

Treading water, Ling scrawled on her wax-covered note board and raised it for Lark to see.

TIME DIFFERENT INSIDE.

He fumbled with his own board, tethered to his waist.

TIME SLOWER?

Her answer was confusing.

PERHAPS.

OR ELSE QUANTIZED.

FRAME-SHIFTED.

His perplexed look conveyed more than written words. Ling wiped the board and scratched again.

DO EXACTLY AS I DO.

He nodded, watching her carefully. Ling swished her arms and legs to turn *away* from the ship. Imitating her, Lark found himself looking across the poor wounded Glade. All the trees had been shattered by ravening beams, left to submerge under the rising lake. Turbid water made everything hazy, but Lark thought he saw *bones* mixed among the splinters. Urrish ribs and hoonish spines, jumbled with grinning human skulls. Not the way bodies ought to be drossed. Not respectful of the dead, or Jijo.

Perhaps the Jophur will let us seed a mulc spider in this new lake, he mused. *Something ought to be done to clean up the mess.*

He was jarred by Ling's nudge. TURN BACK NOW, her wax board said. Lark copied her maneuver again . . . and stared in surprise for a second time.

They had moved!

As before, statues stood in the hatchway. Only now their poses were all changed! One human pointed outward wearing an amazed look. Another seemed to peer straight at Lark, as if frozen in midrealization.

They did all this while we were turned away?

Time's flow within the golden shell was stranger than he could begin to comprehend.

THIS MAY TAKE SOME DOING, Ling wrote.

Lark met her eyes, noting they held tense, hopeful irony. He nodded.

You could say that again.

Alvin

I SPENT MOST OF THE RETURN TRIP WITH MY NOSE buried in my journal, reviewing all the things that I've seen and heard since *Wuphon's Dream* plunged below Terminus Rock. Pincer kindly chewed my pencil to a point for me. Then I lay down and wrote down the section before this one.

What began as a guess grew into reinforced conviction. Concentration also diverted attention from nervous anticipation and the pain in my slowly healing spine. My friends tried wheedling me, but I lapsed into hoonish stubbornness, refusing to confide in them. After all, the phuvnthus had gone to great lengths to hide their identity.

The spinning voice said it was to protect us. Maybe that was just patronizing glaver dreck. Typical from grown-ups. But what if he told the truth? How can I risk my friends?

When the time comes, I'll confront the voice alone.

Sara

SHE DRIFTED IN A CLOUD OF MATHEMATICS.

All around her floated arcs and conic sections, glowing, as though made of enduring fire. Meteors streaked past, coruscating along paths smoothly ordained by gravity.

Then more stately shapes joined the frolicking figures and she guessed they might be planets whose routes were elliptical, not parabolic. Each had its own reference frame, around which all other masses seemed to move.

Rising, falling . . .
Rising, falling . . .

The dance spoke of a lost science she had studied once, in an obscure text from the Biblos Archive. Its name floated through her delirium—*orbital mechanics*—as if managing the ponderous gyres of suns and moons were no more complex than maintaining a windmill or waterwheel.

Dimly, Sara knew physical pain. But it came to her as if through a swaddling of musty clothes, like something unpleasant tucked in a bottom pantry drawer. The strong scent of traeki unguents filled her nostrils, dulling every agony except one . . . the uneasy knowledge—*I've been harmed.*

Sometimes she roused enough to hear speech . . . several lisping urrish voices . . . the gruff terseness of Kurt the Exploser . . . and one whose stiff, pedantic brilliance she knew from happier days.

Purofsky. Sage of mysteries . . .
But what is he doing here?
. . . and where is here?

At one point she managed to crack her eyelids in hopes of solving the riddle. But Sara quickly decided she must still be dreaming. For no place could exist like the one she witnessed through a blurry haze—a world of spinning glass. A universe of translucent saucers, disks and wheels, tilting and rolling against each other at odd angles, reflecting shafts of light in rhythmic bursts.

It was all too dizzying. She closed her eyes against the maelstrom, yet it continued in her mind, persisting in the form of abstractions.

A sinusoidal wave filled her mental foreground, but no longer the static shape she knew from inked figures in books. Instead, this one undulated like ripples on a pond, with time the apparent free variable.

Soon the first wave was joined by a second, with twice the frequency, then a third with the peaks and troughs compressed yet again. New cycles merged, one after an-

other, combining in an endless series—*a transform*—
whose sum built toward a new complex figure, an entity
with jagged peaks and valleys, like a mountain range.

Out of order . . . chaos . . .

Mountains brought to mind the last thing Sara had seen,
before spilling off the volcano's narrow path, tumbling
over sharp stones toward a river of fire.

*Flashes from a distant peak . . . long-short, short-long,
medium-short-short . . .*

*Coded speech, conveyed by a language of light, not un-
like GalTwo . . .*

Words of urgency, of stealth and battle . . .

Her mind's fevered random walk was broken now and
then by soft contact on her brow—a warm cloth, or else a
gentle touch. She recognized the long, slender shape of
Prity's fingers, but there was another texture as well, a
man's contact on her arm, her cheek, or just holding her
hand.

When he sang to her, she knew it was the Stranger . . .
Emerson . . . by his odd accent and the way the lyrics
flowed, smoothly from memory, as a liquid stream, without
thought to any particular word or phrase. Yet the song was
no oddly syncopated Earthling ballad, but a Jijoan folk ballad, familiar as a lullaby. Sara's mother sang it to her, whenever she was ill—as Sara used to murmur it to the man
from space, soon after he crashed on Jijo, barely clinging to
life.

> "One comes from an umbling sac, a
>   song for you to keep,
> Two is for a pair of hands, to spin you
>   happy sleep,
> Three fat rings will huff and puff out
>   clouds of happy steam,
> Four eyes wave and dance about, to
>   watch over your dream,
>
> "Five claws will carve your new hope
>   box, all without a seam,

> *Six will bring you flashing hooves to*
> *cross the prairie plain,*
> *Seven is for hidden thoughts, waiting*
> *in the deep,*
> *But eight comes from a giant stone,*
> *whose patterns gently creep."*

Even half-conscious, she knew something important. He could not sing unless the words were stored deep within, beyond the scarred part of his brain. It meant she must have touched him, when their roles were reversed.

Not all the unguents in the world—nor the cool beauty of mathematics—could do as much for Sara. What finally called her back was knowing someone missed her, when she was gone.

Ewasx

THERE WAS AN ENJOYABLE SENSE OF IMPORTANCE TO our task, was there not, My rings? There we stood, this stack of shabby-looking, retread toruses, deputized with a noble job—explaining to envoys of six races the new order of life on this world.

FIRST—they should not hope for great judges to come from those Institutes who mediate among ten thousand starfaring races. Passions run too high, throughout the Five Galaxies. Institute forces have withdrawn, along with timid, so-called moderate clans, a dithering, ineffectual majority. Only great religious alliances show nerve nowadays, battling over which way the Galactic wheels shall turn during a time of changes.

WE ARE YOUR JUDGES, I told the ambassadors. Out of kindness, we the *Polkjhy* crew have volunteered to serve as both posse and jury, chastening the seven races who invaded this world's fallow peace.

To demonstrate this benevolence, we have delayed by

many days the important work that originally brought us here, even though it means leaving our comrades to make their own repairs in that eastern swamp, while our remaining corvette tours the Slope, photographing and recording evidence. It also gives us an opportunity to demonstrate the irresistible majesty of our power. We did this by destroying egregious structures that sooners should not use, if their goal truly is racial redemption.

IT IS NOTED THAT YOU WERE NOT MUCH HELP IN THIS WORK, MY RINGS. (Accept these reproaching jolts, as tokens of loving guidance.) Asx melted many memories, before capture and conversion, yet we/I did recall certain abominations. We gained credit, for instance, by helping target the Bibur River steamboats, and a refinery tower in Tarek Town, an edifice called the Palace of Stinks.

DON'T WORRY. In time, we of the *Polkjhy* will find all pathetic objects-of-sin prized by headstrong sooners. We shall help erase the flagrant hypocrisy of tool use among those who chose the Downward Path!

SECOND comes our unstoppable demand for justice. The High Sages showed surprising good sense by swiftly emitting a call, soon after our last meeting. A flicker of computer cognizance, leading our corvette to Dooden Mesa. But this token gesture will not suffice for long. We want every living member of the g'Kek race accounted for. That should not be too hard. Stranded on a roadless planet, they are singularly immobile beings.

"Please do not destroy our wheeled brethren," the envoys entreat. "Let the g'Kek seek holy shelter down Redemption's Path. For is it not said that all debts and vendettas stop, once innocence is resumed?"

At first we see this as yet more lawyerly blather. But then, surprisingly, our senior Priest-Stack agrees! Moreover, that august pile makes an unusual, innovative suggestion—

HERE IS THE QUESTION posed by the Priest-Stack:

What kind of revenge on the g'Kek would transcend even extinction?

ANSWER: to see the g'Kek race become once again eligible for adoption, *and for their new patrons to be Jophur*!

In their second sequence of uplift, we might transform them as we see fit—into creatures their former selves would have disdained!

Vengeance is best when executed with imagination. This justifies bringing a priest along. Indeed, that stack variety has uses.

Of course this daring plan carries complications. It means refraining from informing the Five Galaxies about this sooner infestation. Instead, our Jophur clan must keep it secret, tending Jijo like our own private garden.

SO WE BECOME CRIMINALS, under Galactic law. But that hardly matters. For those laws will change, once our alliance assumes leadership during the next phase of history.

Especially if the Progenitors have indeed returned.

THIRD comes opportunity for profit. Perhaps the Rothen gene raiders were onto something. Jijo seems exceptionally rich for a fallow world. (The Buyur were good caretakers who left the planet filled with biopossibilities.) Might the Rothen have discovered a likely presentient race already? One ripe for uplift? Should we have bought off the gene raiders so we might have access to their data, instead of sealing them away in time?

REJECT THE NOTION. They are known blackmailers and double-crossers. We will bring in our own biologists to survey Jijo.

AND WHO KNOWS? Perhaps we might accelerate the sooner races along the path they seek! Glavers are already far progressed toward innocence. Hoons, urs, and qheuens have living star cousins who might object if we adopt too soon. But that may change as battle fires burn across the galaxies. As for human wolflings, at last word their homeworld was under siege, in desperate straits.

Perhaps those on Jijo are already the sole remnant of their kind.

THAT LEAVES OUR TRAEKI RELATIVES TO CONSIDER. The rebel stacks who came here sought to reject the gift of the Oailie—the specialized rings that give us purpose and destiny. It is wrenching to see traeki stumbling about like our pathetic ancestors. Such ungainly beings, so placid and unambitious! We should at once commence a program to create master rings in large quantities. Once converted, our cousins will be ideal instruments of dominance and control, able to knowledgeably run this planet for us without further cost to the clan.

ALL THESE CONCERNS SEEMED PARAMOUNT. Yet from the start, some members of the crew chafed at talk of vengeance, or profit, or redemption. Even the fate of local traeki seemed unimportant, compared with the matter that brought the *Polkjhy* here in the first place.

Hints by the Rothen that they knew the whereabouts of the missing prey ship.

The prey ship carrying news of the Progenitors' return.

DROP ALL OTHER CONCERNS AT ONCE! these stacks insisted. Send the remaining corvette east! Do not wait for the first boat's crew to make repairs on their own. Fetch and interrogate the human-slaves-of-Rothen. Search deep-water places where the prey ship might be hiding. Delay no longer!

But our Captain-Leader and Priest-Stack agreed that a few more days would not matter. Our hold on this world is total. The prey cannot escape.

Lark

PALE DAYLIGHT PENETRATED THE LAKE TO WHERE A few drowned trees wafted their branches, as if to a gusting breeze. The rewq over his eyes helped him see, amplifying the dim glow, but Lark found the resulting shadows creepy, adding to a feeling that none of this could possibly be real.

Working underwater alongside Rann and Ling, he took part in an odd ritual, communicating with the trapped inhabitants of the preservation bubble. Since the process began, the hatchway of the imprisoned ship had filled with humans and Rothen, pressing eagerly against the gold barrier. Yet, from the outside no motion was seen. Those within were as still as statues, like wax effigies, depicting people with worried expressions.

Only when Lark and the other swimmers turned away, averting their gaze, did the "statues" change, shifting positions at incredible speed.

According to Ling's terse explanation, scribbled on her wax board, the captives lived in a QUANTUM SEPARATED WORLD. She added something about COGNIZANCE INTERFERENCE BY ORGANIC OBSERVERS and seemed to think that explained it. But Lark failed to see why not-looking should make any difference. No doubt Sara would understand better than her brother, the backwoods biologist. *I used to tease her that the books she loved best were filled with useless abstractions. Concepts no Jijoan would need again. Guess it just shows how little I knew.*

To Lark the whole thing smacked of a particularly inconvenient kind of magic, as if the capricious goddess, Ifni, had invented the gold barrier to test the patience of mortals.

Fortunately, their micro–traeki rings provided the human swimmers with all the air they needed. When pressurized supplies ran out, the little toruses unfolded great feathery fans that waved through the lake water like lazy wings, sieving fresh oxygen for Lark and the others to breathe. Another impressive feature of the ever-adaptable ringed ones. Combined with the skink-skin wet suits and rewqs, it made the swimmers look like bizarre sea monsters to those inside the bubble. Finally, though, the prisoners set up an electronic message plaque that flashed words through the translucent barrier in shining Anglic letters.

WE MUST MAKE COMMON CAUSE, they sent.

So far, Lark's idea had been fruitful. Unlike at tragic Dooden Mesa, these prisoners had been sealed within an airtight hull that kept the golden liquor from swamping their bodies and life-support machinery. Moreover, the chill lake carried away enough heat so their idle engines did not broil them. They were surrounded, enmeshed in strange time. But they were alive.

When Lark stared at one of the Rothen masters, he easily made out the creature's facade. Rewq-generated colors divided its charismatic features, so noble in human terms, into two parts, each with its own aura. Across the upper half lay a fleshy symbiont beast, shaped to provide the regal brow, high cheeks and trademark stately nose. A gray deadness told that some kind of synthetic lens insert lay over the Rothen's eyeballs, and the fine white teeth were artificially capped.

It's an impressive disguise, he thought. Yet even without masks the Rothen were remarkably humanoid, a resemblance that no doubt originally spurred their cunning plan to win over some impressionable Earthlings back in the frantic, naive days soon after contact, turning those converts into a select tribe of loyal aides—the Daniks. If handled right, it would let the Rothen pull quite a few capers using human intermediaries to do the dirty work. And if Daniks were caught in the act, *Earth* would get the blame.

All told, those inside the trapped ship had a destiny they deserved. Lark might have voted to leave them till Jijo reclaimed their dross. Only now an even greater danger loomed, and there was no other place to turn for allies against the Jophur.

The captives inside the shell seemed eager enough. The last line of their message expressed this.

GET US OUT OF HERE!

Floating in the gentle current, Lark saw Rann, the tall Danik leader, write on his wax board.

WE MAY HAVE A WAY.

YOU MUST PREPARE A FORMULA.

IT IS

Lark grabbed for the board, but Ling got there first, snatching the stylus right out of Rann's meaty hand. Surprise, then anger, flared across the part of his face visible between the rewq and breathing ring. But the big man was outnumbered, and knew that Jeni Shen had lethal darts in her underwater crossbow. The militia sergeant watched from a vantage point where her vigilance would not interfere with the time-jerked conversation.

•

Ling replaced Rann's message with another.

HOW DO YOU SUGGEST WE DO THAT?

She slung the sign's strap over her neck so the board rested against her *back*, message outward. At her nodded signal, Rann and Lark joined her turning around. A spooky feeling swarmed Lark's spine as he imagined a flurry of activity taking place behind them. Without observers peering at them, the Rothen-Danik crew were liberated from frozen time, free to read Ling's message, deliberate, and shape a reply.

I never read much physics, Lark thought. *But something feels awful screwy about how this works.*

The swimmers let momentum carry them around. Only a few duras passed before they faced the hatch once more, but most of the Rothen and human figures had moved in that narrow moment. The electric placard now glimmered with new writing.

PREFERRED METHOD: DESTROY THE JOPHUR.

Bubbles burst past Lark's breathing tube as he choked back a guffaw. Ling glanced his way, conveying agreement with a shake of her head. The second half of the message was more serious.

OTHER POSSIBILITY: OFFER JOPHUR WHAT THEY WANT.

BUY OUR FREEDOM!

Lark scanned the crowded statues, where many human faces wore expressions of desperation. He could not help feeling moved as they pleaded for their lives. *In a way it's not their fault. Their ancestors made a stupid deal on their behalf, just as mine did. People must have been both crazed and gullible in those days, right after Earthlings first met Galactic culture.*

It took effort to harden his heart, but Lark knew he must.

Again, Rann tried for the big writing tablet, but Ling wrote fiercely.

WHAT CAN YOU OFFER US, IN RETURN?

On seeing her message, Lark and Rann both stared at her. But Ling seemed unaware that her words carried a personal as well as general meaning. They turned again, giving the prisoners a chance to read and react to Ling's demand. While sweeping the slow circle, Lark glanced toward her, but living goggles made direct eye contact impossible. Her rewq-mediated aura conveyed grim resolve.

Lark expected to find the captives in turmoil, upset by Ling's implied secession. Then he realized. *They only see us when our backs are turned. They may not even know it's Rann and Ling out here, after all!*

WHATEVER WE HAVE.

That was the frank answer, arrayed in shining letters.

Ling's next message was as straight to the point.

RO-KENN RELEASED QHEUEN AND HOON PLAGUES.

MAYBE OTHERS.

CURE THEM, OR ROT.

At this resumed accusation, Rann nearly exploded. Strangled anger echoed in his pharynx, escaping as bubbles that Lark feared might carry his curses all the way to the far surface of the lake. The starman tried to grab the message board, briefly struggling with Ling. But when Lark made slashing motions across his throat, Rann glanced back as Jeni approached from the ship's curved flank, brandishing her deadly bow, accompanied by two strong young qheuens.

Rann's shoulders slumped. He went through the next turning time sweep mechanically. Lark heard a low, grating sound, and knew the big Danik was grinding his teeth.

Lark expected protestations of innocence from the imprisoned starfarers, and sure enough, when they next looked, the signboard proclaimed—

PLAGUES? WE KNOW NOTHING OF SUCH.

But Ling was adamant to a degree that clearly surprised Rann. Using forceful language, she told the captives—her former friends and comrades—to answer truthfully next time, or be abandoned to their fate.

That brought grudging admission, at last.

RO-KENN HAD OPTIONS,

HIS CHOICE TO USE SUCH MEANS.

GET US OUT.

WE CAN PROVIDE CURES.

Lark stared at the woman next to him, awed by the blazing intensity of her rewq aura. Till that moment, she must have held a slim hope that it was all a mistake . . . that

Lark's indictment of her Rothen gods had a flaw in it some-where. That there was some alternative explanation.

Now every complicating what-if vanished. The flame of her anger made Rann's seem like a pale thing.

While both Daniks fumed, each for different reasons, Lark took the wax board, wiped it, and wrote a reply.

PREPARE CURES AT ONCE.

BUT THERE IS MORE.

WE MUST HAVE ONE MORE THING.

It made sense that the Jophur used this weird weapon—pouring chemically synthesized time-stuff over their ene-mies. It suited their racial genius for manipulating organic materials. But in their contempt, the master rings had for-gotten something.

They have cousins on Jijo, who are loyal to the Six.

True, local traekis lacked ambitious natures, and were unschooled in advanced Galactic science. Regardless, a team of talented local pharmacists had analyzed the sub-stance—a viscous, quasi-living tissue—by taste alone. Without understanding its arcane temporal effects, they managed to secrete a counteragent from their gifted glands.

Unfortunately, it was no simple matter of applying the formula, then rubbing away the golden cocoon surround-ing the Rothen ship. For one thing, the antidote was misci-ble with water. Applying it under a lake presented problems.

But there was a possible way. At Dooden Mesa, they found that the old mulc spider's preservation beads could be pushed against the golden wall and made to *merge* with it, flowing into the barrier like stones sinking in soft clay.

Lark had more beads brought from the ancient treasure hoard of the being Dwer called One-of-a-Kind. Agile, five-clawed blues pushed several egg-shaped objects against the section of wall he indicated, opposite the hatch. These beads had been hollowed out and turned into *bottles,* stop-pered at one end with plugs of traeki wax. Within each could be seen machines and other relics of the Buyur era, gleaming like insects caught in amber. Only now those relics seemed to float inside, sloshing in a frothy foam.

At first there were few visible results to the qheuens' effort. The water resonated with bumps and clanks, but no merging occurred. Lark scribbled a command.

EVERYBODY DON'T LOOK!

Ling nodded vigorously. When earlier experiments were performed at the devastated g'Kek settlement, there had not been observers on the *inside*. No living ones, that is. Here, the scene was being watched, in a weird alternating manner, by people on both sides of the enclosure. Perhaps the unsymmetrical quantum effects meant that nothing would happen while people observed.

It took a while to make those within the ship understand that they should turn around, as well. But soon all the Rothen and humans on both sides swiveled away. Young qheuens pushed blindly, with vision cupolas drawn inside their horny shells. *This has got to be the strangest way to get anything done,* Lark thought, staring across a suffocated landscape, once the Festival Glade of the Commons of Six Races. All his life, teachers and leaders said *if you want a job to go well, pay attention to what you are doing.* But this reversed way of acting—where inattention was a virtue— reminded him how some Nihanese mystics in the Vale practiced "Zen arts" such as archery while blindfolded, cultivating detachment and readiness for the Path of Redemption.

Again he glanced at Ling, the star-voyaging biologist. Her aura still seethed, though now in cooler shades. *She's declared an end to her old allegiance. Does she have a new one yet? Other than revenge, that is?* He wished they could go somewhere private—and dry—to talk, without the guarded gamesmanship of their earlier conversations. But Lark wasn't sure she'd want the same thing. Just because his allegations had proved right, that did not mean she should bless him for smashing her childhood idols.

After counting a long interval, Ling nodded and they turned around again.

Rann grunted satisfaction, and Lark felt his heart race.

The beads had penetrated most of the way into the glowing cage! Hardworking blues bubbled satisfaction, then hurried toward the boo grove, fetching air from their makeshift snorkel.

Lark wrote a message to those inside the Rothen airlock.

EVERYBODY CLEAR OUT

BUT 2 SMALL HUMANS.

WEAR AIR SUPPLY.

BRING CURES!

When next he and his companions turned back toward the lock, it was nearly empty. Two women stood on the other side. Petite, though even through their swim-coverings he saw well-developed figures—buxom and wasp-waisted. Clearly, they must have taken advantage of the same cosmetic biosculpting that had made Ling, and the late Besh, so striking. *It's a different universe out there, where you can design yourself like a god.*

Lark swam to where the tip of a mulc capsule protruded from the Jophur barrier. Most of the bead lay deep inside. At its far end the makeshift bottle's hole was plugged by a thick wax seal.

From his thigh pouch Lark drew a tool provided by one of Lester Cambel's techie assistants. A *can opener* the fellow called it.

"Our problem is to deliver dissolving fluid into contact with the barrier, but not lake water," the tech had explained. *"Our answer is to use the new traeki fluid to hollow out some mulc beads. Then we coat these cavities with neutral wax, and refill them with more of the antidote fluid. The hole is plugged, so we have a sealed vessel—"*

"I see you left an old Buyur machine inside," Lark had observed.

"The fluid won't affect it, and we need the machine inside. It doesn't matter what it did in Buyur days, so long as we can signal-activate it to move again, pulling a string attached to the plug. When the plug goes pop!—the contents pour into contact with the Jophur wall! It's foolproof."

Lark wasn't so sure. There was no telling if clever, home-made electrical devices would work underwater, surrounded by time-warped fields. *Here goes everything,* he thought, squeezing the activator.

To his relief, the Buyur device began moving right away

. . . unfolding an appendage, all coiled and springy like a shambler's tail.

I wonder what you used to do, he pondered, watching the machine writhe and gyre. *Are you aware enough to puzzle over where you are? Where your masters have gone? Do you have an internal clock, to know half a million years have passed? Or did time stop for you inside the bead?*

The coiled arm flailed as the machine sought to right itself, yanking a cord attached to the stopper at the far end. The plug slipped, caught, then slipped some more.

It was hard to follow events in the region of "quantum separated time." Things seemed to happen in fits and starts. Sometimes effect seemed to precede cause, or he saw the far side of a rotating object while closer parts remained somehow obscured. It was a strange, *sideways* manner of seeing that reminded Lark of "Cubist" artworks, depicted in an ancient book his mother loved borrowing from the Biblos Archive.

Finally, the stopper slid free. At once reddish foam spread from the nozzle of the makeshift bottle, where its contents met the golden wall. Lark's heart pounded, and he felt his amulet, the fragment of the Holy Egg, react with growing heat. His left hand clawed at the skink-skin wrappers, but could not gain entry to grab the vibrating stone. So, like an itch that could not be scratched, he endured the palpitation as his breastbone was rubbed from both sides.

Grunts of satisfaction escaped Rann as the foamy stain spread, eroding the Jophur barrier from within. The widening hole soon met a neighboring "bottle," embedded in the wall near the first. In moments, fresh supplies of dissolving fluid gushed. The material of the barrier seemed to shiver, as if it were alive. As though in pain. Waves of color rippled around the growing cavity, as his rewq tried reading strange emotions.

So fixed was everyone on the process, for long intervals no one looked beyond, to the airlock and its two inhabitants, until a stray current tugged Lark aside. Lacking outside observers, the Danik women must have experienced time's passage in a somewhat linear fashion. They looked tense, hunching away from the red foam, crouching near the airlock's sealed inner door as the bubble slowly approached. Fear showed through their transparent face masks. No one knew what would happen when the hissing effervescence broke through.

It was also getting closer to Lark's side of the wall. He backpedaled toward the others . . . only to find they had retreated farther still. Ling grabbed his arm.

Apparently, if they succeeded in making a tunnel, it would be wide in the middle but awfully narrow at both ends. Also, the wall material wasn't solid, but a very viscous liquid. Fresh toporgic could already be seen slumping toward the wound. Any passage was bound to be temporary.

If we didn't estimate right . . . if the two ends open in the wrong order . . . we might have to start all over again. There are more bottles of fluid, back at the cave. But how many times can we try?

Yet he could not talk himself out of feeling pride.

We're not helpless. Faced with overwhelming power, we innovate. We persevere.

The realization was ironic confirmation of the heresy he had maintained all his adult life.

We aren't meant for the Path of Redemption. No matter how hard we try, we'll never tread its road to innocence.

That is why our kind should never have come to Jijo.

We're meant for the stars. We simply don't belong here.

Nelo

THE OLD MAN DID NOT KNOW WHICH WAS THE SADdest sight.

At times he wished the boat had capsized during that wretched, pell-mell running of the rapids so he would not have lived to see such things.

It took half a day of hard labor at the oars to climb back upstream to Dolo Village. By the time they reached the timber pile that had been the town dock, all the young rowers were exhausted. Villagers rushed down a muddy bank to help them drag the boat ashore, and carried Ariana Foo to dry ground. A stout hoon ignored Nelo's protests, picking him up like a baby, until he stood safely by the roots of a mighty garu tree.

Many survivors milled listlessly, though others had formed work gangs whose first task was collecting dross. Especially bodies. Those must be gathered quickly and mulched, as required by sacred law.

Nelo saw corpses gathered in a long row—mostly human, of course. Numbly he noted the master carpenter and Jobee the Plumber. Quite a few craft workers lay muddy and broken along a sodden patch of loam, and many more were missing, carried downstream when the lake came crashing through the millrace and workshops. Tree farmers, in contrast, had suffered hardly a loss. Their life on the branch tops did not expose them when the dam gave way.

No one spoke, though stares followed the papermaker as Nelo moved down the line, allowing a wince or a grunt when he recognized the face of an employee, an apprentice, or a lifelong friend. When he reached the end, he did not turn but kept walking in the same direction, toward what had been the center of his life.

The lake was low. Maybe the flood didn't destroy everything.

Disorientation greeted Nelo, for it seemed at first he was transported far from the village of his birth. Where placid water once glistened, mudflats now stretched for most of a league. A river poured through the near side of his beloved dam.

To local qheuens, dam and home were one and the same. Now the hive lay sliced open, in cross section. The collapse had sheared the larva room in half. Teams of stunned blue adults struggled to move their surviving grubs to safety, out of the harsh sunlight.

With reluctant dread, Nelo dropped his gaze to where the famed paper mill had been, next to a graceful power wheel.

Of his house, his workshops, and pulp vats, nothing more remained than foundation stumps.

The sight tore his heart, but averting his gaze did not help. Just a short distance downstream Nelo saw more blue qheuens working listlessly by the shore, trying to extricate one of their own from a net of some kind. By their lack of haste, one knew the victim must be dead, perhaps trapped in the shallows and drowned.

Unhappily, he recognized the corpse, an older female— Log Biter herself—by markings on her shell. Another lost friend, and a blow to everyone along the upper Roney who valued her good wisdom.

Then he recognized the trap that had pinned her down long enough to smother even a blue qheuen. It was a tangle of wood and metal wires. Something from Nelo's own home.

Melina's precious piano, that I ordered built at great cost.

A moan escaped his throat, at last. In all the world, he had but one thing left to live for—the hope, frail as it was, that his children were safe somewhere, and would not have to see such things.

But where was somewhere? What place could possibly be safe, when starships could plunge from the sky, blasting five generations' work in a single instant?

Words jarred him from dour thoughts of suicide.

"I didn't do this, Nelo."

He turned to see another human standing nearby. A fellow craftsman, almost his own age. Henrik the Exploser, whose young son had accompanied Sara and the Stranger on their journey to far lands. At first, Henrik's words confused Nelo. He had to swallow before finding the strength to reply.

"Of course you didn't do it. They say a skyship came—"

The exploser shook his head. "Fools or liars. Either they have no sense of timing, or else they were in on it."

"What do you mean?"

"Oh, a ship passed overhead all right, and gave us a look-over. Then it went on its way. 'Twas most of a midura *later* that a gang of 'em came down, farmers mostly. They knocked the seals off some of my charges, under one of the piers of the dam, and laid a torch against it."

Nelo blinked. "What did you say?" He stared, then blinked again. "But who . . . ?"

Henrik had a one-word answer.

"Jop."

Lark

THE EXPLORERS EMERGED TRIUMPHANT, RESURFAC-ing from the chill lake into the cave, having brought back almost everything they sought. But bad news awaited them.

Fatigue lay heavily on Lark, while helpers stripped the diving gear and toweled him off.

Tense sadness filled the voice of the human corporal, reporting what had happened in Lark's absence.

"It hit our grays all at once—wheezing up lots of bubbly phlegm. Then a couple of young blues got it, too. We sent 'em to a pharmacist topside, but word says the plague is getting worse up there. There may not be much time."

Attention turned to the Danik women who had just barely escaped from the trapped ship. They still looked woozy from their experience—starting with a blast of high-pressure water that had burst into the airlock when the fissure broke through at last. After that came a hurried, nightmarish squeeze through the briefly dilated opening, squirming desperately before the tunnel could close and immure their bodies in liquid time like the poor g'Keks of Dooden Mesa.

Watching quantum-shifted images of that tight passage nearly unnerved Lark. Instead of two human figures, they looked like jumbled body parts, writhing through a tube that kept shifting around them. One woman he briefly saw with her *insides* on the *outside,* offering unwanted knowl-edge about her latest meal.

Yet here they were, alive in front of him. Overcoming residual nausea, the two escapees kept their side of the bargain, setting to work right away on a small machine they had brought along. In exchange for a cure, Jijoans would help more of their crew mates break out of the trapped ship, then coordinate joint action against the Jophur—no doubt something quite desperate, calling for a pooling of both groups' slim knowledge and resources, plus a generous dollop of Ifni's luck.

This whole enterprise had been Lark's idea . . . and he gave it the same odds as a ribbit walking unscathed through a ligger's den.

"Symptoms?" asked the first woman, with hair a shade of red Lark had never seen on any Jijoan.

"Don't you know already what bug it is?" Jeni Shen demanded.

"A variety of pathogens were kept in stock aboard the research station," answered the other one, a stately brunette who seemed older than any other Danik Lark had seen. She looked a statuesque forty, and might be two centuries old.

"If Ro-kenn did release an organism from that supply," she continued, "we must pin down which one."

Even having stripped off his rewq, he had no trouble reading fatalistic reluctance in her voice. By helping solve the plague, she was in effect confessing that Ro-kenn had attempted genocide . . . and that their ship routinely carried the means for such a crime. Perhaps, like Ling, she had been in the dark about all that till now. Only utter helplessness would have forced the Rothen to reveal so much to their human servants, as well as to the sooners of Jijo.

From the look on Rann's face, the tall star warrior disagreed with the decision, and Lark knew why.

It goes beyond mere morality and crimes against Galactic law. Our local qheuens and hoons have relatives out there, among the stars. If word of this gets out, those home populations might declare vendettas against the Rothen. Or else, with this evidence, Earth might file suit to reclaim the Danik population group that the Rothen have kept secreted away for two centuries.

Of course that assumes Earth still lives. And there's still law in the Five Galaxies.

Rann clearly felt the risk too great. Ship and crew should have been sacrificed to keep the secret.

Tough luck, Rann, Lark thought. *Apparently your fellow spacers would rather live.*

While Ling described the disease that ravaged Uthen before her eyes, Lark overheard Rann whisper impatiently to Jeni Shen.

"If we are to get the others out, it must be a complete job! There are weapons to transfer, and supplies. The traeki formula must be duplicated aboard ship, in order to make a durable passageway—"

Jeni interrupted sharply.

"After we verify a cure, starman. Or else your compadres and their master race can sit in their own dung till Jijo grows cold, for all we care."

Colorful, Lark thought, smiling grimly.

Soon the machine was programmed with all the relevant facts.

"Many hoons are showing signs of a new sickness, too," Ling reminded.

"We'll get to that," said the redhead. "This will take a min or two."

Lark watched symbols flash across the tiny screen. *More computers,* he mulled unhappily. Of course it was a much smaller unit than the big processor they used near Dooden Mesa. This "digital cognizance" might be shielded by geologic activity in the area, plus fifty meters of solid rock.

But can we be sure?

The device issued a high-pitched chime.

"Synthesis complete," said the older Danik, taking a small, clear vial from its side, containing a greenish fluid. "This is just two or three doses, but that should suffice to test it. We can mass-produce more aboard the ship. Which means we'll need a permanent channel through the barrier, of course."

Clearly, she felt her side now had a major bargaining chip. Holding up the tube with three fingers, she went on. "Now might be a good time to discuss how each group will help the other, your side with manpower and sheer numbers, and our side providing—"

Her voice cut off when Ling snatched the capsule from her grasp, swiveling to put it in Jeni Shen's hand.

"Run," was all Ling said.

Jeni took off with a pair of excited noor beasts yapping at her heels.

•   •   •

Any return to the imprisoned ship would have to wait for dawn. Even a well-tuned rewq could not amplify light that was not there.

Ling wanted to keep the two rescued Daniks busy producing antidotes against every pathogen listed in the little Library, in case other plagues were loose that no one knew about, but Lark vetoed the idea. Since the Dooden disaster, all computers made him nervous. He wanted this one turned on as little as possible. Let the Rothen produce extra vaccines inside their vessel and bring them out along with other supplies, he said, if and when a new tunnel was made. Ling seemed about to argue the point, but then her lips pressed hard and she shrugged. Taking one of the lanterns, she retreated to a corner of the cave, far from Rann and her former comrades.

Lark spent some time composing a report to the High Sages, requesting more bottles of the traeki dissolving fluid and describing the preliminary outlines of an alliance between the Six Races and their former enemies. Not that he had much confidence in such a coalition.

They promise weapons and other help, he wrote. *But I urge caution. Given Phwhoon-dau's description of the Rothen as Galactic "petty criminals," and the relative ease with which they were overwhelmed, we should prefer almost any advantageous deal that can be worked out with the Jophur, short of letting them commit mass murder.*

Insurrection ought to be considered a last resort.

The sages might find his recommendation odd, since his own plan made the Rothen alliance possible in the first place. But Lark saw no contradiction. Unlocking a door did not mean you had to walk through it. He just believed in exploring alternatives.

There was little to do then but wait, hoping news from the medics would be happy and swift. The party could not even light a fire in the dank cavern.

"It's cold," Ling commented when Lark passed near her niche. He had been looking for a place to unroll his sleeping bag . . . not so close he'd seem intrusive, yet nearby in case she called. Now he paused, wondering what she meant.

Was that an invitation? Or an accusation?

The latter seemed more likely. Ling might have been much better off remaining forever in the warmth of high-tech habitats, basking in the glow of a messianic faith.

"It is that," he murmured. "Cold."

It was hard to move closer. Hard to expect anything but rejection. For months, their relationship had been based on a consensual game, a tense battle of wits that was part inquisition and part one-upmanship . . . with moments of intense, semierotic flirting stirred in. Eventually he won that game, but not through any credit of his own. The sins of her Rothen gods gave him a weapon out of proportion to personal traits either of them possessed, leaving him just one option—to lay waste to all her beliefs. Ever since, they had labored together toward shared goals without once trading a private word.

In effect, he had conquered her to become Jijo's ally, only to lose what they had before.

Lark did not feel like a conqueror.

"I can see why they call you a heretic," Ling said, breaking the uncomfortable silence.

Either out of shyness or diffidence, Lark had not looked at her directly. Now he saw she had a book open on her lap, with one page illuminated by the faint beam of her glow lamp. It was the Jijoan biology text he had written with Uthen. His life's work.

"I . . . tried not to let it interfere with the research," he answered.

"How could it not interfere? Your use of cladistic taxonomy clashes with the way Galactic science has defined and organized species for a billion years."

Lark saw what she was doing, and felt gladdened by it. Their shared love of biology was neutral ground where issues of guilt or shame needn't interfere. He moved closer to sit on a stony outcrop.

"I thought you were talking about my *Jijoan* heresy. I used to be part of a movement"—he winced, remembering his friend Harullen—"whose goal was to persuade the Six Races to end our illegal colony . . . by voluntary means."

She nodded. "A virtuous stance, by Galactic standards. Though not easy for organic beings, who are programmed for sex and propagation."

Lark felt his face flush, and was grateful for the dim light.

"Well, the question is out of our hands now," he said. "Even if Ro-kenn's plagues are cured, the Jophur can wipe us out if they like. Or else they'll hand us over to the Institutes, and we'll have the Judgment Day described in the Sacred Scrolls. That might come as a relief, after the last few months. At least it's how we always imagined things would end."

"Though your people hoped it wouldn't happen till you'd been redeemed. Yes, I know that's your Jijoan orthodoxy. But I was talking about a heresy of *science*—the way you and Uthen organized animal types in your work—by species, genus, phylum, and so on. You use the old cladistic system of pre-contact Earthling taxonomy."

He nodded. "We do have a few texts explaining Galactic nomenclature. But most of our books came from Earth archives. Few human biologists had changed over to Galactic systematics by the time the *Tabernacle* took off."

"I never saw cladistics used in a real ecosystem," Ling commented. "You present a strong argument for it."

"Well, in our case it's making a virtue out of necessity. We're trying to understand Jijo's past and present by studying a single slice of time—the one we're living in. For evidence, all we have to go on are the common traits of living animals . . . and the fossils we dig up. That's comparable to mapping the history of a continent by studying layers of rocks. Earthlings did a lot of that kind of science before contact, like piecing together evidence of a crime, long after the body has grown cold. Galactics never needed those interpolative techniques. Over the course of eons they simply *watch* and record the rise and fall of mountains, and the divergence of species. Or else they make new species through gene-splicing and uplift."

Ling nodded, considering this. "We're taught contempt for wolfling science. I suppose it affected the way I treated you, back when . . . well, you know."

If that was an apology, Lark accepted it gladly.

"I wasn't exactly honest with you either, as I recall."

She laughed dryly. "No, you weren't."

Another silence stretched. Lark was about to talk some more about biology, when he realized that was exactly the wrong thing to do. What had earlier served to bridge an uncomfortable silence would now only maintain a reserve, a neutrality he did not want anymore. Awkwardly, he moved to change the subject.

"What kind of . . ." He swallowed and tried again. "I have a brother, and a sister. I may have mentioned them before. Do you have family . . . back at . . ."

He let the question hang, and for a moment Lark worried he had dredged a subject too painful and personal. But her relieved look showed Ling, too, wanted to move on.

"I had a baby brother," she said. "And a share daughter, whose up-parents were very nice. I miss them all very much."

For the next midura, Lark listened in confusion to the complex Danik way of life on far-off Poria Outpost. Mostly, he let Ling pour out her sadness, now that even her liberated crew mates were like aliens to her, and nothing would ever be the same.

Later, it seemed wholly natural to stretch his sleeping bag next to hers. Divided by layers of cloth and fluffy torg, their bodies shared warmth without touching. Yet, in his heart, Lark felt a comfort he had lacked till now.

She doesn't hate me.

It was a good place to start.

The second dive seemed to go quicker, at first. They had a better knack for underwater travel now, though several human volunteers had to fill in for blue qheuens who were sick.

About the illness, recent word from topside was encouraging. The vaccine samples seemed to help the first few victims. Better yet, the molecules could be traeki-synthesized. Still, it was too soon for cheers. Even in the event of a complete cure, there were problems of distribution. Could cures reach all the far-flung communities before whole populations of qheuens and hoons were devastated?

Back at the Rothen ship, they found the airlock already occupied by crew members wearing diving gear—three humans and a Rothen—along with slim crates of supplies. Like wax figures, they stood immobile while Lark and Ling

trained new assistants in the strange art they had learned
the day before. Then it was time to begin making another
tunnel through the golden time-stuff.

Again, they went through turnaround sweeps, letting
those inside the hatch prepare. Again, volunteers swam
close with mulc preservation beads that had been hollowed and turned into bottles for the special dissolving
fluid. Once more, the actual act of embedding had to take
place in a shroud of nescience, without anyone watching
directly. Nothing happened the first few tries . . . until
Jeni caught one of the new helpers *peeking,* out of curiosity. Despite watery resistance, she smacked him so hard
the sound traveled as a sharp crack.

Finally, they got the hang of it. Six beads lay in place, at
varying distances inside the barrier. As yesterday, Lark applied the "can opener," turning on an ancient Buyur machine, which in turn pulled a wax plug, setting in motion a
chain reaction to eat a gap through the viscous material. He
backed up, fascinated again by creepy visions as the red
foam spread and a cavity began to form.

Someone abruptly tapped his shoulder.

It was Jeni, the young militia sergeant, urgently holding a
wax board.

WHERE IS RANN?

He blinked, then joined Ling in a shrug. The tall Danik
leader had been nearby till a moment ago. Jeni's expression was anguished. Lark wrote on his own board.

WE'RE NOT NEEDED NOW.

LING AND I WILL LOOK NORTH.

SEND OTHERS SOUTH, EAST.

YOU STAY.

Grudgingly, Jeni accepted the logic. Lark's job was
largely done. If the tunnel opened as planned, another
batch of escapees would wriggle through and Jeni must
coordinate moving them and their baggage back to the
caves.

With a nod, Ling assented. They headed off together,
kicking hard. United, they should be a match for Rann if he
put up a fight. Anyway, where would the big man go? It
wasn't as if he had much choice, these days.

Still, Lark worried. With a head start, Rann might reach

the lakeshore and make good an escape. He could cause mischief, or worse, be caught and questioned by the Jophür. Rann was tough, but how long could he hold out against Galactic interrogation techniques?

Ling caught his arm. Lark turned to follow her jabbing motion *up* toward the surface of the lake. There he saw a pair of flippers, waving slowly at the end of two strong legs.

What's he doing up there? Lark wondered as they propelled after the absconded Danik. Getting close, they saw Rann had actually broached the surface! His head and shoulders were out of the water. *Is he taking a look at the Jophur ship? We all want to, but no one dared.*

Lark felt acutely the shadow of the giant vessel as they kicked upward. For the first time, he got a sense of its roughly globular shape and mammoth dimensions, completely blocking the narrow Festival Glade, creating this lake with its bulk. Having grown up next to a dam, Lark had a sense of the pressure all this water exerted. There would be an awful flood when the ship took off, returning to its home among the stars.

The tube in his mouth squirmed disconcertingly. The traeki air ring struggled as they rose upward, hissing and throbbing to adapt to changing pressure. But Lark was more worried about Rann being spotted by the Jophur.

With luck, the skink skins will make him look like a piece of flotsam . . . which is what he'll feel like once I'm through with him! Lark felt a powerful wrath build as he reached to seize the big man's ankle.

The leg gave a startled twitch . . . then kicked savagely, knocking his hand away.

Ling tugged Lark's other arm, pointing a second time.

Rann had an object in front of him—*the Rothen minicomputer!* He was tapping away at the controls, even as he tread water.

Bastard! Lark thrust toward the surface, grabbing for the device, no longer caring if his mere body happened to be visible from afar. Rann might as well have been waving a searchlight while beating a drum!

As soon as Lark broke through, the starman aimed a punch at him—no doubt a well-trained, expert blow, if delivered on dry land. Here, watery reaction threw Rann off balance and the clout glanced stingingly off Lark's ear.

Amid a shock of pain, he sensed Ling erupt behind her former colleague, throwing her arms around his neck. Lark took advantage of the distraction, planting his feet against Rann's chest and hauling back until the computer popped free of the big man's grasp.

Alas, that wasn't enough to end the danger. The screen was still lit. He cried to Ling: "I don't know how to turn the damned thing off!"

She had troubles of her own, with Rann's powerful arms reaching around to pummel and yank at her. Lark realized the Danik must be put out of commission, and quickly. So with both hands he raised the computer as high as he could—and brought it down hard on Rann's crew cut.

Without leverage, it struck less forcefully than he hoped, but the blow pulled Rann's attention away from Ling.

The second impact was better, giving a resounding smack. Rann groaned, slumping in the water.

Unfortunately, the jolt did not break the durable computer, which kept shining, even after Lark landed a final blow.

Rann floated, arms spread wide, breathing shallowly but noisily from his traeki ring. Ling thrashed toward Lark, gasping as she threw an arm over his shoulder for support. Finally, she reached out to stroke a precise spot on the computer's case, turning it off.

That's better . . . though it's said Galactics can trace digital cognizance, even when a machine is unpowered.

Lark closed the cover, letting the machine drop from his grasp. He needed both hands to hold Ling.

Especially when a new, umbral shadow fell across them, causing her body to stiffen in his arms.

Suddenly, things felt very cold.

Tremulously, they turned together, looking up to see what had come for them.

Dwer

THAT NIGHT WAS AMONG THE STRANGEST OF Dwer's life, though it started in the most natural way—bickering with Rety.

"I *ain't* goin' there!" She swore.

"No one asked you to. When I start downhill, you'll take off the other way. Go half a league west, to that forested rise we passed on the way here. I saw good game signs. You can set snares, or look for clamette bubbles on the beach. They're best roasted, but you oughtn't trust a fire—"

"I'm supposed to wait for you, I s'pose? Have a nice meal ready for the great hunter, after he finishes takin' on the whole dam' universe, single-handed?"

Her biting sarcasm failed to mask tremors of real fear. Dwer didn't flatter himself that Rety worried about *him*. No doubt she hated to face being alone.

Dusk fell on the dunes and mudflats, and mountains so distant they were but a jagged horizon cutting the bloated sun. Failing light gave the two of them a chance at last to worm out from the sand, then slither beyond sight of the crashed ships. Once safely over the verge, they brushed grit out of clothes and body crevices while arguing in heated whispers.

"I'm telling you, we don't haveta *do* anything! I'm sure Kunn had time to holler for help before he went down. The Rothen ship was due back soon, and musta heard him. Any dura now it's gonna swoop down, rescue Kunn, and pick up its prize. All we gotta do then is stand and shout."

Rety had been thinking during the long, uncomfortable wait. She held that the fighter craft full of untraeki rings was the very target Kunn had been looking for, dropping depth bombs to flush his prey out of hiding. By that logic, the brief sky battle was a desperate lashing out by a cornered foe. But Kunn got his own licks in, and now the quarry lay helpless in the swamp, where frantic efforts at repair had so far failed to dislodge it.

Soon, by Rety's reasoning, the Rothen lords would come

to complete the job, taking the untraeki into custody. The Rothen would surely be pleased at this success. Enough to overlook Dwer's earlier mistakes. And hers.

It was a neat theory. But then, why did the untraeki ship attack from the *west,* instead of rising out of the water where Kunn dropped his bombs? Dwer was no expert on the way star gods brawled among themselves, but instinct said Kunn had been caught with his pants down.

"In that case, what I'm about to try should put me in good with your friends," he told Rety.

"If you survive till they come, which I doubt! Those varmints down there will spot you, soon as you go back over the dune."

"Maybe. But I've been watching. Remember when a herd of bog stompers sloshed by, munching tubers torn up by the crash? Large critters passed both hulls and were ignored. I'm guessing the guard robots will take me for a crude native beast—"

"You got *that* right," Rety muttered.

"—and leave me alone, at least till I'm real close."

"And then what? You gonna attack a starship with your *bow and arrows?*"

Dwer held back from reminding Rety that his bow once seemed a treasure to her—a prize worth risking her life to steal.

"I'm leaving the arrows with you," he said. "They have steel tips. If I take 'em, they'll know I'm not an animal."

"They should ask *me.* I'd tell 'em real fast that you're—"

"wife, enough!"

The reedy voice came from Rety's tiny urrish "husband," who had been grooming her, flicking sand grains with his agile tongue.

"have sense, wife! brave boy make ship eyes look at him so you and me can get away! all his other talk-talk is fake stuff. nice-lies to make us go be safe. be good to brave boy-man! least you can do!"

While Rety blinked at yee's rebuke, Dwer marveled. Did all urrish males treat their wives this way, chiding them from within the heavy folds of their brood pouches? Or was yee special? Did some prior mate eject him for scolding?

"Iz' at true, Dwer?" Rety asked. "You'd sacr'fice yourself for me?"

He tried reading her eyes, to judge which answer would make her do as she was told. Fading light forced him to guess.

"No, it's not true. I *do* have a plan. It's risky, but I want to give it a try."

Rety watched him as carefully as he had scanned her. Finally, she gave a curt laugh.

"What a liar. yee's right about you. Too dam' decent to survive without someone to watch over you."

Huh? Dwer thought. He had tried telling the truth, hoping it would convince her to go. Only Rety reacted in a way he did not expect.

"It's decided then," she affirmed with a look of resolve he knew too well. "I'm coming along, Dwer, *whichever* way you head. So if you want to save me, we better both get on west."

"This *ain't* west!" she whispered sharply, half a midura later.

Dwer ignored Rety as he peered ahead through the swampy gloom with water sloshing past his navel. *Too bad we had to leave yee behind with our gear,* he thought. The little urrish male provided his "wife" with a healthy dose of prudence and good judgment. But he could not stand getting wet.

Soon, Dwer hoped Rety's survival instincts would kick in and she'd shut up on her own.

They were nearly naked, wading through the reedy marsh toward a pair of rounded silhouettes, one larger—its smooth flanks glistening except where a sooty stain marred one side. The other lay beyond, crumpled and half-sunk amidships. Both victor and vanquished were silent under the pale yellow glow of Passen, Jijo's smallest moon.

Colonies of long-necked wallow swans nested in the thickets, dozing after a hard day spent hunting through the shallows and tending their broods. The nearest raised spear-shaped heads to blink at the two humans, then lowered their snouts as Dwer and Rety waded on by.

Mud covered Dwer and the sooner girl from head to toe, concealing some of their heat sign with steady evaporation. According to ancient lore, that should make the patrolling guard machine see them as smaller than they really were. Dwer also took a slow, meandering route, to foster the impression of foraging beasts.

Slender shapes with luminous scales darted below the water's surface, brushing Dwer's thighs with their flicking tails. A distant burst of splashing told of some nocturnal hunter at work among the clumps of sword-edged grass. Hungry things moved about in this wet jungle. Rety seemed to grasp this, and did not speak again for some time.

If only she knew how vague Dwer's plan was, Rety might howl loud enough to send all the sleeping waterfowl flapping for the sky. In fact, he was working from a hunch. He wanted to have a closer look at the untraeki ship . . . and to check out his impression of this swamp. In order to test his idea, he needed to attain a particular frame of mind.

What was I thinking about, that day when I first contacted—or hallucinated—the voice of One-of-a-Kind?

It happened some years ago. He had been on his first solo trek over the Rimmers, excited to be promoted from apprentice to master hunter, filled with a spirit of freedom and adventure, for now he was one of the few Sixers licensed to roam wherever he wished, even far beyond the settled Slope. The world had seemed boundless.

And yet . . .

And yet, he still vividly recalled the moment, emerging from a narrow trail through the boo forest—a cathedral aisle as narrow as a man and seemingly high as a moon. Suddenly, the boo just *stopped,* spilling him onto a bowl-shaped rocky expanse, under a vast blue sky. Before Dwer lay a mulc lake, nestled in the mountain's flank, surrounded by fields of broken stone.

What he felt during that moment of disorienting transition was much more than welcome release from a closed space. A sense of *opening up* seemed to fill his mind, briefly expanding his ability to see—especially the tumulus of Buyur ruins. Abruptly, he beheld the ancient towers as they must have stood long ago, shimmering and proud. And for an instant, Dwer had felt strangely at home.

That was when he first heard the spider's voice, whispering, cajoling, urging him to accept a deal. A fair trade. With its help, Dwer might cease living, but he would never die. He could become one with the glorious past, and join the spider on a voyage into time.

Now, while sloshing under starlight through a murky bog, Dwer tried again for that feeling, that *opening* sensation. He could tell from the texture of this place—from its smell and feel—that mighty spires had also pierced the sky, only here they were much grander than at any mountain site. The job of demolition was far advanced—little remained to tear down or erase. Yet somehow he knew what stood where, and when.

Here a row of pure-white obelisks once greeted the sun, both mystical and pragmatic in their mathematically precise alignment.

Over there, Buyur legs once ponderously strode down a shopping arcade, filled with exotic goods.

Near *that* translucent fountain, contemplative Buyur minds occupied themselves with a multitude of tasks beyond his reckoning. And through the sky passed commerce from ten thousand worlds.

Down the avenues were heard voices . . . not just of Buyur, but a myriad of other types of thinking beings.

Surely it was a glorious time, though also *fatiguing* for any planet whose flesh must feed such an eager, busy civilization. After a million years of heavy use, Jijo badly needed rest. And the forces of wisdom granted it. All the busy voices moved on. The towers tumbled and a different kind of life took over here, one dedicated to erasing scars—a more patient, less frenzied type of being. . . .

> . . . ?
> *Yes?*
> *Who . . . goes . . . ?*

Words slithered through Dwer's mind, hesitantly at first.

> *Who calls . . . rousing me from . . . drowsy musing?*

Dwer's first urge was to dismiss it as merely his imagination. Had not his nervous system been palped and bruised from carrying the robot across icy streams? Delusions would be normal after that battering, followed by days of near starvation. Anyway, his habitual defense against One-of-a-Kind had been to dismiss the mulc spider's voice as a phantasm.

> *Who is a phantasm?*
> *I, a being who serenely outlasts empires?*
> *Or you, a mayfly, living and dying in the*
> *time it takes for me to dream a dream?*

Dwer held off acknowledging the voice, even casually. First he wanted to be sure. Wading cautiously, he sought some of the vines he had glimpsed earlier, from the dune heights. A nearby hummock seemed likely. Despite covering vegetation, it had the orderly outlines of some ruined structure. Sure enough, Dwer soon found his way blocked by cables, some as thick as his wrist, all converging on the ancient building site. His nose twitched at the scent of dilute corrosive fluids, carried by the twisted vines.

"Hey, this is a mulc swamp! We're walkin' right into a spider!"

Dwer nodded, acknowledging Rety's comment without words. If she wanted to leave, she knew the way back.

Spiders were common enough on the Slope. Youngsters went exploring through mulc dens, though you risked getting acid burns if you weren't careful. Now and then, some village child died of a foolish mistake while venturing too deep, yet the attraction held. High-quality Buyur relics were often found where vine beasts slowly etched the remains of bygone days.

Folk legends flourished about the creatures, whose bodies were made up by the vines themselves. Some described them *talking* to rare members of the Six, though Dwer had never met anyone else who admitted that it happened to them. He especially never heard of another mulc spider like One-of-a-Kind, who actively lured living prey into its web, sealing "unique" treasures away in coffins of hardening jell.

> *You met that one? The mad spider of the heights?*
> *You actually shared thoughts with it? And escaped?*
> *How exceptionally interesting.*

> *Your mind patterns are very clear for an ephemeral.*
> *That is rare, as mayflies go. . . .*
> *How singular you are.*

Yes, that was the way One-of-a-Kind used to speak to him. This creature was consistent. Or else Dwer's imagination was.

The words returned, carrying a note of pique.

> *You flatter yourself to think you could imagine an entity as sublime as myself! Though I admit, you are intriguing, for a transitory being.*
> *So you need verification of my objective reality? How might I prove myself?*

Rather than answer directly, Dwer kept his thoughts reserved. Languidly, he contemplated that it would be interesting to see the vines in front of him move.

> *As if at your command? An amusing concept.*
> *But why not?*
> *Come back in just five days. In that brief time, you will find all of them shifted to new locales!*

Dwer chuckled contemptuously, under his breath.

> *Not quickly enough, my wanton friend? You have seen a mulc being move faster?*

> *Ah, but that one was crazed, driven mad by isolation, high altitude, and a diet of psi-drenched stone. It grew unwholesomely obsessed with mortality and the nature of time. Surely you do not expect such undignified haste from me?*

Like One-of-a-Kind, this spider could somehow tap Dwer's human memory, using it to make better sentences—more articulate speech—than he ever managed on his own. But Dwer knew better than to bandy words. Instead, he willed himself to turn around.

> *Wait! You intrigue me. The conversations our kind share among ourselves are so languid. Torpid, you might say, featuring endless comparisons of the varied dross we eat. The slow-talk grows ever more tedious as we age. . . .*
> *Tell me, are you from one of the frantic races who have lately settled down to a skittering life beyond the mountains? The ones who talk and talk, but almost never build?*

Behind Dwer, Rety murmured, "What's goin' on!" But he only motioned for her to follow him away from the mulc cords.

> *All right! On a whim, I'll do it. I shall move for you!*
> *I'll move as I have not done in ages.*
> *Watch me, small flickering life-form. Watch this!*

Dwer glanced back, and saw several vines tremble. The tremors strengthened, dura after dura, tightening and releasing till several of the largest bunched in a knotty tangle. More duras passed . . . then one loop *popped up* out of the water, rising high, dripping like some amphibious being, emerging from its watery home.

It was confirmation, not only of the spider's mental reality, but of Dwer's own sane perception. Yet he quashed all sense of acknowledgment or relief. Rather, Dwer let a feeling of disappointment flow across his surface thoughts.

A fresh shoot of lesser boo moves that much, in the course of a day's growth, he pondered, without bothering to project the thought at the spider.

> *You compare me to boo?*
> *Boo?*
> *Insolent bug! It is you who are a figment of my imagination! You may be nothing but an undigested bit of concrete, or a piece of bad steel, perturbing my dreams. . . .*

> *No, wait! Don't leave yet. I sense there is something that would convince you.*
> *Tell me what it is. Tell me what would make you acknowledge me, and talk awhile.*

Dwer felt an impulse to speak directly. To make his wishes known in the form of a request. But no. His experience with One-of-a-Kind had taught him. That mulc beast might have been mad, but it clearly shared some properties of personality with its kind.

Dwer knew the game to play was "hard to get." So he let his idea leak out in the form of a fantasy . . . a daydream. When Rety tried to interrupt again, he made a slashing motion for quiet while he went on picturing what a spider might do to convince him it was real. The sort of thing Dwer would find impressive.

The mulc being's next message seemed intrigued.

> *Truly?*
> *And why not?*
> *The new dross to which you refer already had me concerned. Those great heaps of refined metal and volatile organic poisons—I have not dealt with such purified essences in a very long time.*
> *Now you worry that the dross might fly away again, to pollute some part of Jijo beyond reach*

*of any mulc being? You fear it may never be
properly disposed of?*

*Then worry no more, my responsible little
ephemeral! It will be taken care of.*

Just leave it to me.

Alvin

I WAS RIGHT! THE PHUVNTHUS ARE EARTHLINGS!

I haven't figured out the little amphibians yet, but the
big six-legged creatures? They are dolphins. Just like the
ones in *King of the Sea* or *The Shining Shore* . . . only
these talk and drive spaceships! How uttergloss.

And there are humans.

Sky humans!

Well, a couple of them, anyway.

I met the woman in charge—Gillian is her name. Among
other things, she said some nice words about my journal.
In fact, if they ever succeed in getting away from here, and
returning to Earth, she promises to find an agent for me
and get it published.

Imagine that. I can't wait to tell Huck.

There's just one favor Gillian wants in return.

Ewasx

OH, HOW THEY PREVARICATE!

Is this what it means to take the Downward Path?

Sometimes a citizen race decides to change course,
rejecting the destiny mapped out for it by patron and clan.
The Civilization of the Five Galaxies allows several tradi-
tional avenues of appeal, but if all other measures fail, one
shelter remains available to all—the road that leads *back,*
from starfaring sapience to animal nature. The route to a
second chance. To start over again with a new patron guiding your way.

This much I/we can understand. But must that path have an intermediate phase, between citizen and dumb beast? A phase in which the half-devolved species becomes *lawyers*?

Their envoys stand before us now, citing points of Galactic law that were handed down in sacred lore. Especially verbose is the g'Kek emissary. Yes, My rings, you identify this g'Kek as Vubben—a "friend and colleague" from your days as Asx the traeki. Oh, how that sage-among-sooners nimbly contorts logic, contending that his folk are not responsible for the debt his kind owes our clan, by rule of vendetta. A debt of extinction.

The senior Priest-Stack aboard our ship insists we must listen to this nonsense, for form's sake, before continuing our righteous vengeance. But most of the *Polkjhy* crew stacks side with our Captain-Leader, whose impatience-with-drivel steams with each throbbing pulse of an angry mulching core. Finally, the Captain-Leader transmits a termination signal to Me/us. To faithful Ewasx.

"ENOUGH!" I interrupt Vubben in loud tones of Oailie decisiveness. All four of his eyestalks quail in surprise at my harsh resonance.

"YOUR CONTENTIOUS REASONINGS ARE BASED ON INVALID ASSUMPTIONS."

They stand before us/Me, frozen silent by our rebuke. A silence more appropriate to half animals than all that useless jabber. Finally, the qheuen sage, Knife-Bright Insight, bows her blue-green carapace and inquires:

"Might we ask what assumptions you refer to?"

Our second cognition ring performs a writhing twitch that I must overcome with savage pain jolts, preventing the rebellious ring's color cells from flashing visibly. *Be thou restrained,* I command, enforcing authority over our component selves. *Do not try to signal your erstwhile comrades. The effort will accomplish nothing.*

The minirebellion robs Me of resources to maintain a pontifical voice. So when I next speak aloud, it is in more normal tones. Yet the message is no less severe.

"Your faulty assumptions are threefold," I answer the thoughtful blue qheuen.

"You assume that law still reigns in the Five Galaxies.

"You assume that we should feel restrained by procedures and precedents from the last ten million years.

"But above all, your most defective assumption is that we should care."

Dwer

IT WAS NOT ENOUGH SIMPLY TO COAX THE MULC beast. Dwer had to creep close and supervise, for the spider had no clear concept of haste.

Dwer could sense its concentration, shifting fluids and gathering forces from a periphery that stretched league after league, along the Rift coast. The sheer size of the thing was mind-boggling, far greater than the mad little alpine spider that nearly consumed Dwer and Rety. This titan was in the final stages of demolishing a vast city, the culmination of its purpose, and therefore its life. Millennia ago, it might have ignored Dwer, as a busy workman disregards the corner scratchings of a mouse. Now boredom made it responsive to any new voice, offering relief from monumental ennui.

Still, Dwer wondered.

Why was I able to communicate with One-of-a-Kind? And now this spider, as well? We are so different—creatures meant for opposite sides of a planet's cycle.

His sensitivity, if anything, had increased . . . perhaps from letting the Danik robot conduct force fields down his spine. But the original knack must be related to what made him an exceptional hunter.

Empathy. An intuitive sense for the needs and desires of living things.

The Sacred Scrolls spoke darkly of such powers. Psi-talents. They were not recommended for the likes of the Six, who must cringe away from the great theater of space. So Dwer never mentioned it, not to Sara and Lark, or even Fallon, though he figured the old chief scout must have suspected.

Have I done this before? He mused on how he coaxed the spider into action. *I always thought my empathy was passive. That I listened to animals, and hunted accordingly.*

But have I been subtly influencing them, all along? When I shoot an arrow, is it my legendary aim that makes it always strike home? Or do I also nudge the flight of the bush quail so it dodges into the way of the shaft? Do I make the taniger swerve left, just as my stone is about to strike?

It made him feel guilty. Unsporting.

Well? What about right now? You're famished. Why not put out a call for nearby fish and fowl to gather round your knees for plucking?

Somehow, Dwer knew it did not work that way.

He shook his head, clearing it for matters close at hand. Just ahead, rounded silhouettes took uneven bites out of the arching star field. Two sky boats, unmoving, yet mysterious and deadly as he drew near. He swished a finger through the water and tasted, wincing at some nasty stuff leaking into the fen from one or both fallen cruisers.

Now Dwer's sensitive ears picked up noise coming from the larger vessel. Clankings and hammerings. No doubt the crew was working around the clock to make repairs. Despite Rety's assurances, he had no faith that the new day would see a Rothen starship looming overhead to claim both its lost comrades and long-sought prey. The opposite seemed rather more likely.

Either way, he had a job to do.

Till I hear otherwise from the sages, I've got to keep acting on Danel Ozawa's orders.

He said we must defend Jijo.

Star gods don't belong here, any more than sooners do. Less, in fact.

The cry of a mud wren made Dwer slide his torso lower in the water.

Rety's mimicked call came from a lookout point on a Buyur ruin near the dunes. He scanned above the reeds, and caught sight of a glimmering shape—a patrol robot sent out by the stranded untraekis, returning from its latest search spiral.

The mulc spider read his concern and expressed curiosity.

> *More dross?*

Maintaining aloof reserve, Dwer suggested the creature concentrate on its present task, while he worried about flying things.

> *Your memories assert one of these hovering mechanisms slew my brother of the highlands. Mad he may have been, but his job was left undone by that untimely end. Now who will finish it?*

A fair enough question. This time, Dwer formed words.

If we survive this time of crisis, the sages will have a mulc bud planted in the old one's lake. It's our way. By helping get rid of Buyur remains, each generation of the Six leaves Jijo a little cleaner, making up for the small harm we do. The scrolls say it may ease our penance, when judges finally come.

But don't worry about this robot now. You have a goal to focus on. Over there, in that hull of the larger ship, there is a rip, an opening. . . .

Dwer felt hairs on his neck prickle. He crouched low while the unmistakable tingle of gravitic fields swept close. Clearly this was a more powerful robot than the unit he nearly defeated back at the sooner village. That one still cowered in a hole under the sand, while he and Rety took on its enemies.

He hunched like an animal, and even tried thinking like one as the humming commotion passed, setting the tense surface of the water trembling like a qheuen drum. Dwer closed his eyes, but an onslaught of images assailed him. Sparks flew from an urrish forge. Stinging spray jetted over a drowned village. Starlight glinted off a strange fish whose noorlike mouth opened in a wry grin. . . .

The creepy force receded. He cracked his eyelids to watch the slab-sided drone move east down a line of phosphorescent surf, then vanish among the dunes.

More vines now clustered and writhed around the base of the larger sky boat, bunching to send shoots snaking higher. This whole crazy idea counted on one assumption—that the ship's defenses, already badly damaged, would be on guard against "unnatural" things, like metals or energy sources. Under normal conditions, mere plants or beasts would pose no threat to a thick-hulled vessel.

In here?

The spider's query accompanied mental images of a jagged recess, slashed in the side of the untraeki vessel . . . the result of Kunn's riposte, even as his air boat plunged in flames. The visual impression reaching Dwer was tenuous as a daydream, lacking all but the most vague visual details. Instead, he felt a powerful scent of *substance*. The spider would not know or care how Galactic machines worked, only what they were made of—and which concocted juices would most swiftly delete this insult to Jijo's fallow peace.

Yes, in there, Dwer projected. *And all over the outside, as well.*

Except the transparent viewing port, he added. No sense warning the creatures by covering their windows with slithering vines. Let them find out in the morning. By then, with Ifni's luck, it would be too late.

Remember—he began. But the spider interrupted.

I know. I shall use my strongest cords.

Mulc monofiber was the toughest substance known to the Six. With his own eyes, Dwer had seen one rare loop of reclaimed filament pull gondolas all the way to the heights of Mount Guenn. Still, a crew of star gods would have tools to cut even that staunch material. Unless they were distracted.

Time passed. By moonlight the marsh seemed alive with movement—ripples and jerky slitherings—as more vines converged on a growing mass surrounding the ship. Snakelike cables squirmed by Dwer, yet he felt none of the heartsick dread that used to come from contact with One-of-a-Kind. *Intent is everything.* Somehow, he knew this huge entity meant him no harm.

At uneven intervals, Rety used clever calls to warn him of the guard robot's return. Dwer worried that it might find the cowardly Danik machine, hiding under the sand. If so, the alerted Jophur might emerge, filling the bog with blazing artificial light.

Dwer moved slowly around the vessel, taking its measure. But as he counted footsteps, his thoughts drifted to the Gray Hills, where Lena Strong and Jenin Worley must be busy right now, uniting Rety's old band with surviving urrish sooners, forging a united tribe.

Not an easy task, but those two can do it, if anyone can.

Still, he felt sad for them. They must be lonely, with Danel Ozawa gone. *And me, carried off in the claws of a Rothen machine. They must think I'm dead, too.*

Jenin and Lena still had Ozawa's "legacy" of books and tools, and an urrish sage to help them. They might make it, if they were left alone. That was Dwer's job—to make sure no one came across the sky to bother them.

He knew this scheme of his was farfetched. Lark would surely have thought of something better, if he were here.

But I'm all there is. Dwer the Wild Boy. Tough luck for Jijo.

The spider's voice caught him as he was checking the other side of the grounded cruiser, where a long ramp led to a closed hatch.

In here, as well?

His mind filled with another image of the vessel's damaged recess. Moonlight shone through a jagged rent in the hull. The clutter of sooty machinery seemed even more crowded as vine after vine crammed through, already dripping caustic nectars. But Dwer felt his attention drawn deeper, to the opposite wall.

Dim light shone through a crack on that side. Not pale illumination, but sharp, blue, and synthetic, coming from some room beyond.

The ship probably isn't even airtight anymore.

Too bad this didn't happen high in the mountains. Traeki

hated cold weather. A glacier wind would be just the thing to send whistling through here!

No, he answered the spider. *Don't go into the lighted space. Not yet.*

The voice returned, pensively serious.

> *This light . . . it could interfere with my work?*

Dwer assented. *Yeah. The light would interfere, all right.*

Then he thought no more of it, for at that moment a trace of movement caught his eye, to the southeast. A dark figure waded stealthily, skirting around the teeming mound of mulc vines.

Rety! But she's supposed to be on lookout duty.

This was no time for her impulsiveness. With a larger moon due to rise in less than a midura, the two of them had to start making their getaway before the untraeki woke to what was happening.

With uncanny courtesy, mulc cables slithered out of his path as he hurried after the girl, trying not to splash too noisily. Her apparent objective was the *other* crashed ship, the once-mighty sky steed Kunn had used to drop bombs into the Rift, chasing mysterious prey. From the dunes, Dwer and Rety had seen the sleek dart overwhelmed and sent plunging to the swamp, its two human passengers taken captive.

That could happen to us, too. More than ever, Dwer regretted leaving behind Rety's urrish "husband," her conscience and voice of good sense.

> *About the interfering light.*
> *I thought you would like to know.*
> *It is being taken care of.*

Dwer shrugged aside the spider's mind touch as he crossed an open area, feeling exposed. Things improved slightly when he detoured to take advantage of two reed-covered hummocks, cutting off direct sight of the untraeki ship. But the robot guardian still patrolled somewhere out

there. Lacking a lookout, Dwer had just his own wary
senses to warn him if it neared.

While wading though a deeper patch, floundering in water up to his armpits, he felt a warning shiver.

I'm being watched.

Dwer slowly turned, expecting to see the glassy weapons of a faceless killer. But no smooth-sided machine
hovered above the reedy mound. Instead, he found *eyes*
regarding him, perched at the knoll's highest point, a ledge
that might have been the wall of a Buyur home. Sharp
teeth grinned at Dwer.

Mudfoot.

.The noor had done it again.

*Someday, I'll get even for the times you've scared me half
to death.*

Mudfoot had a companion this time, a smaller creature,
held between his paws. Some recent prey? It did not struggle, but tiny greenish eyes seemed to glow with cool interest. Mudfoot's grin invited Dwer to guess what this new
friend might be.

Dwer had no time for games. "Enjoy yourselves," he
muttered, and moved on, floundering up a muddy bank.
He was just rounding the far corner, seeking Rety in the
shadows of the Rothen wreck, when a clamor erupted
from behind. Loud bangs and thumps reverberated as
Dwer crouched, peering back at the large vessel.

This side appeared undamaged—a glossy chariot of
semidivine star gods, ready at an instant to leap into the
sky.

But then a rectangular crack seamed its flank above the
ramp, releasing clots of smoke, like foul ghosts charging
into the night.

The interference is taken care of.

The spider's mind touch seemed satisfied, even proud.

Dark figures spilled through the roiling soot, then down
the ramp, wheezing in agony. Dwer counted three untraeki
. . . then two shambling biped forms, leaning on each
other as they fled the noxious billows.

What followed nauseated Dwer—solitary doughnut

shapes, slithering traeki rings shorn from the waxy moorings that once united them as sapient beings. One large torus burst from the murk, galloping on pulsating legs without guidance or direction, trailing mucus and silvery fibers as it plunged off the ramp into deep water. Another hapless circle bumped along unevenly, staring in all directions with panicky eye patches until surging black vapors overtook it.

> *I have not acted thus—with such vigor and decisiveness—since the early days, when still-animate Buyur servant machines sometimes tried to hide and reproduce amid the ruins, after their masters departed. Back then, we were fierce, we mulc agents of deconstruction, before the long centuries of patient erosion set in.*

> *Now do you see how efficient my kind can be, when we feel a need? And when we have a worthy audience? Now will you acknowledge me, O unique young ephemeral?*

Dwer turned and fled, kicking spray as he ran.

The Rothen scout boat was a wreck, split in the middle, its wings crumpled. He found an open hatch and clambered inside. The metal deck felt chill and alien beneath his bare feet.

The interior lacked even pale moonlight, so it took time to find Rety in a far corner, taking treasures from a cabinet and stuffing them in a bag. *What's she looking for? Food? After all the star-god poisons that've spilled here since the crash?*

"There's no time for that," he shouted. "We've got to get out of here!"

"Gimme a dura," the girl replied. "I know it's here. Kunn kept it on one o' these shelfs."

Dwer craned his head back through the hatch to look outside. The robot guardian had reappeared, hovering over the stricken untraeki vessel, shining stark light on the survivors mired below. As the thick smoke spread out,

Dwer whiffed something that felt sweet in the front of his mouth, yet made the back part gag.

Abruptly, a new thing impacted the senses—sound. A series of twanging notes shook the air. *Lines* stretched across the water as hundreds of cables tautened, surrounding the skycraft like the tent lines of a festival pavilion. Some vines snapped under the strain, whipping across the landscape. One whirling cord sliced through a surviving stack-of-rings, flinging upper toruses into the swamp while the lower half lurched blindly. Other survivors beat a hasty retreat, deeper into the bog.

The robot descended, its spotlight narrowing to a slender, cutting beam. One by one, straining mulc cables parted under the slashing attack. But it was too little, too late. Something or somebody must already have undermined the muck beneath the ship, for it began sliding into a slimy crypt, gurgling as a muddy slurry poured in through the hatch.

"Found it!" Rety cried, rare happiness invading her voice. She joined Dwer at the door, cradling her reclaimed prize. Her metal bird. Since the first time he laid eyes on it, the thing had gone through a lot of poking and prodding, till it could hardly be mistaken for a real creature anymore, even in dim light. *Another damned robot,* he thought. The Ifni-cursed thing had caused Dwer more trouble than he could count. Yet to the sooner girl it was an emblem of hope. The first harbinger of freedom in her life.

"Come on," he muttered. "This wreck is the only shelter hereabouts. The survivors'll be coming this way. We've got to go."

Rety had only agreeable smiles descending back into the swamp. She followed his every move with the happy compliance of one who had no further need to rebel.

Dwer knew he ought to be pleased, as well. His plan had worked beyond all expectation. Yet his sole emotion was emptiness.

Maybe it's on account of I've been wounded, beat up, exhausted, and starved till I'm too numb to care.

Or else, it's that I never really enjoyed one part of hunting.

The killing part.

They retreated from both ruined sky boats to the nearest concealing thicket. Dwer was trying to select a good route back to the dunes, when a voice spoke up.

"Hello. I think we ought to talk."

Dwer was grateful to the mulc spider. He owed it the conversation it desired, and acknowledgment of its might. But, he felt too drained for the mental effort. *Not now,* he projected. *Later, I promise, if I survive the night.*

But the voice was persistent. And Dwer soon realized—the words weren't echoing *inside* his head, but in the air, with a low, familiar quality and tone. They came from just overhead.

"Hello? Humans in the swamp? Can you hear me?"

Then the voice went muffled, as if the speaker turned aside to address someone else.

"Are you sure this thing is working?" it asked.

Bewildered, and against his better judgment, Dwer found himself answering.

"How the hell should *I* know what's working, an' what ain't? Who on Jijo *are* you?"

The words returned more clearly, with evident eagerness.

"Ah! Good. We're in contact, then. That's great."

Dwer finally saw where the words were coming from. *Mudfoot* squatted just above, having followed to pester him from this new perch. And the noor had his new companion—the one with green eyes.

Rety gasped, and Dwer abruptly realized—the second creature bore a family resemblance to Rety's bird!

"All right," Dwer growled, his patience wearing thin with Mudfoot's endless games. "We're footprints, unless you tell me what's goin' on."

The creature with green eyes emitted a low, rumbling sound, surprising for one so small. Dwer blinked, startled by the commonplace resonance of a hoonish umble.

"Hr-r-rm . . . Well, for starters, let me introduce myself.

"The formal name my folks gave me is Hph-wayuo—

"But you can call me Alvin."

PART SEVEN

A PARABLE

"MASTER," THE STUDENT ASKED. "The Universe is so complex, surely the Creator could not have used volition alone to set it in motion. In crafting His design, and in commanding the angels to carry out His will, He must have used *computers*."

The great savant contemplated this for several spans before replying in the negative.

"You are mistaken. No reality can be modeled completely by a calculating engine that is contained within and partaking of that same reality. God did not use a computer to create the world. He used *mathematics*."

The student pondered this wisdom for a long time, then persisted in his argument.

"That may have been the case when it came to envisioning and creating the world, Master—and to foreseeing future consequences in revealed destiny—but what of *maintenance*? The cosmos is a vast, intricate network of decisions. Choices are made every femtosecond, and living beings win accordingly, or else lose.

"How can the Creator's assistants

carry out these myriad local branchings, unless they use computer models?"

But once again, the great savant turned his gaze away in rebuke.

"It is Ifni, the chief deputy, who decides such things. But she has no need for elaborate tools for deciding local events.

"In the Creator's name she runs the world by using dice."

Streakers

Kaa

THE SUBSEA HABITAT FELT CROWDED AS FIVE DOL-
phins gathered before a small holo display, watching a
raid unfold in real time. Images of the distant assault
were blurry, yet they stirred the heart.

While Brookida, Zhaki, and Mopol jostled near Kaa's left
side, he felt more acutely aware of Peepoe on his right—
fanning water with her pectorals in order to keep one eye
aimed at the monitor. Her presence disturbed his mental
and hormonal equilibrium—especially whenever a stray
current brushed her against him. To Kaa, this ironically
proved the multiple nature of his sapient mind—that the
individual he most desired to see was the same one he
dreaded being near.

Fortunately, the on-screen spectacle offered distraction—transmitted by a slender fiber strand from a spy camera located hundreds of kilometers away, on a sandy bluff
overlooking the Rift. Banks of heavy clouds glowered low,
making twilight out of day. But with enhanced contrast, an
observer could just make out shadows flicking beneath
blue water, approaching the shore.

Abruptly, the line of surf erupted armored figures—six-legged monsters with horizontal cylinders for bodies, flared widely at the back—charging past the beach then through a brackish swamp, firing lasers as they came. Three slim flying robots accompanied the attackers, still dripping seawater as they swooped toward the surprised foe.

The enemy encampment was little more than a rude fabric tent propped against the lee side of a shattered spaceship. A single hovering guardian drone shrieked, rising angrily as it sighted the new arrivals . . . then became a smoldering cinder, toppling to douse in the frothy swamp. Jophur survivors could only stand helpless as the onslaught swept over them. Eye cells throbbed unhappily atop tapered sap rings, staring in dazed wonder, unable to grasp this humiliation. August beings, taken prisoner by mere dolphins.

By the youngest race of the wolfling clan of Terra.

Kaa felt good, watching his crew mates turn the tables on those hateful stacks of greasy doughnuts. The Jophur alliance had been relentless in pursuing *Streaker* across the star lanes. This small victory was almost as satisfying as that other raid, on Oakka World, where resolute action took an enemy base from behind, releasing *Streaker* from yet another trap.

Only that time I didn't have to watch from afar. I piloted the boat to pick up Engineer D'Anite, dodging fire all the way.

In those days, he had still been "Lucky" Kaa.

Alongside Peepoe and the others, he watched Lieutenant Tsh't gesture right and left with the metal arms of her walker unit, ordering members of the raiding party to herd their captives toward the shore, where a whalelike behemoth erupted from the surf, spreading mighty jaws.

Despite thick clouds, the raiders had to make this phase brief to avoid detection.

One Jophur captive stumbled in the surf. Its component rings throbbed, threatening to split their mucusy bindings. Mopol chittered delight at the enemy's discomfiture, thrashing his flukes to splatter the habitat's low ceiling.

Peepoe sent Kaa a brief sonar click, drawing attention to Mopol's behavior.

See what I mean? she remarked in clipped Trinary.

Kaa nodded agreement. All trace of illness was gone, replaced by primal exultation. No doubt Mopol longed to be on the raid, tormenting the tormentors.

Peepoe was naturally irked to have come all this way, driving a one-dolphin sled through unfamiliar waters where frightening sound shadows lurked, just to diagnose a case of kingree fever. The name had roots in an Anglic word—*malingering*. Dolphin spacers knew many clever ways to induce symptoms of food poisoning, in order to feign illness and avoid duty.

"I thought-t so from the beginning," Kaa had told her earlier. "It was Makanee's choice to send a nurse, just in case."

That hardly mollified Peepoe.

"A leader's job is to motivate," she had scolded. "If the work is hard, you're supposed to motivate even harder."

Kaa still winced from her chiding. Yet the words also provoked puzzlement, for Mopol had no apparent reason to fake illness. Despite his other faults, the crewfin wasn't known for laziness. Anyway, conditions at this outpost were more pleasant than back at *Streaker,* where you had to breathe irksome oxy-water much of the time, and struggle for sleep with the weird sonic effects of a high-pressure abyss surrounding you. Here, the waves felt silky, the prey fish were tasty, while the task of spying was varied and diverting. Why should Mopol pretend illness, if it meant being cooped up in a cramped habitat with just old Brookida for company?

On-screen, half a dozen bewildered Jophur were being ushered aboard the submarine, while onshore Lieutenant Tsh't consulted with two native humans draped in muddy rags—a young man and an even younger girl—who looked quite tattered and fatigued. The male moved with a limp, clutching a bow and quiver of arrows while his companion held a small broken robot.

Brookida let out a shout, recognizing a spy probe of his own design, fashioned months ago to send ashore, snooping in the guise of a Jijoan bird.

The young man pointed toward a nearby dune and spoke words the camera could not pick up. Almost at once, the three Earthling war drones darted to surround that hillock, hovering cautiously. Moments later, sand spilled from a hole and a larger robot emerged, visibly scarred from past violent encounters. Hesitantly, it paused as if unsure whether to surrender or self-destruct. Finally, the damaged machine glided to the beach, where two more humans were being carried on stretchers by dolphin warriors in exo-suits. These men were also mud-splashed. But under a grime coating, the bigger one wore garments of Galactic manufacture. The captive robot took a position next to that man, accompanying him aboard the sub.

Last to board were Tsh't and the two walking humans. The young man held back for a moment, awed by the entry hatch, gaping like the jaws of some ravenous beast. But the girl radiated delight. Her legs could barely carry her fast enough through the surf as she plunged inside.

Then only Lieutenant Tsh't remained, staring down at a small creature who lounged indolently on the beach, grooming its sleek fur, pretending it had all the time in the world. Through her exo-suit speakers, Tsh't addressed the strange being.

"Well? If you're coming, this is your lassst chance."

Kaa still found it hard to reconcile. For two weeks he had spied on hoonish sailing ships operating out of Wuphon Port, and watched as tiny figures scampered across the rigging. Not once did he associate the fuzzy shapes with *tytlal*—a Galactic client species whose patrons, the Tymbrimi, were Earth's greatest friends.

Who could blame me? With hoons they act like clever animals, not sapient beings. According to the journal of the young hoon adventurer Alvin, Jijoans called the creatures *noor beasts.* And noor never spoke.

But the one on the beach had! And with a Tymbrimi accent, at that.

Could six races live here all this time without knowing that another band of sooners were right in their midst? Could tytlal play dumb the entire time, without giving themselves away?

The small creature seemed complacently willing to outwait Tsh't, perhaps testing dolphin patience . . . until abruptly a new voice broke in, coming from the sub's open hatch. The camera eye swung that way, catching in its field a tall figure, gangly and white, with scaly arms and a bellowslike organ throbbing below its jaw, emitting a low, resonant hum.

Alvin, Kaa realized. The young author of the memoir that had kept Kaa up late several nights, reading about the strange civilization of refugees.

He must be "umbling" at the tytlal.

In moments the sleek creature was seen perched atop the lieutenant's striding exo-suit, as Tsh't hurried aboard. Its grinning expression seemed to say, *Oh, well. If you positively insist . . .*

The hatch swung shut and the sub backed away swiftly, sinking beneath the waves. But the images did not stop.

Left alone at last, *Streaker*'s little scout robot turned its spy eye back toward the field of dunes. Sandy terrain swept past as it sought a vantage point—some ideal site to watch over two blasted wrecks that had once been small spacecraft, but now lay mired by mud and embraced by corrosive vines.

No doubt Gillian Baskin and the ship's council were deeply interested in who might next visit this place of devastation.

Gillian

THE INITIAL EXERCISES ARE COMPLETE. A WARM TINgling pervades her floating body, from tip to toes.

Now Gillian is ready for the first deep movement. It is *Narushkan*—"the starfish"—an outreach of neck, arms, and legs, extending toward the five planar compass points.

Physique discipline lies at the core of weightless yoga, the way Gillian learned it on Earth, when she and Tom studied Galactic survival skills from Jacob Demwa. *"Flesh partici-*

pates in everything we do," the aged spy master once explained. *"We humans like to think we're rational beings. But feelings always precede reason."*

It is a delicate phase. She needs to release her tense body, allowing the skin itself to become like a sensitive antenna. Yet she cannot afford a complete letting go. Not if it means unleashing the grief and loneliness pent up inside.

Floating in a shielded nul-gee zone, Gillian lets her horizontal torso respond to the tug of certain objects located *outside* of the suspension tank, elsewhere in the ship, and beyond. Their influence penetrates the walls, making her sensitized nerves throb and twitch.

"Articles of Destiny"—that was how an enigmatic Old One described such things, during *Streaker*'s brief visit to the Fractal System.

She never got to meet the one who spoke those words. The voice came a great distance, far across that gargantuan edifice of spiky hydrogen ice. The Fractal System was one huge habitat, as wide as a solar system, with a tiny red sun gleaming in its heart. No pursuer could possibly find *Streaker* in such a vast place, if sanctuary were given.

"Your ship carries heavy freight," the voice had said. *"As fate-laden a cargo as we ever detected."*

"Then you understand why we came," Gillian replied as *Streaker*'s lean hull passed jutting angles of fantastic crystal, alternating with planet-sized hollows of black shadow. The ship seemed like a pollen grain lost in a giant forest.

"Indeed. We comprehend your purpose. Your poignant request is being considered. Meanwhile, can you blame us for refusing your invitation to come aboard in person? Or even to touch your vessel's hull? A hull so recently stroked by dire light?

"We who dwell here have retired from the ferment of the Five Galaxies. From fleets and star battles and political intrigues. You may or may not receive the help you seek—that has yet to be decided. But do not expect glad welcome. For your cargo reawakens many of the hungers, the urgencies, and irksome obsessions of youth."

She tried to play innocent. *"The importance of our cargo*

is overrated. We'll hand it over gladly, to those who prove impartial and wise."

"Speak not so!" the speaker scolded. *"Do not add temptation to the poisons you already bring in our midst!"*

"Poisons?"

"You carry blessings in your hold . . . and curses." The voice concluded, *"We fear what your presence will do to our ancient peace."*

As it turned out, *Streaker*'s time of sanctuary lasted just a few slim weeks before convulsions began to shake the Fractal System, sending awful sparks crackling along an immense structure built to house quadrillions. Crystal greenhouses, as wide as Earth's moon, blew apart, exposing sheltered biomass to hard vacuum. Jupiter-sized slivers cracked loose, diffuse as cardboard, though glittering with lighted windows. Like icicles knocked by a violent wind, these tumbled, then collided with other protrusions, exploding into hurricanes of silent dust. Meanwhile, a cacophony of voices swarmed—

The poor wolfling children . . . we must help the Terrans. . . .

No! Erase them so we may return to quiet dreaming. . . .

Objection! Let us instead squeeze them for what they know. . . .

Yes. Then we'll share the knowledge with our younger brethren of the Awaiter Alliance. . . .

No! The Inheritors . . .

The Abdicators! . . .

Gillian recalls marveling at the unleashed storm of pettiness.

So much for the vaunted detachment of old age.

But then, when all seemed lost, sympathetic forces briefly intervened.

This icy realm is not the place you seek.

Advice you need, dispassionate and sage. Seek it from those who are older and wiser, still.

Where tides curl tightly, warding off the night.

Hurry, youngsters. Take this chance. Flee while you can.

•   •   •

Abruptly, an escape path opened for the Earth vessel—a crevice in the vast maze of hydrogen ice, with star-speckled blackness just beyond. *Streaker* had only moments to charge through . . . an egress too sudden and brief for Emerson D'Anite, who had already set forth in a brave, desolate sacrifice.

Poor Emerson. Fought over by resentful factions until his scout craft was swallowed by enfolding light.

All of this comes back to Gillian, not in sequence, but whole, timeless, and entire as she recalls that one phrase—

"Articles of Destiny."

Immersed in a trance state, she can feel those tugging objects. The same ones that caused so much trouble in the Fractal System.

They stroke her limbs—the limbs of *Narushkan*—not with physical force, but with awful import of their existence.

Abruptly, *Narushkan* gives way to *Abhusha*—"the pointer"—and her left hand uncurls toward a massive cube—a portable branch of the great Galactic Library, squatting in a cool mist, two corridors away. With fingers of thought, Gillian traces one of its gemlike facets, engraved with a rayed spiral symbol. Unlike the minimally programmed units that wolfling upstarts could afford, this one was designed to serve a mighty starfaring clan. Had *Streaker* returned home with this prize alone, her costly voyage might be called worthwhile.

Yet the cube seems least among *Streaker*'s cargoes.

Abhusha shifts to her right hand, turning palm out, like a flower seeking warmth to counter the Library's ancient cold.

Toward youth, the antithesis of age.

Gillian hears her little servant, Kippi, move about her private sanctum, straightening up. The Kiqui amphibian, a native of waterlogged Kithrup, uses all six agile limbs impartially while tidying. A cheerful music of syncopated chirps and trills accompanies his labor. Kippi's surface thoughts prove easy to trace, even with Gillian's limited psi-talent. Placid curiosity fills the presapient mind. Kippi seems blithely unaware that his young race is embroiled in a great crisis, spanning five galaxies.

> ## *What comes next?—I wonder what?*
> ## *What comes?*
> ## *What comes next?—I hope it's something good.*

Gillian shares that fervent wish. For the sake of the Kiqui, *Streaker* must find a corner of space where Galactic traditions still hold. Ideally some strong, benevolent star lineage, able to embrace and protect the juvenile amphibian race while hot winds of fanaticism blow along the starry lanes.

Some race worthy to be their patrons . . . to help them . . . as humans never were helped . . . until the Kiqui can stand on their own.

She had already given up hope of adopting the Kiqui into Terra's small family of humans, neo-dolphins, and neo-chimps, the initial idea, when *Streaker* quickly snatched aboard a small breeding population on Kithrup. Ripe presapient species were rare, and this one was a real find. But right now Earthclan could hardly protect itself, let alone take on new responsibilities.

Abhusha shifts again, transmuting into *Poposh* as one of Gillian's feet swarms with prickliness, sensing a new presence in the room. Smug irony accompanies the intruder, like an overused fragrance. It is the Niss Machine's spinning hologram, barging into her exclusive retreat with typical tactlessness.

Tom had thought it a good idea to bring along the Tymbrimi device, when this ill-fated expedition set forth from Earth. For Tom's sake—because she misses him so—Gillian quashes her natural irritation with the smooth-voiced artificial being.

"The submarine, with our raiding party aboard, is now just hours from returning with the prisoners," the Niss intones. *"Shall we go over plans for interrogation, Dr. Baskin? Or will you leave that chore to a gaggle of alien children?"*

The insolent machine seems piqued, ever since Gillian transferred to Alvin and Huck the job of interpreting. But things are going well so far. Anyway, Gillian already knows what questions to ask the human and Jophur captives.

Moreover, she has her own way to prepare. As old Jake used to say, *"How can one foresee, without first remembering?"*

She needs time alone, without the Niss, or Hannes Suessi, or a hundred nervous dolphins nagging at her as if she were their mother. Sometimes the pressure feels heavier than the dark abyss surrounding *Streaker*'s sheltering mountain of dead starships.

To answer verbally would yank her out of the trance, so Gillian instead calls up *Kopou,* an empathy glyph. Nothing fancy—she lacks the inbuilt talent of a Tymbrimi—just a crude suggestion that the Niss go find a corner of cybernetic space and spend the next hour in simulated self-replication, till she calls for it.

The entity sputters and objects. There are more words. But she lets them wash by like foam on a beach. Meanwhile Gillian continues the exercise, shifting to another compass point. One that seems quiet as death.

Abhusha resumes, now reaching toward a cadaver, standing in a far corner of her office like a pharaoh's mummy, surrounded by preserving fields that still cling after three years and a million parsecs, keeping it as it was. As it had been ever since Tom wrested the ancient corpse from a huge derelict ship, adrift in the Shallow Cluster.

Tom always had a knack for acquiring expensive souvenirs. But this one took the cake.

Herbie.

An ironic name for a Progenitor . . . if that truly was its nature . . . perhaps two billion years old, and the cause of *Streaker*'s troubles.

Chief cause of war and turmoil across a dozen spiral arms.

We could have gotten rid of him on Oakka World, she knew. Handing Herbie over to the Library Institute was officially the right thing to do. The safe thing to do.

But sector-branch officials had been corrupted. Many of the librarians had cast off their oaths and fell to fighting among themselves—race by race, clan by clan—each seeking *Streaker*'s treasure for its own kind.

Fleeing once again became a duty.

No one Galactic faction can be allowed to own your secret.

So commanded Terragens Council, in the single long-range message *Streaker* had received. Gillian knew the words by heart.

To show any partiality might lead to disaster.
It could mean extinction for Earthclan.

Articles of Destiny tug at her limbs, reorienting her floating body. Facing upward, Gillian's eyes open but fail to see the metal ceiling plates. Instead, they look to the past.

To the Shallow Cluster. A phalanx of shimmering globes, deceptively beautiful, like translucent moons, or floating bubbles in a dream.

Then the Morgran ambush . . . fiery explosions amid mighty battleships, as numerous as stars, all striving for a chance to snare a gnat.

To Kithrup, where the gnat fled, where so much was lost, including the better part of her soul.

Where are you, Tom? Do you still live, somewhere in space and time?

Then Oakka, that green betraying place, where the Institutes failed.

And the Fractal System, where Old Ones proved there is no age limit on perfidy.

Herbie seems amused by that thought.

"Old Ones? From my perspective, those inhabitants of a giant snowflake are mere infants, like yourself!"

Of course the voice comes from her imagination, putting words in a mouth that might have spoken when Earth's ocean was innocent of any life but bacteria . . . when Sol's system was half its present age.

Gillian cracks a smile and *Abhusha* transforms into *Kuntatta*—laughter amid a storm of sleeting vacuum rays.

Soon, she must wrestle with the same quandary—how to arrange *Streaker*'s escape one more time, just ahead of baying hounds. It would take a pretty neat trick this time, with a Jophur dreadnought apparently already landed on Jijo, and *Streaker*'s hull still laden with refractory soot.

It would take a miracle.

How did they follow us? she wonders. *It seemed a perfect hideout, with all trails to Jijo quantum collapsed but one, and that one passing through the atmosphere of a giant carbon star. The sooner races all did it successfully, arriving without leaving tracks. What did we do wrong?*

Recrimination has no place in weightless yoga.

It spoils the serenity.

Sorry, Jake, she thinks. Gillian sighs, knowing this trance is now forfeit. She might as well emerge and get back down to business. Perhaps the *Hikahi* will bring useful news from its raid on the surface.

I'm sorry, Tom. Maybe a time will come when I can clear my mind enough to hear you . . . or to cast a piece of myself to wherever you have gone.

Gillian won't let herself imagine the more likely probability—that Tom is dead, along with Creideiki and all the others she was forced to abandon on Kithrup, with little more than a space skiff to convey them home again.

The emergence process continues, drawing meditation en-forms back into their original abstractions, easing her toward the world of unpleasant facts.

And yet . . .

In the course of preparing to exit, Gillian abruptly grows aware of a *fifth* tug on her body, this one stroking the back of her neck, prickling her occipital vertebrae, and follicles along the middle of her scalp. It is familiar. She's felt it before, though never this strong. A presence, beckoning not from nearby, or even elsewhere in the ship, but somewhere beyond *Streaker*'s scarred hull. Somewhere else on the planet.

There is a rhythmic, resonant solidity to the sensation, like vibration in dense stone.

If only Creideiki were here, he could probably relate to it, the way he did with those poor beings who lived underground on Kithrup. Or else Tom might have figured out a way to decipher this thing.

And yet, she begins to suspect this time it is something different. Correcting her earlier impression, Gillian realizes—

It is not a presence *on* this world, or beneath it, but something *of* the planet. An aspect of Jijo itself.

Narushkan orients her like the needle of a compass, and abruptly she feels a strange, unprovoked commotion within. It takes her some time to sort out the impression. But recognition dawns at last.

Tentatively—like a long-lost friend unsure of its welcome—*hope* sneaks back into her heart, riding on the stony cadence.

Ewasx

ABRUPTLY COMES NEWS. TOO SOON FOR YOU RINGS to have interpreted the still-hot wax. So let me relate it directly.

WORD OF DISASTER! WORD OF CALAMITY!

Word of ill-fated loss, just east beyond this range of mountain hills. Our grounded corvette—destroyed!

Dissension tears the *Polkjhy* crew. Chem-synth toruses vent fumes of blame while loud recriminations pour from oration rings.

Could this tragedy be the work of the dolphin prey ship, retaliating against its pursuers? For years its renown has spread, after cunning escapes from other traps.

But it cannot be. Long-range scans show no hint of gravitic emanations or energy weapons. Early signs point to some kind of onboard failure.

And yet, clever wolflings are not to be underrated. I/we can read waxy memories left by the former Asx—historical legends of the formative years of the Jijoan Commons, especially tales of urrish-human wars. These stories demonstrate how both races have exceptional aptitudes for improvisation.

Until now, we thought it was coincidence—that there were Earthling sooners here, that the Rothen had human servants, and the prey ship also came from that wolfling world. The three groups seem to have nothing in common, no motives, goals, or capabilities.

But what if there is a pattern?

I/we must speak of this to the Captain-Leader . . . as soon as higher-status stacks pause their ventings and let us get a puff in edgewise.

Prepare, My rings. Our first task will surely be to interrogate the prisoners.

Tsh't

WHAT AM I GOING TO DO?

She fretted over her predicament as the submarine made its way back to the abyssal mountain of dead starships. While other members of the *Hikahi* team exulted over their successful raid, looking forward to reunion with their crew mates on the *Streaker,* Tsh't anticipated docking with a rising sense of dread.

To outward appearances, all was well. The prisoners were secure. The young adventurers, Alvin and Huck, were debriefing Dwer and Rety—human sooners who had managed somehow to defeat a Jophur corvette. Once *Hikahi* leveled its plunge below the thermocline, Tsh't knew she and her team had pulled it off—striking a blow for Earth without being caught.

The coup reflected well on the mission commander.

Some might call Tsh't a hero. Yet disquiet churned her sour stomach.

Ifni must hate me. The worst of all possible combinations of events has caught me in a vise.

"Wait a minute," snapped the female g'Kek, who had assumed the name of an ancient Earthling literary figure. As her spokes vibrated with agitation, she pointed one eyestalk at the young man whose bow and arrows lay across his knees. "You're saying that you walked all the way from the Slope to find *her* hidden tribe . . . while *she* flew back home aboard the Dakkin sky boat . . ."

The human girl, Rety, interrupted.

"That's *Danik,* you dumb wheelie. And what's so surprisin' about that? I had Kunn an' the others fooled down to their scabs, thinkin' I was ready to be one of 'em. O' course I was just keepin' my eyes peeled fer my first chance to . . ."

Tsh't had already heard the story once through, so she paid scant attention this time, except to note that "Huck" spoke far better Anglic than the human child. Anyway, she had other matters on her mind. Especially one of the prisoners lying in a cell farther aft . . . a captive starfarer who could reveal her deepest secret.

Tsh't sent signals down the neural tap socketed behind her left eye. The mechanical walker unit responded by swiveling on six legs to aim her bottle-shaped beak away from the submarine's bridge. Unburdened by armor or life-support equipment, it maneuvered gracefully past a gaggle of dolphin spectators. The fins seemed captivated by the sight of two humans so disheveled, and the girl bearing scars on her cheek that any Earth hospital could erase in a day. Their rustic accents and overt wonder at seeing real live dolphins seemed poignantly endearing in members of the patron race.

The two seemed to find nothing odd about chatting with Alvin and Huck, though, as if wheeled beings and Anglic-speaking hoons were as common as froth on a wave. Common enough for Rety and Huck to bicker like siblings.

"Sure I led Kunn out this way. But only so's I could find

out where the bird machine came from!" Rety stroked a miniature urs, whose long neck coiled contentedly around her wrist. "And my plan worked, didn't it? I found you!"

Huck reacted with a rolling twist of all four eyestalks, a clear expression of doubt and disdain. "Yes, though it meant revealing the Earthship's position, enabling your *Danik* pilot to target its site from the air."

"So? What's yer point?"

From the door, Tsh't saw the male human glance at the big adolescent hoon. Dwer and Alvin had just met, but they exchanged commiserating grins. Perhaps they would compare notes later, how each managed life with such a "dynamic" companion.

Tsh't found all the varied voices too complicated. *It feels like a menagerie aboard this tub.*

The argument raged on while Tsh't exited the bridge. Perhaps recordings would prove useful when Gillian and the Niss computer analyzed every word. Preparations were also under way to interrogate the Jophur survivors using techniques found in the Thennanin Library cube—sophisticated data from a clan that had been fighting Jophur since before Solomon built his temple.

Tsh't approved . . . so far.

But Gillian will also want to question Kunn. And she knows her own kind too well to be fooled.

The *Hikahi* was a makeshift vessel, built out of parts salvaged from ancient hulks lining the bottom of the Rift. Tsh't passed down corridors of varied substance, linked by coarsely welded plates, until she reached the cell where two human prisoners were held. Unfortunately, the guard on duty turned out to be Karkaett, a disciple of former Captain Creideiki's *keeneenk* mental training program. Tsh't couldn't hope to send Karkaett off on some errand and have him simply forget. Any slip in regulations would be remembered.

"The doughnuts are sedated," the guard reported. "Also, we z-zapped the damaged Rothen battle drone and put it in a freezer. Hannes and I can check its memory store later."

"That-t's fine," she replied. "And the tytlal?"

Karkaett tossed his sleek gray head. "You mean the one

that talks? Isolated in a cabin, as you instructed. Alvin's pet is just a *noor*, of course. I assume you didn't mean to lock her up, t-too."

Actually, Tsh't wasn't sure she grasped the difference between a *noor* and a *tytlal*. Was it simply the ability to talk? What if they all could, but were good at keeping it secret? Tytlal were legendary for one trait—going to any length for a joke.

"I'll see the human prisoners now," she told the guard.

Karkaett transmitted a signal to open the door. Following rules, he accompanied her inside, weapons trained on the captives.

Both men lay on cots with medical packs strapped to their arms. Already they seemed much improved over their condition in the swamp, where, coughing and desperate for breath, they had clutched a reed bank, struggling to keep their heads above water. The younger one looked even more grubby and half-starved than Rety—a slightly built young man with wiry muscles, black hair, and a puckered scar above one eye. *Jass,* Rety had identified him—a sooner cousin, and far from her favorite person.

The other man was much larger. His uniform could still be recognized beneath the caked filth. Steely gray eyes drilled Tsh't the moment she entered.

"How did you follow us to Jijo?"

That was what Gillian would surely ask the Danik voyager. It was the question Tsh't feared most.

Calm down, she urged herself. *The Rothen only know that someone sent a message from the Fractal System. They can't know who.*

Anyway, would they confide in their Danik servants? This poor fellow is probably just as bewildered as we are.

Yet Kunn's steady gaze seemed to hold the same rock-solid faith she once saw in the Missionary . . . the disciple who long ago brought a shining message-of-truth to the small dolphin community of Bimini-Under, back when Tsh't was still a child gliding in her mother's slipstream wake.

"Humans are beloved patrons of the neo-dolphin race, it's true," the proselytizer explained, during one secret meeting, in a cave where scuba-diving tourists never ven-

tured. *"Yet, just a few centuries ago, primitive men in boats hunted cetaceans to the verge of extinction. They may act better today, but who can deny their new maturity is fragile, untested? Without meaning disloyalty, many neo-fins feel discomfort, wondering if there might not be something or somebody greater and wiser than humankind. Someone the entire clan can turn to, in dangerous times."*

"You mean God?" one of the attending dolphins asked. And the Missionary responded with a nod.

"In essence, yes. All the ancient legends about divine beings who intervene in Earth's affairs . . . all the great teachers and prophets . . . can be shown to have their basis in one simple truth.

"Terra is not just an isolated forlorn world—home to bizarre wolflings and their crude clients. Rather, it is part of a wonderful experiment. Something I have come from afar to tell you about.

"We have been watched over for a very long time. Lovingly guarded throughout our long time of dreaming. But soon, quite soon, it will be time to waken."

Kaa

MOPOL'S FEVER SHOWED NO SIGN OF RETURNING. In fact, he seemed quite high in spirits when he left the next morning, swimming east with Zhaki, resuming their reconnaissance of Wuphon Port.

"You see? All he needed was a stern talking-to," Peepoe explained with evident pride. "Mopol just had to be reminded of his duty."

Kaa sensed the implied rebuke in her words, but chose to ignore it.

"You have a persuasive bedside manner," he replied. "No doubt they teach it in medical school."

In fact, he was quite sure that Mopol's recovery had little to do with Peepoe's lecture. The half-stenos male had agreed too readily with everything the young nurse said, tossing his mottled gray head and chittering "Yessss!" repeatedly.

He and Zhaki are up to something, Kaa thought, as he watched the two swim off toward the coastal hoon settlement.

"I need to be heading back to the ship soon," Peepoe said, causing Kaa to dip his narrow jaw.

"But I thought you'd stay a few days. You agreed to come see the volcano."

Her expression seemed wary. "I don't know. . . . When I left, there was talk of shifting *Streaker* to another hiding place. Searchers were getting too damned c-close."

Not that moving the ship a few kilometers would make much difference, if Galactic fleets already had her pinned. Even hiding under a great pile of discarded starcraft would not help, once pursuers had the site narrowed down close enough to use chemical sniffers. Earthling DNA would lure them, like male moths to a female's pheromones.

Kaa shrugged by twisting his flukes.

"Brookida will be disappointed. He was so looking forward to showing off his collection of dross from all six sooner races."

Peepoe stared at Kaa, scanning him with penetrating sound till she found the wryness within.

Her blowhole sputtered laughter.

"Oh, all right. Let's see this mountain of yours. Anyway, I've been aching for a swim."

As usual, the water felt terrific. A little saltier than Earth sea, but with a fine mineral flavor and a gentle ionic oiliness that helped it glide over your skin. The air's rich oxygen level made it seem as if you could keep going well past the horizon.

It was a far friendlier ocean than on Kithrup or Oakka, where the oceans tasted poisonously foul. Friendlier, that is, unless you counted the groaning sounds that occasionally drifted from the Midden, as if a tribe of mad whales lived down there, singing ballads without rhyme or reason.

According to *Alvin's Journal,* their chief source on Jijo, some natives believed that ancient beings lived beyond the continental shelf, fierce and dangerous. Such hints prompted Gillian Baskin to order the spying continued.

So long as Streaker *doesn't need a pilot, I might as well play secret agent. Anyway, it's a job Peepoe might respect.*

Beyond all that, Kaa relearned how fine it was to cruise in tandem with another strong swimmer, jetting along on powerful fluke strokes, building momentum each time you plunged, then soaring through each upper arc, like flying. The true peak of exhilaration could never be achieved alone. Two or more dolphins must move in unison, each surf-riding the other's wake. When done right, surface tension nearly vanished and the planet merged seamlessly, from core to rock, from sea to sky.

And then . . . to bitter-clear vacuum?

A modern poet might make that extrapolation, but it never occurred to natural cetaceans—not even species whose eyesight could make out stars—not until humans stopped hunting and started teaching.

They changed us. Showed us the universe beyond sun, moon, and tides. They even turned some of us into pilots. Wormhole divers. I guess that makes up for their ancestors' crimes.

Still, some things never change. Like the semierotic stroke of whitecaps against flesh, or the spume of hot breath meeting air. The raw, earthy pleasure of this outing offered much that he felt lacking aboard *Streaker*.

It also made a terrific opening to courtship.

Assuming she thinks the same way I do.

Assuming I can start winning her esteem.

They were approaching shore. He could tell by the echoes of rock-churned surf up ahead. A mist-shrouded mountain could be glimpsed from the top of each forward leap. Soon they would reach the hidden cave where his spy equipment lay. Then Kaa must go back to dealing with Peepoe in awkward, inadequate words.

I wish this could just go on without end, he thought.

A brief touch of sonar, and he knew Peepoe felt the same. She, too, yearned for this moment of primitive release to last.

Kaa's sonic sense picked out a school of pseudo-tunny, darting through nearby shoals, tempting after a pallid breakfast of synthi flesh. The tunny weren't quite in their path—it would mean a detour. Still, Kaa squirted a burst of Trinary.

> * In summer sunlight,
> * Fish attract like edible
> * Singularities! *

Kaa felt proud of the haiku—impulsive, yet punning as it mixed both space- and planet-bound images. Of course, free foraging was still not officially sanctioned. He awaited Peepoe's rejection.

> * Passing an abyss, or bright reef,
> * Or black hole—what sustains us?
> * Our navigator! *

Her agreement filled Kaa's pounding heart, offering a basis for hope.

Peepoe's strong, rhythmic strokes easily kept pace alongside as he angled toward a vigorous early lunch.

Sooners

Lark

'VE BEEN ABOARD A FLYING MACHINE BEFORE, HE told himself. *I'm no simple nature child, astonished by doors, metal panels, and artificial light.*
This place should not terrify me.
The walls aren't about to close in.

His body wasn't convinced. His heart raced and he could not rest. Lark kept experiencing a disturbing impression that the little room was getting *smaller*.

He knew it must be an illusion. Neither Ling nor Rann showed outward concern over being crushed in a diminishing space. They were used to hard gray surfaces, but the metal enclosure seemed harsh to one who grew up scampering along the branch-top skyways of a garu forest. The floor plates brought a distant vibration, rhythmic and incessant.

Lark suddenly realized what it reminded him of—the machinery of his father's paper mill—the grinders and pulping hammers—designed to crush scrap cloth into a fine white slurry. That pounding noise used to drive him away into the wilderness, on long journeys seeking living things to study.

"Welcome to a starship, sooner," Rann mumbled, nursing both a headache and a grudge after their fight in the lake. "How do you like it?"

All three human prisoners still wore their damp underwear, having been stripped of their tools and wet suits. For some reason, the Jophur let them keep their rewq symbionts, though Rann had torn his off, leaving red welts at his temples where the crumpled creature had had no time to withdraw its feeding suckers.

At least no one had been injured during the swift capture, when a swarm of tapered cone beings swept down from the mammoth ship, each Jophur riding its own platform of shimmering metal. Suspensor fields pressed the lake, surrounding the human swimmers between disklike watery depressions. Hovering robots crackled with restrained energy—one even dived beneath the surface to cut off escape—crowding the captives toward one of the antigravity sleds, and then to prison.

To Lark's surprise, they were put in the same cell. By accounts from Earth's dark ages, it used to be standard practice to separate prisoners, to break their spirits. Then he realized.

If Jophur are like traeki, they can't quite grasp the notion of being alone. A solitary traeki would be happy arguing among its rings till the Progenitors came home.

"They are probably at a loss, trawling through their database for information about Earthlings," Ling explained. "Till recently, there wasn't much available."

"But it's been three hundred years since contact!"

"That may seem long to us, Lark. But Earth was minor news for most of that time—a back-page sensation. By now the first detailed Institute studies of our homeworld have barely made it through the sector-branch Library, on Tanith."

"Then why not . . ." He sought a word she had used several times. "Why not *upload* Earthling books. Our encyclopedias, medical texts, self-analyses . . . the knowledge we spent thousands of years accumulating about ourselves?"

She lifted her eyes. "*Wolfling superstitions.* Even we Daniks are taught to think that way." She glanced at Rann. "It took your thesis, Lark—the one you wrote with Uthen—to convince me things might be different."

Though flushed at the compliment, Lark reined in his imagination. He tried not to let his eyes drop to her nearly bare figure. Skimpy underclothes would not hide his physical arousal. Besides, this was hardly the time.

"I still find their attitude hard to credit. The Galactics would rather wait centuries for a formal report on us?"

"Oh, I'm sure the great powers—like the Soro and Jophur—got access to early drafts. And they've urgently sought more data since the *Streaker* crisis began. Their strategic agencies almost certainly kidnapped and dissected some humans, for instance. But they could hardly update every star cruiser with illicit data. That would risk contaminating the onboard Library cubes. I'd have to guess this crew has been improvising—not a skill much encouraged in Galactic society."

"But humans are known for it. Is that why your ship came to Jijo? Improvising an opportunity?"

Ling nodded, rubbing her bare shoulders. "Our Rothen lor . . ." She paused, then chose another phrasing. "The Inner Circle received a message. A time-drop capsule, tuned for pickup by anyone with a Rothen cognition wave."

"Who sent it?"

"Apparently, a secret believer living among the crew of the dolphin ship. Or one desperate enough to break from Terragens orders, and summon help from a higher source."

"A believer . . ." Lark mused. "In the Danik faith, you mean. But Daniks teach that *humans* are the secret recipients of Rothen patronhood."

"And by tradition, that means a dolphin crew could also call on Rothen help, in case of dire need . . . which those poor creatures surely face."

"Like running to your grandparents, if your own folks can't handle a problem. Hrm."

Lark had already picked up parts of the story. How the

first dolphin-crewed starship set forth on a survey mission, assigned to check the accuracy of the small planetary branch Earth had received from the Library Institute. Most civilized clans simply accepted the massive volumes of information stored by past generations, especially concerning far corners of space, where little profit could be gained by exploration.

It was supposed to be routine. A shakedown cruise. But then, somewhere off the beaten track, Earthship *Streaker* confronted something unexpected—a discovery that made the great alliances crazy. Clues to a time of transition, perhaps, when ancient verities of the known galaxies might abruptly change.

"It is said that when this happens, just one race in ten shall make the passage to a new age," the hoonish High Sage, Phwhoon-dau, had explained one night by a campfire, just after the fall of Dooden Mesa, drawing on his deep readings of the Biblos Archive. *"Those bent on surviving into the next long phase of stability would naturally want to learn as much as possible. Hr-r-r-rm. Yes, even a sooner can understand why this Earthling ship found itself in trouble."*

"A dolphin Danik." Lark marveled. "So this . . . *believer* sent a secret message to the Rothen. . . ."

"To is the wrong word. You might better use *at.* In fact, nothing in Anglic adequately describes the skewed logic of communicating by time drop." Ling kept running her fingers through her hair. It had grown since the Battle of the Glade, and was still tangled from their long dive under the lake.

"But yes, the message from the dolphin believer explained where the *Streaker* ship was—in one of the hydrogen-ice habitat zones where many older races huddle close to stellar tides, after retiring from active Galactic affairs.

"More important—it hinted where the Earthship commander next planned to flee." Ling shook her head. "It turned out to be a clever version of the Sooner Path. A difficult passage, uncomfortably close to fiery Izmunuti. No wonder you Six were left undetected for so long."

"Hr-rm," Lark umbled contemplatively. "Unlike our ancestors, you let yourselves be followed."

This drew a reaction from Rann, sullenly holding his aching head in the opposite corner of the cell.

"Fool. We did no such thing!" the tall Danik muttered sourly. "Are you saying we cannot easily repeat any feat accomplished by a gaggle of cowardly sooners?"

"Putting insults aside, I agree," Ling said. "It seems unlikely we were followed. That is, not the *first* time our ship came to Jijo."

"What do you mean?" Lark asked.

"When our comrades left us—four humans and two Rothen, with the job of doing a bioassay on Jijo—I thought the others were going to cruise nearby space, in case the dolphin ship was hiding on some nearby planetoid. But that was not their aim at all.

"Their real intent was to go find a buyer."

Lark frowned in puzzlement. "A *Buyur*? But aren't they extinct? You mean the Rothen wanted to hire one as a guide, to come back to Jijo and—"

"No . . . a *buyer*!" Ling laughed, though it was not a happy sound. "You were right about the Rothen, Lark. They live by bartering unusual or illicit information, often using human Daniks as agents or intermediaries. It was an exciting way of life . . . till you made me realize how we've been used." Ling's expression turned dark. Then she shook her head.

"In this case, they must have realized Jijo was worth a fortune to the right customer. There are life-forms on this planet whose development seems ahead of schedule, rapidly approaching presapience. And there are the Six Races. Surely someone would pay to know about such a major infestation of criminal sooners . . . no offense."

"None taken. And of course, the clue to the dolphin ship was worth plenty. So . . ." He blew an airy sigh through his nostrils, like a disgusted urs. "Your masters decided to sell us all."

Ling nodded, but her eyes bored into Rann. "Our patrons sold us all."

The big Danik did not meet her gaze. He pressed both hands against his temples, emitting a low moan that seemed half from pain and half disgust at her treason. He turned toward the wall, but did not touch the oily surface.

"After all we've seen, you still think the Rothen are patrons of humanity?" Lark asked.

Ling shrugged her shoulders. "I cannot easily dismiss the evidence I was shown while growing up—evidence dating back thousands of years. Anyway, it might explain our bloody, treacherous history. The Rothen lords claim it's because our dark souls kept drifting from the Path. But maybe we are exactly what they uplifted us to be. Raised to be shills for a gang of thieves."

"Hrm. That might relieve us of some of the responsibility. Still, I'd rather be wolflings, with ignorance our only excuse."

Ling nodded, lapsing into silence, perhaps contemplating the great lie her life had revolved around. Meanwhile, Lark found a new perspective on the tale of humanity. It went beyond a dry litany of events, recited from dusty tomes in the Biblos Archive.

The Daniks claim that we had guidance all along . . . that Moses, Jesus, Buddha, Fuller, and others were teachers in disguise. But if we were helped—by the Rothen or anybody else—then our helpers clearly did a lousy job.

Like a problem child who needs open, honest, personal attention, we could have used a lot more than a few ethical nostrums. Vague hints like, "Have faith" and "Be nice to each other." Moralizing platitudes aren't enough to guide a rowdy tyke . . . and they sure did not prevent dark ages, slavery, the twentieth-century Holocaust, or the despots of the twenty-first.

All those horrors reflect as poorly on the teacher as the students. Unless . . .

Unless you suppose we actually did it all alone . . .

Lark was struck by the same feeling as when he and Ling spoke beside the mulc spider's lake. His mind filled with an image of poignant, awful beauty. A tapestry spanning thousands of years—human history seen from afar. A tale of frightened orphans, floundering in ignorance. Of creatures smart enough to stare in wonder at the stars, asking questions of a night that never answered, except with terrifying silence.

Sometimes, from desperate imaginations, the silence provoked roaring hallucinations, fantastic rationalizations, or self-serving excuses for any crime the strong might choose to commit against the weak. Deserts widened as men ignorantly cut forests. Species vanished as farmers burned and plowed. Wars spread ruin in the name of noble causes.

Yet, amid all that, humanity somehow began pulling together, learning the arts of calmness, peering forward in time, like a neglected infant teaching itself to crawl and speak.

To stand and think.

To walk and read.

To care . . . and then become a loving parent to others.

The kind of parent poor orphans never had.

Born on a refuge world whose crude safety had vanished, imprisoned in the bowels of an alien starship, Lark nevertheless felt drawn away from worrying about his own fate, or even the six exile clans of Jijo. After all, on the vast scale of things, his life hardly mattered. The Five Galaxies would spin on, even if every last Earthling vanished.

Yet he found his heart torn by the tragic story of *Homo sapiens,* the self-taught wolflings of Terra. It was a bittersweet tale, pulling from his reluctant eyes trickles of tart brine that tasted like the sea.

The voice was familiar . . . horrifyingly so.

"Tell us now."

When all three humans kept silent, the Jophur interrogator edged closer, towering over them. Anglic words hissed from atop the swaying stack of fatty rings, accompanied by liquid burblings and mucusy pops.

"Explain to us; why did you transmit the signal that led to your capture? Did you sacrifice yourselves in order to buy time for unseen comrades? Those we most eagerly pursue?"

It had introduced itself as "Ewasx," and part of Lark's horror lay in recognizing torus markings of the former traeki High Sage, Asx. One major difference appeared at the bottom of the stack, where a new, agile torus-of-legs let the composite being move about more quickly than before. And silvery fibers now laced the doughy tubes, leading up to a glistening young ring that had no apparent features or appendages. Yet Lark sensed it was the chief thing turning the old traeki sage into a Jophur.

"We detected a disturbance in the toporgic time field, imprisoning the Rothen vessel below the lake," it said. "But these tremors were well within noise variance levels, and our leaders were otherwise too busily engaged to investigate. However, we/I now clearly discern what you were trying to accomplish with this trick."

The declaration left Lark unsurprised. Once alerted, the mighty aliens would naturally pierce his jury-rigged scheme for letting Daniks out of the trapped vessel. He only hoped that Jeni Shen, and Jimi, and the others made it out before hunter robots swarmed around the Rothen time cocoon, then through the network of caves.

While all three humans kept silent, Ewasx continued.

"The chain of logic is apparent, revealing a persistent effort on the part of you sooners to divert us from our main purpose on this world.

"In short, you have been attempting to distract us."

Now Lark looked up, baffled. He shared a glance with Ling.

What is the Jophur talking about?

"It began several Jijo rotations ago," Ewasx went on. "Although no other crew stack thought it unusual, *I* was perplexed when the High Sages acceded so swiftly to our Captain-Leader's demand. I did not expect Vubben and Lester Cambel to obey so quickly, revealing the coordinates of the chief g'Kek encampment."

Lark spoke at last. "You mean Dooden Mesa."

He still felt guilty over how a stray computer resonance betrayed the secret colony's location. Apparently, Ewasx thought the transmission had been made on purpose.

"Dooden Mesa, correct. The timing of the signal now seems too convenient, too out of character. Memory stacks inherited from *Asx* indicate a disgusting level of interspecies loyalty among the mongrel races of Jijo. Loyalty that should have delayed compliance with our demand. Normally the sages would have dithered, in hopes of evacuating the g'Keks before giving in."

"Why did you have to wait for a signal at all?" Lark

asked. "If you've got memories from Asx, you knew all along where Dooden was! Why bother asking the High Sages?"

For the first time, Lark saw signs of what might be called an emotional response. Uneven ripples coursed several Ewasx rings, as if they were writhing from unpleasant sensations within. When it spoke next, the voice seemed briefly labored.

"Reasons for incomplete data retrieval access are not your concern. Suffice it to say that the immurement of Dooden Mesa was gratifying to our *Polkjhy* Ship Commanders . . . yet I/we nursed brooding reservations within this stack of restless rings. The timing seemed too convenient."

"What do you mean?"

"I mean that the signal came *just* as we were about to launch our remaining corvette to succor another, which had made a forced landing beyond the mountains. That mission was postponed on learning where the chief g'Kek hideout lay. The corvette was outfitted with toporgic, to attack our sworn feud enemies, lest any escape that nest of wheeled vipers."

Lark caught Rann glancing at Ling, meaningfully. *Beyond the mountains.* The Daniks had sent Kunn's scout vessel out that way, just before the Battle of the Glade. And now the Jophur reported losing a corvette in the same direction?

Not lost. A forced landing. Still, they have strange priorities. Vengeance before rescue.

"After dealing with Dooden Mesa, there were other delays. Then, just as we were resuming preparations to send aid to our grounded cousins, this new distraction came about. I refer to your activity below the lake. You cleverly found some rude way to vibrate the toporgic seal around the Rothen ship. We ignored this at first, since mere sooners could never actually penetrate the cocoon—"

Another tremor crossed the creature's rings, though this time the voice did not pause.

"Soon, however, there came a distraction we could *not* ignore. The appearance of three humans at the surface of the lake, deep within our perimeter! This event triggered alarms, concentrating our attention for a lengthy period.

"I/we are now quite certain that was your intent all along."

Lark stared in astonishment.

Just after they were captured, he and Ling had speculated in whispers about Rann's betrayal, swimming to the surface and using the portable computer to blatantly attract Jophur attention. Ling had illuminated a likely motive.

"Rann is more loyal to our masters than I ever imagined. He knows the Six Races possess evidence that can blow the lid off the grand Rothen deception. Helping our crew mates escape the trapped ship would just make matters worse, by exposing more Daniks to your arguments, Lark. Your evidence of genocide and other wrongs. Like me, they might be converted away from our lords.

"Before allowing that to happen, Rann would rather let the Jophur wipe out everybody, and leave our crew sealed forever. At least that way the Rothen home clan might be safe."

Ling's explanation had rocked Lark. But *this* one from Ewasx was weirder still.

"You're saying we . . . uh, *vibrated* the golden shell around the submerged ship . . . *in order* to attract your attention? And when that didn't work, we swam up to the surface to make even more noise, trying to draw your gaze our way?"

As he said the words, Lark realized in surprise that the scenario made more sense than what had actually happened! In comparison, it did seem improbable that primitive sooners would find a way to pierce the toporgic trap . . . or that a Danik would betray his crew mates in order to keep them buried forever. There was just one logical problem.

"But . . ." he went on. "But *why* would we be desperate enough to do such a thing? What aim could make such a sacrifice worthwhile?"

The Jophur emitted an aggravated sigh.

"You know perfectly well what aim. However, in order to establish a clear basis for interrogation, I will explain.

"I/we know your secret," it told Lark.

"You must certainly be in communication with the Earthling ship."

Alvin

THE DOLPHINS HAVEN'T GIVEN A NAME TO THIS mountain of abandoned starships. This heap of discards from a lost civilization, moldering at the bottom of the Midden.

Huck wants to call it *Atlantis*. But for once I find her suggestion lacking imagination.

I prefer that mythical place described so hauntingly by the great Clarke. The *Seven Suns*. Where my namesake found ancient relics long forgotten by titans who had moved on, leaving their obsolete servants behind.

Remnants of a mighty past, now lost between the city and the stars.

We don't spend much time together anymore. We four from Wuphon Port. We four comrades and adventurers. We've gone off in different directions, led by our own obsessions.

Ur-ronn spends her time where you'd expect—in the engine room, eagerly learning about the hardware of a starship and getting thick as thieves with Hannes Suessi. I get an impression these dolphins aren't as good at delicate hand-eye work as an urs, so Suessi seems glad to have her around.

It's also the *driest* place aboard this waterlogged cruiser. Still, I figure Ur-ronn would spend time down there even if it meant sloshing through knee-deep slush. It's where a smith belongs.

Suessi hoped we might offer clues toward ridding *Streaker*'s hull of a thick carbon coating. Oral traditions speak of *star soot,* weighing down each sneakship that reached Jijo after passing close by Izmunuti. But I never heard of a clan trying to remove it. Why would our ancestors bother, since they scuttled their arks soon after arriving?

Anyway, why not just refurbish one of the old hulks lying under the Midden, and use it to make an escape?

Ur-ronn says Suessi and Dr. Baskin considered the idea. But the ships are junk, after all. If the wrecks could fly well, wouldn't the Buyur have taken them along?

For helping the engineers, Ur-ronn hopes to get some cooperation in return . . . fulfilling the assignment we were given when our little homemade *Wuphon's Dream* first dropped to the sea by Terminus Rock. Uriel had asked us to find a hidden cache—equipment to help the High Sages deal with intruding starships.

Now that we know more about those invaders—a *Rothen* cruiser, followed later by a *Jophur* battleship—it seems unlikely that cache would help against forces so godlike and lofty. Anyway, Uriel and our parents must have given us up for dead, ever since the air hose tore away from *Wuphon's Dream*.

Still, Ur-ronn's right. An oath is an oath.

I can see why Dr. Gillian Baskin prefers we don't contact our folks. But I must persuade her to try.

Pincer-Tip spends most of his time with the Kiqui—those six-limbed amphibians we once thought to be masters of this ship. Instead, they are something even more revered in the Five Galaxies—honest-to-goodness presapient beings. Pincer seems to have an affinity for them, since his red qheuen race is also adapted to live where waves meet a rocky coast. But that may just begin to cover Pincer's attraction to them.

He talks of building a new bathy to explore the Midden. Not just this mound of dead starcraft, but some of the vast jumbled cities, filled with wonders discarded by the departing Buyur.

Clearly he enjoyed his brief stint as captain of *Wuphon's Dream*. Only this time he hopes for a new crew. Agile, obedient, water-loving Kiqui may be ideal, compared to a too-tall hoon, a prolix g'Kek, and a hydrophobic urs.

Maybe Pincer still hopes to find real monsters.

Huck refuses to believe anything important can take place without her. As soon as we returned with Lieutenant Tsh't, she got involved in the serious business of questioning the Jophur prisoners, taken from the wrecked scoutship.

According to spy and adventure novels, the art of interrogation has a lot to do with language trickery. Fooling the other guy into blurting out something he never intended. That's just the kind of stuff Huck thinks she's oh so clever at. So what if Jophur are different from traeki. She expected to break their obstinate silence and get them talking.

So imagine her shock when she rolled into their chamber and the very sight of her sent them into a fit, throwing themselves against the restraining field trying to get at her! The room filled with a stench of pure hatred.

Strangely enough, that proved useful! For the Jophur abruptly lost their sullen muteness and started babbling. Mostly, their GalTwo and GalFive utterance streams were steeped with fuming anger. But soon the sneaky Niss Machine popped in, making insinuations and smooth-voiced hints. . . .

Huck turned all four eyestalks to stare at the whirling hologram when it suggested the Jophur might be given this tasty g'Kek, if they cooperated! Soon, mixed among the vengeance vows and retribution exclamatives were bits of useful information, such as the name of their ship and the rank of its Captain-Leader. And one further crucial fact. Although their battlecruiser is a giant compared to outmatched *Streaker,* the Jophur ship came to Jijo alone.

Huck says she knew all along that the Niss was bluffing about handing her over. In fact, she claimed a triumph, as if it had been her plan all along.

I knew better than to comment on the green sweat coating her eye hoods. After the interview, she needed a bath.

•   •   •

Unlike the others, I can't banish all doubt.

Have we chosen the right side?

Oh, there seem to be good reasons for throwing our fate in with these fugitives. Humans are members of the Six, and that makes the dolphins sort of cousins, I guess. And it's true that *Streaker* seems more like one of our sooner sneakships than those arrogant dreadnoughts, up in the Rimmer Range. Anyway, I was brought up reading Earthling tall tales. My sentiments are drawn to the underdog.

Still, I must keep at least one mental corner detached and uncommitted. My loyalty lies ultimately with family, sept, and clan . . . and with the High Sages of the Commons of Jijo.

Among the four of us, someone must remember our true priorities. A time may come when they clash with our hosts'.

How have I kept busy all this time?

For one thing, I've been learning to skim the ship's database, extracting historical summaries of what's taken place since the Great Printing. The distilled tale is a treat to a born info hound like me.

And yet, I still can't get that big, mist-shrouded cube out of my mind. Sometimes I hanker to sneak into that cold room and ask questions of the Branch Library—a storehouse so great that the Biblos Archive might as well be a primer for a two-year old.

On our way back from the surface I got to know Rety—the irascible, proud human girl whose illegal tribe of savages would have shaken the Commons with a sensational scandal, in normal times. I also talked to Dwer the Hunter, who I recall visiting Wuphon, a few years back. Dwer chatted about his adventures while Physician Makanee treated his wounds, till he fell into exhausted slumber. Soon Rety collapsed, too, with her little "husband" curled alongside, a slim urrish head draped across her chest.

•   •   •

For the most part, my job has been to umble.

Yeah, that's right. To umble for a noor.

My own pet, Huphu, doesn't know what to make of the newcomer—the one called *Mudfoot*. On first spying him, she hissed . . . and he hissed back, exactly like a regular noor. It was such a normal reaction that I started to doubt my own memory. Did I really hear and see Mudfoot *talk*?

My assigned task is to keep him happy till he decides to talk again.

I guess I owe these people—Gillian Baskin and Tsh't and the dolphins.

They saved us from the abyss . . . though maybe we wouldn't have fallen at all, if it hadn't been for their interference.

They fixed my broken back . . . though it was injured when *they* smashed *Wuphon's Dream*.

They turned a mere adventure into an epic . . . but won't let us go home for fear we'd tell the tale.

All right, dammit. I'll umble for the silly noor. He preens and acts starved for sound anyway, after months with just humans for company.

Up close I *can* sense a difference in him. I used to glimpse the same thing now and then, in the eyes of a few strange noor lounging on the Port Wuphon docks.

A sleek arrogance.

A kind of lazy smugness.

The impression that he's in on a great joke. One *you* won't figure out till there's egg all over your face.

Ewasx

THE HUMAN CAPTIVES SEEM OBDURATE, MY RINGS, refusing to answer questions. Or else they obfuscate with blatant lies.

•   •   •

QUERY/INTERROGATIVE:

Is there similarity between their behavior and the way *you* misled *Me*?

The way you rings have blurred so many of the waxy memories we coinherited from Asx?

The way our union oscillates between grudging cooperation and intermittent passive resistance?

It is enough to provoke unpleasant questions.

DON'T YOU LIKE BEING PART OF OUR MUCH-IMPROVED SHARED WHOLE? OUR AMBITIOUS ONENESS?

Yes, the majority of you claim gladness to be part of a great Jophur entity, instead of a tepid traeki mélange. But can I/we really be sure that you/we love Me/us?

The question is, in itself, a possible symptom of madness. What naturally cojoined Jophur would allow itself to entertain such doubts? The *Polkjhy* Priest-Stack predicted this hybridization experiment would fail. The priest foretold it would be useless to impose a master torus onto traeki rings already set in their ways.

A metaphor floats upward, along abused trails of half-molten wax.

Are you trying to make a comparison, O second ring-of-cognition?

Ah, yes. I/we see it.

Forging a noble Jophur out of disparate traeki cells *might* seem like trying to tame a herd of wild beasts. It is an apt analogy.

Too bad the metaphor does nothing to help solve My/our problem.

WHAT SECRETS LIE BURIED in the melted areas? What memories did the traeki High Sage purposely destroy, during those stressful moments before Asx was converted? I/we can tell, important evidence once glimmered in those layers that lined our common core. Something Jophur were not meant to know.

But know it we/I shall.

I must!

• • • •

SUGGESTION:

Perhaps we can tear information out of these recently seized humans.

The ones bearing the name attributes *Lark, Ling,* and *Rann.*

REBUTTAL:

The Priest-Stack vents frustrated steam, upset to learn how little data about Earthlings is contained in our shipboard Library. We have many detailed prescriptions for truth serums or coercion drugs effective against other races and species who are foes of the Great Jophur, but the archives carry no record of any substance that is human-specific. Our Library clearly needs updating, despite the fact that it is a relatively new unit, less than a thousand years old.

One tactician stack, assigned to our shipboard planning staff, proposed that we use interrogation techniques designed against *Tymbrimi.* Those devil tricksters are close allies of Earthlings, and appear similar in ways that go beyond bipedal locomotion. Trying out that suggestion, we tried projecting psi–compulsion waves at the prisoners, tuned to Tymbrimi empathic frequencies.

But the humans seemed deaf to the pulses, showing no reaction at all.

Meanwhile, the Captain-Leader vents irate fumes—acrid vapors that send all off-duty personnel fleeing from its presence.

What is the cause of such rancor, My rings?

Recent news from beyond the nearby hills.

Bitter news confirming our fears.

Disaster to the east.

AT LAST, our remaining corvette reached the site where its twin fell silent, two days ago. Aboard the *Polkjhy,* I/we all stared in dismay at relayed images of devastation.

Hull wreckage lay sunk beneath swampy waters—the sort of marshland morass where a traeki might find it pleasant to wallow while contemplating wax drippings. Wind-blown rain swept the area while searchers scanned for survivors, but all they found were remnants—mostly singleton rings, reverting to a feral animal state, instinctively gathering nests of rotting vegetation, as if they were no more than primitive pretraeki.

Several of these surviving toruses were harvested. By scraping their cores, we managed to download a few blurry memory tracks. Enough to suggest that *dolphins* did this deed, emerging from the sea to play havoc with our brethren.

HOW WERE THEY ABLE TO DO THIS?

The downed corvette had reported defense systems functional at a forty percent level. More than adequate, if concentrated against just such a sortie by the desperate Earthling quarry. Even amid a lightning-charged thunderstorm, it should not have been possible for the cornered prey to mount a surprise attack. Yet, not even an alarm signal escaped our grounded boat before it was mysteriously overwhelmed.

Again, doubts rise to disturb us. The wolflings are said to be primitives, not much more capable than the sooner savages whose coward ancestors settled this world. Yet these same Earthers have sent all Five Galaxies into turmoil, repeatedly escaping mighty fleets sent after them.

Perhaps it was a mistake for our *Polkjhy* ship commune to take on this mission alone, with just our one mighty battlecruiser to seize destiny for our kind.

SCENT RUMORS SPREAD THROUGH *POLKJHY* NOW, alleging the Captain-Leader was deficiently stacked. Subversive pheromones suggest that flawed decision-processing toruses brought us to this unsavory state. Our commander was blinded by obsession with vengeance on the g'Kek, ignoring higher priorities.

Furious to find mutinous molecules wafting through the air ducts, our Captain-Leader seeks to overwhelm them with his own chemical outpourings—a steamy concoction of smoldering rejection. Perfumes of domineering essence flood all decks.

What is it now, My ring?

Ah. Our second torus-of-cognition has come up with another metaphor, this time comparing the Captain-Leader to the skipper of a hoonish sailboat, who tries shouting down his worried crew, using a loud voice to substitute for real leadership.

Very interesting, My ring—making parallels between alien behavior and Jophur ship politics. Such insights make this irksome union seem almost worthwhile.

Unless . . .

Surely you do not ALSO apply this metaphor to your own master ring?

Do not provoke Me. Be warned. It would be a mistake.

OUR PROBLEM REMAINS.

Unlike the tactician stacks, I/we do not attribute wolfling success against our corvette to anomalous technology, or luck. The timing was too coincidental. I am convinced the dolphins knew exactly the right moment to attack, when our attention was diverted by events close by.

CONCLUSION: The savage races MUST be in communication with the Earthship!

The captive humans deny knowing of any contact with the dolphin ship. They claim their activities at the lake surface were strictly a manifestation of interhuman dominance struggles, having nothing to do with the prey ship.

They must be lying. Ways must be found to increase their level of cooperation.

(If only I could lace their apelike cores with silvery fibers, the way a master ring shows other components of a stack how to cooperate in joyful oneness!)

We must, it seems, fall back on classic, barbarous interrogation techniques.

Shall we threaten the humans with bodily damage?

Shall we assail them with metaphysical torment?

Overruling My/our expertise, the Captain-Leader has decided on a technique that is known to be effective against numerous warm-blooded races.

We shall use *atrocity*.

Sara

TRAEKI UNGUENTS FILLED HER SINUSES WITH PLEAS-
ant numbness, as if she'd had several glasses of wine.
Sara felt the chemicals at work, chasing pain, making
room for *herself* to reemerge.

A day after rejoining the world, she let Emerson push her
wheelchair onto the stone veranda at Uriel the Smith's
sanctuary, watching dawn break over a phalanx of royal
peaks, stretching north and east. West of the mountains,
dusty haze muted the manicolored marvel of the Spectral
Flow, and the Plain of Sharp Sand beyond.

The view helped draw Sara's attention from the
handheld mirror on her lap—lent her by Uriel—which she
had examined all through breakfast. Jijo's broad vista made
clear Emerson's quiet sermon.

The world is bigger than all our problems.

Sara handed the looking glass over to the starman, who
performed sleight-of-hand motions, causing it to vanish up
one sleeve of his floppy gown. Emerson grinned when
Sara laughed out loud.

What's the point in dwelling on my stitches and scrapes,
she thought. *Scars won't matter in the days to come. Any
survivors will scratch their living from the soil. Pretty
women won't have advantages. Tough ones will.*

Or was this complacence another result of chemicals in
her veins? Potions tailored by Tyug, master alchemist of
Mount Guenn Forge. Jijo's traekis had learned a lot about
healing other races while qheuens, urs, hoons, and men
fought countless skirmishes before the Great Peace. In recent years, texts from Biblos helped molecule maestros like
Tyug supplement practical lore with fresh insights, using
Anglic words like *peptide* and *enzyme*, reclaiming some of
the knowledge their settler ancestors had abandoned.

*Only not by looking it up in some Library. Earthling texts
served as a starting point. A basis for fresh discoveries.*

Which illustrated her controversial thesis. Six Races

climbing back upward, not via Redemption's Path, the route their forebears used . . . *but on a trail all our own.*

Other examples filled the halls behind this stony parapet, in workshops and labs where Uriel's staff labored near lava heat, wresting secrets from nature. Despite her suffering, Sara was glad to see more evidence on Mount Guenn that Jijoan civilization had begun heading in new directions.

Until starships came.

Sara winced, recalling what they had witnessed last night, from this same veranda. She and her friends were being regaled at a feast under the stars, celebrating her recovery. Hoonish sailors from the nearby seaport boomed festive ballads and Uriel's apprentices cavorted in an intricate dance while diminutive husbands perched on their backs, mimicking each twist and gyre. Gray qheuens, their broad chitin shells embellished with gemstone cloisonné, sculpted wicked impromptu caricatures of the party guests, using their adroit mouths to carve statuettes of solid stone.

Even Ulgor was allowed to take part, playing the violus, drawing rich vibrato tones as Emerson joined in with his dulcimer. The wounded starman had another unpredictable outburst of song, each verse pouring whole from some recessed memory.

> *"In a cottage of Fife,*
> *lived a man and wife,*
> *   who, believe me, were comical folk;*
> *For to people's surprise,*
> *they both saw with their eyes,*
> *   and their tongues moved whenever*
> *   they spoke!"*

Then, as the feast was hitting its stride, there came a rude interruption. Staccato flashes lit the northwest horizon, outlining the distant bulk of Blaze Mountain, drawing everyone to the balcony rim.

Duras passed before sounds arrived, smeared by distance to murmuring growls. Sara pictured lightning and thunder—like the storm that had drenched the badlands lately, drumming at her pain-soaked delirium. But then a chill coursed her spine, and she felt glad to have Emerson nearby. Some apprentices counted intervals separating each flash from its long-retarded echo.

Young Jomah voiced her own thoughts.

"Uncle, is Blaze Mountain erupting?"

Kurt's face had been gaunt and bleak. But it was Uriel who answered, shaking her long head.

"No, lad. It's not an erufshun. I think . . ."

She peered across the poison desert.

"I think it is Ovoon Town."

Kurt found his voice. The words were grim.

"Detonations. Sharp. Well-defined. Bigger than my guild could produce."

Realization quenched all thought of revelry. The biggest city on the Slope was being razed, and they could only watch, helplessly. Some prayed to the Holy Egg. Others muttered hollow vows of vengeance. Sara heard one person explain dispassionately why the outrage was taking place on a clear night—so the violence would be visible from much of the Slope, a demonstration of irresistible power.

Awed by the lamentable spectacle, Sara had been incapable of coherent thought. What filled her mind were images of *mothers*—hoonish mothers, g'Kek mothers, humans, and even haughty qheuen queens—clutching their children as they abandoned flaming, collapsing homes. The visions stirred round her brain like a cyclone of ashes, till Emerson gave her a double dose of traeki elixir.

Dropping toward a deep, dreamless sleep, she had one last thought.

Thank God that I never accepted Sage Taine's proposal of marriage. . . . I might have had a child of my own by now.

This is no time . . . to allow so deep a love.

Now, by daylight, Sara found her mind functioning as it had before her accident—rapidly and logically. She was even able to work out a context for last night's calamity.

Jop and Dedinger will preach we should never have had

cities in the first place. They'll say the Galactics did us a favor by destroying Ovoom Town.

Sara recalled legends her mother used to read aloud, from books of folklore covering many pre-contact Earthling traditions. *Most Earth cultures told sagas of some purported golden age in the past, when people knew more. When they had more wisdom and power.*

Many myths went on to describe angry gods, vengefully toppling the works of prideful mortals, lest men and women think themselves worthy of the sky. No credible evidence ever supported such tales, yet the story seemed so common it must reflect something deep and dour within the human psyche.

Maybe my personal heresy was always a foolish dream, and my notion of "progress" based on concocted evidence. Even if Uriel and others had begun to embark on a different path, the point seems moot now.

Dedinger proved right, after all.

As in those legends, the gods have resolved to pound us down.

Confirmation of the outrage came later by semaphore—the same system of flashing mirrors that had surprised Sara days ago, when a stray beam caught her eye during the steep climb from Xi. Using a code based on simplified GalTwo, the jittering signal followed a twisty route from one Rimmer peak to the next, carrying clipped reports of devastation by the River Gentt.

Then, a few miduras later, an *eyewitness* arrived, swooping out of the sky like some fantastic beast of fable, landing on Uriel's stone parapet. A single human youth emerged beneath shuddering wings, unstrapping himself after a daring journey across the wide desert, skimming from one thermal updraft to the next in a feat that would have caused a sensation during normal times.

But heroism and miraculous deeds are routine during war, Sara thought as crowds gathered around the young man. His limbs trembled with exhaustion as he peeled off the rewq that had protected his eyes above the Spectral

Flow. He gave the Smith a militia salute when Uriel trotted out of the workshop grottoes.

"Before attacking Ovoom Town, the Jophur issued a two-part ultimatum," he explained in a hoarse voice. "Their first demand is that all g'Keks and traekis must head to special gathering zones."

Uriel blew air through her nostril fringe, a resigned blast, as if she had expected something along these lines.

"And the second fortion of the ultinatun?"

She had to wait for her answer. Kepha, the horsewoman from Xi, arrived bearing a glass of water, which the pilot slurped gratefully, letting streams run down his chin. Most urrish eyes turned from the unpleasant sight. But Uriel stared patiently till he finished.

"Go on," she prompted again, when the youth handed the empty glass back to Kepha with a smile.

"Um," he resumed. "The Jophur insist that the High Sages must give up the location of the dolphin ship."

"The dolphin shif?" Uriel's hooves clattered on the flag-stones. "We heard vague stories of this thing. Gossif and conflicting hints told vy the Rothen. Have the Jophur now revealed what it's all avout?"

The courier tried to nod, only now *Tyug* had come forward, gripping the youth's head with several tentacles. He winced as the traeki alchemist secreted ointment for his sun- and windburns.

"It seems . . . Hey, watch it!" He pushed at the ada-mant tendrils, then tried ignoring the traeki altogether.

"It seems these dolphins are the prey that brought both the Rothen and the Jophur to Galaxy Four in the first place. What's more, the Jophur say the sages must be in contact with the Earthling ship. Either we give up its location, or face more destruction, starting with Tarek Town, then lesser hamlets, until no building is left standing."

Kurt shook his head. "They're bluffin'. Even Galactics couldn't find all our wood structures, hidden under blur cloth."

The courier seemed less sure. "There are fanatics every-where who think the end is here. Some believe the Jophur are agents of destiny, come to set us back on the Path. All such fools need do is start a fire somewhere near a building and throw some phosphorus on the flame. The Jophur can sniff the signal using their rainbow finder."

Rainbow finder . . . Sara pondered. *Oh, he means a spectrograph.*

Jomah was aghast. "People would do that?"

"It's already happened in a few places. Some folks have taken their local explosers hostage, forcing them to set off their charges. Elsewhere, the Jophur have established base camps, staffed by a dozen stacks and thirty or so robots, gathering nearby citizens for questioning." His tone was bleak. "You people don't know how lucky you have it here."

Yet Sara wondered. How could the High Sages possibly give in to such demands? The g'Kek weren't being taken off-planet in order to restore their star-god status. As for the traeki, death might seem pleasant compared with the fate planned for them.

Then there was the "dolphin ship." Even the learned Uriel could only speculate if the High Sages truly were in contact with a bunch of fugitive Terran clients.

Perhaps it was emotional fatigue, or a lingering effect of Tyug's drug, but Sara's attention drifted from the litany of woes recited by the pilot. When he commenced describing the destruction and death at Ovoom, Sara steered her wheelchair to join Emerson, standing near the courier's glider.

The starman stroked its lacy wings and delicate spars, beaming with appreciation of its ingenious design. At first Sara thought it must be the same little flier she had seen displayed in a Biblos museum case—the last of its kind, left over from those fabled days just after the *Tabernacle* arrived, when brave aerial scouts helped human colonists survive their early wars. Over time, the art had been lost for lack of high-tech materials.

But this machine is new!

Sara recognized g'Kek weaving patterns in the fine fabric, which felt slick to the touch.

"It is a traeki secretion," explained Tyug, having also abandoned the crowd surrounding the young messenger. The alchemist shared Emerson's preference for physical things, not words.

"i/we sample-tasted a thread. The polymer is a clever filamentary structure based on mulc fiber. No doubt it will find other uses in piduras to come, as our varied schemes converge."

There it was again. Hints of a secret stratagem. A scheme no one had yet explained, though Sara was starting to have suspicions.

"Forgive us/me for interrupting your contemplation, honored Saras and Emersons," Tyug went on. "But a scent message has just activated receptor sites on my/our fifth sensory torus. The simplified meaning is that Sage Purofsky desires your presences, in proximity to his own."

Sara translated Tyug's awkward phrasing.

In other words, no more goofing off. It's time to get back to work.

Back to Uriel's den of mysteries.

Sara saw that the Smith had already departed, along with Kurt, leaving Chief Apprentice Urdonnol to finish de-briefing the young pilot. Apparently, even such dire news was less urgent than the task at hand.

Calculating problems in orbital mechanics, Sara pondered. *I still don't see how that will help get us out of this fix.*

She caught Emerson's eye, and with some reluctance he turned away from the glider. But when the star voyager bent over Sara to tuck in the corners of her lap blanket, he made eye contact and shared an open smile. Then his strong hands aimed her wheelchair down a ramp into the mountain, toward Uriel's fantastic Hall of Spinning Disks.

I feel like a g'Kek, rolling along. Perhaps all humans should spend a week confined like this, to get an idea what life is like for others.

It made her wonder how the g'Kek used to move about in their "natural" environment. According to legend, those were artificial colonies floating in space. Strange places, where many of the assumptions of planet-bound existence did not hold.

Emerson skirted ruts countless generations of urrish hooves had worn in the stone floor. He picked up the pace when they passed a vent pouring fumes from the main forge, keeping his body between her and waves of volcanic heat.

In fact, Sara was almost ready to resume walking on her own. But it felt strangely warming to wallow for a time in their reversed roles.

. She had to admit, he was good at it. Maybe he had a good teacher.

Normally, Prity would have been the one pushing Sara's chair. But the little chimp was busy, perched on a high stool in Uriel's sanctuary with a pencil clutched in one furry hand, drawing arcs across sheets of ruled graph paper. Beyond Prity's work easel stretched a vast underground chamber filled with tubes, pulleys, and disks, all linked by gears and leather straps—a maze of shapes whirling on a timber frame, reaching all the way up to a vaulted ceiling. In the sharp glare of carboacetylene lanterns, tiny figures could be seen scurrying about the scaffolding, tightening and lubricating—nimble urrish males, among the first ever to find useful employment outside their wives' pouches, earning a good income by tending the ornate "hobby" of Uriel the Smith.

When Sara first saw the place, squinting through her fever, she had thought it a dream vision of hell. Then a wondrous thing happened. The spinning glass shapes began *singing* to her.

Not in sound, but light. As they turned, rolling their rims against one another, narrow beams reflected from mirrored surfaces, glittering like winter moonbeams on the countless facets of a frozen waterfall. Only there was more to it than mere gorgeous randomness. Patterns. Rhythms. Some flashes came and went with the perfect precision of a clock, while others performed complex, wavelike cycles, like rolling surf. With the fey sensitivity of a bared subconscious, she had recognized an overlapping harmony of shapes. Ellipses, parabolas, catenaries . . . a nonlinear serenade of geometry.

It's a computer, she had realized, even before regaining the full faculties of her searching mind. And for the first time since departing her Dolo Village tree house, she had felt at home.

It is another world.

My world.

Mathematics.

Blade

HE MIGHT HAVE STAYED DOWN LONGER. BUT AFTER three or four miduras, the air in his leg bladders started growing stale. Even a full-size blue qheuen needs to breathe at least a dozen times a day. So by the time filtered sunlight penetrated to his murky refuge, Blade knew he must abandon the cool river bottom that had sheltered him through the night's long firestorm. He fought the Gentt's current, digging all five claws into the muddy bank, climbing upward till at last it was possible to raise his vision cupola above the water's smeary surface.

It felt as if he had arrived at damnation day.

The fabled towers of Ovoom Town had survived the deconstruction age, then half a million years of wind and rain. Vanished were the sophisticated machines that made it a vibrant Galactic outpost. Those had been taken long ago by the departing Buyur, along with nearly every windowpane. Yet, even despite ten thousand gaping openings, the surviving shells had been luxury palaces to the six exile races—providing room for hundreds of apartments and workshops—all linked by shrewd wooden bridges, ramps, and camouflage lattices.

Now only a few jagged stumps protruded through a haze of dust and soot. Sunshine beat down from a glaring sky, showing how futile every cautious effort at concealment had been.

Picking his way along the riverbank, now cluttered with blocks of shattered stone, Blade encountered a more gruesome kind of debris—*bodies* floating in back eddies of the river, along with varied dismembered parts . . . biped limbs, g'Kek wheels, and traeki toruses. In the qheuen manner, he did not wince or experience revulsion while claw-stepping past the drifting corpses, but hoped that someone would organize a collection of the remains for proper mulching. Little was gained by maundering over the dead.

Blade felt more disturbed by the chaos at the docks, where several collapsing spires had fallen across the riverside piers and warehouses. Not a single ship or coracle appeared untouched.

Pausing to watch one crew of disconsolate hoons examine their once-beautiful craft, Blade felt a brief surge of hope when he recognized the ship, and saw its gleaming wooden hull had survived intact! Then he realized—all the masts and rigging were gone. Bubbles of disappointment escaped three of five leg vents.

Just yesterday, Blade had booked passage aboard that vessel. Now he might as well toss the paper ticket from his moisture pouch to join the other flotsam drifting out to sea.

Much of that dross had been alive till last night, when the starry sky lit up with the spectacle of a Galactic god ship, arriving well ahead of its own shock wave, announcing its sudden arrival instead with a blare of braking engines. Then it glided a complacent circle above Ovoom Town, as gracefully imperturbable as a fat, predatory fish.

The sight had struck Blade as both beautiful and terrible.

At last, an amplified voice boomed forth, declaring a ritual ultimatum in a dense, traekilike dialect of Galactic Two.

Blade had already been through too many adventures to stand and gawk. The lesson taught by experience was simple—when someone much bigger and nastier than you starts making threats, get out! He barely listened to the roar of alien words as he joined an exodus of the prudent. Racing toward the river, Blade made it with kiduras to spare.

Even when ten meters of turbulent brown liquid lay overhead, he could not shut out what followed. Searing blasts, harsh flashes, and screams.

Especially the screams.

Now, under the sun of a new day, Blade found all the concept facets of his mind overwhelmed by a scene of havoc. The biggest population center on the Slope, a once-vibrant community of art and commerce, lay in complete ruins. At the center of devastation, buildings had not simply been toppled, but pulverized to a fine dust that trailed eastward, riding the prevailing breeze.

Had similar evil already befallen Tarek Town, where the pleasant green Roney met the icy Bibur? Or Dolo Village, whose fine dam sheltered the prosperous hive of his aunts and mothers? Though Blade had grown up near humans, he now found that stress drove Anglic out of his mind. For now, the logic of his private thoughts worked better in Galactic Six.

My situation—it seems hopeless.

To Mount Guenn—there is no longer a path by ocean ship.

With Sara and the others—I cannot now rendezvous.

So much for my promise . . . So much for my vow.

Other qheuens were rising out of the water nearby, their cupolas bobbing to the surface like a scattering of corks. Some venturesome blues had already reached the ruined streets ahead of Blade, offering their strong backs and claws to assist rescue parties, searching through the rubble of fallen towers for survivors. He also saw a few reds and several giant grays, who must have somehow survived the night of horrors without a freshwater refuge. Some appeared wounded and all were dust-coated, but they set to work alongside hoons, humans, and others.

A qheuen feels uneasy without a duty to fulfill. Some obligation that can be satisfied, like a scratched itch, through service. On the original race homeworld, gray matrons used to exploit that instinct ruthlessly. But Jijo had changed things, promoting a different kind of fealty. Allegiance to more than a particular hive or queen.

Seeing no chance that he could accomplish his former goal and catch up with Sara, Blade consciously rearranged his priority facets, assigning himself a new short-term agenda.

Corpses meant nothing to him. He was unmoved by the dead majority of Ovoom Town. Yet he roused his bulk, pumping five legs into rapid motion, rushing to help those left with a spark of life.

•   •   •

Survivors and rescuers picked through the wreckage with exaggerated care, as if each overturned stone might conceal danger.

Like most settlements, this one had been mined by a chapter of the Explosers Guild, preparing the city for deliberate razing if ever the long-prophesied Judgment Day arrived. But when it finally came, the manner was not as foreseen by the scrolls. There were no serene, dispassionate officials from the great Institutes, ordaining evacuation and tidy demolition, then weighing the worth of each race by how far it had progressed along the Path of Redemption. Instead there had poured down an abrupt and cruelly impartial cascade of raging flame, efficient only at killing, igniting some of the carefully placed charges that the explosers had reverently tended for generations . . . and leaving others smoldering like booby traps amid the debris.

When the explosers' local headquarters blew up, a huge fireball had risen so high that it briefly licked the underbelly of the Jophur corvette, forcing a hurried retreat. Even now, several miduras after the attack, delayed blasts still rocked random parts of town, disrupting mercy efforts, setting rubble piles tottering.

Matters improved when urrish volunteers from a nearby caravan galloped into town. With their sensitive nostrils, the urs sniffed for both unexploded charges and living flesh. They proved especially good at finding unconscious or hidden humans, whose scent they found pungent.

Miduras of hard labor merged into a blur. By late afternoon, Blade was still at it, straining on a rope, helping clear the stubborn obstruction over a buried basement. The rescue team's ad hoc leader, a hoonish ship captain, boomed out rhythmic commands.

"Hr-r-rm, now *pull,* friends! . . . *Again,* it's coming! . . . And *again!*"

Blade staggered as the stone block finally gave way. A pair of nimble lorniks and a lithe chimpanzee dived through the exposed opening, and soon dragged out a g'Kek with two smashed wheel rims. The braincase was intact, however, and all four eyestalks waved a dance of astounded gratitude. The survivor looked young and strong. Rims could be repaired, and spokes would reweave all by themselves.

But where will he live until then? Blade wondered, knowing that g'Keks preferred city life, not the nearby jungle where many of Ovoom's citizens had fled. *Will it be a world worth rolling back to, or one filled with Jophur-designed viruses and hunter robots, programmed to satisfy an ancient vendetta?*

The work crew was about to resume its unending task when a shrill cry escaped the traeki who had been assigned lookout duty, perched on a nearby rubble pile with its ring-of-sensors staring in all directions at once.

"Observe! All selves, alertly turn your attentions in the direction indicated!"

A pair of tentacles aimed roughly south and west. Blade lifted his heavy carapace and tried bringing his cupola to bear, but it was dust-coated and he had no water to clean it. *If only qheuens had been blessed with better eyesight.*

By Ifni, right now I'd settle for tear ducts.

An object swam into view, roughly spherical, moving languidly above the forested horizon, as if bobbing like a cloud. Lacking any perspective for such a strange sight, Blade could not tell at first how big it was. Perhaps the titanic Jophur battleship had come, instead of dispatching its little brother! Were the Jophur returning to finish the job? Blade remembered tales of Galactic war weapons far worse than the corvette had used last night. Weapons capable of melting a continent's crust. A mere river would prove no refuge, if the aliens meant to use such tools.

But no. He saw the globelike surface *ripple* in an unsteady breeze. It appeared to be made of fabric, and much smaller than he had thought.

Two more globelike forms followed the leader into view, making a threesome convoy. Blade instinctively switched organic filters in his cupola, observing them in infrared. At once he saw that each flying thing carried a sharp heat glow beneath, suspended by cables from the globe itself.

Others standing nearby—those with sharper eyesight— passed through several reactions. First anxious dread, then puzzlement, and finally a kind of joyful wonder they expressed with shrill laughter or deep, umbling tones.

"What is it?" asked a nearby red qheuen, even more dust-blind than Blade.

"I think—" Blade began to answer. But then a human cut in, shading his eyes with both hands.

"They're balloons! By Drake and Ur-Chown . . . they're hot air balloons!"

A short time later, even the qheuens could make out shapes hung beneath the bulging gasbags. Urrish figures standing in wicker baskets, tending fires that intermittently flared with sudden, near-volcanic heat. Blade then realized who had come, as if out of the orange setting sun.

The smiths of Blaze Mountain must have seen last night's calamity from their nearby mountain sanctum. The smiths were coming to help succor their neighbors.

It seemed blasphemous, in a strange way. For the Sacred Scrolls had always spoken of *doom* arriving from the fearsome open sky.

Now it seemed the cloudless heavens could also bring virtue.

Lester Cambel

H E WAS TOO BUSY NOW TO FEEL RACKED WITH conscience pangs. As commotion at the secret base neared a fever pitch, Lester had no time left for wallowing in guilt. There were slurry tubes to inspect—a pipeline threading its meandering way through the boo forest, carrying noxious fluids from the traeki synthesis gang to tall, slender vats where it congealed into a paste of chemically constrained hell.

Lester also had to approve a new machine for winding league after league of strong fiber cord around massive trunks of greatboo, multiplying their strength a thousandfold.

Then there was the matter of *kindling beetles*. One of his assistants had found a new use for an old pest—a dangerous, Buyur-modified insect that most Sixers grew up loathing, but one that might now solve an irksome technical problem. The idea seemed promising, but needed more tests before being incorporated in the plan.

Piece by piece, the scheme progressed from Wild-Eyed Fantasy all the way to Desperate Gamble. In fact, a local hoonish bookie was said to be covering bets at only sixty to one against eventual success—the best odds so far.

Of course, each time they overcame a problem, it was replaced by three more. That was expected, and Lester even came to look upon the growing complexity as a blessing. Keeping busy was the only effective way to fight off the same images that haunted his mind, replaying over and over again.

A golden mist, falling on Dooden Mesa. Only immersion in work could drive out the keening cries of g'Kek citizens, trapped by poison rain pouring from a Jophur cruiser.

A cruiser *he* had carelessly summoned, by giving in to his greatest vice—curiosity.

"Do not blame yourself Lester," Ur-Jah counseled in a dialect of GalSeven. *"The enemy would have found Dooden soon anyway. Meanwhile, your research harvested valuable information. It helped lead to cures for the qheuen and hoonish plagues. Life consists of trade-offs, my friend."*

Perhaps. Lester admitted things might work that way on paper. Especially if you assumed, as many did, that the poor g'Kek were doomed anyway.

That kind of philosophy comes easier to the urrish, who know that only a fraction of their offspring can or should survive. We humans wail for a lifetime if we lose a son or daughter. If we find urs callous, it's good to recall how absurdly sentimental we seem to them.

Lester tried to think like an urs.

He failed.

Now came news from the commandos who so bravely plumbed the lake covering the Glade of Gathering. Sergeant Jeni Shen reported partial success, freeing some Daniks from their trapped ship . . . only to lose others to the Jophur, including the young heretic sage, Lark Koolhan. A net loss, as far as Lester was concerned.

What might the aliens be doing to poor Lark right now? *I never should have agreed to his dangerous plan.*

Lester realized, he did not have the temperament to be a war leader. He could not *spend* people, like fuel for a fire, even as a price for victory.

When all this was over, assuming anyone survived, he planned to resign from the Council of Sages and become the most reclusive scholar in Biblos, creeping like a specter past dusty shelves of ancient tomes. Or else he might resume his old practice of meditation in the narrow Canyon of the Blessed, where life's cares were known to vanish under a sweet ocean of detached oblivion.

It sounded alluring—a chance to retreat from life.

But for now, there was simply too much to do.

The council seldom met anymore.

Phwhoon-dau, who had made a lifelong study of the languages and ways of fabled Galactics, had responsibility for negotiating with the Jophur. Unfortunately, there seemed little to haggle about. Just futile pleading for the invaders to change their many-ringed minds. Phwhoon-dau sent repeated entreaties to the toroidal aliens, protesting that the High Sages knew nothing about the much-sought "dolphin ship."

Believe us, O great Jophur lords, the hoonish sage implored. *We have no secret channel of communication with your prey. The events you speak of were all unrelated . . . a series of coincidences.*

But the Jophur were too angry to believe it.

In attempting to negotiate, Phwhoon-dau was advised by Chorsh, the new traeki representative. But that replacement for Asx the Wise had few new insights to offer. As a member of the Tarek Town Explosers Guild, Chorsh was a valued technician, not an expert on distant Jophur cousins.

What Chorsh did have was a particularly useful talent—a *summoning torus*.

Shifting summer winds carried the traeki's scent message

all over the Slope—a call from Chorsh to all qualified ring stacks.

Come . . . come now to where you/we are needed. . . .

Hundreds of them already stood in single file, a chain of fatty heaps that stretched on for nearly a league, winding amid the gently bending trunks of boo. Each volunteer squatted on its own feast of decaying matter that work crews kept stoked, like feeding logs to a steam engine. Chuffing and smoking from exertion, the chem-synth gang dripped glistening fluids into makeshift troughs made of split and hollowed saplings, contributing to a trickle that eventually became a rivulet of foul-smelling liquor.

Immobile and speechless, they hardly looked like sentient beings. More like tall, greasy beehives, laid one after another along a twisty road. But that image was deceiving. Lester saw swathes of color flash across the body of one nearby traeki—a subtle interplay of shades that rippled first between the stack's component rings, as if they were holding conversations among themselves. Then the pattern coalesced, creating a unified shape of light and shadows at the points that lay nearest to the traeki's neighbors, on either side. Those stacks, in turn, responded with changes in their own surfaces.

Lester recognized the wavelike motif—traeki *laughter.* The workers were sharing jokes, among their own rings and from stack to stack.

They are the strangest of the Six, Lester thought. *And yet we understand them . . . and they, us.*

I doubt even the sophisticates of the Five Galaxies can say the same thing about the Jophur. Out there, none of their advanced science could achieve what we have simply by living next to traeki, day in and day out.

It was pretty crude humor, Lester could tell. Many of these workers were pharmacists, back in their home villages all over the Slope. The one nearest Lester had been speculating about alternative uses of the stuff they were making—perhaps how it might also serve as a cure for the perennial problem of hoonish constipation . . . especially if accompanied by liberal applications of heat. . . .

At least that was how Lester interpreted the language of

color. He was far from expert in its nuances. Anyway, these workers were welcome to a bit of rough-edged drollery. Their hard labor lasted day in, day out, and still production lagged behind schedule.

But more traeki arrived with each passing midura, following the scent trail emitted by their sage.

Now we have to hope that the Jophur are too advanced and urbane to use the same technique, and trace our location by reading the winds.

The qheuen sage, Knife-Bright Insight, bore all the duties of civil administration on her broad blue back.

There were refugees to relocate, food supplies to organize, and militia units to dispatch, quashing outbreaks of civil war among the Six. One clear success came lately in subduing foreign plagues, duplicating the samples Jeni Shen brought from the Glade Lake, then using a new network of glider couriers to distribute vaccines.

Yet despite such successes, the social fabric of the Commons continued dissolving. News arrived telling of sooner bands departing across the official boundaries of the Slope, seeking to escape the doom threatened for the Six Races. The Warril Plain was aflame with fighting among hot-tempered urrish clans. And more bad news kept rolling in.

Recent reports told of several hives of Gray Queens declaring open secession from the Commons, asserting sovereignty over their ancient domains. Spurred by the devastation of Ovoom Town, some rebel princesses even rejected their own official High Sage.

"We accept no guidance from a mere blue," came word from one gray hive, snubbing Knife-Bright Insight and resurrecting ancient bigotry.

"Come give us advice when you have a real name."

Of course no red or blue qheuen ever used a *name,* as such. It was cruel and haughty to mention the handicap, inherited from ancient days and other worlds.

Worse, rumors claimed that some gray hives had started negotiating with the Jophur on their own.

•   •   •

A crisis can tear us apart, or draw us together.

Lester checked on the mixed team of qheuens and hoons who were erecting spindly scaffolding around selected spires of greatboo. Only a small fraction of the designated trunks had been trimmed and readied, but the crews were getting better at their unfamiliar task. Some qheuens brought expertise learned from their grandmothers, who in olden times used to maintain fearsome catapults at Tarek Town, dominating two rivers until a great siege toppled that ancient reign.

So much activity might be detectable by prying sky eyes. But taller trunks surrounded each chosen one, drowning the tumult in a vast sea of Brobdingnagian grass.

Or so we hope.

Guiding the work, urrish and human craft workers pored over ancient designs found in a single rare Biblos text, dating from pre-contact days, dealing with an obscure wolfling technology that no Galactic power had needed or used for a billion years. Side by side, men and women joined their urs colleagues, adapting the book's peculiar concepts, translating its strange recipes to native materials and their own cottage skills.

Conditions were spartan. Many volunteers had already suffered privation, hiking great distances along steep mountain trails to reach this tract of tall green columns, stretching like a prairie as far as any eye could see.

All recruits shared a single motive—finding a way for the Commons of Six Races to fight back.

Amid the shouting throng, it was *Ur-Jah* who brought order out of chaos, galloping from one site to the next, making sure the traeki synthesists had food and raw material, and that every filament was wound tight. Of all the High Sages, Ur-Jah was most qualified to share Lester's job of supervision. Her pelt might be ragged with age and her brood pouches dry, but the mind in that narrow skull was sharp—and more pragmatic than Lester's had ever been.

Of the High Sages, that left only *Vubben*.

Judicious and knowing. Deep in perception. Leader of a sept that had been marked long ago for destruction by foes who never forgot, and never gave up. Among Jijo's exile races, Vubben's folk had been first to brave Izmunuti's stiffening winds, seeking Jijo's bright shoal almost two thousand years ago.

The wheeled g'Kek—both amiable and mysterious.

Neighborly, if weird.

Elfin but reliable.

Faceless, yet as open as a book.

How lessened the universe would be without them!

Despite their difficulty on rough trails, some g'Kek had made it to this remote mountain base, laboring to weave fabric, or applying their keen eyes to the problem of making small parts. Yet their own sage was nowhere in sight.

Vubben had gone south, to a sacred place dangerously near the Jophur ship. There, he was attempting in secret to commune with Jijo's highest power.

Lester worried about his wise friend with the squeaky axles, venturing down there all alone.

But someone has to do it.

Soon we'll know if we have been fools all along . . . or if we've put our faith in something deserving of our love.

Fallon

A DOMAIN OF BLINDING WHITENESS MARKED THE border of the Spectral Flow, where that slanting shelf of radiant stone abruptly submerged beneath an ocean of sparkling grains. North of this point commenced a different kind of desert—one that seemed less hard on the brain and eyes, but just as unforgiving. A desert where hardy lifeforms dwelled.

Dangerous life-forms.

The escaped heretic's footprints transformed as they crossed the boundary. No longer did they *glow,* each with a unique lambency of oil-slick colors, telling truths and lies. Plunging ahead without pause, the tracks became mere impressions on the Plain of Sharp Sand—indentations that grew blurrier as gusty winds stroked the dunes—

revealing only that someone recently came this way, a humanoid biped, favoring his left leg with a limp.

Fallon could tell one more thing—the hiker had been in an awful hurry.

"We can't follow anymore," he told his young companions. "Our mounts are spent, and this is Dedinger's realm. He knows it better than we do."

Reza and Pahna stared at the sandy desert, no less dismayed than he. But the older one dissented—a sturdy redhead with a rifle slung over her shoulder.

"We must go on. The heretic knows everything. If he reaches his band of ruffians, they'll soon follow him back to Xi, attacking us in force. Or else he might trade our location to the aliens. The man must be stopped!"

Despite her vehemence, Fallon could tell Reza's heart was heavy. For several days they had chased Dedinger across the wasteland they knew—a vast tract of laminated rock so poisonous, a sliver under the skin might send you into thrashing fever. A place almost devoid of life, where daylight raised a spectacle of unlikely marvels before any unprotected eye—waterfalls and fiery pits, golden cities and fairy dust. Even night offered no rest, for moonbeams alone could make an unwary soul shiver as ghost shadows flapped at the edge of sight. Such were the terrible wonders of the Spectral Flow—in most ways a harsher territory than the mundane desert just ahead. So harsh that few Jijoans ever thought to explore its fringes, allowing the secret of Xi to remain safe.

Reza was right to fear the consequences, should Dedinger make good his escape—especially if the fanatic managed to reforge his alliance with the horse-hating clan of urrish cultists called the *Urunthai*. The fugitive should have succumbed to the unfamiliar dangers of the Flow by now. The three pursuers had expected to catch up with him yesterday, if not the day before.

It's my fault, Fallon thought. *I was too complacent. Too deliberate. My old bones can't take a gallop and I would not let the women speed on without me.*

Who would guess Dedinger could ride so well after so little practice, driving his stolen horse with a mixture of care and utter brutality, so the poor beast expired just two leagues short of this very boundary?

Even after that, his jogging pace kept the gap between them from closing fast enough. While the Illias preserved their beloved mares, the madman managed to cross ground that should have killed him first.

We are chasing a strong, resourceful adversary. I'd rather face a hoonish ice hermit, or even a Gray Champion, than risk this fellow with his back cornered against a dune.

Of course Dedinger must eventually run out of reserves, pushing himself to the limit. Perhaps the man lay beyond the next drift, sprawled in exhausted stupor.

Well, it did no harm to hope.

"All right." Fallon nodded. "We'll go. But keep a sharp watch. And be ready to move quick if I say so. We'll follow the trail till nightfall, then head back whether he's brought down or not."

Reza and Pahna agreed, nudging their horses to follow. The animals stepped onto hot sand without enthusiasm, laying their ears back and nickering unhappily. Color-blind and unimaginative, their breed was largely immune to the haunting mirages of the Spectral Flow, but they clearly disliked this realm of glaring brightness. Soon, the three humans removed their rewq symbionts, pulling the living veils from over their eyes, trading them for urrish-made dark glasses with polarized coatings made of stretched fish membranes.

Ifni, this is a horrid place, Fallon thought, leaning left in his saddle to make out the renegade's tracks. *But Dedinger is at home here.*

In theory, that should not matter. Before ceding the position to his apprentice, Dwer, Fallon had been chief scout for the Council of Sages—an expert who supposedly knew every hectare of the Slope. But that was always an exaggeration. Oh, he *had* spent some time on this desert, getting to know the rugged, illiterate men who kept homes under certain hollow dunes, making their hard living by spear hunting and sifting for spica granules.

But I was much younger in those days, long before Dedinger began preaching to the sandmen, flattering and con-

vincing them of their righteous perfection. Their role as leaders, blazing a way for humanity down the Path of Redemption.

I'd be a fool to think I still qualify as a "scout" in this terrain.

Sure enough, Fallon was taken by surprise when their trail crossed a stretch of booming sand.

The fugitive's footprints climbed up the side of a dune, following an arc that would have stressed the mounts to follow. Fallon decided to cut inside of Dedinger's track, saving time and energy . . . but soon the sandy surface ceased cushioning the horse's hoofbeats. Instead, low groans echoed with each footfall, resonating like the sound of tapping on a drum. Cursing, he reined back. As an apprentice he once took a dare to jump in the center of a booming dune, and was lucky when it did not collapse beneath him. As it was, he spent the next pidura nursing an aching skull that kept on ringing from the reverberations he set off.

After laborious backtracking, they finally got around the obstacle.

Now Dedinger knows we're still after him. Fallon chided himself. *Concentrate, dammit! You have experience, use it!*

Fallon glanced back at the young women, whose secret clan of riders chose him to spend pleasant retirement in their midst, one of just four men dwelling in Xi's glades. Pahna was still a lanky youth, but Reza had already shared Fallon's bed on three occasions. The last time she had been kind, overlooking when he fell asleep too soon.

They claim experience and thoughtfulness are preferable traits in male companions—qualities that make up for declining stamina. But I wonder if it's a wise policy. Wouldn't they be better off keeping a young stallion like Dwer around, instead?

Dwer was far better equipped for this kind of mission. The lad would have brought Dedinger back days ago, all tied up in a neat package.

Well, you don't always have the ideal man on hand for every job. I just hope old Lester and the sages found a good use for Dwer. His gifts are rare.

Fallon had never been quite the "natural" that his apprentice was. In times past, he used to make up for it with discipline and attention to detail. He had never been one to let his mind wander during a hunt.

But times change, and a man loses his edge. These days, he could not help drifting away to the past. Something always reminded him of other days, his past was so filled with riches.

Oh, the times he used to have, running across the steppe with Ul-ticho, his plains hunting companion whose grand life was heartbreakingly short. Her fellowship meant more to Fallon than any human's, before or since. No one else understood so well the silences within his restless heart.

Ul-ticho, be glad you never saw this year when things fell apart. Those times were better, old friend. Jijo was ours, and even the sky held no threat you and I couldn't handle.

Dedinger's tracks still lay in plain sight, turning the rim of a great dune. The marks grew steadily fresher, and his limp grew worse with every step. The fugitive was near collapse. Assuming he kept going, it would be a half midura, at most, before the mounted party caught him.

And still some distance short of the first shelter well. Not bad. We may pull this off yet.

Assumptions are a luxury that civilized folk can afford. But not warriors or people of the land. In those staggered footprints, Fallon read a reassuring story, and so violated a rule that he used to pound into his apprentice.

They were riding in the same direction as the wind, so no scent warned the animals before they turned, slanting down to the shadowed north side of the dune. Abruptly, a murmur of voices greeted them—shouts, filled with wrath and danger. Before Fallon's blinking eyes could adjust to the changed light, he and the women found themselves staring down the shafts of a dozen or more cocked arbalests, all aimed their way, held by grizzled men wearing cloaks, turbans, and membrane goggles.

Now he made out a structure just ahead, shielded from the elements, made of piled stones. Fallon caught a belated sniff of water.

A new well? Built since I last came here as a young man? Or did I forget this one?

More likely, the desert men never told the visiting chief

scout all their secret sites. Far better, from their point of view, to let the High Sages think their maps complete, while holding something in reserve.

Lifting his hands slowly and carefully away from the pistol at his belt, Fallon now saw Dedinger, sunburned and shaking as he clutched devoted followers—who tenderly poured water over the prophet's broken lips.

We came so close!

The hands holding Dedinger right now should have been Fallon's. They would have been, if only things had gone just a little differently.

I'm sorry, Fallon thought, turning in silent apology to Reza and Pahna. Their faces looked surprised and bleak. *I'm an old man . . . and I let you down.*

Nelo

THE BATTLE FOR DOLO VILLAGE INVOLVED LARGER issues, but the principal thing decided was who would get to sleep indoors that night.

Most of the combatants were quite young, or very old.

In victory, the winners took possession of ashes.

In defeat, the losers marched forth singing.

Aided by a few qheuen allies, the craft workers started the fight evenly matched against the fanatical followers of Jop the Zealot. Both sides were angry, determined, and poorly armed with sticks and cudgels. Every man, woman, and qheuen of fighting age was away on militia duty, taking the swords and other weapons with them.

Even so, it was a wonder no one died in the melee.

Combatants swelled around the village meeting tree in a sweaty, disorderly throng, pushing and flailing at men who had been their neighbors and friends, raising a bedlam that blocked out futile orders by leaders of both sides. It might have gone on till everyone collapsed in hoarse exhaustion, but the conflict was abruptly decided when one side got unexpected reinforcements.

Brown-clad men dropped from the overhanging branches of the garu forest, where gardens of luscious, protein-rich moss created a rich and unique niche for agile human farmers. Suddenly outflanked and outnumbered, Jop and his followers turned and fled the debris-strewn valley.

"The zealots went too far," said one gnarled tree farmer, explaining why his people dropped their neutrality to intervene. "Even if they had an excuse to blow up the dam without guidance from the sages . . . they should've warned the poor qheuens first! A murder committed in the name of reverence is still a crime. It's too high a toll to pay for following the Path."

Nelo was still catching his breath, so Ariana Foo expressed thanks on the craft workers' behalf. "There has already been enough blood spilled down the Bibur's waters. It is well past time for neighbors to care for one another, and heal these wounds."

Despite confinement to her wheelchair, Ariana had been worth ten warriors during the brief struggle, without ever aiming or landing a blow. Her renowned status as the former High Sage of human sept meant that no antagonist dared confront her. It was as if a bubble of sanity moved through the mob, interrupting the riot, which resumed again as soon as she had passed. The sight of her helped the majority of farmers decide to come down off the garu heights and assist.

No one pursued Jop's forces as they retreated on canoes and makeshift rafts to the Bibur's other bank, re-forming on a crest of high ground separating the river from a vast swamp. There the zealots chanted passages from the Sacred Scrolls, still defiant.

Nelo labored for breath. It felt as if his ribs were half torn loose from his side, and he could not tell for some time which pains were temporary, and which were from some fanatic's baton or quarterstaff. At least nothing seemed broken, and he grew more confident that his heart wasn't about to burst out of his chest.

So, Dolo has been won back, he thought, finding little to rejoice over in the triumph. Log Biter was dead, as well as Jobee and half of Nelo's apprentices. With his paper mill gone, along with the dam and qheuen rookery, the battle had been largely to decide who would take shelter in the remaining dwellings.

A makeshift infirmary was set up surrounding the traeki pharmacist, on a stretch of leaf-covered loam. Nelo spent some time sewing cuts with boiled thread, and laying plaster compresses on bruised comrades and foes alike.

The task of healing and stitching was hardly begun when a messenger dropped down from the skyway of rope bridges that laced the forest in all directions. Nelo recognized the lanky teenager, a local girl whose swiftness along the branch-top ways could not be matched. Still short of breath, she saluted Ariana Foo and recited a message from the commander of the militia base concealed some distance downriver.

"Two squads will get here before nightfall," she relayed proudly. "They'll send tents and other gear by tomorrow morn . . . assuming the Jophur don't blow the boats up."

It was fast action, but a resigned murmur was all the news merited. Any help now was too little, and far too late to save the rich, united community Dolo Village had been. No wonder Jop's people had been less tenacious, more willing to retreat. In their eyes, they had already won.

The Path of Redemption lies before us.

Nelo walked over to sit on a tree stump near the town exploser, whose destructive charges were commandeered and misused by Jop's mob. Henrik's shoulders slumped as he stared over the Bibur, past the shattered ruins of the craft shops, at the zealots chanting on the other side.

Nelo wondered if his own face looked as bleak and haggard as Henrik's.

Probably not. To his own great surprise, Nelo found himself in a mood to be philosophical.

"Never have seen such a mess in all my days," he said, with a resigned sigh. "I guess we're gonna have our hands full, rebuilding."

Henrik shook his head, as if to say, *It can't be done.*

This, in turn, triggered a flare of resentment from Nelo. What business did *Henrik* have, wallowing in self-pity? As an exploser, his professional needs were small. Assisted by his guild, he could be back in business within a year. But even if Log Biter's family got help from other qheuen hives, and held a dam-raising to end all dam-raisings, it would still be years before a waterwheel, turbine, and power train could convert lake pressure into industrial muscle. And that would just begin the recovery. Nelo figured he would devote the rest of his life to building a papery like his former mill.

Was Henrik ashamed his charges had been misused by a panicky rabble? How could anyone guard against such times as these, when all prophecy went skewed and awry? Galactics had indeed come to Jijo, but not as foreseen. Instead, month after month of ambiguity had mixed with alien malevolence to sow confusion among the Six Races. Jop represented one reaction. Others sought ways to fight the aliens. In the long run, neither policy would make any difference.

We should have followed a third course—wait and see. Go on living normal lives until the universe decides what to do with us.

Nelo wondered at his own attitude. The earlier shocked dismay had given way to a strange feeling. Not numbness. Certainly not elation amid such devastation.

I hate everything that was done here.

. . . and yet . . .

And yet, Nelo found a spirit of *anticipation* rising within. He could already smell fresh-cut timber and the pungency of boiling pitch. He felt the pulselike pounding of hammers driving joining pegs, and saws spewing dust across the ground. In his mind were the beginnings of a sketch for a better workshop. A better mill.

All my life I tended the factory my ancestors left me, making paper in the time-honored way.

It was a prideful place. A noble calling.

But it wasn't mine.

Even if the original design came from settlers who stepped off the *Tabernacle*, still wearing some of their mantle as star gods, Nelo had always known, deep inside—*I could do a better job*.

Now, when his years were ripe, he finally had a chance to prove it. The prospect was sad, daunting . . . and thrilling. Perhaps the strangest thing of all was how young it made him feel.

"Don't blame yourself, Henrik," he told the exploser, charitably. "You watch and see. Everything'll be better'n ever."

But the exploser only shook his head again. He pointed across the river, where Jop's partisans were now streaming toward the northeastern swamp, carrying canoes and other burdens on their backs, still singing as they went.

"They've got my reserve supply of powder. Snatched it from the warehouse. I couldn't stop 'em."

Nelo frowned.

"What good'll it do 'em? Militia's coming, by land and water. Jop can't reach anywhere else along the river that's worth blowing up."

"They aren't heading along the river," Henrik replied, and Nelo saw it was true.

"Then where?" he wondered aloud.

Abruptly, Nelo knew the answer to his own question, even before Henrik spoke. And that same instant he also realized there were far more important matters than rebuilding a paper mill.

"Biblos," the exploser said, echoing Nelo's thought.

The papermaker blinked silently, unable to make his brain fit around the impending catastrophe.

"The militia . . . can they cut 'em off?"

"Doubtful. But even if they do, it's not Jop alone that has me worried."

He turned to show his eyes for the first time, and they held bleakness.

"I'll bet Jop's bunch ain't the only group heading that way, even as we speak."

Rety

THE MORE SHE LEARNED ABOUT STAR GODS, THE less attractive they seemed.

None of 'em is half as smart as a dung-eating glaver, she thought, while making her way down a long corridor toward the ship's brig. *It must come from using all those computers and smarty-ass machines to cook your food, make your air, tell you stories, kill your enemies, tuck you in at night, and foretell your future for you. Count on 'em too much, and your brain stops working.*

Rety had grown more cynical since those early days when Dwer and Lark first brought her down off the Rimmer Mountains, a half-starved, wide-eyed savage, agog over the simplest crafts produced on the so-called civilized Slope—all the way from pottery to woven cloth and paper books. Of course that awe evaporated just as soon as she sampled *real* luxury aboard the Rothen station, where Kunn and the other Daniks flattered her with promises that sent her head spinning.

Long life, strength and beauty . . . cures for all your aches and scars . . . a clean, safe place to live under the protection of our Rothen lords . . . and all the wonders that come with being a lesser deity, striding among the stars.

There she had met the Rothen patrons of humankind. *Her* patrons, they said. Gazing on the benevolent faces of Ro-kenn and Ro-pol, Rety had allowed herself to see wise, loving parents—unlike those she knew while growing up in a wild sooner tribe. The Rothen seemed so perfect, so noble and strong, that Rety almost gave in. She very nearly pledged her heart.

But it proved a lie. Whether or not they really were humanity's patrons did not matter to her at all. What counted was that the Rothen turned out to be less mighty than they claimed. For that she could never forgive them.

What use was a protector who couldn't protect?

For half a year, Rety had fled one band of incompetents after another—from her birth tribe of filthy cretins to the Commons of Six Races. Then from the Commons to the Rothen. And when the Jophur corvette triumphed over Kunn's little scout boat, she had seriously contemplated heading down to the swamp with both hands upraised, offering her services to the ugly ringed things. Now wouldn't *that* have galled old Dwer!

At one point, while *he* was floundering in the muck, talking to his crazy mulc-spider friend, she had actually started toward the ramp of the grounded spaceship, intending to hammer on the door. Surely the Jophur were like everybody else, willing to deal for information that was important to them.

At a critical moment, only their stench held her back—an aroma that reminded her of festering wounds and gangrene . . . fortunately, as it turned out, since the Jophur also proved unable to defend themselves against the unexpected.

So I got to just keep looking for another way off this mud ball. And who cares what Dwer thinks of me? At least I don't make fancy excuses for what I do.

Rety's tutor had been the wilderness, whose harsh education taught just one lesson—to survive, at all cost. She grew up watching as some creatures ate others, then were eaten by something stronger still. Lark referred to the "food chain," but Rety called it the *who-kills mountain.* Every choice she made involved trying to climb higher on that mountain, hoping the next step would take her to the top.

So when the Jophur were beaten and captured by mythical *dolphins,* it seemed only natural to hurry aboard the submarine and claim sanctuary with her "Earth cousins." *Only now look where I am, buried under a trash heap at the bottom of the sea, hiding with a bunch of chattering Earthfish who have every monster and star god in space chasing them.*

In other words, back at the bottom of the mountain again. Doomed always to be prey, instead of the hunter.

Crax! I sure do got a knack for picking 'em.

• • •

There were a few small compensations.

For one thing, dolphins seemed to hold humans in awe—the same kind as the Daniks had for their Rothen patrons. Furthermore, the *Streaker* crew considered Rety and Dwer "heroes" for their actions in the swamp against the Jophur sky boat. As a result, she had free run of the ship, including a courtesy password that let her approach a sealed entrance to the *Streaker*'s brig.

For a brief time both airlock doors were closed, and she knew guards must be examining her with instruments. *Prob'ly checkin' my innards, to see if I'm smugglin' a laser or something.* Rety took a breath and exhaled deeply, washing away her body's instinctive panic over confinement in a cramped metal space. *It'll pass . . . it'll pass. . . .*

That trick had helped her endure years of frustration in her feral tribe, whenever defeat and brutality seemed to press in from all sides.

Don't react like a savage. If others can stand living in boxes, you can, too . . . for a little while.

The second hatch opened at last, showing Rety a ramp that dropped steeply to a chamber that was flooded, chest-high, with water.

Ugh.

She disliked the mixed compartments making up a large part of this weird vessel—half-immersed rooms that were spanned above by dry catwalks, allowing access to both striding and swimming beings. The liquid felt warm as Rety sloshed downslope, reminding her of volcanic springs back home in the Gray Hills, but with an added *fizzy* quality that left trails of tiny bubbles wherever she moved. Feigning relaxed confidence, Rety approached the guard station, where two sentries were assisted by a globular robot whose whirring antennae watched her acutely. One of the dolphins rode a six-legged walker unit—without the bug-eyed body armor—enabling it to stride about dry areas of the ship. The other "fin" wore just a tool harness, using languid motions of his flippers to face a set of monitor displays.

"May we help you, missss?" the latter one asked, with a tail splash added for punctuation.

"Yeh. I came to question Kunn an' Jass again. I figure I'll get more out of 'em if I try it alone."

The guard focused one eye back at her with a dubious expression. The first attempt had not gone well, when Rety accompanied Lieutenant Tsh't to interrogate the human prisoners. They had been groggy and unhelpful, still wearing bandages and medic pacs for their various injuries. While the dolphin officer tried grilling Kunn about matters back in the Five Galaxies, Rety endured a hot glare of hatred from her cousin Jass, who murmured the word *traitor* and spat on the floor.

Who'd you figure I betrayed, Jass? she had wondered, eyeing him coldly until his stare broke first. *The Daniks? Even Kunn isn't surprised I switched sides, after the way he treated me.*

Or do you mean I've turned against our home clan? The band of grubby savages that birthed me, then never showed me a day's kindness since?

Before looking away, his eyes showed it was personal. She had arranged for Jass to be seized, tormented, and pressed into service as Kunn's guide. His being locked in this metal cage was also her doing.

That thought cheered her up a bit. *You gotta admit, Jass, I finally made an impression on you.*

But soon things are gonna get even worse.

I'm gonna make you grateful.

Meanwhile, Kunn told Tsh't that the siege of Earth went on, though eased somewhat by a strange alliance with the Thennanin.

"But to answer your chief question, there has been no amnesty call by the Institutes. Several great star clans have blocked a safe-conduct decree to let your ship come home."

Rety wasn't sure what that meant, but clearly the news was bitter to the dolphins.

Then a new voice intruded from thin air, where a spinning abstract figure suddenly whirled.

"Lieutenant, please recall instructions. Have the prisoner explain how his vessel tracked us to this world."

Rety recalled seeing a tremor course down the dolphin's sleek gray flank, perhaps from irritation over the machine's snide tone. But Tsh't snapped her jaw in a gesture of submission, and sent her walker unit looming closer to Kunn's bunk. The human star voyager had nowhere to retreat as her machine pressed close, threateningly. Rety recalled sweat popping out on the Danik warrior's brow, giving lie to his false air of calm. Having watched him intimidate others, she was pleased to see the tables turned.

Then it happened. Some piece of equipment failed, or else the lieutenant's walker took a misstep. The right front ankle abruptly snapped, sending the dolphin's great mass crashing forward.

Only lightning reflexes enabled Kunn to scramble out of the way and avoid being crushed. By the time guards arrived to help Tsh't untangle herself, the dolphin officer was bruised, angry, and in no humor to continue the interview.

But I'm ready now, Rety thought later, as one of the brig wardens prepared to escort her down a narrow passage with numbers etched on every hatch. *I've got a plan . . . and this time Kunn and Jass better do as I say.*

"Are you sure you want-t to do this now, miss?" the guard asked. "It's night cycle and the prisoners are asleep."

"That's just how I want 'em. Groggy an' logy. They may blab more."

In fact, Rety hardly cared if Kunn named the admirals of all the fleets in the Five Galaxies. Her questions would only serve as cover for communication on another level.

She had been busy in the room the Streakers assigned her—a snug chamber once occupied by a human named Dennie Sudman, whose clothes fit her pretty well. Pictures on the wall portrayed a young woman with dark hair, who was said to have gone missing on some foreign planet years ago, along with several human and dolphin crew mates. On her cluttered desk Dennie had left a clever machine that spoke in a much friendlier manner than the sarcastic Niss. It seemed eager to assist Rety, telling her all about the Terran ship and its surroundings.

I've studied the passages leading from this jail to the OutLock. I can name what kind of skiffs and star boats they keep there. And most important, these Earthfish trust me. My passwords should let us out.

All I need is a pilot . . . and someone strong and mean enough to do any fighting, if we run into trouble.

And luck. Rety had carefully timed things so there was little chance of running into Dwer along the way.

Dwer knows not to trust me . . . and I can't be sure that both Jass and Kunn together would be enough to bring him down.

Anyway, all else being equal, she'd rather Dwer didn't get hurt.

Maybe I'll even think about him now and then, while I'm livin' high on some far galaxy.

There wasn't much else about Jijo that she planned on remembering.

Dwer

I DON'T BELONG HERE," HE TRIED TO EXPLAIN. "AND neither does Rety. You've got to help us get back."

"Back where?" The woman seemed honestly perplexed. "To that seaside swamp, with toxic engine waste and dead Jophur rings for company? And more Jophur surely on the way?"

Once again, Dwer was having trouble with words. He found it difficult to concentrate in these sealed spaces they called "starship cabins," where the air felt so dead. Especially this one, a dimly lit chamber filled with strange objects Dwer could not hope to understand.

Lark or Sara would do fine here, but I feel lost. I miss the news that comes carried on the wind.

It didn't help settle his nerves that the person sitting opposite him was the most beautiful human being Dwer had ever seen, with dark yellow hair and abiding sadness in her pale eyes.

"No, of course not," he answered. "There's another place where I'm needed. . . . And Rety, too."

Fine lines crinkled at the edges of her eyes.

"The young hoon, Alvin, wants to let his parents know he's alive, and report to the urrish sage who sent the four of them on their diving mission. They want help getting home."

"Will you give it?"

"How can we? Aside from putting our own crewfolk in danger, and perhaps giving our position away to enemies, it seems unfair to endanger your entire culture with knowledge that's a curse to any who possess it.

"And yet . . ."

She paused. Her scrutiny made Dwer feel like a small child.

"Yet, there is a reticence in your voice. A wariness about your destination that makes me suspect you're *not* talking about going home. Not to the tranquil peace you knew among friends and loved ones, in the land you call the Slope."

There seemed little point in trying to conceal secrets from Gillian Baskin. So Dwer silently shrugged.

"The girl's tribe, then," the woman guessed. "Rety's folk, in the northern hills, where you were wounded fighting a war bot with your bare hands."

He looked down, speaking in a low voice.

"There's . . . things that still need to be done there."

"Mm. I can well imagine. Obligations, I suppose? Duties unfulfilled?" Her sigh was soft and distant sounding. "You see, I know how it is with your kind. Where your priorities lie."

That made him look up, wondering. *What did she mean by that?* There was resigned melancholy in her face . . . plus something like recognition, as if she saw something familiar in him, wakening affectionate sadness.

"Tell me about it, Dwer. Tell me what you must accomplish.

"Tell me who depends on you."

Perhaps it was the way she phrased her question, or the power of her personality, but he found himself no longer able to withhold the remaining parts of the story. The parts he had kept back till now.

—about his job as chief scout of the Commons, seeing to it that no colonist race moved east of the Rimmers—sparing the rest of Jijo from further infestation. Enforcing sacred law.

—then how he was ordered to break that law, guiding a mission to tame Rety's savage cousins—a gamble meant to ensure human survival on Jijo, in case the Slope was cleansed of sapient life.

—how the four of them—Danel Ozawa, Dwer, Lena, and Jenin—learned the Gray Hills were no longer a sanctuary when Rety guided a Danik sky chariot to her home tribe.

—how Dwer and the others vowed to gamble their forfeit lives to win a chance for the sooner tribe . . . four humans against a killer machine . . . a gamble that succeeded, at great cost.

"And against all odds, I'd say," Gillian Baskin commented. She turned her head, addressing the third entity sharing the room with them.

"I take it *you* were there, as well. Tell me, did you bother to help Dwer and the others? Or were you always a useless nuisance?"

After relating his dour tale, Dwer was startled by a sudden guffaw escaping his own gut. Fitting words! Clearly, Gillian Baskin understood noor.

Mudfoot lay grooming himself atop a glass-topped display case. Within lay scores of strange artifacts, backlit and labeled like treasures in the Biblos Museum. Some light spilled to the foot of another exhibit standing erect nearby—a *mummy*, he guessed. When they were boys, Lark once tried to scare Dwer with spooky book pictures of old-time Earth bodies that had been prepared that way, instead of being properly mulched. This one looked vaguely human, though he knew it was anything but.

At Gillian's chiding, Mudfoot stopped licking himself to reply with a panting grin. Again, Dwer imagined what the look might mean.

Who, me, lady? Don't you know I fought the whole battle and saved everybody's skins, all by myself?

After his experience with telepathic mulc spiders, Dwer did not dismiss the possibility that it was more than imagination. The noor showed no reaction when he tried mind speaking, but that proved nothing.

Gillian had also tried various techniques to make the noor talk—first asking Alvin to smother the creature with umble songs, then keeping Mudfoot away from the young hoon, locking it instead in this dim office for miduras, with only the ancient mummy for company. The Niss Machine had badgered the noor in a high-pitched dialect of Gal-Seven, frequently using the phrase *dear cousin*.

"Danel Ozawa tried talkin' to it, too," Dwer told Gillian.

"Oh? And did that seem strange to you?"

He nodded. "There are folktales about talking noor . . . and other critters, too. But I never expected it from a sage."

She slapped the desktop.

"I think I get it."

Gillian stood up and began pacing—a simple act that she performed with a hunter's grace, reminding him of the prowl of a she-ligger.

"We call the species *tytlal,* and where I come from, they talk a blue streak. They *are* cousins of the Niss Machine, after a fashion, since the Niss was made by our allies, the Tymbrimi."

"The Tymb . . . I think I heard of 'em. Aren't they the first race Earth contacted, when our ships went out—"

Gillian nodded. "And a lucky break that turned out to be. Oh, there are plenty of honorable races and clans in the Five Galaxies. Don't let the present crisis make you think they're all evil, or religious fanatics. It's just that most of the moderate alliances have conservative mind-sets. They ponder caution first, and act only after long deliberation. Too long to help us, I'm afraid.

"But not the Tymbrimi. They are brave and loyal friends. Also, according to many of the great clans and Institutes, the Tymbrimi are considered quite mad."

Dwer sat up, both intrigued and confused. "Mad?"

Gillian laughed. "I guess a lot of humans would agree. A legend illustrates the point. It's said that one day the Great Power of the Universe, in exasperation over some Tymbrimi antic, cried out, 'These creatures must be the most outrageous beings imaginable!'

"Now, Tymbrimi like nothing better than a challenge. So they took the Great Power's statement as a dare. When they won official patron status, with license to uplift new species, they traded away two perfectly normal client races for the rights to one presapient line that no one else could do anything with."

"The noor," Dwer guessed. Then he corrected himself. "The tytlal."

"The very same. Creatures whose chief delight comes from thwarting, surprising, or befuddling others, making the Tymbrimi seem staid by comparison. Which brings us to our quandary. How did they get to Jijo, and why don't they speak?"

"Our Jijo chimpanzees don't speak either, though your Niss-thing showed me moving pictures of them talking on Earth."

"Hmm. But that's easily explained. Chims were still not very good at it when the *Tabernacle* left, bringing your ancestors here. It would be easy to suppress the talent at that point, in order to let humans pretend . . ."

Gillian snapped her fingers. "Of course." For a moment, her smile reminded Dwer of *Sara,* when his sister had been working on some abstract problem and abruptly saw the light.

"Within a few years of making contact with Galactic civilization, the leaders of Earth knew we had entered an incredibly dire phase. At best, we might barely hang on while learning the complex rules of an ancient and dangerous culture. At worst—" She shrugged. "It naturally seemed prudent to set up an insurance policy. To plant a seed where humanity might be safe, in case the worst happened."

Her expression briefly clouded, and Dwer did not need fey sensitivity to understand. Out there, beyond Izmunuti, the worst *was* happening, and now it seemed the fleeing *Streaker* had exposed the "seed," as well.

That's what Danel was talking about, when he said, "Humans did not come to Jijo to tread the Path of Redemption." He meant we were a survival stash . . . like the poor g'Kek.

"When humans brought chimps with them, they naturally downplayed *pans* intelligence. In case the colony were ever found, chims might miss punishment. Perhaps they could even blend into the forest and survive in Jijo's wilderness, unnoticed by the judges of the great Institutes."

Gillian whirled to look at Mudfoot. "And that must be what the Tymbrimi did, as well! They, too, must have snuck down to Jijo. Only, unlike glavers and the other six races, they planted no colony of their own. Instead, they deposited a secret cache . . . of tytlal."

"And like we did with chimps, they took away their speech." Dwer shook his head. "But then . . ." He pointed to Mudfoot.

Gillian's eyebrows briefly pursed. "A hidden race *within* the race? Fully sapient tytlal, hiding among the others? Why not? After all, your own sages kept secrets from the rest of you. If Danel Ozawa tried speaking to Mudfoot, it means someone must have already known about the tytlal, even in those early days, and kept the confidence all this time."

Absently, she reached out to stroke the noor's sleek fur. Mudfoot rolled over, presenting his belly.

"What is the key?" she asked the creature. "Some code word? Something like a Tymbrimi empathy glyph? Why did you talk to the Niss once, then clam up?"

And why did you follow me across mountains and deserts? Dwer added, silently, enthralled by the mystery tale, although the complexity combined with his ever-present claustrophobia to foster a growing headache.

"Excuse me," he said, breaking into Gillian's ruminations. "But can we go back to the thing I came here about? I know the problems you're wrestling with are bigger and more important than mine, and I'd help you if I could. But I can't see any way to change your star-god troubles with my bow and arrows.

"I'm not asking you to risk your ship, and I'm sorry about being a pest. . . . But if there's any way you could just let me . . . well . . . try to *swim* ashore, I really do have things I've got to do."

That was when the tytlal rolled back onto his feet, wearing a look of evident surprise on his narrow face. Spines that normally lay hidden in the fur behind his ears now stood in stiff bristles. Moreover, Dwer felt sure he glimpsed *something* take shape briefly, in the air above Mudfoot. A ghostly wisp, less than vapor, which seemed to speak of its own accord.

So do I, it said, evidently responding to Dwer's statement.

Things to do.

Dwer rubbed his eyes and would gladly have dismissed the brief specter as another imagining . . . another product of the pummeling his nervous system had gone through.

Only Gillian must have noted the same event. She blinked a few times, pointed at the now-worried expression on Mudfoot's face . . . and burst out laughing.

Dwer stared at her, then found himself breaking up, as well. Till that moment, he had not yet decided about the beautiful Earthwoman. But anyone who could set Mudfoot back like that must be all right.

Rety

AS THE GUARD ESCORTED HER TO THE CAPTIVES' cell, she eyed several air-circulation grates. Schematics showed the system to be equipped with many safety valves, and the ducts were much too small for prisoners to squeeze through.

But not for a little urrish male, armed with borrowed laser cutters.

Rety's plan was chancy, and she hated sending her "husband" into the maze of air pipes. But yee seemed confident that he would not get lost.

"this maze no worse than stinky passages under the grass plain," he had sniffed while examining a holographic chart. *"it easier than dodging through root tunnels where urrish grubs and males must scurry, when we have no sweet wife pouch to lie in."* yee curled his long neck in a shrug. *"don't you worry, wife! yee take tools to locked-up men. we do this neat!"*

That would be the critical phase. Once Kunn and Jass were beyond the brig airlock, all the other obstacles should quickly fall. Rety felt positive.

Two prison cells had red lights glaring above reinforced

hatches. The far one, she knew, contained Jophur rings that had been captured in the swamp. The little g'Kek named Huck was helping the Niss Machine interrogate those captives. Rety had racked her brain to come up with a way they might fit her plan, but finally deemed it best to leave them where they were.

This Streaker *ship won't dare chase us, once we get a star boat outside . . . but the Jophur ship might. Especially if those rings had a way to signal their crew mates.*

As the guard approached Kunn's cell, Rety fondled a folded scrap of paper on which she had laboriously printed instructions, sounding out the words letter by letter, stretching her newborn literacy to the limit. She knew it must look wrong, but no one could afford to be picky these days.

KUN I KAN GIT U OT UV HIR WANT TU GO?

So went the first line of the note she planned slipping him, while pretending to ask questions. If the Danik pilot understood and agreed to the plan, she would depart and set yee loose to worm his small, lithe body through *Streaker*'s ducting system. Meanwhile Rety had selected good places to set fires—in a ship lounge and a cargo locker—to distract the *Streaker* crew away from this area while Kunn used smuggled tools to break out. If all went well, they could then dash for the OutLock, steal a star boat, and escape.

There's just one condition, Kunn. You gotta agree that we get away from here. Away from these Earthers, away from Daniks and Rothens and Jophur monsters and all that crap. Away from Jijo.

Rety felt sure he'd accept. *Anyway, if he or Jass give me any trouble, they'll find they're dealin' with a different Rety now.*

The guard maneuvered his walker unit carefully in the narrow hallway. The gangly machine had to bend in order for him to bring a key against the door panel. Finally, it slid aside. Rety glimpsed two bunks within, each supporting a blanket-covered human form.

"Hey, Kunn," she said, crossing the narrow distance and nudging his shoulder. "Wake up! No more delayin' or foolin' now. These folks want t'know how you followed 'em. . . ."

The blanket slipped off, revealing his shock of glossy hair, but there was no tremor of movement.

They must have him doped, she thought. *I hope he's not too far under. This can't wait!*

Rety shook harder, rolling Kunn toward her—

And jumped back with a gasp of surprise.

The Danik's face was purple. His eyes bulged from their sockets, and his tongue had swollen to fill his mouth.

The dolphin guard chattered a dismayed squeal in the instinctive animal language of his kind.

Rety struggled with shock. She had grown up with death, but it took all her force of will to quash the horror rising in her gorge.

Somehow, she made herself turn toward the other bunk.

Sara

*"Oh, Doctor Faustus was a good man,
He whipped his scholars now and then;
When he whipped them he made them dance,
Out of Scotland into France,
Out of France, and into Spain,
Then he whipped them back again!"*

Emerson's song resonated through the Hall of Spinning Disks, where dust motes sparkled in narrow shafts of rhythmic light.

Sara winced at the violent lyrics, but the starman clearly enjoyed these outbursts, gushing from unknown recesses of his scarred brain. He laughed, as did a crowd of urrish males who followed him, clambering through the scaffolding of Uriel's fantastic machine, helping him fine-tune each delicate part. The little urs cackled at Emerson's rough humor, and showed their devotion by diving between whirling glass plates to tighten a strap here, or a pulley there, wherever he gestured with quick hand signs.

Once an engineer, always an engineer, Sara thought. At times, Emerson resembled her own father, who might go silent for days while tending his beloved paper mill, drawing more satisfaction from the poetry of pulping hammers and rollers than the white sheets that made literacy possible on a barbaric world.

A parallel occurred to her.

Paper suited the Six Races, who needed a memory storage system that was invisible from space. But Uriel's machine has similar traits—an analog computer that no satellite or spaceship can detect, because it uses no electricity and has no digital cognizance. Above all, Galactics would never imagine such an ornate contraption.

And yet it was beautiful in a bizarre way. No wonder she had dreamed shapes and equations when her eyes first glimpsed this marvel through cracks in her delirium. Each time a disk turned against a neighbor's rim, its own axle rotated at a speed that varied with the radial point of contact. If that radius shifted as an independent variable, the rotation changed in response, describing a nonlinear function. It was a marvelously simple concept . . . and hellishly hard to put into practice without years of patient trial and error.

Uriel first saw the idea in an old Earth book—a quintessentially wolfling concept, briefly used in an old-time Amero-Eurasian war. Soon after, humans discovered digital computers and abandoned the technique. But here on Mount Guenn, the urrish smith had extended it to levels never seen before. Much of her prodigious wealth and passion went into making the concept work.

And urrish haste. Their lives are so short, Uriel must have feared she'd never finish before she died. In that case, what would her successor do with all this?

An array of pillars, arches, and boo scaffolding held the turning shafts in proper alignment, forming a three-dimensional maze that stretched away from Sara, nearly filling the vast chamber. Long ago, this cavity spilled liquid magma down the mountain's mighty flanks. Today it throbbed with a different kind of creative force.

Light rays played a clever role in the dance of mathematics. Glancing off selected disks, pulselike reflections fell onto a stretch of black sand that had been raked smooth across the floor. Each flash affected the grains, causing a slight spray or rustle. Hillocks grew wherever glimmers landed most often.

Uriel even found a use for lightning crabs, Sara marveled.

On Jijo, some shorelines were known to froth during electrical storms, as these tiny creatures kicked up sand in frenzied reaction. *We thought it might be static charges in the air, making them behave so. But clearly it is light. I must tell Lark about this, someday.*

And Sara realized something else.

The crabs may be another Buyur gimmick species. Bioengineered servants, reverted to nature, but keeping their special trait, even after the gene meddlers left.

Whatever their original function, the crabs now served Uriel, whose hooves clattered nervously as the sandscape swirled under a cascade of sparkling light. Individual flashes mattered little. It was the summed array over area and time that added up to solving a complex numerical problem. Near Uriel, the little chimp, Prity, perched on a high stool with her drawing pad. Prity's tongue stuck out as she sketched, copying the sand display. Sara had never seen her little assistant happier.

Despite all this impressive ingenuity, the actual equations being solved were not profound. Sara had already worked out rough estimates, within a deviance of ten percent, by using a few simple Delancy approximations. But Lester Cambel needed both precision and accuracy under a wide range of boundary conditions, including atmospheric pressure varying with altitude. For that, machine-derived tables offered advantages.

At least now I understand what it's all for. In her mind, she pictured bustling activity beneath the towering stems of a boo forest, throngs of workers laboring, the flow of acrid liquids, and discussions in the hushed, archaic dialect of science.

They may be crazy—Lester especially. Probably the effort will backfire and make the aliens more vicious than ever. Dedinger would look at this—along with all the sema-

*phores, gliders, balloons, and other innovations—and call
it the futile thrashing of the damned.*

*Yet the attempt is glorious. If they pull it off, I'll know I
was right about the Six. Our destiny was not foretold by the
scrolls, or Dedinger's orthodoxy . . . or Lark's, for that
matter.*

It was unique.

*Anyway, if we're to be damned, I'd rather it be for try-
ing.*

Just one thing still puzzled her. Sara shook her head and
murmured aloud.

"Why me?"

Kurt, the Tarek Town exploser, had acted as if this project desperately needed Sara, for her professional expertise.
But Uriel's machine was already nearly functional by the
time the party arrived from Xi. Prity and Emerson were
helpful at making the analog computer work, and so were
books Kurt hand-carried from Biblos. But Sara found herself with little to contribute.

"I only wish I knew why Uriel asked for me."

Her answer came from the entrance to the computer
vault.

"Is that truly the *only* thing you wish to understand? But
that one is easy, Sara. *Uriel* did not ask for you at all!"

The speaker was a man of middling stature with a shock
of white hair and a stained beard that stood out as if he
were constantly thunderstruck. *Kawsh* leaves smoldered in
his pipe, a habit chiefly indulged in by male hoons, since
the vapors were too strong for most humans. Politely, Sage
Purofsky stood in the draft of the doorway, and turned
away from Sara when exhaling.

She bowed to the senior scholar, known among his
peers as the best mind in the Commons.

"Master, if Uriel doesn't need my help, why was I urged
to come? Kurt made it sound vital."

"Did he? Vital. Well, I suppose it is, Sara. In a different
way."

Purofsky's eyes tracked the glitter of rays glancing off
spinning disks. His gaze showed appreciation of Uriel's
accomplishment. "Math must pay its way with useful
things," the sage once said. "Even though mere computa-

tion is like bashing down a door because you cannot find
the key."

Purofsky had spent his life in search of keys.

"It was *I* who sent for you, my dear," the aged savant
explained after a pause. "And now that you're recovered
from your ill-advised spill down a mountainside, I think it's
high time that I showed you why."

It was still daytime outside, but a starscape spread before
Sara. Clever lenses projected glass photoslides onto a
curved wall and ceiling, recreating the night sky in a wondrous planetarium built by Uriel's predecessor so that even
poor urrish eyesight might explore constellations in detail.
Sage Purofsky wore stars like ornaments on his face and
gown, while his shadow cast a man-shaped nebula across
the wall.

"I should start by explaining what I've been up to since
you left Biblos . . . has it really been more than a year,
Sara?"

"Yes, Master."

"Hmm. An eventful year. And yet . . ."

He worked his jaw for a moment, then shook his head.

"Like you, I had grown discouraged with my former field
of study. At last, I decided to extend the classical, pre-
contact geometrodynamic formalisms beyond the state
they were in when the *Tabernacle* left the solar system."

Sara stared.

"But I thought you wanted to *reconcile* pre-contact Earth
physics with Galactic knowledge. To prove that Einstein
and Lee had made crude but correct approximations . . .
the way Newton preapproximated Einstein."

That in itself would have been a daunting task—some
might say hopeless. According to reports brought by the
Tabernacle, space-time relativity was ill regarded by those
alien experts hired by the Terragens Council to teach modern science to Earthlings. Galactic instructors disdained as
superstition the homegrown cosmology humans formerly
relied on—the basis of crude star probes, crawling along at
sublight speeds. Until the Earthship *Vesarius* fell through
an undetected hyperanomaly, ending humanity's long iso-

lation, Einstein's heirs had never found a useful way to go faster—although some methods had been recorded in the Galactic Library for over a billion years.

After contact, humans scrimped to buy some thirdhand hyperships, and the old mathemetric models of Hawking, Purcell, and Lee fell by the wayside. In trying to show validity for pre-contact physics, Purofsky had taken on a strange, perhaps forlorn, task.

"I had some promising results at first, when I restated the Serressimi Exalted Transfer Shunt in terms compatible with old-fashioned tensor calculus."

"Indeed?" Sara leaned forward in her chair. "But how did you renormalize all the quasi-simultaneous infinities? You'd almost *have* to assume—"

But the elder sage raised a hand to cut her off, unwilling to be drawn into details.

"Plenty of time for that later, if you're still interested. For now let's just say that I soon realized the futility of that approach. Earth must by now have specialists who understand the official Galactic models better than I'll ever hope to. They have units of the Great Library, and truly modern computer simulators to work with. Suppose I did eventually manage to demonstrate that our Old Physics was a decent, if limited, approximation? It might win something for pride, showing that wolflings had been on the right track, on our own. But nothing *new* would come of it."

Purofsky shook his head. "No, I decided it was time to go for broke. I'd *plunge ahead* with the old space-time approach, and see if I could solve a problem relevant to Jijo—the Eight Starships Mystery."

Sara blinked.

"You mean *seven*, don't you? The question of why so many sooner races converged on Jijo within a short time, without getting caught? But isn't that settled?" She pointed at the most brilliant point on the wall. "Izmunuti started flooding nearby space with carbon chaff twenty centuries ago. Enough to seed the hollow hail and change our weather patterns, more than a light-year away. Once the storm wrecked all the watch robots left in orbit by the Migration Institute, sneakships could get in undetected."

"Hr-rm . . . yes, but not good enough, Sara. From wall

inscriptions found in a few Buyur ruins, we know *two* transfer points used to serve this system. The other must have collapsed after the Buyur left."

"Well? That's why the Izmunuti gambit works! A single shrouded access route, and the great Institutes not scheduled to resurvey the area for another eon. It must be a fairly unique situation."

"Unique. Hrm, and convenient. So convenient, in fact, that I decided to acquire fresh data."

Purofsky turned toward the planetarium display, and a distant expression crossed his shadowed face. After a few duras, Sara realized he must be drifting. That kind of absentmindedness might be a prerogative of genius back in the cloistered halls of Biblos, but it was infuriating when he had her keyed up so! She spoke in a sharp tone.

"Master! You were saying you needed data. Is there really something relevant you can see with Uriel's simple telescope?"

The scholar blinked, then cocked his head and smiled. "You know, Sara . . . I find it striking that we both spent the last year chasing unconventional notions. You, a sideline into languages and sociology—yes, I followed your work with interest. And me, thinking I could pierce secrets of the past using coarse implements made of reforged Buyur scrap metal and melted sand.

"Did you know, while taking pictures of Izmunuti, I also happened to snap shots of those *starships*? The ones causing so much fuss, up north? Caught them entering orbit . . . though my warning didn't reach the High Sages in time." Purofsky shrugged. "But to your question. Yes, I managed to learn a few things, using the apparatus here on Mount Guenn.

"Think again about Jijo's unique conditions, Sara. The collapse of the second transfer point . . . the carbon flaring of Izmunuti . . . the inevitable attractiveness of an isolated, shrouded world to sooner refugees.

"Now ponder this—how could beings with minds as agile as the Buyur fail to notice advance symptoms of these changes, about to commence in nearby space?"

"But the Buyur departed half a million years ago! There

may not have been any symptoms back then. Or else they were subtle."

"Perhaps. And that's where my research comes in. Plus your expertise, I hope. For I strongly suspect that space-time anomalies would have been noticeable, even back then."

"Space-time . . ." Sara realized his use of the archaic Earth-physics term was intentional. Now it was her turn to spend several silent duras staring at a blur of stars, sorting implications.

"You're . . . talking about lensing effects, aren't you?"

"Sharp lass," the sage answered approvingly. "And if *I* can see them—"

"Then the Buyur must have, and foreseen—"

"Like reading an open book! Nor is that all. I asked you here to help confirm another, more ominous suspicion."

Sara felt a frisson, climbing her spine like some insect with a million ice-cold feet.

"What do you mean?"

Sage Purofsky briefly closed his eyes. When he re-opened them, his gaze seemed alight with fascination.

"Sara, I believe they planned it this way, from the very start."

PART EIGHT

ILLEGAL RESETTLEMENT OF FALLOW WORLDS has been a predicament in the Five Galaxies for as far back as records exist. There are many causes for this recurring problem, but its most enduring basis is the Paradox of Reproductive Logic.

ORGANIC beings from countless diverse worlds tend to share one common trait—self-propagation. In some species, this manifests as a conscious desire to have offspring. Among other races, individuals respond to crude instinctive drives for either sex or xim, and spare little active attention to the consequences.

However different the detailed mechanisms may be, the net effect remains the same. Left to their own inclinations, organic life-forms will reproduce their kind in numbers exceeding the replacement rate. Over periods of time that are quite brief (by stellar standards) the resulting population increase can swiftly overburden the carrying capacity of any self-sustaining ecosystem. (SEE: AT-TACHED SORTED EXAMPLES.)

Species do this because each fecund individual is the direct descendant of a long chain of successful reproducers. Simply stated; those who lack traits that enable breeding do not become ancestors. Traits that encourage reproduction are the traits that get reproduced.

To the best of our knowledge, this evolutionary imperative extends even to the eco-matrix of hydrogen-based life-forms that shares real space in parallel with our oxygen-breathing civilization. As for the Third Order—autonomous machines—only the relentless application of stringent safeguards has prevented these nonorganic species from engaging in exponential reproduction, threatening the basis of all life in the Five Galaxies.

For the vast majority of nonsapient animal species in natural ecosystems, this tendency to overbreed is kept in check by starvation, predation, or other limiting factors, resulting in quasi-stable states of pseudo-equilibrium. However, presapient life-forms often use their newfound cleverness to eliminate competition and indulge in orgiastic breeding frenzies, followed by overutilization of resources. Left for too long without proper guidance, such species can bring about their own ruin through ecological collapse.

This is one of the Seven Reasons why naive life-forms cannot self-evolve to fully competent sapience. The Paradox of Reproductive Logic means that short-term self-interest will always prevail over long-range planning, unless wisdom is imposed from the outside by an adoptive patron line.

One duty of a patron is to make certain that its client race achieves conscious control over its self-replicating drives, before it can be granted adult status. And yet, despite such precautions, even fully ranked citizen species have been known to engage in breeding spasms, especially during intervals when lawful order temporarily breaks down. (SEE REF: "TIMES OF CHANGE.") Hasty, spasmodic episodes of colonization/exploitation have left entire galactic zones devastated in their wake.

By law, the prescribed punishment for races who perpetrate

such eco-holocausts can be complete extinction, down to the racial rootstock.

IN comparison, illegal resettlement of fallow worlds is a problem of moderate-level criminality. Penalties depend on the degree of damage done, and whether new presapient forms safely emerge from the process.

Nevertheless, it is easy to see how the Paradox of Reproductive Logic applies here, as well. Or else why would individuals and species sacrifice so much, and risk severe punishment, in order to dwell in feral secrecy on worlds where they do not belong?

OVER the course of tens of millions of years, only one solution has ever been found for this enduring paradox. This solution consists of the continuing application of pragmatic foresight in the interests of the common good.

In other words—civilization.

—from *A Galactographic Tutorial for Ignorant Wolfling Terrans,* a special publication of the Library Institute of the Five Galaxies, year 42 EC, in partial satisfaction of the debt obligation of 35 EC

Streakers

Kaa

THEY MADE LOVE IN A HIDDEN CAVE, NESTLED BE-
neath seaside cliffs, while tidal currents pounded nearby,
shooting spume fountains high enough to rival the
craggy promontories.

At last! Booming echoes seemed to shout each time a
wave dashed against the bluffs, as if everything leading up
to that moment had been prelude, a mere transport of momentum across the vast ocean, passed from one patch of
salt water to the next. As if a wave may only become real
by spending itself against stone.

Rolling echoes reverberated in the sheltered cave. *That's
me*, Kaa thought, listening to the breakers cry out their
brief reification. As a coast fulfills a tide, he now felt completed by contact with another.

Water sloshed through his open mouth, still throbbing
with their passion. The secret pool had her flavor.

Peepoe rolled along Kaa's side, stroking with her pectoral fins, making his skin tingle. He responded with a brush
of his tail flukes, pleased at how she quivered with un-

guarded bliss. This postcoital affection had even deeper meaning than the brief glory dance of mating. It was like the difference between mere need and choice.

> * Can the burning stars
> * Shout their joy more happily
> * Than this simple fin? *

His Trinary haiku came out as it should, almost involuntarily, not mulled or rehearsed by the frontal lobes that human gene crafters had so thoroughly palped and reworked during neo-dolphin uplift. The poem's clicks and squeals diffracted through the cave's grottoes at the same moment they first resonated in his skull.

Peepoe's reply emerged the same way, candidly languid, with a natural openness that brooked no lies.

> * Simplicity is not
> * Your best-known trait, dear Kaa.
> * Don't you feel Lucky? *

Her message both thrilled and validated, in a way she must have known he'd treasure. *I have my nickname back,* Kaa mused happily.

All would have been perfection then—a flawless moment—except that something else intruded on his pleasure. A tremor, faint and glimmering, like the sound shadow made by a moray eel, passing swiftly in the night, leaving fey shivers in its wake.

Yes, you have won back your name, whispered a faint voice, as if from a distant seaquake. Or an iceberg, groaning, a thousand miles away.

But to keep it, you will have to earn it.

When Kaa next checked the progress of his spy drone, it had nearly reached the top of the Mount Guenn funicular.

At the beginning, Peepoe's decision to stay with him had been more professional than personal, helping Kaa pilot the special probe up a hollow wooden monorail that climbed the rutted flank of an extinct volcano. While the bamboolike track was a marvel of aboriginal engineering, Kaa found it no simple matter guiding the little robot past sections filled with dirt or debris. He and Peepoe wound up having to camp in the cave, to monitor it round the clock, instead of returning to Brookida and the others. A fully autonomous unit could have managed the journey on its own, but Gillian Baskin had vetoed sending any machine ashore that might be smart enough to show up on Jophur detectors.

A moment of triumph came as the camera eye finally emerged from the rail, passed through a camouflaged station, then proceeded down halls of chiseled stone, trailing its slender fiber comm line like a hurried spider. Kaa had it crawl along the ceiling—the safest route, offering a good view of the native workshops.

Other observers tuned in at this point. From the *Streaker,* Hannes Suessi and his engineering chiefs remarked on the spacious chambers where urrish and qheuen smiths tapped ominous heat from lava pools, dipping ladles into nearby pits for melting, alloying, and casting. Most questions were answered by Ur-ronn, one of the four young guests whose presence on the *Streaker* posed such quandaries. Ur-ronn explained the forge in thickly accented Anglic, revealing tense reserve. Her service as guide was part of a risky bargain, with the details still being worked out.

"I do not see Uriel at the hearths." Ur-ronn's voice came tinnily from Kaa's receiver. *"Ferhafs she is ufstairs, in her hovvy roon."*

Uriel's hobby room. From the journal of Alvin Hphwayuo, Kaa envisioned an ornately useless toy gadget of sticks and spinning glass, something to hypnotize away the ennui of existence on a savage world. He found it puzzling that a leader of this menaced society would spare time for the arty Rube Goldberg contraption Alvin had described.

Ur-ronn told Kaa to send the probe down a long hall, past several mazelike turns, then through an open door into a dim chamber . . . where at last the fabled apparatus came into view.

Peepoe let out an amazed whistle.

> * *Advance description*
> * *Leaves the unwary stunned by*
> * *Serendipity!* *

Yeah, Kaa agreed, staring at a vaulted chamber that would have been impressive even on Earth, filled with crisscrossing timbers and sparkling lights. Alvin's account did the place injustice, never conveying the complex *unity* of all the whirling, spinning parts—for even at a glance one could tell that an underlying rhythm controlled it all. Each ripple and turn was linked to an elegant, ever-changing whole.

The scene was splendid, and ultimately baffling. Dim figures could be glimpsed moving about the scaffolding, making adjustments—several small, scurrying shapes and at least one bipedal silhouette that looked tentatively human. But Kaa could not even judge scale properly because most of the machine lay in deep shadows. Moreover, holovision had been designed to benefit creatures with two forward-facing eyes. A panel equipped with sono-parallax emitters would have better suited dolphins.

Even the normally wry Hannes Suessi was struck silent by this florid, twinkling palace of motion.

Finally, Ur-ronn cut in.

"I see Uriel! She is second fron the right, in that group standing near the chinfanzee."

Several four-footed urs nervously watched the machine whirl, next to a chimp with a sketchpad. Random light pulses dappled their flanks, resembling fauns in a forest, but Kaa could tell that gray-snouted Uriel must be older than the rest. As they watched, the chimp showed the smith an array of abstract curves, commenting on the results with hand signs instead of words.

"How we gonna do this, *Streaker?*" Kaa asked. "Just barge in and start t-talking?"

Until lately, it had seemed best for all concerned that *Streaker* keep her troubles separate. But now events made a meeting seem inevitable—even imperative.

"Let's listen before announcing ourselves," Gillian Baskin instructed. *"I'd rather conditions were more private."*

In other words, she preferred to contact *Uriel,* not a

whole crowd. Kaa sent the robot creeping forward. But before any urrish words became audible, another speaker interrupted from *Streaker*'s end.

"Allow me this indulgence," fluted the refined voice of the Niss Machine. *"Kaa, will you again focus the main camera on Uriel's contraption? I wish to pursue a conjecture."*

When Gillian did not object, Kaa had the probe look at the expanse of scaffolding a second time.

"Note the stretch of sand below," the Niss urged. *"Neat piles accumulate wherever light falls most frequently. These piles correlate with the drawings the chimpanzee just showed Uriel. . . ."*

Kaa's attention jerked away, caught by a slap of Peepoe's tail.

"Someone's c-coming. Peripheral scanner says approaching life signs are Jophur!"

Despite objections from the Niss, Kaa made the probe swivel around. There, framed in the doorway, they saw a silhouette *Streaker*'s crew had come to loathe—like a tapered cone of greasy doughnuts.

Gillian Baskin broke in. *"Calm down, everyone. . . . I'm sure it's just a traeki."*

"Of course it is," confirmed Ur-ronn. *"That stack is Tyug."*

Kaa recalled. This was the "chief alchemist" of Mount Guenn Forge. Uriel's master of chemical synthesis. Kaa brushed reassuringly against Peepoe, and felt her relax a bit. According to Alvin's journal, traeki were docile beings quite unlike their starfaring cousins.

So he was caught completely off guard when Tyug turned a row of jewel-like sensor patches *upward,* toward the tiny spy probe. Thoughtful curls of orange vapor steamed from its central vent. Then the topmost ring bulged outward . . .

. . . and abruptly spewed a jet of flying objects, swarming angrily toward the camera eye! Kaa and the others had time for a brief glimpse of *insects*—or some local equivalent—creating a confusing buzz of light and sound with their compound eyes and fast-beating wings. A horde of blurry creatures converged, surrounding Kaa's lenses and pickups.

Moments later, all that reached his console was a smear of dizzying static.

Gillian

A MAGNIFIED IMAGE FLOATED ABOVE THE CONFERence table—depicting a small creature, frozen in flight, whose wings were a rainbow-streaked haze, painful to the eye. By contrast, the Niss Machine's compact mesh of spiral lines seemed drab and abstruse. A strain of pique filled its voice.

"Might any of you local children be able to identify this bothersome thing for us?"

The words were polite enough, though Gillian winced at its insolent manner.

Fortunately, Alvin Hph-wayuo showed no awareness of being patronized. The young hoon sat near his friends, throbbing his throat sac in the subsonic range for both noor beasts, one lounging on each broad shoulder. To the machine's sardonic question, Alvin nodded amiably, a human gesture that seemed completely unaffected.

"Hrm. That's easy enough. It is a privacy wasp."

"Gene-altered toys of the Vuyur," lisped Ur-ronn. "A well-known nuisance."

Huck's four eyestalks waved, peering at the image. "Now I see how they got their name. They normally move so fast, I never got a good look before. It looks kind of like a tiny rewq, with the membranes turned into wings."

Hannes Suessi grunted, tapping the tabletop with his prosthetic left arm.

"Whatever the origins of these critters, it seems Uriel was armed against the possibility of being spied upon. Our probe's been rendered useless. Will she now assume that it was sent by the Jophur?"

Ur-ronn shrugged, an uncertain twist of her long neck.

"Who else? How would Uriel have heard of you guys . . .
unless the Jophur thenselves sfoke of you?"

Gillian agreed. "Then she may destroy the drone, unless
we make it speak Anglic words right away. Niss, can you
and Kaa get a message through?"

*"We are working to accomplish that. Commands rise
from the control console, but the bedlam given off by these
so-called wasps appears to swamp all bands, thwarting
confirmation. The probe may be effectively inoperable."*

"Damn. It would take days to send another. Days we
don't have." Gillian turned to Ur-ronn. "This might make
our promise hard to keep."

She hated saying it. Part of her had looked forward to
meeting the legendary smith of Mount Guenn. By all accounts, Uriel was an individual of shrewdness and insight,
whose sway on Jijoan society was notable.

"There is another off-shun," Ur-ronn suggested. "Fly
there in ferson."

"An option we must set aside for now," replied Lieutenant Tsh't. "Since any aircraft sent beyond these shielding
waters would be detected instantly, by the enemy battle-
ship-p."

The dolphin officer lay on the cushioned pad of a six-
legged walker. Her long, sleek body took up the end of the
conference room farthest from the sooner youths, her left
eye scanning the members of the ship's council. "Believe it
or not-t, and despite our disappointment over the·loss of
Kaa's probe, there are other agenda items left to cover."

Gillian understood the lieutenant's testy mood. Her report on the apparent suicide of the two human prisoners
had left many unanswered questions. Moreover, discipline
problems were also on the rise, with a growing faction of
the dolphin crew signing what they called the "Breeding
Petition."

Gillian had tried boosting morale by getting out and talking to the dolphins, listening to their concerns, encouraging them with a patron's touch. *Tom had the knack, like
Captain Creideiki. A joke here, a casual parable there.
Most fins grew more inspired and devoted the worse things
got.*

I don't have the same talent, I guess. Or else this poor crew is just tired after all the running.

Anyway, the best workers were all outside the ship now, in gangs that labored round the clock, while she spent hours closeted with the Niss Machine, eliminating one desperate plan after another.

At last, one of her schemes seemed a bit less awful than the rest.

"Tasty," the Niss had called it. *"Though a rash gamble. Our escape from Kithrup had more going for it than this ploy."*

Ship's Physician Makanee raised the next agenda item. Unlike Tsh't, the elderly dolphin surgeon did not like to ride around strapped to a machine. Naked, except for a small tool harness, she took part in the meeting from a clear tube that ran along one wall of the conference room. Makanee's body glistened with tiny bubbles from the oxygen-packed fluid that filled *Streaker*'s waterways.

"There is the matter of the Kiqui," she said. "It must be settled, especially if we are planning to move the ship-p."

Gillian nodded. "I'd hoped to consult about this matter with—" She glanced at the staticky display from Kaa's lost spy probe, and sighed. "A final decision must wait, Doctor. Continue preparations and I'll let you know."

Hannes Suessi next reported on the state of *Streaker*'s hull.

"Weighed down like this, she'll be as slow as when we carried around that hollowed-out Thennanin cruiser, wearing it like a suit of armor. *Slower,* with all the probability arrays gummed up by carbon gunk."

"So we must consider transferring to one of the wrecks outside?"

That would be hard. None had the modifications that made *Streaker* usable by an aquatic race.

The mirrored dome containing Suessi's brain and skull nodded.

"I have crews preparing the best of the drossed starships." A chuckle then escaped the helmet speaker vent. "Cheer up, everybody! With Ifni's luck, some of us may yet make it out of here."

Perhaps, Gillian thought. *But if we get away from the Jijo system, where will we go? Where else can we run?*

The meeting broke up. Everyone, including the sooner kids, had jobs to do.

And Dwer Koolhan will be waiting in my quarters, asking again for passage ashore. Or to swim, if necessary.

To go back to a savage place where he's needed.

Ambivalence filled her. Dwer was hardly more than a boy. Still, in all the years since *Streaker* was forced to abandon Tom on Kithrup, this was the first time she felt anything like physical attraction to another.

Naturally. I've always been a sucker for hero types.

It brought to mind the last time she had felt Tom's touch—one final night together on a metal island, set amid a poison sea. The night before he flew away on a solar-powered glider, determined to mislead great battle fleets, thwart mighty foes, and make an opening for *Streaker* to get away. Gillian's left thigh still tingled, from time to time . . . the site of his last loving squeeze as he lay prone on the flimsy little aircraft, grinning before taking off.

"I'll be back before you know it," Tom said—a metaphysically strange expression, when you thought about it. And she often had.

Then he was gone, winging north, barely skimming the waves, just above the contrary tides of Kithrup.

I should never have let him go. Sometimes you have to tell a hero that enough is enough.

Let someone else save the world.

As Gillian made ready to leave the conference room, she saw Alvin, the young hoon, trying to collect both noors. The female was his longtime pet, to all appearances a bright nonsapient being, probably derived from natural tytlal rootstock, dating from before their species' uplift. *The Tymbrimi must have stockpiled a gene pool of their beloved clients here on Jijo, as insurance in case the worst happened to their clan. A wise precaution, given the number of enemies they've made.*

As for the other one, Mudfoot, Dwer's bane and traveling companion across half a continent, scans of his brain showed uplift traces throughout.

A race hidden within a race, retaining all the traits the Tymbrimi worked hard to foster in their clients.

In other words, the tytlal were true sooners, another wave of illegal settlers, but guarded by added layers of camouflage. So disguised, they might even escape whatever ruin lay in store for the relatives of Alvin, Huck, Urronn, and Pincer.

But that can't be the whole story. Caution isn't a paramount trait in Tymbrimi, or their clients. They wouldn't go to so much trouble just to hide. Not unless it was part of something bigger.

Alvin had trouble gathering Mudfoot, who ignored the boy's umble calls while wandering across the conference table, poking a whiskered nose into debris from the meeting. Finally, the tytlal stood up on his hind legs to peer at the frozen projection last sent by Kaa's probe, the image of a privacy wasp. Mudfoot purred with curiosity.

"Niss," Gillian said in a low voice.

With an audible pop, the pattern of whirling, shifting lines came into being nearby.

"Yes, Dr. Baskin? Have you changed your mind about hearing my tentative conjectures about Uriel's intricate device of spinning disks?"

"Later," she said, and gestured at Mudfoot. Gillian now realized the tytlal was peering *past* the blurry display of the privacy wasp, at something in the scene beyond.

"I'd like you to do some enhancements. Find out what that little devil is looking at."

She did not add that she had detected something on her own. Something only a psi-sensitive would notice. For the second time, a faint *presence* could be felt—vague and ephemeral—floating ever so briefly above Mudfoot's agitated cranial spines. She could not be sure, but whatever it was had a distinctly familiar flavor.

Call it Essence of Tymbrimi.

Kaa

THERE WAS NO MORE TO ACCOMPLISH IN THE CAVE. The probe appeared to be dead.

Even if it came back to life, any conversation with the natives would be handled from *Streaker*'s end. Meanwhile, it was past time to return to the habitat. Kaa had a team he had not seen in days.

A human couple might have paused before exiting the little grotto, looking around to imprint the site of their first lovemaking. But not dolphins. Neo-fins experienced nostalgia, just like their human patrons, but they could store sonar place images in ways humans had to mimic with recording devices. Streaking outside, joining Peepoe under bright sunshine, Kaa knew the two of them could revisit the cave anytime they chose, simply by bringing their arched foreheads together—re-creating its unique echoes in that ancient gulf of memory some called the Whale Dream.

It felt good to dash across the wide sea again, with Peepoe's lithe body sharing every kick and leap in perfect unison. Motion equaled joy after any long confinement to machinery and closed spaces.

On the outward trip, their swim had been exquisite, but tempered by a taut, sexual tension. Now there were no secrets, no conflicting desires. Most of the return journey was spent in silent bliss—like a simple mated pair from presapient days, free of the gifts and burdens of uplift.

Finally, with the habitat drawing near, Kaa felt his mind slip reluctantly back into Anglic-using rhythms. Compelled to speak, he used the informal click-squeal dialect fins preferred while swimming.

"Well, here it comes," he sonar-cast during the underwater phase of their next splash-and-surge cycle. "Back to home and family . . . such as they are."

"Family?" she replied skeptically. "Brookida, perhaps. As for Mopol and Zhaki, wouldn't you rather be related to a penguin?"

Is my opinion of them so obvious? After breaching for air, Kaa tried making light of things with a joke.

"Oh, I give those two some credit. With luck, they won't have set the ocean on fire while we're gone."

Peepoe laughed, then added, "Do you think they'll be jealous?"

Good question. Dolphins could not conceal interpersonal matters like humans, with their complex games of emotional deceit. By sonar-scanning each other's viscera, one seldom had to guess who slept with whom.

Envy wouldn't be a problem if I established clear authority from the start, both as an officer and as senior-ranking male.

Unfortunately, chain of command was a recent, human-imposed concept. Underneath, bull dolphins still felt ancient drives to jostle over status and breeding rights.

In fact, Peepoe's choice might reinforce Kaa's position atop the little local hierarchy. *Though I shouldn't need help. Not if I were a real leader.*

"Jealous." He pondered, thrusting harder with his flukes, till his beak pushed their shared shock wave, drawing her along in his wake. "Those two are highly sexed, so maybe they will be. But at least this way Zhaki and Mopol should stop bothering you with hopeless propositions."

The young males had made relentless crude suggestions toward Peepoe from the first day she arrived, even brushing lewdly against her until Kaa had to rebuke them. While it was true that dolphins had a far different scale of tolerance for such behavior than humans—and Peepoe was capable of taking care of herself—in this case the pair were so persistent that Kaa had to dish out tail whacks to make them back off.

"Hopeless?" Peepoe asked in a teasing tone. "Now you're making assumptions. How do you know I'm monogamous? Maybe a little harem would suit me fine."

Kaa spread his jaws and aimed a nip at her nearest pectoral fin . . . slow enough for her to slip aside, laughing, before his teeth snapped.

"Good," she commented. "Pacific Tursiops go in for that kinky stuff. But I prefer a nice and conservative Atlantean.

You're from Miami-Under, no? Born into an old-fashioned line marriage, I bet."

Kaa grunted. Even the sonar-based dialect of Anglic wasn't easy while speeding at full throttle.

"One of the Heinlein family variants," he conceded. "The style works better for dolphins than humans. Why? You looking for a line to marry into?"

"Mnn. I'd rather start a *new* one. Always hankered to be the founding matriarch of a nice little lineage—if the masters of uplift allow it."

That was the eternal Big If. No neo-dolphin could legally breed without permission from the Terragens Uplift Board. Despite the unusual freedoms humans had given their clients—voting rights and the trappings of citizenship—Earthclan was still bound by ancient Galactic law.

Improve your clients, went the basic code of uplift. . . . *Or lose them.*

"You gotta be kidding," he answered. "If any of us *Streaker* fins ever do make it home somehow from this crazed voyage, we'll never face another sapiency exam from the masters. We may be sterilized on the spot, for all the trouble we caused. Or else we're heroes, and it'll be sperm-and-seed donations for the rest of our lives, fostering almost the whole next neo-fin generation.

"Either way, it won't be cozy family life for any of us. Not ever."

He hadn't expected it to come out that way, with an edge of ironic bitterness. But Peepoe must have seen he was telling the truth. She continued keeping pace alongside, but her silence told Kaa how much it stung.

Great. Everything felt so fine . . . this wonderful water, the fish we snatched for breakfast, our lovemaking. Would it have hurt to let her stay in denial for a while, dreaming of happy endings? Holding on to the fantasy that we might yet go home, and lead normal lives?

"Kaa!" Brookida's cry made the tiny habitat reverberate. "I'm glad you're back. Did your mission go well? Wait till you hear what I discovered by correlating passive seismic echo scans from here to *Streaker*'s sssite. I fed the raw data into one of Charles Dart's old programs to get tomography images of the subcrustal zone!"

All that, on a single breath. It was what humans would call a "mouthful."

"That's great, Brookida. But to answer your question, our mission didn't go as well as we hoped. In fact, we have orders to pack everything up and break camp. Gillian and Tsh't plan to move the ship."

Brookida shook his mottled gray head. "Won't that risk giving away *Streaker's* position?"

"The site's already compromised. Dr. Baskin suspects the Jophur may be p-preoccupied, but that can't last."

It had been Kaa's mission to find out what the sooners knew about such things. Perhaps Uriel the Smith had some idea what the Jophur were up to. No one had blamed Kaa for the failure—not out loud. But he knew the ship's council was disappointed.

I warned them to send someone better trained at spying.

He looked around. "Where are the others?"

Brookida let out a warbled sigh.

"Off joyriding on Peepoe's sled. Or else vandalizing the fishing nets of local hoons and qheuens."

Damn! Kaa cursed. He had ordered Zhaki and Mopol to stay within a kilometer of the dome, and restrict themselves to monitoring spy eyes already in place at Wuphon Port. Above all, they were supposed to avoid direct contact with the sooners.

"They got bored," Brookida explained. "Now that *Streaker* has Alvin and other local experts aboard, our team is a bit redundant. It's why I've been tracing the subduction-zone magma flows. My first chance since Kithrup to test out an idea I had, based on Charles Dart's old research. You recall those strange beings who lived deep under Kithrup's crust? The ones with the weird, unpronounceable species name?"

Peepoe spoke up. "You mean the *Karrank-k%*?"

She did a creditable job of expressing the double-aspirated slide tone at the end, sounding like a steam kettle about to explode.

"Yes, quite. Well, I'd been wondering what kind of

ecosystem could support them down there. And it got me thinking . . ."

Brookida halted. Then all three dolphins whirled around as the wall segment behind them began emitting a low, scraping hum. The grating vibration hurt Kaa's jaw.

Soon, the entire habitat groaned to a rasping sonic frequency Kaa recognized.

It's a saser! Someone's attacking the dome!

"Harnesses!"

At his shouted command, they all dived toward the rack where heavy-duty tool kits were hung, ready for use. Kaa streaked through the open end of his well-worn apparatus, and felt its many control surfaces slide smoothly into place. A control cable snaked toward the neural tap behind his left eye. Robotic arms whirred as he jerked the harness free of its rack. Peepoe's unit popped loose just half an instant later.

A rough rectangle crept across the opposite wall, above and below the waterline, glowing hot.

"They're cutting through!" Peepoe cried.

"Breathers!" Kaa shouted. From the back of his harness, a hose swarmed over his blowhole, covering it with a moist kiss and tight seal. A blast of canned air tasted even more tinny than the recycled stuff within the dome. Kaa sent a neural command activating his torch cutter and saser, tools that could second as weapons in close combat. . . .

But they didn't respond!

"Peepoe!" He shouted. "Check your—"

"I'm helping Brookida!" she cut in. "His harness is stuck!"

Kaa slashed the water with his flukes, squealing a cry of frustration. With no better options, he interposed his body between theirs and the far wall . . .

. . . which abruptly collapsed in a wave of pummeling froth.

Gillian

I HAVE DISCOVERED SEVERAL THINGS OF INTEREST," the Niss Machine told Gillian, after she wakened from a brief induced sleep. *"The first has to do with that wonderfully ostentatious native machine, built and operated by the urrish tinkerer, Uriel."*

Sitting in her darkened office, she watched a recorded holo image of wheels, pulleys, and disks, whirling in a flamboyant show of light and action. Not far from Gillian, the ancient cadaver, *Herbie,* seemed to regard the same scene. A trick of shadows made the enigmatic, mummified face seem amused.

"Let me guess. Uriel created a computer."

The Niss reacted with surprise. Its spiral of meshed lines tightened to a knot.

"You knew?"

"I suspected. From the kids' reports, Uriel wouldn't waste time on anything useless or abstract. She'd want to give her folk something special. The one thing her founding ancestors absolutely had to throw away."

"Possession of computers. Good point, Dr. Baskin. Uriel could aim no higher than to be like Prometheus. Bringing her people the fire of calculation."

"But without digital cognizance," she pointed out. "An undetectable computer."

"Indeed. I found no reference to such a thing in our captured Galactic Library unit. So I turned to the precontact 2198 edition of the Encyclopedia Britannica. *There I learned about analog computation with mechanical components, which actually had a brief ascendancy on Earth, using many of the same techniques we see in Uriel's hall of spinning glass!"*

"I remember hearing about this. Maybe Tom mentioned it."

"Did he also mention that the same thing can be achieved using simple electronic circuits? Networks of resistors, capacitors, and diodes can simulate a variety of

equations. By interconnecting such units, solutions can be worked out for limited problems.

"It provokes one to consider the military potential of such a system. For instance, operating sneak-attack weapons without digital controls, using undetectable guidance systems."

The Niss holo performed a twist that Gillian interpreted as a shrug.

"But then, if the notion were feasible, it would have found its way into the Library by now."

There it was again. Even Tymbrimi suffered from the same all-pervading supposition—that anything worth doing must have been done already, over the course of two billion years. The assumption nearly always proved *true*. Still, wolfling humans resented it.

"So," Gillian prompted. "Have you figured out what Uriel is trying to compute?"

"Ah, yes." The line motif spun contemplatively.

"That is, perhaps.

"Or rather . . . no, I have not."

"What's the problem?"

The Niss showed spiky irritation.

"My difficulty is that all the algorithms used by Uriel are of Terran origin."

Gillian nodded.

"Naturally. Her math books came from the so-called Great Printing, when human learning flooded this world, most of it in the form of pre-contact texts. A mirror image of what Galactic society did to Earth. On Jijo, *we* were the ones to unleash an overpowering wealth of knowledge, engulfing prior beliefs."

Hence also Gillian's recent, weird experience—debating the literary merits of Jules Verne with a pair of distinctly unhuman youngsters named "Alvin" and "Huck," whose personalities had little in common with the stodgy Galactic norm.

The Niss agreed, bowing its tornado of laced lines.

"You grasp my difficulty, Doctor. Despite Tymbrimi sympathy toward Earthlings, my makers were uplifted as Galactic citizens, with a shared tradition. While details of my

programming are exceptional, I was designed according to proven principles, after eons of Galactic experience refining digital computers. These precepts clash with Terran superstitions—"

Gillian coughed behind her hand. The Niss bowed.

"Forgive. I meant to say, Terran lore."

"Can you give an example?"

"I can. Consider the contrast between the word/concepts discrete *and* continuous.

"According to Galactic science, anything and everything can be accomplished by using arithmetic. By counting and dividing, using integers and rational fractions. Sophisticated arithmetic algorithms enable us to understand the behavior of a star, for instance, by partitioning it into ever-smaller pieces, modeling those pieces in a simple fashion, then recombining the parts. That is the digital way."

"It must call for vast amounts of memory and raw computing power."

"True, but these are cheaply provided, enough for any task you might require.

"Now look back at pre-contact human wolflings. Your race spent many centuries as semicivilized beings, mentally ready to ask sophisticated questions, but completely lacking access to transistors, quantum switches, or binary processing. Until your great savants, Turing and Von Neumann, finally expressed the power of digital computers, generations of mathematicians had to cope by using pencil and paper.

"The result? A mix of the brilliant and the inane. Abstract differential analysis and cabalistic numerology. Algebra, astrology, and geometrical topology. Much of this amalgam was based on patently absurd concepts, such as continuity, *or aptly named* irrational numbering, *or the astonishing notion that there are layered infinities of the divisibly small."*

Gillian sighed an old frustration.

"Earth's best minds tried to explain our math, soon after contact. Again and again we showed it was self-consistent. That it worked."

"Yet it accomplished nothing that could not be out-matched in moments by calculating engines like myself. Galactic seers dismissed all the clever equations as trickery and shortcuts, or else the abstract ravings of savages."

She acceded with a nod.

"This happened once before, you know. In Earth's twentieth century, after the Second World War, the victors quickly split into opposing camps. Those experts you mentioned—Turing and von Whoever—they worked in the west, helping set off our own digital revolution.

"Meanwhile, the east was ruled by a single dictator, I think his name was Steel."

"Accessing the Britannica . . . *You mean 'Stalin'? Yes, I see the connection. Until his death, Stalin obstructed Russo-Soviet science for ideological reasons. He banished work on genetics because it contradicted notions of communist perfectibility. Moreover, he quashed work on computers, calling them 'decadent.' Even after his passing, many in the east held that calculation was crude, inelegant . . . only good for quick approximations. For truth, one needed pure mathematics."*

"So that's why many practitioners in the Old Math still come from Russia." Gillian chuckled. "It sounds like yet another inverted image of what happened to Earth, after contact."

The Niss pondered this for a moment.

"What are you implying, Doctor? That Stalin was partly right? That you Terrans were right? That you were onto something the rest of the universe has missed?"

"It seems unlikely, eh? And yet, isn't that slim possibility the very reason why your makers assigned you to this ship?"

Again, the meshed lines whirled.

"Point well taken, Dr. Baskin."

Gillian stood up to start moving her body through a series of stretching exercises. The brief sleep period had helped. Still, there were a hundred problems to address.

"Look," she asked the Niss Machine. "Is there some point where all this is heading? Haven't you a clue what problem Uriel is trying to solve?"

She gestured toward the recorded image of pulleys, leather straps, and spinning disks.

"In a word, Doctor? No.

"Oh, I can tell that Uriel is modeling a set of simultaneous differential equations—to use old wolfling terminology. The range of numerical values being considered appears to be simple, even trivial. I could outcalculate her so-called computer with a mere one quadrillionth of my processing power."

"Then why don't you?"

"Because to me the problem first calls for unlocking the code of a lost language. I need an opening, a Rosetta stone, after which all should be instantly clear.

"In short, I need help from an Earthling, to suggest what the expressions might be for."

Gillian shrugged.

"Another tough break, then. We've plumb run out of mathematicians aboard this crate. Creideiki and Tom both used to play with the Old Math. I know Charles Dart dabbled, and Takkata-Jim. . . ."

She sighed.

"And Emerson D'Anite. He was the last one who could have helped you."

Gillian moved toward her reference console. "I suppose we can scan the personnel files to see if there's anyone else—"

"That may not be necessary," the Niss cut in. *"It might be possible to access one of the experts you already mentioned."*

Gillian blinked, unable to believe she heard right.

"What are you talking about?"

"You assigned me another problem—to find out what the feral-sapient tytlal named 'Mudfoot' was staring at, after the council meeting. To achieve that, I enhanced the spy camera's last scene, before the privacy wasps closed in.

"Please watch carefully, Doctor."

The big display now showed the final clear picture sent by the lost probe. Gillian found it physically painful to watch the insect's beating wings, and felt relief when the Niss zoomed toward a corner of the field, pushing the privacy wasp off-screen. What ballooned outward was a section of the ornate contraption of Uriel the Smith—a marvel of pure ingenuity and resourcefulness.

I did take one course in the Old Math, before heading to medical school. I could try to help. The Niss can supply pre-contact texts. All it wants is insight. Some wolfling intuition . . .

Her thoughts veered, distracted by the vivid enhancement. Looming around her now was a maze of improvised scaffolding, filled with shadows that were split; here and there, by glaring points of light.

All this incredible activity must add up to something important.

Gillian saw the apparent goal sought by the Niss—a set of shadows that had the soft curves of life-forms, precariously balanced in the crisscrossing trusswork. Some figures were small, with snakelike torsos and tiny legs, brandishing tools with slim, many-jointed hands.

Miniature urs, she realized. *The maintenance crew?*

A larger silhouette loomed over these. Gillian gasped when she saw it must be human! Then she recalled.

Of course. Humans are among Uriel's allies, and skilled technicians. They're also good climbers, perfect to help keep things running.

The Niss must now be straining its ability to enhance the grainy image. The rate of magnification slowed, and remaining shadows peeled grudgingly before the onslaught of computing power. But soon she knew the human was male, from the shape of neck and shoulders. He was pointing, perhaps indicating a task for the little urs to perform.

Gillian saw that he had long hair, brushed left over a cruel scar. For an instant she stared at the puckered wound in his temple.

A moment later, the image clarified to show a *smile*.

Recognition hit like a blast of chill water.

"My God . . . It can't be!"

The Niss crooned, expressing both satisfaction and intrigue.

"You confirm the resemblance?

"It does appear to be engineer Emerson D'Anite.

"Our crew mate whom we thought killed by the Old Ones, back at the Fractal System.

"He whose scout vessel was enveloped by a globe of devouring light, as the Streaker *made its getaway, fleeing by a circuitous route toward Jijo."*

The Tymbrimi machine shared one trait with its makers, a deep love of surprise. That pleasure it now expressed in a hum of satisfaction.

"You ask frequently how anyone could have followed us to this forlorn corner of the universe, Dr. Baskin.

"I believe the question just acquired new levels of cogency."

Kaa

HE NEVER GOT TO PUT UP MUCH OF A FIGHT.

How could he, with all his weapons sabotaged from the start? Besides, Kaa wasn't sure he could bring himself to harm one of his own kind.

Clearly, the assailants who attacked the dome had fewer scruples.

The ruined habitat lay far below, its pieces strewn across the continental shelf. Along with Peepoe and Brookida, Kaa barely dodged being pinned by the collapsing walls, escaping the maelstrom of metal and froth only to face the gun barrels of well-armed captors. Herded to the surface, he and the others panted in nervous exhaustion under the waning afternoon sun.

In contrast, Mopol's sleek form rested almost languidly atop the speed sled that Peepoe had brought from *Streaker*'s hiding place, governing the engines and armaments with impulses sent down his neural tap. Swimming nearby—wearing a fully charged tool harness—Zhaki explained the situation.

"It's like this, p-pilot-t. . . ." He slurred the words in his eagerness. "The three of you are gonna do what we sssay, or else."

Kaa tossed his head, using his lower jaw to splash water at Zhaki's eye.

> * Silly threats from one
> * Who's watched too many movies!
> * Just say it, fool. Now! *

Mopol hissed angrily, but Peepoe laughed at Zhaki's predicament. To continue his menacing speech now would be an act of obedience to Kaa's command. It was a minor matter—not exactly a logical checkmate. But Kaa felt it valuable to recover even a little initiative.

"We . . ." Zhaki blew air and tried again. "Mopol and I are resigning from the *Streaker* crew. We're not going back-k, and you can't make us."

So that's what it's about, Kaa thought.

"Desertion!" Brookida sputtered indignantly. "Letting your crew mates down when they need you mossst!"

Mopol let out a skirl of rejection.

"Our legal term of ssservice ended almossst two years ago."

"Right-t," Zhaki agreed. "Anyway, we never signed on for this insanity . . . fleeing like wounded mullet across the galaxies."

"You plan to go *sooner,*" Peepoe fluted, her voice bemused. "Living wild, in this sea."

Mopol nodded. "Some were already talkin' about it, before we left-t the ship. This world's a paradise for our kind. The whole crew oughta do it!"

"But even if they don't-t," Zhaki added, "we're gonna."

Then he added a haiku for emphasis.

> * Six or seven clans
> * Did this already, on shore.
> * We have precedent! *

Kaa realized there was nothing he could do to change their minds. The sea would answer his best arguments with its fine mineral smoothness and the enticing echoes of tasty fish. In time, the deserters would come to miss the comforts of civilized life, or grow bored, or realize there are dangers even on a world without big predators. The water had a faint, prescient choppiness, and Kaa wondered if either of the rebel fins had ever been outside during a truly vicious storm.

But then, hadn't other waves of settlers faced the same choice? The g'Keks, qheuens, and even human beings?

"The Jophur may make it hard on you," he told them.

"We'll take our chancess."

"And if you're caught by the Institutes?" Brookida asked. "Your presence here would be a crime, reflecting badly on—"

Mopol and Zhaki laughed. Even Kaa found that argument easy to dismiss. Humans and chimps were already on Jijo. If Earthclan suffered collective punishment for that crime, a few dolphins living offshore could hardly make things worse.

"So, what do you plan to do with us?" Kaa asked.

"Why, nothing much-ch. You and Brookida are free to swim back to your precious Gillian Basssskin, if you like."

"That could take a week!" Brookida complained. But Kaa struggled against involuntary spasms in his harness arms, set off by Zhaki's implication. Before he could unstrangle his speech centers, Peepoe expressed his dread.

"Jusssst Kaa and Brookida? You're insisting that I stay?"

Mopol chittered assent with such glee that it came out sounding more like gutter Primal Delphin than Trinary.

"That's the p-plan," Zhaki confirmed. "We'd make a poor excuse for a c-colony without at least one female."

Kaa abruptly saw their long-term scheme. Mopol's spell of malingering sickness had been meant to draw one of Makanee's nurses out here from the ship. Most were young females, with Peepoe the best catch of all.

"Will you add kidnap-ping to the crime of desertion?" she asked, sounding as fascinated as fearful.

Kaa's blood surged hot as Zhaki flipped around to streak past Peepoe, gliding along her belly, upside down.

"You won't call it that-t after a while," Zhaki promised, leaving a trail of bubbles as he rolled suggestively. "In time, you'll c-call this your luckiessst day."

At that point, Kaa reached the limit of his endurance. With a lashing of flukes, he charged—

• • •

There was a blank time after that . . . and some more that went by all in a haze—half-numb and half-pained.

Drifting, Kaa was sustained by instinct as his body performed the needed motions. Staying upright. Kicking to bring his blowhole above the watery surface. Breathing. Submerging once again. Allowing his unraveled self to knit slowly back together.

"C-come on now, my boy," the helper told him. "It'sss only a bit farther."

Dutifully, Kaa swam alongside, doing as he was told. You learned this at an early age . . . when injured, always obey the helper. It might be your mother, or an auntie, or even some older male in the pod. Someone always was the helper . . . or else the sea would claim you.

In time, he recalled this helper's name—*Brookida*. He also began recognizing the peculiar lap and texture of littoral water, not far from shore. Kaa even recalled part of what put him in this condition . . . a state so dazed that all speech thoughts were driven from his mind.

There had been a fight. He had charged against harsh odds, hoping to take his enemies by surprise . . . by the sheer audacity of the attack.

It took just one blast of concentrated sound to knock him in a double flip, with tremors shaking every muscle. Paralyzed, he distantly sensed the two male foes move off . . . taking his love with them.

"You feeling better now?" Brookida asked. The older dolphin cast a sonar sweep through Kaa's innards, checking on his progress. Some mental clouds were parting. Enough to recall a few more facts. The shattered habitat—not worth revisiting. The hopelessness of pursuing a speed sled, even one burdened with three passengers, since night was soon approaching.

Both arms of his harness twitched as his rattled brain sent spasmodic commands down the neural link. Kaa managed to lift his head a bit, the next time he breathed, and recognized the shape of nearby coastal hills. Brookida was herding him closer to the native fishing town.

"Mopol and Zhaki wrecked the cables and transmittersss, back at the dome. But-t I figure we can find the lines leading to the spy drones in Wuphon Port, tap into those, and contact the ship-p."

Some order was slipping into Kaa's chaotic thoughts. Enough to comprehend a bit of what the old fin said. This return of sapiency left him with mixed feelings—relieved that the loss was not permanent, plus regretful longing for the simplicity that must now go away, replaced by urgent, hopeless needs.

Trinary came back more easily than Anglic.

> * We must pursue the—
>   * Spawn of syphilitic worms,
>   * While their sound spoor's fresh! *

"Yes, of course. I agree. How awful for Peepoe, poor lass. But first let's contact *Streaker*. Maybe our crew mates can help."

Kaa hearkened to the sense in that. One of the first principles of human legality that dolphins clearly understood was that of a *posse,* which had analogies in natural cetacean society. When an offense is committed against the pod, you can call for help. You should not face trouble alone.

He let Brookida lead him to the site where fiber cables from the onshore spy eyes all converged below. Booming surf reminded Kaa unhappily of this morning's lovemaking. The sound made him squeal a Primal protest, railing against the unfairness of it all. To find a mate and lose her on the same day.

The water tasted of qheuens and hoons . . . plus wooden planks and tar. Kaa rested at the surface, sifting his mind back together while Brookida dived down to establish the link.

A saser . . . Zhaki shot me with a saser beam.

Dimly he realized that Zhaki might have saved his life. If that bolt hadn't stopped him, Mopol would surely have fired next, using the more powerful unit on the sled.

But saved me . . . for what?

Ifni tell me . . . what's the point?

Kaa didn't figure he still had his nickname anymore.

A few hours . . . now it's gone again. She took it with her.

Brookida surfaced next to him, sputtering elation, having achieved quick success.

"Got it-t! Come on, Kaa. I've got Gillian on the line. She wants to talk to you."

Sometimes life is filled with choices. You get to select which current to ride, which tide to pull your destiny.

Other times leave you torn . . . wrenched apart . . . as if two orcas had a grip on you, one biting hard on your flukes while the other plays tug-of-war with your snout.

Kaa heard the order. He understood it.

He wasn't at all sure he could obey.

"I'm sorry about Peepoe," Gillian Baskin said, her voice crackling over the makeshift comm line, conveyed directly to Kaa's auditory nerves. *"We'll rescue her, and deal with the deserters, when opportunity permits. Believe me, it's a high priority.*

"But this other task is crucial. Our lives may depend on it, Kaa."

The human paused.

"I want you to head straight into Wuphon Harbor.

"It's time one of us went to town."

Sooners

Ewasx

MY RINGS, IT HAS FINALLY HAPPENED.
Rejoice! Your master torus has ultimately managed to
recover some of the fatty memories you/we/I had
thought forever lost! Those valuable recall tracks that were
erased when brave-foolish Asx melted the wax!

That act of wrong loyalty stymied the usefulness of this
hybrid ring stack for much too long. Some of the *Polkjhy*
crew called us/Me a failed experiment. Even the Captain-
Leader questioned this effort . . . this attempt to convert a
wild traeki into our loyal authority on Jijoan affairs.

Admittedly, our/My expertise about the Six Races has
been uneven and fitful. Mistakes were made despite/
because of our advice.

BUT NOW I/WE HAVE REACQUIRED THIS SECRET!
This conviction that once filled the mulch center of the
diffuse being called *Asx*.

Deep beneath the melted layers, a few memory tracks
remained.

DO NOT SQUIRM SO! Instead you should exult in this recovery of something so important.

The Egg.

So far, we have seen only insolence from the sooner races—delays and grudging cooperation with the survey teams we send forth.

No voluntary gathering of g'Kek vermin at designated collection points.

No migration of traeki stacks for appraisal-and-conversion.

Swarms of supervised robots have begun sifting the countryside for groups of g'Kek and traeki, herding them toward enclosures where their numbers can be concentrated at higher density. But this task proves laborious and inefficient. It would be far more convenient if the locals were persuaded to perform the task on their own.

Worse, these fallen beings still refuse to admit any knowledge of the Earthling prey ship.

IT PROVES DIFFICULT TO COERCE GREATER COOPERATION.

Attacks on population centers are met with resignation and dispersal.

Their dour religion confounds us with stoic passivity. It is hard to deprive hope from a folk that never had much.

BUT NOW WE HAVE A NEW TARGET!

One more meaningful to the Six Races than any of their campsite villages. A target to convince them of our ruthless resolve.

We already knew something of this *Great Egg*. Its throbbing radiations were an irritant, disrupting our instruments, but we dismissed it as a geophysical anomaly. Psi-resonant formations exist on some worlds. Despite local mythology, our onboard Library cube can cite other cases. A rare phenomenon, but understood.

Only now we realize how deeply this stone is rooted in

the savages' religion. It is their central object of reverence. Their "soul."

How amusing.
How pathetic.
And how very convenient.

Vubben

THE LAST TIME HIS AGED WHEELS HAD ROLLED along this dusty trail, it was in the company of twelve twelves of white-robed pilgrims—the finest eyes, minds, and rings of all six races—winding their way past sheer cliffs and steam vents in a sacred quest to seek guidance from the Holy Egg. For a time, that hopeful procession had made the canyon walls reverberate with fellowship vibrations—the Commons united and at peace.

Alas, before reaching its goal, the company fell into a maelstrom of fire, bloodshed, and despair. Soon the sages and their followers were too busy with survival to spend time meditating on the ineffable. But during the weeks since, Vubben could never shake a sense of unfinished business. Of something vital, left undone.

Hence this solitary return journey, even though it brought his frail wheels all too near the Jophur foe ship. Vubben's axles and motive spindles throbbed from the cruel climb, and he longingly recalled that a brave qheuen had volunteered to carry him all the way here, riding in comfort on a broad gray back.

But he could not accept. Despite creakiness and age, Vubben had to come alone.

At last he reached the final turn before entering the Nest. Vubben paused to catch his breath and smooth his ruffled thoughts in preparation for the trial ahead. He used a soft rag to wipe green sweat off all four eye hoods and stalks.

It is said that g'Kek bodies could never have evolved on a planet. Our wheels and whiplike limbs better suit the artifi-

cial worlds where our star-god ancestors dwelled, before they gambled a great-wager, won their bet, and lost everything.

He often wondered what it must have been like to abide in some vast spinning city whose inner space was spanned by countless slender roadways that arched like ribbons of spun sugar. *Intelligent* paths that would twist, gyre, and reconnect at your command, so the way between any two points could be just as straight or deliciously curved as you liked. To live where a planet's grip did not press you relentlessly, every dura from birth till death, squashing your rims and wearing away your bearings with harsh grit.

More than any other sooner race, the g'Kek had to work hard in order to love Jijo. *Our refuge. Our purgatory.*

Vubben's eyestalks contracted involuntarily as the Egg once again made its presence known. A surge of *tywush* vibrations seemed to rise from the ground. The sporadic patterning tremors had grown more intense, the nearer he came to the source. Now Vubben shivered as another wave front stroked his tense spokes, making his brain resound in its hard case. Words could not express the sensation, even in Galactic Two or Three. The psi-effect provoked no images or dramatic emotions. Rather, a feeling of *expectation* seemed to build, slowly but steadily, as if some long-awaited plan were coming to fruition at long last.

The episode peaked . . . then passed quickly away, still lacking the coherence he hoped for.

Then let us begin in earnest, Vubben thought. His motor spindles throbbed, helped along by slender pusher legs, as both wheels turned away from the sunset's dimming glow, toward mystery.

The Egg loomed above, a rounded shelf of stone that stretched ahead for half an arrowflight before curving out of sight. Although a century of pilgrimages had worn a trail of packed pumice, it still took almost a midura for Vubben to roll his first circuit around the base of the ovoid, whose mass pressed a deep basin in the flank of a dormant volcano. Along the way, he raised slender arms and eyestalks, lofting them in gentle benediction, supplementing his mental entreaty with the language of motion.

Help your people. . . . Vubben urged, seeking to atune his thoughts, harmonizing them with the cyclical vibrations.

Rise up. Waken. Intervene to save us. . . .

Normally, an effort at communion involved more than one suppliant. Vubben would have merged his contribution with a hoon's patience, the tenacity of a qheuen, a traeki's selfless affinity, plus that voracious will to know that made the best urs and humans seem so much alike. But such a large group might be detected moving about close to the Jophur. Anyway, he could not ask others to risk being caught in the company of a g'Kek.

With each pass around the Egg, he sent one eye wafting up to peer at Mount Ingul, whose spire was visible beyond the crater's rim. There, Phwhoon-dau had promised to station a semaphore crew to alert Vubben in case of any approaching threat—or if there were changes in the tense standoff with the aliens. So far, no warnings were seen flashing from that western peak.

But he faced other distractions, just as disturbing to his train of thought.

Loocen hovered in the same western quarter of the sky, with a curve of bright pinpoints shining along the moon's crescent-shaped terminator, dividing sunlit and shadowed faces. Tradition said those lights were domed cities. The departing Buyur left them intact, since Loocen had no native ecosystem to recycle and restore. Time would barely touch them until this fallow galaxy and its myriad star systems were awarded to new legal tenants, and the spiral arms once more teemed with commerce.

How those lunar cities must have tempted the first g'Kek exiles, fleeing here from their abandoned space habitats, just a few sneak jumps ahead of baying lynch mobs. Feeling safe at last, after passing through the storms of Izmunuti, those domes would have enticed them with reminders of home. A promise of low gravity and clean, smooth surfaces.

But such places offered no reliable, long-term shelter

against relentless enemies. A planet's surface was better for
fugitives, with a life-support system that needed no computer regulation. A natural world's complex *messiness*
made it a fine place to hide, if you were willing to live as
primitives, scratching a subsistence like animals.

In fact, Vubben had few clues of what passed through
the original colonists' minds. The Sacred Scrolls were the
only written records from that time, and they mostly ignored the past, preaching instead how to live in harmony
on Jijo, and promising salvation to those following the Path
of Redemption.

Vubben was renowned for skill at reciting those hal-
lowed texts. *But in truth, we sages stopped relying on the
scrolls a century ago.*

He resumed the solitary pilgrimage, commencing his
fourth circuit just as another *tywush* wave commenced.
Vubben now felt certain the cycles were growing more
coherent. Yet there was also a feeling that much more
power lay quiescent, far below the surface—power he desperately needed to tap.

Hoon and qheuen grandparents passed on testimony
that the patterns were more potent in the last days of
Drake the Younger, when the Egg was still warm with birth
heat, fresh from Jijo's womb. Compelling dreams used to
flood all six races back then, convincing all but the most
conservative that a true revelation had come.

Politics also played a role in the great orb's acceptance.
Drake and Ur-Chown made eager proclamations, interpret-
ing the new omen in ways that helped consolidate the
Commons.

*"This stone-of-wisdom is Jijo's gift, a portent, sanctifying
the treaties and ratifying the Great Peace,"* they declared,
with some success. From then on, hope became part of the
revised religion. Though in deference to the scrolls, the
word itself was seldom used.

Now Vubben sought some of that hope for himself, for
his race, and all the Six. He sought it in signs that the great
stone might be stirring once again.

*I can feel it happening! If only the Egg rouses far
enough, soon enough.*

But the increasing activity seemed to follow its own

pace, with a momentum that made him feel like an insect, dancing next to some titanic being.

Perhaps, Vubben suspected, *my presence has nothing to do with these changes.*

What happens next may not involve me at all.

Blade

THE WINDS WERE BLOWING HIM THE WRONG WAY.

No real surprise there. Weather patterns on the Slope had been contrary for more than a year. Anyway, metaphorically, the Six Races were being buffeted by gales of change. Still, at the end of a long, eventful day, Blade had more than enough reason to curse the stubbornly perverse breeze.

By late afternoon, slanting sunshine combed the forests and boo groves into a panorama of shadows and light. The Rimmers were a phalanx of giant soldiers, their armored shells blushing before the lowering sun. Below, a vast marsh had given way to prairie, which in turn became forested hills. Few signs of habitation could be seen from his great height, though Blade was handicapped by a basic inability to look directly *down*. The chitinous bulk of his wide body blocked any direct view of the ground.

How I would love, just once in my life, to see what lies below my own feet!

His five legs weren't doing much at the moment. The claws dangled over open space, snapping occasionally in reflex spasms, trying futilely to get a grip on the clear air. Even more disconcerting, the sensitive feelers around his mouth had no earth or mud to brush against, probing the many textures of the ground. Instead, they, too, hung uselessly. Blade felt numb and bare in the direction a qheuen least liked being exposed.

That had been the hardest part to get used to, after takeoff. To a qheuen, life's texture is determined by its *medium.* Sand and salt water to a red. Freshwater and mud to a blue. A world of stony caverns to imperial grays. Although their ancestors had starships, Jijo's qheuens seemed poor candidates for flight.

As open country glided majestically past, Blade pondered being the first of his kind in hundreds of years to soar.

Some adventure! It will be worth telling Log Biter and the other matrons about, when I return to that homey lodge behind Dolo Dam. The grubs, in their murky den, will want to hear the story at least forty or fifty times.

If only this voyage would get a little *less* adventurous, and more predictable.

I hoped to be communicating with Sara by now, not drifting straight toward the enemy's toothy maw.

Above Blade's cupola and vision strip, he heard valves open with a preliminary hiss—followed by a roaring burst of heat. Unable to shift or turn his suspended body, he could only envision the urrish contraptions in a wicker basket overhead, operating independently, using jets of flame to replenish the hot-air bag, keeping his balloon to a steady altitude.

But not a steady heading.

Everything was as automatic as the smiths' technology allowed, but there was no escaping the tyranny of the wind. Blade had just one control to operate—a cord attached to a distant knife that would rip the balloon open when he pulled, releasing the buoyant vapors and dropping him out of the sky at a smooth rate—so the smiths assured—fast, but not too fast. As pilot, he had one duty, to time his plummet so it ended in a decent-sized body of water.

Even arriving at a fair clip, no mere splash should harm his armored, disklike form. If a tangle of rope and torn fabric pinned his legs, dragging him down, Blade could hold his breath long enough to chew his way free and creep ashore.

Nevertheless, it had been hard to convince the survivors' council, ruling over the ruins of Ovoom Town, to let him try this crazy idea. They naturally doubted his claim that a blue qheuen should be their next courier.

But too many human boys and girls have died in recent days, rushing about in flimsy gliders. Urrish balloonists have been breaking necks and legs. All I have to do is crash into liquid and I'm guaranteed to walk away. Today's crude circumstances make me an ideal aviator!

There was just one problem. While hooking Blade into this conveyance, the smiths had assured him the afternoon breeze was reliable this time of year, straight up the valley of the Gentt. It should waft him all the way to splashdown at Prosperity Lake within a few miduras, leaving more than enough time to dash at a rapid qheuen gait and reach the nearest semaphore station by nightfall. His packet of reports about conditions at ravaged Ovoom would then slide into the flashing message stream. And then Blade could finally scratch his lingering duty itch, restoring contact with Sara as he had vowed. Assuming she was at Mount Guenn, that is.

Only the winds changed, less than a midura after takeoff. The promised quick jaunt east became a long detour north.

Toward home, he noted. Unfortunately, the enemy lay in between. At this rate he'd be shot down before Dolo Village ever hove into view.

To make matters worse, he was starting to get thirsty.

This situation—it is ridiculous, Blade grumbled as sunset brought forth stars. The breeze broke up into rhythmic, contrary gusts. Several times, these bursts raised his hopes by shoving the balloon toward peaks where he spied other semaphore stations, passing soft flashes down the mountain chain. There was apparently a lot of message activity tonight, much of it heading north.

But whenever some large lake seemed about to pass below the bulging gasbag, another hard gusset blew in, pushing him at an infuriating angle, back over jagged rocks and trees. Frustration only heightened his thirst.

If this keeps up, I'll be so dehydrated that I'd dive for a little puddle.

Blade soon realized how far he had come. As the last light of day vanished from the tallest peaks, he spied a cleft in the mountains that any Sixer would recognize—the pass leading to Festival Glade, where each year the Commons of Six Races gathered to celebrate—and mourn—another year of exile. For some time after the sun was gone,

Loocen's bright crescent kept him company, illuminating the foothills. Blade expected the surface to draw closer as he was pushed northeast, but the simpleminded urrish altimeter somehow sensed changing ground levels and reacted with another jet of flame, preventing the balloon from meeting the valley floor.

Then Loocen sank as well, abandoning him to a world of shadows. The mountains became little more than black bites, torn out of the starry heavens. It left Blade all alone with his imagination, speculating how the Jophur were going to deal with him.

Would there be a flash of cold flame, as he had seen darting from the belly of the cruel corvette that devastated Ovoom Town? Would they rip him to bits with scalpels of sound? Or were he and the balloon destined for vaporization upon making contact with some defensive force field? The kind of barrier often described in garish Earthling novels?

Worst of all, he pictured a "tractor beam," seizing and dragging him down to torment in some Jophur-designed hell.

The cord—should I pull it now? he wondered. *Lest our foes learn the secret of hot-air balloons?*

Qheuens never used to laugh before coming to Jijo. But somehow the blue variety picked up the habit, infuriating their Gray Queens, even before hoons and humans could be blamed as bad influences. Blade's legs now contracted, quivering as a calliope of whistles escaped his breathing vents.

Right! We mustn't allow this "technology" to fall into the wrong hands . . . or rings. Why, the Jophur might make balloons of their own, to use against us!

The upland canyons answered with faint repetitions of his laughter—echoes that cheered him up a little, as if there were an audience for his imminent parting from the universe. *No qheuen likes to die alone,* Blade thought, tightening his grip on the cord that would send him plunging to Jijo's dark embrace. *I only hope someone finds enough shell fragments to dross. . . .*

At that moment, a faint glimmer made him pause. It came from dead ahead, farther up the narrowing valley, below the mountain pass. Blade tried focusing his visor, but again had to curse the poor vision his race inherited from ancient times. He peered at the pale shine.

Could it be . . . ?

The soft rays reminded him of starlight, glancing off water, making him hold off yanking the cable for a few duras. If it *was* an alpine lake, he might have just a little time to estimate the distance, include his rate of drift, and guess the right moment to pull. *With my luck, it will turn out to be a mulc spider's acid pit. At least that would take care of the mulching problem.*

The glimmer drew nearer, but its outline seemed strangely smooth, unlike a natural body of water. Its profile was *oval,* and the reflections had a convex quality that—

Ifni and the ancestors! Blade cursed in surprised dismay. *It is the Jophur ship!*

He stared in blank awe at the size of the globular thing. *So huge, I thought it was part of the landscape.*

Worse, he measured his course and heading.

Soon, I'll be right on top of it.

If anything, the wind stiffened from behind, accelerating his approach.

At once, Blade had an idea. One that changed his mind about the cruelty of fate.

This is better, he decided. *It will be like that novel I read last winter, by that pre-contact human, Vonnegut. The book ended with the hero making a bold, personal gesture toward God.*

The point seemed apropos then, and even more so now. When faced with casual extinction by an omnipotent force, sometimes the only option left to a poor mortal is to go out with defiance.

That proved remarkably feasible. Qheuen mouth parts served many functions, including sexual. So Blade made a virtue of his exposed posture, and got ready to present himself to the enemy in the most deliberately offensive manner possible.

Look THIS up in your Galactic Library! he thought, waving his sensor feelers suggestively. Perhaps, before he was vaporized, the Jophur would call up reference data dealing with starfaring qheuens, and realize the extent of his insolence. Blade hoped his life would count for at least that much. To be killed in anger, not as an afterthought.

Waves of tingling sensation coursed his feelers, and Blade wondered if danger was provoking some perverted version of the mating urge. *Well, after all, here I am, veering toward a big, armored, dominant entity with my privates bared.*

Log Biter would not approve of the comparison, I suppose.

As the wind pushed him toward the battleship—a thing so huge it rivaled nearby mountains—all sight of it vanished beneath the forward edge of his chitin carapace. It would be out of sight during final approach, an irony Blade did not find amusing.

Then, to his great surprise, there rushed into sight the very thing he had been longing for—a *lake*. A large one, dammed up behind the great cruiser, drowning the Festival Glade under hectares of cool snowmelt.

If they don't shoot me down, he could not help speculating. *If they fail to notice me, I might yet reach . . .*

But how could they not spy this approaching gasbag? Surely they must already have him pinned by star-god instruments.

Sure enough, the tingling of Blade's exposed feelers multiplied in rapid waves, as if they were being stroked—then stung—by a host of squirming shock worms. Not a sexual stirring, though. Instead the sensation triggered foraging instincts, causing his diamond-tipped incisors to snap reflexively, as if grabbing through mud at armored prey.

The feelers pick up magnetic and electric vibrations from hidden muck crawlers, he recalled.

Electromagnetic . . . I'm being scanned!

Each time he panted breath through a leg vent, another dura passed. The lake swelled, and he knew the ship *must* be almost directly below by now. What were they waiting for?

Then a new thought occurred to Blade.

I'm being scanned . . . but can they see me?

If only he had studied more science at the Tarek Town academy. Although grays tended to be better at abstractions—the reason why they took real names—Blade knew he should have insisted on taking that basic physics course.

Let's see. In human novels, they speak of "radar" . . . *radio waves sent out to bounce off distant objects, giving away the location of intruders, for instance.*

But you only get a good echo if it's something radio will bounce off. Metal, or some other hard stuff.

Blade quickly pulled his teeth back in. Otherwise, his bottom was his softest part, featuring multifaceted planes that might deflect incoming rays in random directions. The gasbag, he figured, must seem hardly more dense than a rain cloud!

Now, if only the urrish altimeter would wait awhile longer before adjusting the balloon's height, shooting hot flame with a roar to fill the night . . .

The tingling peaked . . . then started to diminish. Moments later, coolness stroked Blade's underside and he sensed the allure of water below. Tentative relief came accompanied by worry, for cold air would increase his rate of sink.

Now? Shall I pull the cord, before the flames turn on and give me away?

Water beckoned. Blade yearned to wash the dust from his vent pores. Yet he held back. Even if his sudden plummet from the sky didn't draw attention, he would land in the worst lake on Jijo, deep inside the Jophur defense perimeter, presumably patrolled by all sorts of hunter machines. Perhaps the robots had missed him till now because the possibility of floating qheuens had never been programmed into them. But a *swimming* qheuen most certainly was.

Anyway, the water gave him a strange feeling. There were flickerings under the surface—eerie flashes that reinforced his decision to hold back.

Each passing dura ratified the choice, as a separation slowly increased between Blade and the giant dreadnought, reappearing behind him as a dark curve with glimmering highlights, divided about a third of the way up by a rippling, watery line. It made him feel distinctly creepy.

Abruptly, a pinpoint of brilliance flared from the side of the globe ship, seeming to stab straight toward him.

Here it comes, Blade thought.

But the flaring light was no heat ray. No death beam, after all. Instead, the pinpoint widened. It became a glowing rectangular aperture. A door.

A mighty big door, Blade realized, wondering what could possibly take up so much room inside a mammoth star cruiser.

Apparently—another star cruiser.

From the gaping hangar, a sleek cigar shape emerged with a low hum, moving gradually at first, then accelerating toward Blade.

All right then. Not extinction. Capture. But why send that big thing after me?

Perhaps they saw his obscene gesture; and understood better than he expected.

Once more, Blade readied the rip cord. At the last moment, he would plummet from their grasp . . . or else they'd shoot him as he fell. Or hunter robots would track him, underwater or overland. Still, it seemed proper to make the effort. *At least I'll get a drink.*

Again, night vision gave him trouble. Estimating the corvette's rate of closure proved futile. In frustration, Blade's thoughts slipped from Anglic and into the easier grooves of Galactic Six.

> *This specter of terror—I have seen it before.*
> *This thing I saw last—as it burned down a city.*
> *A city of felons—of sooners—my people.*

His legs flexed spasmodically as the ship rushed toward him without slowing . . .

What the—

. . . and kept going, sweeping past with a roar of displaced air.

Blade felt hooks of urrish steel yank his carapace at all five suspension points. One anchor broke free, tearing chitin armor like paper, then flinging wildly as the balloon was sucked after the skyship's wake.

The world passed in a blur, teaching him what *real* flying was about.

Then the Jophur vessel was gone, ignoring balloon and passenger with contempt, or else indifference. He glimpsed it once more, still climbing steadily toward the Rimmer peaks, leaving him swirling in a backwash of confusion and disturbed air.

Vubben

AFTER A TIME, VUBBEN FINALLY SUCCEEDED IN quelling his busy thoughts, allowing the tywush resonance to pervade his soul, washing away distractions and doubts. Another midura passed, and another prayer circuit, while his meditation deepened. After Loocen set, a vast skyscape of constellations and nebulae passed overhead. Twinkling abode of the gods.

As he rounded back to the west side, another kind of winking light caught one of Vubben's eyes—a syncopated flash unlike any gleaming star. Still wrapped in his trance, Vubben had to labor just to lift a second stalk and recognize the flicker as coded speech.

It took more effort, and yet a third eye, to decipher it.

JOPHUR SMALLSHIP/DEATHSHIP IN MOTION, flashed the lantern on Mount Ingul. HEADING TOWARD EGG.

The message repeated. Vubben even glimpsed a distant sparkle, echoing the words on a farther peak, and realized that other semaphore stations must be relaying the message. Still, his brain was tuned to another plane, preventing him from quite grasping its significance.

Instead, he went back to the sensory phantasm that had been drawing him inward—an impression of being perched atop a swaying ribbon, one that slowly yawed and pitched like some undulating sea.

It was not an unpleasant feeling. Rather, he felt almost like a youngster again, growing up in Dooden Mesa, zooming recklessly along a swaying suspension bridge, feeling its planks rattle beneath his rims, swooping and banking without a safety rail while lethal drops gaped on both sides. His taut spokes hummed as he sped like a bullet, with all four eyestalks stretched wide for maximum parallax.

The moment came back to him whole—not as a distant, fond memory, but in all its splendor. It was the closest thing to paradise he had ever experienced on Jijo's rough orb.

Amid the exhilaration, part of Vubben knew he must have crossed some boundary. He was *with* the Egg now, sensing the approach of a massive object from the west. A deadly thing, complacent and terrible, cruising at a leisurely pace uphill from the Glade.

Leisurely—according to those aboard, that is.

Somehow, Vubben could sense gravitic fields pressing down, tearing leaves from trees, scraping and penetrating Jijo's soil, disturbing ancient rocks. He even knew intuitive things about the crew within—multiringed entities, far more self-assured and unified than traeki.

Strange rings. Egotistical and driven.

Determined to wreak havoc.

Blade

THE BALLOON'S ALTIMETER MUST BE MALFUNCTIONing, he realized. Or else the fuel tank was running low. Either way, the automatic adjustments were growing more sporadic. Unnerving sputtering sounds accompanied each burst of heat, and the pulses came less frequently.

Finally, they halted altogether.

The lake had vanished behind him during those frantic duras when the spaceship's wake dragged the balloon behind it, past the ruined Glade into a narrow pass, toward the Rimmer heights. Also gone was Blade's last chance to pull the rip cord and land in deep water. Instead, trees spired around him, like teeth of a comb you used to pluck fleas from your pet lornik.

And I am the flea.

Assuming he survived when a forest giant snatched him from the sky, someone might hear his cries and come. *But then, what will they think when they find a qheuen in a tree?*

The phrase was a popular metaphor for unlikeliness—a contradiction in terms—like a swimming urs, or a modest human, or an egotistical traeki.

This appears to be the year for contradictions.

A branch top brushed one of his claw tips. Blade yanked back so reflexively that his whole body spun around. All five legs were kept drawn in after that. Still, he expected another impact at any moment.

Instead, the forest abruptly ended. Blade had an impression of craggy cliffs, and a sulfurous odor stroked his tongue. Then came a sensation of upward motion!

And heat. His mouth feelers curled in reaction to a blast from below.

Of course, he realized. *Go east from the Glade for a few leagues, and you're in geyser country.*

The balloon soared, its drooping canopy now buoyed by a warm updraft.

The Jophur ship must have dragged me into a particular canyon. The Pilgrimage Track.

The path leading to the Egg.

Blade's body kept spinning, even as the gasbag climbed. To other beings, it might have been disconcerting, but qheuens had no preferred orientation. It never mattered which way he was "facing." So Blade was ready when the object he sought came into view.

There it is!

The corvette lay dead ahead. It had stopped motionless and was now shining a searchlight downward, circling a site that Blade realized could only be the Nest.

What is it planning to do?

He recalled Ovoom Town, where the aliens chose to attack at night for maximum terror and visual effect. Could that be the intent, once again?

But surely the Jophur would not harm the Egg!

Blade had never shown the slightest psi-ability. Yet it seemed that feelings now crept inward from his extremities to the flexing lymph pump at his body center. Expectation came first. Then something akin to intrigued curiosity.

Finally, in rapid succession, he felt recognition, realization, and a culminating sense of disappointed ennui. All these impressions swept over him in a matter of moments, and he somehow knew they weren't coming from the Jophur.

Indeed, whatever had just happened—a psi-insult or failed communication—it seemed to anger those aboard the cruiser, goading them to action. The searchlight narrowed from a diffuse beam to a needle of horrific brilliance that stabbed down viciously. It took duras for sound to follow . . . a staccato series of crackling booms. Blade could not see the obscured target, but glowing smoke billowed from the point of impact.

A shrill, involuntary whistle escaped Blade's vents and his legs tightened spasmodically. Yet there was no impression of pain, or even surprise. *It will take more than that,* he thought proudly. *A lot more.*

Of course, the Jophur could dish out whatever it took to turn the defenseless Egg into a molten puddle. Their intent was now clear. This act, more even than the slaying at Ovoom Town, would tear the morale of the Six.

Blade urged his windblown vehicle onward, hoping to arrive in time.

Lark

THREE HUMANS IN A PRISON CELL WATCHED A PANorama of destruction, reacting in quite different ways.

Lark stared at the holoscene with the same superstitious thrill he felt months ago, encountering Galactic tech for the first time. The images seemed to demand habits, ways of seeing, learned at an early age. Things he should recognize—the Rimmer mountains, for instance—possessed a *slippery* quality. Odd perspective foldings conveyed far more than you'd see through a window the same size . . . especially when the scene hovered over the Holy Egg.

"Your obstinacy—joint and particular—brought your people to this juncture," the tall stack of rings said.

"Destroying mere towns did not sway you, since your so-called Sacred Scrolls preach the futility of tangible assets.

"But now, observe as our corvette strikes a blow at your true underpinnings."

A glaring needle struck the Egg. Almost at once, waves of pain engulfed Lark's chest. Falling back with a cry, he tore at his clothes, trying to fling away the stone amulet hanging from a thong around his neck. Ling tried to help, but could not grasp the meaning of his agony.

The ordeal might have killed him, but then it ended as suddenly as it began. The cutting ray vanished, leaving a smoking scar along the Egg's flank.

Ewasx burbled glad exhalations about "a signal" and "gratifying surrender."

Lark bunched the fabric of his undershirt around the Egg fragment, wrapping it to prevent contact with his skin. Only then did he notice that Ling had his head on her lap, stroking his face, telling him that everything was going to be all right.

Yeah, sure it is, Lark thought, recognizing a well-meant lie. But the gesture, the warm contact, was appreciated.

As his eyes unblurred, Lark saw Rann looking his way. The big Danik had cool disdain in his eyes. Scorn that Lark would react so to the superficial wounding of rock. Contempt that Ling would soil her hands on a native. And derision that the Six Races would give in so easily, surrendering to the Jophur in order to salvage a mere lump of psi-active stone. Rann had already proved willing to sacrifice himself and all his comrades, to protect his patron race. Clearly, he thought any lesser courage unworthy.

Go kiss a Rothen's feet, Lark thought. But he did not speak aloud.

The corvette had turned away from the Egg. Its transmission now showed the camera gaining altitude, sweeping above dark ridgelines.

The country was familiar. Lark ought to recognize it.

Lester Cambel . . . They're heading straight toward Lester . . . and the boo forest. . . .

So. The sages had chosen to give up whatever mystery project kept them so busy at their secret base—the work of months—just in order to safeguard the Egg.

It shouldn't be surprising. It is our holy site, after all. Our prophet. Our seer.

And yet, he *was* surprised.

In fact, it was the last thing he would have expected.

Blade

SILENTLY, BLADE URGED HIS WINDBLOWN VEHICLE onward, hoping to arrive in time. . . .

To do what? To distract the Jophur for a few duras while they burned him to a cinder, giving the Egg just that much respite before the main assault resumed? Or worse, to float on by, screaming and waving his legs, trying futilely to attract attention from beings who thought him no more important than a cloud?

Frustration boiled. Combat hormones triggered autonomic reactions, causing his cupola to pull inward, taking the vision strip down beneath his carapace, leaving just a smooth, armored surface above.

That instinct response might have made sense long ago, when presentient qheuens fought their battles claw to claw in seaside marshes, on the distant planet where their patrons later found and uplifted them. But now it was a damned nuisance. Blade struggled for calm, schooling his breathing to follow a steady rhythm, sequentially clockwise from leg to leg, instead of random stuttering gasps. It took a count of twenty before the cupola relaxed enough to rise and restore sight.

His vision strip whirled, taking in the dim canyons that made a maze of this part of the Rimmers. At once, he realized two things.

The balloon had climbed considerably in that brief time, widening his field of view.

And the Jophur ship was gone!

But . . . where . . . ?

Blade wondered if it might be right below, in his blind spot. That provoked a surging fantasy. He saw himself slashing the balloon and dropping onto the cruiser from above! Landing with a thump, he would scoot along the top until he reached some point of entry. A hatch that could be forced, or a glass window to smash. Once aboard, in close quarters, he'd show them. . . .

Oh, there it is.

The heroic dream image evaporated like dew when he spied the corvette, diminishing rapidly, heading roughly northwest.

Could it have already finished off the Egg?

Scanning nearer at hand, he spied the great ovoid at last, some distance in the opposite direction. It lay in full view now, a savage burn scarring one flank. The stone glowed along that jagged, half-molten line, casting ocher light across jumbled debris lining the bottom of the Nest. Still, the Egg looked relatively intact.

Why did they leave before finishing the job?

He tracked the corvette by its glimmer of reflected starlight.

Northwest. It's heading northwest.

Blade tried to think.

That's where home is. Dolo Village. Tarek Town.

And Biblos, he then realized, hoping he was wrong.

Things might have just gone from bad to worse.

Ewasx

THE THREAT WORKED, MY RINGS!

Now our expertise is proven. Our/My worth is vindicated before the Captain-Leader and our fellow crew stacks. As I/we predicted, just as our bomber began slicing at their holy psychic rock, a signal came!

It was the same digital radiance they used last time, to reveal the g'Kek city. Thus, the savages attempt once more to placate us. They will do anything to protect their stone deity.

OBSERVE THE HUMAN CAPTIVES, MY RINGS! ONE OF them—the local male whom we/Asx once knew as Lark Koolhan—quailed and moaned to see the "Egg" under attack, while the other two seemed unaffected. Thus, a controlled experiment showed that I/we were right about the primitives and their religion.

Now the female comforts Lark as our cruiser speeds away from the damaged Egg, toward the signal-emanation point.

What will they offer us, this time? Something as satisfying as the g'Kek town, now frozen with immured samples of hated vermin?

The chief-tactician stack calculates that the sooners will not sacrifice the thing we desire most—the dolphin ship. Not yet. First they will try buying us off with lesser things. Perhaps their fabled archive—a pathetic trove of primitive lore, crudely scribed on plant leaves or some barklike substance. A paltry cache of lies and superstitions that simpletons dare call a *library*.

You tremor in surprise, O second ring-of-cognition? You did not expect Me to learn of this other thing treasured by the Six Races?

Well be assured, Asx did a thorough job of melting that particular memory. The information did not come from this reforged stack.

Did you honestly believe that our *Ewasx* stack was the only effort at intelligence gathering ordained by the Captain-Leader? There have been other captives, other interrogations.

It took too long to learn about this pustule of contraband Earthling knowledge—this *Biblos*—and the exact location remained uncertain. But now we/I speculate. Perhaps Biblos is the thing they hope to bribe us with, exchanging their archive for the "life" of their Holy Egg.

If that is their intent, they will learn.

We will burn the books, but that won't suffice.

NOTHING WILL SUFFICE.

In the long run, not even the dolphin ship will do. Though it will make a good start.

Blade

NORTHWEST. WHAT TARGET MIGHT ATTRACT THE aliens' attention that way?

Nearly everything I know or care about, Blade concluded. Dolo Village, Tarek Town, and Biblos.

As pale Torgen rose behind the Rimmer peaks, he watched the slim ship glide on, knowing he would lose sight of it long before the raider arrived at any of those destinations. Blade no longer cared where the contrary winds blew him, so long as he did not have to watch destruction rain down on the places he loved.

A chain of tiny, flickering lights followed the cruiser as scouts stationed on mountain peaks passed reports of its progress. He deciphered a few snatches of GalTwo, and saw they weren't words, but numbers.

Wonderful. We are good at describing and measuring our downfall.

With combat hormones ebbing, Blade grew more aware of physical discomfort. Nerves throbbed where one of the urrish hooks had ripped away skin plates, exposing fleshy integuments to cold air. Thirst gnawed at him, making Blade wish he were a hardy gray.

The balloon passed beyond the warm updraft and stopped climbing. Soon the descent would resume, sending him spinning toward a landscape of jagged shadows.

Wait a dura.

Blade tried to focus his vision strip, peering at the distant Jophur vessel.

Has it stopped?

Soon he knew it had. The ship was hovering again, casting its search beam to scan the ground below.

Was I wrong? The next target may not be Biblos or Tarek, after all.

But . . . there's nothing here! These hills are wilderness. Just a useless tract of boo—

He was staring in perplexity when something happened to the mountain below the floating ship. Reddish flickers erupted, like marsh gas lit by static charges, at the swampy border of a lake. Sparklike ripples seemed to spread amid the dense stands of towering boo.

What are the Jophur doing now? he wondered. *What weapon are they using?*

The flickers brightened, flaring beneath scores of giant greatboo stems. The ship's searchlight still roamed, as if bemused to find slender tubes of native vegetation emitting fire from their bottoms . . . then starting to rise.

The first thunder reached Blade as he realized.

It's not the Jophur at all! It's—

The corvette finally showed alarm, starting to back away. Its beam narrowed to a slicing needle, sweeping through one rising column.

An instant later, the entire northwest was alight. Volley after volley of blazing tubes jetted skyward in a roar that shook the night.

Rockets, Blade thought. *Those are rockets!*

The vast majority missed their apparent target. But accuracy seemed of no concern, so dense was the missile swarm. The retreating corvette could not blast them fast enough before three in a row made glancing blows.

Then a fourth projectile struck head-on. The warhead failed, but sheer momentum crumpled one section of starship hull, tossing it spinning.

Other warheads kept going off ahead of schedule, or tumbling to explode on the ground, filling the night with brilliant, fruitless incandescence. So great was the wastage that it looked as if the Jophur ship might actually limp away.

Then a late-rising rocket took off. It turned, and with apparent deliberation, drove itself straight through the groaning corvette.

A dazzling explosion ripped its belly open, cleaving the skyship apart. Blade had to spin a different part of his half-blinded visor around to witness the two halves plummet, like twin cups filled with fire, to the forest floor.

More dross to clean up, Blade observed, as fires spread across several mountainsides. But his body was content to live in the moment, shrieking celebration whistles from all his breathing vents, competing with the gaudy fireworks to shout at the stars.

With qheuen vision, he could witness the corvette's destruction while also following as most of the missiles continued their flight—those that did not veer off course, or explode on their own. Dozens still thrust noisily into the upper sky, spouting red, flickering tails.

Blade screamed even louder when they finished their brief arc and turned back toward Jijo, plummeting like hail toward Festival Glade.

Lester Cambel

THE FOREST ERUPTED IN FLAME AROUND LESTER. Failed missiles crashed back amid the secret launching sites, setting off explosions of withering heat and igniting tall columns of boo. South, a searing glow told where the shattered spaceship fell. Still, Lester held fast to the clearing where he and a g'Kek assistant had come to watch the flickering sky.

An urrish corporal galloped to report. "Fires surround us. Sage, you must flee!"

But Lester stayed rooted, peering at the fuming heavens. His voice was choked and dry.

"I can't see! Did any make it to burnout? Are they on their way?"

The young g'Kek answered, all four eyes waving upward.

"Many flew true, O sage," she answered. "Several score are airborne. Your design was valid. Now there's nothing more to do. It's time to go."

Reluctantly, Lester let himself be pulled away from the clearing, into the planned escape route through the boo.

Only they soon found the way blocked by fierce tongues of fire. Lester and his companions had to retreat, back past sheltered work camps whose blur-cloth canopies were ablaze, where vats of traeki paste exploded one after another . . . along with some of the traeki themselves. Other figures could be seen fleeing through the clots of smoke as all the labor of months, spent creating a hidden center of industry, was consumed in a roiling maelstrom.

"There is no way out," the urs sighed.

"Then save yourself. I command it!"

Lester pushed her resisting flank, repeating the order until the corporal let out a moan and plunged toward a place where the flames seemed least intense. An urs just might survive the passage. Lester knew better than to try.

Alone with his young assistant, he huddled in the center of the clearing, holding one of her trembling wheels.

"It's all right," he told her, between hacking coughs. "We did what we set out to do.

"All things come to an end.

"Now it all lies with Ifni."

Lark

THE EARLIER HOLOSCENES HAD BEEN CONFUSING, but these new images left Lark stunned, breathless, confused. He had no way to grasp the blazing spectacle . . . mighty tubes of boo, their bottoms explosing in flame . . . scores of them, jetting upward like a swarm of angry fire bees.

The distant camera veered as the corvette struggled to evade a volley of makeshift rockets. The view lurched so suddenly, Lark's stomach reeled and he had to look away.

The others seemed just as amazed. *Ling* laughed aloud, clapping both hands, while Rann's face mixed astonishment with dismay. *Then what's happening must be good.* Lark allowed a spark of hope to rise within.

Ewasx, the Jophur, vented gurgling sounds, along with snatches of Galactic Two.

"Outrageous . . . treacherous . . . unexpected . . . unforeseen!"

Tremors shook its composite body, quivering from the peak down to its basal segment. Most of the elderly, waxy toroids were familiar to Lark. Once, they composed a friend, a sage, wise and good. But a newcomer had taken over—a glistening young collar, black and featureless, without appendages or sensory organs.

Both Ling and Rann cried out. But when Lark turned around, the holoscene was all white—a blank slate.

"The corvette," Ling explained, her voice awed. "It's been destroyed!"

A shrill sigh escaped the Jophur. The tremors turned into convulsions.

Ewasx is having some kind of fit, Lark thought. *Should I attack now? Strike the master ring with all my might?*

Ling was babbling excitedly about "the other rockets—" But Lark had decided, striding toward the shuddering Jophur. His sole weapons were his hands, but so what?

Lester, you pulled off a fantastic wolfling trick. Asx would have been proud of you.

Just as old Asx would have wanted me to do this.

He brought back a fist, aimed at the shivering master ring.

Someone seized his arm, holding it back in a fierce grip. Lark swiveled, cocking his other fist at Rann. But the bull-headed Danik only shook his head.

"What will it prove? You'd just make them angry, native boy. We remain trapped here, at their mercy."

"Get out of my way," Lark growled. "I'm gonna free my traeki friend."

"Your friend is long gone. If you kill a master ring, the whole stack dissolves! I *know* this, young savage. I've put it in practice."

Lark was angry enough to turn his attack on the burly Danik. Sensing it, Rann released Lark and stepped back, raising both hands in a combatant's stance.

Yeah, Lark thought, dropping to a crouch. *You're a star-god soldier. But maybe a savage knows some tricks you don't.*

"Stop it, you two!" Ling shouted. "We've got to get ready—"

She cut off as a chain of low vibrations throbbed the metal floor—mighty forces at work, growling elsewhere in the vast ship.

"Defensive cannon," Rann identified the din. "But what could they be firing—?"

"The rockets!" Ling replied. "I *told* you, they're coming this way!"

Realization dawned on Rann, that sooners might actually threaten a starship. He cursed, diving for a corner of the cell.

Lark allowed Ling to lead him as the battleship shivered, its weapons firing frantically. A mutter of distant detonations crept closer as they held each other. The moment had a heady vividness, a hormonal rush, mixing the pleasure of Ling's touch with sharp awareness of onrushing death.

Yet Lark found himself hoping, praying, that the next few moments would end his life.

Come on. You can do it, Lester. Finish the job!

The fragment of the Egg lay against his chest, where its last outburst had left seething weals. He clutched the stone amulet with his free hand, expecting throbbing heat. Instead, Lark felt an icy cold. A brittleness that breath would shatter.

PART NINE

FROM THE NOTES
OF GILLIAN BASKIN

WE'RE ALL FEELING rather down right now. Suessi called from the second dross pile where his work crew just had an accident. They were trying to clear the area around an old Buyur ore-hauler when a subsea quake hit. The surrounding heap of junk ships shifted and an ancient hulk came rolling down on a couple of workers—Satima and Sup-peh. Neither of them had time to do more than stare at the onrushing wall before it crushed them.

So we keep getting winnowed down where it hurts most. Our best colleagues— the skilled and dedicated—inevitably pay the price.

Then there's Peepoe, everyone's delight. A terrible loss, kidnapped by Zhaki and his pal. If only I could get my hands on that pair!

I had to lie to poor Kaa, though. We cannot spare time to go hunting across the ocean for Peepoe.

That doesn't mean she'll be abandoned. Friends will win her freedom, someday. This I vow.

But our pilot won't be one of them.

Alas, I fear Kaa will never see her again.

MAKANEE finished her autopsies of Kunn and Jass. The prisoners apparently took poison rather than answer our questions. Tsh't blames herself for not searching the Danik agent more carefully, but who would have figured Kunn would be so worried about our amateur grilling?

And did he really have to take the hapless native boy with him? Rety's cousin could hardly know secrets worth dying for.

Rety herself can shed no light on the matter. Without anyone to interrogate, she volunteered to help Suessi, who can certainly use a hand. Makanee recommends work as good therapy for the poor kid, who had to see those gruesome bodies firsthand.

I wonder. What secret was Kunn trying to protect? Normally, I'd drop everything to puzzle it out. But too much is going on as we prepare to make our move.

Anyway, from the Jophur prisoners we know the Rothen ship is irrelevant. We have more immediate concerns.

THE Library cube reports no progress on that symbol—the one with nine spirals and eight ovals. The unit is now sifting its older files, a job that gets harder the further back it goes.

In compensation, the cube has flooded me with records of other recent "sooner outbreaks"—secret colonies established on fallow worlds.

It turns out that most are quickly discovered by guardian patrols of the Institute of Migration. Jijo is a special case, with limited access and the nearby shrouding of Izmunuti. Also, this time an entire galaxy was declared fallow, making inspection a monumental task.

I wondered—why set aside a whole galaxy, when the basic unit of ecological recovery is a planet, or at most a solar system?

The cube explained that much larger areas of space are usually quarantined, all at once. Oxygen-breathing civilization evacuates an entire sector or spiral arm, ceding it to the parallel culture of hydrogen breathers—those mysterious creatures sometimes generically called Zang. This helps keep both societies separated in physical space, reducing the chance of friction.

It also helps the quarantine. The Zang are unpredictable, and often ignore minor incursions, but they can be fierce if large numbers of oxy-sapients appear where they don't belong.

We detected what must have been Zang ships, before diving past Izmunuti. I guess they took us for a "minor incursion," since they left us alone.

The wholesale trading of sectors and zones makes more sense now. Still, I pressed the Library cube.

Has an entire galaxy ever been declared off-limits before?

The answer surprised me.

Not for a very long time . . . at least one hundred and fifty million years.

Now, where have I heard that number before?

WE'RE told there are eight orders of sapience and quasi-sapience. Oxy-life is the most vigorous and blatant—or as Tom put it, "strutting around, acting like we own the place." In fact, though, I was surprised to learn that hydrogen breathers far outnumber oxygen breathers. But Zang and their relatives spend most of their time down in the turbid layers of Jovian-type worlds.

Some say this is because they fear contact with oxy-types.

Others say they could crush us anytime, but have never gotten around to it. Perhaps they will, sometime in the *next* billion years.

The other orders are Machine, Memetic, Quantum, Hypothetical, Retired, and Transcendent.

Why am I pondering this now?

Well, our plans are in motion, and soon *Streaker* will be, too. It's likely that in a few days we'll be dead, or else taken captive. With luck, we may buy something worthwhile with our lives. But our chances of actually getting away seem vanishingly small.

And yet . . . what if we *do* manage it? After all, the Jophur may get engine trouble at just the right moment. They might decide we're not worth the effort.

The sun might go nova.

In that case, where can *Streaker* go next?

We've tried seeking justice from our own oxy-culture—the Civilization of the Five Galaxies—but the Institutes proved untrustworthy. We tried the Old Ones, but those members of the Retired Order proved less impartial than we hoped.

In a universe filled with possibilities, there remain half a dozen other "quasi-sapient" orders out there. Alien in both thought and substance. Rumored to be dangerous.

What have we got to lose?

Streakers

Kaa

GLEAMING MISSILES STRUCK THE WATER WHENEVER he surfaced to breathe. The spears were crude weapons—hollow wooden shafts tipped with slivers of volcanic glass—but when a keen-edged harpoon grazed his flank, Kaa lost half his air in a reflexive cry. The harbor—now a cramped, exitless trap—reverberated with his agonized moan.

The hoonish sailors seemed to have no trouble moving around by torchlight, rowing their coracles back and forth, executing complex orders shouted from their captains' bulging throat sacs. The water's tense skin reverberated like a beaten drum as the snare tightened around Kaa. Already, a barrier of porous netting blocked the narrow harbor mouth.

Worse, the natives had reinforcements. Skittering sounds announced the arrival of clawed feet, scampering down the rocky shore south of town. Chitinous forms plunged underwater, reminding Kaa of some horror movie about giant crabs. *Red qheuens,* he realized, as these new allies helped the hoon sailors close off another haven, the water's depths.

Ifni! What did Zhaki and Mopol do to make the locals so mad at the mere sight of a dolphin in their bay? How did they get these people so angry they want to kill me on sight?

Kaa still had some tricks. Time and again he misled the hoons, making feints, pretending sluggishness, drawing the noose together prematurely, then slipping beneath a gap in their lines, dodging a hail of javelins.

My ancestors had practice doing this. Humans taught us lessons, long before they switched from spears to scalpels.

Yet he knew this was a contest the cetacean could not win. The best he could hope for was a drawn-out tie.

Diving under one hoonish coracle, Kaa impulsively spread his jaws and snatched the rower's oar in his teeth, yanking it like the tentacle of some demon octopus. The impact jarred his mouth and tender gums, but he added force with a hard thrust of his tail flukes.

The oarsman made a mistake by holding on—even a hoon could not match Kaa, strength to strength. A surprised bellow met a resounding splash as the mariner struck salt water far from the boat. Kaa released the oar and kicked away rapidly. That act would not endear him to the hoon. On the other hand, what was there left to lose? Kaa had quite given up on his mission—to make contact with the Commons of Six Races. All that remained was fighting for survival.

I should have listened to my heart.
I should have gone after Peepoe, instead.

The decision still bothered Kaa with nagging pangs of guilt. How could he obey Gillian Baskin's orders—no matter how urgent—instead of striking off across the dark sea, chasing after the thugs who had kidnapped his mate and love?

What did duty matter—or even his oath to Terra—compared with that?

After Gillian signed off, Kaa had listened as the sun set, picking out distant echoes of the fast-receding speed sled, still faintly audible to the northwest. Sound carried far in Jijo's ocean, without the myriad engine noises that made Earth's seas a cacophony. The sled was already so far away—at least a hundred klicks by then—it would seem forlorn to follow.

But so what? So the odds were impossible? That never mattered to the heroes one found in storybooks and holosims! No audience ever cheered a champion who let mere impossibility stand in the way.

Maybe that was what swayed Kaa, in an agonized moment. The fact that it was such a cliché. *All* the movie heroes—whether human or dolphin—would routinely forsake comrades, country, and honor for the sake of love. Relentless propaganda from every romantic tale urged him to do it.

But even if I succeeded, against all odds, what would Peepoe say after I rescued her?

I know her. She'd call me a fool and a traitor, and never respect me again.

So it was that Kaa found himself entering Port Wuphon as ordered, long after nightfall, with all the wooden sailboats shrouded beneath camouflage webbing that blurred their outlines into cryptic hummocks. Still hating himself for his decision, he had approached the nearest wharf, where two watchmen lounged on what looked like walking staffs, beside a pair of yawning noor. By starlight, Kaa had reared up on his churning flukes to begin reciting his memorized speech of greeting . . . and barely escaped being skewered for his trouble. Whirling back into the bay, he dodged razor-tipped staves that missed by centimeters.

"Wait-t-t!" he had cried, emerging on the other side of the wharf. *"You're mak-ing a terrible mistake! I bring news from your own lossssst ch-ch-children! F-from Alvi—"*

He barely escaped a second time. The hoon guards weren't listening. Darkness barely saved Kaa as growing numbers of missiles hurled his way.

His big mistake was trying a third time to communicate. When that final effort failed, Kaa tried to depart . . . only to find belatedly that the door had shut. The harbor mouth was closed, trapping him in a tightening noose.

So much for my skill at diplomacy, he pondered, while skirting silently across the bottom muck . . . only to swerve when his sonar brushed armored forms ahead, approaching with scalloped claws spread wide.

Add that to my other failures . . . as a spy, as an officer . . . Mopol and Zhaki would never have antagonized the locals so, with senseless pranks and mischief, if he had led them properly.

. . . and as a lover. . . .

In fact, Kaa knew just one thing he was good at. And at this rate, he'd never get another chance to ply his trade.

A strange, thrashing sound came from just ahead, toward the bottom of the bay. He nearly swung around again, dodging it to seek some other place, dreading the time when bursting lungs would force him back to the surface. . . .

But there was something peculiar about the sound. A softness. A resigned, *melodious* sadness that seemed to fill the water. Curiosity overcame Kaa as he zigzagged, casting sonar clicks through the murk to perceive—

A hoon!

But what was one of them doing down here?

Kaa nosed forward, ignoring the growing staleness of his air supply, until he made out a tall biped amid clouds of churned-up mud. Diffracted echoes confirmed his unbelieving eyes. The creature was *undressing,* carefully removing articles of clothing, tying them together in a string.

Kaa guessed it was a female, from the fact that it was a bit smaller and had only a modest throat sac.

Is it the one I pulled overboard? But why doesn't she swim back to the boat? I assumed . . .

Kaa was struck by a wave of image-rupture alienation— a sensation all too familiar to Earthlings since contact— when some concept that had seemed familiar abruptly made no sense anymore.

Hoons can't swim!

The journal of Alvin Hph-wayuo never mentioned this. In fact, Alvin implied that his people passionately loved boats and the sea. Nor were they cavalier about their lives, but mourned the loss of loved ones even more deeply than a human or dolphin would. Kaa suddenly knew he'd been fooled by Alvin's writings, sounding so much like an Earth kid, never mentioning things that he simply assumed.

Aliens. Who can figure?

He stared as the hoon tied the string of clothes around

her left wrist and held the other end to her mouth, calmly exhaling her last air, inflating a balloonlike fold of cloth. It floated upward, no more than two meters, stopping far short of the surface.

She's not signaling for help, he fathomed as the hoon sat down in the mud, humming a dirge. *She's making sure they can drag the bottom and retrieve her body.* Kaa had read Alvin's account of death rituals the locals took quite seriously.

By now his own lungs burned fiercely. Kaa deeply regretted that the breather unit on his harness had burned out after Zhaki shot him.

He heard the qheuens approaching from behind, clacking their claws, but Kaa sensed a hole in their line, confident he could streak past, just out of reach. He tried to turn . . . to seize the brief opportunity.

Oh, hell, he sighed, and kicked the other way, aiming for the dying hoon.

It took some time to get her to the surface. When they broke through, her entire body shook with harsh, quivering gasps. Water jetted from nostril orifices at the same time as air poured in through her mouth, a neat trick that Kaa kind of envied.

He pushed her close enough to throw one arm over a drifting oar, then he whirled around to peer across the bay, ready to duck onrushing spears.

None came. In fact, there seemed a curious absence of boats nearby. Kaa dropped his head down to cast suspicious sonar beams through his arched brow—and confirmed that all the coracles had backed off some distance.

A moon had risen. One of the big ones. He could make out silhouettes now . . . hoons standing in their rowboats, all of them turned to face north . . . or maybe northwest. The males had their sacs distended, and a steady thrumming filled the air. They seemed oblivious to the sudden reappearance of one of their kind from a brush with drowning.

I'd have thought they'd be all over this area, dropping weighted ropes, trying to rescue her. It was another example of alien thinking, despite all the Terran books these hoons had read. Kaa was left with the task of shoving her with the tip of his rostrum, a creepy feeling coursing his spine as he pushed the bedraggled survivor toward one of the docks.

More villagers stood along the wharf, their torches flickering under gusts of stiffening wind. They seemed to be watching . . . or listening . . . to something.

A dolphin can both see and hear things happening above the water's surface, but not as well as those who live exclusively in that dry realm. With his senses still in an uproar, Kaa could discern little in the direction they faced. Just the hulking outline of a mountain.

The computerized insert in his right eye flexed and turned until Kaa finally made out a flickering star near the mountain's highest point. A star that *throbbed,* flashing on and off to a staccato rhythm. He could not make anything of it at first . . . though the cadence seemed reminiscent of Galactic Two.

"Ex-x-xcuse me . . ." he began, trying to take advantage of the inactivity. Whatever else was happening, this seemed a good chance to get a word in edgewise. "I'm a dolphin . . . cousin to humansss . . . I've been sssent with-th a message for Uriel the—"

The crowd suddenly erupted in a moan of emotion that made Kaa's sound-sensitive jaw throb. He made out snatches of individual speech.

"Rockets!" one onlooker sighed in Anglic. "The sages made rockets!"

Another spoke GalSeven in tones of wonder. *"One small enemy spaceship destroyed . . . and now the big one is targeted!"*

Kaa blinked, transfixed by the villagers' tension.

Rockets? Did I hear right? But—

Another cry escaped the crowd.

"They plummet!" someone cried. "They strike!"

Abruptly, the mountain-perched star paused its twinkling bulletin. All sound seemed to vanish with it. The hoons stood in dead silence. Even the oily water of the bay was hushed, lapping softly against the wharf.

The flashing resumed, and there came from the crowd a moan of shaken disappointment.

"It survives, exists. The mother battleship continues," went the GalTwo mutter of a traeki, somewhere in the crowd.

"Our best effort has failed.

"And now comes punishment."

Sooners

Lark

THE MOMENT LARK PRAYED FOR NEVER CAME. THE walls did not shatter, torn by native-made warheads or screaming splinters of greatboo. Instead, the sound of detonations remained distant, then diminished. The floor-throbbing vibration of Jophur defense guns changed tenor now that the element of surprise was gone, from frantic to complacent, as if the incoming missiles were mere nuisances.

Then silence fell. It was over.

He let go of the Egg fragment, and released Ling, as well. Lark pulled his knees in, wrapped both arms around them, and rocked miserably. He had never felt so disappointed to be alive.

"Woorsh, that was close!" Ling exhaled, clearly savoring survival. Not that Lark blamed her. She might still nurse hopes of escape, or of being swapped in some Galactic prisoner exchange. All this might become just another episode in her memoirs. *An episode, like me,* he thought. *The clever jungle boy she once met on Jijo.*

His old friend Harullen might have seen a bright side to

this failure. Now the angered Jophur might extinguish all sapient life on the planet, not only their g'Kek blood enemies. Wouldn't that fit in with Lark's beliefs? His heresy?

The Six Races don't belong here, but neither do they deserve annihilation. I wanted us to do the right thing peacefully, honorably, and of our own accord. Without violence. All this burning of forests and valleys.

"Look!"

He glanced at Ling, who had stood up and was pointing at Ewasx. The ring stack still quaked, but one torus in the middle was undergoing full-scale convulsions. Throbbing indentations formed on opposite sides, distending its round shape.

Both men joined Ling, staring with unbelieving eyes as the dents deepened and spread into circular bulges, straining outward until a sheer membrane was all that restrained them. The Jophur's basal legs started pumping and flexing.

The humans jumped back when Ewasx abruptly skittered across the floor, first toward the armored door, then away again, zigging and zagging three times before finally sagging back down, like a heap of flaccid tubes.

The middle ring continued to throb and swell.

"What is it doing?" Ling asked in awe.

Lark had to swallow before answering.

"It's *vlenning*. Giving birth, you'd say. Traekis don't do this often, 'cause it endangers the union of the stack. Mostly they bud embryos and let 'em grow in a mulch pile, on their own."

Rann gaped. "Giving birth? Here?" Clearly, he knew more about killing Jophur than about the rest of their life cycle.

Lark realized—the catatonia of Ewasx was *not* caused simply by the surprise rocket attack. That shock had triggered a separate convulsion just waiting to happen.

Membranes started tearing. One of the new rings, almost the size of Lark's head and colored a deep shade of purple, began writhing through. The other was smaller and crimson, emerging through a mucusy pustule, trailing streamers of rank, oily stuff. Both infant toruses slithered down the flanks of the parent stack, then across the metal floor, seeking shadows.

"Lark, you'd better have a look at this," Ling said.

He could barely yank his gaze away from the nauseating, bewitching sight of the greasy newborns. Upon stumbling over to join Ling, he found her pointing downward.

"When it ran back and forth, a dura ago . . . it left this trail on the floor."

So what? he thought. Lark saw smears, like grease stains on the metal plating. *Traeki often do that.*

Then he blinked, recognizing Anglic letters. One, two, three . . . four of them.

R E W Q

"What the . . . ?" Rann puzzled aloud.

Lark raised a hand to his forehead, where his rewq symbiont lay waiting for its next duty while supping lightly from his veins. At a touch, it swarmed over his eyes, recasting the colors in the room.

At once, everything changed. Till that moment, the still-quivering flanks of the Jophur had seemed a mottled jumble of distorted shades. But now, rows of *letters* could be seen, crisscrossing several older rings.

lark, the first series began. ***one ring opens doors. use it. rejoin the six. . . .***

A squeal of pain interrupted from Lark's right, unlike any shouted by a mammal. He whirled, and cried, "Stop!"

Rann stood over one of the newly vlenned rings, his foot raised to stomp on it a second time. The small creature shook, bleeding waxy fluids from a rent along one flank.

"Why?" the Danik demanded. "You sooners signed our death warrants with that crude missile attack. We might as well get in some of our own."

Ling confronted her former colleague hotly. "Fool! Hypocrite! You stopped Lark earlier, and now do this? Don't you want to get out of here?"

She bent over the quivering ring and reached toward it nervously, tentatively.

Lark turned back toward the ring stack . . . the composite being that had somehow managed to become Asx again, in a strange, limited way. The letters were already fading as he read the second line.

Give other to Phwhoon-dau/Lester. he/you/they must

This time, the scream was human.

Ling! He spun around and rushed to her aid.

She held the little wounded torus in one hand while the other clawed over her shoulder at Rann. The male Danik throttled her from behind, his forearm around her throat, closing her windpipe, and possibly her arteries.

Rann heard Lark's irate bellow and swiveled lightly, using Ling's body as a shield while he kept choking her. Rann's face was contorted with pleasure as Lark feinted right, then launched himself at the star warrior's other side. There was no time for finesse as they all toppled together, a grappling mass of arms and legs.

It might have been an even match, if Ling hadn't passed out. But when her body slumped, insensate, Lark had to face Rann's trained fury alone. He managed to get a few blows in, but soon had his hands full just preventing the Rothen agent from striking a vital spot. Finally, in desperation, he threw his arms around Rann, seizing his broad torso in a wrestler's embrace.

His opponent felt confident enough to spare some strength for taunts.

"Darwinist savage . . ." Rann jeered, close to Lark's ear. ". . . devolved ape . . ."

Lark managed an insult of his own—

"The . . . Rothen . . . are . . . pigs. . . ."

Rann snarled and tried to bite his ear. Lark swung his head aside just in time, then slammed it back into Rann's face, breaking his lip.

Abruptly, a *stench* seemed to swell around their heads, filling Lark's nostrils with a cloying, sickening tang. For an instant he wondered if it was the Danik's body odor. Or else the smell of death.

Rann managed to free a hand and used it to pummel Lark's side. But the pain seemed distant, and the blows vague, unsteady. Vision wavered as the awful smell increased . . . and Lark grew aware that his opponent was being affected, as well.

More so.

In moments, Rann's iron grip let go and the man collapsed away from him. Lark backed up, gasping. Through a haze of wavering consciousness, he noted the source of the stench. The wounded traeki ring had climbed onto Rann's shoulder and was squirting yet another dose of some noxious substance straight into the star god's face.

Should . . . make it . . . stop, now, Lark thought. An excess might not just knock Rann out, but kill him.

Life had priorities, though. Fighting exhaustion and the tempting refuge of sleep, Lark rolled over to seek Ling, hoping enough life still lingered to be coaxed back into the world.

Blade

". . . THE MOST EFFECTIVE WARHEADS WERE THE ones tipped with toporgic capsules, filled with traeki formula type sixteen an' powdered Buyur metal. Kindle beetles were useful in settin' off the solid rocket cores. A lot of the ones that didn't use beetles either fizzled or blew up on their launchpads. . . ."

Blade listened to the young human recite her report to an urrish telegraph operator, whose keystrokes became fast-departing beams of light. Jeni Shen winced as a pharmacist applied unguents to her singed skin. Her face was soot-covered and the left side of her jerkin gave off smoldering fumes. Jeni's voice was dry as slate and it must have been painful for her to speak, but the recitation continued, nonstop, as if she feared this mountaintop semaphore station might be the first target of any Jophur retaliation.

". . . Observers report that the best targeting happened in rockets that had message-ball critters aboard. Usin' 'em that way was just a whim of Phwhoon-dau's, so there weren't many. But it seemed to work. Before everything blew up, Lester said we should reexamine all the Buyur critters we know about, in case they have other uses. . . ."

The stone hut was crowded. The missile assault, and subsequent fires, had sent refugees pouring through the passes. Blade was forced to wade through the tide of fugitives in order to reach this militia outpost, where he might make a report of his adventure.

He found the semaphore already tied up with frenzied news—about the successful downing of the last Jophur corvette . . . and then the failure of a single rocket even to dent the mother ship. That night of soaring hopes crashed further when casualties became known, including at least one of the High Sages of the Six.

Yet a low level of elation continued. Bad news was only expected. But a taste of victory came amplified by sheer surprise.

Blade recalled vividly the fiery plummet of both burning halves of the ruined starship, setting off firestorms. *I'm glad it only landed in boo,* he thought. According to the scrolls, Jijo's varied ecosystems weren't equal. Greatboo was a trashy alien invader—like the Six themselves. The planet was not badly wounded by tonight's conflagration.

Me neither, Blade added, wincing as a g'Kek medic tried to set one of his broken legs.

"Just cut it off," he told the doctor. "The other one, too."

"But that will leave you with just three," the g'Kek complained. "How will you walk?"

"I'll manage. Anyway, new ones grow back faster if you cut all the way to the bud. Just get it over with, will you?"

Fortunately, he had managed to land on two legs spread apart at opposite sides of his body. That left a tripod of them to use, dragging himself from the fluttering tangle of fabric and gondola parts. The moonlit mountainside had been rocky and steep, a horrid place for a blue qheuen to find himself stranded on a chill night. But the beckoning glimmer of flashed messages, darting from peak to peak, encouraged him to limp onward until he reached this sanctuary.

So, I'll be able to tell Log Biter my tale, after all. Maybe I'll even write about it. Nelo should provide backing for a small print run, since half of my story involves his daughter. . . .

Blade knew his mind was drifting from thirst, pain, and lack of sleep. But if he rested now he would lose his place in line, right after Jeni Shen. The station commander, hear-

ing of his balloon adventure, had given him a priority just
after the official report on the rocket attack.

*I should be flattered. But in fact, the rockets are used up.
Even if there are some left, the element of surprise is gone.
They'll never succeed against the Jophur again.*

*But my idea's not been tried yet. And it'd work! I'm liv-
ing proof.*

The smiths of Blaze Mountain have got to be told.

So he sat and fumed, half listening to Jeni's lengthy,
jargon-filled report, trying to be patient.

When the amputation began, Blade's cupola withdrew
instinctively, shielding his eye strip under thick chitin,
preventing him from looking around. So he tried pulling
his mind back to the time when he briefly flew through the
sky . . . the first of his kind to do so since the sneakship
came, so long ago.

But a qheuen's memories aren't strong enough to use as
a bulwark against pain.

It took three strong hoons to keep the leg straight
enough for the medic to do it cleanly.

Lark

A SECOND STENCH MET HIM WHEN HE WAKED.
The first one had smothered cloyingly. When it filled
the little room, the world erased under a blanket of
sweet pungency.

The new smell was bitter, tangy, repellent, cleaving the
insensate swaddling of unconsciousness. There was no
transitory muzziness or confusion. Lark jerked upright
while his body convulsed through a series of sharp
sneezes. All at once he knew the cell, its metal floor and
walls, the cramped despair of this place.

A greasy doughnut shape—purple and still covered with
mucus—sent a final stream of misty liquid jetting toward
his face. Lark gagged, backing away.

"I'm up! Cut it out, dung eater!"

The room wavered as he turned, searching . . . and

found Ling close behind, wheezing at the effort of sitting up. Livid marks showed where Rann had throttled her, nearly taking her life.

Lark turned again, scanning for his enemy.

In moments, he spied the Danik agent's bare feet, jutting from beyond the rotund bulk of Ewasx.

Ewasx? Or is it still Asx?

The ring stack shivered. Trails of waxy pus trickled from twin wounds on either side, where the vlenned rings had made their escape.

I could try to find out. . . . Try talking to—

But Lark saw an *orderliness* to the trembling toruses. A systematic rhythm. Almost regimented. Warbling sounds escaped the speaking vent.

"H-h-h-alt, humans. . . . I/WE COMMAND . . . obedience. . . ."

The voice wavered unevenly, but gained strength with each passing dura.

Ling met his eyes. There was instant rapport.

Asx had gone to a lot of trouble to provide gifts.

Time to give them a try.

"STOP THAT!" Ewasx adjured. "You are required to . . . desist. . . ."

Fortunately, the Jophur's limbs were still locked in rigor. The lowermost set shivered with resistance when the master ring tried to make them move.

Asx is still fighting for us, Lark realized, knowing it could not last.

"Use the purple one," he told Ling, who cradled the larger newborn torus. "Asx said it opens locks."

She lifted her eyes doubtfully, but presented the ring to a flat plate beside the door. They had seen Ewasx touch it whenever the Jophur wanted to leave the cell. Meanwhile, Lark used his frayed shirt as a sling to carry the smaller, crimson traeki. The one cruelly injured by Rann. The one Lark was supposed to deliver to the High Sages—an impossible task, even if the mangled thing survived.

A moan echoed from behind Ewasx. It was the Danik warrior, rousing at last. *Come on!* Lark urged silently, though Ling almost surely had never used such a key to force a lock.

The purple ring oozed a clear fluid from pores near the plate. Clickety sounds followed, as the door mechanism seemed to consider. . . .

Then, with a faint hiss, it opened!

He hurried through with Ling, ignoring bitter Jophur curses that followed them until the portal shut again.

"Where now?" Ling asked.

"You're asking me?" He laughed. "You said Galactic ships are standardized!"

She frowned. "The Rothen don't have any battlecruisers like this beast. Neither does Earth. We'd be lucky to glimpse one from afar . . . and even luckier to escape after seeing it."

Lark felt spooky, standing half-naked in an alien passageway filled with weird aromas. A Jophur might enter this stretch of corridor at any moment, or else a war robot, come to hunt them down.

The floor plates began vibrating, low at first, but with a rising mechanical urgency.

"Just guess," he urged, trying to offer an encouraging smile.

Ling answered with a shrug. "Well, if we keep going in one direction, sooner or later we're bound to reach hull. Come on, then. Standing still is the worst thing we can do."

The hallways were deserted.

Occasionally, they hurried past some large chamber and glimpsed Jophur forms within, standing before oddly curved instrument stations, or mingled in swaying groups, communing with clouds of vapor. But the stacks rarely moved. As a biologist, Lark could not help speculating.

They're descended from sedentary creatures, almost sessile. Even with the introduction of master rings, they'd retain some traeki ways, like preferring to work in one place, relatively still.

Lark found it bizarre, striding past closed doors for more than an arrowflight—then another, and a third—using their passkey ring to open armored hatches along the way, meeting no one. *Asx must have taken this into account, giving us even odds of reaching an airlock and . . .*

Lark wondered.

And then what? If there are sky boats or hover plates, Ling might understand their principles, but how will she operate controls made for Jophur tentacles?

Maybe we should just head for the engine room. Try to break some machinery. Cause some inconvenience before they finally shoot us down.

Ling picked up the pace, a growing eagerness in her steps. Perhaps she sensed something in the thickness of the armored doors, or the subtly curved wall joins, indicating they were close.

The next hatch slid aside—and without warning they suddenly faced their first Jophur.

Ling gasped and Lark's knees almost failed him. He felt an overpowering impulse to spin around and run away, though it was doubtless already too late. The thing was bigger than Ewasx, with component rings that shimmered a glossy, extravagant health he had never seen on a Jijoan traeki.

The way Rann compares to me, Lark thought numbly.

During that brief instant, his companion lifted the purple ring, aiming it like a gun at the big Jophur.

A stream of scent vapor jetted toward the stack.

It hesitated . . . then raised up on a dozen insectoid legs and sidled past the two humans, proceeding down the hall.

Lark stared after it, numbly.

What was that? A recognition signal? A forged safe-conduct pass?

He could imagine that Asx—wherever the traeki sage had concealed a sliver of self—must have observed all the chemical codes a Jophur used to get around the ship. What Lark could not begin to picture was what kind of consciousness that implied. How could one deliberately hide a personality within a personality, when the new master ring was in charge, pulling all the strings?

The Jophur rounded a corner, moving on about its business.

Lark turned to look at Ling. She met his eyes and together they both let out a hard sigh.

The airlock was filled with machinery, though no boats or hover plates. They closed the inner door and hurried to the other side, applying the trusty passkey ring, eager to see blue sky and smell Jijo's fresh wind. If they were lucky, and this portal faced the lake, it might even be possible to leap down to the water. Surviving that, their escape could be cut off at any point, once they passed into the Jophur defense perimeter. But none of that seemed to matter right now. The two of them felt eager, indomitable.

Lark still cradled the injured red ring, wondering what the sages were supposed to do with it.

Perhaps Asx expects us to recruit commandos and return with exploser bombs, using these rings to gain entry. . . .

His thoughts arrested as the big hatch rolled aside. Their first glimpse was not of daylight, but stars.

An instant's shivering worry passed through his mind before he realized—this was not outer space, but nighttime in the Rimmers. A flood of bracing, cool air made Lark instantly ebullient. *I could never leave Jijo,* he knew. *It's my home.*

A pale glow washed out the constellations where a serrated border crossed the sky—the outline of eastern mountains. It would be dawn soon. A time of hopeful beginnings?

Ling held out her free hand for Lark to take as they strode to the edge and looked down.

"So far, so good," she said, and he shared her gladness at the sight of glinting moonlight, sparkling on water. "It's still dim outside. The lake will mask our heat sign. And this time there will be no computer cognizance to give us away."

Nor convenient breathing tubes, to let us stay safe underwater, he almost added, but Lark didn't want to dampen her enthusiasm.

"Let's see if there's anything we can use to get down to the lake, without having to jump," Ling added. Together they inspected the equipment shelves lining one wall of the airlock, until she cried out excitedly. "I found a standard cable reel! Now if only I can figure out the altered controls . . ."

While Ling examined the metal spool, Lark felt a change in the low vibration that had been growling in the background ever since they escaped their prison cell. The resonance began to rise in pitch and force, until it soon filled the air with a harsh keening.

"Something's happening," he said. "I think—"

Just then the battleship took a sudden jerk, almost knocking them both to the floor. Ling dropped the cable, barely missing her foot.

A second noise burst in through the open door of the airlock. An awful *grinding* din, as if Jijo herself were complaining. Lark recognized the scraping of metal against rock.

"Ifni!" Ling cried. "They're taking off!"

Helping each other, fighting for balance, they reached the outer hatch and looked down again, staring aghast at a spectacle of pent-up nature, suddenly unleashed.

Well, so much for jumping in the lake, he thought. The Jophur ship was rising glacially, but the first few dozen meters were crucial, removing the dam that had drowned the valley under a transient reservoir. At once, the Festival Glade was transformed into a roiling tempest. Submerged trees tore loose from their sodden roots. Stones fell crashing into the maelstrom as mud banks were undermined. While the battlecruiser climbed complacently, a vast flood of murky water and debris rushed downstream, pummeling everything in its path, pouring toward distant, unsuspecting plains.

Too late, Lark realized. *We were too late making our escape. Now we're trapped inside.*

As if to seal the fact, a light flashed near the open hatch, which began to close. An automatic safety measure, he figured, for a starship taking off. Lark barely suppressed an overpowering temptation to dive through the narrowing gap, despite the deadly chaos waiting below.

Ling squeezed his hand fiercely as they caught a passing glimpse of something shiny and round-shouldered—a slick, elongated dome, uncovered by retreating waters. Even under pale predawn light, they recognized the Rothen-Danik ship, still shut within a prison of quantum time.

Then the armored portal sealed with a boom and hiss, cutting off the all-too-fleeting breeze. Trapped inside, they stared at the cruel hatch.

"We're heading north," Lark said. It was the one last thing he had noticed, watching the ravaged valley pass below.

"Come on," Ling answered pragmatically. "There must be someplace to hide aboard this bloated ship."

Nelo

STILL A FEW LEAGUES SHORT OF THEIR GOAL, THE zealots realized they were surrounded. They spent the night huddled in the marsh, counting the campfires of regiments loyal to the High Sages. Squeezed between militia units from Biblos and Nelo's pursuing detachment, the rebels surrendered at first light.

There was little ceremony, and few weapons for the rabble to give up. Most of their fanatical ardor had been used up by the hard slog across a quagmire where mighty Buyur towers once reared toward the sky. Already bedraggled, Jop and his followers marched in a ragged column toward the Bibur, enduring taunts from former neighbors.

"Go ahead an' look!" Nelo pushed the tree farmer toward a bluff where everyone could look across the wide river at shimmering cliffs, still immersed in dawn's long shadows. Oncoming daylight revealed a vast cave underneath, chiseled centuries ago by the Earthship *Tabernacle*. Two dozen huge pillars supported the Fist of Stone, hovering like a suspended sentence, just above a cluster of quaint wooden buildings, each fashioned to resemble some famed structure of Terran heritage—such as the Taj Mahal, the Great Pyramid of Cheops, and the Main Library of San Diego, California.

"The Archive stands," Nelo told his enemy. "You wanted to bring the Fist crashing down, but it ain't gonna happen. And in a couple o' years I'll be makin' paper again. It was all for nothin', Jop. The lives you wasted, and the property. You achieved nothing."

Nelo saw Jop's bitterness redouble when they reached a new semaphore station, set up directly across the water from Biblos, where they learned about the rocket attack, the destruction of one Jophur ship, and the rumored damage of another. Young militia soldiers shouted jubilation to learn that last night's distant "thunderstorm" had instead been the unleashed fury of the Six Races, taking vengeance for the poor g'Kek.

A few older faces were grim. The militia captain warned that this was but a single battle in a war the Commons of Jijo could hardly hope to win.

Nelo refused to think about that. Instead, he kept his promise to Ariana Foo, by handing over her message for transmission. Light-borne signals flew better at night, but the operator refired his lamp when he saw Ariana's name on the single sheet of paper. While that bulletin went out, the captain looked into getting transportation across the Bibur, where showers and clean clothes waited.

And sleep, Nelo thought. Yet, despite fatigue, he somehow felt younger than he had in ages, as if the tiring chase through swamplands had stripped years away, leaving him a virile warrior of long ago.

Leaning against a tree, Nelo let his eyes close for a little while, his mind turning back to plans for a rebuilt paper mill.

Our first job will be helping the blues put their dam back together. Do it right, this time. Less worrying about camouflage and more about getting good power output. As long as I'm at Biblos, I might as well look into copying some designs. . . .

Nelo's head jerked up when a carpentry apprentice from Dolo shouted his name. The lad had been reading last night's semaphore messages, affixed on the wall of the relay post.

"I just saw your daughter's name," the young man told him. "She's on Mount Guenn!"

Nelo took three jerky steps forward . . . as *Jop* did exactly the same thing. The farmer's expression showed the same surprise. His shock and dismay contrasted with Nelo's joy at hearing that one of his children lived.

Sara! The papermaker's mind whirled. *In the name of the founders, how did she find herself on Mount Guenn?*

He hurried over to the shed, eager to learn more. Perhaps there would be word of Dwer and Lark, as well!

At that moment, a shout erupted from one of the operators inside the semaphore hut. While the sender kept on clicking his key, transmitting Ariana Foo's message, the *receiver* burst out through the door, a middle-aged woman waving a paper covered with hurried scrawls.

"Mess . . . mess . . ." She ran for the militia captain, gasping urgently.

"Message from lookouts," she cried. "The Jophur . . . the Jophur ship is coming this way!"

It did not swoop or plummet. The star vessel was far too vast for that.

A haze of suspended dust accompanied its passage above forest or open ground, but when the immense sky mountain moved ponderously over the Bibur, the waters went ominously still. The glassy-smooth footprint spread even wider than its shadow.

Keep going, Nelo prayed. *Just pass us by. Keep going. . . .*

But the great cruiser evidently had plans right here, arresting its forward momentum directly over the river, in plain sight of the Great Archive.

Now it was Nelo's turn to glower as he glimpsed grim satisfaction pass over Jop's face. *Someone must've snitched,* he thought. Rumors told of Jophur emissaries, establishing outposts in tiny hamlets, imperiously demanding information. Sooner or later some zealot or scroll thumper would have blabbed about this place.

No slashing rays fell from the mighty battleship. No rain of bombs, taking vengeance for its little brother, lost the night before.

Instead, a few small portals opened in its side. About

two dozen *robots* descended, fluttering lazily until they reached hoon height above the water, where they turned in formation and streaked toward Biblos.

A second wave emerged from the great ship, floating down more slowly on wide plates of burnished black. Tapered cones rode those flat conveyances, like stacks of glossy pancakes, each pile on its own flying skillet.

Even before the Jophur party reached the walls of the hidden city, the space dreadnought began moving again, turning its massive bulk to head back the way it came, roughly south by southeast, gaining altitude at an accelerating pace. By the time Nelo lost it in the glare of the rising sun, the cruiser had climbed above the highest clouds.

Crowds gathered at the riverbank, peering at the opposite shore. Biblos still lay immersed in nightlike shadows. By contrast, the robots glittered till they passed under the Fist of Stone, followed by their Jophur masters.

After that, Nelo and the others had to rely on the militia captain, peering through binoculars, to relate what was happening.

"Each Jophur is entering a different building, guarded by several robots. Some use the front door . . . but one just sent its servants to smash open a wall and go in that way.

"They're all inside now . . . and people are running out! Humans, hoons, qheuens . . . there's a g'Kek . . . his left wheel is smoking. I think he's been shot."

The crowd murmured frustration, but there was nothing to do. Nothing anybody could do.

"I see militia squads! Mostly humans with some urs and hoons. They've got rifles . . . the new kind with mulc-tipped bullets. They're running toward the Science Building!

"They're splitting up, skirmish style, using opposite doors to sneak in from both sides at once."

Nelo clenched his hands as he stared across the Bibur. At the same time, he wondered why the great battleship would come all this way, yet not tarry to destroy the center of Jijoan intellectual life.

I guess the cruiser had other matters to attend to. Anyway, it'll be back to pick up their foray party.

There was one hope. *Maybe there are some rockets left*

after last night. Perhaps they'll catch the cruiser, before it can return.

There was always that hope—though it seemed unlikely the Jophur would be fooled a second time.

Across the river he could see a flood of refugees—scholars, librarians, and students—pouring out of sally ports and over the battlements. There weren't many g'Kek among the fugitives. Nor traeki. Both races appeared doomed to stay within, destined for different fates, both of them unpleasant.

He wondered, *What do the aliens want with our Library? To check out some books and take 'em back home to read?*

In fact, that bizarre notion made sense.

I'll bet the rocket attack made 'em realize we have tricks up our sleeve. Suddenly they're interested in what we know, and how we know it. They'll scan our books to find out what other nasty surprises we might come up with.

Something was happening in the shadowed cave. Distant popping sounds carried across the river, doubtless from within the Hall of Science.

"They're coming out!" the captain announced. His grip on the binoculars stiffened. "The rifle squads . . . they're in retreat . . . dragging their wounded, trying to cover each other. They're . . ."

He lowered the glasses. The officer's eyes were bleak and he stood silently, completely overcome.

A corporal gently took the binoculars and resumed reporting.

"Dead," was the first word she said.

"I see dead soldiers. They're all down."

A hush settled over the crowd. Across the Bibur nothing seemed to be moving anymore, except an occasional sharp-edged machine shape, flitting underneath the Fist of Stone.

The explosers . . . Nelo wondered. *Why didn't they set off their charges?*

The greatest secret of the Six Races. The most secure fortress of humankind on Jijo. Biblos had been captured in a matter of duras. Its treasured archive lay in the tight grip of Jophur invaders.

Ewasx

IS IT SETTLED THEN, MY RINGS? HAVE WE ROOTED out the last corners of your clandestine resistance? Can we assume there will be no more episodes of surreptitious rebellion?

The Priest-Stack threatened to dismantle us/Me after the last embarrassment, when you silly rings foolishly/cleverly managed to perform a vlenning without your master torus knowing. The priest aimed to scrape every drip trail of waxy memory lining our core, seeking clues to the whereabouts of the pair of wolfling vermin you (briefly, mutinously) released into our glorious *Polkjhy* ship.

But then the stack in change of psychological tactics reported telemetry showing that Lark and Ling almost surely departed the ship when instruments showed an airlock hatch anomalously opening.

Humans are good with water. No doubt they imagined themselves safe after entering the lake, never suspecting that they were about to be swept downstream into a vortex of ruin when our majestic *Polkjhy* took off!

The droll appropriateness of this fate—the dramatic irony—so pleased the Captain-Leader that a ruling was made, overturning the Priest-Stack's desire. For the time being, then, our/My union is safe.

DO NOT COUNT ON CONTINUED TEMPERANCE/ FORGIVENESS, MY RINGS!

Forgiveness for *what,* you ask?

Now you worry Me. Is the shared wax so badly melted? Did the Asx personality so damage us, with its second attempt at suicide-by-amnesia? Must I provide memory of recent events through the demi-electronic processes of the master torus?

Very well, My rings, I shall do so. Then we will begin again, restoring the expertise that made us useful to the Jophur cause.

•   •   •

Together we watched while a party from our ship took possession of the so-called Library used by the savage Six Races. Though it contains a pathetically small amount of bit-equivalent data, this is the source/font of their wolfling trickery.

Feral scheming that has cost us dearly.

A fine thing happened when we/I caught sight of those crude buildings made from sliced trees, sheltered in an artificial cave. Many hidden waxy trails resonated with sudden recognition! Accessing these recovered tracks, we were able to tell the Captain-Leader many secrets of this trove of pseudo-knowledge. Secrets Asx had meant to render inaccessible.

Slowly, we regain our former reputation and esteem. Does that make you glad, My rings?

How gratifying to feel your agreement come so readily now! That brief rebellion, followed by a second suicide amnesia, appears to have left you more docile than before. No longer sovereign traeki rings, but parts of a greater whole.

Now regard! Leaving a force behind to secure Biblos, our *Polkjhy* turns to its main task. Too long have we let ourselves be diverted/delayed. There will be no more negotiating with Rothen sneak thieves. No more dickering with savage races. Those six will meet their varied fates from land forces already scattered across the Slope.

As for *Polkjhy*, we cruise toward that continental cleft, that ocean abyss. Estimated locale of the dolphin ship.

IT IS DECIDED. THE ROTHEN HAD THE RIGHT IDEA, AFTER ALL.

We'll bombard the depths, putting the fugitive Earthlings in peril. To preserve their lives, they will have no choice but to rise up and surrender.

Until now, the Captain-Leader preferred patience over rash action. We did not want to destroy the very thing we seek! Not before learning its secrets. Since no competing clan or fleet has come to Jijo, we appeared to have a wealth of time.

But that was before we lost both corvettes. Before postponements stretched on and on.

Now we are resolved to take the chance!

With depth bombs ready in great store, we plunge toward the zone known as the Rift.

WHAT IS THIS? ALREADY?

DETECTORS BLARE.

IN THE WATERS AHEAD OF US—MOTION!

Joyous hunt lust fills the bridge. It must be the *prey,* giving away their location as they scurry in search of a new hiding place.

Then remote perceptors cry out upsetting news.

No single ship is making the vibrations we detect.

THERE ARE SCORES OF EMISSION SITES . . . HUNDREDS!

Sara

EMERSON SEEMED CHEERFUL DURING THE LONG ride down from Mount Guenn, pressing his face against the warped window of the little tram, gazing at the sea.

How would he feel if he knew whom we were meeting? Sara wondered as the car zoomed down ancient lava flows, swifter than a galloping urs.

Would he be ecstatic, or try to jump out and flee?

Far below, a myriad bright sun glints stretched from the surf line all the way to a cloud-fringed western horizon. Jijo's waters seemed placid, but Sara still felt daunted by the sight. A mere one percent ripple in that vastness would erase every tree and settlement along the coast. The ocean's constancy proved the ample goodness of this life world—a nursery of species.

I always hoped to see this, before my bones went to the Midden as dross. I just never figured I'd come by horseback, across the Spectral Flow, over a volcano . . . and finally by fabulous cable car, all toward confronting creatures out of legend.

Sara felt energized, despite the fact that nobody on Mount Guenn slept much lately.

Uriel had finished using her analog computer barely in time. Just miduras after sending the ballistics calculations north, semaphore operators reported breathless news about the consequences.

Stunning rocket victories.

Discouraging rocket failures.

Forest fires, dead sages, and the Egg—wounded, silent, possibly forever.

Flash floods below Festival Glade, leaving countless dead or homeless.

Nor was that all. Throughout the night, tucked amid other tidings from across the Slope, came clipped summaries of events bearing hard on Sara.

Elation surged when she learned of Blade's unqheuenish aerial adventures. Then her father's report triggered overpowering images of the destruction of Dolo Village, forcing her to seek a place to sit, burying her head in her hands. Nelo lived—that was something. But others she had known were gone, along with the house she grew up in.

Lark and Dwer . . . we dreamed what it might be like when the dam blew. But I never really thought it could happen.

Waves of sorrow kept Sara withdrawn for a time, till someone told her an urgent message had come, addressed specifically for her, under the imprimatur of a former High Sage of the Six.

Ariana Foo, Sara realized, scanning the brief missive. *Ifni, who cares about the dimensions of the ship that crashed Emerson into the swamp? Does it matter what kind of chariot he used, when he was a star god? He's a wounded soul now. Crippled. Trapped on Jijo, like the rest of us.*

Or was he?

After so many shocks that eventful night, Sara was just lying down for a blotting balm of sleep when events close at hand rocked Uriel and her guests.

At dawn, the captains of Wuphon Port sent word of a monster in their harbor. A fishlike entity who, after some misunderstandings, claimed relatedness to human beings.

Moreover, the creature said it bore a message for the smith.

Uriel was overjoyed.

"The little sneak canera that scared us so . . . the device cane fron the Earthling shif! Ferhafs the Jophur have not found us, after all!"

That mattered. The sky battleship was said to be on the move, perhaps heading in their direction. But Uriel could not evacuate the forge with several projects still under way. Her teams had never been busier.

"I'll go see the Terran at once," the smith declared.

There was no lack of volunteers to come along. Riding the first tram, Sara watched Prity flip through Emerson's wrinkled sketchpad, lingering over a page where sleek figures with finned backs and tails arched ecstatically through crashing waves. An image drawn from memory.

"They look other than I inagined," commented Uriel, curling her long neck past the chimp's shoulder. "Till now, I only knew the race fron descrifshuns in vooks."

"You should read the kind with pictures in 'em." Kurt the Exploser laughed, nudging his nephew. But Jomah kept his face pressed to the window next to Emerson, taking turns pointing at features of the fast-changing landscape. Ever-cheerful, the starman showed no awareness of what this trip was about.

Sara knew what tugged her heart. Beyond all other worries and pangs, she realized, *It may be time for the bird to fly back to his own kind.*

Watching the robust person she had nursed from the brink of death, Sara saw no more she could offer him. No cure for a ravaged brain, whose sole hope lay back in the Civilization of the Five Galaxies. Even with omnipotent foes in pursuit, who wouldn't choose that life over a shadow existence, huddling on a stranded shore?

The ancestors, that's who. The Tabernacle *crew, and all the other sneakships.*

Sara recalled what Sage Purofsky said, only a day ago.

"There are no accidents, Sara. Too many ships came to Jijo, in too short time."

"The scrolls speak of destiny," she had replied.

"Destiny!" The sage snorted disdain. *"A word made up*

by people who don't understand how they got where they are, and are blind to where they're going."

"Are you saying you know how we got here, Master?"

Despite all the recent commotion and tragedy, Sara found her mind still hooked by Purofsky's reply.

"Of course I do, Sara. It seems quite clear to me.

"We were invited."

Ewasx

"FOOLS!" THE CAPTAIN-LEADER DECLARES. "ALL BUT one of these emanations must come from decoy torpedoes, tuned to imitate the emission patterns of a starship. It is a standard tactical ruse in deep space. But such artifice cannot avail if we linger circumspectly at short range!

"Use standard techniques to sift the emanations.

"FIND THE TRUE VESSEL WE SEEK!"

Ah, My rings. Can you discern the colors swarming down the glossy flanks of our Captain-Leader? See how glorious, how lustrous they are. Witness the true dignity of Jophur wrath in its finest form.

Such indignation! Such egotistic rage! The Oailie would be proud of this commander of ours, especially as we all hear impossible news.

THESE ARE NOT DECOY DRONES AT ALL.

The myriad objects we detect . . . moving out of the Rift toward open ocean . . . EVERY ONE OF THEM IS A REAL STARSHIP!

The bridge mists with fearful vapors. A great fleet of ships! How did the Earthers acquire such allies?

Even our *Polkjhy* is no match for this many.

We will be overwhelmed!

Dwer

I AM SORRY," GILLIAN BASKIN TOLD HIM. "THE DECI-
sion came suddenly. There was no time to arrange a special ride to shore."

She seemed irked, as if his request were unexpected.
But in fact, Dwer had asked for nothing else since his second day aboard this vessel.

The two humans drifted near each other in a spacious,
water-filled chamber, the control center of starship
Streaker. Dolphins flew past them across the spherical
room, breathing oxygen-charged fluid with lungs that had
been modified to make it almost second nature. At consoles and workstations, they switched to bubble domes or
tubes attached directly to their blowholes. It seemed as
strange an environment as Dwer had ever dreamed, yet the
fins seemed in their element. By contrast, Dwer and Gillian
wore balloonlike garments, seeming quite out of place.

"I'm not doing any good here," he repeated, hearing the
words narrowly projected by his globe helmet. "I got no
skills you can use. I can hardly breathe the stuff you call
air. Most important, there are folks waiting for me. Who
need me. Can't you just cut me loose in some kind of a
boat?"

Gillian closed her eyes and sighed—a brief, eerie set of
clicks and chuttering moans. "Look, I understand your predicament," she said in Anglic. "But I have over a hundred
lives to look after . . . and a lot more at stake, in a larger
sense. I'm sorry, Dwer. All I can hope is that you'll understand."

He knew it useless to pursue the matter further. A dol-
phin at one of the bridge stations called for attention, and
Gillian was soon huddled with that fin and Lieutenant
Tsh't, solving the latest crisis.

The groan of *Streaker*'s engines made Dwer's head
itch—a residual effect, perhaps, of the way his brain was
palped and bruised by the Danik robot. He had no proof
things would really be any better if he found his way back

to shore. But his legs, arms, and lungs all pined for wilderness—for wind on his face and the feel of rough ground underfoot.

A ghostly map traced its way across the bridge. The realm of dry land was a grayish border rimming both sides of a submerged canyon—the Rift—now filled with moving lights, dispersing like fire bees abandoning their hives. So it seemed to Dwer as over a hundred ancient Buyur vessels came alive after half a million years, departing the trash heap where they were consigned long ago.

The tactic was familiar. Many creatures used flocking to confuse predators. He approved the cleverness of Gillian and her crew, and wished them luck.

But I can't help them. I'm useless here. She ought to let me go.

Most of the salvaged ships were under robotic control, programmed to follow simple sets of instructions. Volunteers rode a few derelicts, keeping close to *Streaker,* performing special tasks. *Rety* had volunteered for one of those teams, surprising Dwer and worrying him at the same time.

She never does anything unless there's an angle.

If he had gone along, there might have been a chance to veer the decoy close to shore, and jump off. . . .

But no, he had no right to mess up Gillian's plan.

Dammit, I'm used to action! I can't handle being a passive observer.

But handle it he must.

Dwer tried to cultivate patience, ignoring an itch where the bulky suit would not let him scratch, watching the lights disperse—most heading for the mouth of the Rift, spilling into the vast oceanic abyss of the Great Midden itself.

"*Starship enginesss!*" The gravitics detector officer announced, thrashing her tail flukes in the water, causing bubbles in the supercharged liquid.

"*P-passive detectors show Nova class or higher . . . it'sss following the path of the Riffft. . . .*"

Ewasx

REALIZATION EMERGES, ALONG WITH A STENCH OF frustration.

The vast fleet of vessels that we briefly feared has proved not to be a threat, after all. They are not warships, but decommissioned vessels, long ago abandoned as useless for efficient function.

Nevertheless, they baffle and thwart our goal/mission.

A blast of leadership pheromones cuts through the disappointed mist.

"TO WORK THEN," our Captain-Leader proclaims.

"WE ARE SKILLED. WE ARE MIGHTY. SO LET US DO YOUR/OUR JOBS WELL.

"PIERCE THIS MYSTERY. FIND THE PREY. WE ARE JOPHUR. WE SHALL PREVAIL."

Dwer

A GLITTERING LIGHT ENTERED THE DISPLAY ZONE, much higher and much larger than any of the others, and cruising well above the imaginary waterline.

That must be the battleship, he thought. His mind tried to come up with an image. Something huge and terrible. Clawed and swift.

Suddenly, the detection officer's voice went shrill.

"They're dropping ordnance!"

Sparks began falling from the big glow.

Bombs, Dwer realized. He had seen this happen before, but not on such a profuse scale.

Lieutenant Tsh't shouted a warning.

"All handsss, prepare for shock waves!"

Sara

A HOONISH WORK CREW SWARMED OVER THE TRAM
after the passengers debarked, filling the car with stacks
of folded cloth. Teams had been sending the stuff up to
the forge since dawn, stripping every ship of its sails. But
the urrish smith hardly glanced at the cargo. Instead, Uriel
trotted off, leading the way down to the cove with a
haughty centauroid gait.

The dense, salty air of sea level affected everybody. Sara
kept an eye on Emerson, who sniffed the breeze and commented in song.

> *"A storm is a-brewin'*
> *You can bet on it tonight.*
> *A blow is a-stewin'*
> *So you better batten tight."*

The khutas and warehouses of the little port were
shaded by a dense lattice of melon vines and nectar creepers, growing with a lush, tropical abundance characteristic
of southern climes. The alleys were deserted though. Everyone was either working for Uriel or else down by the
bay, where a crowd of hoons and qheuens babbled excitedly. Several hoons—males and females with beards of seniority—knelt by the edge of a quay, conversing toward
the water, using animated gestures. But the town officials
made way when Uriel's party neared.

Sara kept her attention on Emerson, whose expression
stayed casually curious until the last moment, when a sleek
gray figure lifted its glossy head from the water.

The starman stopped and stared, blinking rapidly.

He's surprised, Sara thought. *Could we be wrong? Perhaps he has nothing to do with the dolphin ship.*

Then the cetacean emissary lifted its body higher, thrashing water with its tail.

"Sssso, it's true. . . ." the fishlike Terran said in thickly accented Anglic, inspecting Emerson with one eye, then the other.

"Glad to see you living, Engineer D-D'Anite. Though it hardly seems possible, after what we saw happen to you back at the Fractal world.

"I confessss, I can't see how you followed us to this whale-forsaken planet."

Powerful emotions fought across Emerson's face. Sara read astonishment, battling surges of both curiosity and frustrated despair.

"K-K-K—"

The dismal effort to speak ended in a groan.

"A-ah-ahh . . ."

The dolphin seemed upset by this response, chuttering dismay over the human's condition.

But then Emerson shook his head, seeking to draw on other resources. At last, he found a way to express his feelings, releasing a burst stream of song.

> *"How quaint the ways of paradox!*
> *At common sense she gaily mocks!*
> *We've quips and quibbles heard in*
> *   flocks,*
> *But none to beat this paradox!"*

Gillian

THE ULTIMATUM BLANKETED ALL ETHERIC WAVE-lengths—a scratchy caterwauling that filled *Streaker*'s bridge, making the oxy-water fizz. Streams of bubbles swelled and popped with each Galactic Four syntax phrase.

Most neo-dolphin crew members read a text translation prepared by the Niss Machine. Anglic letters and GalSeven glyphs flowed across the main holo screen.

HEAR AND COMPREHEND OUR FINAL COMMAND/OFFER!

•   •   •

Gillian listened for nuance in the original Jophur dialect, hoping to glean something new. It was the third repetition since the enemy dreadnought began broadcasting from high in the atmosphere.

"YOU WHOM WE SEEK—YOU HAVE PERFORMED CLEVER MANEUVERS, WORTHY OF RESPECT. AT THIS JUNCTURE, WE SHALL NO LONGER WASTE BOMBS. WE SHALL CEASE USELESSLY INSPECTING DECOYS."

The change in tactics was expected. At first, the foe had sent robots into the lightless depths, to examine and eliminate reactivated Buyur ships, one by one. But it was a simple matter for Hannes Suessi's team to fix booby traps. Each derelict would self-destruct when a probe approached, taking the automaton along with it.

The usual hierarchy of battle was thus reversed. Here in the Midden, big noisy ships were far cheaper than robots to hunt them. Suessi had scores more ready to peel off from widely separated dross piles. It was doubtful the Jophur could spend drones at the same rate.

There was a downside. The decoy ships were discards, in ill repair when abandoned, half a million years ago. Only the incredible hardiness of Galactic manufacture left them marginally useful, and dozens had already burned out, littering the Midden once more with their dead hulks.

"FAILING TO COERCE YOU BY THAT MEANS, WE ARE NOW PREPARED TO OFFER YOU GENEROUS TERMS. . . ."

This was the part Gillian paid close attention to, the first couple of times it played. Unfortunately, Jophur "generosity" wasn't tempting. In exchange for *Streaker*'s data, charts, and samples, the Captain-Leader of the Greatship *Polkjhy* promised cryonic internment for the crew, with a guarantee of revival and free release in a mere thousand years. "After the present troubles have been resolved."

In other words, the Jophur wanted to have *Streaker's* secrets . . . *and* to make sure no one else shared them for a long time to come.

While the message laid out this offer, Gillian's second-in-command swam alongside.

"We've managed to c-come up with most of the sup-pliesss the local wizard asked for," Tsh't reported. One of the results of making contact with the Commons of Six Races had been a shopping list of items desperately wanted by the urrish smith, Uriel.

"Several decoy ships are being diverted close to shore, as you requested. Kaa and his new t-team can strip them of the stuff Uriel wants, as they swing by."

The dolphin lieutenant paused. "I suppose I needn't add that this increases our danger? The enemy might detect a rhythm in these movementsss, and target their attention on the hoonish seaport-t."

"The Niss came up with a swarming pattern to prevent that," Gillian answered. "What about the crew separation? How are Makanee's preparations coming along?"

Tsh't nodded her sleek head. Taking a break from the laborious, underwater version of Anglic, she replied in Trinary.

> * *Seasons change the tides,*
> > * *That tug us toward our fates,*
> > > * *And divide loved ones . . .* *

To which she added a punctuating coda:

> * *. . . forever. . . .* *

Gillian winced. What she planned—least awful of a dozen grievous options—would sever close bonds among a crew that had shared great trials. An epic journey Earthlings might sing about for ages to come.

Providing there are still Earthlings, after the Time of Changes.

In fact, she had no choice. Half of *Streaker's* neo-dolphin complement were showing signs of stress atavism—a decay of the faculties needed for critical thought. Fear and exhaustion had finally taken their toll. No client race as young as *Tursiops amicus* had ever endured so much for so long, almost alone.

It's time to make the sacrifice we all knew would someday come.

The chamber still vibrated with Jophur threats. Coming from some other race, she might have factored in an element of bluster and bravado, but she took these adversaries precisely at their word.

The holo display glowed with menacing letters.

WE ARE THE ONLY GALACTIC WARSHIP IN THIS REGION. NO ONE IS COMING TO HELP YOU. NOR WILL ANY COMPETITORS DISTRACT US, AS HAPPENED ON OTHER OCCASIONS.

WE CAN AFFORD TO WAIT YOU OUT, INVESTIGATING AND ELIMINATING DECOYS FROM SAFE RANGE. OR ELSE, IF NECESSARY, THIS NOBLE SHIP WILL FORGO SOLE HONOR AND SEND FOR HELP FROM THE VAST JOPHUR ARMADA.

DELAY MERELY INCREASES OUR WRATH. IT AUGMENTS THE HARM WE SHALL DO TO YOUR TERRAN COUSINS, AND THE OTHER SOONERS WHO DWELL ILLICITLY ON FORBIDDEN LAND. . . .

Gillian thought of Alvin, Huck, and Ur-ronn, listening in a nearby dry cabin—and Pincer-Tip, who represented them on the bridge, darting to and fro with flicks of his red claws.

We already drew hell down on the locals, when the Rothen somehow tracked us to Jijo. There must be a way to spare them further punishment on our account.

Soon it will be time to end this.

Gillian turned back to Tsh't. "How much longer before it's our turn?"

The lieutenant communed with the tactics-and-movement officer.

"We'll slip in to shore between the fourth and fifth decoys . . . about eight hours from now."

Gillian glanced at Pincer, his reddish carapace covered with oxy-water bubbles, the qheuen visor spinning madly, taking in everything with the avidness of adolescence. The local youths should be glad about what was about to happen. *And so will Dwer Koolhan. I hope this pleases him . . . though it's not quite what he wanted.*

Gillian admitted to herself she would miss the young man who reminded her so much of Tom.

"All right, then," she told Tsh't. "Let's take the kids home."

Lark

TOGETHER, THEY PROVED ONLY HALF-BLIND, STUM-bling down the musty corridors of a vast alien ship filled with hostile beings. Ling knew more than he did about starships, but Lark was the one who kept them from getting completely lost.

For one thing, there were few symbols on the walls, so their knowledge of several Galactic dialects proved almost useless. Instead, each closed aperture or intersection seemed to project its own, unique *smell,* effective at short range. As a Jijoan, Lark could sniff some of these and dimly grasp the simplest pheromone indicators—about as well as a bright human four-year-old might read street signs in a metropolis.

One bitter tang reminded him of the scent worn by traeki proctors at Gathering Festival, when they had to break up a fight or subdue a belligerent drunk.

SECURITY, the odor seemed to say. He steered Ling around that hallway.

She had a goal, however, which was one up on him. With his head full of fragrant miasmas, Lark gladly left the destination up to her. No doubt any path they chose would eventually lead to the same place—their old prison cell.

Three more times, they encountered solitary Jophur. But

puffs from the purple ring caused them to be ignored. Doors continued sliding open on command. The gift from Asx was incredible. A little too good, in fact.

I can't believe this trick will work for long, he thought as they hurried deeper into the battleship's heart. *Asx probably expected us to need it for a midura or so, just till we made it outside.* Once the crew was alerted about escaped prisoners, the ruse must surely fail. The Jophur would use countermeasures, wouldn't they?

Then he realized.

Maybe there's been no alert. The Jophur may assume we already fled the ship!

Perhaps.

Still, each encounter with a gleaming ring stack in some dank passage left him feeling eerie. Lark had lived among traeki all his life, but till this moment he never grasped how different their consciousness must be. How strange for a sapient being to look right at you and not *see,* simply because you gave off the right safe-conduct aroma. . . .

At the next intersection, he sniffed all three corridor branches carefully, and found the indicator Ling wanted—a simple scent that meant LIFE. He pointed, and she nodded.

"As I thought. The layout isn't too different from a type-seventy cargo ship. They keep it at the center."

"Keep *what* at the center?" Lark asked, but she was already hurrying ahead. Two human fugitives, bearing their only tools—she cradling the wounded red traeki ring, while he carried the purple one.

When the next door opened, Ling stepped back briefly from a glare. The place was more brightly lit than the normal dim corridors. The air smelled better, too. Less cloying with meanings he could not comprehend. Lark's first impression was of a large chamber, filled with color.

"As I hoped," Ling said, nodding. "The layout's standard. We may actually have a chance."

"A chance for what?"

She turned back to look into the vault, which Lark now saw to be quite vast, filled with a maze of crisscrossing support beams . . . all of them draped with varied types of vegetation.

"A chance to survive," she answered, and took his hand, drawing him inside.

A jungle surrounded them, neatly organized and regimented. Tier after tier of shelves and platforms receded from view, serviced by machines moving slowly along tracks. Arrayed on this vast network there flourished a riot of living forms, broad leaves and hanging vines, creepers and glistening tubers. Water dripped along some of the twisted green cables, and the two of them rushed to the nearest trickle, lapping eagerly.

Now Lark understood the meaning of the aroma symbol that had led them here.

In the middle of hell, they had found a small oasis. At that moment, it felt like paradise.

Emerson

HE DID NOT LIKE GOING DOWN TO THE WATER. THE harbor was too frenzied.

It hardly seemed like a joyous reunion to see Kaa and other friends again. He recognized good old Brookida, and Tussito, and Wattaceti. They all seemed glad to see him, but far too busy to spend time visiting, or catching up.

Perhaps that was just as well. Emerson felt ashamed.

Shame that he could not greet them with anything more than their names . . . and an occasional snippet of song.

Shame that he could not help them in their efforts—hauling all sorts of junk out of the sea, instructing Uriel's assistants, and sending the materials up by tram to the peak of Mount Guenn.

Above all, he felt shame over the failure of his sacrifice, back at that immense space city made of snow—that fluffy metropolis, the size of a solar system—called the Fractal System.

Oh, it seemed so noble and brave when he set forth in a salvaged Thennanin scout, extravagantly firing to create a diversion and help *Streaker* escape. With his last glimpse—as force fields closed in all around him—he had seen the beloved, scarred hull slip out through an opening in the vast shell of ice, and prayed she would make it.

Gillian, he had thought. Perhaps she would think of him, now. The way she recalled her Tom.

Then the Old Ones took him from the little ship, and had their way with him. They prodded and probed. They made him a cripple. They gave him forgetfulness.

And they sent him here.

The outlines are still hazy, but Emerson now saw the essential puzzle.

Streaker had escaped to this forlorn planet, only to be trapped. More hard luck for a crew that never got a break.

But . . . why . . : send . . . me . . . here?

That action by the Old Ones made no sense. It seemed crazy.

Everyone would be better off if he had died, the way he planned.

The whole population of the hoonish seaport was dashing about. Sara seemed preoccupied, spending much of her time talking rapidly to Uriel, or else arguing heatedly with the gray-bearded human scholar whose name Emerson could not recall.

Often a messenger would arrive, bearing one of the pale paper strips used for transcribing semaphore bulletins. Once, the urrish courier came at a gallop, panting and clearly shaken by the news she bore. An eruption of dismayed babble swelled as Emerson made out a single repeated word—"Biblos."

Everyone was so upset and distracted, nobody seemed to mind when he indicated a wish to take the tram back up to Uriel's forge. Using gestures, Sara made clear that he must come back before sunset, and he agreed. Clearly something was going to happen then. Sara made sure Prity went along to look after him.

Emerson didn't mind. He got along well with Prity. They were both of a kind. The little chim's crude humor, expressed with hand-signed jokes, often broke him up.

Those fishie things are cousins? she signaled at one

point, referring to the busy, earnest dolphins. *I was hoping they tasted good!*

Emerson laughed. Earth's two client-level races had an ongoing rivalry that seemed almost instinctive.

During the ride upslope, he examined some of the machinery Kaa and the others had provided at Uriel's request. Most of it looked like junk—low-level Galactic computers, ripped out of standard consoles that might be hundreds or millions of years old. Many were stained or slimy from long immersion. The mélange of devices seemed to share just one trait—they had been refurbished enough to be turned on. He could tell because the power leads were all wrapped in tape to prevent it. Otherwise, it looked like a pile of garbage.

He longed to squat on the floor and tinker with the things. Prity shook her head though. She was under orders to prevent it. So instead Emerson looked out through the window, watching distant banks of dense clouds roll ominously closer from the west.

He fantasized about running away, perhaps to Xi, the quiet, pastoral refuge hidden in a vast desert of color. He would ride horses and practice his music . . . maybe fix simple, useful tools to earn his keep. Something to help fool himself that his life still had worth.

For a while he had felt valued here, helping Uriel get results from the Hall of Spinning Disks, but no one seemed to need him anymore. He felt like a burden.

It would be worse if he returned to *Streaker,* a shell. A fragment. The chance of a cure beckoned. But Emerson was smart enough to know the prospects weren't promising. Captain Creideiki once had an injury like his, and the ship's doctor had been helpless to correct such extensive damage to a brain.

Perhaps at home, though . . . On Earth . . .

He painted the blue globe in his mind, a vision of beauty that ached his heart.

Deep inside, Emerson knew he would never see it again.

The tram docked at last. His mood lifted for a little while, helping Uriel's staff unload cargo. Along with Prity, he followed the urs and qheuens down a long, twisty corridor toward a flow of warm air. At last they reached a big underground grotto—a cave with an opening at the far end, facing north. Hints of color gleamed far beyond, reminding him of the Spectral Flow.

Workers scurried about. Emerson saw g'Kek teams busy sewing together great sheets of strong, lightweight cloth. He watched urs delicately adjust handmade valves as gray qheuens bent lengths of pipe with their strong claws. Already, breaths of volcanically heated air were flowing into the first of many waiting canopies, creating bulges that soon joined together, forming a globe-ended bag.

Emerson looked across the scene, then back at the salvaged junk the dolphins had donated.

Slowly, a smile spread across his face.

To his great satisfaction, the urrish smiths seemed glad when he silently offered to lend a hand.

Kaa

THE SKIES OPENED AROUND NIGHTFALL, LETTING down both rain and lightning.

The whale sub *Hikahi* delayed entering Port Wuphon until the storm's first stinging drizzle began peppering the wharves and huts. The sheltered bay speckled with the impact of dense droplets as the submersible glided up a slanted coastal shelf toward an agreed rendezvous.

Kaa swam just ahead, guiding her through the narrow channel, between jagged shoals of demicoral. No one would have denied him the honor. *I am still chief pilot,* he thought. *With or without my nickname.*

The blunt-nosed craft mimicked his long turn around the sheltering headland, following as he showed the way with powerful, body-arching thrusts of his tail. It was an older piloting technique than wormhole diving, not highly technical. But Kaa's ancestors used to show human sailors the way home in this manner, long before the oldest clear memory of either race.

"Another two hundred meters, Hikahi,*"* he projected us-

ing sonar speech. *"Then a thirty-degree turn to port. After that, it's three hundred and fifty meters to full stop."*

The response was cool, professional.

"Roger. Preparing for debarkation."

Kaa's team—Brookida and a half-dozen neo-fins who had come out earlier to unload Uriel's supplies—moored the vessel when it reached the biggest dock. A small crowd of dignitaries waited on the pier, under heavy skies. Umbrellas sheltered the urrish delegates, who pressed together in a shivering mass, swaying their long necks back and forth. Humans and hoons made do with cloaks and hats, while the others simply ignored the rain.

Kaa was busy for a time, giving instructions as the helmsman fine-tuned her position, then cut engines. Amid a froth of bubbles, the *Hikahi* brought her bow even with the wharf. Clamshell doors opened, like a grinning mouth.

Backlit by the bright interior, a single human being strode forward. A tall female whose proud bearing seemed to say that she had little left to lose—little that life could take from her—except honor. For a long moment, Gillian Baskin looked on the surface of Jijo, inhaling fresh air for the first time in years.

Then she turned back toward the interior, beckoning with a smile and an extended arm.

Four silhouettes approached—one squat, one gangly, one wheeled, and the last clattering like a nervous colt. Kaa knew the tall one, although they had never met. *Alvin,* the young "humicking" writer, lover of Verne and Twain, whose journal had explained so much about the strange mixed culture of sooner races.

A moan of overjoyed release escaped those waiting, who flowed forward in a rush.

So—embraced by their loved ones, and pelted by rain—the adventurous crew of *Wuphon's Dream* finally came home.

There were other reunions . . . and partings.

Kaa went aft to help Makanee debark her patients. *Streaker*'s chief physician seemed older than Kaa remembered, and very tired, as she supervised a growing throng of neo-dolphins, splashing and squealing beyond the *Hikahi*'s starboard flank. While some appeared listless, others dashed about with antic, explosive energy. Two nurses helped Makanee keep the group herded together at the south end of the harbor, using occasional low-voltage discharges from their harnesses to prevent their patients from dashing off. The devolved ones wore nothing but skin.

Kaa counted their number—forty-six—and felt a shiver of worry. Such a large fraction of *Streaker*'s crew! Gillian must be desperate indeed, to contemplate abandoning them here. Many were probably only experiencing fits of temporary stress atavism, and would be all right if they just had peace and quiet for a time.

Well, maybe they'll get it, on Jijo, he thought. *Assuming this planet sea turns out to be as friendly as it looks. And assuming the Galactics leave us alone.*

In becoming Jijo's latest illegal settler race, dolphins had an advantage over those who preceded them. Fins would not need buildings, or much in the way of tools. Only the finest Galactic detectors might sieve their DNA resonance out of the background organic stew of a life world, and just at close range.

There are advantages, he admitted. *This way, some of our kind may survive, even if Earth and her colonies don't. And if dolphins are caught here, so what? How could we Terragens get into any more trouble than we already are?*

Kaa had read about local belief in *Redemption*. A species that found itself in trouble might get a second chance, returning to the threshold state, so that some new patron might adopt and guide them to a better destiny. *Tursiops amicus* was less than three hundred years old as a tool-using life-form. Confronted by a frolicking mob of his own kind—former members of an elite starship crew, now screeching like animals—Kaa knew it shouldn't take fins long to achieve "redemption."

He felt burning shame.

Kaa joined Brookida, unloading Makanee's pallet of supplies. He did not want to face the nurses, who might reproach him for "losing" Peepoe. *At least now there's a chance to find her. With our own colony in place, I can serve Makanee as a scout, patrolling and exploring . . . in time I'll catch up with Zhaki and Mopol. Then we'll have a reckoning.*

The aft hatch kept cycling after the last dolphin was through. Excited squeaks resonated across the bay as another set of émigrés followed Makanee to an assembly point, on a rocky islet in the middle of the harbor. Eager six-limbed amphibian forms, with frilly gill fringes waving about their heads. Transplanted from their native Kithrup, the Kiqui would not qualify as *sooners,* exactly. They were already a ripe, presapient life-form—a real treasure, in fact. It would have been good to bring them home to Earth in triumph and lay a claim of adoption with the Galactic Uplift Institute. But now Gillian clearly thought it better to leave them here, where they had a chance.

According to plan, the dolphin-Kiqui colony would stay in Port Wuphon for a few days, while a traeki pharmacist analyzed the newcomers' dietary needs. If necessary, new types of traeki stacks would be designed to create symbiotic supplements. Then both groups would head out to find homes amid islands offshore.

I'm coming, Peepoe, Kaa thought. *Once we get everyone settled, nothing on Jijo or the Five Galaxies will keep me from you.*

A happy musing. Yet another thought kept nagging at him.

Gillian isn't just stripping the ship of nonessential personnel. She's putting everyone ashore she can spare . . . for their own safety.

In other words, the human Terragens agent was planning something desperate . . . and very likely fatal.

Kaa had an uneasy feeling that he knew what it was.

•

Alvin

GUESS REUNIONS CAN BE KIND OF AWKWARD, EVEN when they're happy ones.

Don't get me wrong! I can't imagine a better moment than when the four of us—Huck, Ur-ronn, Pincer, and me—stepped out of the metal whale's yawning mouth to see the hooded lanterns of our own hometown. My senses were drenched with familiarity. I heard the creaking dross ships and the lapping tide. I smelled the melon canopies and smoke from a nearby cookstove—someone making *chubvash* stew. My magnetic earbones tickled to the familiar presence of Mount Guenn, invisible in the dark, yet a powerful influence on the hoonish shape-and-location sense.

Then there came my father's umble cry, booming from the shadows, and my mother and sister, rushing to my arms.

I confess, my first reaction was hesitant. I was glad to be home, to see and embrace them, but also embarrassed by the attention, and a little edgy about moving around without a cane for the first time in months. When there came a free moment, I bowed to my parents and handed them a package, wrapped in complex folds of the best paper I could find on the *Streaker*, containing my baby vertebrae. It was an important moment. I had gone away a disobedient child. Now I was returning, an adult, with work to do.

My friends' homecomings were less emotional. Of course Huck's hoonish adoptive parents were thrilled to have her back from the dead, but no one expected them to feel what my own folks did after giving up their only son for lost, months ago.

Pincer-Tip touched claws briefly with a matron from the qheuen hive, and that was it for him.

As for Ur-ronn, she and Uriel barely exchanged greetings. Aunt and niece had one priority—to get out of the rain. They fled the drizzle to a nearby warehouse, swiftly immersing themselves in some project. Urs don't believe in wasting time.

Does it make me seem heartless to say that I could not give complete attention to my family? Even as they clasped me happily, I kept glancing to see what else was going on. It will be up to me—and maybe Huck—to tell later generations about this event. This fateful meeting on the docks.

For one thing, there were other reunions.

My new human friend, Dwer Koolhan, emerged from the *Hikahi,* a tall silhouette, as sturdy looking as a preteen hoon. When he appeared, a shout pealed from the crowd of onlookers, and a young woman rushed to him, her arms spread wide. Dwer seemed stunned to see her . . . then equally enthused, seizing her into a whirling hug. At first, I thought she might be some long-separated lover, but now I know it is his sister, with adventures of her own to recount.

The rain let up a bit. Uriel returned, wearing booties and a heavy black waterproof slicker that covered all but the tip of her snout. Behind came several hoons, driving a herd of ambling, four-footed creatures. *Glavers.* At least two dozen of the bulge-eyed brutes swarmed down the pier, their opal skins glistening. A few carried cloth-wrapped burdens in their grasping tails. They did not complain, but trotted toward the opening of the whale sub without pause.

This part of the transaction, I did not—and still do not—understand. Why Earthling fugitives would want glavers is beyond me.

Gillian Baskin had the hoons carry out several large crates in exchange. I had seen the contents and felt an old hunger rise within me.

Books. There were hundreds of paper books, freshly minted aboard the *Streaker.* Not a huge amount of material, compared with the Galactic Library unit, or even the Great Printing, but included in the boxes were updates about the current state of the Five Galaxies, and other subjects Uriel requested. More than enough value to barter for a bunch of grub-eating glavers!

Later, I connected the trade with the dolphins and Kiqui who also debarked in Wuphon Harbor, and I realized, *There's more to this deal than meets the eye.*

•   •   •

Did I mention the tall prisoner? As everybody moved off to the great hall for a hurried feast, I looked back and glimpsed a hooded figure being led down the pier toward the submarine, guarded by two wary-looking urs. It was a biped, but did not move like a human or hoon, and I could tell both hands were tied. Whoever the prisoner was, he vanished into the *Hikahi* in a hurry, and I never heard a word about it.

The last reunion took place half a midura later, when we were all gathered in the town hall.

According to a complex plan worked out by the Niss Machine, the whale sub did not have to depart for some time, so a banquet was held in the fashion of our Jijoan Commons. Each race claimed a corner of the hexagonal chamber for its own food needs, then individuals migrated round the center hearth, chatting, renewing acquaintance, or discussing the nature of the world. While Gillian Baskin was engrossed in deep conversation with my parents and Uriel, my sister brought me up to date on happenings in Wuphon since our departure. In this way I learned of school chums who had marched north to war, joining militia units while we four adventurers had childish exploits in the cryptic deep. Some were dead or missing in the smoldering ruins of Ovoom Town. Others, mostly qheuens, had died in the plagues of late spring.

The hoonish disease never had a chance to take hold here in the south. But before the vaccines came, one ship *had* been kept offshore at anchor—in quarantine—because a sailor showed symptoms.

Within a week, half the crew had died.

Despite the gravity of her words, it was hard to pay close attention. I was trying to screw up my courage, you see. Somehow, I must soon tell my family the news they would least want to hear.

Amid the throng, I spotted Dwer and his sister huddled near the fire, each taking turns amazing the other with tales about their travels. Their elation at being reunited was clearly muted by a kind of worry familiar to all of us—concern about loved ones far away, whose fates were still unknown. I had a sense that the two of them knew, as I did, that there remained very little time.

Not far away I spied Dwer's noor companion, Mudfoot—the one Gillian called a "tytlal"—perched on a rafter, communing with others of his kind. In place of their normal, devil-may-care expressions, the creatures looked somber. Now we Six knew their secret—that the tytlal are a race hidden within a race, another tribe of sooners, fully alert and aware of their actions. Might some victims of past pranks now scheme revenge on the little imps? That seemed the least of their worries, but I wasted no sympathy on them.

Welcome to the real world, I thought.

Tyug squatted in a corner of the hall, furiously puffing away. Every few duras, the traeki's synthi ring would pop out another glistening ball of some substance whose value the Six Races had learned after long experience. Supplements to keep glavers healthy, for instance, and other chemical wonders that might serve Gillian's crew, if some miracle allowed them to escape. If Tyug finished soon, Uriel hoped to keep her alchemist. But I would lay bets that the traeki meant to go along when the Earthlings departed.

The occasion was interrupted when a pair of big hoons wearing proctors' badges pushed through leather door strips into the feasting hall, gripping the arms of a male human I had never seen before. He was of middle height for their kind, with a dark complexion and an unhappy expression. He wore a rewq on his forehead, and hair combed to hide a nasty scar near his left ear. A small chimp followed close behind, her appearance rueful.

I wasn't close enough to hear the details firsthand, but later I pieced together that this was a long-lost crew mate of the Streakers, whose appearance on Jijo had them mystified. He had been on Mount Guenn, helping Uriel's smiths work on some secret project, when he suddenly up and tried to escape by stealing some kind of flying machine!

As the guards brought him forward, Gillian's face washed with recognition. She smiled, though he cringed, as if dreading this meeting. The dark man turned left to hide his mutilation, but Gillian insistently took his hands.

She expressed pleasure at seeing him by leaning up to kiss one cheek.

Perhaps later I'll learn more about where he fits in all this. But time is short and I must close this account before the *Hikahi* sets sail to rejoin the dolphin-crewed ship. So let me finish with the climax of an eventful evening.

A herald burst in. His vibrating sac boomed an alert umble.

"Come! Come and see the unusual!"

Hurrying outside, we found the rain had stopped temporarily. A window opened in the clouds, wide enough for Loocen to pour pale, liquid luminance across a flank of Mount Guenn. Swathes of brittle stars shone through, including one deep red, cyclopean eye.

In spite of this lull, the storm was far from over. Lightning flickered as clouds grew denser still. The west was one great mass of roiling blackness amid a constant background of thunder. In miduras, the coast was really going to get hit.

People started pointing. Huck rolled up near my right leg and gestured with all four agile eyestalks, directing my gaze toward the volcano.

At first, I couldn't tell what I was seeing. Vague, ghostlike shapes seemed to bob and flutter upward, visible mostly as curved silhouettes that blocked sporadic stars. Sometimes lightning caused one of the objects to glow along a rounded flank, revealing a globelike outline, tapered at the bottom. They seemed big, and very far away.

I wondered if they might be starships.

"Balloons," Huck said at last, her voice hushed in awe. "Just like *Around the World in Eighty Days!*"

Funny. Huck seemed more impressed at that moment than she ever had been aboard *Streaker,* by all the glittering consoles and chattering machines. I stared at the flotilla of fragile gasbags, wondering what kind of volunteers were brave enough to pilot them on a night like this, surrounded by slashing electricity, and with ruthless foes prowling higher still. We watched as scores wafted from Mount Guenn's secret caves. One by one, they caught the stiff west wind and flowed past the mountain, vanishing from sight.

I happened to be standing near Gillian Baskin, so I know what the Earthwoman said when she turned to Uriel the Smith.

"All right. You kept your side of the bargain. Now it's time to keep ours."

PART TEN
Vubben

SMASHED UP. Wheels torn or severed. His braincase leaking lubricant. Motivator spindles shredded and discharging slowly into the ground.

Vubben lies crumpled next to his deity, feeling life drain away.

That he still lives seems remarkable. When the Jophur corvette slashed brutally at the Holy Egg, he had been partway around the great stone's flank, almost on the other side. But the moatlike channel of the Nest funneled explosive heat like a river, outracing his fruitless effort at retreat.

Now Vubben lies in a heap, aware of two facts.

Any surviving g'Keks would need a new High Sage.

And something else.

The Egg still lives.

He wonders about that. Why didn't the Jophur finish it off? Surely they had the power.

Perhaps they were distracted.

Perhaps they would be back.

Or else, were they subtly *persuaded* to go away?

The Egg's patterning rhythms seem subdued, and yet more clear than ever. He ponders whether it might be an artifact of his approaching death. Or perhaps his frayed spindles—draped across the stony face—are picking up vibrations that normal senses could not.

Crystalline lucidity calls him, but Vubben feels restrained by the tenacious hold of life. *That* was what always kept sages and mystics from fully communing with the sacred ovoid, he now sees. Mortal beings—even traeki—have to care about continuing, or else the game of existence cannot properly be played. But the caring is also an impediment. It biases the senses. Makes you receptive to noise.

He lets go of the impediment, with a kind of gladness. Surrender clears the way, opening a path that he plunges along, like a youth just released from training wheels, spinning ecstatically down a swooping ramp he never knew before, whose curves change in delightfully ominous ways.

Vubben feels the world grow transparent around him. And with blossoming clarity, he begins to perceive *connections*.

In legend, and in human lore, gods were depicted *speaking* to their prophets, and those on the verge of death. But the great stone does not vocalize. No words come to Vubben, or even images. Yet he finds himself able to trace the Egg's form, its vibrating unity. Like a funnel, it draws him *down*, toward the bowels of Jijo.

That is the first surprise. From its shape alone, the Six Races assumed the Egg was self-contained, an oval stone birthed out of Jijo's inner heat, now wholly part of the upper world.

Apparently it still maintains links to the world below.

Vubben's dazed mind beholds the realm beneath the Slope . . . not as a picture but in its gestalt, as a vast domain threaded by dendritic patterns of lava heat, like branches of a magma forest, feeding and maintaining a growing mountain range.

The forest roots sink into liquefied pools, unimaginably deep and broad—measureless chambers where molten rock strains under the steady grinding of an active planet.

Yet, even here the pattern formations persist. Vubben finds himself amazed by their revealed source.

Dross!

Deep beneath the Slope, there plunges a great sheet of heavier stone . . . an oceanic plate, shoving hard against the continent and then diving deeper still, dragging eons-old basalt down to rejoin slowly convecting mantle layers. The process is not entirely mysterious to Vubben. He has seen illustrations in Biblos texts. As it scrapes by, the plunging ocean plate leaves behind a scum, a frothy mix of water and light elements . . .

. . . and also patterns.

Patterns of dross! Of ancient buildings, implements, machines, all discarded long ago, ages before the Buyur won their leasehold on this world. Before even their predecessors.

The things themselves are long gone, melted, smeared out, their atoms dispersed by pressure and heat. Yet somehow a remnant persists. The magma does not quite forget.

Dross is supposed to be cleansed, Vubben thinks, shocked by the implications. *When we dump our bones and tools in the Midden, it should lead to burial and purification by Jijo's fire. There isn't supposed to be anything left!*

And yet . . . who is he to question, if Jijo chooses to remember something of each tenant race that abides here for a while, availing itself of her resources, her varied life-forms, then departing according to Galactic law?

Is that what you are? He inquires of the Holy Egg. *A distillation of memory? The crystallized essence of species who came before, and are now extinct?*

A transcendent thought, yet it makes him sad. Vubben's own unique race verges on annihilation. He yearns for some kind of preservation, some refuge from oblivion. But in order to leave such a remnant, sophonts must dwell for a long time on a tectonic world.

For most of its sapiency period, his kind had lived in space.

Then you don't care about us living beings, after all, he accuses the Egg. *You are like that crazed mulc spider of the hills, your face turned to the past.*

Again, there is no answer in word or image. What Vubben feels instead is a further extension of the sense of connectedness, now sweeping *upward,* through channels of friction heat, climbing against slow cascades of moist, superheated rock, until his mind emerges in a cool dark kingdom——the sea's deep, most private place.

The Midden. Vubben feels around him the great dross piles of more recent habitation waves. Even here, amid relics of the Buyur, the Egg seems linked. Vubben senses that the graveyard of ancient instrumentalities has been disturbed. Heaps of archaic refuse still quiver from some late intrusion.

There is no anger over this. Nor anything as overt as interest. But he does sense a reaction, like some prodigious reflex.

The sea is involved. Disturbance in the dross piles has provoked shifts in the formation of waves and tides. Of heat and evaporation. Like a sleeping giant, responding heavily to a tiny itch. A massive storm begins roiling both the surface and the ocean floor, sweeping things back where they belong.

Vubben has no idea what vexed the Midden so. Perhaps the Jophur. Or else the end of dross shipments from the Six Races? Anyway, his thoughts are coming more slowly as death swarms in from the extremities. Worldly concerns matter less with each passing dura.

Still, he can muster a few more cogencies.

Is that all we are to you? he inquires of the planet. *An itch?*

He realizes now that Drake and Ur-Chown had pulled a fast one when they announced their "revelation," a century ago. The Egg is no god, no conscious being. Ro-kenn was right, calling it a particle of psi-active stone, more compact and well ordered than the Spectral Flow. A distillation that had proved helpful in uniting the Six Races.

Useful in many ways . . . but not worthy of prayer.

We sensed what we desperately wanted to sense, because the alternative was unacceptable—to face the fact that we sooners are alone. We always were alone.

That might have been Vubben's last thought. But at the final moment there comes something else. A glimmer of meaning that merges with his waning neuronic flashes. In that narrow moment, he feels a wave of overwhelming certainty.

More layers lie beneath the sleeping strata. Layers that are aware.

Layers that know.

Despair is not his final companion. Instead, there comes in rapid succession—

expectation . . .

satisfaction . . .

awareness of an ancient plan, patiently unfolding. . . .

Kaa

"CAN'T-T YOU USE SOMEBODY ELSE?"

"Who else? There is no one."

"What about Karkaett-t?"

"Suessi needs him to help nurse the engines. This effort will be hopeless unless they operate above capacity."

Hopeless; Kaa used to think it such a simple word. But like the concept of infinity, it came freighted with a wide range of meanings. He slashed the water in frustration. *Ifni, will you really trap me this way? Dragging me across the universe again, when all I want to do is stay?*

Gillian Baskin knelt on the quay nearby, her raincoat glistening. Distant lightning flashes periodically lit up the bay, revealing that the *Hikahi* had already closed her clam-shell doors, preparing to depart.

"Besides," Gillian added. "You are our chief pilot. Who could be as well qualified?"

Gratifying words, but in fact *Streaker used* to have a better pilot, by far.

"Keepiru ought to've stayed with the crew, back on Kithrup-p. I should have been the one who went on the skiff with Creideiki."

The woman shrugged. "Things happen, Kaa. I have confidence in your ability to get us off this world in one piece."

And after that? He chuttered a doubt-filled raspberry. Everyone knew this would be little more than a suicide venture. The odds had also seemed bad on Kithrup, but at least there the eatee battle fleets chasing *Streaker* had been distracted, battling each other. Fleeing through that maelstrom of combat and confusion, it proved possible to fool their pursuers by wearing a disguise—the hollowed-out shell of a Thennanin dreadnought. All that ploy took was lots of skill . . . and *luck*.

Here in Jijo space there was no sheltering complexity. No concealing jumble of warfare to sneak through. Just one pursuer—giant and deadly—sought one bedraggled prey.

For the moment, *Streaker* was safe in Jijo's sea, but what chance would she have once she tried to leave?

"You don't have to worry about Peepoe," Gillian said, reading the heart of his reluctance. "Makanee has some solid fins with her. Many are Peepoe's friends. They'll scan relentlessly till they find Zhaki and Mopol, and make them let her go.

"Anyway," the blond woman went on, "isn't Peepoe better off here? Won't you use your skill to keep her safe?"

Kaa eyed Gillian's silhouette, knowing the Terragens agent would use any means to get the job done. If that meant appealing to Kaa's sense of honor . . . or even chivalry . . . Gillian Baskin was not too proud.

"Then you admit it-t," he said.

"Admit what?"

"That we're heading out as bait, nothing elsssse. Our aim is to sacrifice ourselves."

The human on the quay was silent for several seconds, then lifted her shoulders in a shrug.

"It seems worthwhile, don't you think?"

Kaa pondered. At least she was being honest—a decent way for a captain to behave with her pilot.

A whole world, seven or eight sapient races, some near extinction, and a unique culture. Can you see giving up your life for all that?

"I guesss so," he murmured, after a pause.

Gillian had won. Kaa would abandon his heart on Jijo, and fly out to meet death with open eyes.

Then he recalled. *She* had made exactly the same choice, long ago. A decision that still must haunt her sleep, though it could have gone no other way.

Yet it surprised Kaa when Gillian slipped off the stone quay, entering the water next to him, and threw her arms around his head. Shivers followed her hands as she stroked him gratefully.

"You make me proud," she said. "The crew will be glad, and not *just* because we have the best pilot in this whole galaxy."

Kaa's flustered confusion expressed itself in a sonar interrogative, casting puzzled echoes through the colonnade of a nearby pier. Gillian wove her Trinary reply through that filtered reverberation, binding his perplexity, braiding a sound fabric whose texture seemed almost like a melody.

> * Amid the star lanes,
>   * Snowballs sometimes thrive near
> flame. . . .
>   * Don't you feel Lucky? *

Rety

THE DOLPHIN ENGINEER SHOUTED AT HER FROM the airlock of the salvaged dross ship.

"C-come on, Rety! We gotta leave now, t-to make the rendezvous!"

Chuchki had reason to be agitated. His walker unit whined and jittered, reacting to nervous signals sent down his neural tap. It was cramped in the airlock, which also held the speed sled to carry them from this ghost ship back to *Streaker*. Providing all went according to plan.

Only I ain't part of the plan anymore, Rety thought.

Stepping in front of Chuchki, with the sill of the hatch between them, she removed the tunic they had given her, as an honorary member of the crew. At first the gesture had pleased Rety—till she saw the Terrans were just another band of losers.

Rety tossed the garment in the airlock.

"Tell Dr. Baskin an' the others thanks, but I'll be makin' my own way from here on. Good luck. Now scram."

Chuchki stared at first, unable to move or speak. Then servos whirred. The walker started to move.

"Hit the button, yee!" Rety shouted over her left shoulder.

Back in the control room, her little "husband" pressed a lever triggering the airlock's emergency cycle. The inner hatch slid shut, severing Chuchki's wail of protest. Soon, a row of purple lights showed the small chamber filling with water as the outer door opened.

A few duras later, she heard engine noise—the now-familiar growl of the speed sled that had brought the two of them here—ebbing with distance as the machine fled. She ordered the outer door closed and locked against the possibility that Chuchki might try something "heroic." Some still thought of her as a child, and many dolphins also had a mystical attachment to their human patrons.

But I'll be just fine. A lot better off than those fools, in fact.

Several low, squat hallways led away from the lock, but only one was lit by a string of glow bulbs. Following this trail, she made her way back toward the control room, sometimes lingering to stroke a panel or gaze into a chamber filled with mysterious machines. For the last few days she had looked over this salvaged starship—once a Buyur packet boat, according to Chuchki. Though a mess, it was one of the "best" recovered derelicts, capable of life support as well as full engine maneuvering, owing its remarkable state to the Midden's chill, sterile waters. Durable Galactic machines might lie there unchanged forever, or until Jijo sucked them underground.

It's mine now, she mused, surveying her prize. *I've got my own starship.*

Of course it was still a hunk of dross. All odds were against her getting anywhere in this moving scrap pile.

But the odds always had been against her, ever since she was born into that filthy tribe of savages, so proud of their sickly ignorance. And especially since she realized she'd rather be whipped for speaking up than be a slave to some bully with rotting teeth and the mind of a beast.

Rety had suffered some disappointments lately. But now she saw what each of the setbacks had in common. They all came about because of trusting others—first the sages of the Commons, then the Rothens, and finally a ragtag band of helpless Earthlings.

But all that was in the past. Now she was back doing what she did best—relying on herself.

The control room spanned roughly thirty paces in width, featuring about a dozen wide instrument consoles. All were dark, except one jury-rigged station festooned with cables and makeshift bypass connections. Lights blazed across that panel. On the floor nearby, a portable holosim display revealed a staticky map of the ancient vessel's surroundings, a dart-shaped glow threading its way through a maze of ridges at the bottom of the great ocean.

Most of the decoy ships cruised with simple autopilots, but a few moved more flexibly, crewed by volunteer teams, making adjustments to the swarm pattern planned by the Niss Machine. In this effort, Rety's intelligence and agile hands had been helpful to Chuchki, making up for her lack of education. She felt justified in having earned her starship.

"hi captain!"

Her sole companion pranced on the instrument console, each footstep barely missing a glowing lever or switch. The little urrish male greeted her with a shrill ululation.

"we did it! like pirates of the plains! like in legends of the battle aunties! now we free. no more noor beasts. no more yuckity ship full of water-loving fish!"

Rety laughed. Whenever loneliness beckoned, there was always yee to cheer her up.

"so where to now, captain?" the diminutive creature asked. "shake free of Jijo? head someplace good and sunny, for a change?"

She nodded.

"That's the idea. Only we gotta be patient a little while longer."

First *Streaker* must collect Chuchki and other scattered workers. Rety had an impression that the Earthlings were waiting for events to happen onshore. But after hearing the Jophur ultimatum she knew—Gillian Baskin would soon be forced to act.

I helped them, she rationalized. *An' I won't interfere with their plan . . . much.*

But in the long run, none o' that'll matter. Everybody knows they're gonna get roasted when they try to get away. Or else the Jophur'll catch 'em, like a ligger snatchin' up a gallaiter faun.

Nobody can blame me for tryin' to find my own way out of a trap like that.

And if someone *did* cast blame her way?

Rety laughed at the thought.

In that case, they can try to outfart a traeki, for all I care. This ship is mine, and there's nothin' anybody can do about it!

She was getting away from Jijo—one way or another.

Dwer

THE NIGHT SKY CRACKLED.

At random intervals his hair abruptly stood on end. Static electricity snapped the balloon's canopy with a basso boom, while pale blue glows moved up and down the rope cables, dancing like frantic imps. Once, a flickering ball of greenish white followed him across the sky for more than a midura, mimicking each rise, fall, or sway in the wind. He could not tell if it was an arrowflight away, or several leagues. The specter only vanished when a rain squall passed between, but Dwer kept checking nervously, in case it returned.

Greater versions of the same power flashed in all directions—though from a safe distance, so far. He made a habit of counting kiduras between each brilliant discharge and the arrival of its rumbling report. When the interval grew short, thunder would shake the balloon like a child's rag doll.

Uriel had set controls to keep Dwer above most of the gale . . . at least according to the crude weather calculations of her spinning-disk computer. The worst fury took place below, in a dense cloud bank stretching from horizon to horizon.

Still, that only meant there were moonlit gaps for his frail craft to drift through. Surrounding him towered the mighty heat engines of the storm—churning thunderheads whose lofty peaks scraped the boundaries of space.

Though insanely dangerous, the spectacle exceeded anything in Dwer's experience—and perhaps even that of any star god in the Five Galaxies. He was tempted to climb the rigging for a better view of nature's majesty. To let the tempest sweep his hair. To shout back when it bellowed.

But he wasn't free. There were duties unfulfilled.

So Dwer did as he'd been told, remaining huddled in a wire cage the smiths had built for him, lashed to a wicker basket that dangled like an afterthought below a huge gasbag. The metal enclosure would supposedly protect him from a minor lightning strike.

And what if a bolt tears the bag instead? Or ignites the fuel cylinder? Or . . .

Low clicks warned Dwer to cover his face just half a dura before the altitude sensor tripped, sending jets of flame roaring upward, refilling the balloon and maintaining a safe distance from the ground.

Of course, "safe" was a matter of comparison.

"In theory, this vehicle should convey you well past the Rinner Range, and then veyond the Foison Flain," the smith had explained. "After that, there should ve an end to the lightning danger. You can leave the Faraday cage and guide the craft as we taught you."

As they taught me in half a rushed midura, Dwer amended, *while running around preparing one last balloon to launch.*

All the others were far ahead of him—a flotilla of flimsy craft, dispersing rapidly as they caught varied airstreams, but all sharing the same general heading. East, driven by near-hurricane winds. Twice he had witnessed flares in that direction, flames that could not have come from lightning alone. Sudden outbursts of ocher fire, they testified to some balloon exploding in the distance.

Fortunately, those others had no crews, just instruments recovered from dross ships. Dwer was the only Jijoan loony enough to go flying on a night like this.

They needed an expendable volunteer. Someone to observe and report if the trick is successful.

Not that he resented Uriel and Gillian. Far from it. Dwer was suited for the job. It was necessary. And the voyage would take him roughly where he wanted to go.

Where I'm needed.

To the Gray Hills.

What might have happened to Lena and Jenin in the

time he'd spent as captive of a mad robot, battling Jophur in a swamp and then trapped with forlorn Terrans at the bottom of the sea? By now, the women would have united the urrish and human sooner tribes, and possibly led them a long way from the geyser pools where Danel Ozawa died. It might take months to track them down, but that hardly mattered. Dwer had his bow and supplies. His skills were up to the task.

All I need is to land in roughly the right area, say within a hundred leagues . . . and not break my neck in the process. I can hunt and forage. Save my traeki paste for later, in case the search lasts through winter.

Dwer tried going over the plan, dwelling on problems he could grasp—the intricacies of exploring and survival in wild terrain. But his mind kept coming back to this wild ride through an angry sky . . . or else the sad partings that preceded it.

For a time, he and Sara had tried using words, talking about their separate adventures, sharing news of friends living and dead. She told what little she knew about Nelo and their destroyed hometown. He described how Lark had saved his life in a snowstorm, so long ago that it seemed another age.

Hanging over the reunion was sure knowledge that it must end. Each of them had places to go. Missions with slim chance of success, but compelled by duty and curiosity. Dwer had lived his entire adult life that way, but it took some effort to grasp that his sister had chosen the same path, only on a vaster scale.

He still might have tried talking Sara out of her intention—perhaps suicidal—to join the Earthlings' desperate breakout attempt. But there was something new in the way she carried herself—a lean readiness that took him back to when they were children, following Lark on fossil hunts, and *Sara* was the toughest of them all. Her mind had always plunged beyond his comprehension. Perhaps it was time for her to stride the same galaxies that filled her thoughts.

"Remember us, when you're a star god," he had told her, before their final embrace.

Her reply was a hoarse whisper.

"Give my love to Lark and . . ."

Sara closed her eyes, throwing her arms around him.

". . . and to Jijo."

They clung together until the urrish smiths said it was the last possible moment to go.

When the balloon took off, Mount Guenn leaped into view around him, a sight unlike any he ever beheld. Lightning made eerie work of the Spectral Flow, sending brief flashes of illusion dancing across his retinas.

Dwer watched his sister standing at the entrance of the cave, a backlit figure. Too proud to weep. Too strong to pretend. Each knew the other was likely heading to oblivion. Each realized this would be their last shared moment.

I'll never know if she lives, he had thought, as clouds swallowed the great volcano, filling the night with flashing arcs. Looking up through a gap in the overcast, he had glimpsed a corner of the constellation Eagle.

Despite the pain of separation, Dwer had managed a smile.

It's better that way.

From now until the day I die, I'll picture her out there. Living in the sky.

Alvin

AS IT TURNED OUT, I DIDN'T HAVE TO EXPLAIN things to my parents. Gillian and Uriel had already laid it out, before it was time to depart.

The Six Races should be represented, they explained. Come what may.

Furthermore, I had earned the right to go. So had my friends.

Anyway, who was better qualified to tell Jijo's tale?

Mu-phauwq and Yowg-wayuo had no choice but to accept my decision. Was *Jijo* any safer than fighting the Jophur in space? Besides, I had spine-molted. I would make my own decisions.

Mother turned her back to me. I stroked her spines, but she spoke without turning around.

"Thank you for returning from the dead," she murmured. "Honor us by having children of your own. Name your firstborn after your great-uncle, who was captain of the *Auph-Vuhoosh*. The cycle must continue."

With that, she let my sister lead her away. I felt both touched and bemused by her command, wondering how it could ever be obeyed.

Dad, bless him, was more philosophical. He thrust a satchel in my arms, his entire collection of books by New Wave authors of Jijo's recent literary revival—the hoon, urs, and g'Kek writers who have lately begun expressing themselves in unique ways on the printed page. "It's to remind you that humans are not in complete command of our culture. There is more than one line to our harmony, my son."

"I know that, Dad," I replied. "I'm not a *complete* humicker."

He nodded, adding a low umble.

"It is told that we hoons were priggish and sour, before our sneakship came to Jijo. Legends say we had no word for 'fun.'

"If that is true—and in case you meet any of our stodgy cousins out there—tell them about the *sea,* Hph-wayuo! Tell them of the way a sail catches the wind, a sound no mere engine can match.

"Teach them to taste the stinging spray. Show them all the things that our patrons never did.

"It will be our gift—we happy damned—to those who know no joy in heaven."

Others had easier leave-takings.

Qheuens are used to sending their males out on risky ventures, for the sake of the hive. Pincer's mothers did emboss his shell with some proud inlay, though, and saw him off in good style.

Urs care mostly about their work, their chosen loyalties, and themselves. Ur-ronn did not have to endure sodden sentimentality. Partly because of the rain, she and Uriel made brief work of their good-byes. Uriel probably saw it as a good business transaction. She lost her best apprentice, but had adequate compensation.

Uriel seemed far more upset about losing Tyug. But there was no helping it. The Earthers need a traeki. And not just any traeki, but the best alchemist we can send. No pile of substance balls can substitute. Besides, it will be good luck for all races to be along.

Huck's adoptive parents tried to express sorrow at her parting, but their genuine fondness for her would not make them grieve. Hoons are not humans. We cannot transfer the full body bond to those not of our blood. Our affections run deeper, but narrower than Earthlings'. Perhaps that is our loss.

So the five of us reboarded as official representatives, and as grown-ups. I had molted and Pincer showed off his cloisonné. Ur-ronn did not preen, but we all noticed that one of her brood pouches was no longer virgin white, but blushed a fresh shade of blue as her new husband wriggled and stretched it into shape.

Huck carried her own emblem of maturity—a narrow wooden tube, sealed with wax at both ends. Though humble looking, it might be the most important thing we brought with us from the Slope.

Huphu rode my shoulder as I stepped inside the whale sub. I noted that the tytlal-style noor, Mudfoot, had also rejoined us, though the creature seemed decidedly unhappy. Had he been exiled by the others, for the crime of letting their ancient secret slip? Or was he being honored, as we were, with a chance to live or die for Jijo?

Sara Koolhan stood between her chimp and the wounded starman as the great doors closed, cutting us off from the wharf lanterns, our village, and the thundering sky.

"Well, at least this is more comfortable than the last time we submerged, inside a dumb old hollow tree trunk," Huck commented.

Pincer's leg vents whistled resentfully. "You want comfy? Poor little g'Kekkie want to ride my back, an' be tucked into her beddie?"

"Shut uf, you two," Ur-ronn snapped. "Trust Ifni to stick ne with a vunch of ignoranuses for confanions."

Huphu settled close as I umbled, feeling a strange, resigned contentment. My friends' bickering was one unchanged feature of life from those naive days when we were youngsters, still dreaming of adventure in our *Wuphon's Dream*. It was nice to know some things would be constant across space and time.

Alas, Huck had not mentioned the true difference between that earlier submergence and this one.

Back then, we sincerely thought there was a good chance we'd be coming home again.

This time, we all knew better.

Ewasx

ALARMS BLARE! INSTRUMENTS CRY OUT SIRENS OF danger!

Behold, My rings, how the Captain-Leader recalls the robots and remote crew stacks who were engaged in probing the deep-sea trench.

Greater worries now concern us!

For days, cognizance detectors have sieved through the deep, trying to separate the prey from its myriad decoys. It even occurred to us/Me that the Earthling ship may not be one of the moving blips at all! It might be sheltering silently in some dross pile. In operating the swarm by remote control, they might bypass all the normal etheric channels, using instead their fiendish talent at manipulating sound.

I/we are/am learning caution. I did not broach this possibility to the Captain-Leader.

Why did I refrain? A datum has come to our attention. Those in power often ask for the "truth," or even the best guesses of their underlings. But in fact, they seldom truly wish to hear contradiction.

Anyway, the tactics stacks estimated improved odds at sifting for the quarry. Only one more day, at worst. We of the *Polkjhy* could easily afford the time.

Until we detected disturbing intruders. Interlopers that could only have come from the Five Galaxies!

"THERE ARE AT LEAST SIX SIXES OF THEM!"

So declares the cognizance detector operator. "Hovering, almost stationary, no more than fifteen planetary degrees easterly. One moment they were not there. The next moment, they appeared!"

The etherics officer vents steam of doubt.

"I/we perceive nothing, nor have our outlying satellites. This provokes a reasonable hypothesis: that your toruses are defective, or else your instruments."

But routine checks discover no faults in either.

"They may have meme-suborned our satellites," suggests one tactician stack. "Combining this with excellent masking technology—"

"Perhaps," interrupts another. "But *gravitics* cannot be fooled so easily. If there are six sixes of ships, they cannot be larger than hull type sixteen. No match for us, then. We can annihilate the entire squadron, forthwith."

"Is that why they operate in stealth?" inquires the Captain-Leader, puffing pheromones of enforced calm into the tense atmosphere. "Might they be lingering, just beyond line of sight, while awaiting reinforcements?"

It is a possibility we cannot ignore. But, lacking corvettes, we must go investigate ourselves.

Reluctantly, gracefully, the *Polkjhy* turns her omnipotence around, heading toward the ghostly flotilla. If they are scouts for an armada—perhaps the Soro or Tandu, our mortal foes—it may be necessary to act swiftly, decisively. Exactly the kind of performance that best justifies the existence of master rings.

Others must not be allowed to win the prize!

As we move ponderously eastward, a new thought burbles upward. A streak of wax, secreted by our once-rebellious second torus-of-cognition.

What is it, My ring?

You recall how the savage sooners called to our corvette, not once, but twice, using minute tickles of digital power to attract our attention?

The first time, they used such a beacon to bribe us with the location of a g'Kek hideout.

The second time? Ah, yes. It was a lure, drawing the corvette to a trap.

VERY CLEVER, MY RING!

Ah, but the comparison does not work.

There are many more sources, this time.

They are stronger, and the cognizance traces have spoor patterns typical of starship computers.

But above all, My poor ring, did you not hear our detection officer stack?

These signals cannot come from benighted sooners.

THEY FLY!

Sara

"GRAVITICSS!"

The detection officer thrashed her flukes.

"Movement signs! The large emitter departss its stationary hover position. Jophur battleship now moving east at two machsss. Ten klickss altitude."

Sara watched Gillian Baskin absorb the news. This was according to plan, yet the blond Earthwoman showed hardly any reaction. "Very good," she replied. "Inform me of any vector change. Decoy operator, please engage swarming program number four. Start the wrecks drifting upward, slowly."

The water-filled chamber was unlike any "bridge" Sara had read about in ancient books—a Terran vessel, controlled from a room humans could only enter wearing breathing masks. This place was built for the convenience of dolphins. It was their ship—though a woman held command.

A musty smell made Sara's nose itch, but when her hand raised to scratch, it bumped the transparent helmet, startling her for the fiftieth time. Fizzy liquid prickled Sara's bare arms and legs with goose bumps. Yet she had no mental space for annoyance, fear, or claustrophobia. This place was much too strange to allow such mundane reactions.

Streaker's overall shape and size were still enigmas. Her one glimpse of the hull—peering through a viewing port while the whale sub followed a searchlight toward its hurried rendezvous—showed a mysterious, studded cylinder, like a giant twelk caterpillar, whose black surface seemed to drink illumination rather than reflect it. The capacious airlock was almost deserted as Kaa and other dolphins debarked from the *Hikahi*, using spiderlike walking machines to rush to their assigned posts. Except for the bridge, most of the ship had been pumped free of water, reducing weight to a minimum.

The walls trembled with the rhythmic vibration of engines—distant cousins to her father's mill, or the Tarek Town steamboats. The familiarity ran deep, as if affinity flowed in Sara's blood.

"Battleship passing over Rimmer mountains. Departing line-of-sight!"

"Don't make too much of that," Gillian reminded the crew. "They still have satellites overhead. Maintain swarm pattern four. Kaa, ease us to the western edge of our group."

"Aye," the sturdy gray pilot replied. His tail and fins wafted easily, showing no sign of tension. "Suessi reports motors operating at nominal. Gravitics charged and ready."

Sara glanced at a row of screens monitoring other parts of the ship. At first, each display seemed impossibly small, but her helmet heeded subtle motions of her eyes, enhancing any image she chose to focus on, expanding it to 3-D clarity. Most showed empty chambers, with walls still moist from recent flooding. But the engine room was a bustle of activity. She spied "Suessi" by his unique appearance—a torso of wedgelike plates topped by a reflective dome, encasing what remained of his head. The arm that was still human gestured toward a panel, reminding a neo-fin operator to make some adjustment.

That same arm had wrapped around Emerson after the *Hikahi* docked, trembling while clutching the prodigal starman. Sara had never seen a cyborg before. She did not know if it was normal for one to cry.

Emerson and Prity were also down there, helping Suessi with their nimble hands. Sara spied them laboring in the shadows, accompanied by Ur-ronn, the eager young urs, fetching and carrying for the preoccupied engineers. Indeed, Emerson seemed a little happier with work to do. After all, these decks and machines had been his life for many years. Still, ever since the reunion on the docks, Sara had not seen his accustomed grin. For the first time, he seemed ashamed of his injuries.

These people must be hard up to need help from an ape, an urrish blacksmith, and a speechless cripple. The other youngsters from Wuphon were busy, too. Running errands and tending the glaver herd, keeping the creatures calm in strange surroundings.

I'm probably the most useless one of all. The Egg only knows what I'm doing here.

Blame it on Sage Purofsky, whose cosmic speculations justified her charging off with desperate Earthlings. *Even if his reasoning holds, what can I do about the Buyur plan? Especially if this mission is suicidal—*

The detection officer squealed, churning bubbles with her flukes.

"Primary gravitics source decelerating! Jophur ship nearing estimated p-position of mobile observer."

Mobile observer, Sara thought. *That would be Dwer.*

She pictured him in that frail balloon, alone in the wide sky, surrounded by nature's fury, with that great behemoth streaking toward him.

Keep your head down, little brother. Here it comes.

Dwer

WITH THE RIMMERS BEHIND HIM AT LAST, THE storm abated its relentless buffeting enough to glimpse some swathes of stars. The gaps widened. In time Dwer spied a pale glow to the west. Gray luminance spread across a vast plain of waving scimitar blades.

Dwer recalled slogging through the same bitter steppe

months ago, guiding Danel, Lena, and Jenin toward the Gray Hills. He still bore scars from that hard passage, when knifelike stems slashed at their clothes, cutting any exposed flesh.

This was a better way of traveling, floating high above. That is, if you survived searing lightning bolts, and thunder that loosened your teeth, and terrifying brushes with mountain peaks that loomed out of the night like giant claws, snatching at a passing morsel.

Maybe walking was preferable, after all.

He drank from his water bottle. Dawn meant it was time to get ready. Dormant machines would have flickered to life when first light struck the decoy balloons, electric circuits closing. Computers, salvaged from ancient starships, began spinning useless calculations.

The Jophur must be on the move, by now.

He reached up to his forehead and touched the rewq he had been given, causing it to writhe over his eyes. At once, Dwer's surroundings shifted. Contrasts were enhanced. All trace of haze vanished from the horizon, and he was able to look close to the rising sun, making out the distant glimmers of at least a dozen floating gasbags, now widely dispersed far to the east, tiny survivors of the tempest that had driven them so far.

Dwer pulled four crystals from a pouch at his waist and jammed them into the gondola wickerwork so each glittered in the slanted light. A hammer waited at his waist, but he left it there for now, scanning past the decoys, straining to see signs of the Gray Hills.

I'm coming, Jenin. I'll be there soon, Lena.

I've just got a few more obstacles to get by.

He tried to picture their faces, looking to the future rather than dwelling on a harsh past. Buried in his backpack was a sensor stone that would come alight on midwinter's eve, if by some miracle the High Sages gave the all clear. If all the starships were gone, and there was reason to believe none would return. By then Dwer must find Lena and Jenin, and help them prepare the secluded tribe for either fate destiny had in store—a homecoming to the Slope, or else a life of perpetual hiding in the wilderness.

Either way, it's the job I'm trained for. A duty I know how to fulfill.

He found it hard to settle his restless mind, though. For some reason Dwer thought instead about *Rety,* the irascible sooner girl who had chosen to stay with the *Streaker* crew. No surprise there; she wanted nothing in life more than to leave Jijo, and that seemed the most likely, if risky, way.

But Dwer's mind roamed back to their adventure together—as captives of the Danik robot, when Dwer used to carry the machine across rivers by wearing it like a hat, conducting its suspensor fields through his own throbbing nervous system. . . .

All at once he realized. The recollection was no accident. No random association.

It was a warning.

Creepy shivers coursed his spine. Eerily familiar.

"Dung!" he cried out, swiveling to the west—

—just in time to spy a tremendous object, blue and rounded, like a demon's face, soar past the Rimmer peaks and hurtle silently toward him, outracing sound.

It was like watching the onrush of an arrow, aimed straight at your nose. In moments the starship grew from a mere speck, burgeoning to fill the world!

Dwer shut his eyes, bracing for erasure. . . .

Kiduras passed, two for each racing heartbeat. After twenty or so, the gondola was struck by a wall of sound, shaking him like thunder.

But sound was all. No impact.

It must have missed me!

He forced an eye open, turning around . . .

. . . and spied it to the east, bearing toward the decoy balloons.

Now he could tell, the behemoth moved at a higher altitude. The imminent collision had been a mirage. It never came within a league of him, or gave Dwer any notice.

But it can't miss the decoys, he thought. *They're in open view.*

Blade, his childhood qheuen playmate, had reported that balloons seemed transparent to Jophur instruments. *But that was at night. It's almost broad daylight now. Surely they see the gasbags by now.*

Or maybe not. Dwer recalled how excited the balloon concept made the Niss Machine, which understood a lot about Jophur ways. Perhaps Gillian Baskin knew what she was doing.

The idea was to get the Jophur confused. To send them searching around for supposed enemy ships they could detect only vaguely.

Sure enough, the space titan decelerated ponderously, descending in a long spiral around the general area. An aura of warped air seemed to bend all light passing within half a radius of the tremendous globe. The rewq made clear this was a shield of some sort—apparent grounds for the Jophur assumption of invincibility.

Dwer reached for the hammer at his waist . . . and waited.

Lark

HE WANTED TO MAKE LOVE AGAIN.

Who wouldn't, after the way Ling had writhed and clutched at him, with animal-like cries that belied her background as an urbane sky god? He, too, had felt a seismic quake of passion. Ardor that reached out of something wild within . . . followed by a release that was blissfully free of any sapient thought.

Despite their dire circumstance, trapped in a ship filled with mortal enemies, Lark felt fine. Better than he had since—

Since ever. Somehow, this climax did not leave him in a state of lassitude, but filled with energy, a postcoital animation he had never experienced before. *So much for my vow of celibacy,* he thought. Of course, that vow had been for the sake of Jijo. *And we're not on Jijo anymore.*

He reached for Ling. But she stopped him with an upraised hand, sitting up, her breasts still glistening with their commingled sweat.

Ling's eyes were distant. Her ears twitched, listening.

A jungle surrounded them—supported by lattice scaffolding that filled a chamber larger than the artificial cave of Biblos. A maze of fantastic, profusely varied vegetation nearly filled the cavity. In this far corner, apparently ill-tended by the maintenance drones, the two fugitive hominids had built a nest. Ling, the trained spatiobiologist, had no trouble spotting several types of fruits and tubers to eat. They might live weeks or months this way . . . or perhaps the rest of their lives. Unless the universe intruded.

Which it did, of course.

"They've turned on their defensive array," she told him. "And I think they're slowing down."

"How can you tell?" Lark listened, but could make out no difference in the mesh of interlacing engine sounds, more complex than the verdant jungle.

Ling slipped into the rag of a tunic that was her sole remaining garment. "Come on," she said.

With a sigh, he put on his own torn shirt. Lark picked up the leather thong holding his amulet—the fragment of the Holy Egg he had chipped off as a child. For the first time in years, he considered not slipping it on. If the ship had left Jijo, might that make him free at last from the love-hate burden?

"Come on!" Ling was already scooting along the latticeway, heading toward the exit. In a torn cloth sling, she carried the wounded red torus—one of the traeki rings provided by Asx.

He slipped the thong around his neck and reached for the crude sack that contained the purple ring and their few other possessions.

"I'm on my way," he murmured, clambering out of the nest, wondering if they would ever be back.

Ling had her bearings now. With Lark to sniff scent indicators at tunnel intersections, and the purple ring serving as a passkey, they had little trouble hurrying "north" up the ship's axis. Twice they sped along by using antigravity drop tubes. Lark's stomach did somersaults as his body went careening up a jet-black tunnel. The landings were always soft, though. Even better, they did not meet a single Jophur or robot along the way.

"They're at battle stations," she explained. "Here. Their control room should be just below this level. If I'm right, there should be an observers' gallery. . . ."

Lark smelled an oddly familiar aroma, much like the fragrance traeki used when they referred to *Biblos*.

Ling pointed to a rare written symbol inscribed on the wall. She crowed. "I was right!"

Lark had seen the glyph before—a rayed spiral with five swirling arms. Even Jijo's fallen races knew what it stood for. The Great Galactic Library. Symbol for both patience and knowledge.

"Hurry!" Ling said as he applied the purple ring to the entrance plate. The barrier slid open, giving access to a dim chamber whose sole illumination came through a broad window, directly opposite the door. It took just a few strides to cross over and stare through the glass at a bright gallery below. A chamber filled with Jophur.

There were scores of the tapered stacks. Taller and more slickly perfect than any Jijoan traeki, they squatted next to instrument stations, many of them surrounded by flashing panels and lighted controls. At the very center, one gleaming torus pile perched on a raised dais, surveying the labors of the crew.

"A lot of big ships have observation decks, like the one we're in," Ling explained in a low voice. "They're for when legates from any of the great Institutes come aboard—say on an inspection tour. Most of the time, though, they just contain a watcher."

"A what?"

She gestured to her left, where Lark now saw a roughly man-sized cube with a single dark lens in the middle, looking over the Jophur control room.

"It's a WOM . . . or Write-Only Memory. A *witness*. Any capital ship from a great clan is supposed to carry one, especially if engaged in some major venture. It takes a record that can then be archived in deep storage so later generations may learn from the experience of each race, after a certain time period expires."

"How long?"

Ling shrugged. "Millions of years, I guess. You hear

about watchers being sent for storage, but I've never
known of a WOM being read during the present epoch.
I guess when you put it that way, it kind of sounds
like a contradiction in terms. A typical Galactic hypocrisy. Or maybe I don't grasp some subtlety of the concept."

You and me, both, Lark thought, dismissing the watcher
from his mind, like a slab of stone.

"Look," he said, pointing toward one end of the Jophur
headquarters chamber. "Those big screens show the outside! Seems we just passed over the Rimmers."

"Toward the sun." Ling nodded. "Either it's morning
or—"

"Nothing on the Slope looks like that prairie. That's poison grass. So it is morning and that's east."

"See the clouds," Ling commented. "They're breaking
up, but it must've been some stor—" She stopped, blinking. "Hear that? The Jophur are excited. Maybe I can adjust
these knobs and—"

Sound abruptly boomed through the observation deck.
A screech and ratchet of accented GalTwo.

*". . . COMMANDED TO CORRECT THE DISSONANCE/
DISAGREEMENTS BETWEEN YOUR VARIED REPORTS! JUS-
TIFY THIS PATTERNED SEARCH! EXPLAIN REASONS WHY
WE SHOULD NOT RETURN TO OUR PRIMARY MISSION—
SIFTING FOR THE WOLFLING CRAFT!"*

Lark saw the Jophur on the central dais gesticulate along
with these word glyphs, so perhaps that one was in command. *If only I had a weapon,* he mused. But the glasslike
barrier was probably too strong for anything as crude as a
Jijoan axe or rifle.

*"We/I cannot recommend departing this area until we
verify/rebuke the possibility of foe ships/smallships,"* replied
a nearby stack, using a less imperious version of the same
dialect. *"Starship cognizances hover nearby, undetectable
on any other band! But how can that be? Flight without
gravitics? The Jophur, great and mighty, must have/pierce
this secret, for safety's sake!"*

Another ring stack edged forward, and Lark felt a shiver
of recognition. That awkward pile of ragged toruses had

once been the former traeki High Sage, though its speech held none of the unassuming gentleness of Asx.

"I/we offer this wisdom—that the scent indicators we pursue have all the stink of an elaborate ruse! Recall the flame-tube weapons that the savage sooners used against our corvette! Now our comrades in the captured Biblos Archive report they have identified the wolfling trick as 'rockets.' Contradicting the tactics officer, I/we must point out that these rockets flew quite successfully without gravitics! I/we further maintain that—"

Another stack interrupted.

"Localization! One of the nearby cognizance sites has remained active long enough to verify its location."

The commander vented compact clots of purple vapor.

"PROCEED ON ATTACK VECTOR! PREPARE A CAPTURE BOX FOR SEIZURE OF SOURCE! WHETHER IT IS A SO-PHISTICATED STAR ENEMY OR ANOTHER SOONER RUSE, WE SHALL SECURE IT FOR LATER INSPECTION, THEN RE-TURN TO OUR PRINCIPAL OBJECTIVE."

The ring piles reacted more swiftly than Lark had ever witnessed traeki move, setting to work in a whirl of base feet and flailing tendrils. Soon the outside monitors showed clouds and prairie rushing by in a blur, depicted in many spectral bands. On some displays, flashing concentric circles closed in.

"Targeting brackets—" Ling explained. But the circles seemed to contain nothing. Only open space.

Lark's right hand drifted under his shirt, stroking the sliver of the Egg. "I feel . . ."

Ling tugged his arm. "Look at the far left screen!"

He squinted, and began to make out something small and round. A ghostly shape, depicted as nearly transparent. *Blur cloth,* he realized, recognizing the effects of that specialized g'Kek weaving. All at once Lark understood. The Jophur were streaking toward an object that was invisible to nearly all their sensors, because it was made of nothing but air and fabric plaited to smear light.

If only his rewq had not lapsed into exhausted hibernation! The hazy globe loomed larger, even as Lark's heart beat faster. His amulet throbbed in response.

"What *is* it?" Ling wondered, perplexed.

Before he could answer, without warning, all the forward viewing screens abruptly went black.

One Jophur let out a shrill wail. Several vented colored steam. The commander flexed and blared.

"HOSTILITIES ALERT! ROBOTIC DEFENSE! ALL STATIONS PREPARE FOR THE DRAWBA—"

Gillian

DETONATION!"

Streaker's detection officer shouted excitedly. "One of our proximity bombs just went off, almost on t-top of the Jophur!"

The bridge filled with neo-dolphin cheers. "Maybe that got the bastardss," someone chittered hopefully.

Gillian called for quiet.

"Keep it down, everyone. That firecracker won't do more than scratch their paint." She took a deep breath. It was the crucial moment of decision, for commitment to the plan.

"Launch the swarm!" she ordered. "Get us up, Kaa. Exactly the way we planned."

"Aye!" The pilot's back showed momentary waves of tension as he sent commands down his neural tap. *Streaker* responded instantly, engines ramping up to full power for the first time in almost a year. The sound was thrilling, though the act would surely give them away once Jophur sensors recovered.

Telemetry showed the motivators running well. Gillian glanced at viewers showing the engine room. Hannes Suessi darted back and forth, checking the work of his well-trained crew. Even Emerson D'Anite seemed engrossed, running his long, dark hands over the prime resonance console, his old duty station during so many other rough scrapes. Speech seemed hardly relevant at this point, when physical insight and tactile skill mattered most.

Perhaps this time, too, the ship would hear Emerson's rich baritone victory yell.

If the repairs all worked. If we get full use out of the spare parts we mined from discarded wrecks. If the decoys run as planned. If the enemy does what we hope . . . if . . . if . . .

Overhead, the stress crystal dome of the control room changed color. The jet black of the abyss faded rapidly as *Streaker* aimed upward, lightening to a royal blue, then a clear pale green. The engine's roar changed tone as Jijo's ocean reluctantly let go its heavy grasp.

Streaker blew out of the sea with explosive force, already traveling faster than a bullet, trailed by a spoor of superheated steam.

From submarine, back to ship of space. Here we go again.

Go, old girl.

Go!

Rety

WAKENED FROM A HALF-MILLION-YEAR SLEEP, THE ancient wreck clattered and shrieked. Forced into furious effort, it howled, like some beast screaming in agony.

Rety screamed back, pressing both hands over her ears. Harsh fists seemed to pummel her against the arching pillar where she had tied herself down. With each shake, strips of rope and electrical cable dug into her skin.

From Rety's belt pouch, yee's head waved toward her face.

"wife! wife don't cry! don't worry, wife!"

But the piping words were lost amid a maelstrom of sound. Soon his calls merged into a wail, an urrish ululation.

Overwhelmed with dread of being trapped, Rety tore at the straps with her nails, struggling for release.

She never noticed the transition from water to air. The

little holosim display showed whitecaps stretching to a sandy shore, then the tops of clouds.

Crawling across the hard metal floor, Rety toiled toward the airlock, seeing only a narrow tunnel through a haze of pain.

Ewasx

THE EFFECTS START TO WEAR OFF.

I emerge from stun state, blind and alone. More duras pass before I coalesce My sense of oneness. Of purpose.

Sending trace signals down the tendrils of control, I reestablish rapport with subservient rings. Soon I have access to their varied senses, staring in all directions with eye buds that flutter and twitch.

HELLO, MY RINGS. Report now and prepare for urgent movement. Clearly we have experienced—and survived—an episode of the Drawback.

The what?

Truly, you do not know, My rings? You have no experience of the chief disadvantage of the Oailie gift?

Certain weapons exist which can render us Jophur insensate for a time, forcing us to rely on robotic protection for the duration of that brief incapacity.

What incapacity? you ask.

I/we look around. We are no longer near the Captain-Leader, but stand instead at the main control panel, our tendrils wrapped around the piloting wheels.

WHAT ARE WE DOING?

I command the tendrils to draw back, and they obey. Viewscreens show a blur of high-speed motion as the *Polkjhy* races across a landscape of jagged, twisty canyons, unlike anything our memory tracks recall from the Slope. Inertial indicators show us racing *east,* ever farther from the sea. Away from the prey.

Other stacks are beginning to stir, as their master rings

rouse from the Drawback. Hurriedly, I send our basal torus in motion, taking us away from the pilot station. We scurry around behind the Captain-Leader, who is just now rousing from torpor.

In all likelihood others will assume that our sophisticated robotic guardians—programmed to serve/protect during a Drawback interlude—had good reason to send *Polkjhy* careening in this unfavorable direction. Feigning innocence, I/we watch as the pilot stacks resume control, arresting this headlong flight, preparing to regain altitude once more.

MY RINGS, WHAT WAS YOUR AIM? WHAT WERE YOU TRYING TO ACCOMPLISH WHILE YOUR MASTER TORUS WAS INCAPACITATED? TO SEND US CRASHING INTO A MOUNTAIN, PERHAPS?

The robots would not have allowed that. But diverting the course of *Polkjhy*—that was in your power, no?

I perceive we are not finished learning the arts of cooperation.

Gillian

THRILLING AS IT WAS TO BE MOVING AGAIN, GILLIAN knew this wasn't the same old *Streaker*. It ran sluggishly for a snark-class survey ship. The nearby landmass receded with disheartening slowness compared with the rabbitlike agility she used to show. Suessi's motors weren't at fault. It was the damned carbon-carbon coating, sealing *Streaker*'s hull under countless tons of dead weight, clogging the probability flanges and gravitics radiators, costing valuable time to gain orbital momentum. Minutes of vulnerability.

Gillian glanced at the swarm display. A scatter of bright dots showed at least twenty decoys out of the water, with a dozen more now rising from their ancient graves, screaming joy—or agony—over this unwonted mass resurrection. Groups of bait ships speared away in different directions, disbanding according to preset plans, though empty of life.

All empty, except one.

Gillian thought of the human girl, Rety, self-exiled aboard one of those glimmering lights. Would it have been better to break into her hijacked ship? Or try to seize control of the computer, reprogramming it to bring Rety ashore?

The Niss didn't think either effort would succeed in the slim time allowed. Anyway, Alvin and Huck had convinced Gillian not to try.

"We know what you Earthlings are trying to do with this breakout attempt," the young g'Kek had said.

"And yet you volunteered to come?"

"Why not? We risked the Midden in a hollow tree trunk. All sooners know life is something you just borrow for a while. Each person must choose how to spend it.

"All our families and all our septs depend on your venture, Dr. Baskin. This Rety person selected her destiny. Let her follow it."

As *Streaker* gradually accelerated, Gillian turned to the dolphin in charge of psi-ops. "Let me know when you get anything at all from the observer," she ordered.

"No sssignal yet-t," the fin answered. "It'sss well past due, if you ask me."

"No one asked," Gillian snapped.

Without wanting to, she glanced at the Jijoan mathematician, Sara Koolhan, whose brother took off in a hot-air balloon, knowing that if the gale did not get him, the Jophur probably would. Sara floated in a swarm of bubbles, watching intently. But behind the visor of her breathing helmet, Gillian saw a single soft tear, running down the young woman's cheek.

Gillian did not need more guilt. She tried hard to think pragmatically.

I just wish the boy hadn't died for nothing. We're going to have to decide . . .

She checked the swarm monitors.

. . . in moments. . . .

Dwer

THE DAZZLING BLAST JOLTED HIS REWQ, CAUSING IT
to retreat, almost comatose. But the creature served its
purpose, saving Dwer's eyes. Except for a few purple
spots, vision soon returned almost to normal.

There'll be a shock wave, he thought. After the abuse of
last night and morning, he wondered if the balloon would
survive another shaking.

Dwer readied his hammer over the row of crystals, each
jammed into the wicker gondola. He peered east, trying to
figure out which message to send.

All the decoy balloons were gone—no surprise there.

But dammit, where's the Jophur ship?

Dwer could not act without data, so he held on and rode
out the explosion's booming echo when it came rolling by,
flattening the serrated grass of the Venom Plain.

The balloon survived. Solid urrish workmanship. Picking
up binoculars, he sought again for the Jophur, scanning the
horizon.

Could it have been blown up by the aerial mine? Gillian
Baskin had thought the prospect nearly impossible. No
weapon in *Streaker's* arsenal could pierce the defense of
such a dreadnought, even with the element of surprise. But
it might be possible to inconvenience the enemy for a crucial time.

Finally, he made out the distant glint. In fact, the ship
seemed to be *receding!* He had the illusion that it was
heading toward the rising sun.

Dwer hesitated over the message crystals. There were
only four. None of the prearranged codes took in this possibility . . . that the foe would flee the scene. Not upward
toward space, or west back to the Midden, or even standing still, but *away* from any chance to spy the Earthling
ship!

If I don't send anything, they'll think I'm dead.

He thought of Sara, and was tempted to smash all the
crystals, just to reassure her.

But then they might make a wrong decision, and she might die instead of me. Because of me.

By now, squadrons of salvaged decoy spaceships would be heading out beyond Jijo's atmosphere, spiraling toward orbit and beyond. Gillian Baskin had to decide which group to go with. Dwer's signal was supposed to help.

Frustration locked him in a rigor of indecision. Raising the binoculars once more, he found the Jophur ship again, a bare pinpoint near the horizon.

Then he noticed something.

The distant dot . . . it had stopped receding. Instead, it seemed to hover beyond a range of craggy highlands.

The Gray Hills, Dwer realized. *If only I can give the right signal, I'll be able to start descending in time to land where I want!*

The glittering pinpoint hesitated, then began to move again. Dwer soon confirmed—it was growing larger. The Jophur were heading back this way!

Now I know what to send, he thought with satisfaction. Dwer raised the hammer and brought it smashing down on the second crystal. That instant, his back swarmed with a curious tingling. The feeling came and left quickly.

His duty done at last, Dwer reached for the gas-discharge rope. The battleship was going to pass close again, and the only way he had to maneuver was to lose height.

Easy does it, he thought. *Let her down slowly. Might as well reach the foothills before you have to . . .*

The great ship loomed rapidly, then streaked westward while gaining altitude, missing him by hundreds of arrow-flights.

Alas, this time it did not ignore Dwer.

As it hurried by, the mighty blue globe dropped a tiny speck. A minuscule dot that arced away and then dropped rapidly, glittering as it came. Dwer did not have to know much about Galactic technology to recognize a missile when he saw one.

Gillian mentioned that I might attract attention when I signaled.

Dwer sighed, watching the fleck turn a gentle curve and then plunge straight toward him.

Ah, well, he thought, picking up his prize possession—the bow made for him by the master carvers of Ovoom Town, in honor of his skill as tracker for the Commons of Six Races.

When the explosion came, it was unlike anything he expected.

Gillian

T HAT'S IT!" SHE CRIED OUT, GLAD OF THE NEWS. Even more elated was Sara, who let out an urrish-sounding yelp, on learning that her brother yet lived.

The signal also confirmed Gillian's best guess. The Jophur had been slow reacting, but they were doing as she hoped.

"They are predictable," commented the Niss, whose whirling hologram passed through oxy-water bubbles unperturbed. *"The delay only means we get more of a head start."*

Gillian agreed, but in her thoughts added:

We'll need ten times this much of a lead, in order to make it all the way.

Aloud, she told the pilot:

"Punch us out of here, Kaa. Stay with swarm number two. Put us second from the front of the pack."

The pilot shouted, "Aye!"

Soon the low, driving harmonies of the motivators notched upward in pitch. Gillian glanced at the engine-room display. Morale seemed high among Suessi's crewfen. As she watched, Emerson D'Anite threw his head back to *sing*! Gillian only picked up a fragment, though the lyrics had Emerson's coworkers in stitches.

> *"Jijo, Jijo . . .*
> *It's off to war we go!"*

Even suffering from brain affliction, his puns were terrible. It was good to have some of the old Emerson back again.

External displays showed the planet swiftly receding, a gentle blue-brown globe, swathed in a slim envelope of life-giving weather. Numerous sharp-bordered green patches testified to where some metropolis once stood, before the site was scoured and seeded. Whether now covered with swamp, forest, or prairie, the regions still showed regular outlines that would take eons to erase.

Earth has such scars, she thought. *In even greater abundance. The difference is that we were ignorant and didn't know better. We had to learn the hard way how to manage a world, by teaching ourselves.*

Gillian glanced at Sara, whose eyes bore pain and wonder, watching her homeworld diminish to a small orb—the first of her sooner line to look down at Jijo, ever since her ancestors fled here, centuries ago.

A place of refuge. A sanctuary for Earthlings and others. They all meant to hunker down, cowering away from the cosmos, each race redeeming its heritage in its own peculiar way.

Then we brought the universe crashing in on them.

She watched Lieutenant Tsh't move among the crewfen at their dome consoles, encouraging them with bursts of sonar, always checking for lapses of attention. The meticulous supervision hardly seemed necessary. Not one of the elite bridge staff had ever shown a trace of stress atavism. All were guaranteed high uplift classifications when they got home.

If we get home.

If there is still a home, waiting for us.

In fact, everyone knew the real reason why half the crew had been left behind on Jijo, along with the Kiqui and copies of *Streaker*'s records.

We don't have much of a chance of escaping . . . but it might be possible to draw the universe away from Jijo. Diverting its attention. Making it forget the sooners, once again.

It would take skill and luck just to achieve that sacrifice. But if successful, what an accomplishment! Preventing the extinction of the g'Kek, or the unwanted transformation of the traeki, or the discovery and blame that would befall Earth, if human sooners were exposed here.

If this works, we'll have a complete cache of Earthlings on Jijo—humans, chimps, and now dolphins, too. A safety reserve, in case the worst happens at home.

That seems worthwhile. A result worth paying for.

Of course, like everything in the cosmos, it would come at a price.

They had passed Loocen—the moon still glittering with abandoned cities—and accelerated about a million kilometers beyond when the detection officer declared:

"Enemy cruiser leaving atmosphere! Vectoring after swarm number one!"

The spatial schematic showed a speck rising from Jijo, larger and brighter than any other, lumbering to accelerate its titanic mass.

We could outrun you, once, Gillian thought. *We still can . . . for a while.*

Even handicapped by the irksome carbon sheathing, *Streaker* would spend some time increasing the gap between her and the pursuing battleship. Newtonian inertia must drag down the heavier Jophur—that is, until it reached speeds adequate for level-zero hyperdrive.

Then the speed advantage would start to shift.

If only a transfer point were nearer. Gillian shook her head, and kept on wishing.

If only Tom and Creideiki were here. They'd get us away without much trouble, I bet. I could retire to sick bay with confidence, treating dolphins for itchy-flake and spending my copious free time contemplating the mysteries of Herbie.

In a moment of decision, she had elected to take along the billion-year-old mummy, despite the high likelihood *Streaker* would be destroyed in a matter of hours or days. She could not part with the relic, which Tom had fought so hard to snatch from a fleet of ghost ships in the Shallow Cluster—back in those heady days before the whole Civilization of the Five Galaxies seemed to turn against *Streaker.*

Back when the naive crew expected *gratitude* for their epochal discovery.

Never surprise a stodgy Galactic, went a Tymbrimi saying. *Unless you're prepared with twelve more surprises in your pocket.*

Good advice.

Unfortunately, her supply of tricks was running low. There were, in fact, only a few left.

The Sages

THE LATEST GROUP OF PILGRIMS UNDERSTOOD more now, about the Holy Egg.

More than Drake and Ur-Chown knew, when they first stared at the newly emerged wonder, glowing white-hot from its fiery emergence. Those two famed heroes conspired to exploit the Egg for their own religious and political purposes, declaring it an omen. A harbinger of unity. A god.

Now the sages have printouts provided by the dolphin ship. The report, downloaded from a unit of the Great Galactic Library, calls the Egg—*a psi-active geomorph. A phenomenon observed on some life worlds whose tectonic restoration processes are smoothly continuous, where past cycles of occupation and renewal had certain temporal and technologic traits . . .*

Phwhoon-dau contemplated this as the newly reassembled Council of Sages approached the sacred site, walking, slithering, and rolling toward the place they had all separately been heading when they heard Vubben's dying call.

In other words, the Egg is a distillation, a condensation of Jijo's past. All the dross deposited by the Buyur . . . and those who came before . . . has combined to contribute patterns.

Patterns that somehow wove their way through magma pressure and volcanic heat.

To the south, these spilled forth chaotically, to become the Spectral Flow. But here, conditions permitted coalescence. A crystalline tip consisting of pure memory and purpose.

At last he understood the puzzle of why every sooner

race settled on the Slope, despite initial jealousies and feuds.

We were summoned.

Some said this knowledge would crush the old ways, and Phwhoon-dau agreed. The former faith—founded in the Sacred Scrolls, then modified by waves of heresy—would never be the same.

The basis of the Commons of Six Races had changed.

But the basis survived.

A re-formed Council of Six entered the scarred canyon circle, where they spent a brief time contemplating the charred remains of their eldest member, a jumble of frail nerves and fibers, plastered against the Egg's pitted, sooty flank.

They buried Vubben there—the only sage ever so honored. Then began their work.

Others would join them soon. A re-formed council meant re-formed duty.

At last we know what you are, Phwhoon-dau thought silently, leaning back to regard the Egg's great curving mass.

But other questions remain. Such as . . . why?

Rety

THE CONTROLS REFUSED TO RESPOND!

"Come on!" she shouted, slamming the holosim box with the palm of her hand, then jiggling more levers.

Not that Rety had much idea what she'd do if she gained mastery over the decoy vessel. At first, the stunning views of Jijo and space sent her brain reeling. It was all so much *bigger* than she ever imagined. Since then, she had left the big visual holo turned off, while continuing to fiddle with other panels and displays.

Wisdom preached that she ought to leave the machinery alone . . . and finally, Rety listened. She forced herself to back away, joining yee at her small stack of supplies, smuggled off the sled when Chuchki wasn't looking. She stroked her little husband while munching a food-concentrate bar, pondering the situation.

Every salvaged decoy ship had been programmed to head out—by a variety of routes—toward the nearest "transfer point." From there, they would jump away from fallow Galaxy Four, aiming for distant, traffic-filled lanes where oxygen-breathing life-forms teemed.

That was good enough for Rety, providing she then found a way to signal some passing vessel.

This old ship may not be worth much, but it oughta pay my passage to their next stop, at least.

What would happen next remained vague in her mind. Getting some kind of job, most likely. She still had the little teaching machine that used to belong to Dennie Sudman, so learning those jabber-talk alien languages shouldn't be too hard.

I'll find a way to make myself useful. I always have.

Of course, everything depended on making it to the transfer point.

Gillian prob'ly set things up so the decoys'll try to lure the Jophur. Maybe they give off some sort of light or noise to make 'em think there are dolphins aboard.

That might work for a while. The stinky rings'll chase around, losin' time while checkin' things out.

But Rety knew what would happen next. Eventually, the Jophur gods would catch on to the trick. They'd figure out what to look for, and realize which ship was the real target.

Suppose by then they've torn apart half the decoys. That still leaves me fitty-fitty odds. Which is Ifni times more than I'd have aboard old Streaker. *Once they figure which one she is, they'll leave the rest of us decoys alone to go about our business.*

At least that was the overall idea. Ever since she had found Kunn and Jass, dead in their jail cells, Rety knew she must get off the Earthling ship as fast as possible and make it on her own.

I'd better be able to send out a signal, when we pop into a civilized galaxy, she thought. *I s'pose it'll take more than just shining a light out through a window. Guess I better study some more about radio and that hyperwave stuff.*

As wonderful and patient as the teaching unit was, Rety

did not look forward to the drudgery ahead . . . nor to relying on the bland paste put out by the ancient food processor, once her supply of *Streaker* food ran out. The machine had taken the sample of fingernail cuticle she gave it, and after a few moments put out a substance that tasted exactly like cuticle.

Chirping tones interrupted her thoughts. A light flashed atop the holosim casing. Rety scooted over to the machine.

"Display on!"

A 3-D image erupted just above the floor plates. For a time, she made little sense of the image, which showed five small groups of amber points spiraling away from a tiny blue disk. It took moments to realize the dot was Jijo, and the decoy swarms had already left the planet far behind. The separation *between* the convoys also grew larger, with each passing dura.

One dot lagged behind, brighter than the others, gleaming red instead of yellow. It crept toward one of the fleeing swarms as she watched.

That must be the Jophur ship, she realized. Squinting closer, she saw that the big dot was trailed by a set of much tinier crimson pinpricks, almost too small to see, following like beads on a string.

The red symbol accelerated, slowly closing the distance to its intended prey.

Boy, I pity whoever's in that swarm, when the stink rings catch up with 'em.

It took Rety a while longer to fathom the unpleasant truth.

That swarm was the one that contained her own ship.

The Jophur were coming for her first.

My usual luck, she complained, knowing better than to think the universe cared.

Dwer

EVERYTHING CHANGED.

One moment, he had been surrounded by sky. Mountains, clouds, and prairies stretched below his wicker gondola. The urrish balloon bulged and creaked overhead.

From the high northwest, a glittering object fell toward him, like a stoop raptor, unstoppable once it has chosen its prey.

That's me, he thought, feeling transfixed, like a grass mouse who, caught in the open, knows there is no escape, and so has little choice but to watch the terrible beauty of Death on the wing.

Death came streaking toward him.

He felt an explosion, a shrill brilliance . . .

. . . and found himself *here*.

A gilded haze surrounded Dwer as he took stock.

I'm alive.

The sensations of a young, strong body accompanied irksome itches and the sting of recent scrapes. His clothes were as they had been. So was the gondola, for that matter—a basket woven out of dried river reeds—its contents undamaged.

The same could not be said of the balloon itself. The great gasbag lay collapsed in a curved heap of blur cloth, its upper half apparently cleaved off. Remnant folds lay spread across the interior of what Dwer came to realize must be a prison of some sort.

A spherical jail. He now saw it clearly. A sphere whose inner surface gave off a pale, golden light, confusing to the eye at first.

"Huh!"

To Dwer's surprise, his principal reaction was intrigue. In those final moments, as the missile fell, he had bid farewell to life. Now each added moment was profit. He could spend it as he chose.

He decided on curiosity.

Dwer clambered out of the basket and eased his moccasins onto the gold surface. He half expected it to be slick, but the material instead *clung* to his soles, so that he had to pull with some effort each time he took a step. After a few tentative strides, he came to yet another startling revelation.

"Down" is wherever I happen to be standing!

From Dwer's new position, it looked as if the gondola was tilted almost sideways, about to topple onto him.

He squatted, looking down at the "floor" between his legs, riding out the expected wave of disorientation. It wasn't too bad.

I'll adapt. It'll be like learning to ice-walk across a glacier. Or probing face caves at the end of a rope, dangling over the Desolation Cliffs.

Then he realized something. Looking down, he saw more than just a sticky golden surface. Something glittered *beneath* it. Like a dusting of tiny diamonds. Gemstones, mixed with dark loam.

He leaned closer, cupping hands on both sides of his eyes to keep out stray light.

All at once Dwer fathomed; the diamonds were stars.

Lark

CROUCHING BEHIND AN AROMATIC OBELISK, TWO humans had an unparalleled chance to view events in the Jophur control room.

Lark would much rather they had stayed in the quiet, safe "observation chamber."

Towering stacks of sappy toruses loomed nearby, puffing steam as each Jophur worked at a luminous instrument station. The density of smells made Lark want to gag. It must be worse for Ling, who hadn't grown up near traeki. Yet she seemed enthralled to be here.

Well, this was a terrific idea, he groused mentally, recall-

ing the impulse that had sent them charging into a pit of
foes.

*Hey, look! The Jophur seem stunned! Let's rush down
from this nice, safe hiding place and sabotage their instruments while they're out!*

Only the Jophur didn't stay out long enough. By the time
he and Ling made it halfway across the wide control room,
several ring piles abruptly started puffing and swaying as
they roused from their torpor. While machine voices reported status to their reviving masters, the two humans
barely managed to leap behind this cluster of spirelike objects, roughly the shape of idealized Jophur, but twice as
tall and made of some moist, fibrous substance.

Lark dropped down to the floor. All he wanted was to
scrunch out of sight, close his eyes, and make objective
reality go away.

Responding to his racing heartbeat, the purple ring
twitched in its cloth bag. Lark put his hand on it and the
thing eventually calmed down.

"I think I can tell what's going on!"

Lark glanced up the twin, tanned columns of Ling's legs,
and saw that she was leaning around one of the soggy
pillars, staring at the Jophur data screens. Reaching up, he
seized her left wrist and yanked her down. She landed on
her bare bottom beside him.

"Make like vermin," was his advice. On matters of concealment and survival, Ling had a lot to learn from a Jijoan
sooner.

"Okay, brother rat." She nodded with surprising cheerfulness, then went on eagerly. "Some of their screens are
set to spectra I can't grok. But I could tell we're in space
now, racing toward Izmunuti."

A wave of nausea struck Lark—a sensation akin to panic.
Unlike his siblings, who used to talk and dream about star-
flight when they were little, he had never wanted to leave
Jijo. The very thought made him feel sick. Sensing his discomfort, Ling took his head and stroked it, but that did not
stop her from talking, describing a complex hunt through
space that Lark failed to visualize, no matter how he tried.

"Apparently there must have been a fleet of ships on or
near Jijo," she explained. "Though I can't imagine how

they got there. Maybe they came snooping from Izmunuti and the Jophur are chasing them away. Anyway, the mystery fleet seems to have split into five groups, all of them heading separately for the flare star. And from there to the transfer point, I suppose.

"There's also a couple of small objects trailing behind this ship . . . connected to it, as far as I can tell, by a slender force string. I don't know what their purpose is. But give me time. . . ."

Lark wanted to laugh out loud. He would give Ling the world. The universe! But right now all he really wanted was their nest. Their little green hideaway, where sweet fruits dangled within reach and no one could find them.

Lark was starting to push the vertigo away at last, when a noise blared from across the room.

"What's that?" he asked, sitting up. He did not try to stop Ling from rising partway and peering around for a look.

"Weapons release," she explained. "The Jophur are firing missiles at the nearest squadron. They must be pretty confident, because they sent just one for each ship."

Lark silently wished the new aliens luck, whoever they were. If any of them got away, they might report what they saw to the Galactic Migration Institute. Although Jijo's Six Races had lived in fear of the law for two thousand years, the intervention of neutral judges would be far better than any fate the Jophur planned to mete out, in private.

"The small ships are trying evasive maneuvers, but it's doing no good," Ling said. "The missiles are closing in."

Rety

SHE CURSED THE DROSS SHIP, FOR NOT GIVING HER control.

She cursed Gillian Baskin and the dolphins, for putting her in a position where she had no choice but to escape from their incompetence into this impossible trap.

She cursed the Jophur for sending missiles after this decoy flotilla, instead of expertly finding the right prey.

Above all, Rety swore an oath at herself. For in the end, she had no one else to blame.

Her teaching unit explained the symbols representing those deadly arrows, now clearly visible in the display, catching up fast.

One by one, the ships behind hers met their own avenging predators. Surprisingly, the amber pinpoints did not snuff out, but turned crimson instead. Each then drifted backward, toward a meeting with the big red dot.

The Jophur did not swallow their captives. That would take too much time. Instead, they were snagged at the end of a chain—like a tadpole's tail—that waved behind the mighty ship.

Rety wondered. *Maybe they don't want to kill, after all. Maybe they just want prisoners!*

If so, Rety would be prepared. She held yee with one arm, and the teaching unit with the other, setting it to begin teaching her Galactic Two—Jophur dialect.

When her own missile arrived, Rety was calmer than she expected.

"Don't worry, yee," she said, stroking her little husband. "We'll find somethin' they want, an' make a deal. Just you wait an' see."

With desperate confidence, she held on as the ancient Buyur vessel suddenly quivered and shook. In moments, the motors' grating drone cut off . . . and then so did the downward tug of the deck beneath her. In its place, a gentler pull seemed to draw her toward the *nose* of the disabled ship.

The lights went out. But Rety could see a bit. Stepping and sliding carefully along the slanted floor and walls, she followed the source of illumination to an unobstructed viewing port, where she peered outside and saw a world of pale yellow dawn.

yee commented dryly.

"beats being dead, i guess."

Rety agreed. "I guess." Then she shrugged.

"At least we'll see, one way or t'other."

Gillian

FOUND A LIBRARY REFERENCE. THEY ARE CALLED *capture boxes,"* the Niss explained. *"This weapon offers a clever solution to the Jophur dilemma."*

"How do you figure?" Gillian asked.

"We thought we had them in an awkward situation, where they must come close and inspect every decoy in order to find us. A cumbersome, time-consuming process.

"But this way, the Jophur need only get near enough to dispatch special missiles. They can then move on, dragging a string of captives behind them."

"Won't all that additional mass slow them down?" asked Kaa, the pilot.

"Yes, and that works in our favor. Alas, not enough to make up for the advantage this technique gives them."

Gillian shook her head. "Too bad we didn't know about this in time to incorporate it in our plans."

The Niss answered with a defensive tone. *"Great clans can access weaponry files spanning a billion years of Galactic history."*

Silence reigned on the bridge, until Sara Koolhan spoke, her voice transposed by the amplifying faceplate of her helmet.

"What happens if we get caught by a missile?"

"It creates a field related to the toporgic cage your Six Races found enveloping the Rothen ship. Of course that one was meters thick, and missiles cannot carry that much pseudo-material. The chief effect of a capture box is to suppress digital cognizance."

Sara looked confused, so Gillian explained.

"Digital computers are detectable at a distance, and can be suppressed by field-effect technologies. A principal reason why organic life-forms dominate the Five Galaxies, instead of machines.

"Unfortunately, this means our decoys can be disabled easily, by enclosing them in a thin shell of warped space-time."

*"Indeed, it seems an ideal weapon to use against resur-
rected starships lacking crews. The Jophur may be malign
and limited in many ways, but they do not lack for skill or
reasoning power."*

Sara nodded. "You mean the method won't work as well
against *Streaker*?"

"Exactly," Gillian said. "We'll prepare our computers to
stand a temporary shutdown without inconvenience—"

"Speak for yourself," the Niss muttered.

"As soon as the capture box surrounds us, organic crew
members can use simple tools to dissolve it from the inside. Estimated period of shutdown, Niss?"

The hologram whirled.

*"I wish we had better data from the expedition the soon-
ers sent to the Rothen vessel. They reported major quantum
effects from a toporgic layer meters thick.*

*"But the Jophur missiles will cast thin bubbles. If pre-
pared, crews should burst us free in mere minutes."*

A happy sigh escaped Kaa and several dolphins. But
then the Niss Machine went on.

*"Unfortunately, when we pop the bubble, it will alert the
Jophur which captured vessel contains living prey. After
that, our restored freedom will be brief, indeed."*

Dwer

THE STUFF FELT STRANGE. IT SEEMED TO REPEL HIS
hand slightly, until he got within a couple of centimeters.
Then it *pulled*. Neither effect was overwhelming. He
could yank his hand back fairly easily.

He could not quite place why it was eerily familiar.

Dwer walked all the way around his circular cage, stopping on occasion to bend down and examine the starscape
beyond. He recognized most of the constellations, except
for one patch that had always been invisible from the
Slope. *So that's what the southern sky is like.* Undimmed by
dust or atmosphere, the entire Dandelion Cluster lay before

him, a vast unwinking spectacle. It would be even more fantastic without the filmy golden barrier in the way.

Thank Ifni for that barrier, he reminded himself. *There is no air out there.*

In one direction lay a tremendously bright star he did not recognize at first.

Then he knew . . . it was the *sun,* much diminished, and getting smaller all the time.

In the opposite direction lay Izmunuti's fierce eye. The red glare grew more pronounced, until he began to make out an actual disk. Yet he realized it must still be farther away than the sun. Izmunuti was said to be a giant among stars.

In time he noticed other objects. Not stars or nebulae, but gleaming dots. At first they all seemed rather distant. But over the course of a midura, they drew ever closer, rounded shapes that revealed themselves more by their glimmering rims, occulting the constellations, than for any brightness they themselves put out.

One of them—a rippled sphere on the side toward Izmunuti—had to be a starship. It loomed larger with each passing dura. Soon he recognized it as the behemoth that had twice crossed the sky over the Poison Plain, shaking his hapless balloon with each passage.

When Dwer crossed his prison to peer through the membrane on the other side, he saw a line of yellowish globes, even closer than the starship. Their color made him realize, *They're other captives, like me.*

Pressing close to the barrier, a tingle coursed his scalp and spine. He felt similarities to when the Danik robot sent its fields through his body, changing his nervous system in permanent, still-uncertain ways.

Well, I was unusual even before that. For instance, no one else I know ever talked to a mulc spider. . . .

Dwer yanked his head back, recalling at last what this stuff reminded him of. The fluid used by the mad old spider of the mountains—One-of-a-Kind—to seal its victims away, storing its treasured collections against the ravages of time. Months back, a coating of that stuff had nearly smothered him, until he escaped the spider's trap.

A strange sensation came over Dwer. An odd idea.

I could talk to spiders, not just in the mountains, but the one in the swamp, too.

I wonder if that means . . .

Once again, he put his hand against the golden material, pushing through the initial resistance, pressing his finger-tips ahead. The resistance was springy. The material seemed adamant.

But Dwer let his mind slide into the same mode of think-ing that used to open him to communion with mulc beings. Always before, he had felt that the spider was the one doing most of the work, but now he realized, *It's my own talent. My own gift. And by the Holy Egg, I think I can—*

Something gave way. Resistance against his fingertips suddenly vanished and they slipped through, as if pene-trating some greasy fluid.

Abrupt *cold* struck the exposed hand, plus a feeling as if a thousand vampire ants were trying to drink his uncov-ered veins through straws. Dwer jerked back his arm and it popped out, the fingers red and numb, but mostly undam-aged. The membrane flowed back instantly, never leaving an opening to space.

Lucky me, he thought.

When Dwer next checked, the starship had grown to mammoth size. A great bull beast, bearing down on him rapidly, with a hunter's complacent confidence.

I'm a fish on a line. It's reeling me in!

On the other side, the captive globes bobbed almost touching, like toy balloons gathered along an invisible string. The separating distances diminished rapidly.

Dwer sat and thought for a while.

Then he started gathering supplies.

The Sages

PHWHOON-DAU LED THE NEW SEXTET, COMMENC-ing the serenade with a low, rolling umble from his reso-nating throat sac.

Knife-Bright Insight followed by rubbing a myrliton drum with her agile tongue, augmenting this with synco-pated calliope whistles from all five leg vents.

Ur-Jah then joined in, lifting her violus against a fold in her long neck, raising stringed harmonies with the double bow.

After that, by seniority, the new sages for traeki, human, and g'Kek septs added their own contributions, playing for a great ovoid-shaped chunk of wounded stone. The har-monies were rough at first, but soon they melded into the kind of union that focused the mind.

So far, the assembly was unexceptional. Other groups of six had performed for the Egg, over the course of a hun-dred years. Some of them more gifted and musical.

Only this time things were fundamentally different. It was no group of *six*, after all.

Two other Jijoan types were present.

The first was a glaver.

The devolved race always had an open invitation to par-ticipate, but it was centuries since any glaver took part in rituals of the Commons—long before Earthlings arrived, and certainly before the coming of the Egg.

But glavers had been acting strangely for months. And today, a small female came out of the brush and began slogging up the Pilgrimage Path, just behind Phwhoon-dau, as if she had the same destination in mind. Now her huge eyes glistened as the music swelled, and strange mewling noises emerged from her grimaced mouth. Sounds vaguely reminiscent of words. With her agile forked tail, she waved a crude rattle made of a stretched animal skin, with stones shaking inside.

Not much of an instrument, but after all, her kind were out of practice.

What must it take, Phwhoon-dau pondered, *to draw them back from the bliss of Redemption's Path?*

Lounging on a nearby boulder, an eighth creature paused licking himself now and then to survey the proceedings. The noor-tytlal had two blemishes on an otherwise jet-black pelt—white patches under each eye—adding to its natural expression of skeptical disdain.

The sages were not fooled. It had arrived just after the others, gaunt, bedraggled, and tired, having run hard for several days. Only urgency, not complacent inquisitiveness could have driven a noor to strive so. The creature's mobile ears flicked restlessly, and pale, spiky hairs waved behind the skull, belying its air of feigned nonchalance.

Now the secret was out. Everyone knew these were clients of the legendary Tymbrimi. Moreover, their patrons had given the tytlal a boon as uniquely personal as music.

Phwhoon-dau noticed a soft agitation start to form above the insouciant creature, as if a pocket of air were thickening, and beginning to shimmer. The sages altered their harmony to resonate with the throbbing disturbance, helping it grow as a look of hesitant surprise spread across the sleek, noorlike face.

Reluctant or not, he was now part of the pattern.

Part of the Council of Eight.

In the narrow, resonant confines of the Egg's abode, they made their art, their music.

And soon, another presence began to make itself known.

Ewasx

BEHOLD, MY RINGS, HOW WELL THE CHASE PRO-gresses!

Already one fugitive convoy is liquidated, its component vessels enjoined to our train of captives. While this growing impediment slows the *Polkjhy* from engaging her best speed of pursuit, our tactics stacks compute that all but the very last convoy should be in reach before the storms of Izmunuti are near.

To help speed progress, the Captain-Leader has ordered that the string of captive ships be reeled in closer behind us. When robots can board them, we will be able to cast aside the decoys, one by one.

Now the detections stack reports data arriving from Jijo, the planet behind us.

"More digital cognizance traces! More engine signs!"

But the Captain-Leader rules that this is but a futile attempt to distract us from our pursuit. The Earthling vessel may have left salvaged wrecks behind, to turn themselves on after a timed delay. Or else living confederates have acted on Jijo to set off this ruse. It does not matter. Once the fleeing vessels are in tow, we will be in between the Earthers and Izmunuti.

Things would be very different if there were more than one route in or out of this system. But matters are quite convenient for one capital ship to blockade Jijo effectively.

There will be no more breakouts.

That much is true. Yet, I/we hesitate to point out that this may not yet be the end. Indeed, the wolflings may have sent us on a "wild-goose chase," pursuing only robot ships while they use this respite to cache themselves in new hiding places, deep beneath Jijo's confused waters. They may even abandon their vessel, taking their vital information ashore, where we will only find it by slay-sifting the entire ecosystem!

The Priest-Stack will not permit so extreme a violation of Galactic law, of course. If such a drastic policy proves necessary, the priest may have to be dismantled, and the watcher-observer destroyed. Then we would be committed irrevocably. In case of failure, we would be labeled bandits and bring shame upon the clan.

How is it possible even to contemplate such measures?

Because all auguries show, with growing certainty, that a Time of Changes has already commenced upon the Five Galaxies. Hence all the desperate activity by so many great clans.

If the Institutes are indeed about to fall, there will be no one to investigate crimes committed on this world.

DO NOT TREMBLE SO, MY RINGS. Have I not assured you, repeatedly, that the mighty Jophur are fated to prevail? And that you/I am destined to be useful toward that end?

Crime and punishment need not be considerations, if we are the ones who will make the new rules.

Anyway, it may not prove necessary to return to Jijo. If the prey ship truly lies before us, the high ambitions of our alliance may soon be within tentacle reach.

We near the second convoy. And now missiles spring forth.

Dwer

WITH THE MIGHTY STARSHIP LOOMING CLOSER ON one side, he had to wait in frustration while the yellow beads clustered on the other, coming together with disheartening slowness. His preparations made, Dwer raced back and forth to check each direction.

In time, he learned a technique to make each crossing go much quicker—kicking off from the wall and flying straight across the open interior.

The Jophur vessel impended, mammothly immense. When its dark mass blocked nearly half the starscape, a door of some sort opened in its curved flank and several tiny octagonal shapes emerged, floating toward Dwer's prison.

He recognized the silhouettes.

Battle robots.

They took their time drifting closer, and he realized there was still a large span to cross. At least twenty arrowflights. Still, only duras remained until they arrived.

On returning to the rear of the prison sphere, he breathed a sigh of relief. The captive bubbles were touching now! Yellow spheres, they ranged widely in size, but none was anywhere near as large as the battleship. Most were much larger than his own little ball.

Dwer sought the place where his bubble touched the second in line. A low drumming sound carried through each time the surfaces pressed together.

He zipped up the coverall the *Streaker* crew had given him—a fine garment that covered all but his feet, hands, and head. It had never occurred to him to ask for more.

But right now space gloves and a helmet would be nice.

No matter. The next time the spheres touched, he concentrated for the right frame of mind, and made his move.

Sara

SHE LEFT THE CONTROL ROOM WHEN HER SKIN started puckering from too much exposure to fizzy water. Anyway, there seemed no point hanging around. The same news could be had in her comfortable suite— once the home of a great Earthling sage named Ignacio Metz.

Sara dried herself and changed into simple shipboard garments, snug pants and a pullover shirt that posed no mystery even to an unsophisticated sooner. They were wonders of softness and comfort nevertheless.

When she asked the room to provide a tactical display, vivid 3-D images burst forth, showing that the Jophur dreadnought had once again chosen the wrong decoy swarm, and was just finishing firing missiles. Meanwhile, its string of earlier victims merged with the red glow, as if it were gobbling them one by one.

At her voice command, the viewscreen showed *Streaker*'s goal, the red giant star, magnified tremendously, the whirling filamentary structure of its inflamed chromosphere extending beyond the width of any normal solar system. Izmunuti's bloated surface seethed, sending out tongues of ionized gas, rich with the heavy elements that made up Sara's own body.

Purofsky thinks the Buyur had ways to meddle with a star.

Even without that awesome thought, it was a stirring

sight to behold. Past those raging fires had come all the sneakships that deposited their illicit seed on Jijo, along with the varied hopes of each founding generation. Their aspirations had ranged from pure survival, for humans and g'Keks, all the way to the hoonish ancestors who apparently came a long way in order to play hooky.

All those hopes will come crashing down, unless Streaker *can make it to Izmunuti's fires.*

Sara still had no idea how Gillian Baskin hoped to save Jijo. Would she let the enemy catch up and then blow this ship up, in order to take the Jophur out, as well?

A brave ploy, but surely the enemy would be prepared for that, and take precautions.

Then what?

It seemed Sara would find out when the time came.

She felt bad about the kids—Huck, Alvin, and the others. But they were adults now, and volunteers.

Anyway, the sages say it's a good omen for members of all six races to be present when something vital is about to happen.

Sara's own reasons for coming went beyond that.

Purofsky said one of us had to take the risk—either him or me—and go with Streaker, *on the slim chance that she makes it.*

One of us should try to find out if it's true. What we figured out about the Buyur.

All her life's work, in mathematical physics *and* linguistics, seemed to agree with Purofsky's conclusion.

Jijo was no accident.

Oh, if she delved into psychology, she might find other motives underlying her insistence on being the one to go.

To continue taking care of Emerson, perhaps?

But the wounded starman was now with those who loved him. Shipmates he had risked death alongside, many times before. After overcoming initial shame, Emerson had found ways to be useful. He did not need Sara anymore.

No one really needs me.

Face it. You're going out of curiosity.

Because you are Melina's child.

Because you want to see what happens next.

Dwer

IT WAS A GOOD THING HE REMEMBERED ABOUT AIR.
There would be none on the other side.

By twisting through the barrier, writhing, and making
his body into a hoop, Dwer managed to create a tunnel
opening from his prison sphere into the next. A brief hurri-
cane swiftly emptied the atmosphere from his former cell
until the pressure equalized. He then pushed through, letting the opening close behind him.

Dwer's ears popped and his pulse pounded. The trick
had severely diluted the available air, taking him from
near-sea-level pressure to the equivalent of a mountaintop
in just half a dura. Speckles danced before his eyes. His
body would not last long at this rate.

There was another reason to hurry. As he departed the
sphere containing the balloon remnants, he had seen shadows touch beyond the far side. Jophur robots. Come to
inspect their first captive.

His gear had settled against the golden surface of his
new cell. Dwer grabbed the makeshift pack and moved
toward the only possible place of refuge—the nose of the
imprisoned starship.

It looked nothing like the massive Jophur vessel, but
resembled a pair of spoons, welded face-to-face, with the
bulbous end forward. Fortunately, the enclosure barely
cleared the ship, fore and aft. A bank of dim windows
nearly touched the golden surface.

And there's a door!

Dwer gathered strength, flexed his legs, and launched
toward the beckoning airlock. He sailed across the gap and
barely managed to snag a protruding bracket with the tip
of his left hand.

If this takes some kind of secret code, I'm screwed.

Fortunately, the dolphin work crews had a standard procedure for entering and converting Buyur wrecks. He had
accompanied them on some trips, lending a hand. Dwer

was glad to see the makeshift locking mechanism still in place, set to work in a fashion that even a Jijoan hunter might understand.

To open . . . turn knob.

Dwer's luck held. It rotated.

If there's air inside, the wind will blow out. If there's none, I'll be blown in . . . and die.

He had to brace his feet against the hull and pull in order to get the hatch moving. Vision narrowed to a tunnel and Dwer knew he was just duras away from blacking out. . . .

A sudden breeze rushed at him, whistling with force from the ship's interior.

Stale air. Stinky, stale, dank, wonderful air.

Gillian

THE BAD NEWS WAS NOT EXACTLY UNANTICIPATED. Still, she had hoped for better.

As the Jophur ship finished adding another swarm of decoys to its prison chain, the cruiser shifted its attention elsewhere, accelerating to pursue the next chosen group.

Soon the truth became clear.

Streaker's luck had just run out.

Well, they chose right this time, she thought. *It had to happen, sooner or later.*

Streaker was square in the enemy's sights, with seven mictaars of hyperspace yet to cross before reaching safety.

The Sages

THERE ARE OTHERS ON JIJO NOW, PHWHOON-DAU thought, knowing that even eight would not be enough for long. *In time, the new dolphin colonists must be invited to join.*

I have read in Earth lore about cetaceans and their glorious Whale Dream. What music might we make, when these strange beings add their voices to our chorus?

And after that, who knew? Lorniks, chimps, and zookirs? The Kiqui creatures the dolphins brought from far away? A mélange of vocalizations, then. Perhaps a civilization worthy of the name.

All that lay ahead, a glimmering possibility, defying all likelihood or reason. For now, the council was made of those who had earned their place by surviving on Jijo. Partaking of the world. Raising offspring whose atoms all came from the renewing crust of their mother planet. This trait pervaded the musical harmony of the Eight.

We inhale Jijo, with each and every breath.

So Phwhoon-dau umbled in the deep, rolling vibrations of his throat sac.

We drink her waters. At death, our loved ones put us into her abyss. There we join the patterned rhythms of the world.

The presence that joined them was at once both familiar and awesome. The council felt it throb in each note of the flute or myrliton. It permeated the clatter of the glaver's rattle, and the wry empathy glyphs of the tytlal.

For generations, their dreams had been brushed by the Egg. Its soft cadences repaid each pilgrimage, helping to unite the Commons.

But during all those years, the sages had known. *It only sleeps. We do not know what will happen when it wakes.*

Was the Egg only rousing now because the council finally had its missing parts? Or had the cruel Jophur ray shaken it from slumber?

Phwhoon-dau liked to think that his old friend Vubben was responsible.

Or else, perhaps, it was simply time.

The echoes steadily increased. Phwhoon-dau felt them with his feet, reverberating beneath the surface, building to a crescendo. An accretion of pent-up power. Of purpose.

Such energy. What will happen when it is liberated? His

sac pulsed with umbles, painful and mightier than he ever produced before.

Phwhoon-dau envisioned the mountain caldera blowing up with titanic force, spilling lava down the tortured aisles of Festival Glade.

As it turned out, the release came with nothing more physical than a slight trembling of the ground.

And yet they all staggered when it flew forth, racing faster than the speed of thought.

The Slope

TO NELO—STANDING IN THE RUINS OF HIS PAPER mill, exhausted and discouraged after a long homeward slog—it came as a rapid series of aromas.

The sweet-sour odor of pulped cloth, steaming as it poured across the drying screens.

The hot-vital skin smell of his late wife, whenever her attention turned his way after a long day spent pouring herself into their peculiar children.

The smell of Sara's hair, when she was three years old . . . addictive as any drug.

Nelo sat down hard on a shattered wall remnant, and though the feelings passed through him for less than a kidura, something shattered within as he broke down and wept.

"My children . . ." Nelo moaned. "Where are they?"

Something told him they were no longer of his world.

To Fallon—staked down and spread-eagled in an underground roul shambler's lair, waiting for death—the sensation arrived as a wave of images. Memories, yanked back whole.

The mysterious spike trees of the Sunrise Plain, farther east than anyone had traveled in a century.

Ice floes of the northwest, great floating mountains with snowy towers, sculpted by the wind.

The shimmering, teasing phantasms of the Spectral Flow
. . . and the oasis of Xi, where the gentle Illias had invited
him to live out his days, sharing their secrets and their
noble horses.

Fallon did not cry out. He knew Dedinger and his fanatics were listening, just beyond this cave in the dunes.
When the beast returned home, they would get no satisfaction from the former chief scout of the Commons.

Still, the flood of memory affected him. Fallon shed a
single tear of gratitude.

A life is made whole only in its own eyes. Fallon looked
back on his, and called it good.

To Uriel—interrupted in a flurry of new projects—the passing wave barged through as an unwelcome interruption. A
waste of valuable time. Especially when all her apprentices
laid down their tools and stared into space, uttering low,
reverent moans, or sighs, or whinnies.

Uriel knew it for what it was. A blessing. To which she
had a simple reply.

So what?

She just had too much on her mind to squander duras on
things that were out of her control.

In GalTwo she commented, dryly.

> *"Glad I am, that you have finally de-*
> *cided.*
> *Pleased that you, O long-lived Egg,*
> *have deigned to act, at last.*
> *But forgive me if I do not pause long to*
> *exult.*
> *For many of us, life is far too short."*

To Ewasx—moments later and half a light-year away—it
came as a brief, agonizing vibration in the wax. Ancient
wax, accumulated over many jaduras by the predecessor
stack—an old traeki sage.

Involuntary steam welled up the shared core of the
stack, bypassing the master ring to waft as a compact cloud
from the topmost opening.

Praised be destiny. . . .

Other ring stacks drew away from Ewasx, unnerved by the singular aromatics, accented with savage traces of Jijoan soil.

But the senior Jophur Priest-Stack responded automatically to the reverent smoke, bowing and adding:

Amen . . .

Lark

LARK, YOUR HAND!"

He trembled, fighting to control the fit that came suddenly, causing him to snatch the amulet from around his neck. He clutched the stone tight, even when it began to burn his flesh.

Crouched behind a set of strange obelisks—their only shelter in the spacious Jophur control room—Lark dared not cry out from pain. He fought not to thrash about as Ling used both hands to pry at his clenched fist. At last, the stone sliver fell free, tumbling across his lap to the floor, leaving a stench of singed flesh. Even now, the heat kept building. They tried backing away, but the stone's temperature continued rising until a fierce glow made it hard to see.

"No!" Lark whispered harshly as Ling dived toward the blaze, reaching for the thong. To his surprise, enough was still attached for her to grab a loop and whirl it once, then twice around her head, as if slinging a piece of flaming sun.

She let go, hurling Lark's talisman in an arc across the busy chamber, toward the center of the room.

Dismayed whistles ensued, accompanied by waves of aromatic stench so overpowering, Lark almost gagged.

"Why the hell did you—" he began, but Ling tugged his arm.

"We need a distraction. Come on, now's our chance!"

Lark blinked, amazed by the power of habit. He was actually *angry* at her for throwing away his amulet, and even had to quash an urge to go chasing after the damned stone!

Leave it, and good riddance, he thought, and nodded to Ling.

"Right, let's go."

Dwer

INSIDE THE DECOY SHIP, HE COLLAPSED ON THE deck and retched, heaving up what little remained in his stomach.

Midway through that unpleasant experience, another, completely different kind of disorientation abruptly swept over Dwer. For a moment, it seemed as if One-of-a-Kind were inside his head, trying to speak again. The strange, heady sensation might have been almost affable, if his body weren't racked with nausea.

It ended before he had a chance to appraise what was happening. Anyway, by then he figured he had wasted enough time.

The Jophur won't take long picking through my little ur-rish balloon. They'll start on this bubble next.

In full gravity, it might have been impossible to climb along the full length of the captured ship and reach the aft end. But Dwer took advantage of conditions as he found them, and soon taught himself to fly.

Lark

THEY WERE DASHING DOWN A SMOKE-FILLED HALL-way, chased by angry shouts and occasional bolts of shimmering lightning, when an abrupt detonation rocked the floor plates. A wall of air struck the two humans from behind, knocking them off their feet.

We've had it, he thought, figuring it must be a weapon, used by the pursuers.

Glancing over his shoulder, however, Lark saw the robots suddenly turn and head the other way! Into a noisome storm of roiling black soot pouring out of the control room.

"Do you think . . . ?" he began.

Ling shook her head. "Jophur are tough. I doubt they were more than knocked around by the explosion."

Well, he thought. *It was only a little piece of rock.*

He felt its absence acutely.

Lark helped her up, still wary of returning robots.

"I guess now they know we're here."

They resumed running. But a few duras later, Ling burst out in laughing agreement.

"Yeah, I guess now they do."

Gillian

A PSI-DISTURBANCE WAS DETECTED, EMANATING briefly from the planet. Soon after that, the detection officer announced a change on the tactics screen.

"Will you looka that-t!"

Gillian saw it. The Jophur configuration was shifting. The bright red disk seemed to shimmer for a moment. Its "tail" of tiny crimson pinpoints, which had been bunching ever closer to the mother ship, now flexed and began to float away.

"It appears the enemy has jettisoned all the decoys they captured. I can only conclude that they figured out how to scan them quickly and eliminate dross ships from consideration. The decoys will now drift independently toward Izmunuti, while the battleship, free of drag, will catch up with us much faster."

Gillian's hopes, which had lifted when the psi-wave came, now sank lower than ever.

"We'd better get ready for our last stand," she said in a low voice.

From the dolphins there was an utter absence of sonar clicks, as if none of them wanted to reify the moment, to make it real by reading it in sound.

"Wait-t a minute," Kaa announced. "The Jophur's decelerating! Coming about to retrieve the jettisoned string!"

"But . . ." Gillian blinked. "Could they have dropped it by accident?"

The Niss hologram whirled, then accepted the possibility with an abstract nod.

"A hypothesis presents itself. The psi-wave we detected was far too weak to have any effect on a war cruiser . . . unless it was direct-causative."

"Explain."

"It might have served as a trigger that—either by accident or design—precipitated the release of potentialities already in place . . . say, aboard the Jophur ship."

"In other words, the wave might have affected them after all. Maybe it set off events that disrupted—"

"Indeed. If this caused the Jophur to lose their control over their string of capture boxes, they would certainly go back and retrieve them, even at the cost of some delay. Because they would suspect the string's release was the intended purpose of the psi-wave."

"In other words, they'll be even more eager to check every box. Hmm."

Gillian pondered, then asked:

"Has their intercept time been delayed much?"

Kaa thrashed his flukes.

"A fair amount. Not-t enough, however. We'll make it to the Izmunuti corona, but the enemy will be close enough to follow easily with detectorsss. The plasma won't make any a-ppreciable difference."

Gillian nodded. "Well, things are a little better. And a trick or two to make the odds better still."

The dolphins snickered knowingly and went back to work, emanating confident clicks. Gillian's last remark was exactly the sort of thing *Tom* would have said in a situation like this.

In fact, though, Gillian did not know if her scheme was even worthy of the name.

Sara

THEY SAID THAT A PSI-WAVE HAD COME FROM JIJO, but Sara didn't feel a thing.

Not surprising. Of Melina's three children, it always seemed that Dwer had some fey sensitivity, while she, the logical one, possessed none. Till recently, Sara had little interest in such matters.

But then she wondered. *Might this be what Purofsky said we should look out for?*

Sitting at the stateroom's worktable, Sara addressed the portable computer.

"About that psi-wave—do we have a fix on its hypervelocity?"

"Only a rough estimate. It traveled at approximately two mictaars per midura."

Sara tried to work out the timing in her head, translating it in terms she knew better, such as light-years. Then she realized the machine could do it for her graphically.

"Show me."

A holo took shape, portraying her homeworld as a blue dot in the lower left quadrant. *Streaker* was a yellow glimmer to the upper right, accompanied by other members of decoy swarm number two. Meanwhile a crimson convoy— the Jophur ship and its reclaimed captives—resumed hot pursuit.

The computer put down an overlay, depicting a cross-hatching of lines that Sara knew to be wave vectors in level-zero hyperspace. The math was simple enough, but it took her some time to figure out the rich, three-dimensional representation. Then she whistled.

"That's not inverse square. It's not even one-over-R. It was directional!"

"A well-conserved, directional wave packet, resonating on the first, third, and eighth bands of—"

The computer lapsed into psi-jargon that Sara could not follow. For her, it was enough to see that the packet was aimed. Its peak had passed right over both *Streaker* and its pursuer.

The coincidence beggared belief. It meant that some great power on Jijo had known precisely where both ships were, and—

Sara stopped herself.

Don't leap to the first conclusion that comes to mind. What if we weren't the beam's objective at all?

What if we just happened to be along its path, between Jijo and . . .

She leaped to her feet.

"Show me Izmunuti and the transfer point!"

The display changed scale, expanding until *Streaker* was shown just over halfway to the supposed safety of the fiery red giant.

And beyond it, a folded place. A twist in reality's fabric. A spot where you go, if you want to suddenly be very far away.

Although computer graphics were needed to make it out clearly, the transfer point was no invisible nonentity. Izmunuti *bulged* in its direction, sending ocher streamers toward the dimple in space.

"When will the psi-wave reach Izmunuti?"

"It has already arrived."

Sara swallowed hard.

"Then show me estimated . . ." She dredged memory for words she had read, but seldom used. "Show me likely hyperdeflection curves, as the psi-wave hits the red giant. Emphasize meta-stable regions of . . . um, inverted energy storage, with potential for . . . uh, stimulated emission on those *bands* you were talking about."

Sara's face flickered as manicolored lines and curves reflected off her forehead and cheekbones.

Her eyes widened, briefly showing white all the way around the irises. She mouthed a single word, without managing to form a voice.

Then Sara clutched for a nearby pad of paper—no better than the premium stock her own father produced—and scrawled down two lines of coordinates.

Gillian Baskin answered her urgent call, though the older woman looked harassed and a little irked.

"Sage Koolhan, I really don't have time—"

"Oh yes you do," Sara told her sternly. "Meet me in your office in forty duras. You are definitely gonna want to hear this!"

———————

Rety

A YOUNG WOMAN SAT IN A LOCKED ROOM, ALL alone in her universe, until someone knocked.

In fact she was not entirely alone—yee was with her. Moreover, the knock wasn't at the door, but rapped loudly on the window below her feet. Still, the element of eerie surprise was there. Rety jumped back, scurrying away from the sound, which grew louder with each hammerlike stroke.

"it comes from over here!" yee wailed, pointing with his long neck.

Rety saw at once the pane he meant. A silhouetted figure squatted below the window, backlit by the golden haze surrounding her useless ship. The figure was distorted, distended, with a grossly bulbous head. An arm turned, holding a blunt object, and swung forward, striking the crystal once again.

This time, tiny cracks spread from the point of impact.

"enemy foe coming in!"

Visions of space monsters filled Rety, but not with fear. She wasn't about to give up her domain to some invader—Jophur, robot, or whatever.

Another blow struck the same spot. Clearly it would take several more for the assailant to seriously damage the window. Emboldened to see what she was up against, Rety scooted toward the shadowy figure. After the next impact, she pressed close to the glass and peered outside.

Things were blurry at first. Then the creature seemed to

notice her presence and leaned forward as well. Rety glimpsed what looked like a billowing dome of clear fabric. A makeshift helmet, she realized.

And within that protective bubble . . .

"Yah!" she cried out, twitching reflexively away, more set back than if she'd seen a monster or ghost.

When Rety went back for another look, the figure on the other side started making frantic gestures, pointing toward the side of the ship.

"Oh, yeah," she sighed. "I did lock the airlock, didn't I?"

Rety nodded vigorously so the visitor could see, and started scurrying along the canted walls to reach the jimmied door. Rety removed the pry bar she had slipped in place, to keep Chuchki from returning.

The airlock cycled slowly, giving Rety time to wonder if her eyes had deceived her. Perhaps this was just a ruse from some mind-reading creature, seeking to gain entrance by sifting her brain for images from her past. . . .

The inner door opened at last, and Dwer Koolhan tumbled through, tearing at the balloonlike covering he had been using as a crude life-support system. His face was rather blue by the time Rety helped him cut the taped fastenings, scavenged from material found on other decoy vessels during his long journey down the captive string. The young hunter gasped deep breaths while Rety stepped back and stared. Finally, he recovered enough to roll aside, lifting his head to meet her unbelieving gaze.

"I . . . should've known . . . it'd be you," Dwer murmured in a resigned voice.

At the exact same moment, Rety muttered:

"Ifni! Ain't I ever gonna be rid o' you?"

Ewasx

WE MUST WEIGH TRADE-OFFS AND OPTIONS.

As Izmunuti commences to roil with an atmospheric storm, our tactics stack declares that we have lost valuable time.

Three target swarms flee ahead of our majestic *Polkjhy*. The first will enter the storm just as we catch up.

We will reach the second as it passes through maximum hyperbolic momentum change.

And the third?

It will make it to the transfer point, with time enough to jump into the next higher level of hyperspace.

The sabotage attack on our control room has thus created serious problems, out of proportion to the damage done to our Captain-Leader, whose incapacity should not last long. Meanwhile, however, tactics has come up with a plan.

WE SHALL JETTISON THE CAPTURE BOXES DRAGGING AT OUR WAKE.

They are now on course for Izmunuti. If the prey ship lies within one of the glowing traps, it must reveal itself soon, or risk immolation.

THUS FREED, OUR *POLKJHY* WILL ACCELERATE DIRECTLY FOR THE TRANSFER POINT!

In this manner we will be able to interpose ourselves between the prey ship and its escape path. There will be some backlash from such rapid maneuvering, but the result should be an end to all hope for the Earthlings, *whichever* swarm they are hiding in. Their subsequent activities should enable us to detect which ship is sapient-guided and which operate on mere automatic programs.

Hunt scents fill our bridge, eagerness for the approaching conclusion to this great endeavor. It will be most gratifying for *Polkjhy* to achieve conquest of the Earthlings without having to call for help from the great clan. To succeed where battle fleets have failed—this will be glorious!

BUT NOW TO OUR ASSIGNED TASK, MY RINGS!

There are vermin loose on our fine dreadnought. Our damaged/soot-stained bridge was dishonored in full view of the librarian/watcher.

The vermin must be found. I/we am the one called upon as qualified to give chase, by virtue of our/My experience with human types.

Our first recourse, My rings?

Collect the remaining human prisoner!

The one called Rann.

He will help us find his former colleagues. He is already so inclined.

REJOICE, MY RINGS!

In this way we will prove useful, avoiding disassembly. If successful, this master torus has been promised a fine reward.

Quiver in anticipation, My rings! As *Polkjhy* chases certain victory through space, we pursue another hunt within.

Emerson

ENGINES SING TO HIM IN A LANGUAGE HE STILL UNderstands.

When he works the calibrators, it seems almost as if he were his old self. Master of machines. Boy mechanic. The man who makes starships fly.

Then something reminds him. A written status report flashes, or a robot voice runs down a list of parameters. Prity can't interpret for him—sign language cannot translate subtleties of hyperwave transformatics.

Emerson's crew mates respect his efforts. They are pleased and surprised by his ability to help.

But, he now realizes, they are also humoring him.

Things will never be the same.

His long shift ends. Suessi orders him to take a break. So he goes up to the hold with Prity and visits the glavers, sensing something in common with the simple creatures, nearly as speechless as himself.

Alvin and Huck trade insults and witticisms in Anglic, his own native tongue, but he can only follow the general tone of camaraderie. They are kind, but here, too, Emerson finds no solace.

He searches for Sara, and finds her at last in the plotting room, surrounded by Gillian's staff. Fiery representations of a bloated giant star fill the center of the room, with varied orbits plotted through its flaming shell. Some paths slip close, using slingshot arcs to fling *Streaker* toward the transfer point—a twisted funnel in space. The tactics look challenging, even to a pilot like Kaa. Yet that approach is the obvious one.

No doubt the enemy expects just such a maneuver.

Other orbits make no sense, skirting the red giant to strike *away* from the bolt-hole. Farther from the only way to exit this dangerous part of a forbidden galaxy.

Letting the enemy reach the transfer point first would seem suicidal.

On the other hand, at the rate the Jophur battleship is catching up, *Streaker* will have little choice. Perhaps Sara and Gillian plan to head for deep space and hide amid the seared rocks that were planets, before Izmunuti burgeoned and consumed its children.

Emerson watches Sara, immersed in work. No one seems to note the presumption—of a Jijo-born savage directing the endeavors of starfaring sophisticates. At times like these, an idea can count for much more than experience.

The incongruity makes him smile at last, recovering some of his good mood. His accustomed optimism.

After all, what have the odds ever mattered before?

There is an observation dome tucked behind the bridge, accessible only by a twisty ladder with rungs set much too close together. The small room is a leftover from whatever race once owned *Streaker,* before Earthclan bought the hull, converting it for dolphin use. It takes some agility to worm into the odd-shaped cubby. Emerson's secret place.

At one end, a thick bubble of adamantine quartz provides a view outside, where the starry vault is bare, unimpeded, nearly surrounding him with everlasting night.

Izmunuti is occulted by the ship's bow, but vast sweeps of the local spiral arm sparkle like diamonds. Globular clusters are like diatoms, phosphorescent on a moonlit sea. Since waking on Jijo, he never expected to experience this again. The naked confrontation. Mind and universe.

It pours through him, a surfeit of beauty. Too much. Agonizing.

Of course, Emerson spent half a year learning about all kinds of pain, until it became a sort of friend. His ally at dislodging memories. And as he ponders stellar fire, it happens again.

He recalls the stench, just after he crashed into Jijo, clothes aflame, quenching the blaze in murky water, dimly aware of having recently fought a battle. A diversion—a sacrifice to win escape for his friends.

But that wasn't the truth.

It was a planted cover story.

Actually, the Old Ones took him from that old Thennanin fighter. They probed and palped him. Over a period of days, weeks, they reamed his mind, then shoved him in a little capsule. A tube that *squeezed* . . .

Emerson moans, recalling how that passage ended in a blazing plummet down to Jijo and the horrid swamp where Sara found him.

He envisions the Old Ones. Or one faction of them. Cold eyes. Hard voices, commanding him to forget. To forget . . . and yet, sentenced to live.

I . . . know . . . your . . . lie. . . .

The command fights back. For a moment, the pain is greater than he ever knew.

Pain that is elemental, like the black vacuum surrounding him.

Like sleeting cosmic rays.

Like all the myriad quantum layers propping up each quark and every lepton in his shaken frame.

Through it all, his eyes can barely focus, squinting past distilled anguish, turning countless stars into slanting needles.

But then, out of those jagged motes there comes a shape. Weaving, thrashing . . . zigging, zagging.

Swimming, he now realizes. Pushing toward him, as if upstream, against the swell of a strong tide. A shape from memory, but instead of bringing more woe, this recollection sweeps all agony before it. Pushed by stalwart flukes, a soothing current washes over him.

A dolphin's face swims into focus.

Captain . . .

. . . *Creideiki* . . .

It is a scarred face, deeply wounded behind the left eye. A wound too much like Emerson's to be coincidence.

The explanation encircles him in sound.

> * *Crooks and foul liars,*
> * *Lacking imagination,*
> * *Cruelly steal ideas!* *

Emerson comprehends the Trinary haiku at once. The Old Ones must have read his mind somehow and learned of Creideiki's injury. It seemed to fit their needs, so they copied it in their captive human. What better way to release him, yet be certain he would tell no tales?

But that still left open the question of *why?* Why release him at all, if it meant consignment to a twilight existence?

What motive could they have?

All . . . *in* . . . *good* . . . *time* . . .

The phrase brings a smile, for he grasps it in a way he might never have before.

A simple, purified meaning.

. . . *good* . . . *time* . . .

Emerson looks back across the galaxies, now cleansed free of pain. Pain he now recognizes to have been illusion, all along. The product of an exaggerated sense of self-importance that his enemies used against him.

In fact, the ocean of night is too vast, too busy to be involved in his agony. An evolving universe can hardly be bothered with the problems of a single individual, a member of one of the lower orders of sapient life.

And why should it?

What a privilege it is, to exist at all! On the great balance sheet, he owes the cosmos everything, and it owes him nothing.

Emerson manages to share a final moment of communion with his captain and comrade—not caring whether the grinning dolphin is a ghost, a mirage, or some miraculous true image. Knowing only that Creideiki's lesson is true.

There is no setback—no wound or blow of cruel fate—that cannot be turned into a song.

For an instant, Emerson can sense music in every ray of starlight.

> * *When the winter's*
> > *Typhoon pounds you,*
> * *Onto sand grains,*
> > *Sharp and gleaming,*
>
> * *And creation*
> > *All-conspiring,*
> * *Breaks you on a*
> > *Time of Changes,*
>
> * *At the moment*
> > *When breath falters,*
> * *And your lifeblood*
> > *Pours out streaming,*
>
> * *Cast around that*
> > *Bright reef, dear friend,*
> * *For a gift to*
> > *Grant another,*
>
> * *For some way to*
> > *Repay forward,*

* *All the favors*
    You were given.

* *For in good time*
    * *Prospects glitter*
        * *Far along Infinity's Shore.* *

THE END OF PART TWO

Cast of Sapient Species

g'Keks—first sooner race to arrive on Jijo, some two thousand years ago. Uplifted by the Drooli, the g'Kek have biomagnetically driven wheels and eyestalks instead of heads. For most of their period of sapiency, they did not live on planets. g'Kek are extinct throughout the Five Galaxies, except on Jijo.

Glavers—third sooner race to reach Jijo. Uplifted by the Tunnuctyur, who were themselves uplifted by the Buyur, glavers are partly bipedal with opalescent skin and large, bulging eyes. Roughly a meter tall, they have a prehensile forked tail to assist their inefficient hands. Since illegally settling Jijo, they devolved to a state of presapience. To some, glavers are shining examples, having shown the way down the Path of Redemption.

Hoons—fifth wave of settlers to arrive on Jijo, bipedal omnivores with pale scaly skin and woolly white leg fur. Their spines are massive, hollow structures that form part of their circulatory system. Hoons' inflatable throat sacs, originally used for mating displays, are now used for "umbling." Since their uplift by the Guthatsa, this race found widespread service as dour, officious bureaucrats in Galactic culture.

Humans—the youngest sooner race, arrived on Jijo less than three hundred years ago. Human "wolflings" evolved on Earth; possibly achieving technological civilization and crude interstellar travel on their own. Their greatest accomplishment: the uplifting of neo-chimpanzees and neo-dolphins.

Jophur—organisms resembling a cone of stacked doughnuts; like their traeki cousins, Jophur consist of interchangeable spongy "sap rings," each with limited intelligence, but combining to form a sapient communal being. Specialized rings give the stack its senses, manipulative organs, and sometimes exotic chemosynthetic abilities. As traeki, this unique species was originally gentle and unaspiring when first uplifted by the Poa. The zealous Oailie later reinvented them by providing "master rings," transforming the traeki into Jophur, willful and profoundly ambitious beings.

Qheuens—fourth sooner race on Jijo. Uplifted by the Zhosh, qheuens are radially symmetric exoskeletal beings with five legs and claws. Their brain is partly contained in a retractable central dome or "cupola." A rebel band of qheuens settled Jijo attempting to hold on to their ancient caste system, with the gray variety providing royal matriarchs while red and blue types were servants and artisans. Conditions on Jijo—including later human intervention—provoked the breakdown of this system.

Rothen—a mysterious Galactic race. One human group (the Dakkins or Daniks) believe the Rothen to be Earth's lost patrons. Rothen are bipeds, somewhat larger than humans but with similar proportions. Believed to be carnivores.

Traeki—second illicit settler race to arrive on Jijo. Traeki are a throwback variant of Jophur, who fled the imposition of master rings.

Tymbrimi—a humanoid species allied with the Earthclan. Known for their cleverness and devilish sense of humor.

Tytlal—a species considered impossible to uplift. Uplifted by the Tymbrimi.

Urs—sixth sooner race on Jijo. Carnivorous, centauroid plains dwellers; they have long, flexible necks, narrow heads, and shoulderless arms ending in dexterous hands. Urs start life as tiny, six-limbed grubs, turned out of their mothers' pouches to fend for themselves. Any that survive to "childhood" may be accepted into an urrish band. Urrish females reach the size of a large deer, and possess twin brood pouches where they keep diminutive mates, smaller than a house cat. A female with prelarval young ejects one or both husbands to make room for the brood. Urs have an aversion to water in its pure form.

GLOSSARY OF TERMS

Anglic—a human language created in the twenty-first century, using many English words, but influenced by other pre-contact tongues and modified according to new understandings of linguistic theory.

Biblos—a fortress containing the archive, or hall of books; a combined university/central lending library with profound influence on Jijoan culture.

Bibur—a river running past Biblos, joining the Roney at Tarek Town.

Buyur—former legal tenants of Jijo, froglike in appearance, and known for wit, foresight, and for gene crafting specialized animal tools. Departed when Jijo was declared fallow, almost half a million years ago.

Chimpanzee or "chim"—a partly uplifted variety that accompanied humans to Jijo, mute but able to communicate readily with sign language.

Client—a race still working out a period of servitude to the patrons that uplifted it from presapient animal status.

Danik—a vulgarized term for Danikenite, a cultural movement dating from soon after humanity's first contact with Galactic civilization. Daniks believe Earthlings were uplifted by a Galactic patron race that chose to remain hidden for unknown reasons. An offshoot cult believes that the

Rothen are this race of wise, enigmatic guides. (Also sometimes "Dakkin")

Day of Judgment—in prophesy, when the Six Races of Jijo will be judged for their crimes. By that time, many hope that their descendants will be like glavers—innocents, far along the Path of Redemption.

Deconstructor—a mechanical device licensed by the Institute of Migration to demolish remnants of technological civilization on a planet declared fallow.

Dolo—a village on the Roney River, famed for papermaking.

Dooden Mesa—oldest and largest g'Kek enclave.

Dross—Any nonbiodegradable waste material, fated to be cast into the Midden, for recycling by Jijo's tectonic fires.

Dura—Approximately one third of a minute.

Earthclan—a small, eccentric Galactic "family" of sapient races consisting of neo-chimpanzee and neo-dolphin clients and their human patrons.

Egg—see Holy Egg.

Er—a genderless pronoun, sometimes used when referring to a traeki.

Exploser—demolitions expert who mines settlements of the Six Races for quick destruction, should The Day arrive. Guild headquarters in Tarek Town.

Fen—plural of "fin"; Anglic shorthand for a neo-dolphin.

Fist of Stone—a huge shelf of stone above Biblos that has been mined by the explosers, and would serve to destroy the fortress on Judgment Day.

Fractal World or Fractal System—a place of retirement for races that have nearly transcended the Civilization of the Five Galaxies. A huge, diffuse edifice made of hydrogen snow, constructed to surround and use all the energy of a small star.

Galactic—a person, race, concept, or technology deriving from the eons-old Civilization of the Five Galaxies.

Galactic Institutes—vast, powerful academies, purportedly neutral and above interclan politics. The Institutes manage or regulate various aspects of Galactic civilization. Some Institutes are over a billion years old.

Galactic Library—a fantastically capacious collection of knowledge gathered over the course of hundreds of millions of years. Quasi-sapient "branch Libraries" are found in most Galactic starships and settlements.

Gathering Festival—annual fair that celebrates and reinforces the Great Peace among Jijo's sooner races. Incorporates a pilgrimage to the Holy Egg.

Gentt—a river just north of Blaze Mountain.

Great Peace—a time of growing understanding among the Six Races, variously credited to the influence of Biblos, or else to the arrival of the Holy Egg and rewq symbionts.

Great Printing—the sudden introduction of paper books by the humans soon after their arrival on Jijo.

Grok—Anglic term, of obscure origin, that denotes understanding a thing or concept in its entirety. Similar to the Scottish "ken."

Guenn Volcano—Location of the hidden forges of Uriel the Smith.

"Heresies"—variant views of Jijoan destiny, held by groups who disagree with the High Sages. One holds that Galactic law is just—and Jijo would be better off without "infestation" by sooner races. Others subscribe to more orthodox interpretations of the Sacred Scrolls, that each exile race should seek separate salvation down the Path of Redemption. One rare heresy is called "progress."

Holy Egg, the—a mysterious mass of psi-active stone that emerged from a volcano a century ago, accompanied by widespread visions and dreaming.

Humicker—slang term for someone who mimics humans, because Earthling texts still dominate literate life of Jijo, long after the Great Printing.

Ifni—probably a vulgarization of "Infinity." In spacer tradition, a name given to the goddess of luck. Personification of chance or Murphy's law.

Illias—a matriarchal tribe of horsewomen living secretly in the Spectral Flow.

Izmunuti—a red giant star, uncomfortably close to Jijo's sun; spews a carbon wind masking Jijo from supervision by the Institute for Migration.

Jadura—Approximately forty-three hours.

Jijo—planet in Galaxy Four. Home of seven sooner races: humans, hoons, qheuen, urs, g'Kek, devolved glavers, and "demodified" Jophur known as traeki.

Jophekka—the homeworld of the Jophur.

Kidura—approximately one half second.

Kiqui—a presapient race of amphibians native to Kithrup.

Kithrup—a water world rich in heavy metals, where the *Streaker* crew lost Captain Creideiki and many others in escaping a dire trap.

Loocen—largest of Jijo's three moons.

Lorniks—a domesticated animal, bred as servants by qheuen. Lorniks are radially symmetrical, have four legs and four three-fingered hands.

Midden—a vast undersea crevasse, or subduction zone, formed by plate tectonics, that runs alongside the Slope. Dross generated by inhabitant races—from skeletal remains to hulls of sooner spacecraft—should eventually be dumped here, where natural forces will carry it below Jijo's crust for melting.

Midura—a unit of time. Approximately seventy-one minutes.

Morgran—a transfer point where *Streaker* was first attacked by warships of the fanatic religious clans.

Mulc spiders—a life-form engineered to destroy buildings and technological artifacts on worlds declared fallow.

Mulching ceremony—reduction of dead bodies, returning flesh to the Jijoan ecosystem. Often involves consumption of flesh by specialized traeki rings. Nondegradable leftovers are treated as dross and sent to the Midden.

Neo-chimp, neo-chimpanzee—uplifted chimpanzees; humanity's first clients. Fully uplifted neo-chimps can speak; the "unfinished" variety that accompanied humans to Jijo are mute.

Neo-dolphin—uplifted dolphins; clients of humanity.

Nihanic—another pre-contact human language, derived from a hybrid of Japanese and Han Chinese.

Noor—bright, dexterous, but mischievous otterlike creatures. Noor cannot be tamed, but the patient and good-natured hoon are able to employ some noor beasts on their ships. Noor are considered pests by the other sooner races.

Oailie—third-stage uplift consorts and "step-patrons" of the Jophur, and fanatical members of the Obeyer Alliance. As expert gene crafters, the Oailie reworked traeki biology and psychology by the addition of master rings, transforming them into Jophur.

Oakka—a planet containing the regional headquarters of the Institute of Navigation, where *Streaker* barely escaped entrapment and betrayal.

Parrot ticks—a peculiar Buyur-engineered insect that can memorize and recite short phrases. The first humans on Jijo doubted their sanity when they kept "hearing voices."

Passen—Jijo's smallest moon.

Path of Redemption—goal of orthodox religious factions of Jijo, who believe the sooner races should devolve to presapience. Only thus can they escape punishment for colonizing a fallow world, offering a second chance at uplift. Glavers have already trod the Path.

Patron—a Galactic race that has uplifted at least one animal species to full sapience.

Phuvnthus—six-legged wood-eating vermin on Jijo.

Pidura—six-to-the-seventh-power duras, or approximately four days.

Polkjhy—Jophur battleship that landed on Jijo in search of the *Streaker*.

Poria Outpost—the Danik headquarters, where a small human population serves Rothen lords.

Primal Delphin—semilanguage used by natural, nonuplifted dolphins on Earth.

Progenitors—legendary first spacefaring race, who began the cycle of uplift two billion years ago.

Rewq—quasi-fungal symbionts that help the Six Races "read" each other's emotions and body language.

Rift—a branch of the Midden located at the southern end of the Slope.

Rimmers—a mountain range marking the eastern boundary of the Slope.

Sacred Scrolls—texts of enigmatic origin, the only written matter on Jijo between the departure of the Buyur and human introduction of paper books. The scrolls taught the g'Kek and later colonists about the need for concealment, planetary care, and "redemption."

Sept—a race or sapient clan of Jijo, e.g., the g'Kek, glavers, hoons, urs, traeki, qheuen, and humans.

Sooners—outlaws who attempt to colonize worlds designated fallow by the Galactic Institute of Migration. On Jijo, the term means those who try to make new illegal settlements, beyond the confines of the Slope.

Spectral Flow—a forbidding desert region in the southcentral area of the Slope, thought to be uninhabitable. Covered with sheets of luridly colored, psi-active volcanic stone and outcrops of photoactive crystal.

Streaker—a neo-dolphin–crewed Terran starship. The Streaker's discoveries led to unprecedented pursuit by dozens of Galactic factions, each seeking advantage by possessing the dolphins' secrets.

Stress atavism—a condition found among newly uplifted species, when individuals lose their higher cognitive functions under stress.

Tabernacle—the sneakship that brought human sooners to Jijo more than 200 years ago.

Tarek Town—the largest town on the Slope, where the Roney and Bibur merge. Headquarters of the Explosers Guild.

Terragens Council—ruling body of humanity's interstellar government, in charge of matters affecting relations between Earthclan and Galactic society.

Toporgic—a pseudo-material substrate made of organically folded time.

Torgen—one of Jijo's moons.

Transfer point—an area of weak space-time that allows faster than light travel for vessels entering in precise ways.

Uplift—the process of turning a presapient animal species into a fully sapient race capable of joining Galactic society. Performed by patron race.

Urchachka—the urrish homeworld.

Urchachkin—urrish clan that gave refuge to human females and horses in the Spectral Flow.

Vlenning—a rare form of traeki reproduction, in which a small, complete stack is budded from an adult.

Wolfling—a derogatory Galactic term for a race that appears to have uplifted itself to spacefaring status without help from a patron.

Wuphon's Dream—the bathyscaphe built by Pincer-Tip, with the help of Alvin, Huck, and Ur-ronn. Outfitted by Uriel the Smith.

Xi—a meadowland in the midst of the Spectral Flow, home of the Illias.

Year of Exile—the epoch that began when the first sooner race arrived on Jijo.

Zang—a hydrogen-breathing race resembling huge squid. They live in the atmospheres of gas giants. Jijo's entire galactic region has been ceded to hydrogen breathers by the Institute of Migration; oxygen-breathing sapients are supposed to stay out for a long fallow period. Zang patrol globes are a rare but feared visitor to Jijo.

Zhosh—the qheuens' patron race.

Zookir—servant animals bred by the g'Kek, able to memorize and recite messages, but not as bright as neo-chimpanzees.

Acknowledgments

The author would express thanks to Stefan Jones, Steinn Sigurdsson, Professor Steven Potts, Greg Smith, Matthew Johnson, Kevin Conod, Anita Gould, Paul Rothemund, Richard Mason, Gerrit Kirkwood, Ruben Krasnopolsky, Damien Sullivan, Will Smit, Grant Swenson, Roian Egnor, Joy Crisp, Jason M. Robertson, Micah Altman, Jeffrey Slostad, Joseph Miller, and Gregory Benford, for their comments and observations on early drafts of *Infinity's Shore*. Kevin Lenagh provided the map of Jijo. Robert Qualkinbush collated the glossary of terms. The novel profited from insight and helpful assistance from my agent, Ralph Vicinanza, and Tom Dupree of Bantam Books. As usual, this tale would have been a far poorer thing without the wise and very human input of my wife, Dr. Cheryl Brigham. Blame for any excess or extravagance rests on me alone.

About the Author

DAVID BRIN is the author of nine previous novels, *Sundiver, The Uplift War, Startide Rising, The Practice Effect, The Postman, Heart of the Comet* (with Gregory Benford), *Earth, Glory Season,* and *Brightness Reef,* as well as the short-story collections *The River of Time* and *Otherness.* He has a doctorate in astrophysics and has been a NASA consultant and a physics professor. He lives in southern California, where he is at work on *Heaven's Reach,* the third novel in the Uplift Storm trilogy, to be published in 1998.

Turn the page for a preview of *Heaven's Reach*, the third and final book of David Brin's highly acclaimed Uplift Storm trilogy.

Sara

There is a word-glyph.

It names a locale where three states of matter coincide—two that are fluid, swirling past a third that is adamant as coral.

A kind of froth can form in such a place. Dangerous, deceptive foam, beaten to a head by fate-filled tides. No one enters such a turmoil voluntarily.

But sometimes a force called desperation drives prudent sailors to set course for ripping shoals.

◆

A slender shape plummets through the outer fringes of a mammoth star. Caterpillar-ribbed, with rows of talonlike protrusions that bite into spacetime, the vessel claws its way urgently against a bitter gale.

Diffuse flames lick the scarred hull of ancient cerametal, adding new layers to a strange soot coating. Tendrils of plasma fire seek entry, thwarted (so far) by wavering fields.

In time, the heat will find its way through.

Midway along the vessel's girth, a narrow wheel turns, like a wedding band that twists around a nervous finger.

Rows of windows pass by as the slim ring rotates. Unlit from within, most of the dim panes only reflect stellar fire.

Then, rolling into view, a single rectangle shines with artificial color.

A pane for viewing in two directions. A universe without, and within.

◆

Contemplating the maelstrom, Sara mused aloud.

"My criminal ancestors took their sneakship through this same inferno on their way to Jijo . . . covering their tracks under the breath of Great Izmunuti."

Pondering the forces at work just a hand's breadth away, she brushed her fingertips against the crystal surface that kept actinic heat from crossing the narrow gap. One part of her—book-weaned and tutored in mathematics—could grasp the physics of a star whose radius was bigger than her homeworld's yearly orbit. A red giant, in its turgid final stage, boiling a rich stew of nuclear-cooked atoms toward the black vacuum of space.

Abstract knowledge was fine. But Sara's spine also trembled with a superstitious shiver, spawned by her upbringing as a savage *sooner* on a barbarian world. This Earthship, *Streaker,* might be hapless prey—desperately fleeing a titanic hunter many times its size—but the dolphin-crewed vessel still struck Sara as godlike and awesome, carrying more mass than all the wooden dwellings of the Slope. In her wildest dreams, dwelling in a treehouse next to a groaning water mill, she never imagined that destiny might take her on such a ride, swooping through the fringes of a hellish star.

Especially Izmunuti, whose very name was fearsome. To the Six Races, huddling in secret terror on Jijo, it stood for the downward path. A door that swung just one way, toward exile.

For two thousand years, emigrants had slinked past the giant star to find shelter on Jijo. First the wheeled g'Kek race, frantically evading genocide. Then came traekis—gentle stacks of waxy rings who were fleeing their own tyrannical relations—followed by qheuens, hoons, urs, and humans, all settling in a narrow realm between the Rimmer Mountains and a surf-stained shore. Each wave of new arrivals abandoned their starships, computers, and other high-tech implements, sending every god-machine down to the sea, tumbling into Jijo's deep midden of forgetfulness. Breaking with their past, all six clans of former skylords settled down to rustic lives, renouncing the sky forever.

Until the Civilization of the Five Galaxies finally stumbled on the commonwealth of outcasts.

The day had to come, sooner or later; the Sacred Scrolls had said so. No band of trespassers could stay hidden perpetually. Not in a cosmos that had been catalogued for over a billion years, where planets such as Jijo were routinely declared fallow, set aside for rest and restoration. Still, the sages of the Commons of Jijo *had* hoped for more time.

Time for the exile races to prepare. To purify themselves. To seek redemption. To forget the galactic terrors that made them outcasts in the first place.

The Scrolls also foresaw that august magistrates from the Galactic Migration Institute would alight to judge the descendants of trespassers. But instead, the starcraft that pierced Jijo's veil this fateful year carried several types of *outlaws*. First gene raiders, then murderous opportunists, and finally a band of Earthling refugees even more ill-fated than Sara's hapless ancestors.

I used to dream of riding a starship, she thought, pondering the plasma storm outside. *But no fantasy was ever like this—fleeing with dolphins through a fiery night, chased by a battleship full of angry Jophur.*

Fishlike cousins of humans, pursued through space by egotistical cousins of traeki.

The coincidence beggared Sara's imagination.

Anglic words broke through her musing, in a voice Sara always found vexingly sardonic.

"I have finished calculating the hyperspatial tensor, oh Sage.

"It appears you were right in your earlier estimate. The mysterious beam that emanated from Jijo a while ago did more than cause disruptions in this giant star. It also triggered a state-change in a fossil dimensional-nexus, lying dormant just half a mictaar away."

Sara mentally translated into terms she was used to, from the archaic texts that had schooled her.

Half a mictaar. In flat space, that would come to roughly a twientieth of a parsec.

Very close, indeed.

"So, the beam reactivated an old transfer point." She nodded. "I knew it."

"Your foresight would be more impressive if I understood your methods. Humans are noted for making lucky guesses."

Sara turned away from the fiery spectacle outside. The office they had given her seemed like a palace, roomier than the reception hall in a qheuen rookery, with lavish fixtures she had only seen described in books two centuries out of date. This suite once belonged to a man named Ignacio Metz—killed during one of *Streaker*'s previous dire encounters—an expert in the genetic-uplifting of dolphins. A true scientist, not a primitive with academic pretensions, like Sara.

From the desk-console, a twisted blue blob drifted closer—a languid, undulating shape she found as insolent as the voice it emitted.

"Your so-called wolfling mathematics hardly seems up to the task of predicting such profound effects on the continuum. Why not just admit that you had a hunch?"

Sara bit her lip. She would not give the Niss Machine the satisfaction of a hot response.

"Show me the tensor," she ordered tersely. "And a chart . . . a *graphic* . . . that includes all three gravity wells."

The billowing holographic creature managed to imply sarcasm with an obedient bow.

"As you wish."

A cubic display two meters on a side lit up before Sara, far more vivid than the illustrations she had grown up with—flat, unmoving diagrams printed on paper pages.

A glowing mass roiled in the center, representing Izmunuti, a fireball glowing the color of wrath. Tendrils of its engorged corona waved like medusan hair, reaching beyond the limits of any normal solar system. But those lacy filaments were fast being drowned under a new disturbance. During the last few miduras, something had stirred the star to an abnormal fit of rage. Abrupt cyclonic storms began throwing up gouts of dense plasma, tornado-like funnels, rushing far into space.

And we're going to pass through some of the worst of it, she thought.

How strange that all this violent upheaval might have originated in a boulder of psi-active stone back home on primitive Jijo. Yet she felt sure it was all triggered somehow by the Holy Egg.

Already half-immersed in this commotion, a green pin-point plunged toward Izmunuti at frantic speed, aimed at a glancing near-passage, its hyperbolic orbit marked by a line that bent sharply around the giant star. In one direction, that slim trace led all the way back to Jijo, where *Streaker*'s escape attempt had begun two exhausting days ago, breaking for liberty amid a crowd of ancient derelicts—reactivated from ocean bottom junk piles for one last, glorious, screaming run through space.

One by one, those decoys had failed, or dropped out, or were snared by the enemy's clever capture-boxes, until only *Streaker* remained, plummeting for the brief shelter of stormy Izmunuti.

As for the *forward* direction . . .

Instrument readings relayed by the bridge crew enabled the Niss Machine to calculate their likely heading. Apparently, Gillian Baskin had ordered a course change, taking advantage of a gravitational slingshot around the star to fling *Streaker* toward galactic north and east.

Sara swallowed hard. The destination had originally been her idea. But as time passed, she grew less certain.

"The new T-point doesn't look very stable," she commented, following the ship's planned trajectory to the top left corner of the holo unit, where a tight mesh of curling lines funneled through an empty-looking zone of interstellar space. Reacting to her close regard, the display monitor enhanced that section. Rows of symbols glowed, showing details of the local hyperspatial matrix.

She had predicted this wonder—the reawakening of something old. Something marvelous. For a brief while, it had seemed like just the miracle they needed. A gift from the Holy Egg. An escape route from a terrible trap.

But on examining the analytical profiles, Sara concluded that the cosmos was not being all that helpful, after all.

"There *are* connection tubes opening up to other space-time locales. But they seem rather . . . scanty."

"Well, what can you expect from a nexus that is only a few miduras old? One that was only recently yanked from slumber by a force neither of us can grasp?"

After a pause, the Niss unit continued. *"Most of the transfer stigmata leading away from this nexus are still on the order of a Planck width. Some promising threads do appear to be coalescing, and may even be safely traversable by a starship, in a matter of weeks. Of course, that will be of little use to us."*

Sara nodded. The pursuing Jophur battleship would hardly give *Streaker* that much time. Already the mighty *Polkjhy* had abandoned its string of captured decoys in order to focus all its attention on the real *Streaker*, keeping the Earthship bathed in long-range scanning rays.

"Then what does Gillian Baskin hope to accomplish by heading toward a useless . . ."

She blinked, as realization lurched within her rib cage.

"Oh. I see."

Sara stepped back, and the display resumed its normal scale. Two meters away, at the opposite corner, neat curves showed the spatial patterns of another transfer point. The familiar, reliably predictable one that every sneakship had used to reach Izmunuti during the last two millennia. The only quick way in or out of this entire region of Galaxy Four.

But not always. Once, when Jijo had been a center of commerce and civilization under the mighty Buyur, traffic used to flux through *two* hyperdimensional nexi. One of them shut down when Jijo went fallow, half a million years ago, coincidentally soon after the Buyur departed.

Sara and her mentor, Sage Purofsky, had nursed a suspicion. That shutdown was no accident.

"Then we concur," said the Niss Machine. *"Gillian Baskin clearly intends to lead the Jophur into a suicidal trap."*

Sara looked elsewhere in the big display, seeking the enemy. She found it several stellar radii behind Izmunuti, a yellow glow representing the hunter—a Jophur dreadnought whose crew coveted the Earthship and its secrets. Having abandoned the distraction of all the old dross ships, the *Polkjhy* had been racing toward the regular

T-point, confident of cutting off *Streaker*'s sole escape route.

Only now, the sudden reopening of *another* gateway must have flummoxed the giant sap-rings who commanded the great warship. The yellow trace turned sharply, as the *Polkjhy* frantically shed momentum, aiming to chase *Streaker* past Izmunuti's flames toward the new door in spacetime.

A door that's not ready for use, Sara thought. Surely the Jophur must also have instruments capable of reading probability flows. They must realize how dangerous it would be to plunge into a newborn transfer point.

On the other hand, could the *Polkjhy* commanders afford to dismiss it? *Streaker* was small, maneuverable, and had dolphin pilots, reputed to be among the best in all five galaxies.

And the Earthlings were desperate.

The Jophur have to assume we know something about this transfer point that they do not. From their point of view, it seems as if we called it into existence with a wave of our hands—or fins. If we plunge inside, it must be because we know a tube or thread we can latch onto and follow to safety.

They're obliged to give chase, or risk losing Streaker *forever.*

Sara nodded.

"Gillian and the dolphins . . . they're sacrificing themselves, for Jijo."

The tightly meshed Niss hologram appeared to shrug in agreement.

"It does seem the best choice out of a wretched set of options.

"Suppose we turn and fight? The only likely outcomes are capture or death, with your Jijoan civilization lost in the bargain. After extracting information about Streaker's *discoveries in the Shallow Cluster, the Jophur will report to their home clan, then take their time organizing a systematic program for Jijo, first annihilating every g'Kek, then turning the planet into their own private breeding colony, developing new types of humans, traekis, and hoons to suit their perverted needs.*

"By forcing the Polkjhy *to follow us into the new transfer*

point, Dr. Baskin makes it likely that no report will ever reach the Five Galaxies about your Six Races. Your fellow exiles may continue wallowing in sublime, planet-bound squalor for a while longer, chasing vague notions of redemption down the muddy generations."

How very much like the Niss it was, to turn a noble gesture into an excuse for insult. Sara shook her head. Gillian's plan was both grand and poignant.

It also meant Sara's own hours were numbered.

"What a waste," the Niss sighed. "This vessel and crew appear to have made the discovery of the age, and now it may be lost."

Things had been so hectic since the rushed departure from Jijo, that Sara was still unclear about the cause of all this ferment—what the *Streaker* crew had done to provoke such ire and determined pursuit by some of the greater powers of the known universe.

"It began when Captain Creideiki took this ship poking through a seemingly unlikely place, looking for relics or anomalies that had been missed by the Great Library," the artificial intelligence explained. "It was a shallow globular cluster, lacking planets or singularities. Creideiki never told his reasons for choosing such a spot. But his hunch paid off beyond all hope or expectation when* Streaker *came upon a great fleet of derelict ships, drifting in splendid silence through open space. Moreover, samples and holos taken of this mystery armada seemed to hint at possible answers to our civilization's most ancient mystery.*

"Of course our findings should have been shared openly by the institutes of the Civilization of Five Galaxies, in the name of all oxygen-breathing life. Immense credit would have come to your frail, impoverished Earthclan, as well as my Tymbrimi makers. But every other race. and alliance might have shared as well, gaining new insight into the origins of our billion-year-old culture.

"Alas, several mighty coalitions interpreted Streaker*'s initial beamcast as fulfillment of dire prophecy. They felt the news presaged a fateful time of commotion and upheaval, in which a decisive advantage would go to anyone monopolizing our discovery. Instead of celebratory welcome,* Streaker *returned from the Shallow Cluster to find battle fleets lying in wait, eager to secure our secrets before we*

reached neutral ground. Several times, we were cornered, and escaped only because hordes of fanatics fought savagely among themselves over the right of capture . . . a compensation lacking in our present situation."

That was an understatement. The Jophur could pursue *Streaker* at leisure, without threat of interference. As far as the rest of civilization was concerned, this whole region was empty and off-limits.

"Was poor Emerson wounded in one of those earlier space battles?"

Sara felt concern for her friend, the silent star voyager, whose cryptic injuries she had treated in her treehouse, before taking him on an epic journey across the Slope and eventually reuniting him with his crewmates.

"No. Engineer D'Anite was captured by members of the Retired Caste, at a place we call the Fractal World. That particular event—"

Suddenly, the blue blob halted its twisting gyration. Hesitating for a few seconds, it trembled before resuming.

"The detection officer reports that something significant has just been perceived.

"It appears that our instruments were too narrowly focused on the Jophur, and the new transfer point. Until this moment, we missed another phenomenon worth noting. One heretofore masked by the flames of Izmunuti."

The display rippled, and abruptly, a swarm of orange pinpoints sparkled into view, residing amid the filaments and stormy prominences of Izmunuti's roiling atmosphere.

Sara leaned forward. "What are they?"

"Condensed objects.

"Artificial, self-propelled spacial motiles.

"In other words, starships."

Sara's jaw opened and closed twice before she could manage speech.

"Ifni, there must be hundreds! How could we have overlooked them before?"

The Niss answered defensively.

"Oh great Sage, one normally does not send probing beams through a red giant's flaming corona in search of spacecraft. Our chief attention was rightfully turned elsewhere. Besides, these vessels were not using gravitic engines until just moments ago, when several began applying

*gravi-temporal force . . . in an apparent effort to escape
these extravagant new solar storms."*

Sara stared in amazement. *Hope* whirled madly.

"These ships, could they help us?"

Again, the Niss paused, consulting remote instruments.

*"It seems doubtful, oh Sage. They will scarcely care
about our struggles. Indeed, these beings are of another
order on the pyramid of life, completely apart from yours
. . . though one might call them distant cousins of mine."*

Sara shook her head, at first confused. Then she cried
out.

"Machines!"

Even Jijo's fallen castaways could recite the Eight Orders
of Sapience, with oxygen-based life being only one of the
most flamboyant. Among the other orders, Jijo's sacred
scrolls spoke darkly of synthetic beings, coldly cryptic,
who designed and built each other in the farthest depths of
space, needing no ground to stand on, nor wind to
breathe.

*"Indeed. Although their presence here is unexplained, it
seems certain to involve matters beyond our concern. In
any event, the mechanoids will surely perceive us as dangerous, and avoid contact, out of cowardly self-interest."*

The voice paused.

*Fresh data is coming in. It seems that some members of
the flotilla are having a hard time with those tempests your
Holy Egg lately provoked through Izmunuti's outer shell. In
fact, some mechaniforms may be more needy of rescue
than we are."*

Sara pointed at one of the orange dots.

"Show me!"

Using data from long-range scans, the display unit
swooped giddily inward. Swirling stellar filaments seemed
to heave around Sara as her point of view plunged toward
the chosen speck—one of the mechanoid vessels—which
began taking form against a backdrop of irate gas.

The blurry enhancement—stretching the limits of magnification—showed a glimmering trapezoidal shape, almost
mirrorlike, that glancingly reflected surrounding solar fire.
The mechanoid's shape grew slimmer as it turned to flee a
plume of hot ions, fast-rising toward it from Izmunuti's
whipped convection zones. The display software compen-

sated for perspective as columns of numbers estimated the vessel's actual measurements—a square whose edges were hundreds of kilometers in length, with a third dimension that was vanishingly small.

Space seemed to ripple just beneath the mechaniform vessel. Though still inexperienced, Sara recognized the characteristic warping effects of a gravi-temporal field. A modest one, indicated the display numbers. Perhaps sufficient for interplanetary speeds, but not enough to escape the devastation climbing to meet it. She could only watch with helpless sympathy as the mechanoid struggled in vain.

The first shock wave ripped the filmy object in half . . . then into shreds that raveled quickly, becoming a swarm of bright, dissolving streamers.

"This is not the only victim. Observe, as fate catches up with other stragglers."

The display returned to its former scale. As Sara watched, several additional orange glitters were overwhelmed by waves of accelerating dense plasma. Others continued to climb, fighting to escape the maelstrom.

"Whoever they are, I hope they get away," Sara murmured. How strange it seemed that machine-vessels would be less sturdy than *Streaker*, whose protective fields could stand full immersion for several miduras in the red star's chromosphere, storm or no storm.

If they can't take on a plasma surge, they'd be useless against Jophur weapons.

Disappointment tasted bitter after briefly-raised hope. Clearly, no rescue would come from that direction.

Sara perceived a pattern to her trials and adventures during the last year—swept away from her dusty study to encounter aliens, fight battles, ride fabled horses, submerge into the sea, and then join a wild flight aboard a starship. The universe seemed bent on revealing wonders at the edge of her grasp or imagining—giant stars, transfer points, talking computers, universal libraries . . . and now a glimpse revealing a completely different order of life. A mysterious phylum, totally apart from the vast, encompassing Civilization of the Five Galaxies.

Such marvels lay far beyond her old life as a savage intellectual on a rustic world.

And yet, a glimpse was clearly all the cosmos planned on giving her.

Go ahead and look, it seemed to say. *But you can't touch.*

For you, time has almost run out.

Saddened, Sara watched orange pinpoints flee desperately before curling tornadoes of stellar heat. In moments, several more laggards were swept up by the rising storm, their frail light quenched like drowning embers.

Gillian and the dolphins seem sure we can stand a brief passage through that hell. But the vanishing sparks made Sara's confidence waver. After all, weren't machines supposed to be stronger than mere flesh?

She was about to ask the Niss about it when, before her eyes, the holo display abruptly changed once more. Izmunuti flickered, and when the image reformed, something new had come into view. Below the retreating orange glimmers, there now appeared *three sparkling forms,* rising with complacent grace, shining a distinct shade of imperial purple as they emerged from the flames to cross near *Streaker*'s path.

"What now?" she asked. "More mechanoids?"

"No," the Niss answered in a tone that seemed almost awed. *"These appear to be something else entirely. I believe they are . . ."*

The computer's holographic personification paused, deforming into jagged shapes, like nervous icicles.

"I believe they are Zang."

Sara's skin crawled with an involuntary shiver. That name was fraught with fear and legend. Back on Jijo, it was never spoken in tones above a whisper.

"But . . . how . . . what could *they* be doing . . ."

Before she finished her question, the Niss spoke again.

"Excuse me for interrupting, Sara. Our acting captain, Dr. Gillian Baskin, has just called an urgent meeting of the Ship's Council to consider these developments.

"You are invited to attend, oh Sage.

"Do you wish me to make excuses on your behalf?"

Sara was already hurrying toward the exit.

"Don't you dare!" she cried over one shoulder as the door folded aside to let her pass.

The hallway curved up and away in both directions, like

a segment of tortured spacetime, rising toward vertical in the distance. The sight always gave Sara qualms of dizziness, whenever she ventured outside her quarters. Nevertheless, this time she ran.

Gillian

For some reason, the tumultuous red giant star reminded her of Venus.

Naturally, that brought Tom to mind.

Everything reminded Gillian of Tom. After two years, his absence was still a wound, an amputation that left her reflexively turning for his warmth each night. By day, she kept expecting his strong voice, offering to help take on the worries. The damned decisions.

Isn't it just like a hero, to die saving the world?

A little voice within her pointed out—*that's what heroes are for.*

Yes, she answered. *But the world goes on, doesn't it? And it keeps needing to be saved.*

Ever since the universe sundered them apart at Kithrup, Gillian told herself that Tom couldn't be dead. *I'd know it,* she would think repeatedly, convincing herself by force of will. *Across galaxies and megaparsecs, I could tell if he were gone. Tom must be out there somewhere still, with Creideiki and Hikahi, and the others we left behind.*

He'll find a way safely home . . . or else back to me.

That certainty helped Gillian bear her burdens during *Streaker*'s first distraught fugitive year . . . until the last few months of steady crisis finally cracked her assurance. Without ever realizing when it happened, a transition took place, and she began thinking of Tom in the past tense.

He loved Venus, she pondered, looking across the raging solar vista that stretched beyond *Streaker*'s hull. Of course there were differences. Izmunuti's atmosphere was bright, while Earth's sister world had been dim beneath perpetual acid clouds. And the planet was microscopic compared to a giant red star. Yet, both locales shared essential traits. Harsh warmth, unforgiving storms, and a paucity of moisture.

Both provoked extremes of hope and despair.

"Isn't this tremendous?" Tom once asked. *"Have you ever seen anything so superb? This great endeavor proves, once and for all, that humans are capable of thinking long thoughts."*

She could see him now, stretching both spacesuited arms to encompass the panorama below Aphrodite Pinnacle, gesturing toward stark lowlands where lighting danced about a phalanx of titanic structures receding toward the warped horizon—one shadowy behemoth after another—vast new devices freshly engaged in the labor of changing Venus. Transforming hell, one step at a time.

Even with borrowed Galactic technology, the task would take humans longer to complete than the period they had known writing or agriculture. Ten thousand years must pass before seas rolled across the sere plains. It was a bold project for poor wolflings to engage in, especially when Sa'ent and Kloornap bookies gave Earthclan slim odds of surviving more than another century or two.

"We have to show the universe that we trust ourselves," Tom said. *"Or else who will believe in us?"*

His words sounded fine. So noble and grand. At the time, Tom almost convinced Gillian.

Only now things had changed.

Half a year ago during *Streaker*'s brief, terrified refuge at the Fractal World, Gillian had managed to pick up the latest rumors about the Siege of Terra, taking place in faraway Galaxy Two. Apparently, the Sa'ent touts were now taking bets on human extinction in mere years or jaduras, not centuries.

In retrospect, the ferment and debate over terraforming Venus seemed moot, like all the other projects that were supposed to win a special place in the cosmos for humans and their clients.

We'd have been better off as farmers, Tom and I. Or teaching school. Or helping settle Calafia.

We should never have listened to Jake Demwa and Ceideiki. This mission has brought ruin on everyone it touched.

Including the poor colonists of Jijo—six exile races who deserved a chance to find their own strange destiny undisturbed. In seeking shelter from the cosmos on that forlorn, forbidden world, *Streaker* had only managed to bring disaster on the tribes of the Slope.

There seemed just one way to redress the balance.

Can we lure the Jophur to follow us into the new transfer point? Kaa will have to pilot a convincing trajectory, as if he can sense a perfect thread to latch onto. A miracle path leading toward safety. If we do it right, the big ugly sap rings will have to follow! They'll have no choice.

Saving Jijo was good enough reason for the suicidal option, especially since there seemed no way to bring *Streaker*'s cargo safely home to Earth.

Another reason tasted bitter, vengeful.

At least we'll take some of our enemies with us.

It has been said that the prospect of impending death clarifies the mind, but Gillian found that it just stirred regret. She shook her head. It would not do to carry such thoughts to the council meeting. She had a duty not to infect the others with pessimism.

I hope Creideiki and Tom aren't too disappointed in me, she pondered at the door of the conference room.

I did my best. I really did.

◆

The Ship's Council had changed since Gillian reluctantly took over the captain's position at the head of the long table, where Creideiki used to preside in happier times. At the opposite end, *Streaker*'s last surviving dolphin officer, Lieutenant Tsh't, expertly piloted the six-legged walker apparatus carrying her sleek gray form into the same niche where Takkata-Jim once nestled his great bulk, before he was killed near Kithrup.

Tsh't exchanged greetings with the human chief engineer, though Hannes Suessi's own mother would hardly recognize him, with so many body parts replaced by cyborg components, and a silver dome where his head used to be. Much of that gleaming surface was now covered with pre-Contact-era motorcycle decals—an irreverent act that endeared Hannes to Gillian and the fins. At least *someone* aboard had kept a sense of humor through the years of relentless crisis.

Gillian felt acutely the absence of one council member, her friend and fellow physician Makanee, who had lately remained behind on Jijo with several dozen members of the dolphin crew—those suffering from devolution fever, or not essential for the breakout attempt. In effect, dolphins had established a seventh illegal colony on that fallow world—yet another secret worth defending with the lives of those left aboard.

Secrets. There are other enigmas, less easily protected.

Gillian's thoughts slipped past the salvaged objects in her office, some of them worth a stellar ransom. Mere hints at their existence had already knocked civilization teetering across five galaxies.

Foremost among the treasures was a corpse, irreverently nicknamed *Herbie.* An alien cadaver so ancient, its puzzling smile might be from a joke told a billion years ago. Other relics were scarcely less provocative—or cursed. Trouble had followed *Streaker,* ever since its crew began picking up objects they didn't understand.

"Articles of Destiny." That was the awed phrase used by one of the Old Ones, referring to *Streaker's* precious load of mysteries, during that dismal visit to the Fractal World.

Maybe this will be a fitting way to go, she thought. *All those irksome treasures will get smashed down to a proton's thickness moments after we dive into the new transfer point.*

At least she might then get the satisfaction of seeing old Herbie's expression finally change, at the last instant, when the bounds of reality closed in rapidly from ten dimensions.

A holo image of Izmunuti took up one wall of the conference room, an expanse of swirling clouds wider than Earth's orbit, surging and shifting as the Niss Machine relayed the latest intelligence in Tymbrimi-accented Galactic Seven.

"The Jophur battleship has jettisoned the last of its capture boxes, releasing all the decoy vessels it had seized, allowing them to drift onward through space. Now freed of their momentum-burden, the Polkjhy *is much more agile, turning its frightful bulk in a course change toward the new transfer point. Their aim is clearly to reach the reborn nexus before* Streaker *arrives."*

"Can they beat us there?" Gillian asked in Anglic.

The Niss hologram whirled thoughtfully. *"It seems un-*

likely, unless they use some risky type of probability drive, which is not typical of Jophur. They wasted a lot of time dashing ahead toward the older T-point. Our tight swing past Izmunuti should offer enough hyperspatial recoil for Streaker *to arrive first at Number Two . . . for whatever good it will do us."*

Gillian ignored the machine's sarcastic tone. Most of the crew seemed in accord with her decision. Lacking other options, death was more bearable if you took an enemy with you.

The Jophur situation appeared stable for a few more miduras, so she changed the subject.

"What can you report about the other ships?"

"You mean the two mysterious flotillas we recently detected in Izmunuti's chromosphere? After consulting with the tactical computer and archives, I now conclude they must have been operating together. Nothing else could explain their close proximity, fleeing together to escape unexpected plasma storms."

Hannes Suessi objected, his voice wavering low and raspy from the silver dome.

"Mechanoids and hydrogen-breathers cooperating? That sounds unlikely."

The whirling blob made a gesture like a nod.

"Indeed. The various orders of life seldom interact. But I queried our captured Library unit, and discovered that it does happen, more often than you might think, especially when there is some project afoot requiring the talents of two or more orders, working together."

One of the newest members of the council whistled for attention, slashing his tail flukes through water that fizzed with bubbles. *Kaa*, the chief pilot, did not ride a walker, since he might have to speed back to duty at any time. Instead, the young dolphin commented from a fluid-filled tunnel that emerged from a wall to pass near one side of the table.

> * *Can any purpose*
> * *Under tide-pulled moons explain*
> * *Such anomalies? **

Gillian turned to translate the popping whistle-poem for Sara Koolhan, who had never learned Trinary.

"Kaa asks what project could be worth the trouble and danger of diving into a star."

To the surprise of everyone, Sara replied with an eager nod.

"I think I can offer a partial answer."

The young Jijoan nervously stroked a black cube on the table in front of her—the personal algorithmic engine Gillian lent her when she came aboard. "Ever since we first spotted these strange ships, I wondered what trait of Izmunuti might attract folks here from some distant system. I thought about how my own ancestors came to Jijo. After passing through the regular T-point, they took a path through this giant star's outer atmosphere. All the sneak-ships of Jijo's other races also used the same method to cover their tracks."

We thought of it too, Gillian pondered, unhappily. *But I must have done something wrong, since the Rothen were able to follow us, betraying both our hiding place and the Six Races.*

Gillian noticed Lieutenant Tsh't was looking at her. With reproach for getting *Streaker* into this fix? The dolphin's eye remained fixed for a long, appraising moment, then turned away as Sara continued.

"Now, according to this teaching unit, stars like Izmunuti pour out immense amounts of heavy atoms from their bloated atmospheres. Carbon is especially rich, condensing on anything solid that happens nearby. All our ancestor ships arrived at Jijo black with the stuff. *Streaker* may be the first vessel ever to try the trick *twice,* both coming and going. I bet the stuff is causing you some problems."

"No bet!" boomed Suessi's amplified voice. Hannes had been battling the growing carbon coating. "The stuff is heavy, it has weird properties, and it's been gumming up the verity flanges."

Sara nodded.

"But consider, what if somebody else has a *use* for such coatings? What would be the best way to accumulate it?"

She nudged her black cube, using a spoken command to transfer data to the main display. Though Sara had been aboard only a few days, she was quickly adapting to the convenience of modern tools.

A mirrorlike rectangle appeared before the council, reflecting fiery prominences from a broad, planar surface.

"Of course I'm just an ignorant native," Sara commented, "but it seems to me the best way to collect atoms out of a stellar wind would be to use something with a lot of surface area and little initial mass. Such a vehicle might not even have to use much energy to depart from the collection site, if it were propelled outward on the pressure of waves of light."

Lieutenant Tsh't murmured.

"A sssolar sail!"

"Is that what you call it?" Sara nodded. "Imagine machines arriving through the transfer point as compact objects, plummeting down to Izmunuti, then unfurling such sails and catching a free ride back to the T-point, gaining layers of this molecularly unique carbon and other stuff along the way. Energy expenditures per ton of yield would be minimal!"

The whirling Niss hologram edged forward.

"Your hypothesis suggests an economical resource-gathering technique, providing the mechanoids needn't make more than one simple hyperspatial transfer, coming or going. Even so, there are cheaper alternatives in industrialized regions of the Five Galaxies. Still, it may be plausible here in Galaxy Four, where industry is currently minimal or nil, due to the recent fallow-migration."

Gillian noted that the word "recent" in this case meant several thousand years.

"If Sage Sara's conjecture is correct," the Niss continued, *"mechanoids would be ideal contractors to hire for the harvesting chore. They would create special versions of themselves tuned to do the job efficiently, with minimal excess mass. That explains why their drive and protective systems were so easily vanquished by the rising storms. They had no margin to spare for the unexpected."*

Gillian glanced at the big display. Just half the orange glitters remained, still struggling to flee Izmunuti's gravity well before burgeoning plasma surges caught them.

The three purple dots had already reached the mechanoid convoy, ascending past them with graceful ease.

"What about the Zang?" she asked.

"I would surmise they are the mechanoids' employers. Our captured Library unit cannot recall another instance of hydrogen breathers being detected so close to a star, but there are clear precedents for Zang groups hiring special services from the Machine Order. Great clans of oxygen-breathers also do it, from time to time."

"Well, it looks like their plans sure have been ripped," commented Suessi. "Ain't gonna be much cargo getting home, this time."

A series of pensive whistle clicks escaped the gray dolphin floating in the nearby water-filled tunnel—not Trinary but the sort of scattered clicks a cetacean gives off when pondering something deeply. Gillian still felt guilty about asking Kaa to volunteer for this mission, since it meant abandoning his lover, Peepoe, to an uncertain fate on Jijo. But *Streaker* could never manage this desperate ploy without a first-class pilot.

"I concur," the whirling hologram concluded. *"The Zang will not be in a good mood, after this setback."*

"Because they suffered economic loss?" Tsh't asked.

"There is more. According to Library records, most hydrogen-breathing races react badly to surprise. This goes beyond their having slower metabolisms than oxy-life. Anything unpredictable is viscerally loathsome to Zang and their relatives.

"Of course, this attitude is incomprehensible to an entity like me, programmed by the Tymbrimi to seek out novelty in any form. Without surprise, how can you tell there is an objective world? You might as well presume the whole universe is one big—"

"Wait a minute," Gillian interrupted, lest the Niss get sidetracked on some long philosophical rumination. "We're all taught to avoid Zang. They may be dangerous, even under ideal circumstances. Contact is best left to experts from the Great Institutes, we're told. But now you're saying they may be *especially* angry? Possibly short-tempered?"

The Niss hologram whirled silently for several duras, coiling with apparent tension.

"After three Earth years together, amid growing familiarity with your voice tones and thought patterns, Dr. Bas-

*kin, I find that your latest inquiry provokes an uneasy
feeling in me. Am I justified to be wary?*

"*Do you find the notion of short-tempered Zang somehow . . . appealing?*"

Gillian refrained from answering right away. But she did
allow the emergence of a grim, enigmatic smile.